H. G. Wells was born in Bromley, Kent in 1866. After working as a draper's apprentice and pupil teacher, he won a scholarship to the Normal School of Science, South Kensington, in 1884, studying under T. H. Huxley. He was awarded a first-class honours degree in biology and resumed teaching, but had to retire after a kick from an ill-natured pupil, at fooball, afflicted his kidneys. He worked in poverty in London as a crammer while experimenting in journalism and stories, and published textbooks on biology and physiography (1893), but it was *The Time Machine* (1895) that launched his literary career. Many scientific romances and short stories began to be paralleled with sociological and political books and tracts, notably *Anticipations* (1901), *Mankind in the Making* (1903), *A Modern Utopia* (1905). His full-length, largely autobiographical novels began with *The Wheels of Chance* (1896), *Love and Mr Lewisham* (1900), *Kipps* (1905), *Tono-Bungay* and *Ann Veronica* (1909), the last promoting the outspoken, socially and sexually liberated 'New Woman'. He married his cousin Isabel in 1891, but later eloped with, and subsequently married, Catherine Robbins, 'Jane'. A constant philanderer, he invited scandal by including his lightly concealed private affairs in *Ann Veronica* and *The New Machiavelli* (1911). Shaw and the Webbs had invited him into the Fabian Society and soon regretted it. Wells increasingly used fiction as a platform for the ideas and visions of a world-state which preoccupied him, but he foresaw that the Novel itself would decline to be replaced by candid autobiography. After about 1920, critical attention was turning towards his natural successors Aldous Huxley and George Orwell, and the 'pure', non-journalistic novels of James Joyce and Virginia Woolf. After World War I Wells was an internationally recognized figure, gaining access to Stalin and Roosevelt to preach his vision of a new World Order. While his novels declined, his career as a popular educator soared with the publication of *The Outline of History* (1920), *The Science of Life* (1930) and *The Work, Wealth and Happiness of Mankind* (1932). It was the latter book which formed the 'workshop' for *The Shape of Things to Come* (1933). With the film version, *Things to Come* (1936), Wells reached the new cinema-going audiences and saw fully the potential of the medium. In 1939 he jointly produced the 'Sankey Declaration of the Rights of Man' which was debated in twenty-nine countries and only failed to become what is now the United Nation's Charter on Human Rights because of the outbreak of World War II. When the atomic bomb was dropped on Japan Wells was heard to comment, 'this thing could destroy us all.' Perhaps his most fitting epitaph was the one he thought up for himself: 'I told you so. You *damned* fools!'

H. G. WELLS

The Science Fiction

Volume 2

The Invisible Man
When the Sleeper Wakes
The Shape of Things to Come

A Phoenix Giant
This collection first published
in Great Britain by J. M. Dent,
a division of the Orion Publishing Group, in 1996

Texts copyright © the Literary Executors of
the Estate of H. G. Wells 1996

J. M. Dent
Orion Publishing Group
Orion House, 5 Upper St Martin's Lane
London WC2H 9EA
and
Charles E. Tuttle Co. Inc.
28 South Main Street
Rutland, Vermont 05701, USA

Printed in Great Britain by
Clays Ltd, St Ives plc

British Library Cataloguing in Publication Data
is available upon request.

ISBN 1 85799 434 5

CONTENTS

THE INVISIBLE MAN

CONTENTS

I

The Strange Man's Arrival

The stranger came early in February, one wintry day, through a biting wind and a driving snow, the last snowfall of the year, over the down, walking as it seemed from Bramblehurst railway station, and carrying a little black portmanteau in his thickly gloved hand. He was wrapped up from head to foot, and the brim of his soft felt hat hid every inch of his face but the shiny tip of his nose; the snow had piled itself against his shoulders and chest, and added a white crest to the burden he carried. He staggered into the Coach and Horses, more dead than alive as it seemed, and flung his portmanteau down. 'A fire,' he cried, 'in the name of human charity! A room and a fire!' He stamped and shook the snow from off himself in the bar, and followed Mrs Hall into her guest parlour to strike his bargain. And with that much introduction, that and a ready acquiescence to terms and a couple of sovereigns flung upon the table, he took up his quarters in the inn.

Mrs Hall lit the fire and left him there while she went to prepare him a meal with her own hands. A guest to stop at Iping in the winter-time was an unheard-of piece of luck, let alone a guest who was no 'haggler', and she was resolved to show herself worthy of her good fortune. As soon as the bacon was well under way, and Millie, her lymphatic aid, had been brisked up a bit by a few deftly chosen expressions of contempt, she carried the cloth, plates, and glasses into the parlour and began to lay them with the utmost *éclat*. Although the fire was burning up briskly, she was surprised to see that her visitor still wore his hat and coat, standing with his back to her and staring out of the window at the falling snow in the yard. His gloved hands were clasped behind him, and he seemed to be lost in thought. She noticed that the melted snow that still sprinkled his shoulders dropped upon her carpet. 'Can I take your hat and coat, sir,' she said, 'and give them a good dry in the kitchen?'

'No,' he said without turning.

She was not sure she had heard him, and was about to repeat her question.

He turned his head and looked at her over his shoulder. 'I prefer to keep them on,' he said with emphasis, and she noticed that he wore big blue spectacles with side-lights, and had a bushy side-whisker over his coat-collar that completely hid his cheeks and face.

'Very well, sir,' she said. '*As* you like. In a bit the room will be warmer.'

He made no answer, and had turned his face away from her again, and Mrs Hall, feeling that her conversational advances were ill-timed, laid the rest of the table things in a quick staccato and whisked out of the room. When she returned he was still standing there, like a man of stone, his back hunched, his collar turned up, his dripping hat-brim turned down, hiding his face and ears completely. She put down the eggs and bacon with considerable emphasis, and called rather than said to him, 'Your lunch is served, sir.'

'Thank you,' he said at the same time, and did not stir until she was closing the door. Then he swung round and approached the table with a certain eager quickness.

As she went behind the bar to the kitchen she heard a sound repeated at regular intervals. Chirk, chirk, chirk, it went, the sound of a spoon being rapidly whisked round a basin. 'That girl!' she said. 'There! I clean forgot it. It's her being so long!' And while she herself finished mixing the mustard, she gave Millie a few verbal stabs for her excessive slowness. She had cooked the ham and eggs, laid the table, and done everything, while Millie (help indeed!) had only succeeded in delaying the mustard. And him a new guest and wanting to stay! Then she filled the mustard pot, and putting it with a certain stateliness upon a gold and black tea-tray, carried it into the parlour.

She rapped and entered promptly. As she did so her visitor moved quickly, so that she got but a glimpse of a white object disappearing behind the table. It would seem he was picking something from the floor. She rapped down the mustard pot on the table, and then she noticed the overcoat and hat had been taken off and put over a chair in front of the fire, and a pair of wet boots threatened rust to her steel fender. She went to these things resolutely. 'I suppose I may have them to dry now,' she said in a voice that brooked no denial.

'Leave the hat,' said her visitor, in a muffled voice, and turning she saw he had raised his head and was sitting and looking at her.

For a moment she stood gaping at him, too surprised to speak.

He held a white cloth – it was a *serviette* he had brought with him – over the lower part of his face, so that his mouth and jaws were completely hidden, and that was the reason of his muffled voice. But it was not that which startled Mrs Hall. It was the fact that all his forehead above his blue glasses was covered by a white bandage, and that another covered his ears, leaving not a scrap of his face exposed excepting only his pink, peaked nose. It was bright, pink, and shiny just as it had been at first. He wore a dark-brown velvet jacket with a high, black, linen-lined collar turned up about his neck. The thick black hair, escaping as it could below and between the cross bandages, projected in curious tails and horns, giving him the strangest appearance conceivable. This muffled and bandaged head was so unlike what she had anticipated, that for a moment she was rigid.

He did not remove the *serviette*, but remained holding it, as she saw now, with a brown gloved hand, and regarding her with his inscrutable blue glasses. 'Leave the hat,' he said, speaking very distinctly through the white cloth.

Her nerves began to recover from the shock they had received. She placed the hat on the chair again by the fire. 'I didn't know, sir,' she began, 'that – ' and she stopped embarrassed.

'Thank you,' he said drily, glancing from her to the door and then at her again.

'I'll have them nicely dried, sir, at once,' she said, and carried his clothes out of the room. She glanced at his white-swathed head and blue goggles again as she was going out of the door; but his napkin was still in front of his face. She shivered a little as she closed the door behind her, and her face was eloquent of her surprise and perplexity. 'I *never*,' she whispered. 'There!' She went quite softly to the kitchen, and was too preoccupied to ask Millie what she was messing about with *now*, when she got there.

The visitor sat and listened to her retreating feet. He glanced inquiringly at the window before he removed his *serviette*, and resumed his meal. He took a mouthful, glanced suspiciously at the window, took another mouthful, then rose and, taking the *serviette* in his hand, walked across the room and pulled the blind down to the top of the white muslin that obscured the lower panes. This left the room in a twilight. This done, he returned with an easier air to the table and his meal.

'The poor soul's had an accident or an opration or something,' said Mrs Hall. 'What a turn them bandages did give me, to be sure!'

She put on some more coal, unfolded the clothes-horse, and extended the traveller's coat upon this. 'And they goggles! Why, he looked more like a divin' helmet than a human man!' She hung his muffler on a corner of the horse. 'And holding that handkercher over his mouth all the time. Talkin' through it! ... Perhaps his mouth was hurt too – maybe.'

She turned round, as one who suddenly remembers. 'Bless my soul alive!' she said, going off at a tangent; 'ain't you done them taters *yet*, Millie?'

When Mrs Hall went to clear away the stranger's lunch, her idea that his mouth must also have been cut or disfigured in the accident she supposed him to have suffered, was confirmed, for he was smoking a pipe, and all the time that she was in the room he never loosened the silk muffler he had wrapped round the lower part of his face to put the mouth piece to his lips. Yet it was not forgetfulness, for she saw he glanced at it as it smouldered out. He sat in the corner with his back to the window-blind and spoke now, having eaten and drunk and being comfortably warmed through, with less aggressive brevity than before. The reflection of the fire lent a kind of red animation to his big spectacles they had lacked hitherto.

'I have some luggage,' he said, 'at Bramblehurst station,' and he asked her how he could have it sent. He bowed his bandaged head quite politely in acknowledgment of her explanation. 'Tomorrow!' he said. 'There is no speedier delivery?' and seemed quite disappointed when she answered, 'No.' Was she quite sure? No man with a trap who would go over?

Mrs Hall, nothing loath, answered his questions and developed a conversation. 'It's a steep road by the down, sir,' she said in answer to the question about a trap; and then, snatching at an opening, said, 'It was there a carriage was upsettled, a year ago and more. A gentleman killed, besides his coachman. Accidents, sir, happen in a moment, don't they?'

But the visitor was not to be drawn so easily. 'They do,' he said through his muffler, eyeing her quietly through his impenetrable glasses.

'But they take long enough to get well, sir, don't they? . . . There was my sister's son, Tom, jest cut his arm with a scythe, tumbled on it in the 'ayfield, and, bless me! he was three months tied up, sir. You'd hardly believe it. It's regular given me a dread of a scythe, sir.'

'I can quite understand that,' said the visitor.

'He was afraid, one time, that he'd have to have an opration – he was that bad, sir.'

The visitor laughed abruptly, a bark of a laugh that he seemed to bite and kill in his mouth. '*Was* he?' he said.

'He was, sir. And no laughing matter to them as had the doing for him, as I had – my sister being took up with her little ones so much. There was bandages to do, sir, and bandages to undo. So that if I may make so bold as to say it, sir – '

'Will you get me some matches?' said the visitor, quite abruptly. 'My pipe is out.'

Mrs Hall was pulled up suddenly. It was certainly rude of him, after telling him all she had done. She gasped at him for a moment, and remembered the two sovereigns. She went for the matches.

'Thanks,' he said concisely, as she put them down, and turned his shoulder upon her and stared out of the window again. It was altogether too discouraging. Evidently he was sensitive on the top of operations and bandages. She did not 'make so bold as to say,' however, after all.

But his snubbing way had irritated her, and Millie had a hot time of it that afternoon.

The visitor remained in the parlour until four o'clock, without giving the ghost of an excuse for an intrusion. For the most part he was quite still during that time; it would seem he sat in the growing darkness smoking in the firelight, perhaps dozing.

Once or twice a curious listener might have heard him at the coals, and for the space of five minutes he was audible pacing the room. He seemed to be talking to himself. Then the armchair creaked as he sat down again.

II

Mr Teddy Henfrey's First Impressions

At four o'clock, when it was fairly dark and Mrs Hall was screwing up her courage to go in and ask her visitor if he would take some tea, Teddy Henfrey, the clock-jobber, came into the bar. 'My sakes! Mrs Hall,' said he, 'but this is terrible weather for thin boots!' The snow outside was falling faster.

Mrs Hall agreed with him, and then noticed he had his bag, and hit upon a brilliant idea. 'Now you're here, Mr Teddy,' said she, 'I'd be glad if you'd give th' old clock in the parlour a bit of a look. 'T is going, and it strikes well and hearty; but the hour-hand won't do nuthin' but point at six.'

And leading the way, she went across to the parlour door and rapped and entered.

Her visitor, she saw as she opened the door, was seated in the armchair before the fire, dozing it would seem, with his bandaged head drooping on one side. The only light in the room was the red glow from the fire – which lit his eyes like adverse railway signals, but left his downcast face in darkness – and the scanty vestiges of the day that came in through the open door. Everything was ruddy, shadowy, and indistinct to her, the more so since she had just been lighting the bar lamp, and her eyes were dazzled. But for a second it seemed to her that the man she looked at had an enormous mouth wide open, a vast and incredible mouth that swallowed the whole of the lower portion of his face. It was the sensation of a moment: the white-bound head, the monstrous goggle eyes, and this huge yawn below it. Then he stirred, started up in his chair, put up his hand. She opened the door wide, so that the room was lighter, and she saw him more clearly, with the muffler held to his face just as she had seen him hold the *serviette* before. The shadows, she fancied, had tricked her.

'Would you mind, sir, this man a-coming to look at the clock, sir?' she said, recovering from her momentary shock.

'Look at the clock?' he said, staring round in a drowsy manner, and speaking over his hand, and then, getting more fully awake, 'certainly.'

Mrs Hall went away to get a lamp, and he rose and stretched himself. Then came the light, and Mr Teddy Henfrey, entering, was confronted by this bandaged person. He was, he says, 'taken aback'.

'Good-afternoon,' said the stranger, regarding him, as Mr Henfrey says, with a vivid sense of the dark spectacles, 'like a lobster'.

'I hope,' said Mr Henfrey, 'that it's no intrusion.'

'None whatever,' said the stranger. 'Though, I understand,' he said, turning to Mrs Hall, 'that this room is really to be mine for my own private use.'

'I thought, sir,' said Mrs Hall, 'you'd prefer the clock – ' She was going to say 'mended'.

'Certainly,' said the stranger, 'certainly – but, as a rule, I like to be alone and undisturbed.'

'But I'm really glad to have the clock seen to,' he said, seeing a certain hesitation in Mr Henfrey's manner. 'Very glad.' Mr Henfrey had intended to apologise and withdraw, but this anticipation reassured him. The stranger stood round with his back to the fireplace and put his hands behind his back. 'And presently,' he said, 'when the clock-mending is over, I think I should like to have some tea. But not till the clock-mending is over.'

Mrs Hall was about to leave the room – she made no conversational advances this time, because she did not want to be snubbed in front of Mr Henfrey – when her visitor asked her if she had made any arrangements about his boxes at Bramblehurst. She told him she had mentioned the matter to the postman, and that the carrier could bring them over on the morrow. 'You are certain that is the earliest?' he said.

She was certain, with a marked coldness.

'I should explain,' he added, 'what I was really too cold and fatigued to do before, that I am an experimental investigator.'

'Indeed, sir,' said Mrs Hall, much impressed.

'And my baggage contains apparatus and appliances.'

'Very useful things, indeed, they are, sir,' said Mrs Hall.

'And I'm naturally anxious to get on with my inquiries.'

'Of course, sir.'

'My reason for coming to Iping,' he proceeded, with a certain deliberation of manner, 'was – a desire for solitude. I do not wish to be disturbed in my work. In addition to my work, an accident – '

'I thought as much,' said Mrs Hall to herself.

' – necessitates a certain retirement. My eyes – are sometimes so weak and painful that I have to shut myself up in the dark for hours together. Lock myself up. Sometimes – now and then. Not at present, certainly. At such times the slightest disturbance, the entry of a stranger into the room, is a source of excruciating annoyance to me – it is well these things should be understood.'

'Certainly, sir,' said Mrs Hall. 'And if I might make so bold as to ask – '

'That, I think, is all,' said the stranger, with that quietly irresistible air of finality he could assume at will. Mrs Hall reserved her question and sympathy for a better occasion.

After Mrs Hall had left the room, he remained standing in front of the fire, glaring, so Mr Henfrey puts it, at the clock-mending. Mr Henfrey not only took off the hands of the clock, and the face, but extracted the works; and he tried to work in as slow and quiet and unassuming a manner as possible. He worked with the lamp close to him, and the green shade threw a brilliant light upon his hands, and upon the frame and wheels, and left the rest of the room shadowy. When he looked up, coloured patches swam in his eyes. Being constitutionally of a curious nature, he had removed the works – a quite unnecessary proceeding – with the idea of delaying his departure and perhaps falling into conversation with the stranger. But the stranger stood there, perfectly silent and still. So still, it got on Henfrey's nerves. He felt alone in the room and looked up, and there, grey and dim, were the bandaged head and huge blue lenses staring fixedly, with a mist of green spots drifting in front of them. It was so uncanny-looking to Henfrey that for a minute they remained staring blankly at one another. Then Henfrey looked down again. Very uncomfortable position! One would like to say something. Should he remark that the weather was very cold for the time of year?

He looked up as if to take aim with that introductory shot. 'The weather' – he began.

'Why don't you finish and go?' said the rigid figure, evidently in a state of painfully suppressed rage. 'All you've got to do is to fix the hour-hand on its axle. You're simply humbugging – '

'Certainly, sir – one minute more, sir. I overlooked – ' And Mr Henfrey finished and went.

But he went off feeling excessively annoyed. 'Damn it!' said Mr Henfrey to himself, trudging down the village through the thawing snow; 'a man must do a clock at times, sure lie.'

And again: 'Can't a man look at you? – Ugly!'

And yet again: 'Seemingly not. If the police was wanting you you couldn't be more wropped and bandaged.'

At Gleeson's corner he saw Hall, who had recently married the stranger's hostess at the Coach and Horses, and who now drove the Iping conveyance, when occasional people required it, to Sidderbridge Junction, coming towards him on his return from that place. Hall had evidently been 'stopping a bit' at Sidderbridge, to judge by his driving. ''Ow do, Teddy?' he said, passing.

'You got a rum un up home!' said Teddy.

Hall very sociably pulled up. 'What's that?' he asked.

'Rum-looking customer stopping at the Coach and Horses,' said Teddy. 'My sakes!'

And he proceeded to give Hall a vivid description of his grotesque guest. 'Looks a bit like a disguise, don't it? I'd like to see a man's face if I had him stopping in *my* place,' said Henfrey. 'But women are that trustful, where strangers are concerned. He's took your rooms and he ain't even given a name, Hall.'

'You don't say so!' said Hall, who was a man of sluggish apprehension.

'Yes,' said Teddy. 'By the week. Whatever he is, you can't get rid of him under the week. And he's got a lot of luggage coming tomorrow, so he says. Let's hope it won't be stones in boxes, Hall.'

He told Hall how his aunt at Hastings had been swindled by a stranger with empty portmanteaux. Altogether he left Hall vaguely suspicious. 'Get up, old girl,' said Hall. 'I s'pose I must see 'bout this.'

Teddy trudged on his way with his mind considerably relieved.

Instead of 'seeing 'bout it,' however, Hall on his return was severely rated by his wife on the length of time he had spent in Sidderbridge, and his mild inquiries were answered snappishly and in a manner not to the point. But the seed of suspicion Teddy had sown germinated in the mind of Mr Hall in spite of these discouragements. 'You wim' don't know everything,' said Mr Hall, resolved to ascertain more about the personality of his guest at the earliest possible opportunity. And after the stranger had gone to bed, which he did about half-past nine, Mr Hall went very aggressively into the parlour and looked very hard at his wife's furniture, just to show that the stranger wasn't master there, and scrutinised closely and a little contemptuously a sheet of mathematical computation the stranger had left. When retiring for the night he instructed Mrs Hall to look very closely at the stranger's luggage when it came next day.

'You mind your own business, Hall,' said Mrs Hall, 'and I'll mind mine.'

She was all the more inclined to snap at Hall because the stranger was undoubtedly an unusually strange sort of stranger, and she was by no means assured about him in her own mind. In the middle of the night she woke up dreaming of huge white heads like turnips, that came trailing after her at the end of interminable necks, and with vast black eyes. But being a sensible woman, she subdued her terrors and turned over and went to sleep again.

III

The Thousand and One Bottles

So it was that on the twenty-ninth day of February, at the beginning of
the thaw, this singular person fell out of infinity into Iping Village. Next
day his luggage arrived through the slush. And very remarkable luggage
it was. There were a couple of trunks indeed, such as a rational man
might need, but in addition there were a box of books – big, fat books,
of which some were just in an incomprehensible handwriting – and a
dozen or more crates, boxes, and cases, containing objects packed in
straw, as it seemed to Hall, tugging with a casual curiosity at the straw
– glass bottles. The stranger, muffled in hat, coat, gloves, and wrapper,
came out impatiently to meet Fearenside's cart, while Hall was having
a word or so of gossip preparatory to helping bring them in. Out he
came, not noticing Fearenside's dog, who was sniffing in a *dilettante*
spirit at Hall's legs. 'Come along with those boxes,' he said. 'I've been
waiting long enough.'

And he came down the steps towards the tail of the cart as if to lay
hands on the smaller crate.

No sooner had Fearenside's dog caught sight of him, however, than
it began to bristle and growl savagely, and when he rushed down the
steps it gave an undecided hop, and then sprang straight at his hand.
'Whup!' cried Hall, jumping back, for he was no hero with dogs, and
Fearenside howled, 'Lie down!' and snatched his whip.

They saw the dog's teeth had slipped the hand, heard a kick, saw the
dog execute a flanking jump and get home on the stranger's leg, and
heard the rip of his trousering. Then the finer end of Fearenside's whip
reached his property, and the dog, yelping with dismay, retreated under
the wheels of the waggon. It was all the business of a swift half-minute.
No one spoke, every one shouted. The stranger glanced swiftly at his
torn glove and at his leg, made as if he would stoop to the latter, then
turned and rushed swiftly up the steps into the inn. They heard him go
headlong across the passage and up the uncarpeted stairs to his
bedroom.

'You brute, you!' said Fearenside, climbing off the waggon with his

whip in his hand, while the dog watched him through the wheel. 'Come
here!' said Fearenside – 'You'd better.'

Hall had stood gaping. 'He wuz bit,' said Hall. 'I'd better go and see
to en,' and he trotted after the stranger. He met Mrs Hall in the passage.
'Carrier's darg,' he said, 'bit en.'

He went straight upstairs, and the stranger's door being ajar, he
pushed it open and was entering without any ceremony, being of a
naturally sympathetic turn of mind.

The blind was down and the room dim. He caught a glimpse of a
most singular thing, what seemed a handless arm waving towards him,
and a face of three huge indeterminate spots on white, very like the face
of a pale pansy. Then he was struck violently in the chest, hurled back,
and the door slammed in his face and locked. It was so rapid that it
gave him no time to observe. A waving of indecipherable shapes, a
blow, and a concussion. There he stood on the dark little landing,
wondering what it might be that he had seen.

A couple of minutes after, he rejoined the little group that had formed
outside the Coach and Horses. There was Fearenside telling about it all
over again for the second time; there was Mrs Hall saying his dog didn't
have no business to bite her guests; there was Huxter, the general dealer
from over the road, interrogative; and Sandy Wadgers from the forge,
judicial; besides women and children, all of them saying fatuities:
'Wouldn't let en bite *me*, I knows;' ''Tasn't right *have* such dargs;'
'Whad '*e* bite'n for then?' and so forth.

Mr Hall, staring at them from the steps and listening, found it
incredible that he had seen anything so very remarkable happen
upstairs. Besides, his vocabulary was altogether too limited to express
his impressions.

'He don't want no help, he says,' he said in answer to his wife's
inquiry. 'We'd better be a-takin' of his luggage in.'

'He ought to have it cauterised at once,' said Mr Huxter, 'especially
if it's at all inflamed.'

'I'd shoot en, that's what I'd do,' said a lady in the group.

Suddenly the dog began growling again.

'Come along,' cried an angry voice in the doorway, and there stood
the muffled stranger with his collar turned up, and his hat-brim bent
down. 'The sooner you get those things in the better I'll be pleased.' It
is stated by an anonymous bystander that his trousers and gloves had
been changed.

'Was you hurt, sir?' said Fearenside. 'I'm rare sorry the darg – '

'Not a bit,' said the stranger. 'Never broke the skin. Hurry up with
those things.'

He then swore to himself, so Mr Hall asserts.

Directly the first crate was, in accordance with his directions, carried
into the parlour, the stranger flung himself upon it with extraordinary

eagerness, and began to unpack it, scattering the straw with an utter disregard of Mrs Hall's carpet. And from it he began to produce bottles – little fat bottles containing powders, small and slender bottles containing coloured and white fluids, fluted blue bottles labelled *Poison*, bottles with round bodies and slender necks, large green-glass bottles, large white-glass bottles, bottles with glass stoppers and frosted labels, bottles with fine corks, bottles with bungs, bottles with wooden caps, wine bottles, salad-oil bottles – putting them in rows on the chiffonnier, on the mantel, on the table under the window, round the floor, on the bookshelf – everywhere. The chemist's shop in Bramblehurst could not boast half so many. Quite a sight it was. Crate after crate yielded bottles, until all six were empty and the table high with straw; the only things that came out of these crates besides the bottles were a number of test-tubes and a carefully packed balance.

And directly the crates were unpacked, the stranger went to the window and set to work, not troubling in the least about the litter of straw, the fire which had gone out, the box of books outside, nor for the trunks and other luggage that had gone upstairs.

When Mrs Hall took his dinner in to him, he was already so absorbed in his work, pouring little drops out of the bottles into test-tubes, that he did not hear her until she had swept away the bulk of the straw and put the tray on the table, with some little emphasis perhaps, seeing the state that the floor was in. Then he half turned his head and immediately turned it away again. But she saw he had removed his glasses; they were beside him on the table, and it seemed to her that his eye sockets were extraordinary hollow. He put on his spectacles again, and then turned and faced her. She ·was about to complain of the straw on the floor when he anticipated her.

'I wish you wouldn't come in without knocking,' he said in the tone of abnormal exasperation that seemed so characteristic of him.

'I knocked, but seemingly – '

'Perhaps you did. But in my investigations – my really very urgent and necessary investigations – the slightest disturbance, the jar of a door – I must ask you – '

'Certainly, sir. You can turn the lock if you're like that, you know – any time.'

'A very good idea,' said the stranger.

'This stror, sir, if I might make so bold as to remark – '

'Don't. If the straw makes trouble put it down in the bill.' And he mumbled at her – words suspiciously like curses.

He was so odd, standing there, so aggressive and explosive, bottle in one hand and test-tube in the other, that Mrs Hall was quite alarmed. But she was a resolute woman. 'In which case, I should like to know, sir, what you consider – '

'A shilling. Put down a shilling. Surely a shilling's enough?'

'So be it,' said Mrs Hall, taking up the table-cloth and beginning to spread it over the table. 'If you're satisfied, of course – '

He turned and sat down, with his coat-collar towards her.

All the afternoon he worked with the door locked and, as Mrs Hall testifies, for the most part in silence. But once there was a concussion and a sound of bottles ringing together as though the table had been hit, and the smash of a bottle flung violently down, and then a rapid pacing athwart the room. Fearing 'something was the matter,' she went to the door and listened, not caring to knock.

'I can't go on,' he was raving. 'I *can't* go on. Three hundred thousand, four hundred thousand! The huge multitude! Cheated! All my life it may take me! Patience! Patience indeed! Fool and liar!'

There was a noise of hobnails on the bricks in the bar, and Mrs Hall had very reluctantly to leave the rest of his soliloquy. When she returned the room was silent again, save for the faint crepitation of his chair and the occasional clink of a bottle. It was all over. The stranger had resumed work.

When she took in his tea she saw broken glass in the corner of the room under the concave mirror, and a golden stain that had been carelessly wiped. She called attention to it.

'Put it down in the bill,' snapped her visitor. 'For God's sake don't worry me. If there's damage done, put it down in the bill;' and he went on ticking a list in the exercise book before him.

'I'll tell you something,' said Fearenside, mysteriously. It was late in the afternoon, and they were in the little beer-shop of Iping Hanger.

'Well?' said Teddy Henfrey.

'This chap you're speaking of, what my dog bit. Well – he's black. Leastways, his legs are. I seed through the tear of his trousers and the tear of his glove. You'd have expected a sort of pinky to show, wouldn't you? Well – there wasn't none. Just blackness. I tell you, he's as black as my hat.'

'My sakes!' said Henfrey. 'It's a rummy case altogether. Why, his nose is as pink as paint!'

'That's true,' said Fearenside. 'I knows that. And I tell ee what I'm thinking. That marn's a piebald, Teddy. Black here and white there – in patches. And he's ashamed of it. He's a kind of half-breed, and the colour's come off patchy instead of mixing. I've heard of such things before. And it's the common way with horses, as any one can see.'

Mr Cuss Interviews the Stranger

I have told the circumstances of the stranger's arrival in Iping with a certain fullness of detail, in order that the curious impression he created may be understood by the reader. But excepting two odd incidents, the circumstances of his stay until the extraordinary day of the Club Festival may be passed over very cursorily. There were a number of skirmishes with Mrs Hall on matters of domestic discipline, but in every case until late in April, when the first signs of penury began, he over-rode her by the easy expedient of an extra payment. Hall did not like him, and whenever he dared he talked of the advisability of getting rid of him; but he showed his dislike chiefly by concealing it ostentatiously, and avoiding his visitor as much as possible. 'Wait till the summer,' said Mrs Hall, sagely, 'when the artisks are beginning to come. Then we'll see. He may be a bit over-bearing, but bills settled punctual is bills settled punctual, whatever you like to say.'

The stranger did not go to church, and indeed made no difference between Sunday and the irreligious days, even in costume. He worked, as Mrs Hall thought, very fitfully. Some days he would come down early and be continuously busy. On others he would rise late, pace his room, fretting audibly for hours together, smoke, sleep in the armchair by the fire. Communication with the world beyond the village he had none. His temper continued very uncertain; for the most part his manner was that of a man suffering under almost unendurable provocation, and once or twice things were snapped, torn, crushed, or broken in spasmodic gusts of violence. He seemed under a chronic irritation of the greatest intensity. His habit of talking to himself in a low voice grew steadily upon him, but though Mrs Hall listened conscientiously she could make neither head nor tail of what she heard.

He rarely went abroad by daylight, but at twilight he would go out muffled up invisibly, whether the weather were cold or not, and he chose the loneliest paths and those most over-shadowed by trees and banks. His goggling spectacles and ghastly bandaged face under the penthouse of his hat came with a disagreeable suddenness out of the darkness upon one or two home-going labourers, and Teddy Henfrey, tumbling out of the Scarlet Coat one night, at half-past nine, was scared shamefully by the stranger's skull-like head (he was walking hat in hand) lit by the sudden light of the opened inn door. Such children as saw him at nightfall dreamt of bogies, and it seemed doubtful whether he disliked boys more than they disliked him, or the reverse, but there was certainly a vivid dislike enough on either side.

It was inevitable that a person of so remarkable an appearance and bearing should form a frequent topic in such a village as Iping. Opinion was greatly divided about his occupation. Mrs Hall was sensitive on the point. When questioned, she explained very carefully that he was an 'experimental investigator', going gingerly over the syllables as one who dreads pitfalls. When asked what an experimental investigator was, she would say with a touch of superiority that most educated people knew such things as that, and would thus explain that he 'discovered things'. Her visitor had had an accident, she said, which temporarily discoloured his face and hands, and being of a sensitive disposition, he was averse to any public notice of the fact.

Out of her hearing there was a view largely entertained that he was a criminal trying to escape from justice by wrapping himself up so as to conceal himself altogether from the eye of the police. This idea sprang from the brain of Mr Teddy Henfrey. No crime of any magnitude dating from the middle or end of February was known to have occurred. Elaborated in the imagination of Mr Gould, the probationary assistant in the National School, this theory took the form that the stranger was an Anarchist in disguise, preparing explosives, and he resolved to undertake such detective operations as his time permitted. These consisted for the most part in looking very hard at the stranger whenever they met, or in asking people who had never seen the stranger, leading questions about him. But he detected nothing.

Another school of opinion followed Mr Fearenside, and either accepted the piebald view or some modiciation of it; as, for instance, Silas Durgan, who was heard to assert that 'if he choses to show enself at fairs he'd make his fortune in no time,' and being a bit of a theologian, compared the stranger to the man with the one talent. Yet another view explained the entire matter by regarding the stranger as a harmless lunatic. That had the advantage of accounting for everything straight away.

Between these main groups there were waverers and compromisers. Sussex folk have few superstitions, and it was only after the events of early April that the thought of the supernatural was first whispered in the village. Even then it was only credited among the women folks.

But whatever they thought of him, people in Iping, on the whole, agreed in disliking him. His irritability, though it might have been comprehensible to an urban brain-worker, was an amazing thing to these quiet Sussex villagers. The frantic gesticulations they surprised now and then, the headlong pace after nightfall that swept him upon them round quiet corners, the inhuman bludgeoning of all the tentative advances of curiosity, the taste for twilight that led to the closing of doors, the pulling down of blinds, the extinction of candles and lamps – who could agree with such goings on? They drew aside as he passed down the village, and when he had gone by, young humourists would up with coat-collars and down with hat-brims, and go pacing nervously after him in imitation of his occult bearing. There was a song popular at that time called the 'Bogey Man'; Miss Statchell sang it at the schoolroom concert (in aid of the church lamps), and thereafter whenever one or two of the villagers were gathered together and the stranger appeared, a bar or so of this tune, more or less sharp or flat, was whistled in the midst of them. Also belated little children would call 'Bogey Man!' after him, and make off tremulously elated.

Cuss, the general practitioner, was devoured by curiosity. The bandages excited his professional interest, the report of the thousand and one bottles aroused his jealous regard. All through April and May he coveted an opportunity of talking to the stranger, and at last, towards Whitsuntide, he could stand it no longer, but hit upon the subscription-list for a village nurse as an excuse. He was surprised to find that Mr Hall did not know his guest's name. 'He give a name,' said Mrs Hall, an assertion which was quite unfounded, 'but I didn't rightly hear it'. She thought it seemed so silly not to know the man's name.

Cuss rapped at the parlour door and entered. There was a fairly audible imprecation from within. 'Pardon my intrusion,' said Cuss, and then the door closed and cut Mrs Hall off from the rest of the conversation.

She could hear the murmur of voices for the next ten minutes, then a cry of surprise, a stirring of feet, a chair flung aside, a bark of laughter, quick steps to the door, and Cuss appeared, his face white, his eyes staring over his shoulder. He left the door open behind him, and without looking at her strode across the hall and went down the steps, and she heard his feet hurrying along the road. He carried his hat in his hand. She stood behind the door, looking at the open door of the parlour. Then she heard the stranger laughing quietly, and then his footsteps came across the room. She could not see his face where she stood. The parlour door slammed, and the place was silent again.

Cuss went straight up the village to Bunting the vicar. 'Am I mad?' Cuss began abruptly, as he entered the shabby little study. 'Do I look like an insane person?'

'What's happened?' said the vicar, putting the ammonite on the loose sheets of his forthcoming sermon.

'That chap at the inn – '

'Well?'

'Give me something to drink,' said Cuss, and he sat down.

When his nerves had been steadied by a glass of cheap sherry, the only drink the good vicar had available, he told him of the interview he had just had. 'Went in,' he gasped, 'and began to demand a subscription for that Nurse Fund. He'd stuck his hands in his pockets as I came in, and he sat down lumpily in his chair. Sniffed. I told him I'd heard he took an interest in scientific things. He said yes. Sniffed again. Kept on sniffing all the time; evidently recently caught an infernal cold. No wonder, wrapped up like that! I developed the nurse idea, and all the while kept my eyes open. Bottles – chemicals – everywhere. Balance, test-tubes in stands, and a smell of – evening primrose. Would he subscribe? Said he'd consider it. Asked him, point-blank, was he researching. Said he was. A long research? Got quite cross. "A damnable long research," said he, blowing the cork out, so to speak. "Oh," said I. And out came the grievance. The man was just on the boil, and my question boiled him over. He had been given a prescription, most valuable prescription – what for he wouldn't say. Was it medical? "Damn you! What are you fishing after?" I apologised. Dignified sniff and cough. He resumed. He'd read it. Five ingredients. Put it down; turned his head. Draught of air from window lifted the paper. Swish, rustle. He was working in a room with an open fireplace, he said. Saw a flicker, and there was the prescription burning and lifting chimney-ward. Rushed towards it just as it whisked up chimney. So! Just at that point, to illustrate his story, out came his arm.'

'Well?'

'No hand, just an empty sleeve. Lord! I thought, *that's* a deformity! Got a cork arm, I suppose, and has taken it off. Then, I thought, there's something odd in that. What the devil keeps that sleeve up and open, if there's nothing in it? There was nothing in it, I tell you. Nothing down it, right down to the joint. I could see right down it to the elbow, and there was a glimmer of light shining through a tear of the cloth. "Good God!" I said. Then he stopped. Stared at me with those black goggles of his, and then at his sleeve.'

'Well?'

'That's all. He never said a word; just glared, and put his sleeve back in his pocket quickly. "I was saying," said he, "that there was the prescription burning, wasn't I?" Interrogative cough. "How the devil," said I, "can you move an empty sleeve like that?" "Empty sleeve?" "Yes," said I, "an empty sleeve."'

'"It's an empty sleeve, is it? You saw it was an empty sleeve?" He stood up right away. I stood up too. He came towards me in three very slow steps, and stood quite close. Sniffed venomously. I didn't flinch, though I'm hanged if that bandaged knob of his, and those blinkers, aren't enough to unnerve any one, coming quietly up to you.

'"You said it was an empty sleeve?" he said. "Certainly," I said. At staring and saying nothing a barefaced man, unspectacled, starts scratch. Then very quietly he pulled his sleeve out of his pocket again, and raised his arm towards me as though he would show it to me again. He did it very, very slowly. I looked at it. Seemed an age. "Well?" said I, clearing my throat, "there's nothing in it." Had to say something. I was beginning to feel frightened. I could see right down it. He extended it straight towards me, slowly, slowly, just like that, until the cuff was six inches from my face. Queer thing to see an empty sleeve come at you like that! And then – '

'Well?'

'Something – exactly like a finger and thumb it felt – nipped my nose.'

Bunting began to laugh.

'There wasn't anything there!' said Cuss, his voice running up into a shriek at the 'there'. 'It's all very well for you to laugh, but I tell you I was so startled, I hit his cuff hard, and turned round, and cut out of the room – I left him – '

Cuss stopped. There was no mistaking the sincerity of his panic. He turned round in a helpless way and took a second glass of the excellent vicar's very inferior sherry. 'When I hit his cuff,' said Cuss, 'I tell you, it felt exactly like hitting an arm. And there wasn't an arm! There wasn't the ghost of an arm!'

Mr Bunting thought it over. He looked suspiciously at Cuss. 'It's a most remarkable story,' he said. He looked very wise and grave indeed. 'It's really,' said Mr Bunting with judicial emphasis, 'a most remarkable story.'

V

The Burglary at the Vicarage

The facts of the burglary at the vicarage came to us chiefly through the medium of the vicar and his wife. It occurred in the small hours of Whit-Monday, the day devoted in Iping to the Club festivities. Mrs Bunting, it seems, woke up suddenly in the stillness that comes before the dawn, with the strong impression that the door of their bedroom had opened and closed. She did not arouse her husband at first, but sat up in bed listening. She then distinctly heard the pad, pad, pad of bare feet coming out of the adjoining dressing-room and walking along the passage towards the staircase. As soon as she felt assured of this, she aroused the Rev. Mr Bunting as quietly as possible. He did not strike a light, but putting on his spectacles, her dressing-gown, and his bath slippers, he went out on the landing to listen. He heard quite distinctly a fumbling going on at his study desk downstairs, and then a violent sneeze.

At that he returned to his bedroom, armed himself with the most obvious weapon, the poker, and descended the staircase as noiselessly as possible. Mrs Bunting came out on the landing.

The hour was about four, and the ultimate darkness of the night was past. There was a faint shimmer of light in the hall, but the study doorway yawned impenetrably black. Everything was still except the faint creaking of the stairs under Mr Bunting's tread, and the slight movements in the study. Then something snapped, the drawer was opened, and there was a rustle of papers. Then came an imprecation, and a match was struck and the study was flooded with yellow light. Mr Bunting was now in the hall, and through the crack of the door he could see the desk and the open drawer and a candle burning on the desk. But the robber he could not see. He stood there in the hall undecided what to do, and Mrs Bunting, her face white and intent, crept slowly downstairs after him. One thing kept up Mr Bunting's courage: the persuasion that this burglar was a resident in the village.

They heard the chink of money, and realised that the robber had found the housekeeping reserve of gold, two pounds ten in half-sovereigns altogether. At that sound Mr Bunting was nerved to abrupt action. Gripping the poker firmly, he rushed into the room, closely followed by Mrs Bunting. 'Surrender!' cried Mr Bunting, fiercely, and then stopped amazed. Apparently the room was perfectly empty.

Yet their conviction that they had, that very moment, heard somebody moving in the room had amounted to a certainty. For half a minute, perhaps, they stood gaping, then Mrs Bunting went across the room and looked behind the screen, while Mr Bunting, by a kindred impulse, peered under the desk. Then Mrs Bunting turned back the window-curtains, and Mr Bunting looked up the chimney and probed it with the poker. Then Mrs Bunting scrutinised the wastepaper basket and Mr Bunting opened the lid of the coal-scuttle. Then they came to a stop and stood with eyes interrogating each other.

'I could have sworn – ' said Mr Bunting.

'The candle!' said Mr Bunting. 'Who lit the candle?'

'The drawer!' said Mrs Bunting. 'And the money's gone!'

She went hastily to the doorway.

'Of all the extraordinary occurrences – '

There was a violent sneeze in the passage. They rushed out, and as they did so the kitchen door slammed. 'Bring the candle,' said Mr Bunting, and led the way. They both heard a sound of bolts being hastily shot back.

As he opened the kitchen door he saw through the scullery that the back door was just opening, and the faint light of early dawn displayed the dark masses of the garden beyond. He is certain that nothing went out of the door. It opened, stood open for a moment, and then closed with a slam. As it did so, the candle Mrs Bunting was carrying from the study flickered and flared. It was a minute or more before they entered the kitchen.

The place was empty. They refastened the back door, examined the kitchen, pantry, and scullery thoroughly, and at last went down into the cellar. There was not a soul to be found in the house, search as they would.

Daylight found the vicar and his wife, a quaintly costumed little couple, still marvelling about on their own ground floor by the unnecessary light of a guttering candle.

VI

The Furniture That Went Mad

Now it happened that in the early hours of Whit-Monday, before Millie was hunted out for the day, Mr Hall and Mrs Hall both rose and went noiselessly down into the cellar. Their business there was of a private nature, and had something to do with the specific gravity of their beer. They had hardly entered the cellar when Mrs Hall found she had forgotten to bring down a bottle of sarsaparilla from their joint-room. As she was the expert and principal operator in this affair, Hall very properly went upstairs for it.

On the landing he was surprised to see that the stranger's door was ajar. He went on into his own room and found the bottle as he had been directed.

But returning with the bottle, he noticed that the bolts of the front door had been shot back, that the door was in fact simply on the latch. And with a flash of inspiration he connected this with the stranger's room upstairs and the suggestions of Mr Teddy Henfrey. He distinctly remembered holding the candle while Mrs Hall shot these bolts over-night. At the sight he stopped, gaping, then with the bottle still in his hand went upstairs again. He rapped at the stranger's door. There was no answer. He rapped again; then pushed the door wide open and entered.

It was as he expected. The bed, the room also, was empty. And what was stranger, even to his heavy intelligence, on the bedroom chair and along the rail of the bed were scattered the garments, the only garments so far as he knew, and the bandages of their guest. His big slouch hat even was cocked jauntily over the bed-post.

As Hall stood there he heard his wife's voice coming out of the depth of the cellar, with that rapid telescoping of the syllables and interrogative cocking up of the final words to a high note, by which the West Sussex villager is wont to indicate a brisk impatience. 'George! You gart what a wand?'

At that he turned and hurried down to her. 'Janny,' he said, over the rail of the cellar steps, "tas the truth what Henfrey sez. 'E's not in uz room, 'e ent. And the front door's unbolted.'

At first Mrs Hall did not understand, and as soon as she did she resolved to see the empty room for herself. Hall, still holding the bottle, went first. 'If 'e ent there,' he said, 'his close are. And what's 'e doin' without his close, then? 'Tas a most curious basness.'

As they came up the cellar steps, they both, it was afterwards ascertained, fancied they heard the front door open and shut, but seeing it closed and nothing there, neither said a word to the other about it at the time. Mrs Hall passed her husband in the passage and ran on first upstairs. Some one sneezed on the staircase. Hall, following six steps behind, thought that he heard her sneeze. She, going on first, was under the impression that Hall was sneezing. She flung open the door and stood regarding the room. 'Of all the curious!' she said.

She heard a sniff close behind her head as it seemed, and, turning, was surprised to see Hall a dozen feet off on the topmost stair. But in another moment he was beside her. She bent forward and put her hand on the pillow and then under the clothes.

'Cold,' she said. 'He's been up this hour or more.'

As she did so, a most extraordinary thing happened, the bed-clothes gathered themselves together, leapt up suddenly into a sort of peak, and then jumped headlong over the bottom rail. It was exactly as if a hand had clutched them in the centre and flung them aside. Immediately after, the stranger's hat hopped off the bed-post, described a whirling flight in the air through the better part of a circle, and then dashed straight at Mrs Hall's face. Then as swiftly came the sponge from the washstand; and then the chair, flinging the stranger's coat and trousers carelessly aside, and laughing drily in a voice singularly like the stranger's turned itself up with its four legs at Mrs Hall, seemed to take aim at her for a moment, and charged at her. She screamed and turned, and then the chair legs came gently but firmly against her back and impelled her and Hall out of the room. The door slammed violently and was locked. The chair and bed seemed to be executing a dance of triumph for a moment, and then abruptly everything was still.

Mrs Hall was left almost in a fainting condition in Mr Hall's arms on the landing. It was with the greatest difficulty that Mr Hall and Millie, who had been roused by her scream of alarm, succeeded in getting her downstairs, and applying the restoratives customary in these cases.

"Tas sperits,' said Mrs Hall. 'I know 'tas sperits. I've read in papers of en. Tables and chairs leaping and dancing!'

'Take a drop more, Janny,' said Hall, "Twill steady ye.'

'Lock him out,' said Mrs Hall. 'Don't let him come in again. I half guessed – I might ha' known. With them goggling eyes and bandaged head, and never going to church of a Sunday. And all they bottles – more'n it's right for any one to have. He's put the sperits into the furniture. My good old furniture! 'Twas in that very chair my poor dear mother used to sit when I was a little girl. To think it should rise up against me now!'

'Just a drop more, Janny,' said Hall. 'Your nerves is all upset.'

They sent Millie across the street through the golden five o'clock sunshine to rouse up Mr Sandy Wadgers, the blacksmith. Mr Hall's compliments and the furniture upstairs was behaving most extraordinary. Would Mr Wadgers come round? He was a knowing man, was Mr Wadgers, and very resourceful. He took quite a grave view of the case. 'Arm darmed ef thet ent witchcraft,' was the view of Mr Sandy Wadgers. 'You want horseshoes for such gentry as he.'

He came round greatly concerned. They wanted him to lead the way upstairs to the room, but he didn't seem to be in any hurry. He preferred to talk in the passage. Over the way Huxter's apprentice came out and began taking down the shutters of the tobacco window. He was called over to join the discussion. Mr Huxter naturally followed over in the course of a few minutes. The Anglo-Saxon genius for parliamentary government asserted itself; there was a great deal of talk and no decisive action. 'Let's have the facts first,' insisted Mr Sandy Wadgers. 'Let's be sure we'd be acting perfectly right in bustin' that there door open. A door onbust is always open to bustin', but ye can't onbust a door once you've busted en.'

And suddenly and most wonderfully the door of the room upstairs opened of its own accord, and as they looked up in amazement, they saw descending the stairs the muffled figure of the stranger staring more blackly and blankly than ever with those unreasonably large blue glass eyes of his. He came down stiffly and slowly, staring all the time; he walked across the passage staring, then stopped.

'Look there!' he said, and their eyes followed the direction of his gloved finger and saw a bottle of sarsaparilla hard by the cellar door. Then he entered the parlour, and suddenly, swiftly, viciously, slammed the door in their faces.

Not a word was spoken until the last echoes of the slam had died away. They stared at one another. 'Well, if that don't lick everything!' said Mr Wadgers, and left the alternative unsaid.

'I'd go in and ask'n 'bout it,' said Wadgers, to Mr Hall. 'I'd d'mand an explanation.'

It took some time to bring the landlady's husband up to that pitch. At last he rapped, opened the door, and got as far as, 'Excuse me – '

'Go to the devil!' said the stranger in a tremendous voice, and 'Shut the door after you.' So that brief interview terminated.

VII

The Unveiling of the Stranger

The stranger went into the little parlour of the Coach and Horses about
half-past five in the morning, and there he remained until near midday,
the blinds down, the door shut, and none, after Hall's repulse, venturing
near him.

All that time he must have fasted. Thrice he rang his bell, the third
time furiously and continuously, but no one answered him. 'Him and
his "go to the devil" indeed!' said Mrs Hall. Presently came an imperfect
rumour of the burglary at the vicarage, and two and two were put
together. Hall, assisted by Wadgers, went off to find Mr Shuckleforth,
the magistrate, and take his advice. No one ventured upstairs. How the
stranger occupied himself is unknown. Now and then he would stride
violently up and down, and twice came an outburst of curses, a tearing
of paper, and a violent smashing of bottles.

The little group of scared but curious people increased. Mrs Huxter
came over; some gay young fellows resplendent in black ready-made
jackets and *piqué* paper ties, for it was Whit-Monday, joined the group
with confused interrogations. Young Archie Harker distinguished himself by going up the yard and trying to peep under the window-blinds.
He could see nothing, but gave reason for supposing that he did, and
others of the Iping youth presently joined him.

It was the finest of all possible Whit-Mondays, and down the village
street stood a row of nearly a dozen booths, a shooting gallery, and on
the grass by the forge were three yellow and chocolate waggons and
some picturesque strangers of both sexes putting up a cocoanut shy.
The gentlemen wore blue jerseys, the ladies white aprons and quite
fashionable hats with heavy plumes. Woodyer, of the Purple Fawn, and
Mr Jaggers, the cobbler, who also sold second-hand ordinary bicycles,
were stretching a string of union-jacks and royal ensigns (which had
originally celebrated the Jubilee) across the road . . .

And inside, in the artificial darkness of the parlour, into which only
one thin jet of sunlight penetrated, the stranger, hungry we must
suppose, and fearful, hidden in his uncomfortable hot wrappings, pored

through his dark glasses upon his paper or chinked his dirty little bottles, and occasionally swore savagely at the boys, audible if invisible, outside the windows. In the corner by the fireplace lay the fragments of half a dozen smashed bottles, and a pungent twang of chlorine tainted the air. So much we know from what was heard at the time and from what was subsequently seen in the room.

About noon he suddenly opened his parlour door and stood glaring fixedly at the three or four people in the bar. 'Mrs Hall,' he said. Somebody went sheepishly and called for Mrs Hall.

Mrs Hall appeared after an interval, a little short of breath, but all the fiercer for that. Hall was still out. She had deliberated over this scene, and she came holding a little tray with an unsettled bill upon it. 'Is it your bill you're wanting, sir?' she said.

'Why wasn't my breakfast laid? Why haven't you prepared my meals and answered my bell? Do you think I live without eating?'

'Why isn't my bill paid?' said Mrs Hall. 'That's what I want to know.'

'I told you three days ago I was awaiting a remittance – '

'I told you two days ago I wasn't going to await no remittances. You can't grumble if your breakfast waits a bit, if my bill's been waiting these five days, can you?'

The stranger swore briefly but vividly.

'Nar, nar!' from the bar.

'And I'd thank you kindly, sir, if you'd keep your swearing to yourself, sir,' said Mrs Hall.

The stranger stood looking more like an angry diving-helmet than ever. It was universally felt in the bar that Mrs Hall had the better of him. His next words showed as much.

'Look here, my good woman – ' he began.

'Don't good woman *me*,' said Mrs Hall.

'I've told you my remittance hasn't come – '

'Remittance indeed!' said Mrs Hall.

'Still, I daresay in my pocket – '

'You told me two days ago that you hadn't anything but a sovereign's worth of silver upon you – '

'Well, I've found some more – '

''Ul-*lo*!' from the bar.

'I wonder where you found it?' said Mrs Hall.

That seemed to annoy the stranger very much. He stamped his foot. 'What do you mean?' he said.

'That I wonder where you found it,' said Mrs Hall. 'And before I take any bills or get any breakfasts, or do any such things whatsoever, you got to tell me one or two things I don't understand, and what nobody don't understand, and what everybody is very anxious to understand. I want know what you been doing t' my chair upstairs, and I want know how't is your room was empty, and how you got in again. Them as stops in this house comes in by the doors, that's the rule of the house, and that you *didn't* do, and what I want know is how you *did* come in. And I want know – '

Suddenly the stranger raised his gloved hands clenched, stamped his foot, and said, 'Stop!' with such extraordinary violence that he silenced her instantly.

'You don't understand,' he said, 'who I am or what I am. I'll show you. By Heaven! I'll show you.' Then he put his open palm over his face and withdrew it. The centre of his face became a black cavity. 'Here,' he said. He stepped forward and handed Mrs Hall something which she, staring at his metamorphosed face, accepted automatically. Then, when she saw what it was, she screamed loudly, dropped it, and staggered back. The nose – it was the stranger's nose! pink and shining – rolled on the floor.

Then he removed his spectacles, and every one in the bar gasped. He took off his hat, and with a violent gesture tore at his whiskers and bandages. For a moment they resisted him. A flash of horrible anticipation passed through the bar. 'Oh, my Gard!' said some one. Then off they came.

It was worse than anything. Mrs Hall, standing open-mouthed and horror-struck, shrieked at what she saw, and made for the door of the house. Every one began to move. They were prepared for scars, disfigurements, tangible horrors, but *nothing*! The bandages and false hair flew across the passage into the bar, making a hobbledehoy jump to avoid them. Every one tumbled on every one else down the steps. For the man who stood there shouting some incoherent explanation, was a solid gesticulating figure up to the coat-collar of him, and then – nothingness, no visible thing at all!

People down the village heard shouts and shrieks, and looking up the street saw the Coach and Horses violently firing out its humanity. They saw Mrs Hall fall down and Mr Teddy Henfrey jump to avoid tumbling over her, and then they heard the frightful screams of Millie, who, emerging suddenly from the kitchen at the noise of the tumult, had come upon the headless stranger from behind. These ceased suddenly.

Forthwith every one all down the street, the sweetstuff seller, cocoanut shy proprietor and his assistant, the swing man, little boys and girls, rustic dandies, smart wenches, smocked elders and aproned gipsies, began running towards the inn, and in a miraculously short space of time a crowd of perhaps forty people, and rapidly increasing swayed and hooted and inquired and exclaimed and suggested, in front of Mrs Hall's establishment. Every one seemed eager to talk at once, and the result was babel. A small group supported Mrs Hall, who was picked up in a state of collapse. There was a conference, and the incredible evidence of a vociferous eye-witness. 'O Bogey!' 'What's he been doin', then?' 'Ain't hurt the girl, 'as 'e?' 'Run at en with a knife, I believe.' 'No 'ed, I tell ye. I don't mean no manner of speaking, I mean *marn 'ithout a 'ed!*' 'Narnsense! 'tas some conjuring trick.' 'Fetched off 'is wrappin's, 'e did – '

In its struggles to see in through the open door, the crowd formed itself into a straggling wedge, with the more adventurous apex nearest the inn. 'He stood for a moment, I heerd the gal scream, and he turned. I saw her skirts whisk, and he went after her. Didn't take ten seconds. Back he comes with a knife in uz hand and a loaf; stood just as if he was staring. Not a moment ago. Went in that there door. I tell 'e, 'e ain't gart no 'ed 't all. You just missed en – '

There was a disturbance behind, and the speaker stopped to step aside for a little procession that was marching very resolutely towards the house, first Mr Hall, very red and determined, then Mr Bobby Jaffers, the village constable, and then the wary Mr Wadgers. They had come now armed with a warrant.

People shouted conflicting information of the recent circumstances. ''Ed or no 'ed,' said Jaffers, 'I got to 'rest en, and 'rest en I *will*.'

Mr Hall marched up the steps, marched straight to the door of the parlour and flung it open. 'Constable,' he said, 'do your duty.'

Jaffers marched in, Hall next, Wadgers last. They saw in the dim light the headless figure facing them, with a gnawed crust of bread in one gloved hand and a chunk of cheese in the other.

'That's him!' said Hall.

'What the devil's this?' came in a tone of angry expostulation from above the collar of the figure.

'You're a damned rum customer, mister,' said Mr Jaffers. 'But 'ed or no 'ed, the warrant says "body", and duty's duty – '

'Keep off!' said the figure, starting back.

Abruptly he whipped down the bread and cheese, and Mr Hall just grasped the knife on the table in time to save it. Off came the stranger's left glove and was slapped in Jaffer's face. In another moment Jaffers, cutting short some statement concerning a warrant, had gripped him by the handless wrist and caught his invisible throat. He got a sounding kick on the shin that made him shout, but he kept his grip. Hall sent the knife sliding along the table to Wadgers, who acted as goalkeeper for the offensive, so to speak, and then stepped forward as Jaffers and the stranger swayed and staggered towards him, clutching and hitting in. A chair stood in the way, and went aside with a crash as they came down together.

'Get the feet,' said Jaffers between his teeth.

Mr Hall, endeavouring to act on instructions, received a sounding kick in the ribs that disposed of him for a moment, and Mr Wadgers, seeing the decapitated stranger had rolled over and got the upper side of Jaffers, retreated towards the door, knife in hand, and so collided with Mr Huxter and the Siddermorton carter coming to the rescue of law and order. At the same moment down came three or four bottles from the chiffonnier and shot a web of pungency into the air of the room.

'I'll surrender,' cried the stranger, though he had Jaffers down, and in another moment he stood up panting, a strange figure, headless and handless, for he had pulled off his right glove now as well as his left. 'It's no good,' he said, as if sobbing for breath.

It was the strangest thing in the world to hear that voice coming as if out of empty space, but the Sussex peasants are perhaps the most matter-of-fact people under the sun. Jaffers got up also and produced a pair of handcuffs. Then he started.

'I say!' said Jaffers, brought up short by a dim realisation of the incongruity of the whole business. 'Damn it! Can't use 'em as I can see.'

The stranger ran his arm down his waistcoat, and as if by a miracle the buttons to which his empty sleeve pointed became undone. Then he said something about his shin, and stooped down. He seemed to be fumbling with his shoes and socks.

'Why!' said Huxter, suddenly, 'that's not a man at all. It's just empty clothes. Look! You can see down his collar and the linings of his clothes. I could put my arm – '

He extended his hand; it seemed to meet something in mid-air, and he drew back with a sharp exclamation. 'I wish you'd keep your fingers out of my eye,' said the aerial voice, in a tone of savage expostulation. 'The fact is, I'm all here: head, hands, legs, and all the rest of it, but it happens I'm invisible. It's a confounded nuisance, but I am. That's no reason why I should be poked to pieces by every stupid bumpkin in Iping, is it?'

The suit of clothes, now all unbuttoned and hanging loosely upon its unseen supports, stood up, arms akimbo.

Several other of the men folks had now entered the room, so that it was closely crowded. 'Invisible, eigh?' said Huxter, ignoring the stranger's abuse. 'Who ever heard the likes of that?'

'It's strange, perhaps, but it's not a crime. Why am I assaulted by a policeman in this fashion?'

'Ah! that's a different matter,' said Jaffers. 'No doubt you are a bit difficult to see in this light, but I got a warrant and it's all correct. What I'm after ain't no invisibility, it's burglary. There's a house been broken into and money took.'

'Well?'

'And circumstances certainly point – '

'Stuff and nonsense!' said the Invisible Man.

'I hope so, sir; but I've got my instructions.'

'Well,' said the stranger, 'I'll come. I'll *come*. But no handcuffs.'

'It's the regular thing,' said Jaffers.

'No handcuffs,' stipulated the stranger.

'Pardon me,' said Jaffers.

Abruptly the figure sat down, and before any one could realise what was being done, the slippers, socks, and trousers had been kicked off under the table. Then he sprang up again and flung off his coat.

'Here, stop that,' said Jaffers, suddenly realising what was happening. He gripped the waistcoat; it struggled, and the shirt slipped out of it and left it limp and empty in his hand. 'Hold him!' said Jaffers, loudly. 'Once he gets they things off – !'

'Hold him!' cried every one, and there was a rush at the fluttering white shirt which was now all that was visible of the stranger.

The shirt-sleeve planted a shrewd blow in Hall's face that stopped his open-armed advance, and sent him backward into old Toothsome the sexton, and in another moment the garment was lifted up and became convulsed and vacantly flapping about the arms, even as a shirt that is being thrust over a man's head. Jaffers clutched at it, and only helped to pull it off; he was struck in the mouth out of the air, and incontinently drew his truncheon and smote Teddy Henfrey savagely upon the crown of his head.

'Look out!' said everybody, fencing at random and hitting at nothing. 'Hold him! Shut the door! Don't let him loose! I got something! Here he is!' A perfect babel of noises they made. Everybody, it seemed, was being hit all at once, and Sandy Wadgers, knowing as ever and his wits sharpened by a frightful blow in the nose, reopened the door and led the rout. The others, following incontinently, were jammed for a moment in the corner by the doorway. The hitting continued. Phipps, the Unitarian, had a front tooth broken, and Henfrey was injured in the cartilage of his ear. Jaffers was struck under the jaw, and, turning, caught at something that intervened between him and Huxter in the mêlée, and prevented their coming together. He felt a muscular chest, and in another moment the whole mass of struggling, excited men shot out into the crowded hall.

'I got him!' shouted Jaffers, choking and reeling through them all, and wrestling with purple face and swelling veins against his unseen enemy.

Men staggered right and left as the extraordinary conflict swayed swiftly towards the house door, and went spinning down the half-dozen steps of the inn. Jaffers cried in a strangled voice, holding tight, nevertheless, and making play with his knee, spun round, and fell heavily undermost with his head on the gravel. Only then did his fingers relax.

There were excited cries of 'Hold him!' 'Invisible!' and so forth, and a young fellow, a stranger in the place whose name did not come to light, rushed in at once, caught something, missed his hold, and fell over the constable's prostrate body. Half-way across the road a woman screamed as something pushed by her; a dog, kicked apparently, yelped and ran howling into Huxter's yard, and with that the transit of the Invisible Man was accomplished. For a space people stood amazed and gesticulating, and then came Panic, and scattered them abroad through the village as a gust scatters dead leaves.

But Jaffers lay quite still, face upward and knees bent.

VIII

In Transit

The eighth chapter is exceedingly brief, and relates that Gibbins, the amateur naturalist of the district, while lying out on the spacious open downs without a soul within a couple of miles of him, as he thought, and almost dozing, heard close to him the sound as of a man coughing, sneezing, and then swearing savagely to himself; and looking, beheld nothing. Yet the voice was indisputable. It continued to swear with that breadth and variety that distinguishes the swearing of a cultivated man. It grew to a climax, diminished again, and died away in the distance, going as it seemed to him in the direction of Adderdean. It lifted to a spasmodic sneeze and ended. Gibbins had heard nothing of the morning's occurrences, but the phenomenon was so striking and disturbing that his philosophical tranquillity vanished; he got up hastily, and hurried down the steepness of the hill towards the village, as fast as he could go.

IX

Mr Thomas Marvel

You must picture Mr Thomas Marvel as a person of copious, flexible visage, a nose of cylindrical protrusion, a liquorish, ample, fluctuating mouth, and a beard of bristling eccentricity. His figure inclined to embonpoint; his short limbs accentuated this inclination. He wore a furry silk hat, and the frequent substitution of twine and shoelaces for buttons, apparent at critical points of his costume, marked a man essentially bachelor.

Mr Thomas Marvel was sitting with his feet in a ditch by the roadside over the down towards Adderdean, about a mile and a half out of Iping. His feet, save for socks of irregular open-work, were bare, his big toes were broad, and pricked like the ears of a watchful dog. In a leisurely manner – he did everything in a leisurely manner – he was contemplating trying on a pair of boots. They were the soundest boots he had come across for a long time, but too large for him; whereas the ones he had were, in dry weather, a very comfortable fit, but too thin-soled for damp. Mr Thomas Marvel hated roomy shoes, but then he hated damp. He had never properly thought out which he hated most, and it was a pleasant day, and there was nothing better to do. So he put the four shoes in a graceful group on the turf and looked at them. And seeing them there among the grass and springing agrimony, it suddenly occurred to him that both pairs were exceedingly ugly to see. He was not at all startled by a voice behind him.

'They're boots, anyhow,' said the voice.

'They are – charity boots,' said Mr Thomas Marvel, with his head on one side regarding them distastefully; 'and which is the ugliest pair in the whole blessed universe, I'm darned if I know!'

'H'm,' said the voice.

'I've worn worse, in fact. I've worn none. But none so owdacious ugly, if you'll allow the expression. I've been cadging boots – in particular – for days. Because I was sick of *them*. They're sound enough, of course. But a gentleman on tramp sees such a thundering lot of his boots. And if you'll believe me, I've raised nothing in the whole blessed

county, try as I would, but THEM. Look at 'em! And a good county
for boots, too, in a general way. But it's just my promiscuous luck. I've
got my boots in this county ten years or more. And then they treat you
like this.'

'It's a beast of a county,' said the voice. 'And pigs for people.'

'Ain't it?' said Mr Thomas Marvel. 'Lord! But them boots! It beats
it.'

He turned his head over his shoulder to the right, to look at the boots
of his interlocutor with a view to comparisons, and lo! where the boots
of his interlocutor should have been were neither legs nor boots. He
turned his head over his shoulder to the left, and there also were neither
legs nor boots. He was irradiated by the dawn of a great amazement.
'Where *are* yer?' said Mr Thomas Marvel over his shoulder and coming
on all fours. He saw a stretch of empty downs with the wind swaying
the remote green-pointed furze bushes.

'Am I drunk?' said Mr Marvel. 'Have I had visions? Was I talking to
myself? What the – '

'Don't be alarmed,' said a voice.

'None of your ventriloquising *me*,' said Mr Thomas Marvel, rising
sharply to his feet. 'Where *are* yer? Alarmed, indeed!'

'Don't be alarmed,' repeated the voice.

'*You'll* be alarmed in a minute, you silly fool,' said Mr Thomas
Marvel. 'Where *are* yer? Lemme get my mark on yer –

'Are you *buried*?' said Mr Thomas Marvel, after an interval.

There was no answer. Mr Thomas Marvel stood bootless and
amazed, his jacket nearly thrown off.

'Peewit,' said a peewit, very remote.

'Peewit, indeed!' said Mr Thomas Marvel. 'This ain't no time for
foolery.' The down was desolate, east and west, north and south; the
road, with its shallow ditches and white bordering stakes, ran smooth
and empty north and south, and, save for that peewit, the blue sky was
empty too. 'So help me,' said Mr Thomas Marvel, shuffling his coat on
to his shoulders again. 'It's the drink! I might ha' known.'

'It's not the drink,' said the voice. 'You keep your nerves steady.'

'Ow!' said Mr Marvel, and his face grew white amidst its patches.
'It's the drink,' his lips repeated noisely. He remained staring about
him, rotating slowly backwards. 'I could have *swore* I heard a voice,' he
whispered.

'Of course you did.'

'It's there again,' said Mr Marvel, closing his eyes and clapping his
hand on his brow with a tragic gesture. He was suddenly taken by the
collar and shaken violently, and left more dazed than ever. 'Don't be a
fool,' said the voice.

'I'm – off – my – blooming – chump,' said Mr Marvel. It's no good.

It's fretting about them blarsted boots. I'm off my blessed blooming chump. Or it's spirits.'

'Neither one thing nor the other,' said the voice. 'Listen!'

'Chump,' said Mr Marvel.

'One minute,' said the voice, penetratingly, tremulous with self-control.

'Well?' said Mr Thomas Marvel, with a strange feeling of having been dug in the chest by a finger.

'You think I'm just imagination? Just imagination?'

'What else *can* you be?' said Mr Thomas Marvel, rubbing the back of his neck.

'Very well,' said the voice, in a tone of relief. 'Then I'm going to throw flints at you till you think differently.'

'But where *are* yer?'

The voice made no answer. Whizz came a flint, apparently out of the air, and missed Mr Marvel's shoulder by a hair's breadth. Mr Marvel, turning, saw a flint jerk up into the air, trace a complicated path, hang for a moment, and then fling at his feet with almost invisible rapidity. He was too amazed to dodge. Whizz it came, and ricochetted from a bare toe into the ditch. Mr Thomas Marvel jumped a foot and howled aloud. Then he started to run, tripped over an unseen obstacle, and came head over heels into a sitting position.

'*Now*,' said the voice, as a third stone curved upward and hung in the air above the tramp. 'Am I imagination?'

Mr Marvel by way of reply struggled to his feet, and was immediately rolled over again. He lay quiet for a moment. 'If you struggle any more,' said the voice, 'I shall throw the flint at your head.'

'It's a fair do,' said Mr Thomas Marvel, sitting up, taking his wounded toe in hand and fixing his eye on the third missile. 'I don't understand it. Stones flinging themselves. Stones talking. Put yourself down. Rot away. I'm done.'

The third flint fell.

'It's very simple,' said the voice. 'I'm an invisible man.'

'Tell us something I don't know,' said Mr Marvel, gasping with pain. 'Where you've hid – how you do it – I *don't* know. I'm beat.'

'That's all,' said the voice. 'I'm invisible. That's what I want you to understand.'

'Any one could see that. There is no need for you to be so confounded impatient, mister. *Now* then. Give us a notion. How are you hid?'

'I'm invisible. That's the great point. And what I want you to understand is this – '

'But whereabouts?' interrupted Mr Marvel.

'Here! Six yards in front of you.'

'Oh, *come*! I ain't blind. You'll be telling me next you're just thin air. I'm not one of your ignorant tramps – '

'Yes, I am – thin air. You're looking through me.'

'What! Ain't there any stuff to you? *Vox et* – what is it? – jabber. Is it that?'

'I'm just a human being – solid, needing food and drink, needing covering too – But I'm invisible. You see? Invisible. Simple idea. Invisible.'

'What, real like?'

'Yes, real.'

'Let's have a hand of you,' said Marvel, 'if you *are* real. It won't be so darn out-of-the-way like, then – *Lord!*' he said, 'how you made me jump! – gripping me like that!'

He felt the hand that had closed round his wrist with his disengaged fingers, and his fingers went timorously up the arm, patted a muscular chest, and explored a bearded face. Marvel's face was astonishment.

'I'm dashed!' he said. 'If this don't beat cock-fighting! Most remarkable! And there I can see a rabbit clean through you, 'arf a mile away! Not a bit of you visible – except – '

He scrutinised the apparently empty space keenly. 'You 'aven't been eatin' bread and cheese?' he asked, holding the invisible arm.

'You're quite right, and it's not quite assimilated into the system.'

'Ah!' said Mr Marvel. 'Sort of ghostly, though.'

'Of course, all this isn't half so wonderful as you think.'

'It's quite wonderful enough for *my* modest wants,' said Mr Thomas Marvel. 'Howjer manage it! How the dooce is it done?'

'It's too long a story. And besides – '

'I tell you, the whole business fair beats me,' said Mr Marvel.

'What I want to say at present is this: I need help. I have come to that – I came upon you suddenly. I was wandering, mad with rage, naked, impotent. I could have murdered. And I saw you – '

'*Lord!*' said Mr Marvel.

'I came up behind you – hesitated – went on – '

Mr Marvel's expression was eloquent.

' – then stopped. "Here," I said, "is an out-cast like myself. This is the man for me." So I turned back and came to you – you. And – '

'*Lord!*' said Mr Marvel. 'But I'm all in a dizzy. May I ask – How is it? And what you may be requiring in the way of help? Invisible!'

'I want you to help me get clothes – and shelter – and then, with other things. I've left them long enough. If you won't – well! But you *will – must.*'

'Look here,' said Mr Marvel. 'I'm too flabbergasted. Don't knock me about any more. And leave me go. I must get steady a bit. And you've pretty near broken my toe. It's all so unreasonable. Empty downs, empty sky. Nothing visible for miles except the bosom of Nature. And then comes a voice. A voice out of heaven! And stones! And a fist – Lord!'

'Pull yourself together,' said the voice, 'for you have to do the job I've chosen for you.'

Mr Marvel blew out his cheeks, and his eyes were round.

'I've chosen you,' said the voice. 'You are the only man except some of those fools down there, who knows there is such a thing as an invisible man. You have to be my helper. Help me – and I will do great things for you. An invisible man is a man of power.' He stopped for a moment to sneeze violently.

'But if you betray me,' he said, 'if you fail to do as I direct you – '

He paused and tapped Mr Marvel's shoulder smartly. Mr Marvel gave a yelp of terror at the touch. '*I* don't want to betray you,' said Mr Marvel, edging away from the direction of the fingers. 'Don't you go a-thinking that, whatever you do. All I want to do is to help you – just tell me what I got to do. (Lord!) Whatever you want done, that I'm most willing to do.'

X

Mr Marvel's Visit to Iping

After the first gusty panic had spent itself Iping became argumentative. Scepticism suddenly reared its head, rather nervous scepticism, not at all assured of its back, but scepticism nevertheless. It is so much easier not to believe in an invisible man; and those who had actually seen him dissolve into air, or felt the strength of his arm, could be counted on the fingers of two hands. And of these witnesses Mr Wadgers was presently missing, having retired impregnably behind the bolts and bars of his own house, and Jaffers was lying stunned in the parlour of the Coach and Horses. Great and strange ideas transcending experience often have less effect upon men and women than smaller, more tangible considerations. Iping was gay with bunting, and everybody was in gala dress. Whit-Monday had been looked forward to for a month or more. By the afternoon even those who believed in the Unseen were beginning to resume their little amusements in a tentative fashion, on the supposition that he had quite gone away, and with the sceptics he was already a jest. But people, sceptics and believers alike, were remarkably sociable all that day.

Haysman's meadow was gay with a tent, in which Mrs Bunting and the other ladies were preparing tea, while, without, the Sunday-school children ran races and played games under the noisy guidance of the curate and the Misses Cuss and Sackbut. No doubt there was a slight uneasiness in the air, but people for the most part had the sense to conceal whatever imaginative qualms they experienced. On the village green an inclined string, down which, clinging to a pulley-swung handle, one could be hurled violently against a sack at the other end, came in for considerable favour among the adolescent, as also did the swings and the cocoanut shies. There was also promenading, and the steam organ attached to the swings filled the air with a pungent flavour of oil and with equally pungent music. Members of the Club, who had attended church in the morning, were splendid in badges of pink and green, and some of the gayer-minded had also adorned their bowler hats with brilliant-coloured favours of ribbon. Old Fletcher, whose conceptions of holiday-making were severe, was visible through the jasmine about his window or through the open door (whichever way you chose to look), poised delicately on a plank supported on two chairs, and whitewashing the ceiling of his front room.

About four o'clock a stranger entered the village from the direction of the downs. He was a short, stout person in an extraordinary shabby top hat, and he appeared to be very much out of breath. His cheeks were alternately limp and tightly puffed. His mottled face was apprehensive, and he moved with a sort of reluctant alacrity. He turned the corner by the church, and directed his way to the Coach and Horses. Among others old Fletcher remembers seeing him, and indeed the old gentleman was so struck by his peculiar agitation that he inadvertently allowed a quantity of whitewash to run down the brush into the sleeve of his coat while regarding him.

This stranger, to the perceptions of the proprietor of the cocoanut shy, appeared to be talking to himself, and Mr Huxter remarked the same thing. He stopped at the foot of the Coach and Horses steps, and, according to Mr Huxter, appeared to undergo a severe internal struggle before he could induce himself to enter the house. Finally he marched up the steps, and was seen by Mr Huxter to turn to the left and open the door of the parlour. Mr Huxter heard voices from within the room and from the bar apprising the man of his error. 'That room's private!' said Hall, and the stranger shut the door clumsily and went into the bar.

In the course of a few minutes he reappeared, wiping his lips with the back of his hand with an air of quiet satisfaction that somehow impressed Mr Huxter as assumed. He stood looking about him for some moments, and then Mr Huxter saw him walk in an oddly furtive manner towards the gates of the yard, upon which the parlour window opened. The stranger, after some hesitation, leant against one of the gate-posts, produced a short clay pipe, and prepared to fill it. His fingers trembled while doing so. He lit it clumsily, and folding his arms began to smoke in a languid attitude, an attitude which his occasional quick glances up the yard altogether belied.

All this Mr Huxter saw over the canisters of the tobacco window, and the singularity of the man's behaviour prompted him to maintain his observation.

Presently the stranger stood up abruptly and put his pipe in his pocket. Then he vanished into the yard. Forthwith Mr Huxter, conceiving he was witness of some petty larceny, leapt round his counter and ran out into the road to intercept the thief. As he did so, Mr Marvel reappeared, his hat askew, a big bundle in a blue table-cloth in one hand, and three books tied together – as it proved afterwards with the Vicar's braces – in the other. Directly he saw Huxter he gave a sort of gasp, and turning sharply to the left, began to run. 'Stop thief!' cried

Huxter, and set off after him. Mr Huxter's sensations were vivid but brief. He saw the man just before him and spurting briskly for the church corner and the hill road. He saw the village flags and festivities beyond, and a face or so turned towards him. He bawled, 'Stop!' again. He had hardly gone ten strides before his shin was caught in some mysterious fashion, and he was no longer running, but flying with inconceivable rapidity through the air. He saw the ground suddenly close to his face. The world seemed to splash into a million whirling specks of light, and subsequent proceedings interested him no more.

XI

In the Coach and Horses

Now in order clearly to understand what had happened in the inn, it is necessary to go back to the moment when Mr Marvel first came into view of Mr Huxter's window. At that precise moment Mr Cuss and Mr Bunting were in the parlour. They were seriously investigating the strange occurrences of the morning, and were, with Mr Hall's permission, making a thorough examination of the Invisible Man's belongings. Jaffers had partially recovered from his fall and had gone home in the charge of his sympathetic friends. The stranger's scattered garments had been removed by Mrs Hall and the room tidied up. And on the table under the window where the stranger had been wont to work, Cuss had hit almost at once on three big books in manuscript labelled 'Diary'.

'Diary!' said Cuss, putting the three books on the table. 'Now, at any rate, we shall learn something.' The Vicar stood with his hands on the table.

'Diary,' repeated Cuss, sitting down, putting two volumes to support the third, and opening it. 'H'm – no name on the fly-leaf. Bother! cypher. And figures.'

The Vicar came round to look over his shoulder.

Cuss turned the pages over with a face suddenly disappointed. 'I'm – dear me! It's all cypher, Bunting.'

'There are no diagrams?' asked Mr Bunting. 'No illustrations throwing light – '

'See for yourself,' said Mr Cuss. 'Some of it's mathematical and some of it's Russian or some such language (to judge by the letters), and some of it's Greek. Now the Greek I thought *you* – '

'Of course,' said Mr Bunting, taking out and wiping his spectacles and feeling suddenly very uncomfortable, for he had no Greek left in his mind worth talking about; 'yes – the Greek, of course, may furnish a clue.'

'I'll find you a place.'

'I'd rather glance through the volumes first,' said Mr Bunting, still wiping. 'A general impression first, Cuss, and *then*, you know, we can go looking for clues.'

He coughed, put on his glasses, arranged them fastidiously, coughed again, and wished something would happen to avert the seemingly inevitable exposure. Then he took the volume Cuss handed him in a leisurely manner. And then something did happen.

The door opened suddenly.

Both gentlemen started violently, looked round, and were relieved to see a sporadically rosy face beneath a furry silk hat. 'Tap?' asked the face, and stood staring.

'No,' said both gentlemen at once.

'Over the other side, my man,' said Mr Bunting. And 'Please shut that door,' said Mr Cuss, irritably.

'All right,' said the intruder, as it seemed, in a low voice curiously different from the huskiness of its first inquiry. 'Right you are,' said the intruder in the former voice. 'Stand clear!' and he vanished and closed the door.

'A sailor, I should judge,' said Mr Bunting. 'Amusing fellows, they are. Stand clear! indeed. A nautical term, referring to his getting back out of the room, I suppose.'

'I daresay so,' said Cuss. 'My nerves are all loose today. It quite made me jump – the door opening like that.'

Mr Bunting smiled as if he had not jumped. 'And now,' he said with a sigh, 'these books.'

'One minute,' said Cuss, and went and locked the door. 'Now I think we are safe from interruption.'

Someone sniffed as he did so.

'One thing is indisputable,' said Bunting, drawing up a chair next to that of Cuss. 'There certainly have been very strange things happen in Iping during the last few days – very strange. I cannot of course believe in this absurd invisibility story – '

'It's incredible,' said Cuss,' – incredible. But the fact remains that I saw – I certainly saw right down his sleeve – '

'But did you – are you sure? Suppose a mirror, for instance – hallucinations are so easily produced. I don't know if you have ever seen a really good conjuror – '

'I won't argue again,' said Cuss. 'We've thrashed that out, Bunting. And just now there's these books – Ah! here's some of what I take to be Greek! Greek letters certainly.'

He pointed to the middle of the page. Mr Bunting flushed slightly and brought his face nearer, apparently finding some difficulty with his glasses. Suddenly he became aware of a strange feeling at the nape of his neck. He tried to raise his head, and encountered an immovable resistance. The feeling was a curious pressure, the grip of a heavy, firm hand, and it bore his chin irresistibly to the table. '*Don't move, little men*,' whispered a voice, '*or I'll brain you both!*' He looked into the face of Cuss, close to his own, and each saw a horrified reflection of his own sickly astonishment.

'I'm sorry to handle you roughly,' said the Voice, 'but it's unavoidable.

'Since when did you learn to pry into an investigator's private memoranda?' said the Voice; and two chins struck the table simultaneously, and two sets of teeth rattled.

'Since when did you learn to invade the private rooms of a man in misfortune?' and the concussion was repeated.

'Where have they put my clothes?

'Listen,' said the Voice. 'The windows are fastened and I've taken the key out of the door. I am a fairly strong man, and I have the poker handy – besides being invisible. There's not the slightest doubt that I could kill you both and get away quite easily if I wanted to – do you understand? Very well. If I let you go will you promise not to try any nonsense and do what I tell you?'

The Vicar and the Doctor looked at one another, and the Doctor pulled a face. 'Yes,' said Mr Bunting, and the Doctor repeated it. Then the pressure on the necks relaxed, and the Doctor and the Vicar sat up, both very red in the face and wriggling their heads.

'Please keep sitting where you are,' said the Invisible Man. 'Here's the poker, you see.

'When I came into this room,' continued the Invisible Man, after presenting the poker to the tip of the nose of each of his visitors, 'I did not expect to find it occupied, and I expected to find, in addition to my books of memoranda, an outfit of clothing. Where is it? No, don't rise. I can see it's gone. Now, just at present, though the days are quite warm enough for an invisible man to run about stark, the evenings are chilly. I want clothing – and other accommodation; and I must also have those three books.'

XII

The Invisible Man Loses His Temper

It is unavoidable that at this point the narrative should break off again, for a certain very painful reason that will presently be apparent. And while these things were going on in the parlour, and while Mr Huxter was watching Mr Marvel smoking his pipe against the gate, not a dozen yards away were Mr Hall and Teddy Henfrey discussing in a state of cloudy puzzlement the one Iping topic.

Suddenly there came a violent thud against the door of the parlour, a sharp cry, and then – silence.

'*Hul*-lo!' said Teddy Henfrey.

'Hul-*lo*!' from the Tap.

Mr Hall took things in slowly but surely. 'That ain't right,' he said, and came round from behind the bar towards the parlour door.

He and Teddy approached the door together, with intent faces. Their eyes considered. 'Summat wrong,' said Hall, and Henfrey nodded agreement. Whiffs of an unpleasant chemical odour met them, and there was a muffled sound of conversation, very rapid and subdued.

'You all raight thur?' asked Hall, rapping.

The muttered conversation ceased abruptly, for a moment silence, then the conversation was resumed, in hissing whispers, then a sharp cry of 'No! no, you don't!' There came a sudden motion and the oversetting of a chair, a brief struggle. Silence again.

'What the dooce?' exclaimed Henfrey, *sotto voce*.

'You – all – raight – thur?' asked Mr Hall, sharply, again.

The Vicar's voice answered with a curious jerking intonation: 'Quite ri – ight. Please don't – interrupt.'

'Odd!' said Mr Henfrey.

'Odd!' said Mr Hall.

'Says, "Don't interrupt,"' said Henfrey.

'I heerd'n,' said Hall.

'And a sniff,' said Henfrey.

They remained listening. The conversation was rapid and subdued. 'I *can't*,' said Mr Bunting, his voice rising; 'I tell you, sir, I *will* not.'

'What was that?' asked Henfrey.

'Says he wi' nart,' said Hall. 'Warn't speakin' to us, wuz he?'

'Disgraceful!' said Mr Bunting, within.

'"Disgraceful,"' said Mr Henfrey. 'I heard it – *distinct*.

'Who's that speaking now?' asked Henfrey.

'Mr Cuss, I s'pose,' said Hall. 'Can you hear – anything?'

Silence. The sounds within indistinct and perplexing.

'Sounds like throwing the table-cloth about,' said Hall.

Mrs Hall appeared behind the bar. Hall made gestures of silence and invitation. This roused Mrs Hall's wifely opposition. 'What yer listenin' there for, Hall?' she asked. 'Ain't you nothin' better to do – busy day like this?'

Hall tried to convey everything by grimaces and dumb show, but Mrs Hall was obdurate. She raised her voice. So Hall and Henfrey, rather crestfallen, tiptoed back to the bar, gesticulating to explain to her.

At first she refused to see anything in what they had heard at all. Then she insisted on Hall keeping silence, while Henfrey told her his story. She was inclined to think the whole business nonsense – perhaps they were just moving the furniture about. 'I heerd'n say "disgraceful"; *that* I did,' said Hall.

'*I* heerd that, Mis' Hall,' said Henfrey.

'Like as not – ' began Mrs Hall.

'Hsh!' said Mr Teddy Henfrey. 'Didn't I hear the window?'

'What window?' asked Mrs Hall.

'Parlour window,' said Henfrey.

Everyone stood listening intently. Mrs Hall's eyes, directed straight before her, saw without seeing the brilliant oblong of the inn door, the road white and vivid, and Huxter's shop front blistering in the June sun. Abruptly Huxter's door opened and Huxter appeared, eyes staring with excitement, arms gesticulating. '*Yap!* cried Huxter. 'Stop thief!' and he ran obliquely across the oblong towards the yard gates, and vanished.

Simultaneously came a tumult from the parlour, and a sound of windows being closed.

Hall, Henfrey, and the human contents of the Tap rushed out at once pell-mell into the street. They saw some one whisk round the corner towards the down road, and Mr Huxter executing a complicated leap in the air that ended on his face and shoulder. Down the street people were standing astonished or running towards them.

Mr Huxter was stunned. Henfrey stopped to discover this, but Hall and the two labourers from the Tap rushed at once to the corner, shouting incoherent things, and saw Mr Marvel vanishing by the corner of the church wall. They appear to have jumped to the impossible conclusion that this was the Invisible Man suddenly become visible, and set off at once along the lane in pursuit. But Hall had hardly run a dozen yards before he gave a loud shout of astonishment and went flying headlong sideways, clutching one of the labourers and bringing him to the ground. He had been charged just as one charges a man at football. The second labourer came round in a circle, stared, and conceiving that Hall had tumbled over of his own accord, turned to resume the pursuit, only to be tripped by the ankle just as Huxter had been. Then, as the first labourer struggled to his feet, he was kicked sideways by a blow that might have felled an ox.

As he went down, the rush from the direction of the village green came round the corner. The first to appear was the proprietor of the cocoanut shy, a burly man in a blue jersey. He was astonished to see the lane empty save for three men sprawling absurdly on the ground. And then something happened to his rear-most foot, and he went headlong and rolled sideways just in time to graze the feet of his brother and partner, following headlong. The two were then kicked, knelt on, fallen over, and cursed by quite a number of over-hasty people.

Now when Hall and Henfrey and the labourers ran out of the house, Mrs Hall, who had been dsciplined by years of experience, remained in the bar next the till. And suddenly the parlour door was opened, and Mr Cuss appeared, and without glancing at her rushed at once down the steps towards the corner. 'Hold him!' he cried. 'Don't let him drop that parcel! You can see him so long as he holds the parcel.' He knew nothing of the existence of Marvel. For the Invisible Man had handed over the books and bundle in the yard. The face of Mr Cuss was angry and resolute, but his costume was defective, a sort of limp white kilt that could only have passed muster in Greece. 'Hold him!' he bawled. 'He's got my trousers! And every stitch of the Vicar's clothes!'

''Tend to him in a minute!' he cried to Henfrey as he passed the prostrate Huxter, and coming round the corner to join the tumult, was promptly knocked off his feet into an indecorous sprawl. Somebody in full flight trod heavily on his finger. He yelled, struggled to regain his feet, was knocked against and thrown on all fours again, and became aware that he was involved not in a capture, but a rout. Everyone was running back to the village. He rose again and was hit severely behind the ear. He staggered and set off back to the Coach and Horses forthwith, leaping over the deserted Huxter, who was now sitting up, on his way.

Behind him as he was halfway up the inn steps he heard a sudden yell of rage, rising sharply out of the confusion of cries, and a sounding smack in someone's face. He recognised the voice as that of the Invisible Man, and the note was that of a man suddenly infuriated by a painful blow.

In another moment Mr Cuss was back in the parlour. 'He's coming back, Bunting!' he said, rushing in. 'Save yourself! He's gone mad!'

Mr Bunting was standing in the window engaged in an attempt to clothe himself in the hearth-rug and a West Sussex Gazette. 'Who's coming?' he said, so startled that his costume narrowly escaped disintegration.

'Invisible Man,' said Cuss, and rushed to the window. 'We'd better clear out from here! He's fighting mad! Mad!'

In another moment he was out in the yard.

'Good heavens!' said Mr Bunting, hesitating between two horrible alternatives. He heard a frightful struggle in the passage of the inn, and his decision was made. He clambered out of the window, adjusted his costume hastily, and fled up the village as fast as his fat little legs would carry him.

From the moment when the Invisible Man screamed with rage and Mr Bunting made his memorable flight up the village, it became impossible to give a consecutive account of affairs in Iping. Possibly the Invisible Man's original intention was simply to cover Marvel's retreat with the clothes and books. But his temper, at no time very good, seems to have gone completely at some chance blow, and forthwith he set to smiting and overthrowing, for the mere satisfaction of hurting.

You must figure the street full of running figures, of doors slamming and fights for hiding-places. You must figure the tumult suddenly striking on the unstable equilibrium of old Fletcher's planks and two chairs, with cataclysmal results. You must figure an appalled couple caught dismally in a swing. And then the whole tumultuous rush has passed and the Iping street with its gauds and flags is deserted save for the still raging Unseen, and littered with cocoanuts, overthrown canvas screens, and the scattered stock in trade of a sweetstuff stall. Everywhere there is a sound of closing shutters and shoving bolts, and the only visible humanity is an occasional flitting eye under a raised eyebrow in the corner of a window pane.

The Invisible Man amused himself for a little while by breaking all the windows in the Coach and Horses, and then he thrust a street lamp through the parlour window of Mrs Gribble. He it must have been who cut the telegraph wire to Adderdean just beyond Higgins' cottage on the Adderdean road. And after that, as his peculiar qualities allowed, he passed out of human perceptions altogether, and he was neither heard, seen, nor felt in Iping any more. He vanished absolutely.

But it was the best part of two hours before any human being ventured out again into the desolation of Iping street.

XIII

Mr Marvel Discusses His Resignation

When the dusk was gathering and Iping was just beginning to peep timorously forth again upon the shattered wreckage of its Bank Holiday, a short, thickset man in a shabby silk hat was marching painfully through the twilight behind the beechwoods on the road to Bramblehurst. He carried three books bound together by some sort of ornamental elastic ligature, and a bundle wrapped in a blue table-cloth. His rubicund face expressed consternation and fatigue; he appeared to be in a spasmodic sort of hurry. He was accompanied by a Voice other than his own, and ever and again he winced under the touch of unseen hands.

'If you give me the slip again,' said the Voice; 'if you attempt to give me the slip again – '

'Lord!' said Mr Marvel. 'That shoulder's a mass of bruises as it is.'

' – on my honour,' said the Voice, 'I will kill you.'

'I didn't try to give you the slip,' said Marvel, in a voice that was not far remote from tears. 'I swear I didn't. I didn't know the blessed turning, that was all! How the devil was I to know the blessed turning? As it is, I've been knocked about – '

'You'll get knocked about a great deal more if you don't mind,' said the Voice, and Mr Marvel abruptly became silent. He blew out his cheeks, and his eyes were eloquent of despair.

'It's bad enough to let these floundering yokels explode my little secret, without *your* cutting off with my books. It's lucky for some of them they cut and ran when they did! Here am I – No one knew I was invisible! And now what am I to do?'

'What am *I* to do?' asked Marvel, *sotto voce*.

'It's all about. It will be in the papers! Everybody will be looking for me; everyone on their guard – ' The Voice broke off into vivid curses and ceased.

The despair of Mr Marvel's face deepened, and his pace slacked.

'Go on!' said the Voice.

Mr Marvel's face assumed a greyish tint between the ruddier patches.

'Don't drop those books, stupid,' said the Voice sharply – overtaking him.

'The fact is,' said the Voice, 'I shall have to make use of you. You're a poor tool, but I must.'

'I'm a *miserable* tool,' said Marvel.

'You are,' said the Voice.

'I'm the worst possible tool you could have,' said Marvel.

'I'm not strong,' he said after a discouraging silence.

'I'm not over strong,' he repeated.

'No?'

'And my heart's weak. That little business – I pulled it through, of course – but bless you! I could have dropped.'

'Well?'

'I haven't the nerve and strength for the sort of thing you want.'

'*I'll* stimulate you.'

'I wish you wouldn't. I wouldn't like to mess up your plans, you know. But I might, out of sheer funk and misery.'

'You'd better not,' said the Voice, with quiet emphasis.

'I wish I was dead,' said Marvel.

'It ain't justice,' he said; 'you must admit – It seems to me I've a perfect right – '

'*Get* on!' said the Voice.

Mr Marvel mended his pace, and for a time they went in silence again.

'It's devilish hard,' said Mr Marvel.

This was quite ineffectual. He tried another tack.

'What do I make by it?' he began again in a tone of unendurable wrong.

'Oh! *shut up*!' said the Voice, with sudden amazing vigour. 'I'll see to you all right. You do what you're told. You'll do it all right. You're a fool and all that, but you'll do – '

'I tell you, sir, I'm not the man for it. Respectfully – but it is so – '

'If you don't shut up I shall twist your wrist again,' said the Invisible Man. 'I want to think.'

Presently two oblongs of yellow light appeared through the trees, and the square tower of a church loomed through the gloaming. 'I shall keep my hand on your shoulder,' said the Voice, 'all through the village. Go straight through and try no foolery. It will be the worse for you if you do.'

'I know that,' sighed Mr Marvel, 'I know all that.'

The unhappy-looking figure in the obsolete silk hat passed up the street of the little village with his burdens, and vanished into the gathering darkness beyond the lights of the windows.

XIV

At Port Stowe

Ten o'clock the next morning found Mr Marvel, unshaven, dirty, and travel-stained, sitting with the books beside him and his hands deep in his pockets, looking very weary, nervous, and uncomfortable, and inflating his cheeks at frequent intervals, on the bench outside a little inn on the outskirts of Port Stowe. Beside him were the books, but now they were tied with string. The bundle had been abandoned in the pine woods beyond Bramblehurst, in accordance with a change in the plans of the Invisible Man. Mr Marvel sat on the bench, and although no one took the slightest notice of him, his agitation remained at fever heat. His hands would go ever and again to his various pockets with a curious nervous fumbling.

When he had been sitting for the best part of an hour, however, an elderly mariner, carrying a newspaper, came out of the inn and sat down beside him. 'Pleasant day,' said the mariner.

Mr Marvel glanced about him with something very like terror. 'Very,' he said.

'Just seasonable weather for the time of year,' said the mariner, taking no denial.

'Quite,' said Mr Marvel.

The mariner produced a toothpick and (saving his regard) was engrossed thereby for some minutes. His eyes meanwhile were at liberty to examine Mr Marvel's dusty figure, and the books beside him. As he had approached Mr Marvel he had heard a sound like the dropping of coins into a pocket. He was struck by the contrast of Mr Marvel's appearance with this suggestion of opulence. Thence his mind wandered back again to a topic that had taken a curiously firm hold of his imagination.

'Books?' he said suddenly, noisily finishing with the toothpick.

Mr Marvel started and looked at them. 'Oh, yes,' he said. 'Yes, they're books.'

'There's some ex-traordinary things in books,' said the mariner.

'I believe you,' said Mr Marvel.

'And some extra-ordinary things out of 'em,' said the mariner.

'True likewise,' said Mr Marvel. He eyed his interlocutor, and then glanced about him.

'There's some extraordinary things in newspapers, for example,' said the mariner.

'There are.'

'In *this* newspaper,' said the mariner.

'Ah!' said Mr Marvel.

'There's a story,' said the mariner, fixing Mr Marvel with an eye that was firm and deliberate; 'there's a story about an Invisible Man, for instance.'

Mr Marvel pulled his mouth askew and scratched his cheek and felt his ears glowing. 'What will they be writing next?' he asked faintly. 'Ostria, or America?'

'Neither,' said the mariner. '*Here*!'

'Lord!' said Mr Marvel, starting.

'When I say *here*,' said the mariner, to Mr Marvel's intense relief, 'I don't of course mean here in this place, I mean hereabouts.'

'An Invisible Man!' said Mr Marvel. 'And what's *he* been up to?'

'Everything,' said the mariner, controlling Marvel with his eye, and then amplifying: 'Every Blessed Thing.'

'I ain't seen a paper these four days,' said Marvel.

'Iping's the place he started at,' said the mariner.

'In-*deed*!' said Mr Marvel.

'He started there. And where he came from, nobody don't seem to know. Here it is: Pe Culiar Story from Iping. And it says in this paper that the evidence is extraordinary strong – extra-ordinary.'

'Lord!' said Mr Marvel.

'But then, it's a extra-ordinary story. There is a clergyman and a medical gent witnesses – saw 'im all right and proper – or leastways, didn't see 'im. He was staying, it says, at the Coach an' Horses, and no one don't seem to have been aware of his misfortune, it says, aware of his misfortune, until in an Alteration in the inn, it says, his bandages on his head was torn off. It was then ob-served that his head was invisible. Attempts were At Once made to secure him, but casting off his garments it says, he succeeded in escaping, but not until after a desperate struggle, In Which he had inflicted serious injuries, it says, on our worthy and able constable, Mr J. A. Jaffers. Pretty straight story, eigh? Names and everything.'

'Lord!' said Mr Marvel, looking nervously about him, trying to count the money in his pockets by his unaided sense of touch, and full of a strange and novel idea. 'It sounds most astonishing.'

'Don't it? Extra-ordinary, *I* call it. Never heard tell of Invisible Men before, I haven't, but nowadays one hears such a lot of extra-ordinary things – that – '

'That all he did?' asked Marvel, trying to seem at his ease.

'It's enough, ain't it?' said the mariner.

'Didn't go Back by any chance?' asked Marvel. 'Just escaped and that's all, eh?'

'All!' said the mariner. 'Why! ain't it enough?'

'Quite enough,' said Marvel.

'I should think it was enough,' said the mariner. 'I should think it was enough.'

'He didn't have any pals – it don't say he had any pals, does it?' asked Mr Marvel, anxious.

'Ain't one of a sort enough for you?' asked the Mariner. 'No, thank Heaven, as one might say, he didn't.'

He nodded his head slowly. 'It makes me regular uncomfortable, the bare thought of that chap running about the country! He is at present At Large, and from certain evidence it is supposed that he has – taken – *took*, I suppose they mean – the road to Port Stowe. You see we're right *in* it! None of your American wonders, this time. And just think of the things he might do! Where'd you be, if he took a drop over and above, and had a fancy to go for you? Suppose he wants to rob – who can prevent him? He can trespass, he can burgle, he could walk through a cordon of policemen as easy as me or you could give the slip to a blind man! Easier! For these here blind chaps hear uncommon sharp, I'm told. And wherever there was liquor he fancied – '

'He's got a tremenjous advantage, certainly,' said Mr Marvel. 'And – well.'

'You're right,' said the Mariner. 'He *has*.'

All this time Mr Marvel had been glancing about him intently, listening for faint footfalls, trying to detect imperceptible movements. He seemed on the point of some great resolution. He coughed behind his hand.

He looked about him again, listened, bent towards the Mariner, and lowered his voice: 'The fact of it is – I happen – to know just a thing or two about this Invisible Man. From private sources.'

'Oh!' said the Mariner, interested. '*You?*'

'Yes,' said Mr Marvel. 'Me.'

'Indeed!' said the Mariner. 'And may I ask – '

'You'll be astonished,' said Mr Marvel behind his hand. 'It's tremenjous.'

'Indeed!' said the Mariner.

'The fact is,' began Mr Marvel eagerly in a confidential undertone. Suddenly his expression changed marvellously. 'Ow!' he said. He rose stiffly in his seat. His face was eloquent of physical suffering. 'Wow!' he said.

'What's up?' said the Mariner, concerned.

'Toothache,' said Mr Marvel, and put his hand to his ear. He caught hold of his books. 'I must be getting on, I think,' he said. He edged in a curious way along the seat away from his interlocutor. 'But you was just agoing to tell me about this here Invisible Man!' protested the Mariner. Mr Marvel seemed to consult with himself. 'Hoax,' said a voice. 'It's a hoax,' said Mr Marvel.

'But it's in the paper,' said the Mariner.

'Hoax all the same,' said Marvel. 'I know the chap that started the lie. There ain't no Invisible Man whatsoever – Blimey.'

'But how 'bout this paper? D'you mean to say – ?'

'Not a word of it,' said Marvel stoutly.

The Mariner stared, paper in hand. Mr Marvel jerkily faced about. 'Wait a bit,' said the Mariner, rising and speaking slowly. 'D'you mean to say – ?'

'I do,' said Mr Marvel.

'Then why did you let me go on and tell you all this blarsted stuff, then? What d'yer mean by letting a man make a fool of himself like that for? Eigh?'

Mr Marvel blew out his cheeks. The Mariner was suddenly very red indeed; he clenched his hands. 'I been talking here this ten minutes,' he said; 'and you, you little pot-bellied, leathery-faced son of an old boot, couldn't have the elementary manners – '

'Don't you come bandying words with *me*,' said Mr Marvel.

'Bandying words! I'm a jolly good mind – '

'Come up,' said a voice, and Mr Marvel was suddenly whirled about and started marching off in a curious spasmodic manner. 'You'd better move on,' said the Mariner. '*Who's* moving on?' said Mr Marvel. He was receding obliquely with a curious hurrying gait, with occasional violent jerks forward. Some way along the road he began a muttered monologue, protests and recriminations.

'Silly devil!' said the Mariner, legs wide apart, elbows akimbo, watching the receding figure. 'I'll show you, you silly ass, hoaxing *me*! It's here – on the paper!'

Mr Marvel retorted incoherently and, receding, was hidden by a bend in the road, but the Mariner still stood magnificent in the midst of the way, until the approach of a butcher's cart dislodged him. Then he turned himself towards Port Stowe. 'Full of extra-ordinary asses,' he said softly to himself. 'Just to take me down a bit – that was his silly game – It's on the paper!'

And there was another extraordinary thing he was presently to hear, that had happened quite close to him. And that was a vision of a 'fistful of money' (no less) travelling without visible agency, along by the wall at the corner of St Michael's Lane. A brother mariner had seen this wonderful sight that very morning. He had snatched at the money forthwith and had been knocked headlong, and when he had got to his feet the butterfly money had vanished. Our mariner was in the mood to believe anything, he declared, but that was a bit *too* stiff. Afterwards, however, he began to think things over.

The story of the flying money was true. And all about that neighbourhood, even from the august London and Country Banking Company, from the tills of shops and inns – doors standing that sunny weather entirely open – money had been quietly and dexterously making off that day in handfuls and rouleaux, floating quietly along by walls and shady places, dodging quickly from the approaching eyes of men. And it had, though no man had traced it, invariably ended its mysterious flight in the pocket of that agitated gentleman in the obsolete silk hat, sitting outside the little inn on the outskirts of Port Stowe.

XV

The Man Who Was Running

In the early evening time Doctor Kemp was sitting in his study in the belvedere on the hill overlooking Burdock. It was a pleasant little room, with three windows, north, west, and south, and bookshelves covered with books and scientific publications, and a broad writing-table, and, under the north window, a microscope, glass slips, minute instruments, some cultures, and scattered bottles of reagents. Doctor Kemp's solar lamp was lit, albeit the sky was still bright with the sunset light, and his blinds were up because there was no offence of peering outsiders to require them pulled down. Doctor Kemp was a tall and slender young man, with flaxen hair and a moustache almost white, and the work he was upon would earn him, he hoped, the fellowship of the Royal Society, so highly did he think of it.

And his eye presently wandering from his work caught the sunset blazing at the back of the hill that is over against his own. For a minute perhaps he sat, pen in mouth, admiring the rich golden colour above the crest, and then his attention was attracted by the little figure of a man, inky black, running over the hill-brow towards him. He was a shortish little man, and he wore a high hat, and he was running so fast that his legs verily twinkled.

'Another of those fools,' said Doctor Kemp. 'Like that ass who ran into me this morning round a corner, with his "'Visible Man a-coming, sir!" I can't imagine what possesses people. One might think we were in the thirteenth century.'

He got up, went to the window, and stared at the dusky hillside, and the dark little figure tearing down it. 'He seems in a confounded hurry,' said Doctor Kemp, 'but he doesn't seem to be getting on. If his pockets were full of lead, he couldn't run heavier.'

'Spurted, sir,' said Doctor Kemp.

In another moment the higher of the villas that had clambered up the hill from Burdock had occulted the running figure. He was visible again for a moment, and again, and then again, three times between the three detached houses that came next, and the terrace hid him.

'Asses!' said Doctor Kemp, swinging round on his heel and walking back to his writing-table.

But those who saw the fugitive nearer, and perceived the abject terror on his perspiring face, being themselves in the open roadway, did not share in the doctor's contempt. By the man pounded, and as he ran he chinked like a well-filled purse that is tossed to and fro. He looked neither to the right nor the left, but his dilated eyes stared straight downhill to where the lamps were being lit, and the people were crowded in the street. And his ill-shaped mouth fell apart, and a glairy foam lay on his lips, and his breath came hoarse and noisy. All he passed stopped and began staring up the road and down, and interrogating one another with an inkling of discomfort for the reason of his haste.

And then presently, far up the hill, a dog playing in the road yelped and ran under a gate, and as they still wondered something – a wind – a pad, pad, pad, a sound like a panting breathing, rushed by.

People screamed. People sprang off the pavement. It passed in shouts, it passed by instinct down the hill. They were shouting in the street before Marvel was halfway there. They were bolting into houses and slamming the doors behind them, with the news. He heard it and made one last desperate spurt. Fear came striding by, rushed ahead of him, and in a moment had seized the town.

'The Invisible Man is coming! *The Invisible Man!*'

XVI

In the Jolly Cricketers

The Jolly Cricketers is just at the bottom of the hill, where the tram-lines begin. The barman leant his fat red arms on the counter and talked of horses with an anaemic cabman, while a black-bearded man in grey snapped up biscuit and cheese, drank Burton, and conversed in American with a policeman off duty.

'What's the shouting about!' said the anaemic cabman, going off at a tangent, trying to see up the hill over the dirty yellow blind in the low window of the inn. Somebody ran by outside, 'Fire, perhaps,' said the barman.

Footsteps approached, running heavily, the door was pushed open violently, and Marvel, weeping and dishevelled, his hat gone, the neck of his coat torn open, rushed in, made a convulsive turn, and attempted to shut the door. It was held half open by a strap.

'Coming!' he bawled, his voice shrieking with terror. 'He's coming. The 'Visible Man! After me! For Gawd's sake! Elp! Elp! Elp!'

'Shut the doors,' said the policeman. 'Who's coming? What's the row?' He went to the door, released the strap, and it slammed. The American closed the other door.

'Lemme go inside,' said Marvel, staggering and weeping, but still clutching the books. 'Lemme go inside. Lock me in – somewhere. I tell you he's after me. I give him the slip. He said he'd kill me and he will.'

'*You're* safe,' said the man with the black beard. 'The door's shut. What's it all about?'

'Lemme go inside,' said Marvel, and shrieked aloud as a blow suddenly made the fastened door shiver and was followed by a hurried rapping and a shouting outside. 'Hullo,' cried the policeman, 'who's there?' Mr Marvel began to make frantic dives at panels that looked like doors. 'He'll kill me – he's got a knife or something. For Gawd's sake!'

'Here you are,' said the barman. 'Come in here.' And he held up the flap of the bar.

Mr Marvel rushed behind the bar as the summons outside was

repeated. 'Don't open the door,' he screamed. '*Please* don't open the door. *Where* shall I hide?'

'This, this Invisible Man, then?' asked the man with the black beard, with one hand behind him. 'I guess it's about time we saw him.'

The window of the inn was suddenly smashed in, and there was a screaming and running to and fro in the street. The policeman had been standing on the settee staring out, craning to see who was at the door. He got down with raised eyebrows. 'It's that,' he said. The barman stood in front of the bar-parlour door which was now locked on Mr Marvel, stared at the smashed window, and came round to the two other men.

Everything was suddenly quiet. 'I wish I had my truncheon,' said the policeman, going irresolutely to the door. 'Once we open, in he comes. There's no stopping him.'

'Don't you be in too much hurry about that door,' said the anaemic cabman, anxiously.

'Draw the bolts,' said the man with the black beard, 'and if he comes – ' He showed a revolver in his hand.

'That won't do,' said the policeman; 'that's murder.'

'I know what country I'm in,' said the man with the black beard. 'I'm going to let off at his legs. Draw the bolts.'

'Not with that thing going off behind me,' said the barman, craning over the blind.

'Very well,' said the man with the black beard, and stooping down, revolver ready, drew them himself. Barman, cabman, and a policeman faced about.

'Come in,' said the bearded man in an undertone, standing back and facing the unbolted doors with his pistol behind him. No one came in, the door remained closed. Five minutes afterwards when a second cabman pushed his head in cautiously, they were still waiting, and an anxious face peered out of the bar-parlour and supplied information. 'Are all the doors of the house shut?' asked Marvel. 'He's going round – prowling round. He's as artful as the devil.'

'Good Lord!' said the burly barman. 'There's the back! Just watch them doors! I say! – ' He looked about him helplessly. The bar-parlour door slammed and they heard the key turn. 'There's the yard door and the private door. The yard door – '

He rushed out of the bar.

In a minute he reappeared with a carving-knife in his hand. 'The yard door was open!' he said, and his fat under-lip dropped. 'He may be in the house now!' said the first cabman.

'He's not in the kitchen,' said the barman. 'There's two women there, and I've stabbed every inch of it with this little beef slicer. And they don't think he's come in. They haven't noticed – '

'Have you fastened it?' said the first cabman.

'I'm out of frocks,' said the barman.

The man with the beard replaced his revolver. And even as he did so the flap of the bar was shut down and the bolt clicked, and then with a tremendous thud the catch of the door snapped and the bar-parlour door burst open. They heard Marvel squeal like a caught leveret, and forthwith they were clambering over the bar to his rescue. The bearded man's revolver cracked and the looking-glass at the back of the parlour started and came smashing and tinkling down.

As the barman entered the room he saw Marvel, curiously crumpled up and struggling against the door that led to the yard and kitchen. The door flew open while the barman hesitated, and Marvel was dragged into the kitchen. There was a scream and a clatter of pans. Marvel, head down, and lugging back obstinately, was forced to the kitchen door, and the bolts were drawn.

Then the policeman, who had been trying to pass the barman, rushed in, followed by one of the cabmen, gripped the wrist of the invisible hand that collared Marvel, was hit in the face and went reeling back. The door opened, and Marvel made a frantic effort to obtain a lodgment behind it. Then the cabman collared something. 'I got him,' said the cabman. The barman's red hands came clawing at the unseen. 'Here he is!' said the barman.

Mr Marvel, released, suddenly dropped to the ground and made an attempt to crawl behind the legs of the fighting men. The struggle blundered round the edge of the door. The voice of the Invisible Man was heard for the first time, yelling out sharply, as the policeman trod on his foot. Then he cried out passionately and his fists flew round like flails. The cabman suddenly whooped and doubled up, kicked under the diaphragm. The door into the bar-parlour from the kitchen slammed and covered Mr Marvel's retreat. The men in the kitchen found themselves clutching at and struggling with empty air.

'Where's he gone?' cried the man with the beard. 'Out?'

'This way,' said the policeman, stepping into the yard and stopping.

A piece of tile whizzed by his head and smashed among the crockery on the kitchen table.

'I'll show him,' shouted the man with the black beard, and suddenly a steel barrel shone over the policeman's shoulder, and five bullets had followed one another into the twilight whence the missile had come. As he fired, the man with the beard moved his hand in a horizontal curve, so that his shots radiated out into the narrow yard like spokes from a wheel.

A silence followed. 'Five cartridges,' said the man with the black beard. 'That's the best of all. Four aces and the joker. Get a lantern, someone, and come and feel about for his body.'

XVII

Doctor Kemp's Visitor

Doctor Kemp had continued writing in his study until the shots aroused him. Crack, crack, crack, they came one after the other.

'Hullo!' said Doctor Kemp, putting his pen into his mouth again and listening. 'Who's letting off revolvers in Burdock? What are the asses at now?'

He went to the south window, threw it up, and leaning out stared down on the network of windows, beaded gas-lamps and shops, with its black interstices of roofs that made up the town at night. 'Looks like a crowd down the hill,' he said, 'by the Cricketers,' and remained watching. Thence his eyes wandered over the town to far away where the ships' lights shone, and the pier glowed, a little illuminated faceted pavilion like a gem of yellow light. The moon in its first quarter hung over the western hill, and the stars were clear and almost tropically bright.

After five minutes, during which his mind had travelled into a remote speculation of social conditions of the future, and lost itself at last over the time dimension, Doctor Kemp roused himself with a sigh, pulled down the window again, and returned to his writing-desk.

It must have been about an hour after this that the front door bell rang. He had been writing slackly, and with intervals of abstraction, since the shots. He sat listening. He heard the servant answer the door, and waited for her feet on the staircase, but she did not come. 'Wonder what that was,' said Doctor Kemp.

He tried to resume his work, failed, got up, went downstairs from his study to the landing, rang, and called over the balustrade to the housemaid as she appeared in the hall below. 'Was that a letter?' he asked.

'Only a runaway ring, sir,' she answered.

'I'm restless tonight,' he said to himself. He went back to his study, and this time attacked his work resolutely. In a little while he was hard at work again, and the only sounds in the room were the ticking of the clock and the subdued shrillness of his quill, hurrying in the very centre of the circle of light his lampshade threw on his table.

It was two o'clock before Doctor Kemp had finished his work for the night. He rose, yawned, and went downstairs to bed. He had already removed his coat and vest, when he noticed that he was thirsty. He took a candle and went down to the dining-room in search of a syphon and whiskey.

Doctor Kemp's scientific pursuits had made him a very observant man, and as he recrossed the hall, he noticed a dark spot on the linoleum near the mat at the foot of the stairs. He went on upstairs, and then it suddenly occurred to him to ask himself what the spot on the linoleum might be. Apparently some subconscious element was at work. At any rate, he turned with his burden, went back to the hall, put down the syphon and whiskey, and bending down, touched the spot. Without any great surprise he found it had the stickiness and colour of drying blood.

He took up his burden again, and returned upstairs, looking about him and trying to account for the blood-spot. On the landing he saw something and stopped astonished. The door-handle of his own room was blood-stained.

He looked at his own hand. It was quite clean, and then he remembered that the door of his room had been open when he came down from his study, and that consequently he had not touched the handle at all. He went straight into his room, his face quite calm – perhaps a trifle more resolute than usual. His glance, wandering inquisitively, fell on the bed. On the counterpane was a mess of blood, and the sheet had been torn. He had not noticed this before because he had walked straight to the dressing-table. On the further side the bed-clothes were depressed as if someone had been recently sitting there.

Then he had an odd impression that he had heard a loud voice say, 'Good Heavens! *Kemp!*' But Doctor Kemp was no believer in Voices.

He stood staring at the tumbled sheets. Was that really a voice? He looked about again, but noticed nothing further than the disordered and blood-stained bed. Then he distinctly heard a movement across the room, near the wash-hand stand. All men, however highly educated, retain some superstitious inklings. The feeling that is called 'eerie' came upon him. He closed the door of the room, came forward to the dressing table, and put down his burdens. Suddenly, with a start, he perceived a coiled and blood-stained bandage of linen rag hanging in mid-air, between him and the wash-hand stand.

He stared at this in amazement. It was an empty bandage, a bandage properly tied but quite empty. He would have advanced to grasp it, but a touch arrested him, and a voice speaking quite close to him.

'Kemp!' said the Voice.

'Eigh?' said Kemp, with his mouth open.

'Keep your nerve,' said the Voice. 'I'm an Invisible Man.'

Kemp made no answer for a space, simply stared at the bandage. 'Invisible Man,' he said.

'I'm an Invisible Man,' repeated the Voice.

The story he had been active to ridicule only that morning rushed through Kemp's brain. He does not appear to have been either very much frightened or very greatly surprised at the moment. Realisation came later.

'I thought it was all a lie,' he said. The thought uppermost in his mind was the reiterated arguments of the morning. 'Have you a bandage on?' he asked.

'Yes,' said the Invisible Man.

'Oh!' said Kemp, and then roused himself. 'I say!' he said. 'But this is nonsense. It's some trick.' He stepped forward suddenly, and his hand, extended towards the bandage, met invisible fingers.

He recoiled at the touch and his colour changed.

'Keep steady, Kemp, for God's sake! I want help badly. Stop!'

The hand gripped his arm. He struck at it.

'Kemp!' cried the Voice. 'Kemp! Keep steady!' and the grip tightened.

A frantic desire to free himself took possession of Kemp. The hand of the bandaged arm gripped his shoulder, and he was suddenly tripped and flung backwards upon the bed. He opened his mouth to shout, and the corner of the sheet was thrust between his teeth. The Invisible Man had him down grimly, but his arms were free and he struck and tried to kick savagely.

'Listen to reason, will you?' said the Invisible Man, sticking to him in spite of a pounding in the ribs. 'By Heaven! you'll madden me in a minute!

'Lie still, you fool!' bawled the Invisible Man in Kemp's ear.

Kemp struggled for another moment and then lay still.

'If you shout I'll smash your face,' said the Invisible Man, relieving his mouth.

'I'm an Invisible Man. It's no foolishness, and no magic. I really am an Invisible Man. And I want your help. I don't want to hurt you, but if you behave like a frantic rustic, I must. Don't you remember me, Kemp? Griffin, of University College?'

'Let me get up,' said Kemp. 'I'll stop where I am. And let me sit quiet for a minute.'

He sat up and felt his neck.

'I am Griffin, of University College, and I have made myself invisible. I am just an ordinary man – a man you have known – made invisible.'

'Griffin?' said Kemp.

'Griffin,' answered the Voice, 'a younger student, almost an albino, six feet high, and broad, with a pink and white face and red eyes, who won the medal for chemistry.'

'I am confused,' said Kemp. 'My brain is rioting. What has this to do with Griffin?'

'I *am* Griffin.'

Kemp thought. 'It's horrible,' he said. 'But what devilry must happen to make a man invisible?'

'It's no devilry. It's a process, sane and intelligible enough – '

'It's horrible!' said Kemp. 'How on earth – ?'

'It's horrible enough. But I'm wounded and in pain, and tired – Great God! Kemp, you are a man. Take it steady. Give me some food and drink, and let me sit down here.'

Kemp stared at the bandage as it moved across the room, then saw a basket chair dragged across the floor and come to rest near the bed. It creaked, and the seat was depressed the quarter of an inch or so. He rubbed his eyes and felt his neck again. 'This beats ghosts,' he said, and laughed stupidly.

'That's better. Thank Heaven, you're getting sensible!'

'Or silly,' said Kemp, and knuckled his eyes.

'Give me some whiskey. I'm near dead.'

'It didn't feel so. Where are you? If I get up shall I run into you? *There!* all right. Whiskey? Here. Where shall I give it you?'

The chair creaked and Kemp felt the glass drawn away from him. He let go by an effort; his instinct was all against it. It came to rest poised twenty inches above the front edge of the seat of the chair. He stared at it in infinite perplexity. 'This is – this *must* be – hypnotism. You must have suggested you are invisible.'

'Nonsense,' said the Voice.

'It's frantic.'

'Listen to me.'

'I demonstrated conclusively this morning,' began Kemp, 'that invisibility – '

'Never mind what you've demonstrated! I'm starving,' said the Voice, 'and the night is – chilly to a man without clothes.'

'Food!' said Kemp.

The tumbler of whiskey tilted itself. 'Yes,' said the Invisible Man rapping it down. 'Have you got a dressing-gown?'

Kemp made some exclamation in an undertone. He walked to a wardrobe and produced a robe of dingy scarlet. 'This do?' he asked. It was taken from him. It hung limp for a moment in mid-air, fluttered weirdly, stood full and decorous buttoning itself, and sat down in his chair. 'Drawers, socks, slippers would be a comfort,' said the Unseen, curtly. 'And food.'

'Anything. But this is the insanest thing I ever was in, in my life!'

He turned out his drawers for the articles, and then went downstairs to ransack his larder. He came back with some cold cutlets and bread, pulled up a light table, and placed them before his guest. 'Never mind knives,' said his visitor, and a cutlet hung in mid-air, with a sound of gnawing.

'Invisible!' said Kemp, and sat down on a bedroom chair.

'I always like to get something about me before I eat,' said the Invisible Man, with a full mouth, eating greedily. 'Queer fancy!'

'I suppose that wrist is all right,' said Kemp.

'Trust me,' said the Invisible Man.

'Of *all* the strange and wonderful – '

'Exactly. But it's odd I should blunder into *your* house to get my bandaging. My first stroke of luck! Anyhow I meant to sleep in this house tonight. You must stand that! It's a filthy nuisance, my blood showing, isn't it? Quite a clot over there. Gets visible as it coagulates, I see. I've been in the house three hours.'

'But how's it done?' began Kemp, in a tone of exasperation. 'Confound it! The whole business – it's unreasonable from beginning to end.'

'Quite reasonable,' said the Invisible Man. 'Perfectly reasonable.'

He reached over and secured the whiskey bottle. Kemp stared at the devouring dressing-gown. A ray of candlelight penetrating a torn patch in the right shoulder, made a triangle of light under the left ribs. 'What were the shots?' he asked. 'How did the shooting begin?'

'There was a fool of a man – a sort of confederate of mine – curse him! who tried to steal my money. *Has* done so.'

'Is *he* invisible too?'

'No.'

'Well?'

'Can't I have some more to eat before I tell you all that? I'm hungry – in pain. And you want me to tell stories!'

Kemp got up. '*You* didn't do any shooting?' he asked.

'Not me,' said his visitor. 'Some fool I'd never seen fired at random. A lot of them got scared. They all got scared at me. Curse them! – I say – I want more to eat than this, Kemp.'

'I'll see what there is more to eat downstairs,' said Kemp. 'Not much, I'm afraid.'

After he had done eating, and he made a heavy meal, the Invisible Man demanded a cigar. He bit the end savagely before Kemp could find a knife, and cursed when the outer leaf loosened. It was strange to see him smoking; his mouth, and throat, pharynx and nares, became visible as a sort of whirling smoke cast.

'This blessed gift of smoking!' he said, and puffed vigorously. 'I'm lucky to have fallen upon you, Kemp. You must help me. Fancy tumbling on you just now! I'm in a devilish scrape. I've been mad, I think. The things I have been through! But we will do things yet. Let me tell you – '

He helped himself to more whiskey and soda. Kemp got up, looked

about him, and fetched himself a glass from his spare room. 'It's wild –
but I suppose I may drink.'

'You haven't changed much, Kemp, these dozen years. You fair men
don't. Cool and methodical – after the first collapse. I must tell you. We
will work together!'

'But how was it all done?' said Kemp, 'and how did you get like this?'

'For God's sake, let me smoke in peace for a little while! And then I
will begin to tell you.'

But the story was not told that night. The Invisible Man's wrist was
growing painful, he was feverish, exhausted, and his mind came round
to brood upon his chase down the hill and the struggle about the inn.
He spoke in fragments of Marvel, he smoked faster, his voice grew
angry. Kemp tried to gather what he could.

'He was afraid of me, I could see he was afraid of me,' said the
Invisible Man many times over. 'He meant to give me the slip – he was
always casting about! What a fool I was!

'The cur!

'I should have killed him – '

'Where did you get the money?' asked Kemp, abruptly.

The Invisible Man was silent for a space. 'I can't tell you tonight,' he
said.

He groaned suddenly and leant forward, supporting his invisible head
on invisible hands. 'Kemp,' he said, 'I've had no sleep for near three
days, except a couple of dozes of an hour or so. I must sleep soon.'

'Well, have my room – have this room.'

'But how can I sleep? If I sleep – he will get away. Ugh! What does it
matter?'

'What's the shot-wound?' asked Kemp, abruptly.

'Nothing – scratch and blood. Oh, God! How I want sleep!'

'Why not?'

The Invisible Man appeared to be regarding Kemp. 'Because I've a
particular objection to being caught by my fellow-men,' he said slowly.

Kemp started.

'Fool that I am!' said the Invisible Man, striking the table smartly.
'I've put the idea into your head.'

XVIII

The Invisible Man Sleeps

Exhausted and wounded as the Invisible Man was, he refused to accept Kemp's word that his freedom should be respected. He examined the two windows of the bedroom, drew up the blinds, and opened the sashes, to confirm Kemp's statement that a retreat by them would be possible. Outside the night was very quiet and still, and the new moon was setting over the down. Then he examined the keys of the bedroom and the two dressing-room doors, to satisfy himself that these also could be made an assurance of freedom. Finally he expressed himself satisfied. He stood on the hearth rug and Kemp heard the sound of a yawn.

'I'm sorry,' said the Invisible Man, 'if I cannot tell you all that I have done tonight. But I am worn out. It's grotesque, no doubt. It's horrible! But believe me, Kemp, in spite of your arguments of this morning, it is quite a possible thing. I have made a discovery. I meant to keep it to myself. I can't. I must have a partner. And you – We can do such things – But tomorrow. Now, Kemp, I feel as though I must sleep or perish.'

Kemp stood in the middle of the room staring at the headless garment. 'I suppose I must leave you,' he said. 'It's – incredible. These things happening like this, overturning all my preconceptions, would make me insane. But it's real! Is there anything more that I can get you?'

'Only bid me good-night,' said Griffin.

'Good-night,' said Kemp, and shook an invisible hand. He walked sideways to the door. Suddenly the dressing-gown walked quickly towards him. 'Understand me!' said the dressing-gown. 'No attempts to hamper me, or capture me! Or – '

Kemp's face changed a little. 'I thought I gave you my word,' he said.

Kemp closed the door softly behind him, and the key was turned upon him forthwith. Then, as he stood with an expression of passive amazement on his face, the rapid feet came to the door of the dressing-room and that too was locked. Kemp slapped his brow with his hand. 'Am I dreaming? Has the world gone mad – or have I?'

He laughed, and put his hand to the locked door. 'Barred out of my own bedroom, by a flagrant absurdity!' he said.

He walked to the head of the staircase, turned and stared at the locked doors. 'It's fact,' he said. He put his fingers to his slightly bruised neck. 'Undeniable fact!

'But – '

He shook his head hopelessly, turned, and went downstairs.

He lit the dining-room lamp, got out a cigar, and began pacing the room, ejaculating. Now and then he would argue with himself.

'Invisible!' he said.

'Is there such a thing as an invisible animal? In the sea, yes. Thousands! millions! All the larvae, all the little nauplii and tornarias, all the microscopic things, the jelly-fish. In the sea there are more things invisible than visible! I never thought of that before. And in the ponds too! All those little pond-life things, specks of colourless translucent jelly! But in air? No!

'It can't be.

'But after all – why not?

'If a man was made of glass he would still be visible.'

His meditation became profound. The bulk of three cigars had passed into the invisible or diffused as a white ash over the carpet before he spoke again. Then it was merely an exclamation. He turned aside, walked out of the room, and went into his little consulting-room and lit the gas there. It was a little room, because Dr Kemp did not live by practice, and in it were the day's newspapers. The morning's paper lay carelessly opened and thrown aside. He caught it up, turned it over, and read the account of a 'Strange Story from Iping' that the mariner at Port Stowe had spelt over so painfully to Mr Marvel. Kemp read it swiftly.

'Wrapped up!' said Kemp. 'Disguised! Hiding it "No one seems to have been aware of his misfortune." What the devil *is* his game?'

He dropped the paper, and his eye went seeking. 'Ah!' he said, and caught up the St James' Gazette, lying folded up as it arrived. 'Now we shall get at the truth,' said Dr Kemp. He rent the paper open; a couple of columns confronted him. 'An Entire Village in Sussex goes Mad' was the heading.

'Good Heavens!' said Kemp, reading eagerly an incredulous account of the events in Iping, of the previous afternoon, that have already been described. Over the leaf the report in the morning paper had been reprinted.

He re-read it. 'Ran through the streets striking right and left. Jaffers insensible. Mr Huxter in great pain – still unable to describe what he saw. Painful humiliation – vicar. Woman ill with terror! Windows smashed. This extraordinary story probably a fabrication. Too good not to print – *cum grano!*'

He dropped the paper and stared blankly in front of him. 'Probably a fabrication!'

He caught up the paper again, and re-read the whole business. 'But when does the Tramp come in? Why the deuce was he chasing a Tramp?'

He sat down abruptly on the surgical couch. 'He's not only invisible,' he said, 'but he's mad! Homicidal!'

When dawn came to mingle its pallor with the lamplight and cigar smoke of the dining-room, Kemp was still pacing up and down, trying to grasp the incredible.

He was altogether too excited to sleep. His servants, descending sleepily, discovered him, and were inclined to think that over-study had worked this ill on him. He gave them extraordinary but quite explicit instructions to lay breakfast for two in the belvedere study – and then to confine themselves to the basement and ground-floor. Then he continued to pace the dining-room until the morning's paper came. That had much to say and little to tell, beyond the confirmation of the evening before, and a very badly written account of another remarkable tale from Port Burdock. This gave Kemp the essence of the happenings at the Jolly Cricketers, and the name of Marvel. 'He has made me keep with him twenty-four hours,' Marvel testified. Certain minor facts were added to the Iping story, notably the cutting of the village telegraph wire. But there was nothing to throw light on the connexion between the Invisible Man and the Tramp; for Mr Marvel had supplied no information about the three books, or the money with which he was lined. The incredulous tone had vanished and a shoal of reporters and inquirers were already at work elaborating the matter.

Kemp read every scrap of the report and sent his housemaid out to get every one of the morning papers she could. These also he devoured.

'He is invisible!' he said. 'And it reads like rage growing to mania! The things he may do! The things he may do! And he's upstairs free as the air. What on earth ought I to do?'

'For instance, would it be a breach of faith if – ? No.'

He went to a little untidy desk in the corner, and began a note. He tore this up half written, and wrote another. He read it over and considered it. Then he took an envelope and addressed it to 'Colonel Adye, Port Burdock'.

The Invisible Man awoke even as Kemp was doing this. He awoke in an evil temper, and Kemp, alert for every sound, heard his pattering feet rush suddenly across the bedroom overhead. Then a chair was flung over and the wash-hand stand tumbler smashed. Kemp hurried upstairs and rapped eagerly.

XIX

Certain First Principles

'What's the matter?' asked Kemp, when the Invisible Man admitted him.

'Nothing,' was the answer.

'But, confound it! The smash?'

'Fit of temper,' said the Invisible Man. 'Forgot this arm; and it's sore.'

'You're rather liable to that sort of thing.'

'I am.'

Kemp walked across the room and picked up the fragments of broken glass. 'All the facts are out about you,' said Kemp, standing up with the glass in his hand; 'all that happened in Iping, and down the hill. The world has become aware of its invisible citizen. But no one knows you are here.'

The Invisible Man swore.

'The secret's out. I gather it was a secret. I don't know what your plans are, but of course I'm anxious to help you.'

The Invisible Man sat down on the bed.

'There's breakfast upstairs,' said Kemp, speaking as easily as possible, and he was delighted to find his strange guest rose willingly. Kemp led the way up the narrow staircase to the belvedere.

'Before we can do anything else,' said Kemp, 'I must understand a little more about this invisibility of yours.' He had sat down, after one nervous glance out of the window, with the air of a man who has talking to do. His doubts of the sanity of the entire business flashed and vanished again as he looked across to where Griffin sat at the breakfast-table, a headless, handless dressing-gown, wiping unseen lips on a miraculously held *serviette*.

'It's simple enough – and credible enough,' said Griffin, putting the *serviette* aside and leaning the invisible head on an invisible hand.

'No doubt, to you, but – ' Kemp laughed.

'Well, yes; to me it seemed wonderful at first, no doubt. But now, great God! But we will do great things yet! I came on the stuff first at Chesilstowe.'

'Chesilstowe?'

'I went there after I left London. You know I dropped medicine and took up physics? *No!* – well, I did. *Light* fascinated me.'

'Ah!'

'Optical density! The whole subject is a network of riddles – a network with solutions glimmering elusively through. And being but two and twenty and full of enthusiasm, I said, "I will devote my life to this. This is worth while." You know what fools we are at two and twenty?'

'Fools then or fools now,' said Kemp.

'As though Knowing could be any satisfaction to a man!

'But I went to work – like a nigger. And I had hardly worked and thought about the matter six months before light came through one of the meshes suddenly – blindingly! I found a general principle of pigments and refraction, a formula, a geometrical expression involving four dimensions. Fools, common men, even common mathematicians, do not know anything of what some general expression may mean to the student of molecular physics. In the books – the books that Tramp has hidden – there are marvels, miracles! But this was not a method, it was an idea, that might lead to a method by which it would be possible, without changing any other property of matter – except, in some instances, colours – to lower the refractive index of a substance, solid or liquid, to that of air – so far as all practical purposes are concerned.'

'Phew!' said Kemp. 'That's odd! But still I don't see quite – I can understand that thereby you could spoil a valuable stone, but personal invisibility is a far cry.'

'Precisely,' said Griffin. 'But consider: Visibility depends on the action of the visible bodies on light. Either a body absorbs light, or it reflects or refracts it, or does all these things. If it neither reflects nor refracts nor absorbs light, it cannot of itself be visible. You see an opaque red box, for instance, because the colour absorbs some of the light and reflects the rest, all the red part of the light, to you. If it did not absorb any particular part of the light, but reflected it all, then it would be a shining white box. Silver! A diamond box would neither absorb much of the light nor reflect much from the general surface, but just here and there where the surfaces were favourable the light would be reflected and refracted, so that you would get a brilliant appearance of flashing reflections and translucencies, a sort of skeleton of light. A glass box would not be so brilliant, not so clearly visible, as a diamond box, because there would be less refraction and reflection. See that? From certain points of view you would see quite clearly through it. Some kinds of glass would be more visible than others, a box of flint glass would be brighter than a box of ordinary window glass. A box of very thin common glass would be hard to see in a bad light, because it would absorb hardly any light and refract and reflect very little. And if you put a sheet of common white glass in water, still more if you put it in some denser liquid than water, it would vanish almost altogether, because light passing from water to glass is only slightly refracted or reflected or indeed affected in any way. It is almost as invisible as a jet of coal gas or hydrogen is in air. And for precisely the same reason!'

'Yes,' said Kemp, 'that is pretty plain sailing.'

'And here is another fact you will know to be true. If a sheet of glass is smashed, Kemp, and beaten into a powder, it becomes much more visible while it is in the air; it becomes at last an opaque white powder. This is because the powdering multiplies the surfaces of the glass at which refraction and reflection occur. In the sheet of glass there are only two surfaces; in the powder the light is reflected or refracted by each grain it passes through, and very little gets right through the powder. But if the white powdered glass is put into water, it forthwith vanishes. The powdered glass and water have much the same refractive index; that is, the light undergoes very little refraction or reflection in passing from one to the other.

'You make the glass invisible by putting it into a liquid of nearly the same refractive index; a transparent thing becomes invisible if it is put in any medium of almost the same refractive index. And if you will consider only a second, you will see also that the powder of glass might be made to vanish in air, if its refractive index could be made the same as that of air; for then there would be no refraction or reflection as the light passed from glass to air.'

'Yes, yes,' said Kemp. 'But a man's not powdered glass!'

'No,' said Griffin. *'He's more transparent!'*

'Nonsense!'

'That from a doctor! How one forgets! Have you already forgotten your physics, in ten years? Just think of all the things that are transparent and seem not to be so. Paper, for instance, is made up of transparent fibres, and it is white and opaque only for the same reason that a powder of glass is white and opaque. Oil white paper, fill up the interstices between the particles with oil so that there is no longer refraction or reflection except at the surfaces, and it becomes as transparent as glass. And not only paper, but cotton fibre, linen fibre, wool fibre, woody fibre, and *bone*, Kemp, *flesh*, Kemp, *hair*, Kemp, *nails* and *nerves*, Kemp, in fact the whole fabric of a man except the red of his blood and the black pigment of hair, are all made up of transparent, colourless tissue. So little suffices to make us visible one to the other. For the most part the fibres of a living creature are no more opaque than water.'

'Great Heavens!' cried Kemp. 'Of course, of course! I was thinking only last night of the sea larvae and all jellyfish!'

'*Now* you have me! And all that I knew and had in mind a year after I left London – six years ago. But I kept it to myself. I had to do my work under frightful disadvantages. Oliver, my professor, was a scientific bounder, a journalist by instinct, a thief of ideas, he was always prying! And you know the knavish system of the scientific world. I simply would not publish, and let him share my credit. I went on working, I got nearer and nearer making my formula into an experiment, a reality. I told no living soul, because I meant to flash my work upon the world with crushing effect – to become famous at a blow. I took up the question of pigments to fill up certain gaps. And suddenly, not by design but by accident, I made a discovery in physiology.'

'Yes?'

'You know the red colouring matter of blood; it can be made white – colourless – and remain with all the functions it has now!'

Kemp gave a cry of incredulous amazement.

The Invisible Man rose and began pacing the little study. 'You may well exclaim. I remember that night. It was late at night – in the daytime one was bothered with the gaping, silly students – and I worked then sometimes till dawn. It came suddenly, splendid and complete into my mind. I was alone; the laboratory was still, with the tall lights burning brightly and silently. In all my great moments I have been alone. "One could make an animal – a tissue – transparent! One could make it invisible! All except the pigments – I could be invisible!" I said, suddenly realising what it meant to be an albino with such knowledge. It was overwhelming. I left the filtering I was doing, and went and stared out of the great window at the stars. "I could be invisible!" I repeated.

'To do such a thing would be to transcend magic. And I beheld, unclouded by doubt, a magnificent vision of all that invisibility might mean to a man – the mystery, the power, the freedom. Drawbacks I saw none. You have only to think! And I, a shabby, poverty-struck, hemmed-in demonstrator, teaching fools in a provincial college, might suddenly become – this. I ask you, Kemp, if *you* – Anyone, I tell you, would have flung himself upon that research. And I worked three years, and every mountain of difficulty I toiled over showed another from its summit. The infinite details! And the exasperation – a professor, a provincial professor, always prying. "When are you going to publish this work of yours?" was his everlasting question. And the students, the cramped means! Three years I had of it –

'And after three years of secrecy and exasperation, I found that to complete it was impossible – impossible.'

'How?' asked Kemp.

'Money,' said the Invisible Man, and went again to stare out of the window.

He turned round abruptly. 'I robbed the old man – robbed my father.

'The money was not his, and he shot himself.'

XX

At the House in Great Portland Street

For a moment Kemp sat in silence, staring at the back of the headless figure at the window. Then he started, struck by a thought, rose, took the Invisible Man's arm, and turned him away from the outlook.

'You are tired,' he said, 'and while I sit, you walk about. Have my chair.'

He placed himself between Griffin and the nearest window.

For a space Griffin sat silent, and then he resumed abruptly:-

'I had left the Chesilstowe cottage already,' he said, 'when that happened. It was last December. I had taken a room in London, a large unfurnished room in a big ill-managed lodging-house in a slum near Great Portland Street. The room was soon full of the appliances I had bought with his money; the work was going on steadily, successfully, drawing near an end. I was like a man emerging from a thicket, and suddenly coming on some unmeaning tragedy. I went to bury him. My mind was still on this research, and I did not lift a finger to save his character. I remember the funeral, the cheap hearse, the scant ceremony, the windy frost-bitten hillside, and the old college friend of his who read the service over him, a shabby, black, bent old man with a snivelling cold.

'I remember walking back to the empty home, through the place that had once been a village and was now patched and tinkered by the jerry builders into the ugly likeness of a town. Every way the roads ran out at last into the desecrated fields and ended in rubble heaps and rank wet weeds. I remember myself as a gaunt black figure, going along the slippery, shiny pavement, and the strange sense of detachment I felt from the squalid respectability, the sordid commercialism of the place.

'I did not feel a bit sorry for my father. He seemed to me to be the victim of his own foolish sentimentality. The current cant required my attendance at his funeral, but it was really not my affair.

'But going along the High Street, my old life came back to me for a space, for I met the girl I had known ten years since. Our eyes met.

'Something moved me to turn back and talk to her. She was a very ordinary person.

'It was all like a dream, that visit to the old places. I did not feel then that I was lonely, that I had come out from the world into a desolate place. I appreciated my loss of sympathy, but I put it down to the general inanity of things. Re-entering my room seemed like the recovery of reality. There were the things I knew and loved. There stood the apparatus, the experiments arranged and waiting. And now there was scarcely a difficulty left, beyond the planning of details.

'I will tell you, Kemp, sooner or later, all the complicated processes. We need not go into that now. For the most part, saving certain gaps I chose to remember, they are written in cypher in those books that tramp has hidden. We must hunt him down. We must get those books again. But the essential phase was to place the transparent object whose refractive index was to be lowered between two radiating centres of a sort of ethereal vibration, of which I will tell you more fully later. No, not these Röntgen vibrations – I don't know that these others of mine have been described. Yet they are obvious enough. I needed two little dynamos, and these I worked with a cheap gas engine. My first experiment was with a bit of white wool fabric. It was the strangest thing in the world to see it in the flicker of the flashes soft and white, and then to watch it fade like a wreath of smoke and vanish.

'I could scarcely believe I had done it. I put my hand into the emptiness, and there was the thing as solid as ever. I felt it awkwardly, and threw it on the floor. I had a little trouble finding it again.

'And then came a curious experience. I heard a miaow behind me, and turning, saw a lean white cat, very dirty, on the cistern cover outside the window. A thought came into my head. "Everything ready for you," I said, and went to the window, opened it, and called softly. She came in, purring – the poor beast was starving – and I gave her some milk. All my food was in a cupboard in the corner of the room. After that she went smelling round the room – evidently with the idea of making herself at home. The invisible rag upset her a bit; you should have seen her spit at it! But I made her comfortable on the pillow of my truckle-bed. And I gave her butter to get her to wash.'

'And you processed her?'

'I processed her. But giving drugs to a cat is no joke, Kemp! And the process failed.'

'Failed!'

'In two particulars. These were the claws and the pigment stuff – what is it? – at the back of the eye in a cat. You know?'

'*Tapetum.*'

'Yes, the *tapetum*. It didn't go. After I'd given the stuff to bleach the blood and done certain other things to her, I gave the beast opium, and put her and the pillow she was sleeping on, on the apparatus. And after

all the rest had faded and vanished, there remained two little ghosts of
her eyes.'

'Odd!'

'I can't explain it. She was bandaged and clamped, of course – so I
had her safe; but she woke while she was still misty, and miaowled
dismally, and someone came knocking. It was an old woman from
downstairs, who suspected me of vivisection – a drink-sodden old
creature with only a white cat to care for in all the world. I whipped
out some chloroform, applied it, and answered the door. "Did I hear a
cat?" she asked. "My cat?" "Not here," said I, very politely. She was a
little doubtful and tried to peer past me into the room; strange enough
to her no doubt – bare walls, uncurtained windows, truckle-bed, with
the gas engine vibrating, and the seethe of the radiant points, and that
faint ghastly stinging of chloroform in the air. She had to be satisfied at
last and went away again.'

'How long did it take?' asked Kemp.

'Three or four hours – the cat. The bones and sinews and the fat were
the last to go, and the tips of the coloured hairs. And, as I say, the back
part of the eye, tough iridescent stuff it is, wouldn't go at all.

'It was night outside long before the business was over, and nothing
was to be seen but the dim eyes and the claws. I stopped the gas engine,
felt for and stroked the beast, which was still insensible, and then, being
tired, left it sleeping on the invisible pillow and went to bed. I found it
hard to sleep. I lay awake thinking weak aimless stuff, going over the
experiment over and over again, or dreaming feverishly of things
growing misty and vanishing about me, until everything, the ground I
stood on, vanished, and so I came to that sickly falling nightmare one
gets. About two, the cat began miaowling about the room. I tried to
hush it by talking to it, and then I decided to turn it out. I remember
the shock I had when striking a light – there were just the round eyes
shining green – and nothing round them. I would have given it milk,
but I hadn't any. It wouldn't be quiet, it just sat down and miaowed at
the door. I tried to catch it, with an idea of putting it out of the window,
but it wouldn't be caught, it vanished. Then it began miaowing in
different parts of the room. At last I opened the window and made a
bustle. I suppose it went out at last. I never saw any more of it.

'Then – Heaven knows why – I fell thinking of my father's funeral
again, and the dismal windy hillside, until the day had come. I found
sleeping was hopeless, and, locking my door after me, wandered out
into the morning streets.'

'You don't mean to say there's an invisible cat at large!' said Kemp.

'If it hasn't been killed,' said the Invisible Man. 'Why not?'

'Why not?' said Kemp. 'I didn't mean to interrupt.'

'It's very probably been killed,' said the Invisible Man. 'It was alive
four days after, I know, and down a grating in Great Titchfield Street;

because I saw a crowd round the place, trying to see whence the miaowing came.'

He was silent for the best part of a minute. Then he resumed abruptly:-

'I remember that morning before the change very vividly. I must have gone up Great Portland Street. I remember the barracks in Albany Street, and the horse soldiers coming out, and at last I found myself sitting in the sunshine and feeling very ill and strange, on the summit of Primrose Hill. It was a sunny day in January – one of those sunny, frosty days that came before the snow this year. My weary brain tried to formulate the position, to plot out a plan of action.

'I was surprised to find, now that my prize was within my grasp, how inconclusive its attainment seemed. As a matter of fact I was worked out; the intense stress of nearly four years' continuous work left me incapable of any strength of feeling. I was apathetic, and I tried in vain to recover the enthusiasm of my first inquiries, the passion of discovery that had enabled me to compass even the downfall of my father's grey hairs. Nothing seemed to matter. I saw pretty clearly this was a transient mood, due to overwork and want of sleep, and that either by drugs or rest it would be possible to recover my energies.

'All I could think clearly was that the thing had to be carried through; the fixed idea still ruled me. And soon, for the money I had was almost exhausted. I looked about me at the hillside, with children playing and girls watching them, and tried to think of all the fantastic advantages an invisible man would have in the world. After a time I crawled home, took some food and a strong dose of strychnine, and went to sleep in my clothes on my unmade bed. Strychnine is a grand tonic, Kemp, to take the flabbiness out of a man.'

'It's the devil,' said Kemp. 'It's the palaeolithic in a bottle.'

'I awoke vastly invigorated and rather irritable. You know?'

'I know the stuff.'

'And there was someone rapping at the door. It was my landlord with threats and inquiries, an old Polish Jew in a long grey coat and greasy slippers. I had been tormenting a cat in the night, he was sure – the old woman's tongue had been busy. He insisted on knowing all about it. The laws of this country against vivisection were very severe – he might be liable. I denied the cat. Then the vibration of the little gas engine could be felt all over the house, he said. That was true, certainly. He edged round me into the room, peering about over his German-silver spectacles, and a sudden dread came into my mind that he might carry away something of my secret. I tried to keep between him and the concentrating apparatus I had arranged, and that only made him more curious. What was I doing? Why was I always alone and secretive? Was it legal? Was it dangerous? I paid nothing but the usual rent. His had always been a most respectable house – in a disreputable neighbourhood. Suddenly my temper gave way. I told him to get out. He began to protest, to jabber of his right of entry. In a moment I had him by the collar; something ripped, and he went spinning out into his own passage. I slammed and locked the door and sat down quivering.

'He made a fuss outside, which I disregarded, and after a time he went away.

'But this brought matters to a crisis. I did not know what he would do, nor even what he had power to do. To move to fresh apartments would have meant delay; all together I had barely twenty pounds left in the world – for the most part in a bank – and I could not afford that. Vanish! It was irresistible. Then there would be an inquiry, the sacking of my room –

'At the thought of the possibility of my work being exposed or interrupted at its very climax, I became angry and active. I hurried out with my three books of notes, my cheque-book – the tramp has them now – and directed them from the nearest Post Office to a house of call for letters and parcels in Great Portland Street. I tried to go out noiselessly. Coming in, I found my landlord going quietly upstairs; he had heard the door close, I suppose. You would have laughed to see him jump aside on the landing as I came tearing after him. He glared at me as I went by him, and I made the house quiver with the slamming of my door. I heard him come shuffling up to my floor, hesitate, and go down. I set to work upon my preparations forthwith.

'It was all done that evening and night. While I was still sitting under the sickly, drowsy influence of the drugs that decolourise blood, there came a repeated knocking at the door. It ceased, footsteps went away and returned, and the knocking was resumed. There was an attempt to push something under the door – a blue paper. Then in a fit of irritation I rose and went and flung the door wide open. "Now then?" said I.

'It was my landlord, with a notice of ejectment or something. He held it out to me, saw something odd about my hands, I expect, and lifted his eyes to my face.

'For a moment he gaped. Then he gave a sort of inarticulate cry, dropped candle and writ together, and went blundering down the dark passage to the stairs. I shut the door, locked it, and went to the looking-glass. Then I understood his terror. My face was white – like white stone.

'But it was all horrible. I had not expected the suffering. A night of racking anguish, sickness and fainting. I set my teeth, though my skin was presently afire, all my body afire; but I lay there like grim death. I understood now how it was the cat had howled until I chloroformed it. Lucky it was I lived alone and untended in my room. There were times when I sobbed and groaned and talked. But I stuck to it. I became insensible and woke languid in the darkness.

'The pain had passed. I thought I was killing myself and I did not care. I shall never forget that dawn, and the strange horror of seeing that my hands had become as clouded glass, and watching them grow clearer and thinner as the day went by, until at last I could see the sickly disorder of my room through them, though I closed my transparent eyelids. My limbs became glassy, the bones and arteries faded, vanished, and the little white nerves went last. I gritted my teeth and stayed there to the end. At last only the dead tips of the fingernails remained, pallid and white, and the brown stain of some acid upon my fingers.

'I struggled up. At first I was as incapable as a swathed infant – stepping with limbs I could not see. I was weak and very hungry. I went and stared at nothing in my shaving glass, at nothing save where an attenuated pigment still remained behind the retina of my eyes, fainter than mist. I had to hang on to the table and press my forehead to the glass.

'It was only by a frantic effort of will that I dragged myself back to the apparatus and completed the process.

'I slept during the forenoon, pulling the sheet over my eyes to shut out the light, and about midday I was awakened again by a knocking. My strength had returned. I sat up and listened and heard a whispering. I sprang to my feet and as noiselessly as possible began to detach the connections of my apparatus, and to distribute it about the room, so as to destroy the suggestions of its arrangement. Presently the knocking was renewed and voices called, first my landlord's, then two others. To gain time I answered them. The invisible rag and pillow came to hand and I opened the window and pitched them out on to the cistern cover. As the window opened, a heavy crash came at the door. Someone had charged it with the idea of smashing the lock. But the stout bolts I had screwed up some days before stopped him. That startled me, made me angry. I began to tremble and do things hurriedly.

'I tossed together some loose paper, straw, packing paper and so forth, in the middle of the room, and turned on the gas. Heavy blows began to rain upon the door. I could not find the matches. I beat my hands on the wall with rage. I turned down the gas again, stepped out of the window on the cistern cover, very softly lowered the sash, and sat down, secure and invisible, but quivering with anger, to watch events. They split a panel, I saw, and in another moment they had broken away the staples of the bolts and stood in the open doorway. It was the landlord and his two step-sons, sturdy young men of three or four and twenty. Behind them fluttered the old hag of a woman from downstairs.

'You may imagine their astonishment to find the room empty. One of the younger men rushed to the window at once, flung it up and stared out. His staring eyes and thick lipped bearded face came a foot from my face. I was half minded to hit his silly countenance, but I arrested my doubled fist. He stared right through me. So did the others as they joined him. The old man went and peered under the bed, and then they all made a rush for the cupboard. They had to argue about it at length in Yiddish and Cockney English. They concluded I had not answered them, that their imagination had deceived them. A feeling of extraordinary elation took the place of my anger as I sat outside the window and watched these four people – for the old lady came in, glancing suspiciously about her like a cat, trying to understand the riddle of my behaviour.

'The old man, so far as I could understand his *patois*, agreed with the old lady that I was a vivisectionist. The sons protested in garbled English that I was an electrician, and appealed to the dynamos and radiators. They were all nervous against my arrival, although I found subsequently that they had bolted the front door. The old lady peered into the cupboard and under the bed, and one of the young men pushed up the register and stared up the chimney. One of my fellow lodgers, a costermonger who shared the opposite room with a butcher, appeared on the landing, and he was called in and told incoherent things.

'It occurred to me that the radiators, if they fell into the hands of some acute well-educated person, would give me away too much, and watching my opportunity, I came into the room and tilted one of the little dynamos off its fellow on which it was standing, and smashed both apparatus. Then, while they were trying to explain the smash, I dodged out of the room and went softly downstairs.

'I went into one of the sitting-rooms and waited until they came down, still speculating and argumentative, all a little disappointed at finding no "horrors", and all a little puzzled how they stood with regard to me. Then I slipped up again with a box of matches, fired my heap of paper and rubbish, put the chairs and bedding thereby, led the gas to the affair, by means of an india-rubber tube, and waving a farewell to the room left it for the last time.'

'You fired the house!' exclaimed Kemp.

'Fired the house. It was the only way to cover my trail – and no doubt it was insured. I slipped the bolts of the front door quietly and went out into the street. I was invisible, and I was only just beginning to realise the extraordinary advantage my invisibility gave me. My head was already teeming with plans of all the wild and wonderful things I had now impunity to do.'

XXI

In Oxford Street

'In going downstairs the first time I found an unexpected difficulty because I could not see my feet; indeed I stumbled twice, and there was an unaccustomed clumsiness in gripping the bolt. By not looking down, however, I managed to walk on the level passably well.

'My mood, I say was one of exaltation. I felt as a seeing man might do, with padded feet and noiseless clothes, in a city of the blind. I experienced a wild impulse to jest, to startle people, to clap men on the back, fling people's hats astray, and generally revel in my extraordinary advantage.

'But hardly had I emerged upon Great Portland Street, however (my lodging was close to the big draper's shop there), when I heard a clashing concussion and was hit violently behind, and turning saw a man carrying a basket of soda-water syphons, and looking in amazement at his burden. Although the blow had really hurt me, I found something so irresistible in his astonishment that I laughed aloud. "The devil's in the basket," I said, and suddenly twisted it out of his hand. He let go incontinently, and I swung the whole weight into the air.

'But a fool of a cabman, standing outside a public house, made a sudden rush for this, and his extending fingers took me with excruciating violence under the ear. I let the whole down with a smash on the cabman, and then, with shouts and the clatter of feet about me, people coming out of shops, vehicles pulling up, I realised what I had done for myself, and cursing my folly, backed against a shop window and prepared to dodge out of the confusion. In a moment I should be wedged into a crowd and inevitably discovered. I pushed by a butcher boy, who luckily did not turn to see the nothingness that shoved him aside, and dodged behind the cabman's four-wheeler. I do not know how they settled the business. I hurried straight across the road, which was happily clear, and hardly heeding which way I went, in the fright of detection the incident had given me, plunged into the afternoon throng of Oxford Street.

'I tried to get into the stream of people, but they were too thick for me, and in a moment my heels were being trodden upon. I took to the gutter, the roughness of which I found painful to my feet, and forthwith the shaft of a crawling hansom dug me forcibly under the shoulder blade, reminding me that I was already bruised severely. I staggered out of the way of the cab, avoided a perambulator by a convulsive movement, and found myself behind the hansom. A happy thought saved me, and as this drove slowly along I followed in its immediate wake, trembling and astonished at the turn of my adventure. And not only trembling, but shivering. It was a bright day in January and I was stark naked and the thin slime of mud that covered the road was freezing. Foolish as it seems to me now, I had not reckoned that, transparent or not, I was still amenable to the weather and all its consequences.

'Then suddenly a bright idea came into my head. I ran round and got into the cab. And so, shivering, scared, and sniffing with the first intimations of a cold, and with the bruises in the small of my back growing upon my attention, I drove slowly along Oxford Street and past Tottenham Court Road. My mood was as different from that in which I had sallied forth ten minutes ago as it is possible to imagine. *This* invisibility indeed! The one thought that possessed me was – how was I to get out of the scrape I was in.

'We crawled past Mudie's, and there a tall woman with five or six yellow-labelled books hailed my cab, and I sprang out just in time to escape her, shaving a railway van narrowly in my flight. I made off up the roadway to Bloomsbury Square, intending to strike north past the Museum and so get into the quiet district. I was now cruelly chilled, and the strangeness of my situation so unnerved me that I whimpered as I ran. At the northward corner of the Square a little white dog ran out of the Pharmaceutical Society's offices, and incontinently made for me, nose down.

'I had never realised it before, but the nose is to the mind of a dog what the eye is to the mind of a seeing man. Dogs perceive the scent of a man moving as men perceive his vision. This brute began barking and leaping, showing, as it seemed to me, only too plainly that he was aware of me. I crossed Great Russell Street, glancing over my shoulder as I did so, and went some way along Montague Street before I realised what I was running towards.

'Then I became aware of a blare of music, and looking along the street saw a number of people advancing out of Russell Square, red shirts, and the banner of the Salvation Army to the fore. Such a crowd, chanting in the roadway and scoffing on the pavement, I could not hope to penetrate, and dreading to go back and farther from home again, and deciding on the spur of the moment, I ran up the white steps of a house facing the museum railings and stood there until the crowd should have passed. Happily the dog stopped at the noise of the band too, hesitated, and turned tail, running back to Bloomsbury Square again.

'On came the band, bawling with unconscious irony some hymn about "When shall we see his Face?" and it seemed an interminable time to me before the tide of the crowd washed along the pavement by me. Thud, thud, thud, came the drum with a vibrating resonance, and for the moment I did not notice two urchins stopping at the railings by me. "See 'em," said one. "See what?" said the other. "Why – them footmarks – *bare*. Like what you makes in mud."

'I looked down and saw the youngsters had stopped and were gaping at the muddy footmarks I had left behind me up the newly whitened steps. The passing people elbowed and jostled them, but their confounded intelligence was arrested. "Thud, thud, thud, When, thud, shall we see, thud, his Face, thud, thud." "There's a barefoot man gone up them steps, or I don't know nothing," said one. "And he ain't never come down again. And his foot was a-bleeding."

'The thick of the crowd had already passed. "Looky there, Ted," quoth the younger of the detectives, with the sharpness of surprise in his voice, and pointed straight to my feet. I looked down and saw at once the dim suggestion of their outline sketched in splashes of mud. For a moment I was paralysed.

'"Why, that's rum," said the elder. "Dashed rum! It's just like the ghost of a foot, ain't it?" He hesitated and advanced with outstretched hand. A man pulled up short to see what he was catching, and then a girl. In another moment he would have touched me. Then I saw what to do. I made a step, the boy started back with an exclamation, and with a rapid movement I swung myself over into the portico of the next house. But the smaller boy was sharp-eyed enough to follow the movement, and before I was well down the steps and upon the pavement, he had recovered from his momentary astonishment and was shouting out that the feet had gone over the wall.

'They rushed round and saw my new footmarks flash into being on the lower step and upon the pavement. "What's up?" asked someone. "Feet! Look! Feet running!" Everybody in the road, except my three pursuers, was pouring along after the Salvation Army, and this blow not only impeded me but them. There was an eddy of surprise and interrogation. At the cost of bowling over one young fellow I got through, and in another moment I was rushing headlong round the circuit of Russell Square, with six or seven astonished people following my footmarks. There was no time for explanation, or else the whole host would have been after me.

'Twice I doubled round corners, thrice I crossed the road and came back on my tracks, and then, as my feet grew hot and dry, the damp impressions began to fade. At last I had a breathing space and rubbed my feet clean with my hands, and so got away altogether. The last I saw of the chase was a little group of a dozen people perhaps, studying with infinite perplexity a slowly drying footprint that had resulted from a puddle in Tavistock Square – a footprint as isolated and incomprehensible to them as Crusoe's solitary discovery.

'This running warmed me to a certain extent, and I went on with a better courage through the maze of less frequented roads that runs hereabouts. My back had now become very stiff and sore, my tonsils were painful from the cabman's fingers, and the skin of my neck had been scratched by his nails; my feet hurt exceedingly and I was lame from a little cut on one foot. I saw in time a blind man approaching me, and fled limping, for I feared his subtle intuitions. Once or twice accidental collisions occurred and I left people amazed, with unaccountable curses ringing in their ears. Then came something silent and quiet against my face, and across the Square fell a thin veil of slowly, falling flakes of snow. I had caught a cold, and do as I would I could not avoid an occasional sneeze. And every dog that came in sight, with its pointing nose and curious sniffing, was a terror to me.

'Then came men and boys running, first one and then others, and shouting as they ran. It was a fire. They ran in the direction of my lodging, and looking back down a street I saw a mass of black smoke streaming up above the roofs and telephone wires. It was my lodging burning; my clothes, my apparatus, all my resources indeed, except my cheque-book and the three volumes of memoranda that awaited me in Great Portland Street, were there. Burning! I had burnt my boats – if ever a man did! The place was blazing.'

The Invisible Man paused and thought. Kemp glanced nervously out of the window. 'Yes?' he said. 'Go on.'

XXII

In the Emporium

'So last January, with the beginnings of a snowstorm in the air about me – and if it settled on me it would betray me! – weary, cold, painful, inexpressibly wretched, and still but half convinced of my invisible quality, I began this new life to which I am committed. I had no refuge, no appliances, no human being in the world in whom I could confide. To have told my secret would have given me away – made a mere show and rarity of me. Nevertheless, I was half minded to accost some passer-by and throw myself upon his mercy. But I knew too clearly the terror and brutal cruelty my advances would evoke. I made no plans in the street. My sole object was to get shelter from the snow, to get myself covered and warm; then I might hope to plan. But even to me, an Invisible Man, the rows of London houses stood latched, barred, and bolted impregnably.

'Only one thing could I see clearly before me, the cold exposure and misery of the snowstorm and the night.

'And then I had a brilliant idea. I turned down one of the roads leading from Gower Street to Tottenham Court Road, and found myself outside Omniums, the big establishment where everything is to be bought – you know the place – meat, grocery, linen, furniture, clothing, oil paintings even, a huge meandering collection of shops rather than a shop. I had thought I should find the doors open, but they were closed, and as I stood in the wide entrance a carriage stopped outside, and a man in uniform – you know the kind of personage with "*Omnium*" on his cap – flung open the door. I contrived to enter, and walking down the shop – it was a department where they were selling ribbons and gloves and stockings and that kind of thing – came to a more spacious region devoted to picnic baskets and wicker furniture.

'I did not feel safe there, however; people were going to and fro, and I prowled restlessly about until I came upon a huge section in an upper floor containing multitudes of bedsteads, and this I clambered, and found a resting-place at last among a huge pile of folded flock mattresses. The place was already lit up and agreeably warm, and I decided to remain where I was, keeping a cautious eye on the two or three sets of shopmen and customers who were meandering through the place, until closing time came. Then I should be able, I thought, to rob the place for food and clothing, and disguised, prowl through it and examine its resources, perhaps sleep on some of the bedding. That seemed an acceptable plan. My idea was to procure clothing to make myself a muffled but acceptable figure, to get money, and then to recover my books and parcels where they awaited me, take a lodging somewhere and elaborate plans for the complete realisation of the advantages my invisibility gave me (as I still imagined) over my fellow-men.

'Closing time arrived quickly enough; it could not have been more than an hour after I took up my position on the mattresses before I noticed the blinds of the windows being drawn, and customers being marched doorward. And then a number of brisk young men began with remarkable alacrity to tidy up the goods that remained disturbed. I left my lair as the crowds diminished, and prowled cautiously out into the less desolate parts of the shop. I was really surprised to observe how rapidly the young men and women whipped away the goods displayed for sale during the day. All the boxes of goods, the hanging fabrics, the festoons of lace, the boxes of sweets in the grocery section, the displays of this and that, were being whipped down, folded up, slapped into tidy receptacles, and everything that could not be taken down and put away had sheets of some coarse stuff like sacking flung over them. Finally all the chairs were turned up on to the counters, leaving the floor clear. Directly each of these young people had done, he or she made promptly for the door with such expression of animation as I have rarely observed in a shop assistant before. Then came a lot of youngsters scattering sawdust and carrying pails and brooms. I had to dodge to get out of the way, and as it was, my ankle got stung with the sawdust. For some time, wandering through the swathed and darkened departments, I could hear the brooms at work. And at last a good hour or more after the shop had been closed, came a noise of locking doors. Silence came upon the place, and I found myself wandering through the vast and intricate shops, galleries, showrooms of the place, alone. It was very still; in one place I remember passing near one of the Tottenham Court Road entrances and listening to the tapping of boot-heels of the passers-by.

'My first visit was to the place where I had seen stockings and gloves for sale. It was dark, and I had the devil of a hunt after matches, which I found at last in the drawer of the little cash desk. Then I had to get a candle. I had to tear down wrappings and ransack a number of boxes and drawers, but at last I managed to turn out what I sought; the box label called them lambswool pants, and lambswool vests. Then socks, a thick comforter, and then I went to the clothing place and got trousers, a lounge jacket, an overcoat and a slouch hat – a clerical sort of hat with the brim turned down. I began to feel a human being again, and my next thought was food.

'Upstairs was a refreshment department, and there I got cold meat. There was coffee still in the urn, and I lit the gas and warmed it up again, and altogether I did not do badly. Afterwards, prowling through the place in search of blankets – I had to put up at last with a heap of down quilts – I came upon a grocery section with a lot of chocolate and candied fruits, more than was good for me indeed – and some white burgundy. And near that was a toy department, and I had a brilliant idea. I found some artificial noses – dummy noses, you know, and I thought of dark spectacles. But Omniums had no optical department. My nose had been a difficulty indeed – I had thought of paint. But the discovery set my mind running on wigs and masks and the like. Finally I went to sleep in a heap of down quilts, very warm and comfortable.

'My last thoughts before sleeping were the most agreeable I had had since the change. I was in a state of physical serenity, and that was reflected in my mind. I thought that I should be able to slip out unobserved in the morning with my clothes upon me, muffling my face with a white wrapper I had taken, purchase, with the money I had taken, spectacles and so forth, and so complete my disguise. I lapsed into disorderly dreams of all the fantastic things that had happened during the last few days. I saw the ugly little landlord vociferating in his rooms; I saw his two sons marvelling, and the wrinkled old woman's gnarled face as she asked for her cat. I experienced again the strange sensation of seeing the cloth disappear, and so I came round to the windy hillside and the sniffing old clergyman mumbling "Dust to dust, earth to earth," and my father's open grave.

'"You also," said a voice, and suddenly I was being forced towards the grave. I struggled, shouted, appealed to the mourners, but they continued stonily following the service; the old clergyman, too, never faltered droning and sniffing through the ritual. I realised I was invisible and inaudible, that overwhelming forces had their grip on me. I struggled in vain, I was forced over the brink, the coffin rang hollow as I fell upon it, and the gravel came flying after me in spadefuls. Nobody heeded me, nobody was aware of me. I made convulsive struggles and awoke.

'The pale London dawn had come, the place was full of a chilly grey light that filtered round the edges of the window blinds. I sat up, and for a time I could not think where this ample apartment, with its counters, its piles of rolled stuff, its heap of quilts and cushions, its iron pillars, might be. Then, as recollection came back to me, I heard voices in conversation.

'Then far down the place, in the brighter light of some department which had already raised its blinds, I saw two men approaching. I scrambled to my feet, looking about me for some way of escape, and even as I did so the sound of my movement made them aware of me. I suppose they saw merely a figure moving quietly and quickly away. "Who's that?" cried one, and "Stop there!" shouted the other. I dashed round a corner and came full tilt – a faceless figure, mind you! – on a lanky lad of fifteen. He yelled and I bowled him over, rushed past him, turned another corner, and by a happy inspiration threw myself flat behind a counter. In another moment feet went running past and I heard voices shouting, "All hands to the doors!" asking what was "up", and giving one another advice how to catch me.

'Lying on the ground, I felt scared out of my wits. But – odd as it may seem – it did not occur to me at the moment to take off my clothes as I should have done. I had made up my mind, I suppose, to get away in them, and that ruled me. And then down the vista of the counters came a bawling of "Here he is!"

'I sprang to my feet, whipped a chair off the counter, and sent it whirling at the fool who had shouted, turned, came into another round a corner, sent him spinning, and rushed up the stairs. He kept his footing, gave a view hallo! and came up the staircase hot after me. Up the staircase were piled a multitude of those bright-coloured pot things – what are they?'

'Art pots,' suggested Kemp.

'That's it! Art pots. Well, I turned at the top step and swung round, plucked one out of a pile and smashed it on his silly head as he came at me. The whole pile of pots went headlong, and I heard shouting and footsteps running from all parts. I made a mad rush for the refreshment place, and there was a man in white like a man cook, who took up the chase. I made one last desperate turn and found myself among lamps and ironmongery. I went behind the counter of this, and waited for my cook, and as he bolted in at the head of the chase, I doubled him up with a lamp. Down he went, and I crouched down behind the counter and began whipping off my clothes as fast as I could. Coat, jacket, trousers, shoes were all right, but a lambswool vest fits a man like a skin. I heard more men coming, my cook was lying quiet on the other side of the counter, stunned or scared speechless, and I had to make another dash for it, like a rabbit hunted out of a wood-pile.

'"This way, policeman!" I heard someone shouting. I found myself in my bedstead storeroom again, and at the end a wilderness of wardrobes. I rushed among them, went flat, got rid of my vest after infinite wriggling, and stood a free man again, panting and scared, as the policeman and three of the shopmen came round the corner. They made a rush for the vest and pants, and collared the trousers. "He's dropping his plunder," said one of the young men. "He *must* be somewhere here."

'But they did not find me all the same.

'I stood watching them hunt for me for a time, and cursing my ill-luck in losing the clothes. Then I went into the refreshment-room, drank a little milk I found there, and sat down by the fire to consider my position.

'In a little while two assistants came in and began to talk over the business very excitedly and like the fools they were. I heard a magnified account of my depredations, and other speculations as to my where-abouts. Then I fell to scheming again. The insurmountable difficulty of the place, especially now it was alarmed, was to get any plunder out of it. I went down into the warehouse to see if there was any chance of packing and addressing a parcel, but I could not understand the system of checking. About eleven o'clock, the snow having thawed as it fell, and the day being finer and a little warmer than the previous one, I decided that the Emporium was hopeless, and went out again, exasper-ated at my want of success, with only the vaguest plans of action in my mind.'

XXIII

In Drury Lane

'But you begin now to realise,' said the Invisible Man, 'the full disadvantage of my condition. I had no shelter, no covering – to get clothing, was to forego all my advantage, to make of myself a strange and terrible thing. I was fasting; for to eat, to fill myself with unassimilated matter, would be to become grotesquely visible again.'

'I never thought of that,' said Kemp.

'Nor had I. And the snow had warned me of other dangers. I could not go abroad in snow – it would settle on me and expose me. Rain, too, would make me a watery outline, a glistening surface of a man – a bubble. And fog – I should be like a fainter bubble in a fog, a surface, a greasy glimmer of humanity. Moreover, as I went abroad – in the London air – I gathered dirt about my ankles, floating smuts and dust upon my skin. I did not know how long it would be before I should become visible from that cause also. But I saw clearly it could not be for long.

'Not in London at any rate.

'I went into the slums towards Great Portland Street, and found myself at the end of the street in which I had lodged. I did not go that way, because of the crowd halfway down it opposite to the still smoking ruins of the house I had fired. My most immediate problem was to get clothing. What to do with my face puzzled me. Then I saw in one of those little miscellaneous shops – news, sweets, toys, stationery, belated Christmas tomfoolery, and so forth – an array of masks and noses. I realised that problem was solved. In a flash I saw my course. I turned about, no longer aimless, and went – circuitously in order to avoid the busy ways, towards the back streets north of the Strand; for I remembered, though not very distinctly where, that some theatrical costumiers had shops in that district.

'The day was cold, with a nipping wind down the northward running streets. I walked fast to avoid being overtaken. Every crossing was a danger, every passenger a thing to watch alertly. One man as I was about to pass him at the top of Bedford Street, turned upon me abruptly and came into me, sending me into the road and almost under the wheel of a passing hansom. The verdict of the cab-rank was that he had had some sort of stroke. I was so unnerved by this encounter that I went into Covent Garden Market and sat down for some time in a quiet corner by a stall of violets, panting and trembling. I found I had caught a fresh cold, and had to turn out after a time lest my sneezes should attract attention.

'At last I reached the object of my quest, a dirty fly-blown little shop in a byway near Drury Lane, with a window full of tinsel robes, sham jewels, wigs, slippers, dominoes and theatrical photographs. The shop was old-fashioned and low and dark, and the house rose above it for four storeys, dark and dismal. I peered through the window and, seeing no one within, entered. The opening of the door set a clanking bell ringing. I left it open, and walked round a bare costume stand, into a corner behind a cheval glass. For a minute or so no one came. Then I heard heavy feet striding across a room, and a man appeared down the shop.

'My plans were now perfectly definite. I proposed to make my way into the house, secrete myself upstairs, watch my opportunity, and when everything was quiet, rummage out a wig, mask, spectacles, and costume, and go into the world, perhaps a grotesque but still a credible figure. And incidentally of course I could rob the house of any available money.

'The man who had entered the shop was a short, slight, hunched, beetle-browed man, with long arms and very short bandy legs. Apparently I had interrupted a meal. He stared about the shop with an expression of expectation. This gave way to surprise, and then anger, as he saw the shop empty. "Damn the boys!" he said. He went to stare up and down the street. He came in again in a minute, kicked the door to with his foot spitefully, and went muttering back to the house door.

'I came forward to follow him, and at the noise of my movement he stopped dead. I did so too, startled by his quickness of ear. He slammed the house door in my face.

'I stood hesitating. Suddenly I heard his quick footsteps returning, and the door reopened. He stood looking about the shop like one who was still not satisfied. Then, murmuring to himself, he examined the back of the counter and peered behind some fixtures. Then he stood doubtful. He had left the house door open and I slipped into the inner room.

'It was a queer little room, poorly furnished and with a number of big masks in the corner. On the table was his belated breakfast, and it was a confoundedly exasperating thing for me, Kemp, to have to sniff his coffee and stand watching while he came in and resumed his meal. And his table manners were irritating. Three doors opened into the little room, one going upstairs and one down, but they were all shut. I could not get out of the room while he was there, I could scarcely move because of his alertness, and there was a draught down my back. Twice I strangled a sneeze just in time.

'The spectacular quality of my sensations was curious and novel, but for all that I was heartily tired and angry long before he had done his eating. But at last he made an end and putting his beggarly crockery on the black tin tray upon which he had had his teapot, and gathering all the crumbs up on the mustard stained cloth, he took the whole lot of things after him. His burden prevented his shutting the door behind him – as he would have done; I never saw such a man for shutting doors – and I followed him into a very dirty underground kitchen and scullery. I had the pleasure of seeing him begin to wash up, and then, finding no good in keeping down there, and the brick floor being cold to my feet, I returned upstairs and sat in his chair by the fire. It was burning low, and scarcely thinking, I put on a little coal. The noise of this brought him up at once, and he stood aglare. He peered about the room and was within an ace of touching me. Even after that examination, he scarcely seemed satisfied. He stopped in the doorway and took a final inspection before he went down.

'I waited in the little parlour for an age, and at last he came up and opened the upstairs door. I just managed to get by him.

'On the staircase he stopped suddenly, so that I very nearly blundered into him. He stood looking back right into my face and listening. "I could have sworn," he said. His long hairy hand pulled at his lower lip. His eye went up and down the staircase. Then he grunted and went on up again.

'His hand was on the handle of a door, and then he stopped again with the same puzzled anger on his face. He was becoming aware of the faint sounds of my movements about him. The man must have had diabolically acute hearing. He suddenly flashed into rage. "If there's anyone in this house," he cried with an oath, and left the threat unfinished. He put his hand in his pocket, failed to find what he wanted, and rushing past me went blundering noisily and pugnaciously down-stairs. But I did not follow him. I sat on the head of the staircase until his return.

'Presently he came up again, still muttering. He opened the door of the room, and before I could enter, slammed it in my face.

'I resolved to explore the house, and spent some time in doing so as noiselessly as possible. The house was very old and tumble-down, damp so that the paper in the attics was peeling from the walls, and rat infested. Some of the door handles were stiff and I was afraid to turn them. Several rooms I did inspect were unfurnished, and others were littered with theatrical lumber, bought second-hand, I judged, from its appearance. In one room next to his I found a lot of old clothes. I began routing among these, and in my eagerness forgot again the evident sharpness of his ears. I heard a stealthy footstep and, looking up just in time, saw him peering in at the tumbled heap and holding an old-fashioned revolver in his hand. I stood perfectly still while he stared about open-mouthed and suspicious. "It must have been her," he said slowly. "Damn her!"

'He shut the door quietly, and immediately I heard the key turn in the lock. Then his footsteps retreated. I realised abruptly that I was locked in. For a minute I did not know what to do. I walked from door to window and back, and stood perplexed. A gust of anger came upon me. But I decided to inspect the clothes before I did anything further, and my first attempt brought down a pile from an upper shelf. This brought him back, more sinister than ever. That time he actually touched me, jumped back with amazement and stood astonished in the middle of the room.

'Presently he calmed a little. "Rats," he said in an undertone, fingers on lip. He was evidently a little scared. I edged quietly out of the room, but a plank creaked. Then the infernal little brute started going all over the house, revolver in hand and locking door after door and pocketing the keys. When I realised what he was up to I had a fit of rage – I could hardly control myself sufficiently to watch my opportunity. By this time I knew he was alone in the house, and so I made no more ado, but knocked him on the head.'

'Knocked him on the head!' exclaimed Kemp.

'Yes – stunned him – as he was going downstairs. Hit him from behind with a stool that stood on the landing. He went downstairs like a bag of old boots.'

'But – ! I say! The common conventions of humanity – '

'Are all very well for common people. But the point was, Kemp, that I had to get out of that house in a disguise without his seeing me. I couldn't think of any other way of doing it. And then I gagged him with a Louis Quatorze vest and tied him up in a sheet.'

'Tied him up in a sheet!'

'Made a sort of bag of it. It was rather a good idea to keep the idiot scared and quiet, and a devilish hard thing to get out of – head away from the string. My dear Kemp, it's no good your sitting and glaring as though I was a murderer. It had to be done. He had his revolver. If once he saw me he would be able to describe me – '

'But still,' said Kemp, 'in England – today. And the man was in his own house, and you were – well, robbing.'

'Robbing! Confound it! You'll call me a thief next! Surely, Kemp, you're not fool enough to dance on the old strings. Can't you see my position?'

'And his too,' said Kemp.

The Invisible Man stood up sharply. 'What do you mean to say?'

Kemp's face grew a trifle hard. He was about to speak and checked himself. 'I suppose, after all,' he said with a sudden change of manner, 'the thing had to be done. You were in a fix. But still –'

'Of course I was in a fix – an infernal fix. And he made me wild too – hunting me about the house, fooling about with his revolver, locking and unlocking doors. He was simply exasperating. You don't blame me, do you? You don't blame me?'

'I never blame anyone,' said Kemp. 'It's quite out of fashion. What did you do next?'

'I was hungry. Downstairs I found a loaf and some rank cheese – more than sufficient to satisfy my hunger. I took some brandy and water, and then went up past my impromptu bag – he was lying quite still – to the room containing the old clothes. This looked out upon the street, two lace curtains brown with dirt guarding the window. I went and peered out through their interstices. Outside the day was bright – by contrast with the brown shadows of the dismal house in which I found myself, dazzlingly bright. A brisk traffic was going by, fruit carts, a hansom, a four-wheeler with a pile of boxes, a fishmonger's cart. I turned with spots of colour swimming before my eyes to the shadowy fixtures behind me. My excitement was giving place to a clear apprehension of my position again. The room was full of a faint scent of benzoline, used, I suppose, in cleaning the garments.

'I began a systematic search of the place. I should judge the hunchback had been alone in the house for some time. He was a curious person. Everything that could possibly be of service to me I collected in the clothes store-room, and then I made a deliberate selection. I found a handbag I thought a suitable possession, and some powder, rouge, and sticking plaster.

'I had thought of painting and powdering my face and all that there was to show of me, in order to render myself visible, but the disadvantage of this lay in the fact that I should require turpentine and other appliances and a considerable amount of time before I could vanish again. Finally I chose a mask of the better type, slightly grotesque but not more so than many human beings, dark glasses, greyish whiskers, and a wig. I could find no underclothing, but that I could buy subsequently, and for the time I swathed myself in calico dominoes and some white cashmere scarfs. I could find no socks, but the hunchback's boots were rather a loose fit and sufficed. In a desk in the shop were three sovereigns and about thirty shillings' worth of silver, and in a locked cupboard I burst in the inner room were eight pounds in gold. I could go forth into the world again, equipped.

'Then came a curious hesitation. Was my appearance really – credible? I tried myself with a little bedroom looking-glass, inspecting myself from every point of view to discover any forgotten chink, but it all seemed sound. I was grotesque to the theatrical pitch, a stage miser, but I was certainly not a physical impossibility. Gathering confidence, I took my looking-glass down into the shop, pulled down the shop blinds, and surveyed myself from every point of view with the help of the cheval glass in the corner.

'I spent some minutes screwing up my courage and then unlocked the shop door and marched out into the street, leaving the little man to get out of his sheet again when he liked. In five minutes a dozen turnings intervened between me and the costumier's shop. No one appeared to notice me very pointedly. My last difficulty seemed overcome.'

He stopped again.

'And you troubled no more about the hunchback?' said Kemp.

'No,' said the Invisible Man. 'Nor have I heard what became of him. I suppose he untied himself or kicked himself out. The knots were pretty tight.'

He became silent and went to the window and stared out.

'What happened when you went out into the Strand?'

'Oh! – disillusionment again. I thought my troubles were over. Practically I thought I had impunity to do whatever I chose, everything – save to give away my secret. So I thought. Whatever I did, whatever the consequences might be, was nothing to me. I had merely to fling aside my garments and vanish. No person could hold me. I could take my money where I found it. I decided to treat myself to a sumptuous feast, and then put up at a good hotel, and accumulate a new outfit of property. I felt amazingly confident – it's not particularly pleasant recalling that I was an ass. I went into a place and was already ordering a lunch, when it occurred to me that I could not eat unless I exposed my invisible face. I finished ordering the lunch, told the man I should be back in ten minutes, and went out exasperated. I don't know if you have ever been disappointed in your appetite.'

'Not quite so badly,' said Kemp, 'but I can imagine it.'

'I could have smashed the silly devils. At last, faint with the desire for tasteful food, I went into another place and demanded a private room. "I am disfigured," I said. "Badly." They looked at me curiously, but of course it was not their affair – and so at last I got my lunch. It was not particularly well served, but it sufficed; and when I had had it, I sat over a cigar, trying to plan my line of action. And outside a snowstorm was beginning.

'The more I thought it over, Kemp, the more I realised what a helpless absurdity an Invisible Man was – in a cold and dirty climate and a crowded civilised city. Before I made this mad experiment I had dreamt of a thousand advantages. That afternoon it seemed all disappointment. I went over the heads of the things a man reckons desirable. No doubt invisibility made it possible to get them, but it made it impossible to enjoy them when they were got. Ambition – what is the good of pride of place when you cannot appear there? What is the good of the love of woman when her name must needs be Delilah? I have no taste for politics, for the blackguardisms of fame, for philanthropy, for sport. What was I to do? And for this I had become a wrapped-up mystery, a swathed and bandaged caricature of a man!'

He paused, and his attitude suggested a roving glance at the window.

'But how did you get to Iping?' said Kemp, anxious to keep his guest busy talking.

'I went there to work. I had one hope. It was a half idea! I have it still. It is a full blown idea now. A way of getting back! Of restoring what I have done. When I choose. When I have done all I mean to do invisibly. And that is what I chiefly want to talk to you about now.'

'You went straight to Iping?'

'Yes. I had simply to get my three volumes of memoranda and my cheque-book, my luggage and underclothing, order a quantity of chemicals to work out this idea of mine – I will show you the calculations as soon as I get my books – and then I started. Jove! I remember the snowstorm now, and the accursed bother it was to keep the snow from damping my pasteboard nose.'

'At the end,' said Kemp, 'the day before yesterday, when they found you out, you rather – to judge by the papers – '

'I did. Rather. Did I kill that fool of a constable?'

'No,' said Kemp. 'He's expected to recover.'

'That's his luck, then. I clean lost my temper, the fools! Why couldn't they leave me alone? And that grocer lout?'

'There are no deaths expected,' said Kemp.

'I don't know about that tramp of mine,' said the Invisible Man, with an unpleasant laugh.

'By Heaven, Kemp, you don't know what rage *is*! To have worked for years, to have planned and plotted, and then to get some fumbling purblind idiot messing across your course! Every conceivable sort of silly creature that has ever been created has been sent to cross me.

'If I have much more of it, I shall go wild – I shall start mowing 'em.

'As it is, they've made things a thousand times more difficult.'

'No doubt it's exasperating,' said Kemp, drily.

XXIV

The Plan That Failed

'But now,' said Kemp, with a side glance out of the window, 'what are we to do?'

He moved nearer his guest as he spoke in such a manner as to prevent the possibility of a sudden glimpse of the three men who were advancing up the hill road – with an intolerable slowness, as it seemed to Kemp.

'What were you planning to do when you were heading for Port Burdock? *Had* you any plan?'

'I was going to clear out of the country. But I have altered that plan rather since seeing you. I thought it would be wise, now the weather is hot and invisibility possible, to make for the South. Especially as my secret was known, and everyone would be on the lookout for a masked and muffled man. You have a line of steamers from here to France. My idea was to get aboard one and run the risks of the passage. Thence I could go by train into Spain, or else get to Algiers. It would not be difficult. There a man might always be invisible – and yet live. And do things. I was using that tramp as a money box and luggage carrier, until I decided how to get my books and things sent over to meet me.'

'That's clear.'

'And then the filthy brute must needs try and rob me! He has hidden my books, Kemp. Hidden my books! If I can lay my hands on him!'

'Best plan to get the books out of him first.'

'But where is he? Do you know?'

'He's in the town police station, locked up, by his own request, in the strongest cell in the place.'

'Cur!' said the Invisible Man.

'But that hangs up your plans a little.'

'We must get those books; those books are vital.'

'Certainly,' said Kemp, a little nervously, wondering if he heard footsteps outside. 'Certainly we must get those books. But that won't be difficult, if he doesn't know they're for you.'

'No,' said the Invisible Man, and thought.

Kemp tried to think of something to keep the talk going, but the Invisible Man resumed of his own accord.

'Blundering into your house, Kemp,' he said, 'changes all my plans. For you are a man that can understand. In spite of all that has happened, in spite of this publicity, of the loss of my books, of what I have suffered, there still remain great possibilities, huge possibilities –

'You have told no one I am here?' he asked abruptly.

Kemp hesitated. 'That was implied,' he said.

'No one?' insisted Griffin.

'Not a soul.'

'Ah! Now – ' The Invisible Man stood up, and sticking his arms akimbo began to pace the study.

'I made a mistake, Kemp, a huge mistake, in carrying this thing through alone. I have wasted strength, time, opportunities. Alone – it is wonderful how little a man can do alone! To rob a little, to hurt a little, and there is the end.

'What I want, Kemp, is a goal-keeper, a helper, and a hiding-place, an arrangement whereby I can sleep and eat and rest in peace, and unsuspected. I must have a confederate. With a confederate, with food and rest – a thousand things are possible.

'Hitherto I have gone on vague lines. We have to consider all that invisibility means, all that it does not mean. It means little advantage for eavesdropping and so forth – one makes sounds. It's of little help, a little help perhaps – in housebreaking and so forth. Once you've caught me you could easily imprison me. But on the other hand I am hard to catch. This invisibility, in fact, is only good in two cases: It's useful in getting away, it's useful in approaching. It's particularly useful, therefore, in killing. I can walk round a man, whatever weapon he has, choose my point, strike as I like. Dodge as I like. Escape as I like.'

Kemp's hand went to his moustache. Was that a movement downstairs?

'And it is killing we must do, Kemp.'

'It is killing we must do,' repeated Kemp. 'I'm listening to your plan, Griffin, but I'm not agreeing, mind. Why killing?'

'Not wanton killing, but a judicious slaying. The point is, they know there is an Invisible Man. And that Invisible Man, Kemp, must now establish a Reign of Terror. Yes – no doubt it's startling. But I mean it. A Reign of Terror. He must take some town like your Burdock and terrify and dominate it. He must issue his orders. He can do that in a thousand ways – scraps of paper thrust under doors would suffice. And all who disobey his orders he must kill, and kill all who would defend them.'

'Humph!' said Kemp, no longer listening to Griffin but to the sound of his front door opening and closing.

'It seems to me, Griffin,' he said, to cover his wandering attention, 'that your confederate would be in a difficult position.'

'No one would know he was a confederate,' said the Invisible Man, eagerly. And then suddenly, '*Hush!* What's that downstairs?'

'Nothing,' said Kemp, and suddenly began to speak loud and fast. 'I don't agree to this, Griffin,' he said. 'Understand me, I don't agree to this. Why dream of playing a game against the race? How can you hope to gain happiness? Don't be a lone wolf. Publish your results; take the world – take the nation at least – into your confidence. Think what you might do with a million helpers – '

The Invisible Man interrupted Kemp – arms extended. 'There are footsteps coming upstairs,' he said in a low voice.

'Nonsense,' said Kemp.

'Let me see,' said the Invisible Man, and advanced, arm extended, to the door.

And then things happened very swiftly. Kemp hesitated for a second and then moved to intercept him. The Invisible Man started and stood still. 'Traitor!' cried the Voice, and suddenly the dressing-gown opened, and sitting down the Unseen began to disrobe. Kemp made three swift steps to the door, and forthwith the Invisible Man – his legs had vanished – sprang to his feet with a shout. Kemp flung the door open.

As it opened, there came a sound of hurrying feet downstairs and voices.

With a quick movement Kemp thrust the Invisible Man back, sprang aside, and slammed the door. The key was outside and ready. In another moment Griffin would have been alone in the belvedere study, a prisoner. Save for one little thing. The key had been slipped in hastily that morning. As Kemp slammed the door it fell noisily upon the carpet.

Kemp's face became white. He tried to grip the door handle with both hands. For a moment he stood lugging. Then the door gave six inches. But he got it closed again. The second time it was jerked a foot wide, and the dressing-gown came wedging itself into the opening. His throat was gripped by invisible fingers, and he left his hold on the handle to defend himself. He was forced back, tripped and pitched heavily into the corner of the landing. The empty dressing-gown was flung on the top of him.

Halfway up the staircase was Colonel Adye, the recipient of Kemp's letter, the chief of the Burdock police. He was staring aghast at the sudden appearance of Kemp, followed by the extraordinary sight of clothing tossing empty in the air. He saw Kemp felled, and struggling to his feet. He saw him rush forward, and go down again, felled like an ox.

Then suddenly he was struck violently. By nothing! A vast weight, it seemed, leapt upon him, and he was hurled headlong down the staircase, with the grip at his throat and a knee in his groin. An invisible foot trod on his back, a ghostly patter passed downstairs, he heard the two police officers in the hall shout and run, and the front door of the house slammed violently.

He rolled over and sat up staring. He saw, staggering down the staircase, Kemp, dusty and dishevelled, one side of his face white from a blow, his lip bleeding, and a pink dressing-gown and some under-clothing held in his arms.

'My God!' cried Kemp, 'the game's up! He's gone!'

XXV

The Hunting of the Invisible Man

For a space Kemp was too inarticulate to make Adye understand the swift things that had just happened. They stood on the landing, Kemp speaking swiftly, the grotesque swathings of Griffin still on his arm. But presently Adye began to grasp something of the situation.

'He is mad,' said Kemp; 'inhuman. He is pure selfishness. He thinks of nothing but his own advantage, his own safety. I have listened to such a story this morning of brutal self-seeking! He has wounded men. He will kill them unless we can prevent him. He will create a panic. Nothing can stop him. He is going out now – furious!'

'He must be caught,' said Adye. 'That is certain.'

'But how?' cried Kemp, and suddenly became full of ideas. 'You must begin at once. You must set every available man to work. You must prevent his leaving this district. Once he gets away, he may go through the countryside as he wills, killing and maiming. He dreams of a reign of terror! A reign of terror, I tell you. You must set a watch on trains and roads and shipping. The garrison must help. You must wire for help. The only thing that may keep him here is the thought of recovering some books of notes he counts of value. I will tell you of that! There is a man in your police station – Marvel.'

'I know,' said Adye, 'I know. Those books – yes.'

'And you must prevent him from eating or sleeping; day and night the country must be astir for him. Food must be locked up and secured, all food, so that he will have to break his way to it. The houses everywhere must be barred against him. Heaven send us cold nights and rain! The whole countryside must begin hunting and keep hunting. I tell you, Adye, he is a danger, a disaster; unless he is pinned and secured, it is frightful to think of the things that may happen.'

'What else can we do?' said Adye. 'I must go down at once and begin organising. But why not come? Yes – you come too! Come, and we must hold a sort of council of war – get Hopps to help – and the railway managers. By Jove! it's urgent. Come along – tell me as we go. What else is there we can do? Put that stuff down.'

In another moment Adye was leading the way downstairs. They found the front door open and the policemen standing outside staring at empty air. 'He's got away, sir,' said one.

'We must go to the central station at once,' said Adye. 'One of you go on down and get a cab to come up and meet us – quickly. And now, Kemp, what else?'

'Dogs,' said Kemp. 'Get dogs. They don't see him, but they wind him. Get dogs.'

'Good,' said Adye. 'It's not generally known, but the prison officials over at Halstead know a man with bloodhounds. Dogs. What else?'

'Bear in mind,' said Kemp, 'his food shows. After eating, his food shows until it is assimilated. So that he has to hide after eating. You must keep on beating – every thicket, every quiet corner. And put all weapons, all implements that might be weapons, away. He can't carry such things for long. And what he can snatch up and strike men with must be hidden away.'

'Good again,' said Adye. 'We shall have him yet!'

'And on the roads,' said Kemp, and hesitated.

'Yes?' said Adye.

'Powdered glass,' said Kemp. 'It's cruel, I know. But think of what he may do!'

Adye drew the air in sharply between his teeth. 'It's unsportsmanlike. I don't know. But I'll have powdered glass got ready. If he goes too far –'

'The man's become inhuman, I tell you,' said Kemp. 'I am as sure he will establish a reign of terror – so soon as he has got over the emotions of this escape – as I am sure I am talking to you. Our only chance is to be ahead. He has cut himself off from his kind. His blood be upon his own head.'

XXVI

The Wicksteed Murder

The Invisible Man seems to have rushed out of Kemp's house in a state of blind fury. A little child playing near Kemp's gateway was violently caught up and thrown aside, so that its ankle was broken, and thereafter for some hours the Invisible Man passed out of human perceptions. No one knows where he went nor what he did. But one can imagine him hurrying through the hot June forenoon, up the hill and on to the open downland behind Port Burdock, raging and despairing at his intolerable fate, and sheltering at last, heated and weary, amid the thickets of Hintondean, to piece together again his shattered schemes against his species. That seems the most probable refuge for him, for there it was he re-asserted himself in a grimly tragical manner about two in the afternoon.

One wonders what his state of mind may have been during that time, and what plans he devised. No doubt he was almost ecstatically exasperated by Kemp's treachery, and though we may be able to understand the motives that led to that deceit, we may still imagine and even sympathise a little with the fury the attempted surprise must have occasioned. Perhaps something of the stunned astonishment of his Oxford Street experiences may have returned to him, for he had evidently counted on Kemp's co-operation in his brutal dream of a terrorised world. At any rate he vanished from human ken about midday, and no living witness can tell what he did until about half-past two. It was a fortunate thing, perhaps, for humanity, but for him it was a fatal inaction.

During that time a growing multitude of men scattered over the countryside were busy. In the morning he had still been simply a legend, a terror; in the afternoon, by virtue chiefly of Kemp's drily worded proclamation, he was presented as a tangible antagonist, to be wounded, captured, or overcome, and the countryside began organising itself with inconceivable rapidity. By two o'clock even he might still have removed himself out of the district by getting aboard a train, but after two that became impossible. Every passenger train along the lines on a great parallelogram between Southampton, Manchester, Brighton, and Horsham, travelled with locked doors, and the goods traffic was almost entirely suspended. And in a great circle of twenty miles round Port Burdock, men armed with guns and bludgeons were presently setting out in groups of three and four, with dogs, to beat the roads and fields.

Mounted policemen rode along the country lanes, stopping at every cottage and warning the people to lock up their houses, and keep indoors unless they were armed, and all the elementary schools had broken up by three o'clock, and the children, scared and keeping together in groups, were hurrying home. Kemp's proclamation – signed indeed by Adye – was posted over almost the whole district by four or five o'clock in the afternoon. It gave briefly but clearly all the conditions of the struggle, the necessity of keeping the Invisible Man from food and sleep, the necessity for incessant watchfulness and for a prompt attention to any evidence of his movements. And so swift and decided was the action of the authorities, so prompt and universal was the belief in this strange being, that before nightfall an area of several hundred square miles was in a stringent state of siege. And before nightfall, too, a thrill of horror went through the whole watching nervous countryside. Going from whispering mouth to mouth, swift and certain over the length and breadth of the county, passed the story of the murder of Mr Wicksteed.

If our supposition that the Invisible Man's refuge was the Hintondean thickets is correct, then we must suppose that in the early afternoon he sallied out again bent upon some project that involved the use of a weapon. We cannot know what the project was, but the evidence that he had the iron rod in hand before he met Wicksteed is to me at least overwhelming.

Of course we can know nothing of the details of the encounter. It occurred on the edge of a gravel pit, not two hundred yards from Lord Burdock's Lodge gate. Everything points to a desperate struggle – the trampled ground, the numerous wounds Mr Wicksteed received, his splintered walking-stick; but why the attack was made – save in a murderous frenzy – it is impossible to imagine. Indeed the theory of madness is almost unavoidable. Mr Wicksteed was a man of forty-five or forty-six, steward to Lord Burdock, of inoffensive habits and appearance, the very last person in the world to provoke such a terrible antagonist. Against him it would seem the Invisible Man used an iron rod dragged from a broken piece of fence. He stopped this quiet man, going quietly home to his midday meal, attacked him, beat down his feeble defences, broke his arm, felled him, and smashed his head to a jelly.

Of course he must have dragged this rod out of the fencing before he met his victim; he must have been carrying it ready in his hand. Only two details beyond what has already been stated seem to bear on the matter. One is the circumstance that the gravel pit was not in Mr Wicksteed's direct path home, but nearly a couple of hundred yards out of his way. The other is the assertion of a little girl to the effect that, going to her afternoon school, she saw the murdered man 'trotting' in a peculiar manner across a field towards the gravel pit. Her pantomime of his action suggests a man pursuing something on the ground before him and striking at it ever and again with his walking-stick. She was the last person to see him alive. He passed out of her sight to his death, the struggle being hidden from her only by a clump of beech trees and a slight depression in the ground.

Now this, to the present writer's mind at least, lifts the murder out of the realm of the absolutely wanton. We may imagine that Griffin had taken the rod as a weapon indeed, but without any deliberate intention of using it in murder. Wicksteed may then have come by and noticed this rod inexplicably moving through the air. Without any thought of the Invisible Man – for Port Burdock is ten miles away – he may have pursued it. It is quite conceivable that he may not even have heard of the Invisible Man. One can then imagine the Invisible Man making off – quietly in order to avoid discovering his presence in the neighbour-hood, and Wicksteed, excited and curious, pursuing this unaccountably locomotive object – finally striking at it.

No doubt the Invisible Man could easily have distanced his middle-aged pursuer under ordinary circumstances, but the position in which Wicksteed's body was found suggests that he had the ill luck to drive his quarry into a corner between a drift of stinging nettles and the gravel pit. To those who appreciate the extraordinary irascibility of the Invisible Man, the rest of the encounter will be easy to imagine.

But this is pure hypothesis. The only undeniable facts – for stories of children are often unreliable – are the discovery of Wicksteed's body, done to death, and of the blood-stained iron rod flung among the nettles. The abandonment of the rod by Griffin, suggests that in the emotional excitement of the affair, the purpose for which he took it – if he had a purpose – was abandoned. He was certainly an intensely egotistical and unfeeling man, but the sight of his victim, his first victim, bloody and pitiful at his feet, may have released some long pent fountain of remorse which for a time may have flooded whatever scheme of action he had contrived.

After the murder of Mr Wicksteed, he would seem to have struck across the country towards the downland. There is a story of a voice heard about sunset by a couple of men in a field near Fern Bottom. It was wailing and laughing, sobbing and groaning, and ever and again it shouted. It must have been queer hearing. It drove up across the middle of a clover field and died away towards the hills.

That afternoon the Invisible Man must have learnt something of the rapid use Kemp had made of his confidences. He must have found houses locked and secured; he may have loitered about railway stations and prowled about inns, and no doubt he read the proclamations and realised something of the nature of the campaign against him. And as the evening advanced, the fields became dotted here and there with groups of three or four men, and noisy with the yelping of dogs. These men-hunters had particular instructions in the case of an encounter as to the way they should support one another. He avoided them all. We may understand something of his exasperation, and it could have been none the less because he himself had supplied the information that was being used so remorselessly against him. For that day at least he lost heart; for nearly twenty-four hours, save when he turned on Wicksteed, he was a hunted man. In the night, he must have eaten and slept; for in the morning he was himself again, active, powerful, angry, and malignant, prepared for his last great struggle against the world.

XXVII

The Siege of Kemp's House

Kemp read a strange missive, written in pencil on a greasy sheet of paper.

'You have been amazingly energetic and clever,' this letter ran, 'though what you stand to gain by it I cannot imagine. You are against me. For a whole day you have chased me; you have tried to rob me of a night's rest. But I have had food in spite of you, I have slept in spite of you, and the game is only beginning. The game is only beginning. There is nothing for it, but to start the Terror. This announces the first day of the Terror. Port Burdock is no longer under the Queen, tell your Colonel of Police, and the rest of them; it is under me – the Terror! This is day one of year one of the new epoch – the Epoch of the Invisible Man. I am Invisible Man the First. To begin with the rule will be easy. The first day there will be one execution for the sake of example – a man named Kemp. Death starts for him today. He may lock himself away, hide himself away, get guards about him, put on armour if he likes; Death, the unseen Death, is coming. Let him take precautions; it will impress my people. Death starts from the pillar box by midday. The letter will fall in as the postman comes along, then off! The game begins. Death starts. Help him not, my people, lest Death fall upon you also. Today Kemp is to die.'

When Kemp read this letter twice, 'It's no hoax,' he said. 'That's his voice! And he means it.'

He turned the folded sheet over and saw on the addressed side of it the postmark Hintondean, and the prosaic detail '2*d. to pay.*'

He got up slowly, leaving his lunch unfinished – the letter had come by the one o'clock post – and went into his study. He rang for his housekeeper, and told her to go round the house at once, examine all the fastenings of the windows, and close all the shutters. He closed the shutters of his study himself. From a locked drawer in his bedroom he took a little revolver, examined it carefully, and put it into the pocket of his lounge jacket. He wrote a number of brief notes, one to Colonel Adye, gave them to his servant to take, with explicit instructions as to her way of leaving the house. 'There is no danger,' he said, and added a mental reservation, 'to you.' He remained meditative for a space after doing this, and then returned to his cooling lunch.

He ate with gaps of thought. Finally he struck the table sharply. 'We will have him!' he said; 'and I am the bait. He will come too far.'

He went up to the belvedere, carefully shutting every door after him. 'It's a game,' he said, 'an odd game – but the chances are all for me, Mr Griffin, in spite of your invisibility. Griffin *contra mundum* – with a vengeance.'

He stood at the window staring at the hot hillside. 'He must get food every day – and I don't envy him. Did he really sleep last night? Out in the open somewhere – secure from collisions. I wish we could get some good cold wet weather instead of the heat.

'He may be watching me now.'

He went close to the window. Something rapped smartly against the brickwork over the frame, and made him start violently back.

'I'm getting nervous,' said Kemp. But it was five minutes before he went to the window again. 'It must have been a sparrow,' he said.

Presently he heard the front-door bell ringing, and hurried downstairs. He unbolted and unlocked the door, examined the chain, put it up, and opened cautiously without showing himself. A familiar voice hailed him. It was Adye.

'Your servant's been assaulted, Kemp,' he said round the door.

'What!' exclaimed Kemp.

'Had that note of yours taken away from her. He's close about here. Let me in.'

Kemp released the chain, and Adye entered through as narrow an opening as possible. He stood in the hall looking with infinite relief at Kemp refastening the door. 'Note was snatched out of her hand. Scared her horribly. She's down at the station. Hysterics. He's close here. What was it about?'

Kemp swore.

'What a fool I was,' said Kemp, 'I might have known. It's not an hour's walk from Hintondean. Already!'

'What's up?' said Adye.

'Look here!' said Kemp, and led the way into his study. He handed Adye the Invisible Man's letter. Adye read it and whistled softly. 'And you – ?' said Adye.

'Proposed a trap – like a fool,' said Kemp, 'and sent my proposal out by a maid servant. To him.'

Adye followed Kemp's profanity.

'He'll clear out,' said Adye.

'Not he,' said Kemp.

A resounding smash of glass came from upstairs. Adye had a silvery glimpse of a little revolver half out of Kemp's pocket. 'It's the window, upstairs!' said Kemp, and led the way up. There came a second smash while they were still on the staircase. When they reached the study they found two of the three windows smashed, half the room littered with splintered glass, and one big flint lying on the writing table. The two men stopped in the doorway, contemplating the wreckage. Kemp swore again, and as he did so the third window went with a snap like a pistol, hung starred for a moment, and collapsed in jagged, shivering triangles into the room.

'What's this for?' said Adye.

'It's a beginning,' said Kemp.

'There's no way of climbing up here?'

'Not for a cat,' said Kemp.

'No shutters?'

'Not here. All the downstairs rooms – Hullo!'

Smash, and then whack of boards hit hard came from downstairs. 'Confound him!' said Kemp. 'That must be – yes – it's one of the bedrooms. He's going to do all the house. But he's a fool. The shutters are up, and the glass will fall outside. He'll cut his feet.'

Another window proclaimed its destruction. The two men stood on the landing perplexed. 'I have it!' said Adye. 'Let me have a stick or something, and I'll go down to the station and get the bloodhounds put on. That ought to settle him! They're hard by – not ten minutes – '

Another window went the way of its fellows.

'You haven't a revolver?' asked Adye.

Kemp's hand went to his pocket. Then he hesitated. 'I haven't one – at least to spare.'

'I'll bring it back,' said Adye, 'you'll be safe here.'

Kemp, ashamed of his momentary lapse from truthfulness, handed him the weapon.

'Now for the door,' said Adye.

As they stood hesitating in the hall, they heard one of the first-floor bedroom windows crack and clash. Kemp went to the door and began to slip the bolts as silently as possible. His face was a little paler than usual. 'You must step straight out,' said Kemp. In another moment Adye was on the doorstep and the bolts were dropping back into the staples. He hesitated for a moment, feeling more comfortable with his back against the door. Then he marched, upright and square, down the steps. He crossed the lawn and approached the gate. A little breeze seemed to ripple over the grass. Something moved near him. 'Stop a bit,' said a Voice, and Adye stopped dead and his hand tightened on the revolver.

'Well?' said Adye, white and grim, and every nerve tense.

'Oblige me by going back to the house,' said the Voice, as tense and grim as Adye's.

'Sorry,' said Adye a little hoarsely, and moistened his lips with his tongue. The Voice was on his left front, he thought. Suppose he were to take his luck with a shot?

'What are you going for?' said the Voice, and there was a quick movement of the two, and a flash of sunlight from the open lip of Adye's pocket.

Adye desisted and thought. 'Where I go,' he said slowly, 'is my own business.' The words were still on his lips, when an arm came round his neck, his back felt a knee, and he was sprawling backward. He drew clumsily and fired absurdly, and in another moment he was struck in the mouth and the revolver wrested from his grip. He made a vain clutch at a slippery limb, tried to struggle up and fell back. 'Damn!' said Adye. The Voice laughed. 'I'd kill you now if it wasn't the waste of a bullet,' it said. He saw the revolver in mid-air, six feet off, covering him.

'Well?' said Adye, sitting up.

'Get up,' said the Voice.

Adye stood up.

'Attention,' said the Voice, and then fiercely, 'Don't try any games. Remember I can see your face if you can't see mine. You've got to go back to the house.'

'He won't let me in,' said Adye.

'That's a pity,' said the Invisible Man. 'I've got no quarrel with you.'

Adye moistened his lips again. He glanced away from the barrel of the revolver and saw the sea far off very blue and dark under the midday sun, the smooth green down, the white cliff of the Head, and the multitudinous town, and suddenly he knew that life was very sweet. His eyes came back to this little metal thing hanging between heaven and earth, six feet away. 'What am I to do?' he said sullenly.

'What am *I* to do?' asked the Invisible Man. 'You will get help. The only thing is for you to go back.'

'I will try. If he lets me in will you promise not to rush the door?'

'I've got no quarrel with you,' said the Voice.

Kemp had hurried upstairs after letting Adye out, and now crouching among the broken glass and peering cautiously over the edge of the study window sill, he saw Adye stand parleying with the Unseen. 'Why doesn't he fire?' whispered Kemp to himself. Then the revolver moved a little and the glint of the sunlight flashed in Kemp's eyes. He shaded his eyes and tried to see the source of the blinding beam.

'Surely!' he said, 'Adye has given up the revolver.'

'Promise not to rush the door,' Adye was saying. 'Don't push a winning game too far. Give a man a chance.'

'You go back to the house. I tell you flatly I will not promise anything.'

Adye's decision seemed suddenly made. He turned towards the house, walking slowly with his hands behind him. Kemp watched him – puzzled. The revolver vanished, flashed again into sight, vanished again, and became evident on a closer scrutiny as a little dark object following Adye. Then things happened very quickly. Adye leapt backwards, swung round, clutched at this little object, missed it, threw up his hands and fell forward on his face, leaving a little puff of blue in the air. Kemp did not hear the sound of the shot. Adye writhed, raised himself on one arm, fell forward, and lay still.

For a space Kemp remained staring at the quiet carelessness of Adye's attitude. The afternoon was very hot and still, nothing seemed stirring in all the world save a couple of yellow butterflies chasing each other through the shrubbery between the house and the road gate. Adye lay on the lawn near the gate. The blinds of all the villas down the hill road were drawn, but in one little green summer-house was a white figure, apparently an old man asleep. Kemp scrutinised the surroundings of the house for a glimpse of the revolver, but it had vanished. His eyes came back to Adye. The game was opening well.

Then came a ringing and knocking at the front door, that grew at last tumultuous, but pursuant to Kemp's instructions the servants had locked themselves into their rooms. This was followed by a silence. Kemp sat listening and then began peering cautiously out of the three windows, one after another. He went to the staircase head and stood listening uneasily. He armed himself with his bedroom poker, and went to examine the interior fastenings of the ground-floor windows again. Everything was safe and quiet. He returned to the belvedere. Adye lay motionless over the edge of the gravel just as he had fallen. Coming along the road by the villas were the housemaid and two policemen.

Everything was deadly still. The three people seemed very slow in approaching. He wondered what his antagonist was doing.

He started. There was a smash from below. He hesitated and went downstairs again. Suddenly the house resounded with heavy blows and the splintering of wood. He heard a smash and the destructive clang of the iron fastenings of the shutters. He turned the key and opened the kitchen door. As he did so, the shutters, split and splintering, came flying inward. He stood aghast. The window frame, save for one cross bar, was still intact, but only little teeth of glass remained in the frame. The shutters had been driven in with an axe, and now the axe was descending in sweeping blows upon the window frame and the iron bars defending it. Then suddenly it leapt aside and vanished. He saw the revolver lying on the path outside, and then the little weapon sprang into the air. He dodged back. The revolver cracked just too late, and a splinter from the edge of the closing door flashed over his head. He slammed and locked the door, and as he stood outside he heard Griffin shouting and laughing. Then the blows of the axe with its splitting and smashing consequences, were resumed.

Kemp stood in the passage trying to think. In a moment the Invisible

Man would be in the kitchen. This door would not keep him a moment, and then –

A ringing came at the front door again. It would be the policemen. He ran into the hall, put up the chain, and drew the bolts. He made the girl speak before he dropped the chain, and the three people blundered into the house in a heap, and Kemp slammed the door again.

'The Invisible Man!' said Kemp. 'He has a revolver, with two shots – left. He's killed Adye. Shot him anyhow. Didn't you see him on the lawn? He's lying there.'

'Who?' said one of the policemen.

'Adye,' said Kemp.

'We came in the back way,' said the girl.

'What's that smashing?' asked one of the policemen.

'He's in the kitchen – or will be. He has found an axe – '

Suddenly the house was full of the Invisible Man's resounding blows on the kitchen door. The girl stared towards the kitchen, shuddered, and retreated into the dining-room. Kemp tried to explain in broken sentences. They heard the kitchen door give.

'This way,' cried Kemp, starting into activity, and bundled the policemen into the dining-room doorway.

'Poker,' said Kemp, and rushed to the fender. He handed the poker he had carried to the policeman and the dining-room one to the other. He suddenly flung himself backward.

'Whup!' said one policeman, ducked, and caught the axe on his poker. The pistol snapped its penultimate shot and ripped a valuable Sidney Cooper. The second policeman brought his poker down on the little weapon, as one might knock down a wasp, and sent it rattling to the floor.

At the first clash the girl screamed, stood screaming for a moment by the fireplace, and then ran to open the shutters – possibly with an idea of escaping by the shattered window.

The axe receded into the passage, and fell to a position about two feet from the ground. They could hear the Invisible Man breathing. 'Stand away, you two,' he said. 'I want that man Kemp.'

'We want you,' said the first policeman, making a quick step forward and wiping with his poker at the Voice. The Invisible Man must have started back, and he blundered into the umbrella stand. Then, as the policeman staggered with the swing of the blow he had aimed, the Invisible Man countered with the axe, the helmet crumpled like paper, and the blow sent the man spinning to the floor at the head of the kitchen stairs. But the second policeman, aiming behind the axe with his poker, hit something soft that snapped. There was a sharp exclamation of pain and then the axe fell to the ground. The policeman wiped again at vacancy and hit nothing; he put his foot on the axe, and struck again. Then he stood, poker clubbed, listening intent for the slightest movement.

He heard the dining-room window open, and a quick rush of feet within. His companion rolled over and sat up, with the blood running down between his eye and ear. 'Where is he?' asked the man on the floor.

'Don't know. I've hit him. He's standing somewhere in the hall. Unless he's slipped past you. Doctor Kemp – sir.'

Pause.

'Doctor Kemp,' cried the policeman again.

The second policeman began struggling to his feet. He stood up. Suddenly the faint pad of bare feet on the kitchen stairs could be heard. 'Yap!' cried the first policeman, and incontinently flung his poker. It smashed a little gas bracket.

He made as if he would pursue the Invisible Man downstairs. Then he thought better of it and stepped into the dining-room.

'Doctor Kemp,' he began, and stopped short –

'Doctor Kemp's a hero,' he said, as his companion looked over his shoulder.

The dining-room window was wide open, and neither housemaid nor Kemp was to be seen.

The second policeman's opinion of Kemp was terse and vivid.

XXVIII

The Hunter Hunted

Mr Heelas, Dr Kemp's nearest neighbour among the villa holders, was asleep in his summer-house when the siege of Kemp's house began. Mr Heelas was one of the sturdy minority who refused to believe 'in all this nonsense' about an Invisible Man. His wife, however, as he was subsequently to be reminded, did. He insisted upon walking about his garden just as if nothing was the matter, and he went to sleep in the afternoon in accordance with the custom of years. He slept through the smashing of the windows, and then woke up suddenly with a curious persuasion of something wrong. He looked across at Kemp's house, rubbed his eyes and looked again. Then he put his feet to the ground, and sat listening. He said he was damned, and still the strange thing was visible. The house looked as though it had been deserted for weeks – after a violent riot. Every window was broken, and every window, save those of the belvedere study, was blinded by the internal shutters.

'I could have sworn it was all right' – he looked at his watch – 'twenty minutes ago.'

He became aware of a measured concussion and the clash of glass, far away in the distance. And then, as he sat open mouthed, came a still more wonderful thing. The shutters of the dining-room window were flung open violently, and the housemaid in her outdoor hat and garments, appeared struggling in a frantic manner to throw up the sash. Suddenly a man appeared beside her, helping her – Dr Kemp! In another moment the window was open, and the housemaid was struggling out; she pitched forward and vanished among the shrubs. Mr Heelas stood up, exclaiming vaguely and vehemently at all these wonderful things. He saw Kemp stand on the sill, spring from the window, and reappear almost instantaneously running along a path in the shrubbery and stooping as he ran, like a man who evades observation. He vanished behind a laburnum, and appeared again clambering a fence that abutted on the open down. In a second he had tumbled over and was running at a tremendous pace down the slope towards Mr Heelas.

'Lord!' cried Mr Heelas, struck with an idea; 'it's that Invisible Man brute! It's right, after all!'

With Mr Heelas to think things like that was to act, and his cook watching him from the top window was amazed to see him come pelting towards the house at a good nine miles an hour. 'Thought he wasn't afraid,' said the cook. 'Mary, just come here!' There was a slamming of doors, a ringing of bells, and the voice of Mr Heelas bellowing like a bull. 'Shut the doors, shut the windows, shut everything! the Invisible Man is coming!' Instantly the house was full of screams and directions, and scurrying feet. He ran himself to shut the french windows that opened on the veranda; as he did so Kemp's head and shoulders and knee appeared over the edge of the garden fence. In another moment Kemp had ploughed through the asparagus, and was running across the tennis lawn to the house.

'You can't come in,' said Mr Heelas, shutting the bolts. 'I'm very sorry if he's after you, but you can't come in!'

Kemp appeared with a face of terror close to the glass, rapping and then shaking frantically at the french window. Then, seeing his efforts were useless, he ran along the veranda, vaulted the end, and went to hammer at the side door. Then he ran around by the side gate to the front of the house, and so into the hill-road. And Mr Heelas staring from his window – a face of horror – had scarcely witnessed Kemp vanish, ere the asparagus was being trampled this way and that by feet unseen. At that Mr Heelas fled precipitately upstairs, and the rest of the chase is beyond his purview. But as he passed the staircase window, he heard the side gate slam.

Emerging into the hill-road, Kemp naturally took the downward direction, and so it was he came to run in his own person the very race he had watched with such a critical eye from the belvedere study only four days ago. He ran it well, for a man out of training, and though his face was white and wet, his wits were cool to the last. He ran with wide strides, and wherever a patch of rough ground intervened, wherever there came a patch of raw flints, or a bit of broken glass shone dazzling, he crossed it and left the bare invisible feet that followed to take what line they would.

For the first time in his life Kemp discovered that the hill-road was indescribably vast and desolate, and that the beginnings of the town far below at the hill foot were strangely remote. Never had there been a slower or more painful method of progression than running. All the gaunt villas, sleeping in the afternoon sun, looked locked and barred; no doubt they were locked and barred – by his own orders. But at any rate they might have kept a lookout for an eventuality like this! The town was rising up now, the sea had dropped out of sight behind it, and people down below were stirring. A tram was just arriving at the hill foot. Beyond that was the police station. Was that footsteps he heard behind him? Spurt.

The people below were staring at him, one or two were running, and his breath was beginning to saw in his throat. The tram was quite near now, and the Jolly Cricketers was noisily barring its doors. Beyond the tram were posts and heaps of gravel – the drainage works. He had a transitory idea of jumping into the train and slamming the doors, and then he resolved to go for the police station. In another moment he had passed the door of the Jolly Cricketers, and was in the blistering fag end of the street, with human beings about him. The tram driver and his helper – arrested by the sight of his furious haste – stood staring with the tram horses unhitched. Further on the astonished features of navvies appeared above the mounds of gravel.

His pace broke a little, and then he heard the swift pad of his pursuer, and leapt forward again. 'The Invisible Man!' he cried to the navvies, with a vague indicative gesture, and by an inspiration leapt the excavation and placed a burly group between him and the chase. Then abandoning the idea of the police station he turned into a little side street, rushed by a greengrocer's cart, hesitated for the tenth of a second at the door of a sweetstuff shop, and then made for the mouth of an alley that ran back into the main Hill Street again. Two or three little children were playing here, and shrieked and scattered running at his apparition, and forthwith doors and windows opened and excited mothers revealed their hearts. Out he shot into Hill Street again, three hundred yards from the tram-line end, and immediately he became aware of a tumultuous vociferation and running people.

He glanced up the street towards the hill. Hardly a dozen yards off ran a huge navvy, cursing in fragments and slashing viciously with a spade, and hard behind him came the tram conductor with his fists clenched. Up the street others followed these two, striking and shouting. Down towards the town, men and women were running, and he noticed clearly one man coming out of a shop-door with a stick in his hand. 'Spread out! Spread out!' cried some one. Kemp suddenly grasped the altered condition of the chase. He stopped, and looked round, panting. 'He's close here!' he cried. 'Form a line across – '

'Aha!' shouted a voice.

He was hit hard under the ear, and went reeling, trying to face round towards his unseen antagonist. He just managed to keep his feet, and he struck a vain counter in the air. Then he was hit again under the jaw, and sprawled headlong on the ground. In another moment a knee compressed his diaphragm, and a couple of eager hands gripped his throat, but the grip of one was weaker than the other; he grasped the wrists, heard a cry of pain from his assailant, and then the spade of the navvy came whirling through the air above him, and struck something with a dull thud. He felt a drop of moisture on his face. The grip at his throat suddenly relaxed, and with a convulsive effort, Kemp loosed himself, grasped a limp shoulder, and rolled uppermost. He gripped the unseen elbows near the ground. 'I've got him!' screamed Kemp. 'Help! Help hold! He's down! Hold his feet!'

In another second there was a simultaneous rush upon the struggle, and a stranger coming into the road suddenly might have thought an exceptionally savage game of Rugby football was in progress. And there was no shouting after Kemp's cry – only a sound of blows and feet and a heavy breathing.

Then came a mighty effort, and the Invisible Man threw off a couple of his antagonists and rose to his knees. Kemp clung to him in front like a hound to a stag, and a dozen hands gripped, clutched, and tore at the Unseen. The tram conductor suddenly got the neck and shoulders and lugged him back.

Down went the heap of struggling men again and rolled over. There was, I am afraid, some savage kicking. Then suddenly a wild scream of 'Mercy! Mercy!' that died down swiftly to a sound like choking.

'Get back, you fools!' cried the muffled voice of Kemp, and there was a vigorous shoving back of stalwart forms. 'He's hurt, I tell you. Stand back!'

There was a brief struggle to clear a space, and then the circle of eager faces saw the doctor kneeling, as it seemed, fifteen inches in the air, and holding invisible arms to the ground. Behind him a constable gripped invisible ankles.

'Don't you leave go of en,' cried the big navvy, holding a bloodstained spade: 'he's shamming.'

'He's not shamming,' said the doctor, cautiously raising his knee; 'and I'll hold him.' His face was bruised and already going red; he spoke thickly because of a bleeding lip. He released one hand and seemed to be feeling at the face. 'The mouth's all wet,' he said. And then, 'Good God!'

He stood up abruptly and then knelt down on the ground by the side of the thing unseen. There was a pushing and shuffling, a sound of heavy feet as fresh people turned up to increase the pressure of the crowd. People now were coming out of the houses. The doors of the Jolly Cricketers were suddenly wide open. Very little was said.

Kemp felt about, his hand seeming to pass through empty air. 'He's not breathing,' he said, and then, 'I can't feel his heart. His side – ugh!'

Suddenly an old woman, peering under the arm of the big navvy, screamed sharply. 'Looky there!' she said, and thrust out a wrinkled finger.

And looking where she pointed, everyone saw, faint and transparent as though it was made of glass, so that veins and arteries and bones and nerves could be distinguished, the outline of a hand, a hand limp and prone. It grew clouded and opaque even as they stared.

'Hullo!' cried the constable. 'Here's his feet a-showing!'

And so, slowly, beginning at his hands and feet and creeping along his limbs to the vital centres of his body, that strange change continued. It was like the slow spreading of a poison. First came the little white nerves, a hazy grey sketch of a limb, then the glassy bones and intricate arteries, then the flesh and skin, first a faint fogginess, and then growing rapidly dense and opaque. Presently they could see his crushed chest and his shoulders, and the dim outline of his drawn and battered features.

When at last the crowd made way for Kemp to stand erect, there lay, naked and pitiful on the ground, the bruised and broken body of a young man about thirty. His hair and beard were white – not grey with age, but white with the whiteness of albinism, and his eyes were like garnets. His hands were clenched, his eyes wide open, and his expression was one of anger and dismay.

'Cover his face!' said a man. 'For Gawd's sake, cover that face!' and three little children, pushing forward through the crowd, were suddenly twisted round and sent packing off again.

Someone brought a sheet from the Jolly Cricketers, and having covered him, they carried him into that house.

The Epilogue

So ends the story of the strange and evil experiment of the Invisible Man. And if you would learn more of him you must go to a little inn near Port Stowe and talk to the landlord. The sign of the inn is an empty board save for a hat and boots, and the name is the title of this story. The landlord is a short and corpulent little man with a nose of cylindrical protrusion, wiry hair, and a sporadic rosiness of visage. Drink generously, and he will tell you generously of all the things that happened to him after that time, and of how the lawyers tried to do him out of the treasure found upon him.

'When they found they couldn't prove whose money was which, I'm blessed,' he says, 'if they didn't try to make me out a blooming treasure trove! Do I *look* like a Treasure Trove? And then a gentleman gave me a guinea a night to tell the story at the Empire Music 'all – just tell 'em in my own words – barring one.'

And if you want to cut off the flow of his reminiscences abruptly, you can always do so by asking if there weren't three manuscript books in the story. He admits there were and proceeds to explain, with asseverations that everybody thinks *he* has 'em! But bless you! he hasn't. 'The Invisible Man it was took 'em off to hide 'em when I cut and ran for Port Stowe. It's that Dr Kemp put people on with the idea of *my* having 'em.'

And then he subsides into a pensive state, watches you furtively, bustles nervously with glasses, and presently leaves the bar.

He is a bachelor man – his tastes were ever bachelor, and there are no women folk in the house. Outwardly he buttons – it is expected of him – but in his more vital privacies, in the matter of braces for example, he still turns to string. He conducts his house without enterprise, but with eminent decorum. His movements are slow, and he is a great thinker. But he has a reputation for wisdom and for a respectable parsimony in the village, and his knowledge of the roads of the South of England would beat Cobbett.

And on Sunday mornings, every Sunday morning, all the year round, while he is closed to the outer world, and every night after ten, he goes into his bar parlour, bearing a glass of gin faintly tinged with water, and having placed this down, he locks the door and examines the blinds, and even looks under the table. And then, being satisfied of his solitude, he unlocks the cupboard and a box in the cupboard and a drawer in that box, and produces three volumes bound in brown leather, and places them solemnly in the middle of the table. The covers are weather-worn and tinged with an algal green – for once they sojourned in a ditch and some of the pages have been washed blank by dirty water. The landlord sits down in an armchair, fills a long clay pipe slowly – gloating over the books the while. Then he pulls one towards him and opens it, and begins to study it – turning over the leaves backwards and forwards.

His brows are knit and his lips move painfully. 'Hex, little two up in the air, cross and a fiddle-de-dee. Lord! what a one he was for intellect!'

Presently he relaxes and leans back, and blinks through his smoke across the room at things invisible to other eyes. 'Full of secrets,' he says. 'Wonderful secrets!

'Once I get the haul of them – *Lord*!

'I wouldn't do what *he* did; I'd just – well!' He pulls at his pipe.

So he lapses into a dream, the undying wonderful dream of his life. And though Kemp has fished unceasingly, and Adye has questioned closely, no human being save the landlord knows those books are there, with the subtle secret of invisibility and a dozen other strange secrets written therein. And none other will know of them until he dies.

WHEN THE SLEEPER WAKES

CONTENTS

PREFACE TO 1921 EDITION

This book, *The Sleeper Awakes*, was written in that remote and comparatively happy year, 1898. It is the first of a series of books which I have written at intervals since that time; *The World Set Free* is the latest, they are all 'fantasias of possibility'; each one takes some great creative tendency, or group of tendencies, and develops its possible consequences in the future. *The War in the Air* did that for example with aviation, and is perhaps, as a forecast, the most successful of them all. The present volume takes up certain ideas already very much discussed in the concluding years of the last century, the idea of the growth of the towns and the depopulation of the countryside and the degradation of labour through the higher organisation of industrial production. 'Suppose these forces go on', that is the fundamental hypothesis of the story.

The 'Sleeper' is of course the average man, who owns everything – did he but choose to take hold of his possessions – and who neglects everything. He wakes up to find himself the puppet of a conspiracy of highly intellectual men in a world which is a practical realisation of Mr Belloc's nightmare of the Servile State. And the book resolves itself into as vigorous an imagination as the writer's quality permitted of this world of base servitude in hypertrophied cities.

Will such a world ever exist? I will confess I doubt it. At the time when I wrote this story I had a considerable belief in its possibility, but later on, in *Anticipations* (1900), I made a very careful analysis of the causes of town aggregation and showed that a period of town dispersal was already beginning. And the thesis of a gradual systematic enslavement of organised labour presupposes an intelligence, a power of combination and a *wickedness* in the class of rich financiers and industrial organisers such as this class certainly does not possess, and probably cannot possess. A body of men who had the character and the largeness of imagination necessary to combine and overcome the natural insubordination of the worker would have a character and largeness of imagination too fine and great for any such plot against humanity. I was young in those days, I was thirty-two, I had met few big business men, and I still thought of them as wicked, able men. It was only later that I realised that on the contrary they were, for the most part, rather foolish plungers, fortunate and energetic rather than capable, vulgar rather than wicked, and quite incapable of worldwide constructive plans or generous combined action. 'Ostrog' in *The Sleeper Awakes*, gave way to reality when I drew Uncle Ponderevo in *Tono-Bungay*. The great city of this story is no more then than a nightmare of Capitalism triumphant, a nightmare that was dreamt nearly a quarter of a century ago. It is a fantastic possibility no longer possible. Much evil may be in store for mankind, but to this immense grim organisation of servitude, our race will never come.

H. G. WELLS
Easton Glebe, Dunmow, 1921.

I

Insomnia

One afternoon, at low water, Mr Isbister, a young artist lodging at Boscastle, walked from that place to the picturesque cove of Pentargen, desiring to examine the caves there. Halfway down the precipitous path to the Pentargen beach he came suddenly upon a man sitting in an attitude of profound distress beneath a projecting mass of rock. The hands of this man hung limply over his knees, his eyes were red and staring before him, and his face was wet with tears.

He glanced around at Isbister's footfall. Both men were disconcerted, Isbister the more so, and, to over-ride the awkwardness of his involuntary pause, he remarked, with an air of mature conviction, that the weather was hot for the time of year.

'Very,' answered the stranger shortly, hesitated a second, and added in a colourless tone, 'I can't sleep.'

Isbister stopped abruptly. 'No?' was all he said, but his bearing conveyed his helpful impulse.

'It may sound incredible,' said the stranger, turning weary eyes to Isbister's face and emphasising his words with a languid hand, 'but I have had no sleep at all for six nights.'

'Had advice?'

'Yes. Bad advice for the most part. Drugs. My nervous system . . . They are all very well for the run of people. It's hard to explain. I dare not take . . . sufficiently powerful drugs.'

'That makes it difficult,' said Isbister.

He stood helplessly in the narrow path, perplexed what to do. Clearly the man wanted to talk. An idea natural enough under the circumstances, prompted him to keep the conversation going. 'I've never suffered from sleeplessness myself,' he said in a tone of commonplace gossip, 'but in those cases I have known, people have usually found something – '

'I dare make no experiments.'

He spoke wearily. He gave a gesture of rejection, and for a space both men were silent.

'Exercise?' suggested Isbister diffidently, with a glance from his interlocutor's face of wretchedness to the turning costume he wore.

'That is what I have tried. Unwisely perhaps. I have followed the coast, day after day – from New Quay. It has only added muscular fatigue to the mental. The cause of this unrest was overwork – trouble. There was something – '

He stopped as if from sheer fatigue. He rubbed his forehead with a lean hand. He resumed speech like one who talks to himself.

'I am a lone wolf, a solitary man, wandering through a world in which I have no part. I am wifeless – childless – who is it speaks of the childless as the dead twigs on the tree of life? I am wifeless, childless – I could find no duty to do. No desire even in my heart. One thing at last I set myself to do.

'I said, I *will* do this, and to do it, to overcome the inertia of this dull body, I resorted to drugs. Great God, I've had enough of drugs! I don't know if *you* feel the heavy inconvenience of the body, its exasperating demand of time from the mind – time – life! Live! We only live in patches. We have to eat, and then comes the dull digestive complacencies – or irritations. We have to take the air or else our thoughts grow sluggish, stupid, run into gulfs and blind alleys. A thousand distractions arise from within and without, and then comes drowsiness and sleep. Men seem to live for sleep. How little of a man's day is his own – even at the best! And then come those false friends, those Thug helpers, the alkaloids that stifle natural fatigue and kill rest – black coffee, cocaine – '

'I see,' said Isbister.

'I did my work,' said the sleepless man with a querulous intonation.

'And this is the price?'

'Yes.'

For a little while the two remained without speaking.

'You cannot imagine the craving for rest that I feel – a hunger and thirst. For six long days, since my work was done, my mind has been a whirlpool, swift, unprogressive and incessant, a torrent of thoughts leading nowhere, spinning round swift and steady – '

He paused. 'Towards the gulf.'

'You must sleep,' said Isbister decisively, and with an air of a remedy discovered. 'Certainly you must sleep.'

'My mind is perfectly lucid. It was never clearer. But I know I am drawing towards the vortex. Presently – '

'Yes?'

'You have seen things go down an eddy? Out of the light of the day, out of this sweet world of sanity – down – '

'But,' expostulated Isbister.

The man threw out a hand towards him, and his eyes were wild, and his voice suddenly high. 'I shall kill myself. If in no other way – at the foot of yonder dark precipice there, where the waves are green, and the white surge lifts and falls, and that little thread of water trembles down. There at any rate is . . . sleep.'

'That's unreasonable,' said Isbister, startled at the man's hysterical gust of emotion. 'Drugs are better than that.'

'There at any rate is sleep,' repeated the stranger, not heeding him.

Isbister looked at him and wondered transitorily if some complex Providence had indeed brought them together that afternoon. 'It's not a cert, you know,' he remarked. 'There's a cliff like that at Lulworth Cove – as high, anyhow – and a little girl fell from top to bottom. And lives to-day – sound and well.'

'But those rocks there?'

'One might lie on them rather dismally through a cold night, broken bones grating as one shivered, chill water splashing over you. Eh?'

Their eyes met. 'Sorry to upset your ideals,' said Isbister with a sense of devil-may-careish brilliance. 'But a suicide over that cliff (or any cliff for the matter of that), really, as an artist – ' He laughed. 'It's so damned amateurish.'

'But the other thing,' said the sleepless man irritably, 'the other thing. No man can keep sane if night after night – '

'Have you been walking along this coast alone?'

'Yes.'

'Silly sort of thing to do. If you'll excuse my saying so. Alone! As you say; body fag is no cure for brain fag. Who told you to? No wonder; walking! And the sun on your head, heat, fag, solitude all the day long, and then, I supposed, you go to bed and try very hard – eh?'

Isbister stopped short and looked at the sufferer doubtfully.

'Look at these rocks!' cried the seated man with a sudden force of gesture. 'Look at that sea that has shone and quivered there for ever! See the white spume rush into darkness under that great cliff. And this blue vault, with the blinding sun pouring from the dome of it. It is your world. You accept, you rejoice in it. It warms and supports and lights you. And for me – '

He turned his head and showed a ghastly face, blood-shot pallid eyes and bloodless lips. He spoke almost in a whisper. 'It is the garment of my misery. The whole world . . . is the garment of my misery.'

Isbister looked at all the wild beauty of the sunlit cliffs about them and back to that face of despair. For a moment he was silent.

He started, and made a gesture of impatient rejection. 'You get a night's sleep,' he said, 'and you won't see much misery out here. Take my word for it.'

He was quite sure now that this was a providential encounter. Only half an hour ago he had been feeling horribly bored. Here was employment the bare thought of which was righteous self-applause. He took possession forthwith. It seemed to him that the first need of this exhausted being was companionship. He flung himself down on the steeply sloping turf beside the motionless figure, and deployed forthwith into a skirmishing line of gossip.

His hearer seemed to have lapsed into apathy; he stared dismally seaward, and spoke only in answer to Isbister's direct questions – and not to all of those. But he made no sign of objection to this benevolent intrusion upon his despair.

In a helpless way he seemed even grateful, and when presently Isbister, feeling that his unsupported talk was losing vigour, suggested that they should reascend the steep and return towards Boscastle, alleging the view into Blackapit, he submitted quietly. Halfway up he began talking to himself, and abruptly turned a ghastly face on his helper. 'What can be happening?' he asked with a gaunt illustrative hand. 'What can be happening? Spin, spin, spin, spin. It goes round and round, round and round for evermore.'

He stood with his hand circling.

'It's all right, old chap,' said Isbister with the air of an old friend. 'Don't worry yourself. Trust to me.'

The man dropped his hand and turned again. They went over the brow in single file and to the headland beyond Penally, with the sleepless man gesticulating ever and again, and speaking fragmentary things concerning his whirling brain. At the headland they stood for a space by the seat that looks into the dark mysteries of Blackapit, and then he sat down. Isbister had resumed his talk whenever the path had widened sufficiently for them to walk abreast. He was enlarging upon the complex difficulty of making Boscastle Harbour in bad weather, when suddenly and quite irrelevantly his companion interrupted him again.

'My head is not like what it was,' he said, gesticulating for want of expressive phrases. 'It's not like what it was. There is a sort of oppression, a weight. No – not drowsiness, would God it were! It is like a shadow, a deep shadow falling suddenly and swiftly across something busy. Spin, spin into the darkness. The tumult of thought, the confusion, the eddy and eddy. I can't express it. I can hardly keep my mind on it – steadily enough to tell you.'

He stopped feebly.

'Don't trouble, old chap,' said Isbister. 'I think I can understand. At any rate, it don't matter very much just at present about telling me, you know.'

The sleepless man thrust his knuckles into his eyes and rubbed them. Isbister talked for awhile while this rubbing continued, and then he had a fresh idea. 'Come down to my room,' he said, 'and try a pipe. I can show you some sketches of this Blackapit. If you'd care?'

The other rose obediently and followed him down the steep.

Several times Isbister heard him stumble as they came down, and his movements were slow and hesitating. 'Come in with me,' said Isbister, 'and try some cigarettes and the blessed gift of alcohol. If you take alcohol?'

The stranger hesitated at the garden gate. He seemed no longer clearly aware of his actions. 'I don't drink,' he said slowly, coming up the garden path, and after a moment's interval repeated absently, 'No – I don't drink. It goes round. Spin, it goes – spin – '

He stumbled at the doorstep and entered the room with the bearing of one who sees nothing.

Then he sat down abruptly and heavily in the easy chair, seemed almost to fall into it. He leant forward with his brows on his hands and became motionless.

Presently he made a faint sound in his throat. Isbister moved about the room with the nervousness of an inexperienced host, making little remarks that scarcely required answering. He crossed the room to his portfolio, placed it on the table and noticed the mantel clock.

'I don't know if you'd care to have supper with me,' he said with an unlighted cigarette in his hand – his mind troubled with a design of the furtive administration of chloral. 'Only cold mutton, you know, but passing sweet. Welsh. And a tart, I believe.' He repeated this after momentary silence.

The seated man made no answer. Isbister stopped, match in hand, regarding him.

The stillness lengthened. The match went out, the cigarette was put down unlit. The man was certainly very still. Isbister took up the portfolio, opened it, put it down, hesitated, seemed about to speak. 'Perhaps,' he whispered doubtfully. Presently he glanced at the door and back to the figure. Then he stole on tiptoe out of the room, glancing at his companion after each elaborate pace.

He closed the door noiselessly. The house door was standing open, and he went out beyond the porch, and stood where the monkshood rose at the corner of the garden bed. From this point he could see the stranger through the open window, still and dim, sitting head on hand. He had not moved.

A number of children going along the road stopped and regarded the artist curiously. A boatman exchanged civilities with him. He felt that possibly his circumspect attitude and position seemed peculiar and unaccountable. Smoking, perhaps, might seem more natural. He drew pipe and pouch from his pocket, filled the pipe slowly.

'I wonder,' ... he said, with a scarcely perceptible loss of complacency. 'At any rate one must give him a chance.' He struck a match in the virile way, and proceeded to light his pipe.

Presently he heard his landlady behind him, coming with his lamp lit from the kitchen. He turned, gesticulating with his pipe, and stopped her at the door of his sitting-room. He had some difficulty in explaining the situation in whispers, for she did not know he had a visitor. She retreated again with the lamp, still a little mystified to judge from her manner, and he resumed his hovering at the corner of the porch, flushed and less at his ease.

Long after he had smoked out his pipe, and when the bats were abroad, his curiosity dominated his complex hesitations, and he stole back into his darkling sitting-room. He paused in the doorway. The stranger was still in the same attitude, dark against the window. Save for the singing of some sailors aboard one of the little slate-carrying ships in the harbour, the evening was very still. Outside, the spikes of monkshood and delphinium stood erect and motionless against the shadow of the hillside. Something flashed into Isbister's mind; he started, and leaning over the table, listened. An unpleasant suspicion grew stronger; became conviction. Astonishment seized him and became – dread!

No sound of breathing came from the seated figure!

He crept slowly and noiselessly round the table, pausing twice to listen. At last he could lay his hand on the back of the armchair. He bent down until the two heads were ear to ear.

Then he bent still lower to look up at his visitor's face. He started violently and uttered an exclamation. The eyes were void spaces of white.

He looked again and saw that they were open and with the pupils rolled under the lids. He was suddenly afraid. Overcome by the strangeness of the man's condition, he took him by the shoulder and shook him. 'Are you asleep?' he said, with his voice jumping into alto, and again, 'Are you asleep?'

A conviction took possession of his mind that this man was dead. He suddenly became active and noisy, strode across the room, blundering against a table as he did so, and rang the bell.

'Please bring a light at once,' he said in the passage. 'There is something wrong with my friend.'

Then he returned to the motionless seated figure, grasped the shoulder, shook it, and shouted. The room was flooded with yellow glare as his astonished landlady entered with the light. His face was white as he turned blinking towards her. 'I must fetch a doctor at once,' he said. 'It is either death or a fit. Is there a doctor in the village? Where is a doctor to be found?'

11

The Trance

The state of cataleptic rigour into which this man had fallen, lasted for an unprecedented length of time, and then he passed slowly to the flaccid state, to a lax attitude suggestive of profound repose. Then it was his eyes could be closed.

He was removed from the hotel to the Boscastle surgery, and from the surgery, after some weeks, to London. But he still resisted every attempt at reanimation. After a time, for reasons that will appear later, these attempts were discontinued. For a great space he lay in that strange condition, inert and still – neither dead nor living but, as it were, suspended, hanging mid-way between nothingness and existence. His was a darkness unbroken by a ray of thought or sensation, a dreamless inanition, a vast space of peace. The tumult of his mind had swelled and risen to an abrupt climax of silence. Where was the man? Where is any man when insensibility takes hold of him?

'It seems only yesterday,' said Isbister. 'I remember it all as though it happened yesterday – clearer perhaps, than if it had happened yesterday.'

It was the Isbister of the last chapter, but he was no longer a young man. The hair that had been brown and a trifle in excess of the fashionable length, was iron grey and clipped close, and the face that had been pink and white was buff and ruddy. He had a pointed beard shot with grey. He talked to an elderly man who wore a summer suit of drill (the summer of that year was unusually hot). This was Warming, a London solicitor and next of kin to Graham, the man who had fallen into the trance. And the two men stood side by side in a room in a house in London regarding his recumbent figure.

It was a yellow figure lying lax upon a water-bed and clad in a flowing shirt, a figure with a shrunken face and a stubby beard, lean limbs and lank nails, and about it was a case of thin glass. This glass seemed to mark off the sleeper from the reality of life about him, he was a thing apart, a strange, isolated abnormality. The two men stood close to the glass, peering in.

'The thing gave me a shock,' said Isbister. 'I feel a queer sort of surprise even now when I think of his white eyes. They were white, you know, rolled up. Coming here again brings it all back to me.'

'Have you never seen him since that time?' asked Warming.

'Often wanted to come,' said Isbister; 'but business nowadays is too serious a thing for much holiday keeping. I've been in America most of the time.'

'If I remember rightly,' said Warming, 'you were an artist?'

'Was. And then I became a married man. I saw it was all up with black and white, very soon – at least for a mediocre man, and I jumped on to process. Those posters on the Cliffs at Dover are by my people.'

'Good posters,' admitted the solicitor, 'though I was sorry to see them there.'

'Last as long as the cliffs, if necessary,' exclaimed Isbister with satisfaction. 'The world changes. When he fell asleep, twenty years ago, I was down at Boscastle with a box of water-colours and a noble, old-fashioned ambition. I didn't expect that some day my pigments would glorify the whole blessed coast of England, from Land's End round again to the Lizard. Luck comes to a man very often when he's not looking.'

Warming seemed to doubt the quality of the luck. 'I just missed seeing you, if I recollect aright.'

'You came back by the trap that took me to Camelford railway station. It was close on the Jubilee, Victoria's Jubilee, because I remember the seats and flags in Westminster, and the row with the cabman at Chelsea.'

'The Diamond Jubilee, it was,' said Warming; 'the second one.'

'Ah, yes! At the proper Jubilee – the Fifty Year affair – I was down at Wookey – a boy. I missed all that ... What a fuss we had with him! My landlady wouldn't take him in, wouldn't let him stay – he looked so queer when he was rigid. We had to carry him in a chair up to the hotel. And the Boscastle doctor – it wasn't the present chap, but the G.P. before him – was at him until nearly two, with me and the landlord holding lights and so forth.'

'It was a cataleptic rigour at first, wasn't it?'

'Stiff! – Wherever you bent him he stuck. You might have stood him on his head and he'd have stopped. I never saw such stiffness. Of course this' – he indicated the prostrate figure by a movement of his head – 'is quite different. And, of course, the little doctor – what was his name?'

'Smithers?'

'Smithers it was – was quite wrong in trying to fetch him round too soon, according to all accounts. The things he did. Even now it makes me feel all – ugh! Mustard, snuff, pricking. And one of those beastly little things, not dynamos – '

'Induction coils.'

'Yes. You could see his muscles throb and jump, and he twisted about. There was just two flaring yellow candles, and all the shadows were shivering, and the little doctor nervous and putting on side, and *him* – stark and squirming in the most unnatural ways. Well, it made me dream.'

Pause.

'It's a strange state,' said Warming.

'It's a sort of complete absence,' said Isbister. 'Here's the body, empty. Not dead a bit, and yet not alive. It's like a seat vacant and marked "engaged". No feeling, no digestion, no beating of the heart – not a flutter. *That* doesn't make me feel as if there was a man present. In a sense it's more dead than death, for these doctors tell me that even the hair has stopped growing. Now with the proper dead, the hair will go on growing – '

'I know,' said Warming, with a flash of pain in his expression.

They peered through the glass again. Graham was indeed in a strange state, in the flaccid phase of a trance, but a trance unprecedented in medical history. Trances had lasted for as much as a year before – but at the end of that time it had ever been a waking or a death; sometimes first one and then the other. Isbister noted the marks the physicians had made in injecting nourishment, for that device had been resorted to to postpone collapse; he pointed them out to Warming, who had been trying not to see them.

'And while he has been lying here,' said Isbister, with the zest of a life freely spent, 'I have changed my plans in life; married, raised a family, my eldest lad – I hadn't begun to think of sons then – is an American citizen, and looking forward to leaving Harvard. There's a touch of grey in my hair. And this man, not a day older not wiser (practically) than I was in my downy days. It's curious to think of.'

Warming turned. 'And I have grown old too. I played cricket with him when I was still only a lad. And he looks a young man still. Yellow perhaps. But that *is* a young man nevertheless.'

'And there's been the War,' said Isbister.

'From beginning to end.'

'And these Martians.'

'I've understood,' said Isbister after a pause, 'that he had some moderate property of his own?'

'That is so,' said Warming. He coughed primly. 'As it happens – I have charge of it.'

'Ah!' Isbister thought, hesitated and spoke: 'No doubt – his keep here is not expensive – no doubt it will have improved – accumulated?'

'It has. He will wake up very much better off – if he wakes – than when he slept.'

'As a business man,' said Isbister, 'that thought has naturally been in my mind. I have, indeed, sometimes thought that, speaking commercially, of course, this sleep may be a very good thing for him. That he knows what he is about, so to speak, in being insensible for so long. If he had lived straight on – '

'I doubt if he would have premeditated as much,' said Warming. 'He was not a far-sighted man. In fact – '

'Yes?'

'We differed on that point. I stood to him somewhat in the relation of a guardian. You have probably seen enough of affairs to recognise that occasionally a certain friction – . But even if that was the case, there is a doubt whether he will ever wake. This sleep exhausts slowly, but it exhausts. Apparently he is sliding slowly, very slowly and tediously, down a long slope, if you can understand me?'

'It will be a pity to lose his surprise. There's been a lot of change these twenty years. It's Rip Van Winkle come real.'

'It's Bellamy,' said Warming. 'There has been a lot of change certainly. And, among other changes, I have changed. I am an old man.'

Isbister hesitated, and then feigned a belated surprise. 'I shouldn't have thought it.'

'I was forty-three when his bankers – you remember you wired to his bankers – sent on to me.'

'I got their address from the cheque book in his pocket,' said Isbister.

'Well, the addition is not difficult,' said Warming.

There was another pause, and then Isbister gave way to an unavoidable curiosity. 'He may go on for years yet,' he said, and had a moment of hesitation. 'We have to consider that. His affairs, you know, may fall some day into the hands of – someone else, you know.'

'That, if you will believe me, Mr Isbister, is one of the problems most constantly before my mind. We happen to be – as a matter of fact, there are no very trustworthy connexions of ours. It is a grotesque and unprecedented position.'

'It is,' said Isbister. 'As a matter of fact, it's a case for a public trustee, if only we had such a functionary.'

'It seems to me it's a case for some public body, some practically undying guardian. If he really is going on living – as the doctors, some of them, think. As a matter of fact, I have gone to one or two public men about it. But, so far, nothing has been done.'

'It wouldn't be a bad idea to hand him over to some public body – the British Museum Trustees, or the Royal College of Physicians. Sounds a bit odd, of course, but the whole situation is odd.'

'The difficulty is to induce them to take him.'

'Red tape, I suppose?'

'Partly.'

Pause. 'It's a curious business, certainly,' said Isbister. 'And compound interest has a way of mounting up.'

'It has,' said Warming. 'And now the gold supplies are running short there is a tendency towards . . . appreciation.'

'I've felt that,' said Isbister with a grimace. 'But it makes it better for *him*.'

'*If* he wakes.'

'If he wakes,' echoed Isbister. 'Do you notice the pinched-in look of his nose, and the way in which his eyelids sink?'

Warming looked and thought for a space. 'I doubt if he will wake,' he said at last.

'I never properly understood,' said Isbister, 'what it was brought this on. He told me something about overstudy. I've often been curious.'

'He was a man of considerable gifts, but spasmodic, emotional. He had grave domestic troubles, divorced his wife, in fact, and it was as a relief from that, I think, that he took up politics of the rabid sort. He was a fanatical Radical – a Socialist – or typical Liberal, as they used to call themselves, of the advanced school. Energetic – flighty – undisciplined. Overwork upon a controversy did this for him. I remember the pamphlet he wrote – a curious production. Wild, whirling stuff. There were one or two prophecies. Some of them are already exploded, some of them are established facts. But for the most part to read such a thesis is to realise how full the world is of unanticipated things. He will have much to learn, much to unlearn, when he wakes. If ever a waking comes.'

'I'd give anything to be there,' said Isbister, 'just to hear what he would say to it all.'

'So would I,' said Warming. 'Aye! so would I,' with an old man's sudden turn to self pity. 'But I shall never see him wake.'

He stood looking thoughtfully at the waxen figure. 'He will never wake,' he said at last. He sighed. 'He will never wake again.'

III

The Awakening

But Warming was wrong in that. An awakening came.

What a wonderfully complex thing! this simple seeming unity – the self! Who can trace its reintegration as morning after morning we awaken, the flux and confluence of its countless factors interweaving, rebuilding, the dim first stirrings of the soul, the growth and synthesis of the unconscious to the sub-conscious, the sub-conscious to dawning consciousness, until at last we recognise ourselves again. And as it happens to most of us after the night's sleep, so it was with Graham at the end of his vast slumber. A dim cloud of sensation taking shape, a cloudy dreariness, and he found himself vaguely somewhere, recumbent, faint, but alive.

The pilgrimage towards a personal being seemed to traverse vast gulfs, to occupy epochs. Gigantic dreams that were terrible realities at the time, left vague perplexing memories, strange creatures, strange scenery, as if from another planet. There was a distinct impression, too, of a momentous conversation, of a name – he could not tell what name – that was subsequently to recur, of some queer long-forgotten sensation of vein and muscle, of a feeling of vast hopeless effort, the effort of a man near drowning in darkness. Then came a panorama of dazzling unstable confluent scenes.

Graham became aware his eyes were open and regarding some unfamiliar thing.

It was something white, the edge of something, a frame of wood. He moved his head slightly, following the contour of this shape. It went up beyond the top of his eyes. He tried to think where he might be. Did it matter, seeing he was so wretched? The colour of his thoughts was a dark depression. He felt the featureless misery of one who wakes towards the hour of dawn. He had an uncertain sense of whispers and footsteps hastily receding.

The movement of his head involved a perception of extreme physical weakness. He supposed he was in bed in the hotel at the place in the valley – but he could not recall that white edge. He must have slept. He remembered now that he had wanted to sleep. He recalled the cliff and waterfall again, and then recollected something about talking to a passer-by.

How long had he slept? What was that sound of pattering feet? And that rise and fall, like the murmur of breakers on pebbles? He put out a languid hand to reach his watch from the chair whereon it was his habit to place it, and touched some smooth hard surface like glass. This was so unexpected that it startled him extremely. Quite suddenly he rolled over, stared for a moment, and struggled into a sitting position. The effort was unexpectedly difficult, and it left him giddy and weak – and amazed.

He rubbed his eyes. The riddle of his surroundings was confusing but his mind was quite clear – evidently his sleep had benefitted him. He was not in a bed at all as he understood the word, but lying naked on a soft and yielding mattress, in a trough of dark glass. The mattress was partly transparent, a fact he observed with a strange sense of insecurity, and below it was a mirror reflecting him greyly. About his arm – and he saw with a shock that his skin was strangely dry and yellow – was bound a curious apparatus of rubber, bound so cunningly that it seemed to pass into his skin above and below. And this strange bed was placed in a case of greenish coloured glass (as it seemed to him), a bar in the white framework of which had first arrested his attention. In the corner of the case was a stand of glittering and delicately made apparatus, for the most part quite strange appliances, though a maximum and minimum thermometer was recognisable.

The slightly greenish tint of the glass-like substance which surrounded him on every hand obscured what lay behind, but he perceived it was a vast apartment of splendid appearance, and with a very large and simple white archway facing him. Close to the walls of the cage were articles of furniture, a table covered with a silvery cloth, silvery like the side of a fish, a couple of graceful chairs, and on the table a number of dishes with substances piled on them, a bottle and two glasses. He realised that he was intensely hungry.

He could see no human being, and after a period of hesitation scrambled off the translucent mattress and tried to stand on the clean white floor of his little apartment. He had miscalculated his strength, however, and staggered and put his hand against the glass-like pane before him to steady himself. For a moment it resisted his hand, bending outward like a distended bladder, then it broke with a slight report and vanished – a pricked bubble. He reeled out into the general space of the hall, greatly astonished. He caught at the table to save himself, knocking one of the glasses to the floor – it rang but did not break – and sat down in one of the armchairs.

When he had a little recovered he filled the remaining glass from the bottle and drank – a colourless liquid it was, but not water, with a pleasing faint aroma and taste and a quality of immediate support and stimulus. He put down the vessel and looked about him.

The apartment lost none of its size and magnificence now that the greenish transparency that had intervened was removed. The archway he saw led to a flight of steps, going downward without the intermediation of a door, to a spacious transverse passage. This passage ran between polished pillars of some white-veined substance of deep ultramarine, and along it came the sound of human movements and voices and a deep undeviating droning note. He sat, now fully awake, listening alertly, forgetting the viands in his attention.

Then with a shock he remembered that he was naked, and casting about him for covering, saw a long black robe thrown on one of the chairs beside him. This he wrapped about him and sat down again, trembling.

His mind was still a surging perplexity. Clearly he had slept, and had been removed in his sleep. But where? And who were those people, the distant crowd beyond the deep blue pillars? Boscastle? He poured out and partially drank another glass of the colourless fluid.

What was this place? – this place that to his senses seemed subtly quivering like a thing alive? He looked about him at the clean and beautiful form of the apartment, unstained by ornament, and saw that the roof was broken in one place by a circular shaft full of light, and, as he looked, a steady, sweeping shadow blotted it out and passed, and came again and passed. 'Beat, beat,' that sweeping shadow had a note of its own in the subdued tumult that filled the air.

He would have called out, but only a little sound came into his throat. Then he stood up, and, with the uncertain steps of a drunkard, made his way towards the archway. He staggered down the steps, tripped on the corner of the black cloak he had wrapped about himself, and saved himself by catching at one of the blue pillars.

The passage ran down a cool vista of blue and purple, and ended remotely in a railed space like a balcony, brightly lit and projecting into a space of haze, a space like the interior of some gigantic building. Beyond and remote were vast and vague architectural forms. The tumult of voices rose now loud and clear, and on the balcony and with their backs to him, gesticulating and apparently in animated conversation, were three figures, richly dressed in loose and easy garments of bright soft colourings. The noise of a great multitude of people poured up over the balcony, and once it seemed the top of a banner passed, and once some brightly coloured object, a pale blue cap or garment thrown up into the air perhaps, flashed athwart the space and fell. The shouts sounded like English, there was a reiteration of 'Wake!' He heard some indistinct shrill cry, and abruptly these three men began laughing.

'Ha, ha, ha!' laughed one – a red-haired man in a short purple robe. 'When the Sleeper wakes – *When*!'

He turned his eyes full of merriment along the passage. His face changed, the whole man changed, became rigid. The other two turned swiftly at his exclamation and stood motionless. Their faces assumed an expression of consternation, an expression that deepened into awe.

Suddenly Graham's knees bent beneath him, his arm against the pillar collapsed limply, he staggered forward and fell upon his face.

IV

The Sound of a Tumult

Graham's last impression before he fainted was of a clamorous ringing of bells. He learnt afterwards that he was insensible, hanging between life and death, for the better part of an hour. When he recovered his senses there was a stirring warmth at heart and throat. The dark apparatus, he perceived, had been removed from his arm, which was bandaged. The white framework was still about him, but the greenish transparent substance that had filled it was altogether gone. A man in a deep violet robe, one of those who had been on the balcony, was looking keenly into his face.

Remote but insistent was a clamour of bells and confused sounds, that suggested to his mind the picture of a great number of people shouting together. Something seemed to fall across this tumult, a door suddenly closed.

Graham moved his head. 'What does this all mean?' he said slowly. 'Where am I?'

He saw the red-haired man who had been first to discover him. A voice seemed to be asking what he had said, and was abruptly stilled.

The man in violet answered in a soft voice, speaking English with a slightly foreign accent, or so at least it seemed to the Sleeper's ears, 'You are quite safe. You were brought hither from where you fell asleep. It is quite safe. You have been here some time – sleeping. In a trance.'

He said something further that Graham could not hear, and a little phial was handed across to him. Graham felt a cooling spray, a fragrant mist played over his forehead for a moment, and his sense of refreshment increased. He closed his eyes in satisfaction.

'Better?' asked the man in violet, as Graham's eyes reopened. He was a pleasant-faced man of thirty, perhaps, with a pointed flaxen beard, and a clasp of gold at the neck of his violet robe.

'Yes,' said Graham.

'You have been asleep some time. In a cataleptic trance. You have heard? Catalepsy? It may seem strange to you at first, but I can assure you everything is well.'

Graham did not answer, but these words served their reassuring purpose. His eyes went from face to face of the three people about him. They were regarding him strangely. He knew he ought to be somewhere in Cornwall, but he could not square these things with that impression.

A matter that had been in his mind during his last waking moments at Boscastle recurred, a thing resolved upon and somehow neglected. He cleared his throat.

'Have you wired my cousin?' he asked. 'E. Warming, 27, Chancery Lane?'

They were all assiduous to hear. But he had to repeat it. 'What an odd *blurr* in his accent!' whispered the red-haired man. 'Wire, sir?' said the young man with the flaxen beard, evidently puzzled.

'He means send an electric telegram,' volunteered the third, a pleasant-faced youth of nineteen or twenty. The flaxen-bearded man gave a cry of comprehension. 'How stupid of me! You may be sure everything shall be done, sir,' he said to Graham. 'I am afraid it would be difficult to – *wire* to your cousin. He is not in London now. But don't trouble about arrangements yet; you have been asleep a very long time and the important thing is to get over that, sir.' (Graham concluded the word was sir, but this man pronounced it 'Sire.')

'Oh!' said Graham, and became quiet.

It was all very puzzling, but apparently these people in unfamiliar dress knew what they were about. Yet they were odd and the room was odd. It seemed he was in some newly established place. He had a sudden flash of suspicion. Surely this wasn't some hall of public exhibition! If it was he would give Warming a piece of his mind. But it scarcely had that character. And in a place of public exhibition he would not have discovered himself naked.

Then suddenly, quite abruptly, he realised what had happened. There was no perceptible interval of suspicion, no dawn to his knowledge. Abruptly he knew that his trance had lasted for a vast interval; as if by some processes of thought reading he interpreted the awe in the faces that peered into his. He looked at them strangely, full of intense emotion. It seemed they read his eyes. He framed his lips to speak and could not. A queer impulse to hide his knowledge came into his mind almost at the moment of his discovery. He looked at his bare feet, regarding them silently. His impulse to speak passed. He was trembling exceedingly.

They gave him some pink fluid with a greenish fluorescence and a meaty taste, and the assurance of returning strength grew.

'That – makes me feel better,' he said hoarsely, and there were murmurs of respectful approval. He knew now quite clearly. He made to speak again, and again he could not.

He pressed his throat and tried a third time. 'How long?' he asked in a level voice. 'How long have I been asleep?'

'Some considerable time,' said the flaxen-bearded man, glancing quickly at the others.

'How long?'

'A very long time.'

'Yes – yes,' said Graham, suddenly testy. 'But I want – Is it – it is – some years? Many years? There was something – I forget what. I feel – confused. But you – ' He sobbed. 'You need not fence with me. How long – ?'

He stopped, breathing irregularly. He squeezed his eyes with his knuckles and sat waiting for an answer.

They spoke in undertones.

'Five or six?' he asked faintly. 'More?'

'Very much more than that.'

'More.'

'More.'

He looked at them and it seemed as though imps were twitching the muscles of his face. He looked his question.

'Many years,' said the man with the red beard.

Graham struggled into a sitting position. He wiped a rheumy tear from his face with a lean hand. 'Many years!' he repeated. He shut his eyes tight, opened them, and sat looking about him from one unfamiliar thing to another.

'How many years?' he asked.

'You must be prepared to be surprised.'

'Well?'

'More than a gross of years.'

He was irritated at the strange word. 'More than a *what*?'

Two of them spoke together. Some quick remarks that were made about 'decimal' he did not catch.

'How long did you say?' asked Graham. 'How long? Don't look like that. Tell me.'

Among the remarks in an undertone, his ear caught six words: 'More than a couple of centuries.'

'*What*?' he cried, turning on the youth who he thought had spoken. 'Who says – ? What was that? A couple of *centuries*!'

'Yes,' said the man with the red beard. 'Two hundred years.'

Graham repeated the words. He had been prepared to hear of a vast repose, and yet these concrete centuries defeated him.

'Two hundred years,' he said again, with the figure of a great gulf opening very slowly in his mind; and then,

They said nothing.

'You – did you say – ?'

'Two hundred years. Two centuries of years,' said the man with the red beard.

There was a pause. Graham looked at their faces and saw that what he had heard was indeed true.

'But it can't be,' he said querulously. 'I am dreaming. Trances. Trances don't last. That is not right – this is a joke you have played upon me! Tell me – some days ago, perhaps, I was walking along the coasts of Cornwall – ?'

His voice failed him.

The man with the flaxen beard hesitated. 'I'm not very strong in history, sir,' he said weakly, and glanced at the others.

'That was it, sir,' said the youngster. 'Boscastle, in the old Duchy of Cornwall – it's in the southwest country beyond the dairy meadows. There is a house there still. I have been there.'

'Boscastle!' Graham turned his eyes to the youngster. 'That was it – Boscastle. Little Boscastle. I fell asleep – somewhere there. I don't exactly remember. I don't exactly remember.'

He pressed his brows and whispered, 'More than *two hundred years*!'

He began to speak quickly with a twitching face, but his heart was cold within him. 'But if it *is* two hundred years, every soul I know, every human being that ever I saw or spoke to before I went to sleep, must be dead.'

They did not answer him.

'The Queen and the Royal Family, her Ministers, Church and State. High and low, rich and poor, one with another –

'Is there England still?

'That's a comfort! Is there London?

'This *is* London, eh? And you are my assistant-custodian; assistant-custodian. And these – ? Eh? Assistant-custodians too!'

He sat with a gaunt stare on his face. 'But why am I here? No! Don't talk. Be quiet. Let me – '

He sat silent, rubbed his eyes, and, uncovering them, found another little glass of pinkish fluid held towards him. He took the dose. It was almost immediately sustaining. Directly he had taken it he began to weep naturally and refreshingly.

Presently he looked at their faces, suddenly laughed through his tears, a little foolishly. 'But – two – hun-dred – years!' he said. He grimaced hysterically and covered up his face again.

After a space he grew calm. He sat up, his hands hanging over his knees in almost precisely the same attitude in which Isbister had found him on the cliff at Pentargen. His attention was attracted by a thick domineering voice, the footsteps of an advancing personage. 'What are you doing? Why was I not warned? Surely you could tell? Someone will suffer for this. The man must be kept quiet. Are the doorways closed?

All the doorways? He must be kept perfectly quiet. He must not be told. Has he been told anything?'

The man with the fair beard made some inaudible remark, and Graham looking over his shoulder saw approaching a very short, fat, and thickset beardless man, with aquiline nose and heavy neck and chin. Very thick black and slightly sloping eyebrows that almost met over his nose and overhung deep grey eyes, gave his face an oddly formidable expression. He scowled momentarily at Graham and then his regard returned to the man with the flaxen beard. 'These others,' he said in a voice of extreme irritation. 'You had better go.'

'Go?' said the red-bearded man.

'Certainly – go now. But see the doorways are closed as you go.'

The two men addressed turned obediently, after one reluctant glance at Graham, and instead of going through the archway as he expected, walked straight to the dead wall of the apartment opposite the archway. And then came a strange thing; a long strip of this apparently solid wall rolled up with a snap, hung over the two retreating men and fell again, and immediately Graham was alone with the new comer and the purple-robed man with the flaxen beard.

For a space the thickset man took not the slightest notice of Graham, but proceeded to interrogate the other – obviously his subordinate – upon the treatment of their charge. He spoke clearly, but in phrases only partially intelligible to Graham. The awakening seemed not only a matter of surprise but of consternation and annoyance to him. He was evidently profoundly excited.

'You must not confuse his mind by telling him things,' he repeated again and again. 'You must not confuse his mind.'

His questions answered, he turned quickly and eyed the awakened sleeper with an ambiguous expression.

'Feel queer?' he asked.

'Very.'

'The world, what you see of it, seems strange to you?'

'I suppose I have to live in it, strange as it seems.'

'I suppose so, now.'

'In the first place, hadn't I better have some clothes?'

'They – ' said the thickset man and stopped, and the flaxen-bearded man met his eye and went away. 'You will very speedily have clothes,' said the thickset man.

'Is it true indeed, that I have been asleep two hundred – ?' asked Graham.

'They have told you that, have they? Two hundred and three, as a matter of fact.'

Graham accepted the indisputable now with raised eyebrows and depressed mouth. He sat silent for a moment, and then asked a question,

'Is there a mill or dynamo near here?' He did not wait for an answer. 'Things have changed tremendously, I suppose?' he said.

'What is that shouting?' he asked abruptly.

'Nothing,' said the thickset man impatiently. 'It's people. You'll understand better later – perhaps. As you say, things have changed.' He spoke shortly, his brows were knit, and he glanced about him like a man trying to decide in an emergency. 'We must get you clothes and so forth, at any rate. Better wait here until some can come. No one will come near you. You want shaving.'

Graham rubbed his chin.

The man with the flaxen beard came back towards them, turned suddenly, listened for a moment, lifted his eyebrows at the older man, and hurried off through the archway towards the balcony. The tumult of shouting grew louder, and the thickset man turned and listened also. He cursed suddenly under his breath, and turned his eyes upon Graham with an unfriendly expression. It was a surge of many voices, rising and falling, shouting and screaming, and once came a sound like blows and sharp cries, and then a snapping like the crackling of dry sticks. Graham strained his ears to draw some single thread of sound from the woven tumult.

Then he perceived, repeated again and again, certain formula. For a time he doubted his ears. But surely these were the words: 'Show us the Sleeper! Show us the Sleeper!'

The thickset man rushed suddenly to the archway.

'Wild!' he cried, 'How do they know? Do they know? Or is it guessing?'

There was perhaps an answer.

'I can't come,' said the thickset man; 'I have *him* to see to. But shout from the balcony.'

There was an inaudible reply.

'Say he is not awake. Anything! I leave it to you.'

He came hurrying back to Graham. 'You must have clothes at once,' he said. 'You cannot stop here – and it will be impossible to – '

He rushed away, Graham shouting unanswered questions after him. In a moment he was back.

'I can't tell you what is happening. It is too complex to explain. In a moment you shall have your clothes made. Yes – in a moment. And then I can take you away from here. You will find out our troubles soon enough.'

'But those voices. They were shouting – ?'

'Something about the Sleeper – that's you. They have some twisted idea. I don't know what it is. I know nothing.'

A shrill bell jetted acutely across the indistinct mingling of remote noises, and this brusque person sprang to a little group of appliances in the corner of the room. He listened for a moment, regarding a ball of crystal, nodded, and said a few indistinct words; then he walked to the wall through which the two men had vanished. It rolled up again like a curtain, and he stood waiting.

Graham lifted his arm and was astonished to find what strength the restoratives had given him. He thrust one leg over the side of the couch and then the other. His head no longer swam. He could scarcely credit his rapid recovery. He sat feeling his limbs.

The man with the flaxen beard re-entered from the archway, and as he did so the cage of a lift came sliding down in front of the thickset man, and a lean, grey-bearded man, carrying a roll, and wearing a tightly-fitting costume of dark green, appeared therein.

'This is the tailor,' said the thickset man with an introductory gesture. 'It will never do for you to wear that black. I cannot understand how it got here. But I shall. I shall. You will be as rapid as possible?' he said to the tailor.

The man in green bowed, and advancing, seated himself by Graham on the bed. His manner was calm, but his eyes were full of curiosity. 'You will find the fashions altered, Sire,' he said. He glanced from under his brows at the thickset man.

He opened the roller with a quick movement, and a confusion of brilliant fabrics poured out over his knees. 'You lived, Sire, in a period essentially cylindrical – the Victorian. With a tendency to the hemisphere in hats. Circular curves always. Now – ' He flicked out a little appliance the size and appearance of a keyless watch, whirled the knob, and behold – a little figure in white appeared kinetoscope fashion on the dial, walking and turning. The tailor caught up a pattern of bluish white satin. 'That is my conception of your immediate treatment,' he said.

The thickset man came and stood by the shoulder of Graham.

'We have very little time,' he said.

'Trust me,' said the tailor. 'My machine follows. What do you think of this?'

'What is that?' asked the man from the nineteenth century.

'In your days they showed you a fashion-plate,' said the tailor, 'but this is our modern development. See here.' The little figure repeated its evolutions, but in a different costume. 'Or this,' and with a click another small figure in a more voluminous type of robe marched on to the dial. The tailor was very quick in his movements, and glanced twice towards the lift as he did these things.

It rumbled again, and a crop-haired anaemic lad with features of the Chinese type, clad in coarse pale blue canvas, appeared together with a complicated machine, which he pushed noiselessly on little castors into the room. Incontinently the little kinetoscope was dropped, Graham was invited to stand in front of the machine and the tailor muttered some instructions to the crop-haired lad, who answered in guttural tones and with words Graham did not recognise. The boy then went to conduct an incomprehensible monologue in the corner, and the tailor pulled out a number of slotted arms terminating in little discs, pulling them out until the discs were flat against the body of Graham, one at each shoulder blade, one at the elbows, one at the neck and so forth, so that at last there were, perhaps, two score of them upon his body and limbs. At the same time, some other person entered the room by the lift, behind Graham. The tailor set moving a mechanism that initiated a faint-sounding rhythmic movement of parts in the machine, and in another moment he was knocking up the levers and Graham was released. The tailor replaced his cloak of black, and the man with the flaxen beard proffered him a little glass of some refreshing fluid. Graham saw over the rim of the glass a pale-faced young man regarding him with a singular fixity.

The thickset man had been pacing the room fretfully, and now turned and went through the archway towards the balcony, from which the noise of a distant crowd still came in gusts and cadences. The crop-headed lad handed the tailor a roll of the bluish satin and the two began fixing this in the mechanism in a manner reminiscent of a roll of paper in a nineteenth-century printing machine. Then they ran the entire thing on its easy, noiseless bearings across the room to a remote corner where a twisted cable looped rather gracefully from the wall. They made some connexion and the machine became energetic and swift.

'What is that doing?' asked Graham, pointing with the empty glass to the busy figures and trying to ignore the scrutiny of the new comer. 'Is that – some sort of force – laid on?'

'Yes,' said the man with the flaxen beard.

'Who is *that*?' He indicated the archway behind him.

The man in purple stroked his little beard, hesitated, and answered in an undertone, 'He is Howard, your chief guardian. You see, Sire, – it's a little difficult to explain. The Council appoints a guardian and assistants. This hall has under certain restrictions been public. In order that people might satisfy themselves. We have barred the doorways for the first time. But I think – if you don't mind, I will leave him to explain.'

'Odd!' said Graham. 'Guardian? Council?' Then turning his back on the new comer, he asked in an undertone, 'Why is this man *glaring* at me? Is he a mesmerist?'

'Mesmerist! He is a capillotomist.'

'Capillotomist!'

'Yes – one of the chief. His yearly fee is sixdoz lions.'

It sounded sheer nonsense. Graham snatched at the last phrase with an unsteady mind. 'Sixdoz lions?' he said.

'Didn't you have lions? I suppose not. You had the old pounds? They are our monetary units.'

'But what was that you said – sixdoz?'

'Yes. Six dozen, Sire. Of course things, even these little things, have altered. You lived in the days of the decimal system, the Arab system – tens, and little hundreds and thousands. We have eleven numerals now. We have single figures for both ten and eleven, two figures for a dozen, and a dozen dozen makes a gross, a great hundred, you know, a dozen gross a dozand, and a dozand dozand a myriad. Very simple?'

'I suppose so,' said Graham. 'But about this cap – what was it?'

The man with the flaxen beard glanced over his shoulder.

'Here are your clothes!' he said. Graham turned round sharply and saw the tailor standing at his elbow smiling, and holding some palpably new garments over his arm. The crop-headed boy, by means of one finger, was impelling the complicated machine towards the lift by which he had arrived. Graham stared at the completed suit. 'You don't mean to say – !'

'Just made,' said the tailor. He dropped the garments at the feet of Graham, walked to the bed on which Graham had so recently been lying, flung out the translucent mattress, and turned up the looking glass. As he did so a furious bell summoned the thickset man to the corner. The man with the flaxen beard rushed across to him and then hurried out by the archway.

The tailor was assisting Graham into a dark purple combination garment, stockings, vest, and pants in one, as the thickset man came back from the corner to meet the man with the flaxen beard returning from the balcony. They began speaking quickly in an undertone, their bearing had an unmistakable quality of anxiety. Over the purple under-garment came a complex but graceful garment of bluish white, and Graham was clothed in the fashion once more and saw himself, sallow-faced, unshaven and shaggy still, but at least naked no longer, and in some indefinable unprecedented way graceful.

'I must shave,' he said regarding himself in the glass.

'In a moment,' said Howard.

The persistent stare ceased. The young man closed his eyes, reopened them, and with a lean hand extended, advanced on Graham. Then he stopped, with his hand slowly gesticulating, and looked about him.

'A seat,' said Howard impatiently, and in a moment the flaxen-bearded man had a chair behind Graham. 'Sit down, please,' said Howard.

Graham hesitated, and in the other hand of the wild-eyed man he saw the glint of steel.

'Don't you understand, Sire?' cried the flaxen-bearded man with hurried politeness. 'He is going to cut your hair.'

'Oh!' cried Graham enlightened. 'But you called him – '

'A capillotomist – precisely! He is one of the finest artists in the world.'

Graham sat down abruptly. The flaxen-bearded man disappeared. The capillotomist came forward with graceful gestures, examined Graham's ears and surveyed him, felt the back of his head, and would have sat down again to regard him but for Howard's audible impatience. Forthwith with rapid movements and a succession of deftly handled implements he shaved Graham's chin, clipped his moustache, and cut and arranged his hair. All this he did without a word, with something of the rapt air of a poet inspired. And as soon as he had finished Graham was handed a pair of shoes.

Suddenly a loud voice shouted – it seemed from a piece of machinery in the corner – 'At once – at once. The people know all over the city. Work is being stopped. Work is being stopped. Wait for nothing, but come.'

This shout appeared to perturb Howard exceedingly. By his gestures it seemed to Graham that he hesitated between two directions. Abruptly he went towards the corner where the apparatus stood about the little crystal ball. As he did so the undertone of tumultuous shouting from the archway that had continued during all these occurrences rose to a mighty sound, roared as if it were sweeping past, and fell again as if receding swiftly. It drew Graham after it with an irresistible attraction. He glanced at the thickset man, and then obeyed his impulse. In two strides he was down the steps and in the passage, and in a score he was out upon the balcony upon which the three men had been standing.

V

The Moving Ways

He went to the railings of the balcony and stared upward. An exclamation of surprise at his appearance, and the movements of a number of people came from the spacious area below.

His first impression was of overwhelming architecture. The place into which he looked was an aisle of Titanic buildings, curving spaciously in either direction. Overhead mighty cantilevers sprang together across the huge width of the place, and a tracery of translucent material shut out the sky. Gigantic globes of cool white light shamed the pale sunbeams that filtered down through the girders and wires. Here and there a gossamer suspension bridge dotted with foot passengers flung across the chasm and the air was webbed with slender cables. A cliff of edifice hung above him, he perceived as he glanced upward, and the opposite facade was grey and dim and broken by great archings, circular perforations, balconies, buttresses, turret projections, myriads of vast windows, and an intricate scheme of architectural relief. Athwart these ran inscriptions horizontally and obliquely in an unfamiliar lettering. Here and there close to the roof cables of a peculiar stoutness were fastened, and drooped in a steep curve to circular openings on the opposite side of the space, and even as Graham noted these a remote and tiny figure of a man clad in pale blue arrested his attention. This little figure was far overhead across the space beside the higher fastening of one of these festoons, hanging forward from a little ledge of masonry and handling some well-nigh invisible strings dependent from the line. Then suddenly, with a swoop that sent Graham's heart into his mouth, this man had rushed down the curve and vanished through a round opening on the hither side of the way. Graham had been looking up as he came out upon the balcony, and the things he saw above and opposed to him had at first seized his attention to the exclusion of anything else. Then suddenly he discovered the roadway! It was not a roadway at all, as Graham understood such things, for in the nineteenth century the only roads and streets were beaten tracks of motionless earth, jostling rivulets of vehicles between narrow footways. But this roadway was three hundred feet across, and it moved; it moved, all save the middle, the lowest part. For a moment, the motion dazzled his mind. Then he understood.

Under the balcony this extraordinary roadway ran swiftly to Graham's right, an endless flow rushing along as fast as a nineteenth-century express train, an endless platform of narrow transverse overlapping slats with little interspaces that permitted it to follow the curvatures of the street. Upon it were seats, and here and there little kiosks, but they swept by too swiftly for him to see what might be therein. From this nearest and swiftest platform a series of others descended to the centre of the space. Each moved to the right, each perceptibly slower than the one above it, but the difference in pace was small enough to permit anyone to step from any platform to the one adjacent, and so walk uninterruptedly from the swiftest to the motionless middle way. Beyond this middle way was another series of endless platforms rushing with varying pace to Graham's left. And seated in crowds upon the two widest and swiftest platforms, or stepping from one to another down the steps, or swarming over the central space, was an innumerable and wonderfully diversified multitude of people.

'You must not stop here,' shouted Howard suddenly at his side. 'You must come away at once.'

Graham made no answer. He heard without hearing. The platforms ran with a roar and the people were shouting. He perceived women and girls with flowing hair, beautifully robed, with bands crossing between the breasts. These first came out of the confusion. Then he perceived that the dominant note in that kaleidoscope of costume was the pale blue that the tailor's boy had worn. He became aware of cries of 'The Sleeper. What has happened to the Sleeper?' and it seemed as though the rushing platforms before him were suddenly spattered with the pale buff of human faces, and then still more thickly. He saw pointing fingers. He perceived that the motionless central area of this huge arcade just opposite to the balcony was densely crowded with blue-clad people. Some sort of struggle had sprung into life. People seemed to be pushed up the running platforms on either side and carried away against their will. They would spring off so soon as they were beyond the thick of the confusion, and run back towards the conflict.

'It is the Sleeper. Verily it is the Sleeper,' shouted voices. 'That is never the Sleeper,' shouted others. More and more faces were turned to him. At the intervals along this central area Graham noted openings, pits, apparently the heads of staircases going down with people ascending out of them and descending into them. The struggle it seemed centred about the one of these nearest to him. People were running down the moving platforms to this, leaping dexterously from platform to platform. The clustering people on the higher platforms seemed to divide their interest between this point and the balcony. A number of sturdy little figures clad in a uniform of bright red, and working methodically together, were employed it seemed in preventing access to this descending staircase. About them a crowd was rapidly accumulating. Their brilliant colour contrasted vividly with the whitish-blue of their antagonists, for the struggle was indisputable.

He saw these things with Howard shouting in his ear and shaking his arm. And then suddenly Howard was gone and he stood alone.

He perceived that the cries of 'The Sleeper!' grew in volume, and that the people on the nearer platform were standing up. The nearer swifter platform he perceived was empty to the right of him, and far across the space the platform running in the opposite direction was coming crowded and passing away bare. With incredible swiftness a vast crowd had gathered in the central space before his eyes; a dense swaying mass of people, and the shouts grew from a fitful crying to a voluminous incessant clamour: 'The Sleeper! The Sleeper!' and yells and cheers, a waving of garments and cries of 'Stop the ways!' They were also crying another name strange to Graham. It sounded like 'Ostrog'. The slower platforms were soon thick with active people, running against the movement so as to keep themselves opposite to him.

'Stop the ways,' they cried. Agile figures ran up swiftly from the centre to the swift road nearest to him, were borne rapidly past him, shouting strange, unintelligible things, and ran back obliquely to the central way. One thing he distinguished: 'It is indeed the Sleeper. It is indeed the Sleeper,' they testified.

For a space Graham stood without a movement. Then he became vividly aware that all this concerned him. He was pleased at his wonderful popularity, he bowed, and, seeking a gesture of longer range, waved his arm. He was astonished at the violence of uproar that this provoked. The tumult about the descending stairway rose to furious violence. He became aware of crowded balconies, of men sliding along ropes, of men in trapeze-like seats hurling athwart the space. He heard voices behind him, a number of people descending the steps through the archway; he suddenly perceived that his guardian Howard was back again and gripping his arm painfully, and shouting inaudibly in his ear.

He turned, and Howard's face was white. 'Come back,' he heard. 'They will stop the ways. The whole city will be in confusion.'

He perceived a number of men hurrying along the passage of blue pillars behind Howard, the red-haired man, the man with the flaxen beard, a tall man in vivid vermilion, a crowd of others in red carrying staves, and all these people had anxious eager faces.

'Get him away,' cried Howard.

'But why?' said Graham. 'I don't see – '

'You must come away!' said the man in red in a resolute voice. His face and eyes were resolute, too. Graham's glances went from face to face, and he was suddenly aware of that most disagreeable flavour in life, compulsion. Some one gripped his arm. . . . He was being dragged away. It seemed as though the tumult suddenly became two, as if half the shouts that had come in from this wonderful roadway had sprung into the passages of the great building behind him. Marvelling and confused, feeling an impotent desire to resist, Graham was half led, half thrust, along the passage of blue pillars, and suddenly he found himself alone with Howard in a lift and moving swiftly upward.

VI

The Hall of the Atlas

From the moment when the tailor had bowed his farewell to the moment when Graham found himself in the lift, was altogether barely five minutes. And as yet the haze of his vast interval of sleep hung about him, as yet the initial strangeness of his being alive at all in this remote age touched everything with wonder, with a sense of the irrational, with something of the quality of a realistic dream. He was still detached, an astonished spectator, still but half involved in life. What he had seen, and especially the last crowded tumult, framed in the setting of the balcony, had a spectacular turn, like a thing witnessed from the box of a theatre. 'I don't understand,' he said. 'What was the trouble? My mind is in a whirl. Why were they shouting? What is the danger?'

'We have our troubles,' said Howard. His eyes avoided Graham's inquiry. 'This is a time of unrest. And, in fact, your appearance, your waking just now, has a sort of connexion – '

He spoke jerkily, like a man not quite sure of his breathing. He stopped abruptly.

'I don't understand,' said Graham.

'It will be clearer later,' said Howard.

He glanced uneasily upward, as though he found the progress of the lift slow.

'I shall understand better, no doubt, when I have seen my way about a little,' said Graham puzzled. 'It will be – it is bound to be perplexing. At present it is all so strange. Anything seems possible. Anything. In the details even. Your counting, I understand, is different.'

The lift stopped, and they stepped out into a narrow but very long passage between high walls, along which ran an extraordinary number of tubes and big cables.

'What a huge place this is!' said Graham. 'Is it all one building? What place is it?'

'This is one of the city ways for various public services. Light and so forth.'

'Was it a social trouble – that – in the great roadway place? How are you governed? Have you still a police?'

'Several,' said Howard.

'Several?'

'About fourteen.'

'I don't understand.'

'Very probably not. Our social order will probably seem very complex to you. To tell you the truth, I don't understand it myself very clearly. Nobody does. You will, perhaps – bye and bye. We have to go to the Council.'

Graham's attention was divided between the urgent necessity of his inquiries and the people in the passages and halls they were traversing. For a moment his mind would be concentrated upon Howard and the halting answers he made, and then he would lose the thread in response to some vivid unexpected impression. Along the passages, in the halls, half the people seemed to be men in red uniform. The pale blue canvas that had been so abundant in the aisle of moving ways did not appear. Invariably these men looked at him and saluted him and Howard as they passed.

He had a clear vision of entering a long corridor, and there were a number of girls sitting on low seats, and as though in a class. He saw no teacher, but only a novel apparatus from which he fancied a voice proceeded. The girls regarded him and his conductor, he thought, with curiosity and astonishment. But he was hurried on before he could form a clear idea of the gathering. He judged they knew Howard and not himself and that they wondered who he was. This Howard it seemed, was a person of importance. But then he was also merely Graham's guardian. That was odd.

There came a passage in twilight, and into this passage a footway hung so that he could see the feet and ankles of people going to and fro thereon, but no more of them. Then vague impressions of galleries and of casual astonished passers-by turning around to stare after the two of them with their red-clad guard.

The stimulus of the restoratives he had taken was only temporary. He was speedily fatigued by this excessive haste. He asked Howard to slacken his speed. Presently he was in a lift that had a window upon the great street space, but this was glazed and did not open, and they were too high for him to see the moving platforms below. But he saw people going to and fro along cables and along strange, frail-looking bridges.

And thence they passed across the street and at a vast height above it. They crossed by means of a narrow bridge closed in with glass, so clear that it made him giddy even to remember it. The floor of it also was of glass. From his memory of the cliffs between New Quay and Boscastle, so remote in time, and so recent in his experience, it seemed to him that they must be near four hundred feet above the moving ways. He stopped, looked down between his legs upon the swarming blue and red multitudes, minute and fore-shortened, struggling and gesticulating still towards the little balcony far below, a littl toy balcony, it seemed, where he had so recently been standing. A thin haze and the glare of the mighty globes of light obscured everything. A man seated in a little openwork cradle shot by from some point still higher than the little narrow bridge, rushing down a cable as swiftly almost as if he were falling. Graham stopped involuntarily to watch this strange passenger vanish in a great circular opening below, and then his eyes went back to the tumultuous struggle.

Along one of the swifter ways rushed a thick crowd of red spots. This broke up into individuals as it approached the balcony, and went pouring down the slower ways towards the dense struggling crowd on the central area. These men in red appeared to be striking and thrusting. A great shouting, cries of wrath, screaming, burst out and came up to Graham, faint and thin. 'Go on,' cried Howard, laying hands on him.

Another man rushed down a cable. Graham suddenly glanced up to see whence he came, and beheld through the glassy roof and the network of cables and girders, dim rhythmically passing forms like the vans of windmills, and between them glimpses of a remote and pallid sky. Then Howard had thrust him forward across the bridge, and he was in a little narrow passage decorated with geometrical patterns.

'I want to see more of that,' cried Graham, resisting.

'No, no,' cried Howard, still gripping his arm. 'This way. You must go this way.' And the men in red following them seemed ready to enforce his orders.

Some negroes in a curious wasp-like uniform of black and yellow appeared down the passage, and one hastened to throw up a sliding shutter that had seemed a door to Graham, and led the way through it. Graham found himself in a gallery overhanging the end of a great chamber. The attendant in black and yellow crossed this, thrust up a second shutter and stood waiting.

This place had the appearance of an ante-room. He saw a number of people in the central space, and, at the opposite end a large and imposing doorway at the top of a flight of steps, heavily curtained but giving a glimpse of some still larger hall beyond. He perceived white men in red and other negroes in black and yellow standing stiffly about those portals.

As they crossed the gallery he heard a whisper from below, 'The Sleeper', and was aware of a turning of heads, a hum of observation. They entered another little passage in the wall of this ante-chamber, and then he found himself on an iron-railed gallery of metal that passed round the side of the great hall he had already seen through the curtains. He entered the place at the corner, so that he received the fullest impression of its huge proportions. The black in the wasp uniform stood aside like a well-trained servant, and closed the valve behind him.

Compared with any of the places that Graham had seen thus far, this second hall appeared to be decorated with extreme richness. On a pedestal at the remoter end, and more brilliantly lit than any other object, was a gigantic white figure of Atlas, strong and strenuous, the globe upon his bowed shoulders. It was the first thing to strike his attention, it was so vast, so patiently and painfully real, so white and simple. Save for this figure and for a dais in the centre, the wide floor of the place was a shining vacancy. The dais was remote in the greatness of the area: it would have looked a mere slab of metal had it not been for the group of seven men who stood about a table on it, and gave an inkling of its proportions. They were all dressed in white robes, they seemed to have arisen that moment from their seats, and they were regarding Graham steadfastly. At the end of the table he perceived the glitter of some mechanical appliances.

Howard led him along the end gallery until they were opposite this mighty labouring figure. Then he stopped. The two men in red who had followed them into the gallery came and stood on either hand of Graham.

'You must remain here,' murmured Howard, 'for a few moments,' and, without waiting for a reply, hurried away along the gallery.

'But, *why* – ?' began Graham.

He moved as if to follow Howard, and found his path obstructed by one of the men in red. 'You have to wait here, Sire,' said the man in red.

'*Why?*'

'Orders, Sire.'

'Whose orders?'

'Our orders, Sire.'

Graham looked his exasperation.

'What place is this?' he said presently. 'Who are those men?'

'They are the lords of the Council, Sire.'

'What Council?'

'*The* Council.'

'Oh!' said Graham, and after an equally ineffectual attempt at the other man, went to the railing and stared at the distant men in white, who stood watching him and whispering together.

The Council? He perceived there were now eight though how the newcomer had arrived he had not observed. They made no gestures of greeting; they stood regarding him as in the nineteenth century a group of men might have stood in the street regarding a distant balloon that had suddenly floated into view. What council could it be that gathered there, that little body of men beneath the significant white Atlas, secluded from every eavesdropper in this impressive spaciousness? And why should he be brought to them, and be looked at strangely and spoken of inaudibly? Howard appeared beneath, walking quickly across the polished floor towards them. As he drew near he bowed and performed certain peculiar movements, apparently of a ceremonious nature. Then he ascended the steps of the dais, and stood by the apparatus at the end of the table.

Graham watched that visible inaudible conversation. Occasionally, one of the white-robed men would glance towards him. He strained his ears in vain. The gesticulation of two of the speakers became animated. He glanced from them to the passive faces of his attendants. . . . When he looked again Howard was extending his hands and moving his head like a man who protests. He was interrupted, it seemed by one of the white-robed men rapping the table.

The conversation lasted an interminable time to Graham's sense. His eyes rose to the still giant at whose feet the Council sat. Thence they wandered at last to the walls of the hall. It was decorated in long painted panels of a quasi-Japanese type, many of them very beautiful. These panels were grouped in a great and elaborate framing of dark metal, which passed into the metallic caryatidae of the galleries, and the great structural lines of the interior. The facile grace of these panels enhanced the mighty white effort that laboured in the centre of the scheme. Graham's eyes came back to the Council, and Howard was descending the steps. As he drew nearer his features could be distinguished, and Graham saw that he was flushed and blowing out his cheeks. His countenance was still disturbed when presently he reappeared along the gallery.

'This way,' he said concisely, and they went on in silence to a little door that opened at their approach. The two men in red stopped on either side of this door. Howard and Graham passed in, and Graham, glancing back, saw the white-robed Council still standing in a close group and looking at him. Then the door closed behind him with a heavy thud, and for the first time since his awakening he was in silence. The floor, even, was noiseless to his feet.

Howard opened another door, and they were in the first of two contiguous chambers furnished in white and green. 'What Council was that?' began Graham. 'What were they discussing? What have they to do with me?' Howard closed the door carefully, heaved a huge sigh, and said something in an undertone. He walked slantingways across the room and turned, blowing out his cheeks again. 'Ugh!' he grunted, a man relieved.

Graham stood regarding him.

'You must understand,' began Howard abruptly, avoiding Graham's eyes, 'that our social order is very complex. A half explanation, a bare unqualified statement would give you false impressions. As a matter of fact – it is a case of compound interest partly – your small fortune, and the fortune of your cousin Warming which was left to you – and certain other beginnings – have become very considerable. And in other ways that will be hard for you to understand, you have become a person of significance – of very considerable significance – involved in the world's affairs.'

He stopped.

'Yes?' said Graham.

'We have grave social troubles.'

'Things have come to such a pass that, in fact, it is advisable to seclude you here.'

'Keep me prisoner!' exclaimed Graham.

'Well – to ask you to keep in seclusion.'

Graham turned on him. 'This is strange' he said.

'Yes?

'No harm will be done to you.'

'No harm!'

'But you must be kept here – '

'While I learn my position, I presume.'

'Precisely.'

'Very well then. Begin. Why *harm*?'

'Not now.'

'Why not?'

'It is too long a story, Sire.'

'All the more reason I should begin at once. You say I am a person of importance. What was that shouting I heard? Why is a great multitude shouting and excited because my trance is over, and who are the men in white in that huge council chamber?'

'All in good time, Sire,' said Howard. 'But not crudely, not crudely. This is one of those flimsy times when no man has a settled mind. Your awakening. No one expected your awakening. The Council is consulting.'

'What council?'

'The Council you saw.'

Graham made a petulant movement. 'This is not right,' he said. 'I should be told what is happening.'

'You must wait. Really you must wait.'

Graham sat down abruptly. 'I suppose since I have waited so long to resume life,' he said, 'that I must wait a little longer.'

'That is better,' said Howard. 'Yes, that is much better. And I must leave you alone. For a space. While I attend the discussion in the Council. . . . I am sorry.'

He went towards the noiseless door, hesitated and vanished.

Graham walked to the door, tried it, found it securely fastened in some way he never came to understand, turned about, paced the room restlessly, made the circuit of the room, and sat down. He remained sitting for some time with folded arms and knitted brow, biting his finger nails and trying to piece together the kaleidoscopic impressions of this first hour of awakened life; the vast mechanical spaces, the endless series of chambers and passages, the great struggle that roared and splashed through these strange ways, the little group of remote unsympathetic men beneath the colossal Atlas, Howard's mysterious behaviour. There was an inkling of some vast inheritance already in his mind – a vast inheritance perhaps misapplied – of some unprecedented importance and opportunity. What had he to do? And this room's secluded silence was eloquent of imprisonment!

It came into Graham's mind with irresistible conviction that this series of magnificent impressions was a dream. He tried to shut his eyes and succeeded, but that time-honoured device led to no awakening.

Presently he began to touch and examine all the unfamiliar appointments of the two small rooms in which he found himself.

In a long oval panel of mirror he saw himself and stopped astonished. He was clad in a graceful costume of purple and bluish-white, with a little greyshot beard trimmed to a point, and his hair, its blackness streaked now with bands of grey, arranged over his forehead in an unfamiliar but graceful manner. He seemed a man of five-and-forty perhaps. For a moment he did not perceive this was himself.

A flash of laughter came with the recognition. 'To call on old Warming like this!' he exclaimed, 'and make him take me out to lunch!'

Then he thought of meeting first one and then another of the few familiar acquaintances of his early manhood, and in the midst of his amusement realised that every soul with whom he might jest had died many score of years ago. The thought smote him abruptly and keenly; he stopped short, the expression of his face changed to a white consternation.

The tumultuous memory of the moving platforms and the huge facade of that wonderful street reasserted itself. The shouting multitudes came back clear and vivid, and those remote, inaudible, unfriendly councillors in white. He felt himself a little figure, very small and ineffectual, pitifully conspicuous. And all about him, the world was – *strange*.

VII

In the Silent Rooms

Presently Graham resumed his examination of his apartments. Curiosity kept him moving in spite of his fatigue. The inner room, he perceived, was high, and its ceiling dome shaped, with an oblong aperture in the centre, opening into a funnel in which a wheel of broad vans seemed to be rotating, apparently driving the air up the shaft. The faint humming note of its easy motion was the only clear sound in that quiet place. As these vans sprang up one after the other, Graham could get transient glimpses of the sky. He was surprised to see a star.

This drew his attention to the fact that the bright lighting of these rooms was due to a multitude of very faint glow lamps set about the cornices. There were no windows. And he began to recall that along all the vast chambers and passages he had traversed with Howard he had observed no windows at all. Had there been windows? There were windows on the street indeed, but were they for light? Or was the whole city lit day and night for evermore, so that there was no night there?

And another thing dawned upon him. There was no fireplace in either room. Was the season summer, and were these merely summer apartments, or was the whole city uniformly heated or cooled? He became interested in these questions, began examining the smooth texture of the walls, the simply constructed bed, the ingenious arrangements by which the labour of bedroom service was practically abolished. And over everything was a curious absence of deliberate ornament, a bare grace of form and colour, that he found very pleasing to the eye. There were several very comfortable chairs, a light table on silent runners carrying several bottles of fluids and glasses, and two plates bearing a clear substance like jelly. Then he noticed there were no books, no newspapers, no writing materials. 'The world has changed indeed,' he said.

He observed one entire side of the outer room was set with rows of peculiar double cylinders inscribed with green lettering on white that harmonised with the decorative scheme of the room, and in the centre of this side projected a little apparatus about a yard square and having a white smooth face to the room. A chair faced this. He had a transitory idea that these cylinders might be books, or a modern substitute for books, but at first it did not seem so.

The lettering on the cylinders puzzled him. At first sight it seemed like Russian. Then he noticed a suggestion of mutilated English about certain of the words.

'*oi* Man huwdbi Kin',

forced itself on him as 'The Man who would be King.' 'Phonetic spelling,' he said. He remembered reading a story with that title, then he recalled the story vividly, one of the best stories in the world. But this thing before him was not a book as he understood it. He puzzled out the titles of two adjacent cylinders 'The Heart of Darkness', he had never heard of before nor 'The Madonna of the Future' – no doubt if they were indeed stories, they were by post Victorian authors.

He puzzled over this peculiar cylinder for some time and replaced it. Then he turned to the square apparatus and examined that. He opened a sort of lid and found one of the double cylinders within, and on the upper edge a little stud like the stud of an electric bell. He pressed this and a rapid clicking began and ceased. He became aware of voices and music, and noticed a play of colour on the smooth front face. He suddenly realised what this might be, and stepped back to regard it.

On the flat surface was now a little picture, very vividly coloured, and in this picture were figures that moved. Not only did they move, but they were conversing in clear small voices. It was exactly like reality viewed through an inverted opera glass and heard through a long tube. His interest was seized at once by the situation, which presented a man pacing up and down and vociferating angry things to a pretty but petulant woman. Both were in the picturesque costume that seemed so strange to Graham. 'I have worked,' said the man, 'but what have you been doing?'

'Ah!' said Graham. He forgot everything else, and sat down in the chair. Within five minutes he heard himself named, heard 'when the Sleeper wakes', used jestingly as a proverb for remote postponement, and passed himself by, a thing remote and incredible. But in a little while he knew those two people like intimate friends.

At last the miniature drama came to an end, and the square face of the apparatus was blank again.

It was a strange world into which he had been permitted to see, unscrupulous, pleasure seeking, energetic, subtle, a world too of dire economic struggle; there were allusions he did not understand, incidents that conveyed strange suggestions of altered moral ideals, flashes of dubious enlightenment. The blue canvas that bulked so largely in his first impression of the city ways appeared again and again as the costume of the common people. He had no doubt the story was contemporary, and its intense realism was undeniable. And the end had been a tragedy that oppressed him. He sat staring at the blankness.

He started and rubbed his eyes. He had been so absorbed in the latter-day substitute for a novel, that he awoke to the little green and white room with more than a touch of the surprise of his first awakening.

He stood up, and abruptly he was back in his own wonderland. The clearness of the kinetoscope drama passed, and the struggle in the vast place of streets, the ambiguous Council, the swift phases of his waking hour, came back. These people had spoken of the Council with suggestions of a vague universality of power. And they had spoken of the Sleeper; it had not really struck him vividly at the time that he was the Sleeper. He had to recall precisely what they had said. . . .

He walked into the bedroom and peered up through the quick intervals of the revolving fan. As the fan swept round, a dim turmoil like the noise of machinery came in rhythmic eddies. All else was silence. Though the perpetual day still irradiated his apartments, he perceived the little intermittent strip of sky was now deep blue – black almost, with a dust of little stars. . . .

He resumed his examination of the rooms. He could find no way of opening the padded door, no bell nor other means of calling for attendance. His feeling of wonder was in abeyance; but he was curious, anxious for information. He wanted to know exactly how he stood to these new things. He tried to compose himself to wait until someone came to him. Presently he became restless and eager for information, for distraction, for fresh sensations.

He went back to the apparatus in the other room, and had soon puzzled out the method of replacing the cylinders by others. As he did so, it came into his mind that it must be these little appliances had fixed the language so that it was still clear and understandable after two hundred years. The haphazard cylinders he substituted displayed a musical fantasia. At first it was beautiful, and then it was sensuous. He presently recognised what appeared to him to be an altered version of the story of Tannhauser. The music was unfamiliar. But the rendering was realistic, and with a contemporary unfamiliarity. Tannhauser did not go to a Venusberg, but to a Pleasure City. What was a Pleasure City? A dream, surely, the fancy of a fantastic, voluptuous writer.

He became interested, curious. The story developed with a flavour of strangely twisted sentimentality. Suddenly he did not like it. He liked it less as it proceeded.

He had a revulsion of feeling. These were no pictures, no idealisations, but photographed realities. He wanted no more of the twenty-second-century Venusberg. He forgot the part played by the model in nineteenth-century art, and gave way to an archaic indignation. He rose, angry and half ashamed at himself for witnessing this thing even in solitude. He pulled forward the apparatus, and with some violence sought for a means of stopping its action. Something snapped. A violet spark stung and convulsed his arm and the thing was still. When he attempted next day to replace these Tannhauser cylinders by another pair, he found the apparatus broken. . . .

He struck out a path oblique to the room and paced to and fro, struggling with intolerable vast impressions. The things he had derived from the cylinders and the things he had seen, conflicted, confused him. It seemed to him the most amazing thing of all that in his thirty years of life he had never tried to shape a picture of these coming times. 'We were making the future,' he said, 'and hardly any of us troubled to think what future we were making. And here it is!'

'What have they got to, what has been done? How do I come into the midst of it all?' The vastness of street and house he was prepared for, the multitudes of people. But conflicts in the city ways! And the systematised sensuality of a class of rich men!

He thought of Bellamy, the hero of whose Socialistic Utopia had so oddly anticipated this actual experience. But here was no Utopia, no Socialistic state. He had already seen enough to realise that the ancient antithesis of luxury, waste and sensuality on the one hand and abject poverty on the other, still prevailed. He knew enough of the essential factors of life to understand that correlation. And not only were the buildings of the city gigantic and the crowds in the street gigantic, but the voices he had heard in the ways, the uneasiness of Howard, the very atmosphere spoke of gigantic discontent. What country was he in? Still England it seemed, and yet strangely 'un-English'. His mind glanced at the rest of the world, and saw only an enigmatical veil.

He prowled about his apartment, examining everything as a caged animal might do. He felt very tired, felt that feverish exhaustion that does not admit of rest. He listened for long spaces under the ventilator to catch some distant echo of the tumults he felt must be proceeding in the city.

He began to talk to himself. 'Two hundred and three years!' he said to himself over and over again, laughing stupidly. 'Then I am two hundred and thirty-three years old! The oldest inhabitant. Surely they haven't reversed the tendency of our time and gone back to the rule of the oldest. My claims are indisputable. Mumble, mumble. I remember the Bulgarian atrocities as though it was yesterday. 'Tis a great age! Ha ha!' He was surprised at first to hear himself laughing, and then laughed again deliberately and louder. Then he realised that he was behaving foolishly. 'Steady,' he said. 'Steady!'

His pacing became more regular. 'This new world,' he said. 'I don't understand it. *Why* . . . But it is all *why*!'

'I suppose they can fly and do all sorts of things. Let me try and remember just how it began.'

He was surprised at first to find how vague the memories of his first thirty years had become. He remembered fragments, for the most part trivial moments, things of no great importance that he had observed. His boyhood seemed the most accessible at first, he recalled school books and certain lessons in mensuration. Then he revived the more salient features of his life, memories of the wife long since dead, her magic influence now gone beyond corruption, of his rivals and friends and betrayers, of the swift decision of this issue and that, then of his last years of misery, of fluctuating resolves, and at last of his strenuous studies. In a little while he perceived he had it all again; dim perhaps, like metal long laid aside, but in no way defective or injured, capable of re-polishing. And the hue of it was a deepening misery. Was it worth re-polishing? By a miracle he had been lifted out of a life that had become intolerable. . . .

He reverted to his present condition. He wrestled with the facts in vain. It became an inextricable tangle. He saw the sky through the ventilator pink with dawn. An old persuasion came out of the dark recesses of his memory. 'I must sleep,' he said. It appeared as a delightful relief from this mental distress and from the growing pain and heaviness of his limbs. He went to the strange little bed, lay down and was presently asleep. . . .

He was destined to become very familiar indeed with these apartments before he left them, for he remained imprisoned for three days. During that time no one, except Howard, entered his prison. The marvel of his fate mingled with and in some way minimised the marvel of his survival. He had awakened to mankind it seemed only to be snatched away into this unaccountable solitude. Howard came regularly with subtly sustaining and nutrititive fluids, and light and pleasant foods, quite strange to Graham. He always closed the door carefully as he entered. On matter of detail he was increasingly obliging, but the bearing of Graham on the great issues that were evidently being contested so closely beyond the soundproof walls that enclosed him, he would not elucidate. He evaded, as politely as possible, every question on the position of affairs in the outer world.

And in those three days Graham's incessant thoughts went far and wide. All that he had seen, all this elaborate contrivance to prevent his seeing, worked together in his mind. Almost every possible interpretation of his position he debated – even as it chanced, the right interpretation. Things that presently happened to him, came to him at last credible, by virtue of this seclusion. When at length the moment of his release arrived, it found him prepared. . . .

Howard's bearing went far to deepen Graham's impression of his own strange importance; the door between its opening and closing seemed to admit with him a breath of momentous happening. His inquiries became more definite and searching. Howard retreated through protests and difficulties. The awakening was unforeseen, he repeated; it happened to have fallen in with the trend of a social convulsion. 'To explain it I must tell you the history of a gross and a half of years,' protested Howard.

'The thing is this,' said Graham. 'You are afraid of something I shall do. In some way I am arbitrator – I might be arbitrator.'

'It is not that. But you have – I may tell you this much – the automatic increase of your property puts great possibilities of interference in your hands. And in certain other ways you have influence, with your eighteenth-century notions.'

'Nineteenth century,' corrected Graham.

'With your old world notions, anyhow, ignorant as you are of every feature of our State.'

'Am I a fool?'

'Certainly not.'

'Do I seem to be the sort of man who would act rashly?'

'You were never expected to act at all. No one counted on your awakening. No one dreamt you would ever awake. The Council had surrounded you with antiseptic conditions. As a matter of fact, we thought that you were dead – a mere arrest of decay. And – but it is too complex. We dare not suddenly – while you are still half awake.'

'It won't do,' said Graham. 'Suppose it is as you say – why am I not being crammed night and day with facts and warnings and all the wisdom of the time to fit me for my responsibilities? Am I any wiser now than two days ago, if it is two days, when I awoke?'

Howard pulled his lip.

'I am beginning to feel – every hour I feel more clearly – a sense of complex concealment of which you are the salient point. Is this Council, or committee, or whatever they are, cooking the accounts of my estate? Is that it?'

'That note of suspicion – ' said Howard.

'Ugh!' said Graham. 'Now, mark my words, it will be ill for those who have put me here. It will be ill. I am alive. Make no doubt of it, I am alive. Every day my pulse is stronger and my mind clearer and more vigorous. No more quiescence. I am a man come back to life. And I want to *live* –

'*Live!*'

Howard's face lit with an idea. He came towards Graham and spoke in an easy confidential tone.

'The Council secludes you here for your good. You are restless. Naturally – an energetic man! You find it dull here. But we are anxious that everything you may desire – every desire – every sort of desire.... There may be something. Is there any sort of company?'

He paused meaningly.

'Yes,' said Graham thoughtfully. 'There is.'

'Ah! *Now!* We have treated you neglectfully.'

'The crowds in yonder streets of yours.'

'That,' said Howard, 'I am afraid – But – '

Graham began pacing the room. Howard stood near the door watching him. The implication of Howard's suggestion was only half evident to Graham. Company? Suppose he were to accept the proposal, demand some sort of *company*? Would there be any possibilities of gathering from the conversation of this additional person some vague inkling of the struggle that had broken out so vividly at his waking moment. He meditated again, and the suggestion took colour. He turned on Howard abruptly.

'What do you mean by company?'

Howard raised his eyes and shrugged his shoulders. 'Human beings,' he said, with a curious smile on his heavy face.

'Our social ideas,' he said, 'have a certain increased liberality, perhaps, in comparison with your times. If a man wishes to relieve such a tedium as this – by feminine society, for instance. We think it no scandal. We have cleared our minds of formulae. There is in our city a class, a necessary class, no longer despised – discreet – '

Graham stopped dead.

'It would pass the time,' said Howard. 'It is a thing I should perhaps have thought of before, but, as a matter of fact, so much is happening – '

He indicated the exterior world.

Graham hesitated. For a moment the figure of a possible woman that his imagination suddenly created dominated his mind with an intense attraction. Then he flashed into anger.

'No!' he shouted.

He began striding rapidly up and down the room. 'Everything you say, everything you do, convinces me – of some great issue in which I am concerned. I do not want to pass the time, as you call it. Yes, I know. Desire and indulgence are life in a sense – and Death! Extinction! In my life before I slept I had worked out that pitiful question. I will not begin again. There is a city, a multitude – . And meanwhile I am here like a rabbit in a bag.'

His rage surged high. He choked for a moment and began to wave his clenched fists. He gave way to an anger fit, he swore archaic curses. His gestures had the quality of physical threats.

'I do not know who your party may be. I am in the dark, and you keep me in the dark. But I know this, that I am secluded here for no good purpose. For no good purpose. I warn you, I warn you of the consequences. Once I come at my power – '

He realised that to threaten thus might be a danger to himself. He stopped. Howard stood regarding him with a curious expression.

'I take it this is a message to the Council,' said Howard.

Graham had a momentary impulse to leap upon the man, fell or stun him. It must have shown upon his face; at any rate Howard's movement was quick. In a second the noiseless door had closed again, and the man from the nineteenth century was alone.

For a moment he stood rigid, with clenched hands half raised. Then he flung them down. 'What a fool I have been!' he said, and gave way to his anger again, stamping about the room and shouting curses. . . . For a long time he kept himself in a sort of frenzy, raging at his position, at his own folly, at the knaves who had imprisoned him. He did this because he did not want to look calmly at his position. He clung to his anger – because he was afraid of Fear.

Presently he found himself reasoning with himself. This imprisonment was unaccountable, but no doubt the legal forms – new legal forms – of the time permitted it. It must, of course, be legal. These people were two hundred years further on in the march of civilisation than the Victorian generation. It was not likely they would be less – humane. Yet they had cleared their minds of formulae! Was humanity a formula as well as chastity?

His imagination set to work to suggest things that might be done to him. The attempts of his reason to dispose of these suggestions, though for the most part logically valid, were quite unavailing. 'Why should anything be done to me?'

'If the worst comes to the worst,' he found himself saying at last, 'I can give up what they want. But what do they want? And why don't they ask me for it instead of cooping me up?'

He returned to his former preoccupation with the Council's possible intentions. He began to reconsider the details of Howard's behaviour, sinister glances, inexplicable hesitations. Then, for a time, his mind circled about the idea of escaping from these rooms; but whither could he escape into this vast, crowded world? He would be worse off than a Saxon yeoman suddenly dropped into nineteenth-century London. And besides, how could anyone escape from these rooms?

'How can it benefit anyone if harm should happen to me?'

He thought of the tumult, the great social trouble of which he was so unaccountably the axis. A text, irrelevant enough and yet curiously insistent, came floating up out of the darkness of his memory. This also a Council had said:

'It is expedient for us that one man should die for the people.'

VIII

The Roof Spaces

As the fans in the circular aperture of the inner room rotated and permitted glimpses of the night, dim sounds drifted in thereby. And Graham, standing underneath, wrestling darkly with the unknown powers that imprisoned him, and which he had now deliberately challenged, was startled by the sound of a voice.

He peered up and saw in the intervals of the rotation dark and dim, the face and shoulders of a man regarding him. Then a dark hand was extended, the swift van struck it, swung round and beat on with a little brownish patch on the edge of its thin blade, and something began to fall therefrom upon the floor, dripping silently.

Graham looked down, and there were spots of blood at his feet. He looked up again in a strange excitement. The figure had gone.

He remained motionless – his every sense intent upon the flickering patch of darkness, for outside it was high night. He became aware of some faint, remote, dark specks floating lightly through the outer air. They came down towards him, fitfully, eddyingly, and passed aside out of the uprush from the fan. A gleam of light flickered, the specks flashed white, and then the darkness came again. Warmed and lit as he was, he perceived that it was snowing within a few feet of him.

Graham walked across the room and came back to the ventilator again. He saw the head of a man pass near. There was a sound of whispering. Then a smart blow on some metallic substance, effort, voices, and the vans stopped. A gust of snowflakes whirled into the room, and vanished before they touched the floor. 'Don't be afraid,' said a voice.

Graham stood under the van. 'Who are you?' he whispered.

For a moment there was nothing but a swaying of the fan, and then the head of a man was thrust cautiously into the opening. His face appeared nearly inverted to Graham; his dark hair was wet with dissolving flakes of snow upon it. His arm went up into the darkness holding something unseen. He had a youthful face and bright eyes, and the veins of his forehead were swollen. He seemed to be exerting himself to maintain his position.

For several seconds neither he nor Graham spoke.

'You were the Sleeper?' said the stranger at last.

'Yes,' said Graham. 'What do you want with me?'

'I come from Ostrog, Sire.'

'Ostrog?'

The man in the ventilator twisted his head round so that his profile was towards Graham. He appeared to be listening. Suddenly there was a hasty exclamation, and the intruder sprang back just in time to escape the sweep of the released fan. And when Graham peered up there was nothing visible but the slowly falling snow.

It was perhaps a quarter of an hour before anything returned to the ventilator. But at last came the same metallic interference again; the fans stopped and the face reappeared. Graham had remained all this time in the same place, alert and tremulously excited.

'Who are you? What do you want?' he said.

'We want to speak to you, Sire,' said the intruder. 'We want – can't hold the thing. We have been trying to find a way to you – these three days.'

'Is it rescue?' whispered Graham. 'Escape?'

'Yes, Sire. If you will.'

'You are my party – the party of the Sleeper?'

'Yes, Sire.'

'What am I to do?' said Graham.

There was a struggle. The stranger's arm appeared, and his hand was bleeding. His knees came into view over the edge of the funnel. 'Stand away from me,' he said, and he dropped rather heavily on his hands and one shoulder at Graham's feet. The released ventilator whirled noisily. The stranger rolled over, sprang up nimbly and stood panting, hand to a bruised shoulder, and with his bright eyes on Graham.

'You are indeed the Sleeper,' he said. 'I saw you asleep. When it was the law that anyone might see you.'

'I am the man who was in the trance,' said Graham. 'They have imprisoned me here. I have been here since I awoke – at least three days.'

The intruder seemed about to speak, heard something, glanced swiftly at the door, and suddenly left Graham and ran towards it, shouting quick incoherent words. A bright wedge of steel flashed in his hand, and he began tap, tap, a quick succession of blows upon the hinges.

'Mind!' cried a voice. 'Oh!' The voice came from above.

Graham glanced up, saw the soles of two feet, ducked, was struck on the shoulder by one of them, and a heavy weight bore him to the earth. He fell on his knees and forward, and the weight went over his head. He knelt up and saw a second man from above seated before him.

'I did not see you, Sire,' panted the man. He rose and assisted Graham to arise. 'Are you hurt, Sire?' he panted. A succession of heavy blows on the ventilator began, something fell close to Graham's face, and a shivering edge of white metal danced, fell over, and lay flat upon the floor.

'What is this?' cried Graham, confused and looking at the ventilator. 'Who are you? What are you going to do? Remember, I understand nothing.'

'Stand back,' said the stranger, and drew him from under the ventilator as another fragment of metal fell heavily.

'We want you to come, Sire,' panted the newcomer, and Graham glancing at his face again, saw a new cut had changed from white to red on his forehead, and a couple of little trickles of blood starting therefrom. 'Your people call for you.'

'Come where? My people?'

'To the hall about the markets. Your life is in danger here. We have spies. We learned but just in time. The Council has decided – this very day – either to drug or kill you. And everything is ready. The people are drilled, the wind-vane police, the engineers, and half the way-gearers are with us. We have the halls crowded – shouting. The whole city shouts against the Council. We have arms.' He wiped the blood with his hand. 'Your life here is not worth – '

'But why arms?'

'The people have risen to protect you, Sire. What?'

He turned quickly as the man who had first come down made a hissing with his teeth. Graham saw the latter start back, gesticulate to them to conceal themselves, and move as if to hide behind the opening door.

As he did so Howard appeared, a little tray in one hand and his heavy face downcast. He started, looked up, the door slammed behind him, the tray tilted sideways, and the steel wedge struck him behind the ear. He went down like a felled tree, and lay as he fell athwart the floor of the outer room. The man who had struck him bent hastily, studied his face for a moment, rose, and returned to his work at the door.

'Your poison!' said a voice in Graham's ear.

Then abruptly they were in darkness. The innumerable cornice lights had been extinguished. Graham saw the aperture of the ventilator with ghostly snow whirling above it and dark figures moving hastily. Three knelt on the van. Some dim thing – a ladder – was being lowered through the opening, and a hand appeared holding a fitful yellow light.

He had a moment of hesitation. But the manner of these men, their swift alacrity, their words, marched so completely with his own fears of the Council, with his idea and hope of a rescue, that it lasted not a moment. And his people awaited him!

'I do not understand,' he said, 'I trust. Tell me what to do.'

The man with the cut brow gripped Graham's arm. 'Clamber up the ladder,' he whispered. 'Quick. They will have heard – '

Graham felt for the ladder with extended hands, put his foot on the lower rung, and, turning his head, saw over the shoulder of the nearest man, in the yellow flicker of the light, the first-comer astride over Howard and still working at the door. Graham turned to the ladder again, and was thrust by his conductor and helped up by those above, and then he was standing on something hard and cold and slippery outside the ventilating funnel.

He shivered. He was aware of a great difference in the temperature. Half a dozen men stood about him, and light flakes of snow touched hands and face and melted. For a moment it was dark, then for a flash a ghastly violet white, and then everything was dark again.

He saw he had come out upon the roof of the vast city structure which had replaced the miscellaneous houses, streets and open spaces of Victorian London. The place upon which he stood was level, with huge serpentine cables lying athwart it in every direction. The circular wheels of a number of windmills loomed indistinct and gigantic through the darkness and snowfall, and roared with a varying loudness as the fitful wind rose and fell. Some way off an intermittent white light smote up from below, touched the snow eddies with a transient glitter, and made an evanescent spectre in the night; and here and there, low down, some vaguely outlined wind-driven mechanism flickered with livid sparks.

All this he appreciated in a fragmentary manner as his rescuers stood about him. Someone threw a thick soft cloak of fur-like texture about him, and fastened it by buckled straps at waist and shoulders. Things were said briefly, decisively. Someone thrust him forward.

Before his mind was yet clear a dark shape gripped his arm. 'This way,' said this shape, urging him along, and pointed Graham across the flat roof in the direction of a dim semicircular haze of light. Graham obeyed.

'Mind!' said a voice, as Graham stumbled against a cable. 'Between them and not across them,' said the voice. And, 'We must hurry.'

'Where are the people?' said Graham. 'The people you said awaited me?'

The stranger did not answer. He left Graham's arms as the path grew narrower, and led the way with rapid strides. Graham followed blindly. In a minute he found himself running. 'Are the others coming?' he panted, but received no reply. His companion glanced back and ran on. They came to a sort of pathway of open metalwork, transverse to the direction they had come, and they turned aside to follow this. Graham looked back, but the snowstorm had hidden the others.

'Come on!' said his guide. Running now, they drew near a little windmill spinning high in the air. 'Stoop,' said Graham's guide, and they avoided an endless band running roaring up to the shaft of the vane. 'This way!' and they were ankle deep in the gutter full of drifted thawing snow, between two low walls of metal that presently rose waist high. 'I will go first,' said the guide. Graham drew his cloak about him and followed. Then suddenly came a narrow abyss across which the gutter leapt to the snowy darkness of the further side. Graham peeped over the side once and the gulf was black. For a moment he regretted his flight. He dared not look again, and his brain spun as he waded through the half liquid snow.

Then out of the gutter they clambered and hurried across a wide flat space damp with thawing snow, and for half its extent dimly translucent to lights that went to and fro underneath. He hesitated at this unstable looking substance, but his guide ran on unheeding, and so they came to and clambered up slippery steps to the rim of a great dome of glass. Round this they went. Far below a number of people seemed to be dancing, and music filtered through the dome. . . . Graham fancied he heard a shouting through the snowstorm, and his guide hurried him on with a new spurt of haste. They clambered panting to a space of huge windmills, one so vast that only the lower edge of its vans came rushing into sight and rushed up again and was lost in the night and the snow. They hurried for a time through the colossal metallic tracery of its supports, and came at last above a place of moving platforms like the place into which Graham had looked from the balcony. They crawled across the sloping transparency that covered this street of platforms, crawling on hands and knees because of the slipperiness of the snowfall.

For the most part the glass was bedewed, and Graham saw only hazy suggestions of the forms below, but near the pitch of the transparent roof the glass was clear, and he found himself looking sheerly down upon it all. For awhile, in spite of the urgency of his guide, he gave way to vertigo and lay spread-eagled on the glass, sick and paralysed. Far below, mere stirring specks and dots, went the people of the unsleeping city in their perpetual daylight, and the moving platforms ran on their incessant journey. Messengers and men on unknown businesses shot along the drooping cables and the frail bridges were crowded with men. It was like peering into a gigantic glass hive, and it lay vertically below him with only a tough glass of unknown thickness to save him from a fall. The street showed warm and lit, and Graham was wet now to the skin with thawing snow, and his feet were numbed with cold. For a space he could not move. 'Come on!' cried his guide, with terror in his voice. 'Come on!'

Graham reached the pitch of the roof by an effort.

Over the ridge, following his guide's example, he turned about and slid backward down the opposite slope very swiftly, amid a little avalanche of snow. While he was sliding he thought of what would happen if some broken gap should come in his way. At the edge he stumbled to his feet ankle deep in slush, thanking heaven for an opaque footing again. His guide was already clambering up a metal screen to a level expanse.

Through the spare snowflakes above this loomed another line of vast windmills, and then suddenly the amorphous tumult of the rotating wheels was pierced with a deafening sound. It was a mechanical shrilling of extraordinary intensity that seemed to come simultaneously from every point of the compass.

'They have missed us already!' cried Graham's guide in an accent of terror, and suddenly, with a blinding flash, the night became day.

Above the driving snow, from the summits of the wind-wheels, appeared vast masts carrying globes of livid light. They receded in illimitable vistas in every direction. As far as his eye could penetrate the snowfall they glared.

'Get on this,' cried Graham's conductor, and thrust him forward to a long grating of snowless metal that ran like a band between two slightly sloping expanses of snow. It felt warm to Graham's benumbed feet, and a faint eddy of steam rose from it.

'Come on!' shouted his guide ten yards off, and, without waiting, ran swiftly through the incandescent glare towards the iron supports of the next range of wind-wheels. Graham, recovering from his astonishment, followed as fast, convinced of his imminent capture. . . .

In a score of seconds they were within a tracery of glare and black shadows shot with moving bars beneath the monstrous wheels. Graham's conductor ran on for some time, and suddenly darted sideways and vanished into a black shadow in the corner of the foot of a huge support. In another moment Graham was beside him.

They cowered panting and stared out.

The scene upon which Graham looked was very wild and strange. The snow had now almost ceased; only a belated flake passed now and again across the picture. But the broad stretch of level before them was a ghastly white, broken only by gigantic masses and moving shapes and lengthy strips of impenetrable darkness, vast ungainly Titans of shadow. All about them, huge metallic structures, iron girders, inhumanly vast as it seemed to him, interlaced, and the edges of wind-wheels, scarcely moving in the lull, passed in great shining curves steeper and steeper up into a luminous haze. Wherever the snow-spangled light struck down, beams and girders, and incessant bands running with a halting, indomitable resolution, passed upward and downward into the black. And with all that mighty activity, with an omnipresent sense of motive and design, this snow-clad desolation of mechanism seemed void of all human presence save themselves, seemed as trackless and deserted and unfrequented by men as some inaccessible Alpine snowfield.

'They will be chasing us,' cried the leader. 'We are scarcely halfway there yet. Cold as it is we must hide here for a space – at least until it snows more thickly again.'

His teeth chattered in his head.

'Where are the markets?' asked Graham staring out. 'Where are all the people?'

The other made no answer.

'*Look!*' whispered Graham, crouched close, and became very still.

The snow had suddenly become thick again, and sliding with the whirling eddies out of the black pit of the sky came something, vague and large and very swift. It came down in a steep curve and swept round, wide wings extended and a trail of white condensing steam behind it, rose with an easy swiftness and went gliding up the air, swept horizontally forward in a wide curve, and vanished again in the steaming specks of snow. And, through the ribs of its body, Graham saw two little men, very minute and active, searching the snowy areas about him, as it seemed to him, with field glasses. For a second they were clear, then hazy through a thick whirl of snow, then small and distant, and in a minute they were gone.

'*Now!*' cried his companion. 'Come!'

He pulled Graham's sleeve, and incontinently the two were running headlong down the arcade of ironwork beneath the wind-wheels. Graham, running blindly, collided with his leader, who had turned back on him suddenly. He found himself within a dozen yards of a black chasm. It extended as far as he could see right and left. It seemed to cut off their progress in either direction.

'Do as I do,' whispered his guide. He lay down and crawled to the edge, thrust his head over and twisted until one leg hung. He seemed to feel for something with his foot, found it, and went sliding over the edge into the gulf. His head reappeared. 'It is a ledge,' he whispered. 'In the dark all the way along. Do as I did.'

Graham hesitated, went down upon all fours, crawled to the edge, and peered into a velvety blackness. For a sickly moment he had courage neither to go on nor retreat, then he sat and hung his leg down, felt his guide's hands pulling at him, had a horrible sensation of sliding over the edge into the unfathomable, splashed, and felt himself in a slushy gutter, impenetrably dark.

'This way,' whispered the voice, and he began crawling along the gutter through the trickling thaw, pressing himself against the wall. They continued along it for some minutes. He seemed to pass through a hundred stages of misery, to pass minute after minute through a hundred degrees of cold, damp, and exhaustion. In a little while he ceased to feel his hands and feet.

The gutter sloped downwards. He observed that they were now many feet below the edge of the buildings. Rows of spectral white shapes like the ghosts of blinddrawn windows rose above them. They came to the end of a cable fastened above one of these white windows, dimly visible and dropping into impenetrable shadows. Suddenly his hand came against his guide's. '*Still!*' whispered the latter very softly.

He looked up with a start and saw the huge wings of the flying machine gliding slowly and noiselessly overhead athwart the broad band of snow-flecked grey-blue sky. In a moment it was hidden again.

'Keep still; they were just turning.'

For awhile both were motionless, then Graham's companion stood up, and reaching towards the fastenings of the cable fumbled with some indistinct tackle.

'What is that?' asked Graham.

The only answer was a faint cry. The man crouched motionless. Graham peered and saw his face dimly. He was staring down the long ribbon of sky, and Graham, following his eyes, saw the flying machine small and faint and remote. Then he saw that the wings spread on either side, that it headed towards them, that every moment it grew larger. It was following the edge of the chasm towards them.

The man's movements became convulsive. He thrust two cross bars into Graham's hand. Graham could not see them, he ascertained their form by feeling. They were slung by thin cords to the cable. On the cord were hand grips of some soft elastic substance. 'Put the cross between your legs,' whispered the guide hysterically, 'and grip the holdfasts. Grip tightly, grip!' Graham did as he was told.

'Jump,' said the voice. 'In heaven's name, jump!'

For one momentous second Graham could not speak. He was glad afterwards that darkness hid his face. He said nothing. He began to tremble violently. He looked sideways at the swift shadow that swallowed up the sky as it rushed upon him.

'Jump! Jump – in God's name! Or they will have us,' cried Graham's guide, and in the violence of his passion thrust him forward.

Graham tottered convulsively, gave a sobbing cry, a cry in spite of himself, and then, as the flying machine swept over them, fell forward into the pit of that darkness, seated on the cross wood and holding the ropes with the clutch of death. Something cracked, something rapped smartly against a wall. He heard the pulley of the cradle hum on its rope. He heard the aeronauts shout. He felt a pair of knees digging into his back. . . . He was sweeping headlong through the air, falling through the air. All his strength was in his hands. He would have screamed but he had no breath.

He shot into a blinding light that made him grip the tighter. He recognised the great passage with the running ways, the hanging lights and interlacing girders. They rushed upward and by him. He had a momentary impression of a great circular aperture yawning to swallow him up.

He was in the dark again, falling, gripping with aching hands, and behold! a clap of sound, a burst of light, and he was in a brightly lit hall with a roaring multitude of people beneath his feet. The people! His people! A proscenium, a stage rushed up towards him, and his cable swept down to a circular aperture to the right of this. He felt he was travelling slower, and suddenly very much slower. He distinguished shouts of 'Saved! The Master. He is safe!' The stage rushed up towards him with rapidly diminishing swiftness. Then – .

He heard the man clinging behind him shout as if suddenly terrified, and this shout was echoed by a shout from below. He felt that he was no longer gliding along the cable but falling with it. There was a tumult of yells, screams and cries. He felt something soft against his extended hand, and the impact of a broken fall quivering through his arm. . . .

He wanted to be still and the people were lifting him. He believed afterwards he was carried to the platform and given some drink, but he was never sure. He did not notice what became of his guide. When his mind was clear again he was on his feet; eager hands were assisting him to stand. He was in a big alcove, occupying the position that in his previous experience had been devoted to the lower boxes. If this was indeed a theatre.

A mighty tumult was in his ears, a thunderous roar, the shouting of a countless multitude. 'It is the Sleeper! The Sleeper is with us!'

'The Sleeper is with us! The Master – the Owner! The Master is with us. He is safe.'

Graham had a surging vision of a great hall crowded with people. He saw no individuals, he was conscious of a froth of pink faces, of waving arms and garments, he felt the occult influence of a vast crowd pouring over him, buoying him up. There were balconies, galleries, great archways giving remoter perspectives, and everywhere people, a vast arena of people, densely packed and cheering. Across the nearer space lay the collapsed cable like a huge snake. It had been cut by the men of the flying machine at its upper end, and had crumpled down into the hall. Men seemed to be hauling this out of the way. But the whole effect was vague, the very buildings throbbed and leapt with the roar of the voices.

He stood unsteadily and looked at those about him. Someone supported him by one arm. 'Let me go into a little room,' he said, weeping; 'a little room', and could say no more. A man in black stepped forward, took his disengaged arm. He was aware of officious men opening a door before him. Someone guided him to a seat. He staggered. He sat down heavily and covered his face with his hands; he was trembling violently, his nervous control was at an end. He was relieved of his cloak, he could not remember how; his purple hose he saw were black with wet. People were running about him, things were happening, but for some time he gave no heed to them.

He had escaped. A myriad of cries told him that. He was safe. These were the people who were on his side. For a space he sobbed for breath, and then he sat still with his face covered. The air was full of the shouting of innumerable men.

IX

The People March

He became aware of someone urging a glass of clear fluid upon his
attention, looked up and discovered this was a dark young man in a
yellow garment. He took the dose forthwith, and in a moment he was
glowing. A tall man in a black robe stood by his shoulder, and pointed
to the half-open door into the hall. This man was shouting close to his
ear and yet what was said was indistinct because of the tremendous
uproar from the great theatre. Behind the man was a girl in a silvery
grey robe, whom Graham, even in this confusion, perceived to be
beautiful. Her dark eyes, full of wonder and curiosity, were fixed on
him, her lips trembled apart. A partially opened door gave a glimpse of
the crowded hall, and admitted a vast uneven tumult, a hammering,
clapping and shouting that died away and began again, and rose to a
thunderous pitch, and so continued intermittently all the time that
Graham remained in the little room. He watched the lips of the man in
black and gathered that he was making some clumsy explanation.

He stared stupidly for some moments at these things and then stood
up abruptly; he grasped the arm of this shouting person.

'Tell me!' he cried. 'Who am I? Who am I?'

The others came nearer to hear his words. 'Who am I?' His eyes
searched their faces.

'They have told him nothing!' cried the girl.

'Tell me, tell me!' cried Graham.

'You are the Master of the Earth. You are owner of half the world.'

He did not believe he heard aright. He resisted the persuasion. He
pretended not to understand, not to hear. He lifted his voice again. 'I
have been awake three days – a prisoner three days. I judge there is
some struggle between a number of people in this city – it is London?'

'Yes,' said the younger man.

'And those who meet in the great hall with the white Atlas? How
does it concern me? In some way it has to do with me. *Why*, I don't
know. Drugs? It seems to me that while I have slept the world has gone
mad. I have gone mad.'

'Who are those Councillors under the Atlas? Why should they try to drug me?'

'To keep you insensible,' said the man in yellow. 'To prevent your interference.'

'But *why*?'

'Because *you* are the Atlas, Sire,' said the man in yellow. 'The world is on your shoulders. They rule it in your name.'

The sounds from the hall had died into a silence threaded by one monotonous voice. Now suddenly, trampling on these last words, came a deafening tumult, a roaring and thundering, cheer crowded on cheer, voices hoarse and shrill, beating, overlapping, and while it lasted the people in the little room could not hear each other shout.

Graham stood, his intelligence clinging helplessly to the thing he had just heard. 'The Council,' he repeated blankly, and then snatched at a name that had struck him. 'But who is Ostrog?' he said.

'He is the organiser – the organiser of the revolt. Our Leader – in your name.'

'In my name? – And you? Why is he not here?'

'He – has deputed us. I am his brother – his half-brother, Lincoln. He wants you to show yourself to these people and then come on to him. That is why he has sent. He is at the wind-vane offices directing. The people are marching.'

'In your name,' shouted the younger man. 'They have ruled, crushed, tyrannised. At last even – '

'In my name! My name! Master?'

The younger man suddenly became audible in a pause of the outer thunder, indignant and vociferous, a high penetrating voice under his red aquiline nose and bushy moustache. 'No one expected you to wake. No one expected you to wake. They were cunning. Damned tyrants! But they were taken by surprise. They did not know whether to drug you, hypnotise you, kill you.'

Again the hall dominated everything.

'Ostrog is at the wind-vane offices ready – . Even now there is a rumour of fighting beginning.'

The man who had called himself Lincoln came close to him. 'Ostrog has it planned. Trust him. We have our organisations ready. We shall seize the flying stages – . Even now he may be doing that. Then – '

'This public theatre,' bawled the man in yellow, 'is only a contingent. We have five myriads of drilled men – '

'We have arms,' cried Lincoln. 'We have plans. A leader. Their police have gone from the streets and are massed in the – ' (inaudible). 'It is now or never. The Council is rocking – They cannot trust even their drilled men – '

'Hear the people calling to you!'

Graham's mind was like a night of moon and swift clouds, now dark and hopeless, now clear and ghastly. He was Master of the Earth, he was a man sodden with thawing snow. Of all his fluctuating impressions the dominant ones presented an antagonism; on the one hand was the White Council, powerful, disciplined, few, the White Council from which he had just escaped; and on the other, monstrous crowds, packed masses of indistinguishable people clamouring his name, hailing him Master. The other side had imprisoned him, debated his death. These shouting thousands beyond the little doorway had rescued him. But why these things should be so he could not understand.

The door opened, Lincoln's voice was swept away and drowned, and a rush of people followed on the heels of the tumult. These intruders came towards him and Lincoln gesticulating. The voices without explained their soundless lips. 'Show us the Sleeper, show us the Sleeper!' was the burden of the uproar. Men were bawling for 'Order! Silence!'

Graham glanced towards the open doorway, and saw a tall, oblong picture of the hall beyond, a waving, incessant confusion of crowded, shouting faces, men and women together, waving pale blue garments, extended hands. Many were standing, one man in rags of dark brown, a gaunt figure, stood on the seat and waved a black cloth. He met the wonder and expectation of the girl's eyes. What did these people expect from him. He was dimly aware that the tumult outside had changed its character, was in some way beating, marching. His own mind, too, changed. For a space he did not recognise the influence that was transforming him. But a moment that was near to panic passed. He tried to make audible inquiries of what was required of him.

Lincoln was shouting in his ear, but Graham was deafened to that. All the others save the woman gesticulated towards the hall. He perceived what had happened to the uproar. The whole mass of people was chanting together. It was not simply a song, the voices were gathered together and upborne by a torrent of instrumental music, music like the music of an organ, a woven texture of sounds, full of trumpets, full of flaunting banners, full of the march and pageantry of opening war. And the feet of the people were beating time – tramp, tramp.

He was urged towards the door. He obeyed mechanically. The strength of that chant took hold of him, stirred him, emboldened him. The hall opened to him, a vast welter of fluttering colour swaying to the music.

'Wave your arm to them,' said Lincoln. 'Wave your arm to them.'

'This,' said a voice on the other side, 'he must have this.' Arms were about his neck detaining him in the doorway, and a black subtly-folding mantle hung from his shoulders. He threw his arm free of this and followed Lincoln. He perceived the girl in grey close to him, her face lit, her gesture onward. For the instant she became to him, flushed and eager as she was, an embodiment of the song. He emerged in the alcove again. Incontinently the mounting waves of the song broke upon his appearing, and flashed up into a foam of shouting. Guided by Lincoln's hand he marched obliquely across the centre of the stage facing the people.

The hall was a vast and intricate space – galleries, balconies, broad spaces of amphitheatral steps, and great archways. Far away, high up, seemed the mouth of a huge passage full of struggling humanity. The whole multitude was swaying in congested masses. Individual figures sprang out of the tumult, impressed him momentarily, and lost definition again. Close to the platform swayed a beautiful fair woman, carried by three men, her hair across her face and brandishing a green staff. Next this group an old careworn man in blue canvas maintained his place in the crush with difficulty, and behind shouted a hairless face, a great cavity of toothless mouth. A voice called that enigmatical word 'Ostrog'. All his impressions were vague save the massive emotion of that trampling song. The multitude were beating time with their feet – marking time, tramp, tramp, tramp, tramp. The green weapons waved, flashed and slanted. Then he saw those nearest to him on a level space before the stage were marching in front of him, passing towards a great archway, shouting 'To the Council!' Tramp, tramp, tramp, tramp. He raised his arm, and the roaring was redoubled. He remembered he had to shout 'March!' His mouth shaped inaudible heroic words. He waved his arm again and pointed to the archway, shouting 'Onward!' They were no longer marking time, they were marching; tramp, tramp, tramp, tramp. In that host were bearded men, old men, youth, fluttering robed bare-armed women, girls. Men and women of the new age! Rich robes, grey rags fluttered together in the whirl of their movement amidst the dominant blue. A monstrous black banner jerked its way to the right. He perceived a blue-clad negro, a shrivelled woman in yellow, then a group of tall fair-haired, white-faced, blue-clad men pushed theatrically past him. He noted two Chinamen. A tall, sallow, dark-haired, shining-eyed youth, white clad from top to toe, clambered up towards the platform shouting loyally, and sprang down again and receded, looking backward. Heads, shoulders, hands clutching weapons, all were swinging with those marching cadences.

Faces came out of the confusion to him as he stood there, eyes met his and passed and vanished. Men gesticulated to him, shouted inaudible personal things. Most of the faces were flushed, but many were ghastly white. And disease was there, and many a hand that waved to him was gaunt and lean. Men and women of the new age! Strange and incredible meeting! As the broad stream passed before him to the right, tributary gangways from the remote uplands of the hall thrust downward in an incessant replacement of people; tramp, tramp, tramp, tramp. The unison of the song was enriched and complicated by the massive echoes of arches and passages. Men and women mingled in the ranks; tramp, tramp, tramp, tramp. The whole world seemed marching. Tramp, tramp, tramp, tramp; his brain was tramping. The garments waved onward, the faces poured by more abundantly.

Tramp, tramp, tramp, tramp; at Lincoln's pressure he turned towards the archway, walking unconsciously in that rhythm, scarcely noticing his movement for the melody and stir of it. The multitude, the gesture and song, all moved in that direction, the flow of people smote downward until the upturned faces were below the level of his feet. He was aware of a path before him, of a suite about him, of guards and dignities, and Lincoln on his right hand. Attendants intervened, and ever and again blotted out the sight of the multitude to the left. Before him went the backs of the guards in black – three and three and three. He was marched along a little railed way, and crossed above the archway, with the torrent dipping to flow beneath, and shouting up to him. He did not know whither he went; he did not want to know. He glanced back across a flaming spaciousness of hall. Tramp, tramp, tramp, tramp.

X

The Battle of the Darkness

He was no longer in the hall. He was marching along a gallery overhanging one of the great streets of the moving platforms that traversed the city. Before him and behind him tramped his guards. The whole concave of the moving ways below was a congested mass of people marching, tramping to the left, shouting, waving hands and arms, pouring along a huge vista, shouting as they came into view, shouting as they passed, shouting as they receded, until the globes of electric light receding in perspective dropped down it seemed and hid the swarming bare heads. Tramp, tramp, tramp, tramp.

The song roared up to Graham now, no longer upborne by music, but coarse and noisy, and the beating of the marching feet, tramp, tramp, tramp, tramp, interwove with a thunderous irregularity of footsteps from the undisciplined rabble that poured along the higher ways.

Abruptly he noted a contrast. The buildings on the opposite side of the way seemed deserted, the cables and bridges that laced across the aisle were empty and shadowy. It came into Graham's mind that these also should have swarmed with people.

He felt a curious emotion – throbbing – very fast! He stopped again. The guards before him marched on; those about him stopped as he did. He saw the direction of their faces. The throbbing had something to do with the lights. He too looked up.

At first it seemed to him a thing that affected the lights simply, an isolated phenomenon, having no bearing on the things below. Each huge globe of blinding whiteness was as it were clutched, compressed in a systole that was followed by a transitory diastole, and again a systole like a tightening grip, darkness, light, darkness, in rapid alternation.

Graham became aware that this strange behaviour of the lights had to do with the people below. The appearance of the houses and ways, the appearance of the packed masses changed, became a confusion of vivid lights and leaping shadows. He saw a multitude of shadows had sprung into aggressive existence, seemed rushing up, broadening, widening, growing with steady swiftness – to leap suddenly back and return reinforced. The song and the tramping had ceased. The unanimous march, he discovered, was arrested, there were eddies, a flow sideways, shouts of 'The lights!' Voices were crying together one thing. 'The lights!' cried these voices. 'The lights!' He looked down. In this dancing death of the lights the area of the street had suddenly become a monstrous struggle. The huge white globes became purple-white, purple with a reddish glow, flickered, flickered faster and faster, fluttered between light and extinction, ceased to flicker and became mere fading specks of glowing red in vast obscurity. In ten seconds the extinction was accomplished, and there was only this roaring darkness, a black monstrosity that had suddenly swallowed up those glittering myriads of men.

He felt invisible forms about him; his arms were gripped. Something rapped sharply against his shin. A voice bawled in his ear, 'It is all right – all right.'

Graham shook off the paralysis of his first astonishment. He stuck his forehead against Lincoln's and bawled, 'What is this darkness?'

'The Council has cut the currents that light the city. We must wait – stop. The people will go on. They will – '

His voice was drowned. Voices were shouting, 'Save the Sleeper. Take care of the Sleeper.' A guard stumbled against Graham and hurt his hand by an inadvertent blow of his weapon. A wild tumult tossed and whirled about him, growing, as it seemed, louder, denser, more furious each moment. Fragments of recognisable sounds drove towards him, were whirled away from him as his mind reached out to grasp them. Voices seemed to be shouting conflicting orders, other voices answered. There were suddenly a succession of piercing screams close beneath them.

A voice bawled in his ear, 'The red police,' and receded forthwith beyond questions.

A crackling sound grew to distinctness, and therewith a leaping of faint flashes along the edge of the further ways. By their light Graham saw the heads and bodies of a number of men, armed with weapons like those of his guards, leap into an instant's dim visibility. The whole area began to crackle, to flash with little instantaneous streaks of light, and abruptly the darkness rolled back like a curtain.

A glare of light dazzled his eyes, a vast seething expanse of struggling men confused his mind. A shout, a burst of cheering, came across the ways. He looked up to see the source of the light. A man hung far overhead from the upper part of a cable, holding by a rope the blinding star that had driven the darkness back. He wore a red uniform.

Graham's eyes fell to the ways again. A wedge of red a little way along the vista caught his eye. He saw it was a dense mass of red-clad men jammed on the higher further way, their backs against the pitiless cliff of building, and surrounded by a dense crowd of antagonists. They were fighting. Weapons flashed and rose and fell, heads vanished at the edge of the contest, and other heads replaced them, the little flashes from the green weapons became little jets of smoky grey while the light lasted.

Abruptly the flare was extinguished and the ways were an inky darkness once more, a tumultuous mystery.

He felt something thrusting against him. He was being pushed along the gallery. Someone was shouting – it might be at him. He was too confused to hear. He was thrust against the wall, and a number of people blundered past him. It seemed to him that his guards were struggling with one another.

Suddenly the cable-hung star-holder appeared again, and the whole scene was white and dazzling. The band of red-coats seemed broader and nearer; its apex was half-way down the ways towards the central aisle. And raising his eyes Graham saw that a number of these men had also appeared now in the darkened lower galleries of the opposite building, and were firing over the heads of their fellows below at the boiling confusion of people on the lower ways. The meaning of these things dawned upon him. The march of the people had come upon an ambush at the very outset. Thrown into confusion by the extinction of the lights they were now being attacked by the red police. Then he became aware that he was standing alone, that his guards and Lincoln were along the gallery in the direction along which he had come before the darkness fell. He saw they were gesticulating to him wildly, running back towards him. A great shouting came from across the ways. Then it seemed as though the whole face of the darkened building opposite was lined and speckled with red-clad men. And they were pointing over to him and shouting. 'The Sleeper! Save the Sleeper!' shouted a multitude of throats.

Something struck the wall above his head. He looked up at the impact and saw a star-shaped splash of silvery metal. He saw Lincoln near him. Felt his arm gripped. Then, pat, pat; he had been missed twice.

For a moment he did not understand this. The street was hidden, everything was hidden, as he looked. The second flare had burnt out.

Lincoln had gripped Graham by the arm, was lugging him along the gallery. 'Before the next light!' he cried. His haste was contagious. Graham's instinct of self-preservation overcame the paralysis of his incredulous astonishment. He became for a time the blind creature of the fear of death. He ran, stumbling because of the uncertainty of the darkness, blundered into his guards as they turned to run with him. Haste was his one desire, to escape this perilous gallery upon which he was exposed. A third glare came close on its predecessors. With it came a great shouting across the ways, an answering tumult from the ways. The red-coats below, he saw, had now almost gained the central passage. Their countless faces turned towards him, and they shouted. The white facade opposite was densely stripped with red. All these wonderful things concerned him, turned upon him as a pivot. These were the guards of the Council attempting to recapture him.

Lucky it was for him that these shots were the first fired in anger for a hundred and fifty years. He heard bullets whacking over his head, felt a splash of molten metal sting his ear, and perceived without looking that the whole opposite facade, an unmasked ambuscade of red police, was crowded and bawling and firing at him.

Down went one of his guards before him, and Graham, unable to stop, leapt the writhing body.

In another second he had plunged, unhurt, into a black passage, and incontinently someone, coming, it may be, in a transverse direction, blundered violently into him. He was hurling down a staircase in absolute darkness. He reeled, and was struck again, and came against a wall with his hands. He was crushed by a weight of struggling bodies, whirled round, and thrust to the right. A vast pressure pinned him. He could not breathe, his ribs seemed cracking. He felt a momentary relaxation, and then the whole mass of people moving together, bore him back towards the great theatre from which he had so recently come. There were moments when his feet did not touch the ground. Then he was staggering and shoving. He heard shouts of 'They are coming!' and a muffled cry close to him. His foot blundered against something soft, he heard a hoarse scream under foot. He heard shouts of 'The Sleeper!' but he was too confused to speak. He heard the green weapons crackling. For a space he lost his individual will, became an atom in a panic, blind, unthinking, mechanical. He thrust and pressed back and writhed in the pressure, kicked presently against a step, and found himself ascending a slope. And abruptly the faces all about him leapt out of the black, visible, ghastly-white and astonished, terrified, perspiring, in a livid glare. One face, a young man's, was very near to him, not twenty inches away. At the time it was but a passing incident of no emotional value, but afterwards it came back to him in his dreams. For this young man, wedged upright in the crowd for a time, had been shot and was already dead.

A fourth white star must have been lit by the man on the cable. Its light came glaring in through vast windows and arches and showed Graham that he was now one of a dense mass flying black figures pressed back across the lower area of the great theatre. This time the picture was livid and fragmentary, slashed and barred with black shadows. He saw that quite near to him the red guards were fighting their way through the people. He could not tell whether they saw him. He looked for Lincoln and his guards. He saw Lincoln near the stage of the theatre surrounded in a crowd of black-badged revolutionaries, lifted up and staring to and fro as if seeking him. Graham perceived

that he himself was near the opposite edge of the crowd, that behind
him, separated by a barrier, sloped the now vacant seats of the theatre.
A sudden idea came to him, and he began fighting his way towards the
barrier. As he reached it the glare came to an end.

In a moment he had thrown off the great cloak that not only impeded
his movements but made him conspicuous, and had slipped it from his
shoulders. He heard someone trip in its folds. In another he was scaling
the barrier and had dropped into the blackness on the further side. Then
feeling his way he came to the lower end of an ascending gangway. In
the darkness the sound of firing ceased and the roar of feet and voices
lulled. Then suddenly he came to an unexpected step and tripped and
fell. As he did so pools and islands amidst the darkness about him leapt
to vivid light again, the uproar surged louder and the glare of the fifth
white star shone through the vast fenestrations of the theatre walls.

He rolled over among some seats, heard a shouting and the whirring
rattle of weapons, struggled up and was knocked back again, perceived
that a number of black-badged men were all about him firing at the reds
below, leaping from seat to seat, crouching among the seats to reload.
Instinctively he crouched amidst the seats, as stray shots ripped the
pneumatic cushions and cut bright slashes on their soft metal frames.
Instinctively he marked the direction of the gangways, the most plausible way of escape for him so soon as the veil of darkness fell again.

A young man in faded blue garments came vaulting over the seats.
'Hullo!' he said, with his flying feet within six inches of the crouching
Sleeper's face.

He stared without any sign of recognition, turned to fire, fired, and,
shouting, 'To hell with the Council!' was about to fire again. Then it
seemed to Graham that the half of this man's neck had vanished. A
drop of moisture fell on Graham's cheek. The green weapon stopped
half raised. For a moment the man stood still with his face suddenly
expressionless, then he began to slant forward. His knees bent. Man
and darkness fell together. At the sound of his fall Graham rose up and
ran for his life until a step down to the gangway tripped him. He
scrambled to his feet, turned up the gangway and ran on.

When the sixth star glared he was already close to the yawning throat
of a passage. He ran on the swifter for the light, entered the passage
and turned a corner into absolute night again. He was knocked
sideways, rolled over, and recovered his feet. He found himself one of a
crowd of invisible fugitives pressing in one direction. His one thought
now was their thought also; to escape out of this fighting. He thrust and
struck, staggered, ran, was wedged tightly, lost ground and then was
clear again.

For some minutes he was running through the darkness along a
winding passage, and then he crossed some wide and open space, passed
down a long incline, and came at last down a flight of steps to a level

place. Many people were shouting. 'They are coming! The guards are coming. They are firing. It will be safe in Seventh Way. Along here to Seventh Way!' There were women and children in the crowd as well as men. Men called names to him. The crowd converged on an archway, passed through a short throat and emerged on a wider space again, lit dimly. The black figures about him spread out and ran up what seemed in the twilight to be a gigantic series of steps. He followed. The people dispersed to the right and left. . . . He perceived that he was no longer in a crowd. He stopped near the highest step. Before him, on that level, were groups of seats and a little kiosk. He went up to this and, stopping in the shadow of its eaves, looked about him panting.

Everything was vague and grey, but he recognised that these great steps were a series of platforms of the 'ways', now motionless again. The platform slanted up on either side, and the tall buildings rose beyond, vast dim ghosts, their inscriptions and advertisements indistinctly seen, and up through the girders and cables was a faint interrupted ribbon of pallid sky. A number of people hurried by. From their shouts and voices, it seemed they were hurrying to join the fighting. Other less noisy figures flitted timidly among the shadows.

From very far away down the street he could hear the sound of a struggle. But it was evident to him that this was not the street into which the theatre opened. That former fight, it seemed, had suddenly dropped out of sound and hearing. And – grotesque thought! – they were fighting for him.

For a space he was like a man who pauses in the reading of a vivid book, and suddenly doubts what he has been taking unquestioningly. At that time he had little mind for details; the whole effect was a huge astonishment. Oddly enough, while the flight from the Council prison, the great crowd in the hall, and the attack of the red police upon the swarming people were clearly present in his mind, it cost him an effort to piece in his awakening and to revive the meditative interval of the Silent Rooms. At first his memory leapt these things and took him back to the cascade at Pentargen quivering in the wind, and all the sombre splendours of the sunlit Cornish coast. The contrast touched everything with unreality. And then the gap filled, and he began to comprehend his position.

It was no longer absolutely a riddle, as it had been in the Silent Rooms. At least he had the strange, bare outline now. He was in some way the owner of half the world, and great political parties were fighting to possess him. On the one hand was the White Council, with its red police, set resolutely, it seemed, on the usurpation of his property and perhaps his murder; on the other, the revolution that had liberated him, with this unseen 'Ostrog' as its leader. And the whole of this gigantic city was convulsed by their struggle. Frantic development of his world! 'I do not understand,' he cried. 'I do not understand!'

He had slipped out between the contending parties into this liberty of the twilight. What would happen next? What was happening? He figured the red-clad men as busily hunting him, driving the black-badged revolutionists before them.

At any rate chance had given him a breathing space. He could lurk unchallenged by the passers-by, and watch the course of things. His eye followed up the intricate dim immensity of the twilight buildings, and it came to him as a thing infinitely wonderful, that above there the sun was rising, and the world was lit and glowing with the old familiar light of day. In a little while he had recovered his breath. His clothing had already dried upon him from the snow.

He wandered for miles along these twilight ways, speaking to no one, accosted by no one – a dark figure among dark figures – the coveted man out of the past, the inestimable unintentional owner of half the world. Wherever there were lights or dense crowds, or exceptional excitement he was afraid of recognition, and watched and turned back or went up and down by the middle stairways, into some transverse system of ways at a lower or higher level. And though he came on more fighting, the whole city stirred with battle. Once he had to run to avoid a marching multitude of men that swept the street. Everyone abroad seemed involved. For the most part they were men, and they carried what he judged were weapons. It seemed as though the struggle was concentrated mainly in the quarter of the city from which he came. Ever and again a distant roaring, the remote suggestion of that conflict, reached his ears. Then his caution and his curiosity struggled together. But his caution prevailed, and he continued wandering away from the fighting – so far as he could judge. He went unmolested, unsuspected through the dark. After a time he ceased to hear even a remote echo of the battle, fewer and fewer people passed him, until at last the Titanic streets became deserted. The frontages of the buildings grew plain and harsh; he seemed to have come to a district of vacant warehouses. Solitude crept upon him – his pace slackened.

He became aware of a growing fatigue. At times he would turn aside and seat himself on one of the numerous seats of the upper ways. But a feverish restlessness, the knowledge of his vital implication in this struggle, would not let him rest in any place for long. Was the struggle on his behalf alone?

And then in a desolate place came the shock of an earthquake – a roaring and thundering – a mighty wind of cold air pouring through the city, the smash of glass, the slip and thud of falling masonry – a series of gigantic concussions. A mass of glass and ironwork fell from the remote roofs into the middle gallery, not a hundred yards away from him, and in the distance were shouts and running. He, too, was startled to an aimless activity, and ran first one way and then as aimlessly back.

A man came running towards him. His self-control returned. 'What have they blown up?' asked the man breathlessly. 'That was an explosion,' and before Graham could speak he had hurried on.

The great buildings rose dimly, veiled by a perplexing twilight, albeit the rivulet of sky above was now bright with day. He noted many strange features, understanding none at the time; he even spelt out many of the inscriptions in Phonetic lettering. But what profits it to decipher a confusion of odd-looking letters resolving itself, after painful strain of eye and mind, into 'Here is Eadhamite,' or, 'Labour Bureau – Little Side'? Grotesque thought, that in all probability some or all of these cliff-like houses were his!

The perversity of his experience came to him vividly. In actual fact he had made such a leap in time as romancers have imagined again and again. And that fact realised, he had been prepared, his mind had, as it were, seated itself for a spectacle. And no spectacle, but a great vague danger, unsympathetic shadows and veils of darkness. Somewhere through the labyrinthine obscurity his death sought him. Would he, after all, be killed before he saw? It might be that even at the next shadowy corner his destruction ambushed. A great desire to see, a great longing to know, arose in him.

He became fearful of corners. It seemed to him that there was safety in concealment. Where could he hide to be inconspicuous when the lights returned? At last he sat down upon a seat in a recess on one of the higher ways, conceiving he was alone there.

He squeezed his knuckles into his weary eyes. Suppose when he looked again he found the dark trough of parallel ways and that intolerable altitude of edifice, gone? Suppose he were to discover the whole story of these last few days, the awakening, the shouting multitudes, the darkness and the fighting, a phantasmagoria, a new and more vivid sort of dream. It must be a dream; it was so inconsecutive, so reasonless. Why were the people fighting for him? Why should this saner world regard him as Owner and Master?

So he thought, sitting blinded, and then he looked again, half hoping in spite of his ears to see some familiar aspect of the life of the nineteenth century, to see, perhaps, the little harbour of Boscastle about him, the cliffs of Pentargen, or the bedroom of his home. But fact takes no heed of human hopes. A squad of men with a black banner tramped athwart the nearer shadows, intent on conflict, and beyond rose that giddy wall of frontage, vast and dark, with the dim incomprehensible lettering showing faintly on its face.

'It is no dream,' he said, 'no dream.' And he bowed his face upon his hands.

XI

The Old Man Who Knew Everything

He was startled by a cough close at hand.

He turned sharply, and peering, saw a small, hunched-up figure sitting a couple of yards off in the shadow of the enclosure.

'Have ye any news?' asked the high-pitched wheezy voice of a very old man.

Graham hesitated. 'None,' he said.

'I stay here till the lights come again,' said the old man. 'These blue scoundrels are everywhere – everywhere.'

Graham's answer was inarticulate assent. He tried to see the old man but the darkness hid his face. He wanted very much to respond, to talk, but he did not know how to begin.

'Dark and damnable,' said the old man suddenly. 'Dark and damnable. Turned out of my room among all these dangers.'

'That's hard,' ventured Graham. 'That's hard on you.'

'Darkness. An old man lost in the darkness. And all the world gone mad. War and fighting. The police beaten and rogues abroad. Why don't they bring some negroes to protect us? . . . No more dark passages for me. I fell over a dead man.'

'You're safer with company,' said the old man, 'if it's company of the right sort,' and peered frankly. He rose suddenly and came towards Graham.

Apparently the scrutiny was satisfactory. The old man sat down as if relieved to be no longer alone. 'Eh!' he said, 'but this is a terrible time! War and fighting, and the dead lying there – men, strong men, dying in the dark. Sons! I have three sons. God knows where they are tonight.'

The voice ceased. Then repeated quavering: 'God knows where they are tonight.'

Graham stood revolving a question that should not betray his ignorance. Again the old man's voice ended the pause.

'This Ostrog will win,' he said. 'He will win. And what the world will be like under him no one can tell. My sons are under the wind-vanes, all three. One of my daughters-in-law was his mistress for a while. His mistress! We're not common people. Though they've sent me to wander tonight and take my chance. . . . I knew what was going on. Before most people. But this darkness! And to fall over a dead body suddenly in the dark!'

His wheezy breathing could be heard.

'Ostrog!' said Graham.

'The greatest Boss the world has ever seen,' said the voice.

Graham ransacked his mind. 'The Council has few friends among the people,' he hazarded.

'Few friends. And poor ones at that. They've had their time. Eh! They should have kept to the clever ones. But twice they held election. And Ostrog – . And now it has burst out and nothing can stay it, nothing can stay it. Twice they rejected Ostrog – Ostrog the Boss. I heard of his rages at the time – he was terrible. Heaven save them! For nothing on earth can now, he has raised the Labour Companies upon them. No one else would have dared. All the blue canvas armed and marching! He will go through with it. He will go through.'

He was silent for a little while. 'This Sleeper,' he said, and stopped.

'Yes,' said Graham. 'Well?'

The senile voice sank to a confidential whisper, the dim, pale face came close. 'The real Sleeper – '

'Yes', said Graham.

'Died years ago.'

'What?' said Graham, sharply.

'Years ago. Died. Years ago.'

'You don't say so!' said Graham.

'I do. I do say so. He died. This Sleeper who's woke up – they changed in the night. A poor, drugged insensible creature. But I mustn't tell all I know. I mustn't tell all I know.'

For a little while he muttered inaudibly. His secret was too much for him. 'I don't know the ones that put him to sleep – that was before my time – but I know the man who injected the stimulants and woke him again. It was ten to one – wake or kill. Wake or kill. Ostrog's way.'

Graham was so astonished at these things that he had to interrupt, to make the old man repeat his words, to re-question vaguely, before he was sure of the meaning and folly of what he heard. And his awakening had not been natural! Was that an old man's senile superstition, too, or had it any truth in it? Feeling in the dark corners of his memory, he presently came on something that might conceivably be an impression of some such stimulating effect. It dawned upon him that he had happened upon a lucky encounter, that at last he might learn something of the new age. The old man wheezed a while and spat, and then the piping, reminiscent voice resumed:

'The first time they rejected him. I've followed it all.'

'Rejected whom?' said Graham. 'The Sleeper?'

'Sleeper? *No.* Ostrog. He was terrible – terrible! And he was promised then, promised certainly the next time. Fools they were – not to be more afraid of him. Now all the city's his millstone, and such as we dust ground upon it. Dust ground upon it. Until he set to work – the workers cut each other's throats, and murdered a Chinaman or a Labour policeman at times, and left the rest of us in peace. Dead bodies! Robbing! Darkness! Such a thing hasn't been this gross of years. Eh! – but 'tis ill on small folks when the great fall out! It's ill.'

'Did you say – there had not been – what? – for a gross of years?'

'Eh?' said the old man.

The old man said something about clipping his words, and made him repeat this a third time. 'Fighting and slaying, and weapons in hand, and fools bawling freedom and the like,' said the old man. 'Not in all my life has there been that. These are like the old days – for sure – when the Paris people broke out – three gross of years ago. That's what I mean hasn't been. But it's the world's way. It had to come back. I know. I know. This five years Ostrog has been working, and there has been trouble and trouble, and hunger and threats and high talk and arms. Blue canvas and murmurs. No one safe. Everything sliding and slipping. And now here we are! Revolt and fighting, and the Council come to its end.'

'You are rather well-informed on these things,' said Graham.

'I know what I hear. It isn't all Babble Machine with me.'

'No,' said Graham, wondering what Babble Machine might be. 'And you are certain this Ostrog – you are certain Ostrog organised this rebellion and arranged for the waking of the Sleeper? Just to assert himself – because he was not elected to the Council?'

'Everyone knows that, I should think,' said the old man 'Except – just fools. He meant to be master somehow. In the Council or not. Everyone who knows anything knows that. And here we are with dead bodies lying in the dark! Why, where have you been if you haven't heard all about the trouble between Ostrog and the Verneys? And what do you think the troubles are about? The Sleeper? Eh? You think the Sleeper's real and woke of his own accord – eh?'

'I'm a dull man, older than I look, and forgetful,' said Graham. 'Lots of things that have happened – especially of late years – . If I was the Sleeper, to tell you the truth, I couldn't know less about them.'

'Eh!' said the voice. 'Old, are you? You don't sound so very old! But it's not everyone keeps his memory to my time of life – truly. But these notorious things! But you're not so old as me – not nearly so old as me. Well! I ought not to judge other men by myself, perhaps. I'm young – for so old a man. Maybe you're older for so young.'

'That's it,' said Graham. 'And I've a queer history. I know very little. And history! Practically I know no history. The Sleeper and Julius

Caesar are all the same to me. It's interesting to hear you talk of these things.'

'I know a few things,' said the old man. I know a thing or two. But – . Hark!'

The two men became silent, listening. There was a heavy thud, a concussion that made their seat shiver. The passers-by stopped, shouted to one another. The old man was full of questions; he shouted to a man who passed near. Graham, emboldened by his example, got up and accosted others. None knew what had happened.

He returned to the seat and found the old man muttering vague interrogations in an undertone. For a while they said nothing to one another.

The sense of this gigantic struggle, so near and yet so remote oppressed Graham's imagination. Was this old man right, was the report of the people right, and were the revolutionaries winning? Or were they all in error, and were the red guards driving all before them? At any time the flood of warfare might pour into this silent quarter of the city and seize upon him again. It behooved him to learn all he could while there was time. He turned suddenly to the old man with a question and left it unsaid. But his motion moved the old man to speech again.

'Eh! but how things work together!' said the old man. 'This Sleeper that all the fools put their trust in! I've the whole history of it – I was always a good one for histories. When I was a boy – I'm that old – I used to read printed books. You'd hardly think it. Likely you've seen none – they rot and dust so – and the Sanitary Company burns them to make ashlarite. But they were convenient in their dirty way. One learnt a lot. These new-fangled Babble Machines – they don't seem newfangled to you, eh? – they're easy to hear, easy to forget. But I've traced all the Sleeper business from the first.'

'You will scarcely believe it,' said Graham slowly, 'I'm so ignorant – I've been so preoccupied in my own little affairs, my circumstances have been so odd – I know nothing of this Sleeper's history. Who was he?'

'Eh!' said the old man. 'I know. I know. He was a poor nobody, and set on a playful woman, poor soul! And he fell into a trance. There's the old things they had, those brown things – silver photographs – still showing him as he lay, a gross and a half years ago – a gross and a half of years.'

'Set on a playful woman, poor soul,' said Graham softly to himself, and then aloud, 'Yes – well! go on.'

'You must know he had a cousin named Warming, a solitary man without children, who made a big fortune speculating in roads – the first Eadhamite roads. But surely you've heard? No? Why? He bought all the patent rights and made a big company. In those days there were grosses of grosses of separate business and business companies. Grosses of grosses! His roads killed the railroads – the old things – in two dozen years; he bought up and Eadhamited the tracks. And because he didn't want to break up his great property or let in shareholders, he left it all to the Sleeper, and put it under a Board of Trustees that he had picked and trained. He knew then the Sleeper wouldn't wake, that he would go on sleeping, sleeping till he died. He knew that quite well! And plump! a man in the United States, who had lost two sons in a boat accident, followed that up with another great bequest. His trustees found themselves with a dozen myriads of lions-worth or more of property at the very beginning.'

'What was his name?'

'Graham.'

'No – I mean – that American's.'

'Isbister.'

'Isbister!' cried Graham. 'Why, I don't even know the name.'

'Of course not,' said the old man. 'Of course not. People don't learn much in the schools nowadays. But I know all about him. He was a rich American who went from England, and he left the Sleeper even more than Warming. How he made it? That I don't know. Something about pictures by machinery. But he made it and left it, and so the Council had its start. It was just a council of trustees at first.'

'And how did it grow?'

'Eh! – but you're not up to things. Money attracts money – and twelve brains are better than one. They played it cleverly. They worked politics with money, and kept on adding to the money by working currency and tariffs. They grew – they grew. And for years the twelve trustees hid the growing of the Sleeper's estate, under double names and company titles and all that. The Council spread by title deed, mortgage, share, every political party, every newspaper, they bought. If you listen to the old stories you will see the Council growing and growing. Billions and billions of lions at last – the Sleeper's estate, and all growing out of a whim – out of this Warming's will, and an accident to Isbister's sons.

'Men are strange,' said the old man. 'The strange thing to me is how the Council worked together so long. As many as twelve. But they worked in cliques from the first. And they've slipped back. In my young days speaking of the Council was like an ignorant man speaking of God. We didn't think they could do wrong. We didn't know of their women and all that! Or else I've got wiser.'

'Men are strange,' said the old man. 'Here are you, young and ignorant, and me – sevendy years old, and I might reasonably be forgetting – explaining it all to you short and clear.

'Sevendy,' he said, 'sevendy, and I hear and see – hear better than I see. And reason clearly, and keep myself up to all the happenings of things. Sevendy!

'Life is strange. I was twaindy before Ostrog was a baby. I remember him long before he'd pushed his way to the head of the Wind-Vanes Control. I've seen many changes. Eh! I've worn the blue. And at last I've come to see this crush and darkness and tumult and dead men carried by in heaps on the ways. And all his doing! All his doing!'

His voice died away in scarcely articulate praises of Ostrog.

Graham thought. 'Let me see,' he said, 'if I have it right.'

He extended a hand and ticked off points upon his fingers. 'The Sleeper has been asleep – '

'Changed,' said the old man.

'Perhaps. And meanwhile the Sleeper's property grew in the hands of Twelve Trustees, until it swallowed up nearly all the great ownership of the world. The Twelve Trustees – by virtue of this property have become virtually masters of the world. Because they are the paying power – just as the old English Parliament used to be – '

'Eh!' said the old man. 'That's so – that's a good comparison. You're not so – '

'And now this Ostrog – has suddenly revolutionised the world by waking the Sleeper – whom no one but the superstitious, common people had ever dreamt would wake again – raising the Sleeper to claim his property from the Council, after all these years.'

The old man endorsed this statement with a cough. 'It's strange,' he said, 'to meet a man who learns these things for the first time tonight.'

'Aye,' said Graham, 'it's strange.'

'Have you been in a Pleasure City?' said the old man. 'All my life I've longed – ' He laughed. 'Even now,' he said 'I could enjoy a little fun. Enjoy seeing things, anyhow.' He mumbled a sentence Graham did not understand.

'The Sleeper – when did he awake?' said Graham suddenly.

'Three days ago.'

'Where is he?'

'Ostrog has him. He escaped from the Council not four hours ago. My dear sir, where were you at the time? He was in the hall of the markets – where the fighting has been. All the city was screaming about it. All the Babble Machines. Everywhere it was shouted. Even the fools who speak for the Council were admitting it. Everyone was rushing off to see him – everyone was getting arms. Were you drunk or asleep? And even then! But you're joking! Surely you're pretending. It was to stop the shouting of the Babble Machines and prevent the people gathering that they turned off the electricity – and put this damned darkness upon us. Do you mean to say – ?'

'I had heard the Sleeper was rescued,' said Graham. 'But – to come back a minute. Are you sure Ostrog has him?'

'He won't let him go,' said the old man.

'And the Sleeper. Are you sure he is not genuine? I have never heard – '

'So all the fools think. So they think. As if there wasn't a thousand things that were never heard. I know Ostrog too well for that. Did I tell you? In a way I'm a sort of relation of Ostrog's. A sort of relation. Through my daughter-in-law.'

'I suppose – '

'Well?'

'I suppose there's no chance of this Sleeper asserting himself. I suppose he's certain to be a puppet – in Ostrog's hands or the Council's, as soon as the struggle is over.'

'In Ostrog's hands – certainly. Why shouldn't he be a puppet? Look at his position. Everything done for him, every pleasure possible. Why should he want to assert himself?'

'What are these Pleasure Cities?' said Graham, abruptly.

The old man made him repeat the question. When at last he was assured of Graham's words, he nudged him violently. 'That's *too* much,' said he. 'You're poking fun at an old man. I've been suspecting you know more than you pretend.'

'Perhaps I do,' said Graham. 'But no! why should I go on acting? No, I do not know what a Pleasure City is.'

The old man laughed in an intimate way.

'What is more, I do not know how to read your letters, I do not know what money you use, I do not know what foreign countries there are. I do not know where I am. I cannot count. I do not know where to get food, nor drink, nor shelter.'

'Come, come,' said the old man, 'if you had a glass of drink, now, would you put it in your ear or your eye?'

'I want you to tell me all these things.'

'He, he! Well, gentlemen who dress in silk must have their fun.' A withered hand caressed Graham's arm for a moment. 'Silk. Well, well! But, all the same, I wish I was the man who was put up as the Sleeper. He'll have a fine time of it. All the pomp and pleasure. He's a queer looking face. When they used to let anyone go to see him, I've got tickets and been. The image of the real one, as the photographs show him, this substitute used to be. Yellow. But he'll get fed up. It's a queer world. Think of the luck of it. The luck of it. I expect he'll be sent to Capri. It's the best fun for a greener.'

His cough overtook him again. Then he began mumbling enviously of pleasures and strange delights. 'The luck of it, the luck of it! All my life I've been in London, hoping to get my chance.'

'But you don't know that the Sleeper died,' said Graham, suddenly.

The old man made him repeat his words.

'Men don't live beyond ten dozen. It's not in the order of things,' said the old man. 'I'm not a fool. Fools may believe it, but not me.'

Graham became angry with the old man's assurance. 'Whether you are a fool or not,' he said, 'it happens you are wrong about the Sleeper.'

'Eh?'

'You are wrong about the Sleeper. I haven't told you before, but I will tell you now. You are wrong about the Sleeper.'

'How do you know? I thought you didn't know anything – not even about Pleasure Cities.'

Graham paused.

'You don't know,' said the old man. 'How are you to know? It's very few men – '

'I *am* the Sleeper.'

He had to repeat it.

There was a brief pause. 'There's a silly thing to say, sir, if you'll excuse me. It might get you into trouble in a time like this,' said the old man.

Graham, slightly dashed, repeated his assertion.

'I was saying I was the Sleeper. That years and years ago I did, indeed, fall asleep, in a little stone-built village, in the days when there were hedgerows, and villages, and inns, and all the countryside cut up into little pieces, little fields. Have you never heard of those days? And it is I – I who speak to you – who awakened again these four days since.'

'Four days since! – the Sleeper! But they've *got* the Sleeper. They have him and they won't let him go. Nonsense! You've been talking sensibly enough up to now. I can see it as though I was there. There will be Lincoln like a keeper just behind him; they won't let him go about alone. Trust them. You're a queer fellow. One of these fun pokers. I see now why you have been clipping your words so oddly, but – '

He stopped abruptly, and Graham could see his gesture.

'As if Ostrog would let the Sleeper run about alone! No, you're telling that to the wrong man altogether. Eh! as if I should believe. What's your game? And besides, we've been talking of the Sleeper.'

Graham stood up. 'Listen,' he said. 'I am the Sleeper.'

'You're an odd man,' said the old man, 'to sit here in the dark, talking clipped, and telling a lie of that sort. But – '

Graham's exasperation fell to laughter. 'It is preposterous,' he cried. 'Preposterous. The dream must end. It gets wilder and wilder. Here am I – in this damned twilight – I never knew a dream in twilight before – an anachronism by two hundred years and trying to persuade an old fool that I am myself, and meanwhile – Ugh!'

He moved in gusty irritation and went striding. In a moment the old man was pursuing him. 'Eh! but don't go!' cried the old man. 'I'm an old fool, I know. Don't go. Don't leave me in all this darkness.'

Graham hesitated, stopped. Suddenly the folly of telling his secret flashed into his mind.

'I didn't mean to offend you – disbelieving you,' said the old man coming near. 'It's no manner of harm. Call yourself the Sleeper if it pleases you. 'Tis a foolish trick – '

Graham hesitated, turned abruptly and went on his way.

For a time he heard the old man's hobbling pursuit and his wheezy cries receding. But at last the darkness swallowed him, and Graham saw him no more.

XII

Ostrog

Graham could now take a clearer view of his position. For a long time yet he wandered, but after the talk of the old man his discovery of this Ostrog was clear in his mind as the final inevitable decision. One thing was evident, those who were at the headquarters of the revolt had succeeded very admirably in suppressing the fact of his disappearance. But every moment he expected to hear the report of his death or of his recapture by the Council.

Presently a man stopped before him. 'Have you heard?' he said.

'No!' said Graham starting.

'Near a dozand,' said the man, 'a dozand men!' and hurried on.

A number of men and girls passed in the darkness, gesticulating and shouting: 'Capitulated! Given up!' 'A dozand of men.' 'Two dozand of men.' 'Ostrog, Hurrah! Ostrog, Hurrah!' These cries receded, became indistinct.

Other shouting men followed. For a time his attention was absorbed in the fragments of speech he heard. He had a doubt whether all were speaking English. Scraps floated to him, scraps like Pigeon English, like negro dialect, blurred and mangled distortions. He dared accost no one with questions. The impression the people gave him jarred altogether with his preconceptions of the struggle and confirmed the old man's faith in Ostrog. It was only slowly he could bring himself to believe that all these people were rejoicing at the defeat of the Council, that the Council which had pursued him with such power and vigour was after all the weaker of the two sides in conflict. And if that was so, how did it affect him? Several times he hesitated on the verge of fundamental questions. Once he turned and walked for a long way after a little man of rotund inviting outline, but he was unable to master confidence to address him.

It was only slowly that it came to him that he might ask for the 'wind-vane offices', whatever the 'wind-vane offices' might be. His first inquiry simply resulted in a direction to go towards Westminster. His second led to the discovery of a short cut in which he was speedily lost.

He was told to leave the ways to which he had hitherto confined himself – knowing no other means of transit – and to plunge down one of the middle staircases into the blackness of a crossway. Thereupon came some trivial adventures; chief of these an ambiguous encounter with a gruffvoiced invisible creature speaking in a strange dialect that seemed at first a strange tongue, a thick flow of speech with the drifting corpses of English words therein, the dialect of the latter-day vile. Then another voice drew near, a girl's voice singing, 'tralala tralala'. She spoke to Graham, her English touched with something of the same quality. She professed to have lost her sister, she blundered needlessly into him he thought, caught hold of him and laughed. But a word of vague remonstrance sent her into the unseen again.

The sounds about him increased. Stumbling people passed him, speaking excitedly. 'They have surrendered!' 'The Council! Surely not the Council!' 'They are saying so in the Ways.' The passage seemed wider. Suddenly the wall fell away. He was in a great space and people were stirring remotely. He inquired his way of an indistinct figure. 'Strike straight across,' said a woman's voice. He left his guiding wall, and in a moment had stumbled against a little table on which were utensils of glass. Graham's eyes, now attuned to darkness, made out a long vista with pallid tables on either side. He went down this. At one or two of the tables he heard a clang of glass and a sound of eating. There were people then cool enough to dine, or daring enough to steal a meal in spite of social convulsion and darkness. Far off and high up he presently saw a pallid light of a semi-circular shape. As he approached this, a black edge came up and hid it. He stumbled at steps and found himself in a gallery. He heard a sobbing, and found two scared little girls crouched by a railing. These children became silent at the near sound of feet. He tried to console them, but they were very still until he left them. Then as he receded he could hear them sobbing again.

Presently he found himself at the foot of a staircase and near a wide opening. He saw a dim twilight above this and ascended out of the blackness into a street of moving Ways again. Along this a disorderly swarm of people marched shouting. They were singing snatches of the song of the revolt, most of them out of tune. Here and there torches flared creating brief hysterical shadows. He asked his way and was twice puzzled by that same thick dialect. His third attempt won an answer he could understand. He was two miles from the wind-vane offices in Westminster, but the way was easy to follow.

When at last he did approach the district of the wind-vane offices it seemed to him, from the cheering processions that came marching along the Ways, from the tumult of rejoicing, and finally from the restoration of the lighting of the city, that the overthrow of the Council must already be accomplished. And still no news of his absence came to his ears.

The re-illumination of the city came with startling abruptness. Suddenly he stood blinking, all about him men halted dazzled, and the world was incandescent. The light found him already upon the outskirts of the excited crowds that choked the Ways near the wind-vane offices, and the sense of visibility and exposure that came with it turned his colourless intention of joining Ostrog to a keen anxiety.

For a time he was jostled, obstructed, and endangered by men hoarse and weary with cheering his name. Some of them bandaged and bloody in his cause. The frontage of the wind-vane offices was illuminated by some moving picture, but what it was he could not see, because in spite of his strenuous attempts the density of the crowd prevented his approaching it. From the fragments of speech he caught, he judged it conveyed news of the fighting about the Council House. Ignorance and indecision made him slow and ineffective in his movements. For a time he could not conceive how he was to get within the unbroken facade of this place. He made his way slowly into the midst of this mass of people, until he realised that the descending staircase of the central Way led to the interior of the buildings. This gave him a goal, but the crowding in the central path was so dense that it was long before he could reach it. And even then he encountered intricate obstruction, and had an hour of vivid argument first in this guard room and then in that before he could get a note taken to the one man of all men who was most eager to see him. His story was laughed to scorn at one place, and wiser for that, when at last he reached a second stairway he professed simply to have news of extraordinary importance for Ostrog. What it was he would not say. They sent his note reluctantly. For a long time he waited in a little room at the foot of the lift shaft, and thither at last came Lincoln, eager, apologetic, astonished. He stopped in the doorway scrutinising Graham, then rushed forward effusively.

'Yes,' he cried. 'It is you. And you are not dead!'

Graham made a brief explanation.

'My brother is waiting,' explained Lincoln. 'He is alone in the wind-vane offices. We feared you had been killed in the theatre. He doubted – and things are very urgent still in spite of what we are telling them *there* – or he would have come to you.'

They ascended a lift, passed along a narrow passage, crossed a great hall, empty save for two hurrying messengers, and entered a comparatively little room, whose only furniture was a long settee and a large oval disc of cloudy, shifting grey, hung by cables from the wall. There Lincoln left Graham for a space, and he remained alone without understanding the shifting smoky shapes that drove slowly across this disc.

His attention was arrested by a sound that began abruptly. It was cheering, the frantic cheering of a vast but very remote crowd, a roaring exultation. This ended as sharply as it had begun, like a sound heard between the opening and shutting of a door. In the outer room was a noise of hurrying steps and a melodious clinking as if a loose chain was running over the teeth of a wheel.

Then he heard the voice of a woman, the rustle of unseen garments. 'It is Ostrog!' he heard her say. A little bell rang fitfully, and then everything was still again.

Presently came voices, footsteps and movement without. The footsteps of some one person detached itself from the other sounds and drew near, firm, evenly measured steps. The curtain lifted slowly. A tall, white-haired man, clad in garments of cream-coloured silk, appeared, regarding Graham from under his raised arm.

For a moment the white form remained holding the curtain, then dropped it and stood before it. Graham's first impression was of a very broad forehead, very pale blue eyes deep sunken under white brows, an aquiline nose, and a heavily-lined resolute mouth. The folds of flesh over the eyes, the drooping of the corners of the mouth contradicted the upright bearing, and said the man was old. Graham rose to his feet instinctively, and for a moment the two men stood in silence, regarding each other.

'You are Ostrog?' said Graham.

'I am Ostrog.'

'The Boss?'

'So I am called.'

Graham felt the inconvenience of the silence. 'I have to thank you chiefly, I understand, for my safety,' he said presently.

'We were afraid you were killed,' said Ostrog. 'Or sent to sleep again – for ever. We have been doing everything to keep our secret – the secret of your disappearance. Where have you been? How did you get here?'

Graham told him briefly.

Ostrog listened in silence.

He smiled faintly. 'Do you know what I was doing when they came to tell me you had come?'

'How can I guess?'

'Preparing your double.'

'My double?'

'A man as like you as we could find. We were going to hypnotise him to save him the difficulty of acting. It was imperative. The whole of this revolt depends on the idea that you are awake, alive, and with us. Even now a great multitude of people has gathered in the theatre clamouring to see you. They do not trust . . . You know, of course – something of your position?'

'Very little,' said Graham.

'It is like this.' Ostrog walked a pace or two into the room and turned. 'You are absolute owner,' he said, 'of more than half the world. As a result of that you are practically King. Your powers are limited in many intricate ways, but you are the figurehead, the popular symbol of government. This White Council, the Council of Trustees as it is called – '

'I have heard the vague outline of these things.'

'I wondered.'

'I came upon a garrulous old man.'

'I see. . . . Our masses – the word comes from your days – you know of course, that we still have masses – regard you as our actual ruler. Just as a great number of people in your days regarded the Crown as the ruler. They are discontented – the masses all over the earth – with the rule of your Trustees. For the most part it is the old discontent, the old quarrel of the common man with his commonness – the misery of work and discipline and unfitness. But your Trustees have ruled ill. In certain matters, in the administration of the Labour Companies, for example, they have been unwise. They have given endless opportunities. Already we of the popular party were agitating for reforms – when your waking came. Came! If it had been contrived it could not have come more opportunely.' He smiled. 'The public mind, making no allowance for your years of quiescence, had already hit on the thought of waking you and appealing to you, and – Flash!'

He indicated the outbreak by a gesture, and Graham moved his head to show that he understood.

'The Council muddled – quarrelled. They always do. They could not decide what to do with you. You know how they imprisoned you?'

'I see. I see. And now – we win?'

'We win. Indeed we win. Tonight, in five swift hours. Suddenly we struck everywhere. The wind-vane people, the Labour Company and its millions, burst the bonds. We got the pull of the aeropiles.'

He paused. 'Yes,' said Graham, guessing that aeropile meant flying machine.

'That was, of course, essential. Or they could have got away. All the city rose, every third man almost was in it! All the blue, all the public services, save only just a few aeronauts and about half the red police. You were rescued, and their own police of the Ways – not half of them could be massed at the Council House – have been broken up, disarmed or killed. All London is ours – now. Only the Council House remains.

'Half of those who remain to them of the red police were lost in that foolish attempt to recapture you. They lost their heads when they lost you. They flung all they had at the theatre. We cut them off from the Council House there. Truly tonight has been a night of victory. Everywhere your star has blazed. A day ago – the White Council ruled as it has ruled for a gross of years, for a century and a half of years, and then, with only a little whispering, a covert among here and there, suddenly – So!'

'I am very ignorant,' said Graham. 'I suppose – . I do not clearly understand the conditions of this fighting. If you could explain. Where is the Council? Where is the fight?'

Ostrog stepped across the room, something clicked, and suddenly, save for an oval glow, they were in darkness. For a moment Graham was puzzled.

Then he saw that the cloudy grey disc had taken depth and colour, had assumed the appearance of an oval window looking out upon a strange unfamiliar scene.

At the first glance he was unable to guess what this scene might be. It was a daylight scene, the daylight of a wintry day, grey and clear. Across the picture and halfway as it seemed between him and the remoter view, a stout cable of twisted white wire stretched vertically. Then he perceived that the rows of great wind-wheels he saw, the wide intervals, the occasional gulfs of darkness, were akin to those through which he had fled from the Council House. He distinguished an orderly file of red figures marching across an open space between files of men in black, and realised before Ostrog spoke that he was looking down on the upper surface of latter-day London. The overnight snows had gone. He judged that this mirror was some modern replacement of the camera obscura, but that matter was not explained to him. He saw that though the file of red figures was trotting from left to right, yet they were passing out of the picture to the left. He wondered momentarily, and then saw that the picture was passing slowly, panorama fashion, across the oval.

'In a moment you will see the fighting,' said Ostrog at his elbow. 'Those fellows in red you notice are prisoners. This is the roof space of London – all the houses are practically continuous now. The streets and public squares are covered in. The gaps and chasms of your time have disappeared.'

Something out of focus obliterated half the picture. Its form suggested a man. There was a gleam of metal, a flash, something that swept across the oval, as the eyelid of a bird sweeps across its eye, and the picture was clear again. And now Graham beheld men running down among the wind-wheels, pointing weapons from which jetted out little smoky flashes. They swarmed thicker and thicker to the right, gesticulating – it might be they were shouting, but of that the picture told nothing. They and the wind-wheels passed slowly and steadily across the field of the mirror.

'Now,' said Ostrog, 'comes the Council House,' and slowly a black edge crept into view and gathered Graham's attention. Soon it was no longer an edge but a cavity, a huge blackened space amidst the clustering edifices, and from it thin spires of smoke rose into the pallid winter sky. Gaunt ruinous masses of the building, mighty truncated piers and girders, rose dismally out of this cavernous darkness. And over these vestiges of some splendid place, countless minute men were clambering, leaping, swarming.

'This is the Council House,' said Ostrog. 'Their last stronghold. And the fools wasted enough ammunition to hold out for a month in blowing up the buildings all about them – to stop our attack. You heard the smash? It shattered half the brittle glass in the city.'

And while he spoke, Graham saw that beyond this area of ruins, overhanging it and rising to a great height, was a ragged mass of white building. This mass had been isolated by the ruthless destruction of its surroundings. Black gaps marked the passages the disaster had torn apart; big halls had been slashed open and the decoration of their interiors showed dismally in the wintry dawn, and down the jagged walls hung festoons of divided cables and twisted ends of lines and metallic rods. And amidst all the vast details moved little red specks, the red-clothed defenders of the Council. Every now and then faint flashes illuminated the bleak shadows. At the first sight it seemed to Graham that an attack upon this isolated white building was in progress, but then he perceived that the party of the revolt was not advancing, but sheltered amidst the colossal wreckage that encircled this last ragged stronghold of the red-garbed men, was keeping up a fitful firing.

And not ten hours ago he had stood beneath the ventilating fans in a little chamber within that remote building wondering what was happening in the world!

Looking more attentively as this warlike episode moved silently across the centre of the mirror, Graham saw that the white building was surrounded on every side by ruins, and Ostrog proceeded to describe in concise phrases how its defenders had sought by such destruction to isolate themselves from a storm. He spoke of the loss of men that huge downfall had entailed in an indifferent tone. He indicated an improvised mortuary among the wreckage, showed ambulances swarming like cheese-mites along a ruinous groove that had once been a street of moving ways. He was more interested in pointing out the parts of the Council House, the distribution of the besiegers. In a little while the civil contest that had convulsed London was no longer a mystery to Graham. It was no tumultuous revolt had occurred that night, no equal warfare, but a splendidly organised *coup d'état*. Ostrog's grasp of details was astonishing; he seemed to know the business of even the smallest knot of black and red specks that crawled amidst these places.

He stretched a huge black arm across the luminous picture, and showed the room whence Graham had escaped, and across the chasm of ruins the course of his flight. Graham recognised the gulf across which the gutter ran, and the wind-wheels where he had crouched from the flying machine. The rest of his path had succumbed to the explosion. He looked again at the Council House, and it was already half hidden, and on the right a hillside with a cluster of domes and pinnacles, hazy, dim and distant, was gliding into view.

'And the Council is really overthrown?' he said

'Overthrown,' said Ostrog.

'And I – . Is it indeed true that I – ?'

'You are Master of the World.'

'But that white flag – '

'That is the flag of the Council – the flag of the Rule of the World. It will fall. The fight is over. Their attack on the theatre was their last frantic struggle. They have only a thousand men or so, and some of these men will be disloyal. They have little ammunition. And we are reviving the ancient arts. We are casting guns.'

'But – help. Is this city the world?'

'Practically this is all they have left to them of their empire. Abroad the cities have either revolted with us or wait the issue. Your awakening has perplexed them, paralysed them.'

'But haven't the Council flying machines? Why is there no fighting with them?'

'They had. But the greater part of the aeronauts were in the revolt with us. They wouldn't take the risk of fighting on our side, but they would not stir against us. We *had* to get a pull with the aeronauts. Quite half were with us, and the others knew it. Directly they knew you had got away, those looking for you dropped. We killed the man who shot at you – an hour ago. And we occupied the flying stages at the outset in every city we could, and so stopped and captured the aeroplanes, and as for the little flying machines that turned out – for some did – we kept up too straight and steady a fire for them to get near the Council House. If they dropped they couldn't rise again, because there's no clear space about there for them to get up. Several we have smashed, several others have dropped and surrendered, the rest have gone off to the Continent to find a friendly city if they can before their fuel runs out. Most of these men were only too glad to be taken prisoner and kept out of harm's way. Upsetting in a flying machine isn't a very attractive prospect. There's no chance for the Council that way. Its days are done.'

He laughed and turned to the oval reflection again to show Graham what he meant by flying stages. Even the four nearer ones were remote and obscured by a thin morning haze. But Graham could perceive they were very vast structures, judged even by the standard of the things about them.

And then as the dim shapes passed to the left there came again the sight of the expanse across which the disarmed men in red had been marching. And then the black ruins, and then again the beleaguered white fastness of the Council. It appeared no longer a ghostly pile, but glowing amber in the sunlight, for a cloud shadow had passed. About it the pigmy struggle still hung in suspense, but now the red defenders were no longer firing.

So, in a dusky stillness, the man from the nineteenth century saw the closing scene of the great revolt, the forcible establishment of his rule. With a quality of startling discovery it came to him that this was his world, and not that other he had left behind; that this was no spectacle to culminate and cease; that in this world lay whatever life was still before him, lay all his duties and dangers and responsibilities. He turned with fresh questions. Ostrog began to answer them, and then broke off abruptly. 'But these things I must explain more fully later. At present there are – duties. The people are coming by the moving ways towards this ward from every part of the city – the markets and theatres are densely crowded. You are just in time for them. They are clamouring to see you. And abroad they want to see you. Paris, New York, Chicago, Denver, Capri – thousands of cities are up and in a tumult, undecided, and clamouring to see you. They have clamoured that you should be awakened for years, and now it is done they will scarcely believe –'

'But surely – I can't go. . . .'

Ostrog answered from the other side of the room, and the picture on the oval disc paled and vanished as the light jerked back again. 'There are kineto-tele-photographs,' he said. 'As you bow to the people here – all over the world myriads of myriads of people, packed and still in darkened halls, will see you also. In black and white, of course – not like this. And you will hear their shouts reinforcing the shouting in the hall.

'And there is an optical contrivance we shall use,' said Ostrog, 'used by some of the posturers and women dancers. It may be novel to you. You stand in a very bright light, and they see not you but a magnified image of you thrown on a screen – so that even the furtherest man in the remotest gallery can, if he chooses, count your eyelashes.'

Graham clutched desperately at one of the questions in his mind. 'What is the population of London?' he said.

'Eight and twaindy myriads.'

'Eight and what?'

'More than thirty-three millions.'

These figures went beyond Graham's imagination.

'You will be expected to say something,' said Ostrog. 'Not what you used to call a Speech, but what our people call a Word – just one sentence, six or seven words. Something formal. If I might suggest – "I have awakened and my heart is with you." That is the sort of thing they want.'

'What was that?' asked Graham.

'"I am awakened and my heart is with you." And bow – bow royally. But first we must get you black robes – for black is your colour. Do you mind? And then they disperse to their homes.'

Graham hesitated. 'I am in your hands,' he said.

Ostrog was clearly of that opinion. He thought for a moment, turned to the curtain and called brief directions to some unseen attendants. Almost immediately a black robe, the very fellow of the black robe Graham had worn in the theatre, was brought. And as he threw it about his shoulders there came from the room without the shrilling of a high-pitched bell. Ostrog turned in interrogation to the attendant, then suddenly seemed to change his mind, pulled the curtain aside and disappeared.

For a moment Graham stood with the deferential attendant listening to Ostrog's retreating steps. There was a sound of quick question and answer and of men running. The curtain was snatched back and Ostrog reappeared, his massive face glowing with excitement. He crossed the room in a stride, clicked the room into darkness, gripped Graham's arm and pointed to the mirror.

'Even as we turned away,' he said.

Graham saw his index finger, black and colossal, above the mirrored Council House. For a moment he did not understand. And then he perceived that the flagstaff that had carried the white banner was bare.

'Do you mean – ?' he began.

'The Council has surrendered. Its rule is at an end for evermore.'

'Look!' and Ostrog pointed to a coil of black that crept in little jerks up the vacant flagstaff, unfolding as it rose.

The oval picture paled as Lincoln pulled the curtain aside and entered.

'They are clamorous,' he said.

Ostrog kept his grip of Graham's arm.

'We have raised the people,' he said. 'We have given them arms. For today at least their wishes must be law.'

Lincoln held the Curtain open for Graham and Ostrog to pass through. . . .

On his way to the markets Graham had a transitory glance of a long narrow white-walled room in which men in the universal blue canvas were carrying covered things like biers, and about which men in medical purple hurried to and fro. From this room came groans and wailing. He had an impression of an empty blood-stained couch, of men on other couches, bandaged and blood-stained. It was just a glimpse from a railed footway and then a buttress hid the place and they were going on towards the markets. . . .

The roar of the multitude was near now: it leapt to thunder. And, arresting his attention, a fluttering of black banners, the waving of blue canvas and brown rags, and the swarming vastness of the theatre near the public markets came into view down a long passage. The picture opened out. He perceived they were entering the great theatre of his first appearance, the great theatre he had last seen as a chequer-work of glare and blackness in his flight from the red police. This time he entered it along a gallery at a level high about the stage. The place was now brilliantly lit again. He sought the gangway up which he had fled, but he could not tell it from among its dozens of fellows; nor could he see anything of the smashed seats, deflated cushions, and such like traces of the fight because of the density of the people. Except the stage the whole place was closely packed. Looking down the effect was a vast area of stippled pink, each dot a still upturned face regarding him. At his appearance with Ostrog the cheering died away, the singing died away, a common interest stilled and unified the disorder. It seemed as though every individual of those myriads was watching him.

XIII

The End of the Old Order

So far as Graham was able to judge, it was near midday when the white
banner of the Council fell. But some hours had to elapse before it was
possible to effect the formal capitulation, and so after he had spoken
his 'Word' he retired to his new apartments in the wind-vane offices.
The continuous excitement of the last twelve hours had left him
inordinately fatigued, even his curiosity was exhausted; for a space he
slept. He was roused by two medical attendants, come prepared with
stimulants to sustain him through the next occasion. After he had taken
their drugs and bathed by their advice in cold water, he felt a rapid
return of interest and energy, and was presently able and willing to
accompany Ostrog through several miles (as it seemed) of passages,
lifts, and slides to the closing scene of the White Council's rule.

The way ran deviously through a maze of buildings. They came at
last to a passage that curved about, and showed broadening before him
an oblong opening, clouds hot with sunset, and the ragged skyline of
the ruinous Council House. A tumult of shouts came drifting up to him.
In another moment they had come out high up on the brow of the cliff
of torn buildings that overhung the wreckage. The vast area opened to
Graham's eyes, none the less strange and wonderful for the remote view
he had had of it in the oval mirror.

This rudely amphitheatral space seemed now the better part of a mile
to its outer edge. It was gold lit on the left hand, catching the sunlight,
and below and to the right clear and cold in the shadow. Above the
shadowy grey Council House that stood in the midst of it, the great
black banner of the surrender still hung in sluggish folds against the
blazing sunset. Severed rooms, halls and passages gaped strangely,
broken masses of metal projected dismally from the complex wreckage,
vast masses of twisted cable dropped like tangled seaweed, and from its
base came a tumult of innumerable voices, violent concussions, and the
sound of trumpets. All about this great white pile was a ring of
desolation; the smashed and blackened masses, the gaunt foundations
and ruinous lumber of the fabric that had been destroyed by the

Council's orders, skeletons of girders, Titanic masses of wall, forests of stout pillars. Amongst the sombre wreckage beneath, running water flashed and glistened, and far away across the space, out in the midst of a vague vast mass of buildings, there thrust the twisted end of a watermain, two hundred feet in the air, thunderously spouting a shining cascade. And everywhere great multitudes of people.

Wherever there was space and foothold, people swarmed, little people, small and minutely clear, except where the sunset touched them to indistinguishable gold. They clambered up the tottering walls, they clung in wreaths and groups about the high-standing pillars. They swarmed along the edges of the circle of ruins. The air was full of their shouting, and they were pressing and swaying towards the central space.

The upper storeys of the Council House seemed deserted, not a human being was visible. Only the drooping banner of the surrender hung heavily against the light. The dead were within the Council House, or hidden by the swarming people, or carried away. Graham could see only a few neglected bodies in gaps and corners of the ruins, and amidst the flowing water.

'Will you let them see you, Sire?' said Ostrog. 'They are very anxious to see you.'

Graham hesitated, and then walked forward to where the broken verge of wall dropped sheer. He stood looking down, a lonely, tall, black figure against the sky.

Very slowly the swarming ruins became aware of him. And as they did so little bands of black-uniformed men appeared remotely, thrusting through the crowds towards the Council House. He saw little black heads become pink, looking at him, saw by that means a wave of recognition sweep across the space. It occurred to him that he should accord them some recognition. He held up his arm, then pointed to the Council House and dropped his hand. The voices below became unanimous, gathered volume, came up to him as multitudinous wavelets of cheering.

The western sky was a pallid bluish green, and Jupiter shone high in the south, before the capitulation was accomplished. Above was a slow insensible change, the advance of night serene and beautiful; below was hurry, excitement, conflicting orders, pauses, spasmodic developments or organisation, a vast ascending clamour and confusion. Before the Council came out, toiling perspiring men, directed by a conflict of shouts, carried forth hundreds of those who had perished in the hand-to-hand conflict within those long passages and chambers. . . .

Guards in black lined the way that the Council would come, and as far as the eye could reach into the hazy blue twilight of the ruins, and swarming now at every possible point in the captured Council House and along the shattered cliff of its circumadjacent buildings, were innumerable people, and their voices even when they were not cheering, were as the soughing of the sea upon a pebble beach. Ostrog had chosen a huge commanding pile of crushed and overthrown masonry, and on this stage of timbers and metal girders was being hastily constructed. Its essential parts were complete, but humming and clangorous machinery still glared fitfully in the shadows beneath this temporary edifice.

The stage had a small higher portion on which Graham stood with Ostrog and Lincoln close beside him, a little in advance of a group of minor officers. A broader lower stage surrounded this quarter deck, and on this were the black-uniformed guards of the revolt armed with the little green weapons whose very names Graham still did not know. Those standing about him perceived that his eyes wandered perpetually from the swarming people in the twilight ruins about him to the darkling mass of the White Council House, whence the Trustees would presently come, and to the gaunt cliffs of ruin that encircled him, and so back to the people. The voices of the crowd swelled to a deafening tumult.

He saw the Councillors first afar off in the glare of one of the temporary lights that marked their path, a little group of white figures blinking in a black archway. In the Council House they had been in darkness. He watched them approaching, drawing nearer past first this blazing electric star and then that; the minatory roar of the crowd over whom their power had lasted for a hundred and fifty years marched along beside them. As they drew still nearer their faces came out weary, white and anxious. He saw them blinking up through the glare about him and Ostrog. He contrasted their strange cold looks in the Hall of Atlas.... Presently he could recognise several of them; the man who had rapped the table at Howard, a burly man with a red beard, and one delicate-featured, short, dark man with a peculiarly long skull. He noted that two were whispering together and looking behind him at Ostrog. Next there came a tall, dark and handsome man, walking downcast. Abruptly he glanced up, his eyes touched Graham for a moment, and passed beyond him to Ostrog. The way that had been made for them was so contrived that they had to march past and curve about before they came to the sloping path of planks that ascended to the stage where their surrender was to be made.

'The Master, the Master! God and the Master,' shouted the people. 'To hell with the Council!' Graham looked at their multitudes, receding beyond counting into a shouting haze, and then at Ostrog beside him, white and steadfast and still. His eye went again to the little group of White Councillors. And then he looked up at the familiar quiet stars overhead. The marvellous element in his fate was suddenly vivid. Could that be his indeed, that little life in his memory two hundred years gone by – and this as well?

XIV

From the Crow's Nest

And so after strange delays and through an avenue of doubt and battle, this man from the nineteenth century came at last to his position at the head of that complex world.

At first when he rose from the long deep sleep that followed his rescue and the surrender of the Council, he did not recognise his surroundings. By an effort he gained a clue in his mind, and all that had happened came back to him, at first with a quality of insincerity like a story he heard, like something read out of a book. And even before his memories were clear, the exultation of his escape, the wonder of his prominence were back in his mind. He was owner of half the world; Master of the Earth. This new great age was in the completest sense his. He no longer hoped to discover his experiences a dream; he became anxious now to convince himself that they were real.

An obsequious valet assisted him to dress under the direction of a dignified chief attendant, a little man whose face proclaimed him Japanese, albeit he spoke English like an Englishman. From the latter he learnt something of the state of affairs. Already the revolution was an accepted fact; already business was being resumed throughout the city. Abroad the downfall of the Council had been received for the most part with delight. Nowhere was the Council popular, and the thousand cities of Western America, after two hundred years still jealous of New York, London, and the East, had risen almost unanimously two days before at the news of Graham's imprisonment. Paris was fighting within itself. The rest of the world hung in suspense.

While he was breaking his fast, the sound of a telephone bell jetted from a corner, and his chief attendant called his attention to the voice of Ostrog making polite inquiries. Graham interrupted his refreshment to reply. Very shortly Lincoln arrived, and Graham at once expressed a strong desire to talk to people and to be shown more of the new life that was opening before him. Lincoln informed him that in three hours' time a representative gathering of officials and their wives would be held in the state apartments of the Wind-Vane Chief. Graham's desire to traverse the ways of the city was, however, at present impossible, because of the enormous excitement of the people. It was, however, quite possible for him to take a bird's eye view of the city from the crow's nest of the wind-vane keeper. To this accordingly Graham was conducted by his attendant. Lincoln, with a graceful compliment to the attendant, apologised for not accompanying them, on account of the present pressure of administrative work.

Higher even than the most gigantic wind-wheels hung this crow's nest, a clear thousand feet above the roofs, a little disc-shaped speck on a spear of metallic filigree, cable stayed. To its summit Graham was drawn in a little wire-hung cradle. Halfway down the frail-seeming stem was a light gallery about which hung a cluster of tubes – minute they looked from above – rotating slowly on the ring of its outer rail. These were the specula, *en rapport* with the wind-vane keeper's mirrors, in one of which Ostrog had shown him the coming of his rule. His Japanese attendant ascended before him and they spent nearly an hour asking and answering questions.

It was a day full of the promise and quality of spring. The touch of the wind warmed. The sky was an intense blue and the vast expanse of London shone dazzling under the morning sun. The air was clear of smoke and haze, sweet as the air of a mountain glen.

Save for the irregular oval of ruins about the House of the Council and the black flag of the surrender that fluttered there, the mighty city seen from above showed few signs of the swift revolution that had, to his imagination, in one night and one day, changed the destinies of the world. A multitude of people still swarmed over these ruins, and the huge openwork stagings in the distance from which started in times of peace the service of aeroplanes to the various great cities of Europe and America, were also black with the victors. Across a narrow way of planking raised on trestles that crossed the ruins a crowd of workmen were busy restoring the connection between the cables and wires of the Council House and the rest of the city, preparatory to the transfer thither of Ostrog's headquarters from the Wind-Vane buildings.

For the rest the· luminous expanse was undisturbed. So vast was its serenity in comparison with the areas of disturbance, that presently Graham, looking beyond them, could almost forget the thousands of men lying out of sight in the artificial glare within the quasi-subterra-nean labyrinth, dead or dying of the overnight wounds, forget the improvised wards with the hosts of surgeons, nurses, and bearers feverishly busy, forget, indeed, all the wonder, consternation and novelty under the electric lights. Down there in the hidden ways of the anthill he knew that the revolution triumphed, that black everywhere carried the day, black favours, black banners, black festoons across the streets. And out here, under the fresh sunlight, beyond the crater of the fight, as if nothing had happened to the earth, the forest of Wind-Vanes that had grown from one or two while the Council had ruled, roared peacefully upon their incessant duty.

Far away, spiked, jagged and indented by the wind-vanes, the Surrey Hills rose blue and faint; to the north and nearer, the sharp contours of Highgate and Muswell Hill were similarly jagged. And all over the countryside, he knew, on every crest and hill, where once the hedges had interlaced, and cottages, churches, inns, and farmhouses had nestled among their trees, wind wheels similar to those he saw and bearing like them vast advertisements, gaunt and distinctive symbols of the new age, cast their whirling shadows and stored incessantly the energy that flowed away incessantly through all the arteries of the city. And underneath these wandered the countless flocks and herds of the British Food Trust with their lonely guards and keepers.

Not a familiar outline anywhere broke the cluster of gigantic shapes below. St Paul's he knew survived, and many of the old buildings in Westminster, embedded out of sight, arched over and covered in among the giant growths of the great age. The Thames, too, made no fall and gleam of silver to break the wilderness of the city; the thirsty water mains drank up every drop of its waters before they reached the walls. Its bed and estuary, scoured and sunken, was now a canal of sea water and a race of grimy bargemen brought the heavy materials of trade from the Pool thereby beneath the very feet of the workers. Faint and dim in the eastward between earth and sky hung the clustering masts of the colossal shipping in the Pool. For all the heavy traffic, for which there was no need of haste, came in gigantic sailing ships from the ends of the earth, and the heavy goods for which there was urgency in mechanical ships of a smaller swifter sort.

And to the south over the hills, came vast aqueducts with sea water for the sewers and in three separate directions, ran pallid lines – the roads, stippled with moving grey specks. On the first occasion that offered he was determined to go out and see these roads. That would come after the flying ship he was presently to try. His attendant officer described them as a pair of gently curving surfaces a hundred yards wide, each one for the traffic going in one direction, and made of a substance called Eadhamite – an artificial substance, so far as he could gather, resembling toughened glass. Along this shot a strange traffic of narrow rubber-shod vehicles, great single wheels, two and four wheeled vehicles, sweeping along at velocities of from one to six miles a minute. Railroads had vanished; a few embankments remained as rust-crowned trenches here and there. Some few formed the cores of Eadhamite ways.

Among the first things to strike his attention had been the great fleets of advertisement balloons and kites that receded in irregular vistas northward and southward along the lines of the aeroplane journeys. No aeroplanes were to be seen. Their passages had ceased, and only one little-seeming aeropile circled high in the blue distance above the Surrey Hills, an unimpressive soaring speck.

A thing Graham had already learnt, and which he found very hard to imagine, was that nearly all the towns in the country, and almost all the villages, had disappeared. Here and there only, he understood, some gigantic hotel-like edifice stood amid square miles of some single cultivation and preserved the name of a town – as Bournemouth, Wareham, or Swanage. Yet the officer had speedily convinced him how inevitable such a change had been. The old order had dotted the country with farmhouses, and every two or three miles was the ruling landlord's estate, and the place of the inn and cobbler, the grocer's shop and church – the village. Every eight miles or so was the country town, where lawyer, corn merchant, wool-stapler, saddler, veterinary surgeon, doctor, draper, milliner and so forth lived. Every eight miles – simply because that eight mile marketing journey, four there and back, was as much as was comfortable for the farmer. But directly the railways came into play, and after them the light railways, and all the swift new motor cars that had replaced waggons and horses, and so soon as the high roads began to be made of wood, and rubber, and Eadhamite, and all sorts of elastic durable substances – the necessity of having such frequent market towns disappeared. And the big towns grew. They drew the worker with the gravitational force of seemingly endless work, the employer with their suggestions of an infinite ocean of labour.

And as the standard of comfort rose, as the complexity of the mechanism of living increased, life in the country had become more and more costly, or narrow and impossible. The disappearance of vicar and squire, the extinction of the general practitioner by the city specialist, had robbed the village of its last touch of culture. After telephone, kinematograph and phonograph had replaced newspaper, book, school-master, and letter, to live outside the range of the electric cables was to live an isolated savage. In the country were neither means of being clothed nor fed (according to the refined conceptions of the time), no efficient doctors for an emergency, no company and no pursuits.

Moreover, mechanical appliances in agriculture made one engineer the equivalent of thirty labourers. So, inverting the condition of the city clerk in the days when London was scarce inhabitable because of the coaly foulness of its air, the labourers now came hurrying by road or air to the city and its life and delights at night to leave it again in the morning. The city had swallowed up humanity; man had entered upon a new stage in his development. First had come the nomad, the hunter, then had followed the agriculturist of the agricultural state, whose towns and cities and ports were but the headquarters and markets of the countryside. And now, logical consequence of an epoch of invention, was this huge new aggregation of men. Save London, there were only four other cities in Britain – Edinburgh, Portsmouth, Manchester and

Shrewsbury. Such things as these, simple statements of fact though they were to contemporary men, strained Graham's imagination to picture. And when he glanced 'over beyond there' at the strange things that existed on the Continent, it failed him altogether.

He had a vision of city beyond city, cities on great plains, cities beside great rivers, vast cities along the sea margin, cities girdled by snow mountains. Over a great part of the earth the English tongue was spoken; taken together with its Spanish American and Hindoo and Negro and 'Pidgin' dialects, it was the everyday language of two-thirds of the people of the earth. On the Continent, save as remote and curious survivals, three other languages alone held sway – German, which reached to Antioch and Genoa and jostled Spanish-English at Cadiz, a Gallicised Russian which met the Indian English in Persia and Kurdistan and the 'Pidgin' English in Pekin, and French still clear and brilliant, the language of lucidity, which shared the Mediterranean with the Indian English and German and reached through a negro dialect to the Congo.

And everywhere now, through the city-set earth, save in the administered 'black belt' territories of the tropics, the same cosmopolitan social organisation prevailed, and everywhere from Pole to Equator his property and his responsibilities extended. The whole world was civilised; the whole world dwelt in cities; the whole world was property. Over the British Empire and throughout America his ownership was scarcely disguised, Congress and Parliament were usually regarded as antique, curious gatherings. And even in the two Empires of Russia and Germany, the influence of his wealth was conceivably of enormous weight. There, of course, came problems – possibilities, but, uplifter as he was, even Russia and Germany seemed sufficiently remote. And of the quality of the black belt administration, and of what that might mean for him he thought, after the fashion of his former days, not at all. That it should hang like a threat over the spacious vision before him could not enter his nineteenth-century mind. But his mind turned at once from the scenery to the thought of a vanished dread. 'What of the yellow peril?' he asked and Asano made him explain. The Chinese spectre had vanished. Chinaman and European were at peace. The twentieth century had discovered with reluctant certainty that the average Chinaman was as civilised, more moral, and far more intelligent than the average European serf, and had repeated on a gigantic scale the fraternisation of Scot and Englishman that happened in the seventeenth century. As Asano put it; 'They thought it over. They found we were white men after all.' Graham turned again to the view and his thoughts took a new direction.

Out of the dim south-west, glittering and strange, voluptuous, and in some way terrible, shone those Pleasure Cities, of which the kinematograph-phonograph and the old man in the street had spoken. Strange places reminiscent of the legendary Sybaris, cities of art and beauty, mercenary art and mercenary beauty, sterile wonderful cities of motion and music, whither repaired all who profited by the fierce, inglorious, economic struggle that went on in the glaring labyrinth below.

Fierce he knew it was. How fierce he could judge from the fact that these latter-day people referred back to the England of the nineteenth century as the figure of an idyllic easy-going life. He turned his eyes to the scene immediately before him again, trying to conceive the big factories of that intricate maze.

Northward he knew were the potters, makers not only of earthenware and china, but of the kindred pastes and compounds a subtler mineralogical chemistry had devised; there were the makers of statuettes and wall ornaments and much intricate furniture; there too were the factories where feverishly competitive authors devised their phonograph discourses and advertisements and arranged the groupings and developments for their perpetually startling and novel kinematographic dramatic works. Thence, too, flashed the world-wide messages, the world-wide falsehoods of the news-tellers, the chargers of the telephonic machines that had replaced the newspapers of the past.

To the westward beyond the smashed Council House were the voluminous offices of municipal control and government; and to the eastward, towards the port, the trading quarters, the huge public markets, the theatres, houses of resort, betting palaces, miles of billiard saloons, baseball and football circuses, wild beast rings and the innumerable temples of the Christian and quasi-Christian sects, the Mahomedans, Buddhists, Gnostics, Spook Worshippers, the Incubus Worshippers, the Furniture Worshippers, and so forth; and to the south again a vast manufacture of textiles, pickles, wines and condiments. And from point to point tore the countless multitudes along the roaring mechanical ways. A gigantic hive, of which the winds were tireless servants, and the ceaseless wind-vanes an appropriate crown and symbol.

He thought of the unprecedented population that had been sucked up by this sponge of halls and galleries – the thirty-three million lives that were playing out each its own brief ineffectual drama below him, and the complacency that the brightness of the day and the space and splendour of the view, and above all the sense of his own importance had begotten, dwindled and perished. Looking down from this height over the city it became at last possible to conceive this overwhelming multitude of thirty-three millions, the reality of the responsibility he would take upon himself, the vastness of the human Maelstrom over which his slender kingship hung.

He tried to figure the individual life. It astonished him to realise how little the common man had changed in spite of the visible change in his conditions. Life and property, indeed, were secure from violence almost all over the world, zymotic diseases, bacterial diseases of all sorts had practically vanished, everyone had a sufficiency of food and clothing, was warmed in the city ways and sheltered from the weather – so much the almost mechanical progress of science and the physical organisation of society had accomplished. But the crowd, he was already beginning to discover, was a crowd still, helpless in the hands of demagogue and organiser, individually cowardly, individually swayed by appetite, collectively incalculable. The memory of countless figures in pale blue canvas came before his mind. Millions of such men and women below him, he knew, had never been out of the city, had never seen beyond the little round of unintelligent grudging participation in the world's business, and unintelligent dissatisfied sharing in its tawdrier pleasures. He thought of the hopes of his vanished contemporaries, and for a moment the dream of London in Morris's quaint old *News from Nowhere*, and the perfect land of Hudson's beautiful *Crystal Age* appeared before him in an atmosphere of infinite loss. He thought of his own hopes.

For in the latter days of that passionate life that lay now so far behind him, the conception of a free and equal manhood had become a very real thing to him. He had hoped, as indeed his age had hoped, rashly taking it for granted, that the sacrifice of the many to the few would some day cease, that a day was near when every child born of woman should have a fair and assured chance of happiness. And here, after two hundred years, the same hope, still unfulfilled, cried passionately through the city. After two hundred years, he knew, greater than ever, grown with the city to gigantic proportions, were poverty and helpless labour and all the sorrows of his time.

Already he knew something of the history of the intervening years. He had heard now of the moral decay that had followed the collapse of supernatural religion in the minds of ignoble man, the decline of public honour, the ascendency of wealth. For men who had lost their belief in God had still kept their faith in property, and wealth ruled a venial world.

His Japanese attendant, Asano, in expounding the political history of the intervening two centuries, drew an apt image from a seed eaten by insect parasites. First there is the original seed, ripening vigorously enough. And then comes some insect and lays an egg under the skin, and behold! in a little while the seed is a hollow shape with an active grub inside that has eaten out its substance. And then comes some secondary parasite, some ichneumon fly, and lays an egg within this grub, and behold! that, too, is a hollow shape, and the new living thing is inside its predecessor's skin which itself is snug within the seed coat. And the seed coat still keeps its shape, most people think it a seed still, and for all one knows it may still think itself a seed, vigorous and alive. 'Your Victorian kingdom,' said Asano, 'was like that – kingship with the heart eaten out.' The landowners – the barons and gentry – began ages ago with King John; there were lapses, but they beheaded King Charles, and ended practically with King George, a mere husk of a king ... the real power in the hands of their parliament. But the Parliament – the organ of the land-holding tenant-ruling gentry – did not keep its power long. The change had already come in the nineteenth century. The franchises had been broadened until it included masses of ignorant men, 'urban myriads', who went in their featureless thousands to vote together. And the natural consequence of a swarming constituency is the rule of the party organisation. Power was passing even in the Victorian time to the party machinery, secret, complex, and corrupt. Very speedily power was in the hands of great men of business who financed the machines. A time came when the real power and interest of the Empire rested visibly between the two party councils, ruling by newspapers and electoral organisations – two small groups of rich and able men, working at first in opposition, then presently together.

There was a reaction of a genteel ineffectual sort. There were numberless books in existence, Asano said, to prove that – the publication of some of them was as early as Graham's sleep – a whole literature of reaction in fact. The party of the reaction seems to have locked itself into its study and rebelled with unflinching determination – on paper. The urgent necessity of either capturing or depriving the party councils of power is a common suggestion underlying all the thoughtful work of the early twentieth century, both in America and England. In most of these things America was a little earlier than England, though both countries drove the same way.

That counter-revolution never came. It could never organise and keep pure. There was not enough of the old sentimentality, the old faith in righteousness, left among men. Any organisation that became big enough to influence the polls became complex enough to be undermined, broken up, or bought outright by capable rich men. Socialistic and Popular, Reactionary and Purity Parties were all at last mere Stock Exchange counters, selling their principles to pay for their electioneering. And the great concern of the rich was naturally to keep property intact, the board clear for the game of trade. Just as the feudal concern had been to keep the board clear for hunting and war. The whole world was exploited, a battlefield of businesses; and financial convulsions, the scourge of currency manipulation, tariff wars, made more human misery during the twentieth century – because the wretchedness was dreary life instead of speedy death – than had war, pestilence and famine, in the darkest hours of earlier history.

His own part in the development of this time he now knew clearly enough. Through the successive phases in the development of this mechanical civilisation, aiding and presently directing its development, there had grown a new power, the Council, the board of his trustees. At first it had been a mere chance union of the millions of Isbister and

Warming, a mere property holding company, the creation of two childless testators' whims, but the collective talent of its first constitution had speedily guided it to a vast influence, until by title deed, loan and share, under a hundred disguises and pseudonyms it had ramified through the fabric of the American and English States.

Wielding an enormous influence and patronage, the Council had early assumed a political aspect; and in its development it had continually used its wealth to tip the beam of political decisions and its political advantages to grasp yet more and more wealth. At last the party organisations of two hemispheres were in its hands; it became an inner council of political control. Its last struggle was with the tacit alliance of the great Jewish families. But these families were linked only by a feeble sentiment, at any time inheritance might fling a huge fragment of their resources to a minor, a woman or a fool, marriages and legacies alienated hundreds of thousands at one blow. The Council had no such breach in its continuity. Steadily, steadfastly it grew.

The original Council was not simply twelve men of exceptional ability; they fused, it was a council of genius. It struck boldly for riches, for political influence, and the two subserved each other. With amazing foresight it spent great sums of money on the art of flying, holding that invention back against an hour foreseen. It used the patent laws, and a thousand half-legal expedients, to hamper all investigators who refused to work with it. In the old days it never missed a capable man. It paid his price. Its policy in those days was vigorous – unerring, and against it as it grew steadily and incessantly was only the chaotic selfish rule of the casually rich. In a hundred years Graham had become almost exclusive owner of Africa, of South America, of France, of London, of England and all its influence – for all practical purposes, that is – a power in North America – then the dominant power in America. The Council bought and organised China, drilled Asia, crippled the Old World empires, undermined them financially, fought and defeated them.

And this spreading usurpation of the world was so dexterously performed – a proteus – hundreds of banks, companies, syndicates, masked the Council's operations – that it was already far advanced before common men suspected the tyranny that had come. The Council never hesitated, never faltered. Means of communication, land, buildings, governments, municipalities, the territorial companies of the tropics, every human enterprise, it gathered greedily. And it drilled and marshalled its men, its railway police, its roadway police, its house guards, and drain and cable guards, its host of land-workers. Their unions it did not fight, but it undermined and betrayed and bought them. It bought the world at last. And, finally, its culminating stroke was the introduction of flying.

When the Council, in conflict with the workers in some of its huge monopolies, did something flagrantly illegal and that without even the ordinary civility of bribery, the old Law, alarmed for the profits of its complaisance, looked about it for weapons. But there were no more armies, no fighting navies; the age of Peace had come. The only possible war ships were the great steam vessels of the Council's Navigation Trust. The police forces they controlled; the police of the railways, of the ships, of their agricultural estates, their time-keepers and order-keepers, outnumbered the neglected little forces of the old country and municipal organisations ten to one. And they produced flying machines. There were men alive still who could remember the last great debate in the London House of Commons – the legal party, the party against the Council was in a minority, but it made a desperate fight – and how the members came crowding out upon the terrace to see these great unfamiliar winged shapes circling quietly overhead. The Council had soared to its power. The last sham of a democracy that had permitted unlimited irresponsible property was at an end.

Within one hundred and fifty years of Graham's falling asleep, his Council had thrown off its disguises and ruled openly, supreme in his name. Elections had become a cheerful formality, a septennial folly, an ancient unmeaning custom; a social Parliament as ineffectual as the convocation of the Established Church in Victorian times assembled now and then; and a legitimate King of England, disinherited, drunken and witless, played foolishly in a second-rate music-hall. So the magnificent dream of the nineteenth century, the noble project of universal individual liberty and universal happiness, touched by a disease of honour, crippled by a superstition of absolute property, crippled by the religious feuds that had robbed the common citizens of education, robbed men of standards of conduct, and brought the sanctions of morality to utter contempt, had worked itself out in the face of invention and ignoble enterprise, first to a warring plutocracy, and finally to the rule of a supreme plutocrat. His Council at last had ceased even to trouble to have its decrees endorsed by the constitutional authorities, and he a motionless, sunken, yellow-skinned figure had lain, neither dead nor living, recognisably and immediately Master of the Earth. And awoke at last to find himself – Master of that inheritance! Awoke to stand under the cloudless empty sky and gaze down upon the greatness of his dominion.

To what end had he awakened? Was this city, this hive of hopeless toilers, the final refutation of his ancient hopes? Or was the fire of liberty, the fire that had blazed and waned in the years of his past life, still smouldering below there? He thought of the stir and impulse of the song of the revolution. Was that song merely the trick of a demagogue, to be forgotten when its purpose was served? Was the hope that still stirred within him only the memory of abandoned things, the vestige of a creed outworn? Or had it a wider meaning, an import interwoven with the destiny of a man? To what end had he awakened, what was there for him to do? Humanity was spread below him like a map. He thought of the millions and millions of humanity following each other unceasingly for ever out of the darkness of non-existence into the darkness of death. To what end? Aim there must be, but it transcended his power of thought. He saw for the first time clearly his own infinite littleness, saw stark and terrible the tragic contrast of human strength and the craving of the human heart. For that little while he knew himself for the petty accident he was, and knew therewith the greatness of his desire. And suddenly his littleness was intolerable, his aspiration was intolerable, and there came to him an irresistible impulse to pray. And he prayed. He prayed vague, incoherent, contradictory things his soul strained up through time and space and all the fleeting multitudinous confusion of being, towards something – he scarcely knew what – towards something that could comprehend his striving and endure.

A man and a woman were far below on a roof space to the southward enjoying the freshness of the morning air. The man had brought out a perspective glass to spy upon the Council House and he was showing her how to use it. Presently their curiosity was satisfied, they could see no traces of bloodshed from their position, and after a survey of the empty sky she came round to the crow's nest. And there she saw two little black figures, so small it was hard to believe they were men, one who watched and one who gesticulated with hands outstretched to the silent emptiness of Heaven.

She handed the glass to the man. He looked and exclaimed:

'I believe it is the Master. Yes. I am sure. It *is* the Master!'

He lowered the glass and looked at her. 'Waving his hands about almost as if he was praying. I wonder what he is up to. Worshipping the sun? There weren't Parsees in this country in *his* time, were there?'

He looked again. 'He's stopped it now. It was a chance attitude, I suppose.' He put down the glass and became meditative. 'He won't have anything to do but enjoy himself – just enjoy himself. Ostrog will boss the show of course. Ostrog will have to, because of keeping all these Labourer fools in bounds. Them and their song! And got it all by sleeping, dear eyes – just sleeping. It's a wonderful world.'

XV

Prominent People

The state apartments of the Wind-Vane Keeper would have seemed astonishingly intricate to Graham had he entered them fresh from his nineteenth-century life, but already he was growing accustomed to the scale of the new time. They can scarcely be described as halls and rooms, seeing that a complicated system of arches, bridges, passages and galleries divided and united every part of the great space. He came out through one of the now familiar sliding panels upon a plateau of landing at the head of a flight of very broad and gentle steps, with men and women far more brilliantly dressed than any he had hitherto seen ascending and descending. From this position he looked down a vista of intricate ornament in lustreless white and mauve and purple, spanned by bridges that seemed wrought of porcelain and filigree, and terminating far off in a cloudy mystery of perforated screens.

Glancing upward, he saw tier above tier of ascending galleries with faces looking down upon him. The air was full of the babble of innumerable voices and of a music that descended from above, a gay and exhilarating music whose source he never discovered.

The central aisle was thick with people, but by no means uncomfortably crowded; altogether that assembly must have numbered many thousands. They were brilliantly, even fantastically dressed, the men as fancifully as the women, for the sobering influence of the Puritan conception of dignity upon masculine dress had long since passed away. The hair of the men, too, though it was rarely worn long, was commonly curled in a manner that suggested the barber, and baldness had vanished from the earth. Frizzy straight-cut masses that would have charmed Rossetti abounded, and one gentleman, who was pointed out to Graham under the mysterious title of an 'amorist', wore his hair in two becoming plaits à la Marguerite. The pigtail was in evidence; it would seem that citizens of Chinese extraction were no longer ashamed of their race. There was little uniformity of fashion apparent in the forms of clothing worn. The more shapely men displayed their symmetry in trunk hose, and here were puffs and slashes, and there a cloak and there a robe.

The fashions of the days of Leo the Tenth were perhaps the prevailing influence, but the aesthetic conceptions of the far east were also patent. Masculine embonpoint, which, in Victorian times, would have been subjected to the tightly buttoned perils, the ruthless exaggeration of tight-legged tight-armed evening dress, now formed but the basis of a wealth of dignity and drooping folds. Graceful slenderness abounded also. To Graham, a typically stiff man from a typically stiff period, not only did these men seem altogether too graceful in person, but altogether too expressive in their vividly expressive faces. They gesticulated, they expressed surprise, interest, amusement, above all, they expressed the emotions excited in their minds by the ladies about them with astonishing frankness. Even at the first glance it was evident that women were in a great majority.

The ladies in the company of these gentlemen displayed in dress, bearing and manner alike, less emphasis and more intricacy. Some affected a classical simplicity of robing and subtlety of fold, after the fashion of the First French Empire, and flashed conquering arms and shoulders as Graham passed. Others had closely-fitting dresses without seam or belt at the waist, sometimes with long folds falling from the shoulders. The delightful confidences of evening dress had not been diminished by the passage of two centuries.

Everyone's movements seemed graceful. Graham remarked to Lincoln that he saw men as Raphael's cartoons walking, and Lincoln told him that the attainment of an appropriate set of gestures was part of every rich person's education. The Master's entry was greeted with a sort of tittering applause, but these people showed their distinguished manners by not crowding upon him nor annoying him by any persistent scrutiny, as he descended the steps towards the floor of the aisle.

He had already learnt from Lincoln that these were the leaders of existing London society; almost every person there that night was either a powerful official or the immediate connexion of a powerful official. Many had returned from the European Pleasure Cities expressly to welcome him. The aeronautic authorities, whose defection had played a part in the overthrow of the Council only second to Graham's were very prominent, and so, too, was the Wind-Vane Control. Amongst others there were several of the more prominent officers of the Food Trust; the controller of the European Piggeries had a particularly melancholy and interesting countenance and a daintily cynical manner. A bishop in full canonicals passed athwart Graham's vision, conversing with a gentleman dressed exactly like the traditional Chaucer, including even the laurel wreath.

'Who is that?' he asked almost involuntarily.

'The Bishop of London,' said Lincoln.

'No – the other, I mean.'

'Poet Laureate.'

'You still – ?'

'He doesn't make poetry, of course. He's a cousin of Wotton – one of the Councillors. But he's one of the Red Rose Royalists – a delightful club – and they keep up the tradition of these things.'

'Asano told me there was a King.'

'The King doesn't belong. They had to expel him. It's the Stuart blood, I suppose; but really – '

'Too much?'

'Far too much.'

Graham did not quite follow all this, but it seemed part of the general inversion of the new age. He bowed condescendingly to his first introduction. It was evident that subtle distinctions of class prevailed even in this assembly, that only to a small proportion of the guests, to an inner group, did Lincoln consider it appropriate to introduce him. This first introduction was the Master Aeronaut, a man whose sun-tanned face contrasted oddly with the delicate complexions about him. Just at present his critical defection from the Council made him a very important person indeed.

His manner contrasted very favourably, according to Graham's ideas, with the general bearing. He made a few commonplace remarks, assurances of loyalty and frank inquiries about the Master's health. His manner was breezy, his accent lacked the easy staccato of latter-day English. He made it admirably clear to Graham that he was a bluff 'aerial dog' – he used that phrase – that there was no nonsense about him, that he was a thoroughly manly fellow and old-fashioned at that, that he didn't profess to know much, and that what he did not know was not worth knowing. He made a manly bow, ostentatiously free from obsequiousness, and passed.

'I am glad to see that type endures,' said Graham.

'Phonographs and kinematographs,' said Lincoln, a little spitefully. 'He has studied from the life.' Graham glanced at the burly form again. It was oddly reminiscent.

'As a matter of fact we bought him,' said Lincoln. 'Partly. And partly he was afraid of Ostrog. Everything rested with him.'

He turned sharply to introduce the Surveyor-General of the Public School Trust. This person was a willowy figure in a blue-grey academic gown, he beamed down upon Graham through *pince-nez* of a Victorian pattern, and illustrated his remarks by gestures of a beautifully mani-cured hand. Graham was immediately interested in this gentleman's functions, and asked him a number of singularly direct questions. The Surveyor-General seemed quietly amused at the Master's fundamental bluntness. He was a little vague as to the monopoly of education his Company possessed; it was done by contract with the syndicate that ran the numerous London Municipalities, but he waxed enthusiastic over educational progress since the Victorian times. 'We have conquered

Cram,' he said, 'completely conquered Cram – there is not an examination left in the world. Aren't you glad?'

'How do you get the work done?' asked Graham.

'We make it attractive – as attractive as possible. And if it does not
attract then – we let it go. We cover an immense field.'

He proceeded to details, and they had a lengthy conversation. The
Surveyor-General mentioned the names of Pestalozzi and Froebel with
profound respect, although he displayed no intimacy with their epoch-
making works. Graham learnt that University Extension still existed in
a modified form. 'There is a certain type of girl, for example,' said the
Surveyor-General, dilating with a sense of his usefulness, 'with a perfect
passion for severe studies – when they are not too difficult you know.
We cater for them by the thousand. At this moment,' he said with a
Napoleonic touch, 'nearly five hundred phonographs are lecturing in
different parts of London on the influence exercised by Plato and Swift
on the love affairs of Shelley, Hazlitt, and Burns. And afterwards they
write essays on the lectures, and the names in order of merit are put in
conspicuous places. You see how your little germ has grown? The
illiterate middleclass of your days has quite passed away.'

'About the public elementary schools,' said Graham. 'Do you control
them?'

The Surveyor-General did, 'entirely'. Now, Graham, in his later
democractic days, had taken a keen interest in these and his questioning
quickened. Certain casual phrases that had fallen from the old man
with whom he had talked in the darkness recurred to him. The Surveyor-
General, in effect, endorsed the old man's words. 'We have abolished
Cram,' he said, a phrase Graham was beginning to interpret as the
abolition of all sustained work. The Surveyor-General became sentimental. 'We try and make the elementary schools very pleasant for the little
children. They will have to work so soon. Just a few simple principles –
obedience – industry.'

'You teach them very little?'

'Why should we? It only leads to trouble and discontent. We amuse
them. Even as it is – there are troubles – agitations. Where the labourers
get the ideas, one cannot tell. They tell one another. There are socialistic
dreams – anarchy even! Agitators *will* get to work among them. I take
it – I have always taken it – that my foremost duty is to fight against
popular discontent. Why should people be made unhappy?'

'I wonder,' said Graham thoughtfully. 'But there are a great many
things I want to know.'

Lincoln, who had stood watching Graham's face throughout the
conversation, intervened. 'There are others,' he said in an undertone.

The Surveyor-General of schools gesticulated himself away. 'Perhaps,'
said Lincoln, intercepting a casual glance, 'you would like to know
some of these ladies?'

The daughter of the Manager of the Piggeries of the European Food Trust was a particularly charming little person with red hair and animated blue eyes. Lincoln left him awhile to converse with her, and she displayed herself as quite an enthusiast for the 'dear old times', as she called them, that had seen the beginning of his trance. As she talked she smiled, and her eyes smiled in a manner that demanded reciprocity.

'I have tried,' she said, 'countless times – to imagine those old romantic days. And to you – they are memories. How strange and crowded the world must seem to you! I have seen photographs and pictures of the old times, the little isolated houses built of bricks made out of burnt mud and all black with soot from your fires, the railway bridges, the simple advertisements, the solemn savage Puritanical men in strange black coats and those tall hats of theirs, iron railway trains on iron bridges overhead, horses and cattle, and even dogs running half wild about the streets. And suddenly, you have come into this!'

'Into this,' said Graham.

'Out of your life – out of all that was familiar.'

'The old life was not a happy one,' said Graham. 'I do not regret that.'

She looked at him quickly. There was a brief pause. She sighed encouragingly. 'No?'

'No,' said Graham. 'It was a little life – and unmeaning. But this – . We thought the world complex and crowded and civilised enough. Yet I see – although in this world I am barely four days old – looking back on my own time, that it was a queer, barbaric time – the mere beginning of this new order. The mere beginning of this new order. You will find it hard to understand how little I know.'

'You may ask me what you like,' she said, smiling at him.

'Then tell me who these people are. I'm still very much in the dark about them. It's puzzling. Are there any Generals?'

'Men in hats and feathers?'

'Of course not. No. I suppose they are the men who control the great public businesses. Who is that distinguished looking man?'

'That? He's a most important officer. That is Morden. He is managing director of the Antibilious Pill Company. I have heard that his workers sometimes turn out a myriad myriad pills a day in the twenty-four hours. Fancy a myriad myriad!'

'A myriad myriad. No wonder he looks proud,' said Graham. 'Pills! What a wonderful time it is! That man in purple?'

'He is not quite one of the inner circle, you know. But we like him. He is really clever and very amusing. He is one of the heads of the Medical Faculty of our London University. All medical men, you know, are shareholders in the Medical Faculty Company, and wear that purple. You have to be – to be qualified. But of course, people who are paid by fees for *doing* something – ' She smiled away the social pretensions of all such people.

'Are any of your great artists or authors here?'

'No authors. They are mostly such queer people – and so preoccupied about themselves. And they quarrel so dreadfully! They will fight, some of them, for precedence on staircases! Dreadful isn't it? But I think Wraysbury, the fashionable capillotomist is here. From Capri.'

'Capillotomist,' said Graham. 'Ah! I remember. An artist! Why not?'

'We have to cultivate him,' she said apologetically. 'Our heads are in his hands.' She smiled.

Graham hesitated at the invited compliment, but his glance was expressive. 'Have the arts grown with the rest of civilised things?' he said. 'Who are your great painters?'

She looked at him doubtfully. Then laughed. 'For a moment,' she said, 'I thought you meant – ' She laughed again. 'You mean, of course, those good men you used to think so much of because they could cover great spaces of canvas with oil-colours? Great oblongs. And people used to put the things in gilt frames and hang them up in rows in their square rooms. We haven't any. People grew tired of that sort of thing.'

'But what did you think I meant?'

She put a finger significantly on a cheek whose glow was above suspicion, and smiled and looked very arch and pretty and inviting. 'And here,' and she indicated her eyelid.

Graham had an adventurous moment. Then a grotesque memory of a picture he had somewhere seen of Uncle Toby and the Widow flashed across his mind. An archaic shame came upon him. He became acutely aware that he was visible to a great number of interested people. 'I see,' he remarked inadequately. He turned awkwardly away from her fascinating facility. He looked about him to meet a number of eyes that immediately occupied themselves with other things. Possibly he coloured a little. 'Who is that talking with the lady in saffron?' he asked, avoiding her eyes.

The person in question he learnt was one of the great organisers of the American theatres just fresh from a gigantic production at Mexico. His face reminded Graham of a bust of Caligula. Another striking-looking man was the Black Labour Master. The phrase at the time made no deep impression, but afterwards it recurred; – the Black Labour Master? The little lady, in no degree embarrassed, pointed out to him a charming little woman as one of the subsidiary wives of the Anglican Bishop of London. She added encomiums on the episcopal courage – hitherto there had been a rule of clerical monogamy – 'neither a natural nor an expedient condition of things. Why should the natural development of the affections be dwarfed and restricted because a man is a priest?'

'And, bye the bye,' she added, 'are you an Anglican?' Graham was on the verge of hesitating inquiries about the status of a 'subsidiary wife', apparently an euphemistic phrase, when Lincoln's return broke off this very suggestive and interesting conversation. They crossed the aisle to where a tall man in crimson, and two charming persons in Burmese costume (as it seemed to him) awaited him diffidently. From their civilities he passed to other presentations.

In a little while his multitudinous impressions began to organise themselves into a general effect. At first the glitter of the gathering had raised all the democrat in Graham; he had felt hostile and satirical. But it is not in human nature to resist an atmosphere of courteous regard. Soon the music, the light, the play of colours, the shining arms and shoulders about him, the touch of hands, the transient interest of smiling faces, the frothing sound of skilfully modulated voices, the atmosphere of compliment, interest and respect, had woven together into a fabric of indisputable pleasure. Graham for a time forgot his spacious resolutions. He gave way insensibly to the intoxication of the position that was conceded him, his manner became less conscious, more convincingly regal, his feet walked assuredly, the black robe fell with a bolder fold and pride ennobled his voice. After all this was a brilliant interesting world.

His glance went approvingly over the shifting colurs of the people, it rested here and there in kindly criticism upon a face. Presently it occurred to him that he owed some apology to the charming little person with the red hair and blue eyes. He felt guilty of a clumsy snub. It was not princely to ignore her advances, even if his policy necessitated their rejection. He wondered if he should see her again. And suddenly a little thing touched all the glamour of this brilliant gathering and changed its quality.

He looked up and saw passing across a bridge of porcelain and looking down upon him, a face that was almost immediately hidden, the face of the girl he had seen overnight in the little room beyond the theatre after his escape from the Council. And she was looking with much the same expression of curious expectation, of uncertain intentness, upon his proceedings. For the moment he did not remember when he had seen her, and then with recognition came a vague memory of the stirring emotions of their first encounter. But the dancing web of melody about him kept the air of that great marching song from his memory.

The lady to whom he was talking repeated her remark, and Graham recalled himself to the quasi-regal flirtation upon which he was engaged.

But from that moment a vague restlessness, a feeling that grew to dissatisfaction, came into his mind. He was troubled as if by some half forgotten duty, by the sense of things important slipping from him amidst this light and brilliance. The attraction that these bright ladies who crowded about him were beginning to exercise ceased. He no longer made vague and clumsy responses to the subtly amorous advances that he was now assured were being made to him, and his eyes wandered for another sight of that face that had appealed so strongly to his sense of beauty. But he did not see her again until he was awaiting Lincoln's return to leave this assembly. In answer to his request Lincoln had promised that an attempt should be made to fly that afternoon, if the weather permitted. He had gone to make certain necessary arrangements.

Graham was in one of the upper galleries in conversation with a bright-eyed lady on the subject of Eadhamite – the subject was his choice and not hers. He had interrupted her warm assurances of personal devotion with a matter-of-inquiry. He found her, as he had already found several other latter-day women that night, less well informed than charming. Suddenly, struggling against the eddying drift of nearer melody, the song of the Revolt, the great song he had heard in the Hall, hoarse and massive, came beating down to him.

He glanced up startled, and perceived above him an *œil de bœuf* through which this song had come, and beyond, the upper courses of cable, the blue haze, and the pendant fabric of the lights of the public ways. He heard the song break into a tumult of voices and cease. But now he perceived quite clearly the drone and tumult of the moving platforms and a murmur of many people. He had a vague persuasion that he could not account for, a sort of instinctive feeling that outside in the ways a huge crowd must be watching this place in which their Master amused himself. He wondered what they might be thinking.

Though the song had stopped so abruptly, though the special music of this gathering reasserted itself, the *motif* of the marching song, once it had begun, lingered in his mind.

The bright-eyed lady was still struggling with the mysteries of Eadhamite when he perceived the girl he had seen in the theatre again. She was coming now along the gallery towards him; he saw her first before she saw him. She was dressed in a faintly luminous grey, her dark hair about her brows was like a cloud, and as he saw her the cold light from the circular opening into the ways fell upon her downcast face.

The lady in trouble about the Eadhamite saw the change in his expression, and grasped her opportunity to escape. 'Would you care to know that girl, Sire?' she asked boldly. 'She is Helen Wotton – a niece of Ostrog's. She knows a great many serious things. She is one of the most serious persons alive. I am sure you will like her.'

In another moment Graham was talking to the girl, and the bright-eyed lady had fluttered away.

'I remember you quite well,' said Graham. 'You were in that little room. When all the people were singing and beating time with their feet. Before I walked across the Hall.'

Her momentary embarrassment passed. She looked up at him, and her face was steady. 'It was wonderful,' she said, hesitated, and spoke with a sudden effort. 'All those people would have died for you, Sire. Countless people did die for you that night.'

Her face glowed. She glanced swiftly aside to see that no other heard her words.

Lincoln appeared some way off along the gallery, making his way through the press towards them. She saw him and turned to Graham strangely eager, with a swift change to confidence and intimacy. 'Sire,' she said quickly. 'I cannot tell you now and here. But the common people are very unhappy; they are oppressed – they are misgoverned. Do not forget the people, who faced death – death that you might live.'

'I know nothing – ' began Graham.

'I cannot tell you now.'

Lincoln's face appeared close to them. He bowed an apology to the girl.

'You find the new world pleasant, Sire?' asked Lincoln, with smiling deference, and indicating the space and splendour of the gathering by one comprehensive gesture. 'At any rate, you find it changed.'

'Yes,' said Graham, 'changed. And yet, after all, not so greatly changed.'

'Wait till you are in the air,' said Lincoln. 'The wind has fallen; even now an aeroplane awaits you.'

The girl's attitude awaited dismissal.

Graham glanced at her face, was on the verge of a question, found a warning in her expression, bowed to her and turned to accompany Lincoln.

XVI

The Aeropile

For a while, as Graham went through the passages of the Wind-Vane offices with Lincoln, he was preoccupied. But, by an effort, he attended to the things which Lincoln was saying. Soon his preoccupation vanished. Lincoln was talking of flying. Graham had a strong desire to know more of this new human attainment. He began to ply Lincoln with questions. He had followed the crude beginnings of aerial navigation very keenly in his previous life; he was delighted to find the familiar names of Maxim and Pilcher, Langley and Chanute, and, above all, of the aerial proto-martyr Lillienthal, still honoured by men.

Even during his previous life two lines of investigation had pointed clearly to two distinct types of contrivance as possible, and both of these had been realised. On the one hand was the great engine-driven aeroplane, a double row of horizontal floats with a big aerial screw behind, and on the other the nimbler aeropile. The aeroplanes flew safely only in a calm or moderate wind, and sudden storms, occurrences that were now accurately predictable, rendered them for all practical purposes useless. They were built of enormous size – the usual stretch of wing being six hundred feet or more, and the length of the fabric a thousand feet. They were for passenger traffic alone. The lightly swung car they carried was from a hundred to a hundred and fifty feet in length. It was hung in a peculiar manner in order to minimise the complex vibration that even a moderate wind produced, and for the same reason the little seats within the car – each passenger remained seated during the voyage – were slung with great freedom of movement. The starting of the mechanism was only possible from a gigantic car on the rail of a specially constructed stage. Graham had seen these vast stages, the flying stages, from the crow's nest very well. Six huge blank areas they were, with a giant 'carrier' stage on each.

The choice of descent was equally circumscribed, an accurately plane surface being needed for safe grounding. Apart from the destruction that would have been caused by the descent of this great expanse of sail and metal, and the impossibility of its rising again, the concussion of an irregular surface, a tree-set hillside, for instance, or an embankment, would be sufficient to pierce or damage the framework, to smash the ribs of the body, and perhaps kill those aboard.

At first Graham felt disappointed with these cumbersome contrivances, but he speedily grasped the fact that smaller machines would have been unremunerative, for the simple reason that their carrying power would be disproportionately diminished with diminished size. Moreover, the huge size of these things enabled them – and it was a consideration of primary importance – to traverse the air at enormous speeds, and so run no risks of unanticipated weather. The briefest journey performed, that from London to Paris, took about three-quarters of an hour, but the velocity attained was not high; the leap to New York occupied about two hours, and by timing oneself carefully at the intermediate stations it was possible in quiet weather to go around the world in a day.

The little aeropiles (as for no particular reason they were distinctively called) were of an altogether different type. Several of these were going to and fro in the air. They were designed to carry only one or two persons, and their manufacture and maintenance was so costly as to render them the monopoly of the richer sort of people. Their sails, which were brilliantly coloured, consisted only of two pairs of lateral air floats in the same plane, and of a screw behind. Their small size rendered a descent in any open space neither difficult nor disagreeable, and it was possible to attach pneumatic wheels or even the ordinary motors for terrestrial traffic to them, and so carry them to a convenient starting place. They required a special sort of swift car to throw them into the air, but such a car was efficient in any open place clear of high buildings or trees. Human aeronautics, Graham perceived, were evidently still a long way behind the instinctive gift of the albatross or the fly-catcher. One great influence that might have brought the aeropile to a more rapid perfection had been withheld; these inventions had never been used in warfare. The last great international struggle had occurred before the usurpation of the Council.

The Flying Stages of London were collected together in an irregular crescent on the southern side of the river. They formed three groups of two each and retained the names of ancient suburban hills or villages. They were named in order, Roehampton, Wimbledon Park, Streatham, Norwood, Blackheath, and Shooter's Hill. They were uniform structures rising high above the general roof surfaces. Each was about four thousand yards long and a thousand broad, and constructed of the compound of aluminium and iron that had replaced iron in architecture. Their higher tiers formed an openwork of girders through which lifts and staircases ascended. The upper surface was a uniform expanse, with portions – the starting carriers – that could be raised and were then able to run on very slightly inclined rails to the end of the fabric. Save for any aeropiles or aeroplanes that were in port these open surfaces were kept clear for arrivals.

During the adjustment of the aeroplanes it was the custom for passengers to wait in the system of theatres, restaurants, news-rooms, and places of pleasure and indulgence of various sorts that interwove with the prosperous shops below. This portion of London was in consequence commonly the gayest of all its districts, with something of the meretricious gaiety of a seaport or city of hotels. And for those who took a more serious view of aeronautics, the religious quarters had flung out an attractive colony of devotional chapels, while a host of brilliant medical establishments competed to supply physical preparatives for the journey. At various levels through the mass of chambers and passages beneath these, ran, in addition to the main moving ways of the city which laced and gathered here, a complex system of special passages and lifts and slides, for the convenient interchange of people and luggage between stage and stage. And a distinctive feature of the architecture of this section was the ostentatious massiveness of the metal piers and girders that everywhere broke the vistas and spanned the halls and passages, crowding and twining up to meet the weight of the stages and the weighty impact of the aeroplanes overhead.

Graham went to the flying stages by the public ways. He was accompanied by Asano, his Japanese attendant. Lincoln was called away by Ostrog, who was busy with his administrative concerns. A strong guard of the Wind-Vane police awaited the Master outside the Wind-Vane offices, and they cleared a space for him on the upper moving platform. His passage to the flying stages was unexpected, nevertheless a considerable crowd gathered and followed him to his destination. As he went along, he could hear the people, shouting his name, and saw numberless men and women and children in blue come swarming up the staircases in the central path, gesticulating and shouting. He could not hear what they shouted. He was struck again by the evident existence of a vulgar dialect among the poor of the city. When at last he descended, his guards were immediately surrounded by a dense excited crowd. Afterwards it occurred to him that some had attempted to reach him with petitions. His guards cleared a passage for him with difficulty.

He found an aeropile in charge of an aeronaut awaiting him on the westward stage. Seen close this mechanism was no longer small. As it lay on its launching carrier upon the wide expanse of the flying stage, its aluminium body skeleton was as big as the hull of a twenty-ton yacht. Its lateral supporting sails braced and stayed with metal nerves almost like the nerves of a bee's wing, and made of some sort of glassy artificial membrane, cast their shadow over many hundreds of square yards. The chairs for the engineer and his passenger hung free to swing by a complex tackle, within the protecting ribs of the frame and well abaft the middle. The passenger's chair was protected by a wind-guard and guarded about with metallic rods carrying air cushions. It could, if desired, be completely closed in, but Graham was anxious for novel experiences, and desired that it should be left open. The aeronaut sat behind a glass that sheltered his face. The passenger could secure himself firmly in his seat, and this was almost unavoidable on landing, or he could move along by means of a little rail and rod to a locker at the stem of the machine, where his personal luggage, his wraps and restoratives were placed, and which also with the seats, served as a makeweight to the parts of the central engine that projected to the propeller at the stern.

The engine was very simple in appearance. Asano, pointing out the parts of this apparatus to him, told him that, like the gas-engine of Victorian days, it was of the explosive type, burning a small drop of a substance called 'fomile' at each stroke. It consisted simply of reservoir and piston about the long fluted crank of the propeller shaft. So much Graham saw of the machine.

The flying stage about him was empty save for Asano and their suite of attendants. Directed by the aeronaut he placed himself in his seat. He then drank a mixture containing ergot – a dose, he learnt, invariably administered to those about to fly, and designed to counteract the possible effect of diminished air pressure upon the system. Having done so, he declared himself ready for the journey. Asano took the empty glass from him, stepped through the bars of the hull, and stood below on the stage waving his hand. Suddenly he seemed to slide along the stage to the right and vanish.

The engine was beating, the propeller spinning, and for a second the stage and the buildings beyond were gliding swiftly and horizontally past Graham's eye; then these things seemed to tilt up abruptly. He gripped the little rods on either side of him instinctively. He felt himself moving upward, heard the air whistle over the top of the wind screen. The propeller screw moved round with powerful rhythmic impulses – one, two, three, pause; one, two, three – which the engineer controlled very delicately. The machine began a quivering vibration that continued throughout the flight, and the roof areas seemed running away to starboard very quickly and growing rapidly smaller. He looked from the face of the engineer through the ribs of the machine. Looking sideways, there was nothing very startling in what he saw – a rapid funicular railway might have given the same sensations. He recognised the Council House and the Highgate Ridge. And then he looked straight down between his feet.

For a moment physical terror possessed him, a passionate sense of insecurity. He held tight. For a second or so he could not lift his eyes. Some hundred feet or more sheer below him was one of the big wind-vanes of south-west London, and beyond it the southernmost flying stage crowded with little black dots. These things seemed to be falling away from him. For a second he had an impulse to pursue the earth. He set his teeth, he lifted his eyes by a muscular effort, and the moment of panic passed.

He remained for a space with his teeth set hard, his eyes staring into the sky. Throb, throb, throb – beat, went the engine; throb, throb, throb, – beat. He gripped his bars tightly, glanced at the aeronaut, and saw a smile upon his sun-tanned face. He smiled in return – perhaps a little artificially. 'A little strange at first,' he shouted before he recalled his dignity. But he dared not look down again for some time. He stared over the aeronaut's head to where a rim of vague blue horizon crept up the sky. For a little while he could not banish the thought of possible accidents from his mind. Throb, throb, throb – beat; suppose some trivial screw went wrong in that supporting engine! Suppose – ! He made a grim effort to dismiss all such suppositions. After a while they did at least abandon the foreground of his thoughts. And up he went steadily, higher and higher into the clear air.

Once the mental shock of moving unsupported through the air was over, his sensations ceased to be unpleasant, became very speedily pleasurable. He had been warned of air sickness. But he found the pulsating movement of the aeropile as it drove up the faint south-west breeze was very little in excess of the pitching of a boat head on to broad rollers in a moderate gale, and he was constitutionally a good sailor. And the keenness of the more rarified air into which they ascended produced a sense of lightness and exhilaration. He looked up and saw the blue sky above fretted with cirrus clouds. His eye came cautiously down through the ribs and bars to a shining flight of white birds that hung in the lower sky. For a space he watched these. Then going lower and less apprehensively, he saw the slender figure of the Wind-Vane keeper's crow's nest shining golden in the sunlight and growing smaller every moment. As his eye fell with more confidence now, there came a blue line of hills, and then London, already to leeward, an intricate space of roofing. Its near edge came sharp and clear, and banished his last apprehensions in a shock of surprise. For the boundary of London was like a wall, like a cliff, a steep fall of three or four hundred feet, a frontage broken only by terraces here and there, a complex decorative facade.

That gradual passage of town into country through an extensive sponge of suburbs, which was so characteristic a feature of the great cities of the nineteenth century, existed no longer. Nothing remained of it but a waste of ruins here, variegated and dense with thickets of the heterogeneous growths that had once adorned the gardens of the belt, interspersed among levelled brown greens. The latter even spread among the vestiges of patches of sown ground, and verdant stretches of winter houses. But for the most part the reefs and skerries of ruins, the wreckage of suburban villas, stood among their streets and roads, queer islands amidst the levelled expanses of green and brown, abandoned indeed by the inhabitants years since, but too substantial, it seemed, to be cleared out of the way of the wholesale horticultural mechanisms of the time.

The vegetation of this waste undulated and frothed amidst the countless cells of crumbling house walls, and broke along the foot of the city wall in a surf of bramble and holly and ivy and teazle and tall grasses. Here and there gaudy pleasure places towered amidst the puny remains of Victorian times, and cable ways slanted to them from the city. That winter day they seemed deserted. Deserted, too, were the artificial gardens among the ruins. The city limits were indeed as sharply defined as in the ancient days when the gates were shut at nightfall and the robber foeman prowled to the very walls. A huge semi-circular throat poured out a vigorous traffic upon Eadhamite Bath Road. So the first prospect of the world beyond the city flashed on Graham, and dwindled. And when at last he could look vertically downward again, he saw below him the vegetable fields of the Thames valley – innumerable minute oblongs of ruddy brown, intersected by shining threads, the sewage ditches.

His exhilaration increased rapidly, became a sort of intoxication. He found himself drawing deep breaths of air, laughing aloud, desiring to shout. After a time that desire became too strong for him, and he shouted.

The machine had now risen as high as was customary with aeropiles, and they began to curve about towards the south. Steering, Graham perceived, was effected by the opening or closing of one or two thin strips of membrane in one or other of the otherwise rigid wings, and by the movement of the whole engine backward or forward along its supports. The aeronaut set the engine gliding slowly forward along its rail and opened the valve of the leeward wing until the stem of the aeropile was horizontal and pointing southward. And in that direction they drove with a slight list to leeward, and with a slow alternation of movement, first a short, sharp ascent and then a long downward glide that was very swift and pleasing. During these downward glides the propeller was inactive altogether. These ascents gave Graham a glorious sense of successful effort; the descents through the rarified air were beyond all experience. He wanted never to leave the upper air again.

For a time he was intent upon the minute details of the landscape that ran swiftly northward beneath him. Its minute, clear detail pleased him exceedingly. He was impressed by the ruin of the houses that had once dotted the country, by the vast treeless expanse of country from which all farms and villages had gone, save for crumbling ruins. He had known the thing was so, but seeing it so was an altogether different matter. He tried to make out places he had known within the hollow basin of the world below, but at first he could distinguish no data now that the Thames valley was left behind. Soon, however, they were driving over a sharp chalk hill that he recognised as the Guildford Hog's Back, because of the familiar outline of the gorge at its eastward end, and because of the ruins of the town that rose steeply on either lip of this gorge. And from that he made out other points, Leith Hill, the sandy wastes of Aldershot, and so forth. The Downs escarpment was set with gigantic slow-moving wind-wheels. Save where the broad Eadhamite Portsmouth Road, thickly dotted with rushing shapes, followed the course of the old railway, the gorge of the Wey was choked with thickets.

The whole expanse of the Downs escarpment, so far as the grey haze permitted him to see, was set with wind-wheels to which the largest of the city was but a younger brother. They stirred with a stately motion before the south-west wind. And here and there were patches dotted with the sheep of the British Food Trust, and here and there a mounted shepherd made a spot of black. Then rushing under the stern of the aeropile came the Wealden Heights, the line of Hindhead, Pitch Hill, and Leith Hill, with a second row of wind-wheels that seemed striving to rob the downland whirlers of their share of breeze. The purple heather was speckled with yellow gorse, and on the further side a drove of black oxen stampeded before a couple of mounted men. Swiftly these swept behind, and dwindled and lost colour, and became scarce moving specks that were swallowed up in haze.

And when these had vanished in the distance Graham heard a peewit wailing close at hand. He perceived he was now above the South Downs, and staring over his shoulder saw the battlements of Portsmouth Landing Stage towering over the ridge of Portsdown Hill. In another moment there came into sight a spread of shipping like floating cities, the little white cliffs of the Needles dwarfed and sunlit, and the grey and glittering waters of the narrow sea. They seemed to leap the Solent in a moment, and in a few seconds the Isle of Wight was running past, and then beneath him spread a wider and wider extent of sea, here purple with the shadow of a cloud, here grey, here a burnished mirror, and here a spread of cloudy greenish blue. The Isle of Wight grew smaller and smaller. In a few more minutes a strip of grey haze detached itself from other strips that were clouds, descended out of the sky and became a coastline – sunlit and pleasant – the coast of northern France. It rose, it took colour, became definite and detailed, and the counterpart of the Downland of England was speeding by below.

In a little time, as it seemed, Paris came above the horizon, and hung there for a space, and sank out of sight again as the aeropile circled about to the north again. But he perceived the Eiffel Tower still standing, and beside it a huge dome surmounted by a pinpoint Colossus. And he perceived, too, though he did not understand it at the time, a slanting drift of smoke. The aeronaut said something about 'trouble in the underways', that Graham did not heed at the time. But he marked the minarets and towers and slender masses that streamed skyward above the city wind-vanes, and knew that in the matter of grace at least Paris still kept in front of her larger rival. And even as he looked a pale blue shape ascended very swiftly from the city like a dead leaf driving up before a gale. It curved round and soared towards them growing rapidly larger and larger. The aeronaut was saying something. 'What?' said Graham, loth to take his eyes from this. 'Aeroplane, Sire,' bawled the aeronaut pointing.

They rose and curved about northward as it drew nearer. Nearer it came and nearer, larger and larger. The throb, throb, throb – beat, of the aeropile's flight, that had seemed so potent and so swift, suddenly appeared slow by comparison with this tremendous rush. How great the monster seemed, how swift and steady! It passed quite closely beneath them, driving along silently, a vast spread of wirenetted translucent wings, a thing alive. Graham had a momentary glimpse of the rows and rows of wrapped-up passengers, slung in their little cradles behind wind-screens, of a white-clothed engineer crawling against the gale along a ladder way, of spouting engines beating together, of the whirling wind screw, and of a wide waste of wing. He exulted in the sight. And in an instant the thing had passed.

It rose slightly and their own little wings swayed in the rush of its flight. It fell and grew smaller. Scarcely had they moved, as it seemed, before it was again only a flat blue thing that dwindled in the sky. This was the aeroplane that went to and fro between London and Paris. In fair weather and in peaceful times it came and went four times a day.

They beat across the Channel, slowly as it seemed now, to Graham's enlarged ideas, and Beachy Head rose greyly to the left of them.

'Land,' called the aeronaut, his voice small against the whistling of the air over the wind-screen.

'Not yet,' bawled Graham, laughing. 'Not land yet. I want to learn more of this machine.'

'I meant – ' said the aeronaut.

'I want to learn more of this machine,' repeated Graham.

'I'm coming to you,' he said, and had flung himself free of his chair and taken a step along the guarded rail between them. He stopped for a moment, and his colour changed and his hands tightened. Another step and he was clinging close to the aeronaut. He felt a weight on his shoulder, the pressure of the air. His hat was a whirling speck behind. The wind came in gusts over his wind-screen and blew his hair in streamers past his cheek. The aeronaut made some hasty adjustments for the shifting of the centres of gravity and pressure.

'I want to have these things explained,' said Graham. 'What do you do when you move that engine forward?'

The aeronaut hesitated. Then he answered, 'They are complex, Sire.'

'I don't mind,' shouted Graham. 'I don't mind.'

There was a moment's pause. 'Aeronautics is the secret – the privilege – '

'I know. But I'm the Master, and I mean to know.'

He laughed, full of this novel realisation of power that was his gift from the upper air.

The aeropile curved about, and the keen fresh wind cut across Graham's face and his garment lugged at his body as the stem pointed round to the west. The two men looked into each other's eyes.

'Sire, there are rules – '

'Not where I am concerned,' said Graham. 'You seem to forget.'

The aeronaut scrutinised his face. 'No,' he said. 'I do not forget, Sire. But in all the earth – no man who is not a sworn aeronaut – has ever a chance. They come as passengers – '

'I have heard something of the sort. But I'm not going to argue these points. Do you know why I have slept two hundred years? To fly!'

'Sire,' said the aeronaut, 'the rules – if I break the rules – '

Graham waved the penalties aside.

'Then if you will watch me – '

'No,' said Graham, swaying and gripping tight as the machine lifted its nose again for an ascent. 'That's not my game. I want to do it myself. Do it myself if I smash for it! No! I will. See. I am going to clamber by this – to come and share your seat. Steady! I mean to fly of my own accord if I smash at the end of it. I will have something to pay for my sleep. Of all other things – . In my past it was my dream to fly. Now – keep our balance.'

'A dozen spies are watching me, Sire.'

Graham's temper was at end. Perhaps he chose it should be. He swore. He swung himself round the intervening mass of levers and the aeropile swayed.

'Am I Master of the earth?' he said. 'Or is your Society? Now. Take your hands off those levers, and hold my wrists. Yes – so. And now, how do we turn her nose down to the glide?'

'Sire,' said the aeronaut.

'What is it?'

'You will protect me?'

'Lord! Yes! If I have to burn London. Now!'

And with that promise Graham bought his first lesson in aerial navigation. 'It's clearly to your advantage, this journey,' he said with a loud laugh – for the air was like strong wine – 'to teach me quickly and well. Do I pull this? Ah! So! Hullo!'

'Back, Sire. Back.'

'Back – right. One – two – three – good God! Ah! Up she goes! But this is living!'

And now the machine began to dance the strangest figures in the air. Now it would sweep round a spiral of scarcely a hundred yards diameter, now it would rush up into the air and swoop down again, steeply, falling like a hawk, to recover in a rushing loop that swept it high again. In one of these descents it seemed driving straight at the drifting park of balloons in the southeast, and only curved about and cleared them by a sudden recovery of dexterity. The extraordinary swiftness and smoothness of the motion, the extraordinary effect of the rarified air upon his constitution, threw Graham into a careless fury.

But at last a queer incident came to sober him, to send him flying down once more to the crowded life below with all its dark insoluble riddles. As he swooped, came a tap and something flying past, and a drop like a drop of rain. Then as he went on down he saw something like a white rag whirling down in his wake. 'What was that?' he asked. 'I did not see.'

The aeronaut glanced, and then clutched at the lever to recover, for they were sweeping down. When the aeropile was rising again he drew a deep breath and replied. 'That,' and he indicated the white thing still fluttering down, 'was a swan.'

'I never saw it,' said Graham.

The aeronaut made no answer, and Graham saw little drops upon his forehead.

They drove horizontally while Graham clambered back to the passenger's place out of the lash of the wind. And then came a swift rush down, with the wide-screw whirling to check their fall, and the flying stage growing broad and dark before them. The sun, sinking over the chalk hills in the west, fell with them, and left the sky a blaze of gold.

Soon men could be seen as little specks. He heard a noise coming up to meet him, a noise like the sound of waves upon a pebbly beach, and saw that the roofs about the flying stage were dark with his people rejoicing over his safe return. A dark mass was crushed together under the stage, a darkness stippled with innumerable faces, and quivering with the minute oscillation of waved white handkerchiefs and waving hands.

XVII

Three Days

Lincoln awaited Graham in an apartment beneath the flying stages. He seemed curious to learn all that had happened, pleased to hear of the extraordinary delight and interest which Graham took in flying. Graham was in a mood of enthusiasm. 'I must learn to fly,' he cried. 'I must master that. I pity all poor souls who have died without this opportunity. The sweet swift air! It is the most wonderful experience in the world.'

'You will find our new times full of wonderful experiences,' said Lincoln. 'I do not know what you will care to do now. We have music that may seem novel.'

'For the present,' said Graham, 'flying holds me. Let me learn more of that. Your aeronaut was saying there is some trades union objection to one's learning.'

'There is, I believe,' said Lincoln. 'But for you – ! If you would like to occupy yourself with that, we can make you a sworn aeronaut tomorrow.'

Graham expressed his wishes vividly and talked of his sensations for a while. 'And as for affairs,' he asked abruptly. 'How are things going on?'

Lincoln waved affairs aside. 'Ostrog will tell you that tomorrow,' he said. 'Everything is settling down. The Revolution accomplishes itself all over the world. Friction is inevitable here and there, of course; but your rule is assured. You may rest secure with things in Ostrog's hands.'

'Would it be possible for me to be made a sworn aeronaut, as you call it, forthwith – before I sleep?' said Graham, pacing. 'Then I could be at it the very first thing tomorrow again. . . .'

'It would be possible,' said Lincoln thoughtfully.

'Quite possible. Indeed, it shall be done.' He laughed. 'I came prepared to suggest amusements, but you have found one for yourself. I will telephone to the aeronautical offices from here and we will return to your apartments in the Wind-Vane Control. By the time you have dined the aeronauts will be able to come. You don't think that after you have dined, you might prefer – ?' He paused.

'Yes,' said Graham.

'We had prepared a show of dancers – they have been brought from the Capri theatre.'

'I hate ballets,' said Graham, shortly. 'Always did. That other – . That's not what I want to see. We had dancers in the old days. For the matter of that, they had them in ancient Egypt. But flying – '

'True,' said Lincoln. 'Though our dancers – '

'They can afford to wait,' said Graham; 'they can afford to wait. I know. I'm not a Latin. There's questions I want to ask some expert – about your machinery. I'm keen. I want no distractions.'

'You have the world to choose from,' said Lincoln; 'whatever you want is yours.'

Asano appeared, and under the escort of a strong guard they returned through the city streets to Graham's apartments. Far larger crowds had assembled to witness his return than his departure had gathered, and the shouts and cheering of these masses of people sometimes drowned Lincoln's answers to the endless questions Graham's aerial journey had suggested. At first Graham had acknowledged the cheering and cries of the crowd by bows and gestures, but Lincoln warned him that such a recognition would be considered incorrect behaviour. Graham, already a little wearied by rhythmic civilities, ignored his subjects for the remainder of his public progress.

Directly they arrived at his apartments Asano departed in search of kinematographic renderings of machinery in motion, and Lincoln despatched Graham's commands for models of machines and small machines to illustrate the various mechanical advances of the last two centuries. The little group of appliances for telegraphic communication attracted the Master so strongly that his delightfully prepared dinner, served by a number of charmingly dexterous girls, waited for a space. The habit of smoking had almost ceased from the face of the earth, but when he expressed a wish for that indulgence, inquiries were made and some excellent cigars were discovered in Florida, and sent to him by pneumatic despatch while the dinner was still in progress. Afterwards came the aeronauts, and a feast of ingenious wonders in the hands of a latter-day engineer. For the time, at any rate, the neat dexterity of counting and numbering machines, building machines, spinning engines, patent doorways, explosive motors, grain and water elevators, slaughter-house machines and harvesting appliances, was more fascinating to Graham than any bayadere. 'We were savages,' was his refrain, 'we were savages. We were in the stone age – compared with this. . . . And what else have you?'

There came also practical psychologists with some very interesting developments in the art of hypnotism. The names of Milne Bramwell,

Fechner, Liebault, William James, Myers and Gurney, he found, bore a value now that would have astonished their contemporaries. Several practical applications of psychology were now in general use; it had largely superseded drugs, antiseptics and anaesthetics in medicine; was employed by almost all who had any need of mental concentration. A real enlargement of human faculty seemed to have been effected in this direction. The feats of 'calculating boys', the wonders, as Graham had been wont to regard them, of mesmerisers, were now within the range of anyone who could afford the services of a skilled hypnotist. Long ago the old examination methods in education had been destroyed by these expedients. Instead of years of study, candidates had substituted a few weeks of trances, and during the trances expert coaches had simply to repeat all the points necessary for adequate answering, adding a suggestion of the post hypnotic recollection of these points. In process mathematics particularly, this aid had been of singular service, and it was now invariably invoked by such players of chess and games of manual dexterity as were still to be found. In fact, all operations conducted under finite rules, of a quasi-mechanical sort that is, were now systematically relieved from the wanderings of imagination and emotion, and brought to an unexampled pitch of accuracy. Little children of the labouring classes, so soon as they were of sufficient age to be hypnotised, were thus converted into beautifully punctual and trustworthy machine minders, and released forthwith from the long, long thoughts of youth. Aeronautical pupils, who gave way to giddiness, could be relieved from their imaginary terrors. In every street were hypnotists ready to print permanent memories upon the mind. If anyone desired to remember a name, a series of numbers, a song or a speech, it could be done by this method, and conversely memories could be effaced, habits removed, and desires eradicated – a sort of psychic surgery was, in fact, in general use. Indignities, humbling experiences, were thus forgotten, amorous widows would obliterate their previous husbands, angry lovers release themselves from their slavery. To graft desires, however, was still impossible, and the facts of thought transference were yet unsystematised. The psychologists illustrated their expositions with some astounding experiments in mnemonics made through the agency of a troupe of pale-faced children in blue.

Graham, like most of the people of his former time, distrusted the hypnotist, or he might then and there have eased his mind of many painful preoccupations. But in spite of Lincoln's assurances he held to the old theory that to be hypnotised was in some way the surrender of his personality, the abdication of his will. At the banquet of wonderful experiences that was beginning, he wanted very keenly to remain absolutely himself.

The next day, and another day, and yet another day passed in such interests as these. Each day Graham spent many hours in the glorious entertainment of flying. On the third day he soared across middle France, and within sight of the snow-clad Alps. These vigorous exercises gave him restful sleep, and each day saw a great stride in his health from the spiritless anaemia of his first awakening. And whenever he was not in the air, and awake, Lincoln was assiduous in the cause of his amusement; all that was novel and curious in contemporary invention was brought to him, until at last his appetite for novelty was well-nigh glutted. One might fill a dozen inconsecutive volumes with the strange things they exhibited. Each afternoon he held his court for an hour or so. He speedily found his interest in his contemporaries becoming personal and intimate. At first he had been alert chiefly for unfamiliarity; and foppishness in their dress, any discordance with his preconceptions of nobility in their status and manners had jarred upon him, and it was remarkable to him how soon that strangeness and the faint hostility that arose from it, disappeared; how soon he came to appreciate the true perspective of his position, and see the old Victorian days remote and quaint. He found himself particularly amused by the red-haired daughter of the Manager of the European Piggeries. On the second day after dinner he made the acquaintance of a latter-day dancing girl, and found her an astonishing artist. And after that, more hypnotic wonders. On the third day Lincoln was moved to suggest that the Master should repair to a Pleasure City, but this Graham declined, nor would he accept the services of the hypnotists in his aeronautical experiments. The link of locality held him to London; he found a perpetual wonder in topographical identifications that he would have missed abroad. 'Here – or a hundred feet below,' he could say, 'I used to eat my midday cutlets during my London University days. Underneath here was Waterloo and the perpetual hunt for confusing trains. Often have I stood waiting down there, bag in hand, and stared up into the sky above the forest of signals, little thinking I shoud walk some day a hundred yards in the air. And now in that very sky that was once a grey smoke canopy, I circle in an aeropile.'

During those three days Graham was so occupied with such distractions that the vast political movements in progress outside his quarters had but a small share of his attention. Those about him told him little. Daily came Ostrog, the Boss, his Grand Vizier, his mayor of the palace, to report in vague terms the steady establishment of his rule; 'a little trouble' soon to be settled in this city, 'a slight disturbance' in that. The song of the social revolt came to him no more; he never learned that it had been forbidden in the municipal limits; and all the great emotions of the crow's nest slumbered in his mind.

But on the second and third of the three days he found himself, in spite of his interest in the daughter of the Pig Manager, or it may be by reason of the thoughts her conversation suggested, remembering the girl Helen Wotton, who had spoken to him so oddly at the Wind-Vane

Keeper's gathering. The impression she had made was a deep one, albeit the incessant surprise of novel circumstances had kept him from brooding upon it for a space. But now her memory was coming to its own. He wondered what she had meant by those broken half-forgotten sentences; the picture of her eyes and the earnest passion of her face became more vivid as his mechanical interest faded. Her beauty came compellingly between him and certain immediate temptations of ignoble passion. But he did not see her again until three full days were past.

XVIII

Graham Remembers

She came upon him at last in a little gallery that ran from the Wind-Vane Offices toward his state apartments. The gallery was long and narrow, with a series of recesses, each with an arched fenestration that looked upon a court of palms. He came upon her suddenly in one of these recesses. She was seated. She turned her head at the sound of his footsteps and started at the sight of him. Every touch of colour vanished from her face. She rose instantly, made a step toward him as if to address him, and hesitated. He stopped and stood still, expectant. Then he perceived that a nervous tumult silenced her, perceived too, that she must have sought speech with him to be waiting for him in this place.

He felt a regal impulse to assist her. 'I have wanted to see you,' he said. 'A few days ago you wanted to tell me something – you wanted to tell me of the people. What was it you had to tell me?'

She looked at him with troubled eyes.

'You said the people were unhappy?'

For a moment she was silent still.

'It must have seemed strange to you,' she said abruptly.

'It did. And yet – '

'It was an impulse.'

'Well?'

'That is all.'

She looked at him with a face of hesitation. She spoke with an effort. 'You forget,' she said, drawing a deep breath.

'What?'

'The people – '

'Do you mean – ?'

'You forget the people.'

He looked interrogative.

'Yes. I know you are surprised. For you do not understand what you are. You do not know the things that are happening.'

'Well?'

'You do not understand.'

'Not clearly, perhaps. But – tell me.'

She turned to him with sudden resolution. 'It is so hard to explain. I have meant to, I have wanted to. And now – I cannot. I am not ready with words. But about you – there is something. It is Wonder. Your sleep – your awakening. These things are miracles. To me at least – and to all the common people. You who lived and suffered and died, you who were a common citizen, wake again, live again, to find yourself Master almost of the earth.'

'Master of the earth,' he said. 'So they tell me. But try and imagine how little I know of it.'

'Cities – Trusts – the Labour Company – '

'Principalities, powers, dominions – the power and the glory. Yes, I have heard them shout. I know. I am Master. King, if you wish. With Ostrog, the Boss – '

He paused.

She turned upon him and surveyed his face with a curious scrutiny. 'Well?'

He smiled. 'To take the responsibility.'

'That is what we have begun to fear.' For a moment she said no more. 'No,' she said slowly. '*You* will take the responsibility. You will take the responsibility. The people look to you.'

She spoke softly. 'Listen! For at least half the years of your sleep – in every generation – multitudes of people, in every generation greater multitudes of people, have prayed that you might awake – *prayed*.'

Graham moved to speak and did not.

She hesitated, and a faint colour crept back to her cheek. 'Do you know that you have been to myriads – King Arthur, Barbarossa – the King who would come in his own good time and put the world right for them?'

'I suppose the imagination of the people – '

'Have you not heard our proverb, "When the Sleeper wakes?" While you lay insensible and motionless there – thousands came. Thousands. Every first of the month you lay in state with a white robe upon you and the people filed by you. When I was a little girl I saw you like that, with your face white and calm.'

She turned her face from him and looked steadfastly at the painted wall before her. Her voice fell. 'When I was a little girl I used to look at your face. . . . it seemed to me fixed and waiting, like the patience of God.

'That is what we thought of you,' she said. 'That is how you seemed to us.'

She turned shining eyes to him, her voice was clear and strong. 'In the city, in the earth, a myriad myriad men and women are waiting to see what you will do, full of strange incredible expectations.'

'Yes?'

'Ostrog – no one – can take that responsibility.'

Graham looked at her in surprise, at her face lit with emotion. She seemed at first to have spoken with an effort, and to have fired herself by speaking.

'Do you think,' she said, 'that you who have lived that little life so far away in the past, you who have fallen into and risen out of this miracle of sleep – do you think that the wonder and reverence and hope of half the world has gathered about you only that you may live another little life? . . . That you may shift the responsibility to any other man?'

'I know how great this kingship of mine is,' he said haltingly. 'I know how great it seems. But is it real? It is incredible – dreamlike. Is it real, or is it only a great delusion?'

'It is real,' she said; 'if you dare.'

'After all, like all kingship, my kingship is Belief. It is an illusion in the minds of men.'

'If you dare!' she said.

'But – '

'Countless men,' she said, 'and while it is in their minds – they will obey.'

'But I know nothing. That is what I had in mind. I know nothing. And these others – the Councillors, Ostrog. They are wiser, cooler, they know so much, every detail. And, indeed, what are these miseries of which you speak? What am I to know? Do you mean – '

He stopped blankly.

'I am still hardly more than a girl,' she said. 'But to me the world seems full of wretchedness. The world has altered since your day, altered very strangely. I have prayed that I might see you and tell you these things. The world has changed. As if a canker had seized it – and robbed life of – everything worth having.'

She turned a flushed face upon him, moving suddenly. 'Your days were the days of freedom. Yes – I have thought. I have been made to think, for my life – has not been happy. Men are no longer free – no greater, no better than the men of your time. That is not all. This city – is a prison. Every city now is a prison. Mammon grips the key in his hand. Myriads, countless myriads, toil from the cradle to the grave. Is that right? Is that to be – for ever? Yes, far worse than in your time. All about us, beneath us, sorrow and pain. All the shallow delight of such life as you find about you, is separated by just a little from a life of wretchedness beyond any telling. Yes, the poor know it – they know they suffer. These countless multitudes who faced death for you two nights since – ! You owe your life to them.'

'Yes,' said Graham, slowly. 'Yes. I owe my life to them.'

'You come,' she said, 'from the days when this new tyranny of the cities was scarcely beginning. It is a tyranny – a tyranny. In your days the feudal war lords had gone, and the new lordship of wealth had still to come. Half the men in the world still lived out upon the free countryside. The cities had still to devour them. I have heard the stories out of the old books – there was nobility! Common men led lives of love and faithfulness then – they did a thousand things. And you – you come from that time.'

'It was not – . But never mind. How is it now – ?'

'Gain and the Pleasure Cities! Or slavery – unthanked, unhonoured, slavery.'

'Slavery!' he said.

'Slavery.'

'You don't mind to say that human beings are chattels.'

'Worse. That is what I want you to know, what I want you to see. I know you do not know. They will keep things from you, they will take you presently to a Pleasure City. But you have noticed men and women and children in pale blue canvas, with thin yellow faces and dull eyes?'

'Everywhere.'

'Speaking a horrible dialect, coarse and weak.'

'I have heard it.'

'They are the slaves – your slaves. They are the slaves of the Labour Company you own.'

'The Labour Company! In some way – that is familiar. Ah! now I remember. I saw it when I was wandering about the city, after the lights returned, great fronts of buildings coloured pale blue. Do you really mean – ?'

'Yes. How can I explain it to you? Of course the blue uniform struck you. Nearly a third of our people wear it – more assume it now every day. This Labour Company has grown imperceptibly.'

'What *is* this Labour Company?' asked Graham.

'In the old times, how did you manage with starving people?'

'There was the workhouse – which the parishes maintained.'

'Workhouse! Yes – there was something. In our history lessons. I remember now. The Labour Company ousted the workhouse. It grew – partly – out of something – you, perhaps, may remember it – an emotional religious organisation called the Salvation Army – that became a business company. In the first place it was almost a charity. To save people from workhouse rigours. Now I come to think of it, it was one of the earliest properties your Trustees acquired. They bought the Salvation Army and reconstructed it as this. The idea in the first place was to give work to starving homeless people.'

'Yes.'

'Nowadays there are no workhouses, no refuges and charities, nothing but that Company. Its offices are everywhere. That blue is its colour. And any man, woman or child who comes to be hungry and weary and with neither home nor friend nor resort, must go to the Company in the end – or seek some way of death. The Euthanasy is beyond their means – for the poor there is no easy death. And at any hour in the day or night there is food, shelter and a blue uniform for all comers – that is the first condition of the Company's incorporation – and in return for a day's shelter the Company extracts a day's work, and then returns the visitor's proper clothing and sends him or her out again.'

'Yes?'

'Perhaps that does not seem so terrible to you. In your days men starved in your streets. That was bad. But they died – men. These people in blue – . The proverb runs: "Blue canvas once and ever." The Company trades in their labour, and it has taken care to assure itself of the supply. People come to it starving and helpless – they eat and sleep for a night and day, they work for a day, and at the end of the day they go out again. If they have worked well they have a penny or so – enough for a theatre or a cheap dancing place, or a kinematograph story, or a dinner or a bet. They wander about after that is spent. Begging is prevented by the police of the ways. Besides, no one gives. They come back again the next day or the day after – brought back by the same incapacity that brought them first. At last their proper clothing wears out, or their rags get so shabby that they are ashamed. Then they must work for months to get fresh. If they want fresh. A great number of children are born under the Company's care. The mother owes them a month thereafter – the children they cherish and educate until they are fourteen, and they pay two years' service. You may be sure these children are educated for the blue canvas. And so it is the Company works.'

'And none are destitute in the city?'

'None. They are either in blue canvas or in prison.'

'If they will not work?'

'Most people will work at that pitch, and the Company has powers. There are stages of unpleasantness in the work – stoppage of food – and a man or woman who has refused to work once is known by a thumb-marking system in the Company's offices all over the world. Besides, who can leave the city poor? To go to Paris costs two lions. And for insubordination there are the prisons – dark and miserable – out of sight below. There are prisons now for many things.'

'And a third of the people wear this blue canvas?'

'More than a third. Toilers, living without pride or delight or hope, with the stories of Pleasure Cities ringing in their ears, mocking their shameful lives, their privations and hardships. Too poor even for the Euthanasy, the rich man's refuge from life. Dumb, crippled millions, countless millions, all the world about, ignorant of anything but limitations and unsatisfied desires. They are born, they are thwarted and they die. That is the state to which we have come.'

For a space Graham sat downcast.

'But there has been a revolution,' he said. 'All these things will be changed. 'Ostrog – '

'That is our hope. That is the hope of the world. But Ostrog will not do it. He is a politician. To him it seems things must be like this. He does not mind. He takes it for granted. All the rich, all the influential, all who are happy, come at last to take these miseries for granted. They use the people in their politics, they live in ease by their degradation. But you – you who come from a happier age it is to you the people look. To you.'

He looked at her face. Her eyes were bright with unshed tears. He felt a rush of emotion. For a moment he forgot this city, he forgot the race, and all those vague remote voices, in the immediate humanity of her beauty.

'But what am I to do?' he said with his eyes upon her.

'Rule,' she answered, bending towards him and speaking in a low tone. 'Rule the world as it has never been ruled, for the good and happiness of men. For you might rule it – you could rule it.'

'The people are stirring. All over the world the people are stirring. It wants but a word – but a word from you – to bring them all together. Even the middle sort of people are restless – unhappy.

'They are not telling you the things that are happening. The people will not go back to their drudgery – they refuse to be disarmed. Ostrog has awakened something greater than he dreamt of – he has awakened hopes.'

His heart was beating fast. He tried to seem judicial, to weigh considerations.

'They only want their leader,' she said.

'And then?'

'You could do what you would; – the world is yours.'

He sat, no longer regarding her. Presently he spoke.

'The old dreams, and these things I have dreamt, liberty, happiness. Are they dreams? Could one man – *one man* – ?' His voice sank and ceased.

'Not one man, but all men – give them only a leader to speak the desire of their hearts.'

He shook his head, and for a time there was silence.

He looked up suddenly, and their eyes met. 'I have not your faith,' he said. 'I have not your youth. I am here with power that mocks me. No – let me speak. I want to do – not right – I have not the strength for that – but something rather right than wrong. It will bring no millennium, but I am resolved now that I will rule. What you have said has awakened me. . . . You are right. Ostrog must know his place. And I will learn – . . . . One thing I promise you. This Labour slavery shall end.'

'And you will rule?'

'Yes. Provided – . There is one thing.'

'Yes?'

'That you will help me.'

'*I!* – a girl!'

'Yes. Does it not occur to you I am absolutely alone?'

She started and for an instant her eyes had pity. 'Need you ask whether I will help you?' she said.

She stood before him, beautiful, worshipful, and her enthusiasm and the greatness of their theme was like a great gulf fixed between them. To touch her, to clasp her hand, was a thing beyond hope. 'Then I will rule indeed,' he said slowly. 'I will rule – ' He paused. 'With you.'

There came a tense silence, and then the beating of a clock striking the hour. She made him no answer. Graham rose.

'Even now,' he said, 'Ostrog will be waiting.' He hesitated, facing her. 'When I have asked him certain questions – . There is much I do not know. It may be, that I will go to see with my own eyes the things of which you have spoken. And when I return – ?'

'I shall know of your going and coming. I will wait for you here again.'

He stood for a moment regarding her.

'I knew,' she said, and stopped.

He waited, but she said no more. They regarded one another steadfastly, questioningly, and then he turned from her towards the Wind-Vane office.

XIX

Ostrog's Point of View

Graham found Ostrog waiting to give a formal account of his day's stewardship. On previous occasions he had passed over this ceremony as speedily as possible, in order to resume his aerial experiences, but now he began to ask quick short questions. He was very anxious to take up his empire forthwith. Ostrog brought flattering reports of the development of affairs abroad. In Paris and Berlin, Graham perceived that he was saying, there had been trouble, not organised resistance indeed, but insubordinate proceedings. 'After all these years,' said Ostrog, when Graham pressed inquiries; 'the Commune has lifted its head again. That is the real nature of the struggle, to be explicit.' But order had been restored in these cities. Graham, the more deliberately judicial for the stirring emotions he felt, asked if there had been any fighting. 'A little,' said Ostrog. 'In one quarter only. But the Senegalese division of our African agricultural police – the Consolidated African Companies have a very well drilled police – was ready, and so were the aeroplanes. We expected a little trouble in the continental cities, and in America. But things are very quiet in America. They are satisfied with the overthrow of the Council. For the time.'

'Why should you expect trouble?' asked Graham abruptly.

'There is a lot of discontent – social discontent.'

'The Labour Company?'

'You are learning,' said Ostrog with a touch of surprise. 'Yes. It is chiefly the discontent with the Labour Company. It was that discontent supplied the motive force of this overthrow – that and your awakening.'

'Yes?'

Ostrog smiled. He became explicit. 'We had to stir up their discontent, we had to revive the old ideals of universal happiness – all men equal – all men happy – no luxury that everyone may not share – ideas that have slumbered for two hundred years. You know that? We had to revive these ideals, impossible as they are – in order to overthrow the Council. And now – '

'Well?'

'Our revolution is accomplished, and the Council is overthrown, and people whom we have stirred up – remain surging. There was scarcely enough fighting. . . . We made promises, of course. It is extraordinary how violently and rapidly this vague out-of-date humanitarianism has revived and spread. We who sowed the seed even, have been astonished. In Paris, as I say – we have had to call in a little external help.'

'And here?'

'There is trouble. Multitudes will not go back to work. There is a general strike. Half the factories are empty and the people are swarming in the Ways. They are talking of a Commune. Men in silk and satin have been insulted in the streets. The blue canvas is expecting all sorts of things from you. . . . Of course there is no need for you to trouble. We are setting the Babble Machines to work with counter suggestions in the cause of law and order. We must keep the grip tight; that is all.'

Graham thought. He perceived a way of asserting himself. But he spoke with restraint.

'Even to the pitch of bringing a negro police,' he said.

'They are useful,' said Ostrog. 'They are fine loyal brutes, with no wash of ideas in their heads – such as our rabble has. The Council should have had them as police of the Ways, and things might have been different. Of course, there is nothing to fear except rioting and wreckage. You can manage your own wings now, and you can soar away to Capri if there is any smoke or fuss. We have the pull of all the great things; the aeronauts are privileged and rich, the closest trades union in the world, and so are the engineers of the wind-vanes. We have the air, and the mastery of the air is the mastery of the earth. No one of any ability is organising against us. They have no leaders – only the sectional leaders of the secret society we organised before your very opportune awakening. Mere busybodies and sentimentalists they are and bitterly jealous of each other. None of them is man enough for a central figure. The only trouble will be a disorganised upheaval. To be frank – that may happen. But it won't interrupt your aeronautics. The days when the People could make revolutions are past.'

'I suppose they are,' said Graham. 'I suppose they are.' He mused. 'This world of yours has been full of surprises to me. In the old days we dreamt of a wonderful democratic life, of a time when all men would be equal and happy.'

Ostrog looked at him steadfastly. 'The day of democracy is past,' he said. 'Past for ever. That day began with the bowmen of Crecy, it ended when marching infantry, when common men in masses ceased to win the battles of the world, when costly cannon, great ironclads, and strategic railways became the means of power. Today is the day of wealth. Wealth now is power as it never was before – it commands earth and sea and sky. All power is for those who can handle wealth. . . . You must accept facts, and these are facts. The world for the Crowd!

The Crowd as Ruler! Even in your days that creed had been tried and condemned. Today it has only one believer – a multiplex, silly one – the man in the Crowd.'

Graham did not answer immediately. He stood lost in sombre preoccupations.

'No,' said Ostrog. 'The day of the common man is past. On the open countryside one man is as good as another, or nearly as good. The earlier aristocracy had a precarious tenure of strength and audacity. They were tempered. There were insurrections, duels, riots. The first real aristocracy, the first permanent aristocracy, came in with castles and armour, and vanished before the musket and bow. But this is the second aristocracy. The real one. Those days of gunpowder and democracy were only an eddy in the stream. The common man now is a helpless unit. In these days we have this great machine of the city, and an organisation complex beyond his understanding.'

'Yet,' said Graham, 'there is something resists, something you are holding down – something that stirs and presses.'

'You will see,' said Ostrog, with a forced smile that would brush these difficult questions aside. 'I have not roused the force to destroy myself – trust me.'

'I wonder,' said Graham.

Ostrog stared.

'*Must* the world go this way?' said Graham, with his emotions at the speaking point. 'Must it indeed go in this way? Have all our hopes been vain?'

'What do you mean?' said Ostrog. 'Hopes?'

'I came from a democratic age. And I find an aristocratic tyranny!'

'Well, – but you are the chief tyrant.'

Graham shook his head.

'Well,' said Ostrog, 'take the general question. It is the way that change has always travelled. Aristocracy, the prevalence of the best – suffering and extinction of the unfit, and so to better things.'

'But aristocracy! those people I met – '

'Oh! not *those*!' said Ostrog. 'But for the most part they go to their death. Vice and pleasure! They have no children. That sort of stuff will die out. If the world keeps to one road, that is, if there is no turning back. An easy road to excess, convenient Euthanasia for the pleasure seekers singed in the flame, that is the way to improve the race!'

'Pleasant extinction,' said Graham. 'Yet – .' He thought for an instant. 'There is that other thing – the Crowd, the great mass of poor men. Will that die out? That will not die out. And it suffers, its suffering is a force that even you – '

Ostrog moved impatiently, and when he spoke, he spoke rather less evenly than before.

'Don't you trouble about these things,' he said. 'Everything will be

settled in a few days now. The Crowd is a huge foolish beast. What if it
does not die out? Even if it does not die, it can still be tamed and driven.
I have no sympathy with servile men. You heard those people shouting
and singing two nights ago. They were taught that song. If you had
taken any man there in cold blood and asked why he shouted, he could
not have told you. They think they are shouting for you, that they are
loyal and devoted to you. Just then they were ready to slaughter the
Council. Today – they are already murmuring against those who have
overthrown the Council.'

'No, no,' said Graham. 'They shouted because their lives were dreary,
without joy or pride, and because in me – in me – they hoped.'

'And what was their hope? What is their hope? What right have they
to hope? They work ill and they want the reward of those who work
well. The hope of mankind – what is it? That some day the Over-man
may come, that some day the inferior, the weak and the bestial may be
subdued or eliminated. Subdued if not eliminated. The world is no place
for the bad, the stupid, the enervated. Their duty – it's a fine duty too!
– is to die. The death of the failure! That is the path by which the beast
rose to manhood, by which man goes on to higher things.'

Ostrog took a pace, seemed to think, and turned on Graham. 'I can
imagine how this great world state of ours seems to a Victorian
Englishman. You regret all the old forms of representative government
– their spectres still haunt the world, the voting councils and parliaments
and all that eighteenth-century tomfoolery. You feel moved against our
Pleasure Cities. I might have thought of that, – had I not been busy. But
you will learn better. The people are mad with envy – they would be in
sympathy with you. Even in the streets now, they clamour to destroy
the Pleasure Cities. But the Pleasure Cities are the excretory organs of
the State, attractive places that year after year draw together all that is
weak and vicious, all that is lascivious and lazy, all the easy roguery of
the world, to a graceful destruction. They go there, they have their time,
they die childless, all the pretty silly lascivious women die childless, and
mankind is the better. If the people were sane they would not envy the
rich their way of death. And you would emancipate the silly brainless
workers that we have enslaved, and try to make their lives easy and
pleasant again. Just as they have sunk to what they are fit for.' He
smiled a smile that irritated Graham oddly. 'You will learn better. I
know those ideas; in my boyhood I read your Shelley and dreamt of
Liberty. There is no liberty, save wisdom and self-control. Liberty is
within – not without. It is each man's own affair. Suppose – which is
impossible – that these swarming yelping fools in blue get the upper
hand of us, what then? They will only fall to other masters. So long as
there are sheep Nature will insist on beasts of prey. It would mean but
a few hundred years' delay. The coming of the aristocrat is fatal and
assured. The end will be the Over-man – for all the mad protests of

humanity. Let them revolt, let them win and kill me and my like. Others will arise – other masters. The end will be the same.'

'I wonder,' said Graham doggedly.

For a moment he stood downcast.

'But I must see these things for myself,' he said, suddenly assuming a tone of confident mastery. 'Only by seeing can I understand. I must learn. That is what I want to tell you, Ostrog. I do not want to be King in a Pleasure City; that is not my pleasure. I have spent enough time with aeronautics – and those other things. I must learn how people live now, how the common life has developed. Than I shall understand these things better. I must learn how common people live – the labour people more especially – how they work, marry, bear children, die – '

'You get that from our realistic-novelists,' suggested Ostrog, suddenly preoccupied.

'I want reality,' said Graham, 'not realism.'

'There are difficulties,' said Ostrog, and thought. 'On the whole perhaps – .'

'I did not expect – .'

'I had thought – . And yet, perhaps – . You say you want to go through the Ways of the city and see the common people.'

Suddenly he came to some conclusion. 'You would need to go disguised,' he said. 'The city is intensely excited, and the discovery of your presence among them might create a fearful tumult. Still this wish of yours to go into this city – this idea of yours – . Yes, now I think the thing over it seems to me not altogether – . It can be contrived. If you would really find an interest in that! You are, of course, Master. You can go soon if you like. A disguise for this excursion Asano will be able to manage. He would go with you. After all it is not a bad idea of yours.'

'You will not want to consult me in any matter?' asked Graham suddenly, struck by an odd suspicion.

'Oh, dear no! No! I think you may trust affairs to me for a time, at any rate,' said Ostrog, smiling. 'Even if we differ – '

Graham glanced at him sharply.

'There is no fighting likely to happen soon?' he asked abruptly.

'Certainly not.'

'I have been thinking about these negroes. I don't believe the people intend any hostility to me, and, after all, I am the Master. I do not want any negroes brought to London. It is an archaic prejudice perhaps, but I have peculiar feelings about Europeans and the subject races. Even about Paris – '

Ostrog stood watching him from under his drooping brows. 'I am not bringing negroes to London,' he said slowly. 'But if – '

'You are not to bring armed negroes to London, whatever happens,' said Graham. 'In that matter I am quite decided.'

Ostrog, after a pause, decided not to speak, and bowed deferentially.

XX

In the City Ways

And that night, unknown and unsuspected, Graham, dressed in the costume of an inferior wind-vane official keeping holiday, and accompanied by Asano in Labour Company canvas, surveyed the city through which he had wandered when it was veiled in darkness. But now he saw it lit and waking, a whirlpool of life. In spite of the surging and swaying of the forces of revolution, in spite of the unusual discontent, the mutterings of the greater struggle of which the first revolt was but the prelude, the myriad streams of commerce still flowed wide and strong. He knew now something of the dimensions and quality of the new age, but he was not prepared for the infinite surprise of the detailed view, for the torrent of colour and vivid impressions that poured past him.

This was his first real contact with the people of these latter days. He realised that all that had gone before, saving his glimpses of the public theatres and markets, had had its element of seclusion, had been a movement within the comparatively narrow political quarter, that all his previous experiences had revolved immediately about the question of his own position. But here was the city at the busiest hours of night, the people to a large extent returned to their own immediate interests, the resumption of the real informal life, the common habits of the new time.

They emerged at first into a street whose opposite ways were crowded with the blue canvas liveries. This swarm Graham saw was a portion of a procession – it was odd to see a procession parading the city *seated*. They carried banners of coarse red stuff with red letters. 'No disarmament,' said the banners, for the most part in crudely daubed letters and with variant spelling, and 'Why should we disarm?' 'No disarming.' 'No disarming.' Banner after banner went by, a stream of banners flowing past, and at last at the end, the song of the revolt and a noisy band of strange instruments. 'They all ought to be at work,' said Asano. 'They have had no food these two days, or they have stolen it.'

Presently Asano made a detour to avoid the congested crowd that gaped upon the occasional passage of dead bodies from hospital to a mortuary, the gleanings after death's harvest of the first revolt.

That night few people were sleeping, everyone was abroad. A vast excitement, perpetual crowds perpetually changing, surrounded Graham; his mind was confused and darkened by an incessant tumult, by the cries and enigmatical fragments of the social struggle that was as yet only beginning. Everywhere festoons and banners of black and strange decorations, intensified the quality of his popularity. Everywhere he caught snatches of that crude thick dialect that served the illiterate class, the class, that is, beyond the reach of phonograph culture, in their common-place intercourse. Everywhere this trouble of disarmament was in the air, with a quality of immediate stress of which he had no inkling during his seclusion in the Wind-Vane quarter. He perceived that as soon as he returned he must discuss this with Ostrog, this and the greater issues of which it was the expression, in a far more conclusive way than he had so far done. Perpetually that night, even in the earlier hours of their wanderings about the city, the spirit of unrest and revolt swamped his attention, to the exclusion of countless strange things he might otherwise have observed.

This preoccupation made his impressions fragmentary. Yet amidst so much that was strange and vivid, no subject, however personal and insistent, could exert undivided sway. There were spaces when the revolutionary movement passed clean out of his mind, was drawn aside like a curtain from before some startling new aspect of the time. Helen had swayed his mind to this intense earnestness of inquiry, but there came times when she, even, receded beyond his conscious thoughts. At one moment, for example, he found they were traversing the religious quarter, for the easy transit about the city afforded by the moving ways rendered sporadic churches and chapels no longer necessary – and his attention was vividly arrested by the facade of one of the Christian sects.

They were travelling seated on one of the swift upper ways, the place leapt upon them at a bend and advanced rapidly towards them. It was covered with inscriptions from top to base, in vivid white and blue, save where a vast and glaring kinematograph transparency presented a realistic New Testament scene, and where a vast festoon of black to show that the popular religion followed the popular politics, hung across the lettering. Graham had already become familiar with the phonotype writing and these inscriptions arrested him, being to his sense for the most part almost incredible blasphemy. Among the less offensive were 'Salvation on the First Floor and turn to the Right.' 'Put you Money on your Maker.' 'The Sharpest Conversion in London, Expert Operators! Look Slippy!' 'What Christ would say to the Sleeper; – Join the Up-to-date Saints!' 'Be a Christian – without hindrance to your present Occupation.' 'All the Brightest Bishops on the Bench tonight and Prices as Usual.' 'Brisk Blessings for Busy Business Men.'

'But this is appalling!' said Graham, as that deafening scream of mercantile piety towered above them.

'What is appalling?' asked his little officer, apparently seeking vainly for anything unusual in this shrieking enamel.

'*This!* Surely the essence of religion is reverence.'

'Oh *that!*' Asano looked at Graham. 'Does it shock you?' he said in the tone of one who makes a discovery. 'I suppose it would, of course. I had forgotten. Nowadays the competition for attention is so keen, and people simply haven't the leisure to attend to their souls, you know, as they used to do.' He smiled. 'In the old days you had quiet Sabbaths and the countryside. Though somewhere I've read of Sunday afternoons that – '

'But, *that*,' said Graham, glancing back at the receding blue and white. 'That is surely not the only – '

'There are hundreds of different ways. But, of course, if a sect doesn't *tell* it doesn't pay. Worship has moved with the times. There are high class sects with quieter ways – costly incense and personal attentions and all that. These people are extremely popular and prosperous. They pay several dozen lions for those apartments to the Council – to you, I should say.'

Graham still felt a difficulty with the coinage, and this mention of a dozen lions brought him abruptly to that matter. In a moment the screaming temples and their swarming touts were forgotten in this new interest. A turn of a phrase suggested, and an answer confirmed the idea that gold and silver were both demonetised, that stamped gold which had begun its reign amidst the merchants of Phoenicia was at last dethroned. The change had been graduated but swift, brought about by an extension of the system of cheques that had even in his previous life already practically superseded gold in all the larger business transactions. The common traffic of the city, the common currency indeed of all the world, was conducted by means of the little brown, green and pink council cheques for small amounts, printed with a blank payee. Asano had several with him, and at the first opportunity he supplied the gaps in his set. They were printed not on tearable paper, but on a semi-transparent fabric of silken flexibility, interwoven with silk. Across them all sprawled a fac-simile of Graham's signature, his first encounter with the curves and turns of that familiar autograph for two hundred and three years.

Some intermediary experiences made no impression sufficiently vivid to prevent the matter of the disarmament claiming his thoughts again; a blurred picture of a Theosophist temple that promised MIRACLES in enormous letters of unsteady fire was least submerged perhaps, but then came the view of the dining hall in Northumberland Avenue. That interested him very greatly.

By the energy and thought of Asano he was able to view this place from a little screened gallery reserved for the attendants of the tables. The building was pervaded by a distant muffled hooting, piping and bawling, of which he did not at first understand the import, but which recalled a certain mysterious leathery voice he had heard after the resumption of the lights on the night of his solitary wandering.

He had grown accustomed now to vastness and great numbers of people, nevertheless this spectacle held him for a long time. It was as he watched the table service more immediately beneath, and interspersed with many questions and answers concerning details, that the realisation of the full significance of the feast of several thousand people came to him.

It was his constant surprise to find that points that one might have expected to strike vividly at the very outset never occurred to him until some trivial detail suddenly shaped as a riddle and pointed to the obvious thing he had overlooked. In this matter, for instance, it had not occurred to him that this continuity of the city, this exclusion of weather, these vast halls and ways, involved the disappearance of the household: that the typical Victorian 'Home', the little brick cell containing kitchen and scullery, living rooms and bedrooms, had, save for the ruins that diversified the countryside, vanished as surely as the wattle hut. But now he saw what had indeed been manifest from the first, that London, regarded as a living place, was no longer an aggregation of houses but a prodigious hotel, an hotel with a thousand classes of accommodation, thousands of dining halls, chapels, theatres, markets and places of assembly, a synthesis of enterprises, of which he chiefly was the owner. People had their sleeping rooms, with, it might be, antechambers, rooms that were always sanitary at least whatever the degree of comfort and privacy, and for the rest they lived much as many people had lived in the new-made giant hotels, of the Victorian days, eating, reading, thinking, playing, conversing, all in places of public resort, going to their work in the industrial quarters of the city or doing business in their offices in the trading section.

He perceived at once how necessarily this state of affairs had developed from the Victorian city. The fundamental reason for the modern city had ever been the economy of co-operation. The chief thing to prevent the merging of the separate households in his own generation was simply the still imperfect civilisation of the people, the strong barbaric pride, passions, and prejudices, the jealousies, rivalries, and violence of the middle and lower classes, which had necessitated the entire separation of contiguous households. But the change, the taming of the people, had been in rapid progress even then. In his brief thirty years of previous life he had seen an enormous extension of the habit of consuming meals from home, the casually patronised horse-box coffee-house had given place to the open and crowded Aerated Bread Shop for instance, women's clubs had had their beginning, and an immense development of reading rooms, lounges and libraries had witnessed to the growth of social confidence. These promises had by this time attained to their complete fulfilment. The locked and barred household had passed away.

These people below him belonged, he learnt, to the lower middle class, the class just above the blue labourers, a class so accustomed in the Victorian period to feed with every precaution of privacy that its members, when occasion confronted them with a public meal, would usually hide their embarrassment under horseplay or a markedly militant demeanour. But these gaily, if lightly dressed people below, albeit vivacious, hurried and uncommunicative, were dexterously man-nered and certainly quite at their ease with regard to one another.

He noted a slight significant thing; the table, as far as he could see, was and remained delightfully neat, there was nothing to parallel the confusion, the broadcast crumbs, the splashes of viand and condiment, the overturned drink and displaced ornaments, which would have marked the stormy progress of the Victorian meal. The table furniture was very different. There were no ornaments, no flowers, and the table was without a cloth, being made, he learnt, of a solid substance having the texture and appearance of damask. He discerned that this damask substance was patterned with gracefully designed trade advertisements.

In a sort of recess before each diner was a complex apparatus of porcelain and metal. There was one plate of white porcelain, and by means of taps for hot and cold volatile fluids the diner washed this himself between the courses; he also washed his elegant white metal knife and fork and spoon as occasion required.

Soup and the chemical wine that was the common drink were delivered by similar taps, and the remaining covers travelled automati-cally in tastefully arranged dishes down the table along silver rails. The diner stopped these and helped himself at his discretion. They appeared at a little door at one end of the table, and vanished at the other. That turn of democratic sentiment in decay, that ugly pride of menial souls, which renders equals loth to wait on one another, was very strong he found among these people. He was so preoccupied with these details that it was only just as he was leaving the place that he remarked the huge advertisement dioramas that marched majestically along the upper walls and proclaimed the most remarkable commodities.

Beyond this place they came into a crowded hall, and he discovered the cause of the noise that had perplexed him. They paused at a turnstile at which a payment was made.

Graham's attention was immediately arrested by a violent, loud hoot, followed by a vast leathery voice. 'The Master is sleeping peacefully,' it vociferated. 'He is in excellent health. He is going to devote the rest of his life to aeronautics. He says women are more beautiful than ever. Galloop! Wow! Our wonderful civilisation astonishes him beyond measure. Beyond all measure. Galloop. He puts great trust in Boss Ostrog, absolute confidence in Boss Ostrog. Ostrog is to be his chief minister; is authorised to remove or reinstate public officers – all patronage will be in his hands. All patronage in the hands of Boss Ostrog! The Councillors have been sent back to their own prison above the Council House.'

Graham stopped at the first sentence, and, looking up, beheld a foolish trumpet face from which this was brayed. This was the General Intelligence Machine. For a space it seemed to be gathering breath, and a regular throbbing from its cylindrical body was audible. Then it trumpeted 'Galloop, Galloop,' and broke out again.

'Paris is now pacified. All resistance is over. Galloop! The black police hold every position of importance in the city. They fought with great bravery, singing songs written in praise of their ancestors by the poet Kipling. Once or twice they got out of hand, and tortured and mutilated wounded and captured insurgents, men and women. Moral – don't go rebelling. Haha! Galloop, Galloop! They are lively fellows. Lively brave fellows. Let this be a lesson to the disorderly banderlog of this city. Yah! Banderlog! Filth of the earth! Galloop, Galloop!'

The voice ceased. There was a confused murmur of disapproval among the crowd. 'Damned niggers.' A man began to harangue near them. 'Is this the Master's doing, brothers? Is this the Master's doing?'

'Black police!' said Graham. 'What is that? You don't mean – '

Asano touched his arm and gave him a warning look, and forthwith another of these mechanisms screamed deafeningly and gave tongue in a shrill voice. 'Yahaha, Yahah, Yap! Hear a live paper yelp! Live paper. Yaha! Shocking outrage in Paris. Yahahah! The Parisians exasperated by the black police to the pitch of assassination. Dreadful reprisals. Savage times come again. Blood! Blood! Yaha!' The nearer Babble Machine hooted stupendously, 'Galloop, Galloop,' drowned the end of the sentence, and proceeded in a rather flatter note than before with novel comments on the horrors of disorder. 'Law and order must be maintained,' said the nearer Babble Machine.

'But,' began Graham.

'Don't ask questions here,' said Asano, 'or you will be involved in an argument.'

'Then let us go on,' said Graham, 'for I want to know more of this.'

As he and his companions pushed their way through the excited crowd that swarmed beneath these voices, towards the exit, Graham conceived more clearly the proportion and features of this room. Altogether, great and small, there must have been nearly a thousand of these erections, piping, hooting, bawling and gabbling in that great space, each with its crowd of excited listeners, the majority of them men dressed in blue canvas. There were all sizes of machines, from the little gossiping mechanisms that chuckled out mechanical sarcasm in odd corners, through a number of grades to such fifty-foot giants as that which had first hooted over Graham.

This place was unusually crowded, because of the intense public interest in the course of affairs in Paris. Evidently the struggle had been much more savage than Ostrog had represented it. All the mechanisms were discoursing upon that topic, and the repetition of the people made the huge hive buzz with such phrases as 'Lynched policemen,' 'Women burnt alive,' 'Fuzzy Wuzzy.' 'But does the Master allow such things?' asked a man near him. 'Is *this* the beginning of the Master's rule?'

Is *this* the beginning of the Master's rule? For a long time after he had left the place, the hooting, whistling and braying of the machines pursued him; 'Galloop, Galloop,' 'Yahahah, Yaha, Yap! Yaha!' Is *this* the beginning of the Master's rule?

Directly there were out upon the ways he began to question Asano closely on the nature of the Parisian struggle. 'This disarmament! What was their trouble? What does it all mean? Asano seemed chiefly anxious to reassure him that it was 'all right'. 'But these outrages!' 'You cannot have an omelette,' said Asano, 'without breaking eggs. It is only the rough people. Only in one part of the city. All the rest is all right. The Parisian labourers are the wildest in the world, except ours.'

'What! the Londoners?'

'No, the Japanese. They have to be kept in order.'

'But burning women alive!'

'A commune!' said Asano. 'They would rob you of your property. They would do away with property and give the world over to mob rule. You are Master, the world is yours. But there will be no Commune here. There is no need for black police here.

'And every consideration has been shown. It is their own negroes – French speaking negroes. Senegal regiments, and Niger and Timbuctoo.'

'Regiments?' said Graham, 'I thought there was only one – .'

'No,' said Asano, and glanced at him. 'There is more than one.'

Graham felt unpleasantly helpless.

'I did not think,' he began and stopped abruptly. He went off at a tangent to ask for information about these Babble Machines. For the most part, the crowd present had been shabbily or even raggedly dressed, and Graham learnt that so far as the more prosperous classes were concerned, in all the more comfortable private apartments of the city were fixed Babble Machines that would speak directly if a lever was pulled. The tenant of the apartment could connect this with the cables of any of the great News Syndicates that he preferred. When he learnt this presently, he demanded the reason of their absence from his own suite of apartments. Asano stared. 'I never thought,' he said. 'Ostrog must have had them removed.'

Graham stared. 'How was I to know?' he exclaimed.

'Perhaps he thought they would annoy you,' said Asano.

'They must be replaced directly I return,' said Graham after an interval.

He found a difficulty in understanding that this news room and the dining hall were not great central places, that such establishments were repeated almost beyond counting all over the city. But ever and again during the night's expedition his ears, in some new quarter would pick out from the tumult of the ways the peculiar hooting of the organ of Boss Ostrog, 'Galloop, Galloop!' or the shrill 'Yahaha, Yaha, Yap! – Hear a live paper yelp!' of its chief rival.

Repeated, too, everywhere, were such *crèches* as the one he now entered. It was reached by a lift, and by a glass bridge that flung across the dining hall and traversed the ways at a slight upward angle. To enter the first section of the place necessitated the use of his solvent signature under Asano's direction. They were immediately attended to by a man in a violet robe and gold clasp, the insignia of practising medical men. He perceived from this man's manner that his identity was known, and proceeded to ask questions on the strange arrangements of the place without reserve.

On either side of the passage, which was silent and padded, as if to deaden the footfall, were narrow little doors, their size and arrangement suggestive of the cells of a Victorian prison. But the upper portion of each door was of the same greenish transparent stuff that had enclosed him at his awakening, and within, dimly seen, lay, in every case, a very young baby in a little nest of wadding. Elaborate apparatus watched the atmosphere and rang a bell far away in the central office at the slightest departure from the optimum of temperature and moisture. A system of such *crèches* had almost entirely replaced the hazardous adventures of the old-world nursing. The attendant presently called Graham's attention to the wet nurses, a vista of mechanical figures, with arms, shoulders and breasts of astonishingly realistic modelling, articulation, and texture, but mere brass tripods below, and having in the place of features a flat disc bearing advertisements likely to be of interest to mothers.

Of all the strange things that Graham came upon that night, none jarred more upon his habits of thought than this place. The spectacle of the little pink creatures, their feeble limbs swaying uncertainly in vague first movements, left alone, without embrace or endearment, was wholly repugnant to him. The attendant doctor was of a different opinion. His statistical evidence showed beyond dispute that in the Victorian times the most dangerous passage of life was the arms of the mother, that there human mortality had ever been most terrible. On the other hand this *crèche* company, the International Crèche Syndicate, lost not one-half per cent of the million babies or so that formed its peculiar care. But Graham's prejudice was too strong even for those figures.

Along one of the many passages of the place they presently came upon a young couple in the usual blue canvas peering through the transparency and laughing hysterically at the bald head of their first-born. Graham's face must have showed his estimate of them, for their merriment ceased and they looked abashed. But this little incident accentuated his sudden realisation of the gulf between his habits of thought and the ways of the new age. He passed on to the crawling rooms and the Kindergarten, perplexed and distressed. He found the endless long playrooms were empty! the latter-day children at least still spent their nights in sleep. As they went through these, the little officer pointed out the nature of the toys, developments of those devised by that inspired sentimentalist Froebel. There were nurses here, but much was done by machines that sang and danced and dandled.

Graham was still not clear upon many points. 'But so many orphans,' he said perplexed, reverting to a first misconception, and learnt again that they were not orphans.

So soon as they had left the *crèche* he began to speak of the horror the babies in their incubating cases had caused him. 'Is motherhood gone?' he said. 'Was it a cant? Surely it was an instinct. This seems so unnatural – abominable almost.'

'Along here we shall come to the dancing place,' said Asano by way of reply. 'It is sure to be crowded. In spite of all the political unrest it will be crowded. The women take no great interest in politics – except a few here and there. You will see the mothers – most young women in London are mothers. In that class it is considered a creditable thing to have one child – a proof of animation. Few middle class people have more than one. With the Labour Company it is different. As for motherhood! They still take an immense pride in the children. They come here to look at them quite often.'

'Then do you mean that the population of the world – ?'

'Is falling? Yes. Except among the people under the Labour Company. They are reckless – .'

The air was suddenly dancing with music, and down a way they approached obliquely, set with gorgeous pillars as it seemed of clear amethyst, flowed a concourse of gay people and a tumult of merry cries and laughter. He saw curled heads, wreathed brows, and a happy intricate flutter of gamboge pass triumphant across the picture.

'You will see,' said Asano with a faint smile. 'The world has changed. In a moment you will see the mothers of the new age. Come this way. We shall see those yonder again very soon.'

They ascended a certain height in a swift lift, and changed to a slower one. As they went on the music grew upon them, until it was near and full and splendid, and, moving with its glorious intricacies they could distinguish the beat of innumerable dancing feet. They made a payment at a turnstile, and emerged upon the wide gallery that overlooked the dancing place, and upon the full enchantment of sound and sight.

'Here,' said Asano, 'are the fathers and mothers of the little ones you saw.'

The hall was not so richly decorated as that of the Atlas, but saving that, it was, for its size, the most splendid Graham had seen. The beautiful white limbed figures that supported the galleries reminded him once more of the restored magnificence of sculpture; they seemed to writhe in engaging attitudes, their faces laughed. The source of the music that filled the place was hidden, and the whole vast shining floor was thick with dancing couples. 'Look at them,' said the little officer, 'see how much they show of motherhood.'

The gallery they stood upon ran along the upper edge of a huge screen that cut the dancing hall on one side from a sort of outer hall that showed through broad arches the incessant onward rush of the city ways. In this outer hall was a great crowd of less brilliantly dressed people, as numerous almost as those who danced within, the great majority wearing the blue uniform of the Labour Company that was now so familiar to Graham. Too poor to pass the turnstiles to the festival, they were yet unable to keep away from the sound of its seductions. Some of them even had cleared spaces, and were dancing also, fluttering their rags in the air. Some shouted as they danced, jests and odd allusions Graham did not understand. Once someone began whistling the refrain of the revolutionary song, but it seemed as though that beginning was promptly suppressed. The corner was dark and Graham could not see. He turned to the hall again. Above the caryatidae were marble busts of men whom that age esteemed great moral emancipators and pioneers; for the most part their names were strange to Graham, though he recognised Grant Allen, Le Gallienne, Nietzsche, Shelley and Goodwin. Great black festoons and eloquent sentiments reinforced the huge inscription that partially defaced the upper end of the dancing place, and asserted that 'The Festival of the Awakening' was in progress.

'Myriads are taking holiday or staying from work because of that, quite apart from the labourers who refuse to go back,' said Asano. 'These people are always ready for holidays.'

Graham walked to the parapet and stood leaning over, looking down at the dancers. Save for two or three remote whispering couples, who had stolen apart, he and his guide had the gallery to themselves. A warm breath of scent and vitality came up to him. Both men and women below were lightly clad, bare-armed, open-necked, as the universal warmth of the city permitted. The hair of the men was often a mass of effeminate curls, their chins were always shaven, and many of them had flushed or coloured cheeks. Many of the women were very pretty, and all were dessed with elaborate coquetry. As they swept by beneath, he saw ecstatic faces with eyes half closed in pleasure.

'What sort of people are these?' he asked abruptly.

'Workers – prosperous workers. What you would have called the middle class. Independent tradesmen with little separate businesses have vanished long ago, but there are store servers, managers, engineers of a hundred sorts. Tonight is a holiday of course, and every dancing place in the city will be crowded, and every place of worship.'

'But – the women?'

'The same. There's a thousand forms of work for women now. But you had the beginning of the independent working-woman in your days. Most women are independent now. Most of these are married more or less – there are a number of methods of contract – and that gives them more money, and enables them to enjoy themselves.'

'I see,' said Graham looking at the flushed faces, the flash and swirl of movement, and still thinking of that nightmare of pink helpless limbs. 'And these are – mothers.'

'Most of them.'

'The more I see of these things the more complex I find your problems. This, for instance, is a surprise. That news from Paris was a surprise.'

In a little while he spoke again:

'These are mothers. Presently, I suppose, I shall get into the modern way of seeing things. I have old habits of mind clinging about me – habits based, I suppose, on needs that are over and done with. Of course, in our time, a woman was supposed not only to bear children, but to cherish them, to devote herself to them, to educate them – all the essentials of moral and mental education a child owed its mother. Or went without. Quite a number, I admit, went without. Nowadays, clearly, there is no more need for such care than if they were butterflies. I see that! Only there was an ideal – that figure of a grave, patient woman, silently and serenely mistress of a home, mother and maker of men – to love her was a sort of worship –'

He stopped and repeated, 'A sort of worship.'

'Ideals change,' said the little man, 'as needs change.'

Graham awoke from an instant reverie and Asano repeated his words. Graham's mind returned to the thing at hand.

'Of course I see the perfect reasonableness of this. Restraint, sober-ness, the matured thought, the unselfish act, they are necessities of the barbarous state, the life of dangers. Dourness is man's tribute to unconquered nature. But man has conquered nature now for all practical purposes – his political affairs are managed by Bosses with a black police – and life is joyous.'

He looked at the dancers again. 'Joyous,' he said.

'There are weary moments,' said the little officer, reflectively.

'They all look young. Down there I should be visibly the oldest man. And in my own time I should have passed as middle-aged.'

'They are young. There are few old people in this class in the work cities.'

'How is that?'

'Old people's lives are not so pleasant as they used to be, unless they are rich to hire lovers and helpers. And we have an institution called Euthanasy.'

'Ah! that Euthanasy!' said Graham. 'The easy death?'

'The easy death. It is the last pleasure. The Euthanasy Company does it well. People will pay the sum – it is a costly thing – long beforehand, go off to some pleasure city and return impoverished and weary, very weary.'

'There is a lot left for me to understand,' said Graham after a pause. 'Yet I see the logic of it all. Our array of angry virtues and sour restraints was the consequence of danger and insecurity. The Stoic, the Puritan, even in my time, were vanishing types. In the old days man was armed against Pain, now he is eager for Pleasure. There lies the difference. Civilisation has driven pain and danger so far off – for well-to-do-people. And only well-to-do people matter now. I have been asleep two hundred years.'

For a minute they leant on the balustrading, following the intricate evolution of the dance. Indeed the scene was very beautiful.

'Before God,' said Graham, suddenly, 'I would rather be a wounded sentinel freezing in the snow than one of these painted fools!'

'In the snow,' said Asano, 'one might think differently.'

'I am uncivilised,' said Graham, not heeding him. 'That is the trouble. I am primitive – Palaeolithic. *Their* fountain of rage and fear and anger is sealed and closed, the habits of a lifetime make them cheerful and easy and delightful. You must bear with my nineteenth-century shocks and disgusts. These people, you say, are skilled workers and so forth. And while these dance, men are fighting – men are dying in Paris to keep the world – that they may dance.'

Asano smiled faintly. 'For that matter, men are dying in London,' he said.

There was a moment's silence.

'Where do these sleep?' asked Graham.

'Above and below – an intricate warren.'

'And where do they work? This is – the domestic life.'

'You will see little work to-night. Half the workers are out or under arms. Half these people are keeping holiday. But we will go to the work places if you wish it.'

For a time Graham watched the dancers, then suddenly turned away. 'I want to see the workers. I have seen enough of these,' he said.

Asano led the way along the gallery across the dancing hall. Presently they came to a transverse passage that brought a breath of fresher, colder air.

Asano glanced at this passage as they went past, stopped, went back to it, and turned to Graham with a smile. 'Here, Sire,' he said, 'is something – will be familiar to you at least – and yet – . But I will not tell you. Come!'

He led the way along a closed passage that presently became cold. The reverberation of their feet told that this passage was a bridge. They came into a circular gallery that was glazed in from the outer weather, and so reached a circular chamber which seemed familiar, though Graham could not recall distinctly when he had entered it before. In this was a ladder – the first ladder he had seen since his awakening – up which they went, and came into a high dark, cold place in which was another almost vertical ladder. This they ascended, Graham still perplexed.

But at the top he understood, and recognised the metallic bars to which he clung. He was in the cage under the ball of St Paul's. The dome rose but a little way above the general contour of the city, into the still twilight, and sloped away, shining greasily under a few distant lights, into a circumambient ditch of darkness.

Out between the bars he looked upon the wind clear nothern sky and saw the starry constellations all unchanged. Capella hung in the west, Vega was rising, and the seven glittering points of the Great Bear swept overhead in their stately circle about the Pole.

He saw these stars in a clear gap of sky. To the east and south the great circular shapes of complaining wind-wheels blotted out the heavens, so that the glare about the Council House was hidden. To the south-west hung Orion, showing like a pallid ghost through a tracery of iron-work and interlacing shapes above a dazzling coruscation of lights. A bellowing and siren screaming that came from the flying stages warned the world that one of the aeroplanes was ready to start. He remained for a space gazing towards the glaring stage. Then his eyes went back to the northward constellations.

For a long time he was silent. 'This,' he said at last, smiling in the shadow, 'seems the strangest thing of all. To stand in the dome of Saint Paul's and look once more upon these familiar, silent stars!'

Thence Graham was taken by Asano along devious ways to the great gambling and business quarters where the bulk of the fortunes in the city were lost and made. It impressed him as a well-nigh interminable series of very high halls, surrounded by tiers upon tiers of galleries into which opened thousands of offices, and traversed by a complicated multitude of bridges, footways, aerial motor rails, and trapeze and cable leaps. And here more than anywhere the note of vehement vitality, of uncontrollable, hasty activity, rose high. Everywhere was violent advertisement, until his brain swam at the tumult of light and colour. And

Babble Machines of a peculiarly rancid tone were abundant and filled the air with strenuous squealing and an idiotic slang. 'Skin your eyes and slide,' 'Gewhoop, Bonanza,' 'Gollipers come and hark!'

The place seemed to him to be dense with people either profoundly agitated or swelling with obscure cunning, yet he learnt that the place was comparatively empty, that the great political convulsion of the last few days had reduced transactions to an unprecedented minimum. In one huge place were long avenues of roulette tables, each with an excited, undignified crowd about it; in another a yelping Babel of white-faced women and red-necked leathery-lunged men bought and sold the wares of an absolutely fictitious business undertaking which, every five minutes, paid a dividend of ten per cent and cancelled a certain proportion of its shares by means of a lottery wheel.

These business activities were prosecuted with an energy that readily passed into violence, and Graham approaching a dense crowd found at its centre a couple of prominent merchants in violent controversy with teeth and nails on some delicate point of business etiquette. Something still remained in life to be fought for. Further he had a shock at a vehement announcement in phonetic letters of scarlet flame, each twice the height of a man, that 'WE ASSURE THE PROPRAIET'R. WE ASSURE THE PROPRAIET'R.'

'Who's the proprietor?' he asked.

'You.'

'But what do they assure me?' he asked. 'What do they assure me?'

'Didn't you have assurance?'

Graham thought. 'Insurance?'

'Yes – Insurance. I remember that was the older word. They are insuring your life. Dozands of people are taking out policies, myriads of lions are being put on you. And further on other people are buying annuities. They do that on everybody who is at all prominent. Look there!'

A crowd of people surged and roared, and Graham saw a vast black screen suddenly illuminated in still larger letters of burning purple. 'Anuetes on the Propraiet'r – × 5 pr. G.' The people began to boo and shout at this, a number of hard breathing, wild-eyed men came running past, clawing with hooked fingers at the air. There was a furious crash about a little doorway.

Asano did a brief calculation. 'Seventeen per cent per annum is their annuity on you. They would not pay so much per cent if they could see you now, Sire. But they do not know. Your own annuities used to be a very safe investment, but now you are sheer gambling, of course. This is probably a desperate bid. I doubt if people will get their money.'

The crowd of would-be annuitants grew so thick about them that for some time they could move neither forward nor backward. Graham noticed what appeared to him to be a high proportion of women among

the speculators, and was reminded again of the economical independence of their sex. They seemed remarkably well able to take care of
themselves in the crowd, using their elbows with particular skill, as he
learnt to his cost. One curly-headed person caught in the pressure for a
space, looked steadfastly at him several times, almost as if she recognised him, and then, edging deliberately towards him, touched his hand
with her arm in a scarcely accidental manner, and made it plain by a
look as ancient as Chaldea that he had found favour in her eyes. And
then a lank, grey-bearded man, perspiring copiously in a noble passion
of self-help, blind to all earthly things save that glaring bait thrust
between them and a cataclysmal rush towards that alluring '× 5 pr. G.'

'I want to get out of this,' said Graham to Asano. 'This is not what I
came to see. Show me the workers. I want to see the people in blue.
These parasitic lunatics –'

He found himself wedged in a struggling mass of people and this
hopeful sentence went unfinished.

XXI

The Under Side

From the Business Quarter they presently passed by the running ways into a remote quarter of the city, where the bulk of the manufactures was done. On their way the platforms crossed the Thames twice, and passed in a broad viaduct across one of the great roads that entered the city from the North. In both cases his impression was swift and in both very vivid. The river was a broad wrinkled glitter of black sea water, overarched by buildings, and vanishing either way into a blackness starred with receding lights. A string of black barges passed seaward, manned by blue-clad men. The road was a long and very broad and high tunnel, along which big-wheeled machines drove noiselessly and swiftly. Here, too, the distinctive blue of the Labour Company was in abundance. The smoothness of the double tracks, the largeness and the lightness of the big pneumatic wheels in proportion to the vehicular body, struck Graham most vividly. One lank and very high carriage with longitudinal metallic rods hung with the dripping carcasses of many hundred sheep arrested his attention unduly. Abruptly the edge of the archway cut and blotted out the picture.

Presently they left the way and descended by a lift and traversed a passage that sloped downward, and so came to a descending lift again. The appearance of things changed. Even the pretence of architectural ornament disappeared, the lights diminished in number and size, the architecture became more and more massive in proportion to the spaces as the factory quarters were reached. And in the dusty biscuit-making place of the potters, among the felspar mills in the furnace rooms of the metal workers, among the incandescent lakes of crude Eadhamite, the blue canvas clothing was on man, woman and child.

Many of these great and dusty galleries were silent avenues of machinery, endless raked out ashen furnaces testified to the revolutionary disclocation, but wherever there was work it was being done by slow-moving workers in blue canvas. The only people not in blue canvas were the overlookers of the work-places and the orange-clad Labour Police. And fresh from the flushed faces of the dancing halls, the voluntary vigours of the business quarter, Graham could note the pinched faces, the feeble muscles, and weary eyes of many of the latter-day workers. Such as he saw at work were noticeably inferior in physique to the few gaily dressed managers and fore-women who were directing their labours. The burly labourers of the old Victorian times had followed the dray horse and all such living force producers, to extinction; the place of his costly muscles was taken by some dexterous machine. The latter-day labourer, male as well as female, was essentially a machine-minder and feeder, a servant and attendant, or an artist under direction.

The women, in comparison with those Graham remembered, were as a class distinctly plain and flat-chested. Two hundred years of emancipation from the moral restraints of Puritanical religion, two hundred years of city life, had done their work in eliminating the strain of feminine beauty and vigour from the blue canvas myriads. To be brilliant physically or mentally, to be in any way attractive or exceptional, had been and was still a certain way of emancipation to the drudge, a line of escape to the Pleasure City and its splendours and delights, and at last to the Euthanasy and peace. To be steadfast against such inducements was scarcely to be expected of meanly-nourished souls. In the young cities of Graham's former life, the newly aggregated labouring mass had been a diverse multitude, still stirred by the tradition of personal honour and a high morality; now it was differentiating into a distinct class, with a moral and physical difference of its own – even with a dialect of its own.

They penetrated downward, ever downward, towards the working places. Presently they passed underneath one of the streets of the moving ways, and saw its platforms running on their rails overhead, and chinks of white lights between the transverse slits. The factories that were not working were sparsely lighted; to Graham they and their shrouded aisles of giant machines seemed plunged in gloom, and even where work was going on the illumination was far less brilliant than upon the public ways.

Beyond the blazing lakes of Eadhamite he came to the warren of the jewellers, and, with some difficulty and by using his signature, obtained admission to these galleries. They were high and dark, and rather cold. In the first a few men were making ornaments of gold filigree, each man at a litte bench by himself, and with a little shaded light. The long vista of light patches, with the nimble fingers brightly lit and moving among the gleaming yellow coils, and the intent face like the face of a ghost, in each shadow, had the oddest effect.

The work was beautifully executed, but without any strength of modelling or drawing, for the most part intricate grotesques or the ringing of the changes on a geometrical *motif*. These workers wore a peculiar white uniform without pockets or sleeves. They assumed this on coming to work, but at night they were stripped and examined before they left the premises of the Company. In spite of every precaution, the Labour policeman told them in a depressed tone, the Company was not infrequently robbed.

Beyond was a gallery of women busied in cutting and setting slabs of artificial ruby, and next these were men and women busied together upon the slabs of copper net that formed the basis of *cloisonné* tiles. Many of these workers had lips and nostrils a livid white, due to a disease caused by a peculiar purple enamel that chanced to be much in fashion. Asano apologised to Graham for the offence of their faces, but excused himself on the score of the convenience of this route. 'This is what I wanted to see,' said Graham; 'this is what I wanted to see,' trying to avoid a start at a particularly striking disfigurement that suddenly stared him in the face.

'She might have done better with herself than that,' said Asano.

Graham made some indignant comments.

'But, Sire, we simply could not stand that stuff without the purple,' said Asano. 'In your days people could stand such crudities, they were nearer the barbaric by two hundred years.'

They continued along one of the lower galleries of this *cloisonné* factory, and came to a little bridge that spanned a vault. Looking over the parapet, Graham saw that beneath was a wharf under yet more tremendous archings than any he had seen. Three barges, smothered in floury dust, were being unloaded of their cargoes of powdered felspar by a multitude of coughing men, each guiding a little truck; the dust filled the place with a choking mist, and turned the electric glare yellow. The vague shadows of these workers gesticulated about their feet, and rushed to and fro against a long stretch of white-washed wall. Every now and then one would stop to cough.

A shadowy, huge mass of masonry rising out of the inky water, brought to Graham's mind the thought of the multitude of ways and galleries and lifts, that rose floor above floor overhead between him and the sky. The men worked in silence under the supervision of two of the Labour Police; their feet made a hollow thunder on the planks along which they went to and fro. And as he looked at this scene, some hidden voice in the darkness began to sing.

'Stop that!' shouted one of the policemen, but the order was disobeyed, and first one and then all the white-stained men who were working there had taken up the beating refrain, singing it defiantly, the Song of the Revolt. The feet upon the planks thundered now to the rhythm of the song, tramp, tramp, tramp. The policeman who had shouted glanced at his fellow, and Graham saw him shrug his shoulders. He made no further effort to stop the singing.

And so they went through these factories and places of toil, seeing many painful and grim things. But why should the gentle reader be depressed? Surely to a refined nature our present world is distressing enough without bothering ourselves about these miseries to come. We shall not suffer anyhow. Our children may, but what is that to us? That walk left on Graham's mind a maze of memories, fluctuating pictures of swathed halls, and crowded vaults seen through clouds of dust, of intricate machines, the racing threads of looms, the heavy beat of stamping machinery, the roar and rattle of belt and armature, of ill-lit subterranean aisles of sleeping places, illimitable vistas of pin-point lights. And here the smell of tanning, and here the reek of a brewery and here, unprecedented reeks. And everywhere were pillars and cross archings of such a massiveness as Graham had never before seen, thick Titans of greasy, shining brickwork crushed beneath the vast weight of that complex city world, even as these anaemic millions were crushed by its complexity. And everywhere were pale features, lean limbs, disfigurement and degradation.

Once and again, and again a third time, Graham heard the song of the revolt during his long, unpleasant research in these places, and once he saw a confused struggle down a passage, and learnt that a number of these serfs had seized their bread before their work was done. Graham was ascending towards the ways again when he saw a number of blue-clad children running down a transverse passage, and presently perceived the reason of their panic in a company of the Labour Police armed with clubs, trotting towards some unknown disturbance. And then came a remote disorder. But for the most part this remnant that worked, worked hopelessly. All the spirit that was left in fallen humanity was above in the streets that night, calling for the Master, and valiantly and noisily keeping its arms.

They emerged from these wandering and stood blinking in the bright light of the middle passage of the platforms again. They became aware of the remote hooting and yelping of the machines of one of the General Intelligence Offices, and suddenly came men running, and along the platforms and about the ways everywhere was a shouting and crying. Then a woman with a face of mute white terror, and another who gasped and shrieked as she ran.

'What has happened now?' said Graham, puzzled, for he could not understand their thick speech. Then he heard it in English and perceived that the thing that everyone was shouting, that men yelled to one another, that women took up screaming, that was passing like the first breeze of a thunderstorm, chill and sudden through the city, was this: 'Ostrog has ordered the Black Police to London. The Black Police are coming from South Africa. . . . The Black Police. The Black Police.'

Asano's face was white and astonished; he hesitated, looked at Graham's face, and told him the thing he already knew. 'But how can they know?' asked Asano.

Graham heard something shouting. 'Stop all work. Stop all work,' and a swarthy hunchback, ridiculously gay in green and gold, came leaping down the platforms toward him, bawling again and again in good English, 'This is Ostrog's doing, Ostrog, the Knave! The Master is betrayed.' His voice was hoarse and a thin foam dropped from his ugly shouting mouth. He yelled an unspeakable horror that the Black Police had done in Paris, and so passed shrieking, 'Ostrog the Knave!'

For a moment Graham stood still, for it had come upon him again that these things were a dream. He looked up at the great cliff of buildings on either side, vanishing into blue haze at last above the lights, and down to the roaring tiers of platforms, and the shouting, running people who were gesticulating past. 'The Master is betrayed!' they cried. 'The Master is betrayed!'

Suddenly the situation shaped itself in his mind real and urgent. His heart began to beat fast and strong.

'It has come,' he said. 'I might have known. The hour has come.'

He thought swiftly. 'What am I to do?'

'Go back to the Council House,' said Asano.

'Why should I not appeal – ? The people are here.'

'You will lose time. They will doubt if it is you. But they will mass about the Council House. There you will find their leaders. Your strength is there – with them.'

'Suppose this is only a rumour?'

'It sounds true,' said Asano.

'Let us have the facts,' said Graham.

Asano shrugged his shoulders. 'We had better get towards the Council House,' he cried. 'That is where they will swarm. Even now the ruins may be impassable.'

Graham regarded him doubtfully and followed him.

They went up the stepped platforms to the swiftest one, and there Asano accosted a labourer. The answers to his questions were in the thick, vulgar speech.

'What did he say?' asked Graham.

'He knows little, but he told me that the Black Police would have arrived here before the people knew – had not someone in the Wind-Vane Offices learnt. He said a girl.'

'A girl? Not – ?'

'He said a girl – he did not know who she was. Who came out from the Council House crying aloud, and told the men at work among the ruins.'

And then another thing was shouted, something that turned an aimless tumult into determinate movements, it came like a wind along the street. 'To your Wards, to your Wards. Every man get arms. Every man to his Ward!'

XXII

The Struggle in the Council House

As Asano and Graham hurried along to the ruins about the Council House, they saw everywhere the excitement of the people rising. 'To your Wards! To your Wards!' Everywhere men and women in blue were hurrying from unknown subterranean employments, up the staircases of the middle path; at one place Graham saw an arsenal of the revolutionary committee besieged by a crowd of shouting men, at another a couple of men in the hated yellow uniform of the Labour Police, pursued by a gathering crowd, fled precipitately along the swift way that went in the opposite direction.

The cries of 'To your Wards!' became at last a continuous shouting as they drew near the Government quarter. Many of the shouts were unintelligible. 'Ostrog has betrayed us,' one man bawled in a hoarse voice, again and again, dinning that refrain into Graham's ear until it haunted him. This person stayed close beside Graham and Asano on the swift way, shouting to the people who swarmed on the lower platforms as he rushed past them. His cry about Ostrog alternated with some incomprehensible orders. Presently he went leaping down and disappeared.

Graham's mind was filled with the din. His plans were vague and unformed. He had one picture of some commanding position from which he could address the multitudes, another of meeting Ostrog face to face. He was full of rage, of tense muscular excitement, his hands gripped, his lips were pressed together.

The way to the Council House across the ruins was impassable, but Asano met that difficulty and took Graham into the premises of the central post-office. The post-office was nominally at work, but the blue-clothed porters moved sluggishly or had stopped to stare through the arches of their galleries at the shouting men who were going by outside. 'Every man to his Ward! Every man to his Ward!' Here, by Asano's advice, Graham revealed his identity.

They crossed to the Council House by a cable cradle. Already in the brief interval since the capitulation of the Councillors a great change had been wrought in the appearance of the ruins. The spurting cascades of the ruptured sea water-mains had been captured and tamed, and huge temporary pipes ran overhead along a flimsy-looking fabric of girders. The sky was laced with restored cables and wires that served the Council House, and a mass of new fabric with cranes and other building machines going to and fro upon it, projected to the left of the white pile.

The moving ways that ran across this area had been restored, albeit for once running under the open sky. These were the ways that Graham had seen from the little balcony in the hour of his awakening, not nine days since, and the hall of his Trance had been on the further side, where now shapeless piles of smashed and shattered masonry were heaped together.

It was already high day and the sun was shining brightly. Out of their tall caverns of blue electric light came the swift ways crowded with multitudes of people, who poured off them and gathered ever denser over the wreckage and confusion of the ruins. The air was full of their shouting, and they were pressing and swaying towards the central building. For the most part that shouting mass consisted of shapeless swarms, but here and there Graham could see that a rude discipline struggled to establish itself. And every voice clamoured for order in the chaos. 'To your Wards! Every man to his Ward!'

The cable carried them into a hall which Graham recognised as the ante-chamber to the Hall of the Atlas, about the gallery of which he had walked days ago with Howard to show himself to the vanished Council, an hour from his awakening. Now the place was empty except for two cable attendants. These men seemed hugely astonished to recognise the Sleeper in the man who swung down from the cross seat.

'Where is Helen Wotton?' he demanded. 'Where is Helen Wotton?'

They did not know.

'Then where is Ostrog? I must see Ostrog forthwith. He has disobeyed me. I have come back to take things out of his hands.' Without waiting for Asano, he went straight across the place, ascended the steps at the further end, and pulling the curtain aside, found himself facing the perpetually labouring Titan.

The hall was empty. Its appearance had changed very greatly since his first sight of it. It had suffered serious injury in the violent struggle of the first outbreak. On the right hand side of the great figure the upper half of the wall had been torn away for nearly two hundred feet of its length, and a sheet of the same glassy film that had enclosed Graham at his awakening had been drawn across the gap. This deadened, but did not altogether exclude the roar of the people outside. 'Wards! Wards! Wards!' they seemed to be saying. Through it there were visible the beams and supports of metal scaffoldings that rose and fell according to the requirements of a great crowd of workmen. An idle building machine, with lank arms of red painted metal that caught the still plastic blocks of mineral paste and swung them neatly into position, stretched gauntly across this green tinted picture. On it were still a number of workmen staring at the crowd below. For a moment he stood regarding these things, and Asano overtook him.

'Ostrog,' said Asano, 'will be in the small offices beyond there.' The little man looked livid now and his eyes searched Graham's face.

They had scarcely advanced ten paces from the curtain before a little panel to the left of the Atlas rolled up, and Ostrog, accompanied by Lincoln and followed by two black and yellow clad negroes, appeared crossing the remote corner of the hall, towards a second panel that was raised and open. 'Ostrog,' shouted Graham, and at the sound of his voice the little party turned astonished.

Ostrog said something to Lincoln and advanced alone.

Graham was the first to speak. His voice was loud and dictatorial. 'What is this I hear?' he asked. 'Are you bringing negroes here – to keep the people down?'

'It is none too soon,' said Ostrog. 'They have been getting out of hand more and more, since the revolt. I under-estimated – '

'Do you mean that these infernal negroes are on the way?'

'On the way. As it is, you have seen the people – outside?'

'No wonder. But – after what was said. You have taken too much on yourself, Ostrog.'

Ostrog said nothing, but drew nearer.

'These negroes must not come to London,' said Graham. 'I am Master and they shall not come.'

Ostrog glanced at Lincoln, who at once came towards them with his two attendants close behind him. 'Why not?' asked Ostrog.

'White men must be mastered by white men. Besides – '

'The negroes are only an instrument.'

'But that is not the question. I am the Master. I mean to be the Master. And I tell you these negroes shall not come.'

'The people – '

'I believe in the people.'

'Because you are an anachronism. You are a man out of the Past – an accident. You are Owner perhaps of half the property in the world. But you are not Master. You do not know enough to be Master.'

He glanced at Lincoln again. 'I know now what you think – I can guess something of what you mean to do. Even now it is not too late to warn you. You dream of human equality – of a socialistic order – you have all those worn-out dreams of the nineteenth century fresh and vivid in your mind, and you would rule this age that you do not understand.'

'Listen!' said Graham. 'You can hear it – a sound like the sea. Not voices – but a voice. Do *you* altogether understand?'

'We taught them that,' said Ostrog.

'Perhaps. Can you teach them to forget it? But enough of this! These negroes must not come.'

There was a pause and Ostrog looked him in the eyes.

'They will,' he said.

'I forbid it,' said Graham.

'They have started.'

'I will not have it.'

'No,' said Ostrog. 'Sorry as I am to follow the method of the Council – . For your own good – you must not side with – Disorder. And now that you are here – . It was kind of you to come here.'

Lincoln laid his hand on Graham's shoulder. Abruptly Graham realised the enormity of his blunder in coming to the Council House. He turned towards the curtains that separated the hall from the ante-chamber. The clutching hand of Asano intervened. In another moment Lincoln had grasped Graham's cloak.

He turned and struck at Lincoln's face, and incontinently a negro had him by the collar and arm. He wrenched himself away, his sleeve tore noisily, and he stumbled back, to be tripped by the other attendant. Then he struck the ground heavily and he was staring at the distant ceiling of the hall.

He shouted, rolled over, struggling fiercely, clutched an attendant's leg and threw him headlong, and struggled to his feet.

Lincoln appeared before him, went down heavily again with a blow under the point of the jaw and lay still. Graham made two strides, stumbled. And then Ostrog's arm was round his neck, he was pulled over backward, fell heavily, and his arms were pinned to the ground. After a few violent efforts he ceased to struggle and lay staring at Ostrog's heaving throat.

'You – are – a prisoner,' panted Ostrog, exulting. 'You – were rather a fool – to come back.'

Graham turned his head about and perceived through the irregular green window in the walls of the hall the men who had been working the building cranes gesticulating excitedly to the people below them. They had seen!

Ostrog followed his eyes and started. He shouted something to Lincoln, but Lincoln did not move. A bullet smashed among the mouldings above the Atlas. The two sheets of transparent matter that had been stretched across this gap were rent, the edges of the torn aperture darkened, curved, ran rapidly towards the framework, and in a moment the Council chamber stood open to the air. A chilly gust blew in by the gap, bringing with it a war of voices from the ruinous spaces without, an elvish babblement, 'Save the Master!' 'What are they doing to the Master?' 'The Master is betrayed!'

And then he realised that Ostrog's attention was distracted, that

Ostrog's grip had relaxed, and wrenching his arms free, he struggled to his knees. In another moment he had thrust Ostrog back, and he was on one foot, his hand gripping Ostrog's throat, and Ostrog's hands clutching the silk about his neck.

But now men were coming towards them from the dais – men whose intentions he misunderstood. He had a glimpse of someone running in the distance towards the curtains of the antechamber, and then Ostrog had slipped from him and these newcomers were upon him. To his infinite astonishment, they seized him. They obeyed the shouts of Ostrog.

He was lugged a dozen yards before he realised that they were not friends – that they were dragging him towards the open panel. When he saw this he pulled back, he tried to fling himself down, he shouted for help with all his strength. And this time there were answering cries.

The grip upon his neck relaxed, and behold! in the lower corner of the rent upon the wall, first one and then a number of little black figures appeared shouting and waving arms. They came leaping down from the gap into the light gallery that had led to the Silent Rooms. They ran along it, so near were they that Graham could see the weapons in their hands. Then Ostrog was shouting in his ear to the men who held him, and once more he was struggling with all his strength against their endeavours to thrust him towards the opening that yawned to receive him. 'They can't come down,' panted Ostrog. 'They daren't fire. It's all right.' 'We'll save him from them yet.'

For long minutes as it seemed to Graham that inglorious struggle continued. His clothes were rent in a dozen places, he was covered in dust, one hand had been trodden upon. He could hear the shouts of his supporters, and once he heard shots. He could feel his strength giving way, feel his efforts wild and aimless. But no help came, and surely, irresistibly, that black, yawning opening came nearer.

The pressure upon him relaxed and he struggled up. He saw Ostrog's grey head receding and perceived that he was no longer held. He turned about and came full into a man in black. One of the green weapons cracked close to him, a drift of pungent smoke came into his face, and a steel blade flashed. The huge chamber span about him.

He saw a man in pale blue stabbing one of the black and yellow attendants not three yards from his face. Then hands were upon him again.

He was being pulled in two directions now. It seemed as though people were shouting to him. He wanted to understand and could not. Someone was clutching about his thighs, he was being hoisted in spite of his vigorous efforts. He understood suddenly, he ceased to struggle. He was lifted up on men's shoulders and carried away from that devouring panel. Ten thousand throats were cheering.

He saw men in blue and black hurrying after the retreating Ostrogites and firing. Lifted up, he saw now across the whole expanse of the hall beneath the Atlas image, saw that he was being carried towards the raised platform in the centre of the place. The far end of the hall was already full of people running towards him. They were looking at him and cheering.

He became aware that a sort of body-guard surrounded him. Active men about him shouted vague orders. He saw close at hand the black moustached man in yellow who had been among those who had greeted him in the public theatre, shouting directions. The hall was already densely packed with swaying people, the little metal gallery sagged with a shouting load, the curtains at the end had been torn away, and the ante-chamber was revealed densely crowded. He could scarcely make the man near him hear for the tumult about them. 'Where has Ostrog gone?' he asked.

The man he questioned pointed over the heads towards the lower panels about the hall on the side opposite the gap. They stood open and armed men, blue clad with black sashes, were running through them and vanishing into the chambers and passages beyond. It seemed to Graham that a sound of firing drifted through the riot. He was carried in a staggering curve across the great hall towards an opening beneath the gap.

He perceived men working with a sort of rude discipline to keep the crowd off him, to make a space clear about him. He passed out of the hall, and saw a crude, new wall rising blankly before him topped by blue sky. He was swung down to his feet; someone gripped his arm and guided him. He found the man in yellow close at hand. They were taking him up a narrow stairway of brick, and close at hand rose the great red painted masses, the cranes and levers and the still engines of the big building machine.

He was at the top of the steps. He was hurried across a narrow railed footway, and suddenly with a vast shouting the amphitheatre of ruins opened again before him. 'The Master is with us! The Master! The Master!' The shout swept athwart the lake of faces like a wave, broke against the distant cliff of ruins, and came back in a welter of cries. 'The Master is on our side.'

Graham perceived that he was no longer encompassed by people, that he was standing upon a little temporary platform of white metal, part of a flimsy seeming scaffolding that laced about the great mass of the Council House. Over all the huge expanse of the ruins, swayed and eddied the shouting people; and here and there the black banners of the revolutionary societies ducked and swayed and formed rare nuclei of organisation in the chaos. Up the steep stairs of wall and scaffolding by which his rescuers had reached the opening in the Atlas Chamber, clung a solid crowd, and little energetic black figures clinging to pillars and projections were strenuous to induce these congested masses to stir.

Behind him, at a higher point on the scaffolding, a number of men struggled upwards with the flapping folds of a huge black standard. Through the yawning gap in the walls below him he could look down upon the packed attentive multitudes in the Hall of the Atlas. The distant flying stages to the south came out bright and vivid, brought nearer as it seemed by an unusual translucency of the air. A solitary aeropile beat up from the central stage as if to meet the coming aeroplanes.

'What had become of Ostrog?' asked Graham, and even as he spoke he saw that all eyes were turned from him towards the crest of the Council House building. He looked also in this direction of universal attention. For a moment he saw nothing but the jagged corner of a wall, hard and clear against the sky. Then in the shadow he perceived the interior of a room and recognised with a start the green and white decorations of his former prison. And coming quickly across this opened room and up to the very verge of the cliff of the ruins came a little white clad figure followed by two other smaller seeming figures in black and yellow. He heard the man beside him exclaim 'Ostrog,' and turned to ask a question. But he never did, because of the startled exclamation of another of those who were with him and a lank finger suddenly pointing. He looked, and behold the aeropile that had been rising from the flying stage when last he had looked in that direction, was driving towards them. The swift steady flight was still novel enough to hold his attention.

Nearer it came, growing rapidly larger and larger, until it had swept over the further edge of the ruins and into view of the dense multitudes below. It drooped across the space and rose and passed overhead, rising to clear the mass of the Council House, a filmy translucent shape with the solitary aeronaut peering down through its ribs. It vanished beyond the skyline of the ruins.

Graham transferred his attention to Ostrog. He was signalling with his hands, and his attendants busy breaking down the wall beside him. In another moment the aeropile came into view again, a little thing far away, coming round on a wide curve and going slower.

Then suddenly the man in yellow shouted: 'What are they doing? What are the people doing? Why is Ostrog left there? Why is he not captured? They will lift him – the aeropile will lift him! Ah!'

The exclamation was echoed by a shout from the ruins. The rattling sound of the green weapons drifted across the intervening gulf to Graham, and, looking down, he saw a number of black and yellow uniforms running along one of the galleries that lay open to the air below the promontory upon which Ostrog stood. They fired as they ran at men unseen, and then emerged a number of pale blue figures in pursuit. These minute fighting figures had the oddest effect; they seemed as they ran like little model soldiers in a toy. This queer appearance of a house cut open gave that struggle amidst furniture and passages a quality of unreality. It was perhaps two hundred yards away from him, and very nearly fifty above the heads in the ruins below. The black and yellow men ran into an open archway, and turned and fired a volley. One of the blue pursuers striding forward close to the edge, flung up his arms, staggered sideways, seemed to Graham's sense to hang over the edge for several seconds, and fell headlong down. Graham saw him strike a projecting corner, fly out, head over heels, and vanish behind the red arm of the building machine.

And then a shadow came between Graham and the sun. He looked up and the sky was clear, but he knew the aeropile had passed. Ostrog had vanished. The man in yellow thrust before him, zealous and perspiring, pointing and blatant.

'They are grounding!' cried the man in yellow. 'They are grounding. Tell the people to fire at him. Tell them to fire at him!'

Graham could not understand. He heard loud voices repeating these enigmatical orders.

Suddenly over the edge of the ruins he saw the prow of the aeropile come gliding and stop with a jerk. In a moment Graham understood that the thing had grounded in order that Ostrog might escape by it. He saw a blue haze climbing out of the gulf, perceived that the people below him were now firing up at the projecting stem.

A man beside him cheered hoarsely, and he saw that the blue rebels had gained the archway that had been contested by the men in black and yellow a moment before, and were running in a continual stream along the open passage.

And suddenly the aeropile slipped over the edge of the Council House and fell. It dropped, tilting at an angle of forty-five degrees, and dropping so steeply that it seemed to Graham, it seemed perhaps to most of those below, that it could not possibly rise again.

It fell so closely past him that he could see Ostrog clutching the guides of the seat, with his grey hair streaming; see the white-faced aeronaut wrenching over the lever that drove the engine along its guides. He heard the apprehensive vague cry of innumerable men below.

Graham clutched the railing before him and gasped. The second seemed an age. The lower van of the aeropile passed within an ace of touching the people, who yelled and screamed and trampled one another below.

And then it rose.

For a moment it looked as if it could not possibly clear the opposite cliff, and then that it could not possibly clear the wind-wheel that rotated beyond.

And behold! it was clear and soaring, still heeling sideways, upward, upward into the wind-swept sky.

The suspense of the moment gave place to a fury of exasperation as the swarming people realised that Ostrog had escaped them. With belated activity they renewed their fire, until the rattling wove into a roar, until the whole area became dim and blue and the air pungent with the thin smoke of their weapons.

Too late! The aeropile dwindled smaller and smaller, and curved about and swept gracefully downward to the flying stage from which it had so lately risen. Ostrog had escaped.

For a while a confused babblement arose from the ruins, and then the universal attention came back to Graham, perched high among the scaffolding. He saw the faces of the people turned towards him, heard their shouts at his rescue. From the throat of the ways came the song of the revolt spreading like a breeze across that swaying sea of men.

The little group of men about him shouted congratulations on his escape. The man in yellow was close to him, with a set face and shining eyes. And the song was rising, louder and louder; tramp, tramp, tramp, tramp.

Slowly the realisation came of the full meaning of these things to him, the perception of the swift change in his position. Ostrog, who had stood beside him whenever he had faced that shouting multitude before, was beyond there – the antagonist. There was no one to rule for him any longer. Even the people about him, the leaders and organisers of the multitude, looked to see what he would do, looked to him to act, awaited his orders. He was King indeed. His puppet reign was at an end.

He was very intent to do the thing that was expected of him. His nerves and muscles were quivering, his mind was perhaps a little confused, but he felt neither fear nor anger. His hand that had been trodden upon throbbed and was hot. He was a little nervous about his bearing. He knew he was not afraid, but he was anxious not to seem afraid. In his former life he had often been more excited in playing games of skill. He was desirous of immediate action, he knew he must not think too much in detail of the huge complexity of the struggle about him lest he should be paralysed by the sense of its intricacy. Over there those square blue shapes, the flying stages, meant Ostrog; against Ostrog he was fighting for the world.

XXIII

While the Aeroplanes Were Coming

For a time the Master of the Earth was not even master of his own mind. Even his will seemed a will not his own, his own acts surprised him and were but a part of the confusion of strange experiences that poured across his being. These things were definite, the aeroplanes were coming, Helen Wotton had warned the people of their coming, and he was Master of the Earth. Each of these facts seemed struggling for complete possession of his thoughts. They protruded from a background of swarming halls, elevated passages, rooms jammed with ward leaders in council, kinematograph and telephone rooms, and windows looking out on a seething sea of marching men. The man in yellow, and men whom he fancied were called Ward Leaders, were either propelling him forward or following him obediently; it was hard to tell. Perhaps they were doing a little of both. Perhaps some power unseen and unsuspected, propelled them all. He was aware that he was going to make a proclamation to the People of the Earth, aware of certain grandiose phrases floating in his mind as the thing he meant to say. Many little things happened, and then he found himself with the man in yellow entering a little room where this proclamation of his was to be made.

This room was grotesquely latter-day in its appointments. In the centre was a bright oval lit by shaded electric lights from above. The rest was in shadow, and the double finely fitting doors through which he came from the swarming Hall of the Atlas made the place very still. The dead thud of these as they closed behind him, the sudden cessation of the tumult in which he had been living for hours, the quivering circle of light, the whispers and quick noiseless movements of vaguely visible attendants in the shadows, had a strange effect upon Graham. The huge ears of a phonographic mechanism gaped in a battery for his words, the black eyes of great photographic cameras awaited his beginning, beyond metal rods and coils glittered dimly, and something whirled about with a droning hum. He walked into the centre of the light, and his shadow drew together black and sharp to a little blot at his feet.

The vague shape of the thing he meant to say was already in his mind. But this silence, this isolation, the sudden withdrawal from that contagious crowd, this silent audience of gaping, glaring machines had not been in his anticipation. All his supports seemed withdrawn together; he seemed to have dropped into this suddenly, suddenly to have discovered himself. In a moment he was changed. He found that he now feared to be inadequate, he feared to be theatrical, he feared the quality of his voice, the quality of his wit, astonished, he turned to the man in yellow with a propritiatory gesture. 'For a moment,' he said, 'I must wait. I did not think it would be like this. I must think of the thing I have to say.'

While he was still hesitating there came an agitated messenger with news that the foremost aeroplanes were passing over Arawan.

'Arawan?' he said. 'Where is that? But anyhow, they are coming. They will be here. When?'

'By twilight.'

'Great God! In only a few hours. What news of the flying stages?' he asked.

'The people of the south-west wards are ready.'

'Ready!'

He turned impatiently to the blank circles of the lenses again.

'I suppose it must be a sort of speech. Would to God I knew certainly the thing that should be said! Aeroplanes at Arawan! They must have started before the main fleet. And the people only ready! Surely . . .

'Oh! what does it matter whether I speak well or ill?' he said, and felt the light grow brighter.

He had framed some vague sentence of democratic sentiment when suddenly doubts overwhelmed him. His belief in his heroic quality and calling he found had altogether lost its assured conviction. The picture of a little strutting futility in a windy waste of incomprehensible destinies replaced it. Abruptly it was perfectly clear to him that this revolt against Ostrog was premature, foredoomed to failure, the impulse of passionate inadequacy against inevitable things. He thought of that swift flight of aeroplanes like the swoop of Fate towards him. He was astonished that he could have seen things in any other light. In that final emergency he debated, thrust debate resolutely aside, determined at all costs to go through with the thing he had undertaken. And he could find no word to begin. Even as he stood, awkward, hesitating, with an indiscrete apology for his inability trembling on his lips, came the noise of many people crying out, the running to and fro of feet. 'Wait,' cried someone, and a door opened. 'She is coming,' said the voices. Graham turned, and the watching lights waned.

Through the open doorway he saw a slight grey figure advancing across a spacious hall. His heart leapt. It was Helen Wotton. Behind and about her marched a riot of applause. The man in yellow came out of the nearer shadows into the circle of light.

'This is the girl who told us what Ostrog had done,' he said.

Her face was aflame, and the heavy coils of her black hair fell about her shoulders. The folds of the soft silk robe she wore streamed from her and floated in the rhythm of her advance. She drew nearer and nearer, and his heart was beating fast. All his doubts were gone. The shadow of the doorway fell athwart her face and she was near him. 'You have not betrayed us?' she cried. 'You are with us?'

'Where have you been?' said Graham.

'At the office of the south-west wards. Until ten minutes since I did not know you had returned. I went to the office of the south-west wards to find the Ward Leaders in order that they might tell the people.'

'I came back so soon as I heard – '

'I knew,' she cried, 'knew you would be with us. And it was I – it was I told them. They have risen. All the world is rising. The people have awakened. Thank God that I did not act in vain! You are Master still.'

'You told them,' he said slowly, and he saw that in spite of her steady eyes her lips trembled and her throat rose and fell.

'I told them. I knew of the order. I was here. I heard that the negroes were to come to London to guard you and to keep the people down – to keep you a prisoner. And I stopped it. I came out and told the people. And you are Master still.'

Graham glanced at the black lenses of the cameras, the vast listening ears, and back to her face. 'I am Master still,' he said slowly, and the swift rush of a fleet of aeroplanes passed across his thoughts.

'And you did this? You, who are the niece of Ostrog.'

'For you,' she cried. 'For you! That you for whom the world has waited should not be cheated of your power.'

Graham stood for a space, wordless, regarding her. His doubts and questionings had fled before her presence. He remembered the things that he had meant to say. He faced the cameras again and the light about him grew brighter. He turned again towards her.

'You have saved me,' he said; 'you have saved my power. And the battle is beginning. God knows what this night will see – but not dishonour.'

He paused. He addressed himself to the unseen multitudes who stared upon him through those grotesque black eyes. At first he spoke slowly.

'Men and women of the new age,' he said; 'You have arisen to do battle for the race! . . . There is no easy victory before us.'

He stopped to gather words. The thoughts that had been in his mind before she came returned, but transfigured, no longer touched with the shadow of a possible irrelevance. 'This night is a beginning,' he cried. 'This battle that is coming, this battle that rushes upon us tonight, is only a beginning. All your lives, it may be, you must fight. Take no thought though I am beaten, though I am utterly overthrown.'

He found the thing in his mind too vague for words. He paused momentarily, and broke into vague exhortations, and then a rush of speech came upon him. Much that he said was but humanitarian commonplace of a vanished age, but the conviction of his voice touched it to vitality. He stated the case of the old days to the people of the new age, to the woman at his side. 'I come out of the past to you,' he said, 'with the memory of an age that hoped. My age was an age of dreams – of beginnings, an age of noble hopes; throughout the world we had made an end of slavery; throughout the world we had spread the desire and anticipation that wars might cease, that all men and women might live nobly, in freedom and peace. . . . So we hoped in the days that are past. And what of those hopes? How is it with man after two hundred years?

'Great cities, vast powers, a collective greatness beyond our dreams. For that we did not work, and that has come. But how is it with the little lives that make up this greater life? How is it with the common lives? As it has ever been – sorrow and labour, lives cramped and unfulfilled, lives tempted by power, tempted by wealth, and gone to waste and folly. The old faiths have faded and changed, the new faith – . Is there a new faith?'

Things that he had long wished to believe, he found that he believed. He plunged at belief and seized it, and clung for a time at her level. He spoke gustily, in broken incomplete sentences, but with all his heart and strength, of this new faith within him. He spoke of the greatness of self-abnegation, of his belief in an immortal life of Humanity in which we live and move and have our being. His voice rose and fell, and the recording appliances hummed their hurried applause, dim attendants watched him out of the shadow. Through all those doubtful places his sense of that silent spectator beside him sustained his sincerity. For a few glorious moments he was carried away; he felt no doubt of his heroic quality, no doubt of his heroic words, he had it all straight and plain. His eloquence limped no longer. And at last he made an end to speaking. 'Here and now,' he cried, 'I make my will. All that is mine in the world I give to the people of the world. I give it to you, and myself I give to you. And as God wills, I will live for you, or I will die.'

He ended with a florid gesture and turned about. He found the light of his present exaltation reflected in the face of the girl. Their eyes met; her eyes were swimming with tears of enthusiasm. They seemed to be urged towards each other. They clasped hands and stood gripped, facing one another, in an eloquent silence. She whispered. 'I knew,' she whispered. 'I knew.' He could not speak, he crushed her hand in his. His mind was the theatre of gigantic passions.

The man in yellow was beside them. Neither had noted his coming. He was saying that the south-west wards were marching. 'I never expected it so soon,' he cried. 'They have done wonders. You must send them a word to help them on their way.'

Graham dropped Helen's hand and stared at him absent-mindedly. Then with a start he returned to his previous preoccupation about the flying stages.

'Yes,' he said. 'That is good, that is good.' He weighed a message. 'Tell them; – well done South West.'

He turned his eyes to Helen Wotton again. His face expressed his struggle between conflicting ideas. 'We must capture the flying stages,' he explained. 'Unless we can do that they will land negroes. At all costs we must prevent that.'

He felt even as he spoke that this was not what had been in his mind before the interruption. He saw a touch of surprise in her eyes. She seemed about to speak and a shrill bell drowned her voice.

It occurred to Graham that she expected him to lead these marching people, that that was the thing he had to do. He made the offer abruptly. He addressed the man in yellow, but he spoke to her. He saw her face respond. 'Here I am doing nothing,' he said.

'It is impossible,' protested the man in yellow. 'It is a fight in a warren. Your place is here.'

He explained elaborately. He motioned towards the room where Graham must wait, he insisted no other course was possible. 'We must know where you are,' he said. 'At any moment a crisis may arise needing your presence and decision.' The room was a luxurious little apartment with news machines and a broken mirror that had once been *en rapport* with the crow's nest specula. It seemed a matter of course to Graham that Helen should stop with him.

A picture had drifted through his mind of such a vast dramatic struggle as the masses in the ruins had suggested. But here was no spectacular battle-field such as he imagined. Instead was seclusion – and suspense. It was only as the afternoon wore on that he pieced together a truer picture of the fight that was raging, inaudibly and invisibly, within four miles of him, beneath the Roehampton stage. A strange and unprecedented contest it was, a battle that was a hundred thousand little battles, a battle in a sponge of ways and channels, fought out of sight of sky or sun under the electric glare, fought out in a vast confusion by multitudes untrained in arms, led chiefly by acclamation, multitudes dulled by mindless labour and enervated by the tradition of two hundred years of servile security against multitudes demoralised by lives of venial privilege and sensual indulgence. They had no artillery, no differentiation into this force or that; the only weapon on either side was the little green metal carbine, whose secret manufacture and sudden distribution in enormous quantities had been one of Ostrog's culminating moves against the Council. Few had had any experience with this weapon, many had never discharged one, many who carried it came unprovided with ammunition; never was wilder firing in the history of warfare. It was a battle of amateurs, a hideous experimental warfare, armed rioters fighting armed rioters, armed rioters swept forward by the words and fury of a song, by the tramping sympathy of their numbers, pouring in countless myriads towards the smaller ways, the disabled lifts, the galleries slippery with blood, the halls and passages choked with smoke, beneath the flying stages, to learn there when retreat was hopeless the ancient mysteries of warfare. And overhead save for a few sharpshooters upon the roof spaces and for a few bands and threads of vapour that multiplied and darkened towards the evening, the day was a clear serenity. Ostrog it seems had no bombs at command and in all the earlier phases of the battle the aeropiles played no part. Not the smallest cloud was there to break the empty brilliance of the sky. It seemed as though it held itself vacant until the aeroplanes should come.

Ever and again there was news of these, drawing nearer, from this Mediterranean port and then that, and presently from the south of France. But of the new guns that Ostrog had made and which were known to be in the city came no news in spite of Graham's urgency, nor any report of successes from the dense felt of fighting strands about the flying stages. Section after section of the Labour Societies reported itself assembled, reported itself marching, and vanished from knowledge into the labyrinth of that warfare. What was happening there? Even the busy ward leaders did not know. In spite of the opening and closing of doors, the hasty messengers, the ringing of bells and the perpetual clitter-clack of recording implements, Graham felt isolated, strangely inactive, inoperative.

Their isolation seemed at times the strangest, the most unexpected of all the things that had happened since his awakening. It had something of the quality of that inactivity that comes in dreams. A tumult, the stupendous realisation of a world struggle between Ostrog and himself, and then this confined quiet little room with its mouth-pieces and bells and broken mirror!

Now the door would be closed and they were alone together; they seemed sharply marked off then from all the unprecedented world storm that rushed together without, vividly aware of one another, only concerned with one another. Then the door would open again, messengers would enter, or a sharp bell would stab their quiet privacy, and it was like a window in a well built brightly lit house flung open suddenly to a hurricane. The dark hurry and tumult, the stress and vehemence of the battle rushed in and overwhelmed them. They were no longer persons but mere spectators, mere impressions of a tremendous convulsion. They became unreal even to themselves, miniatures of personality, indescribably small, and the two antagonistic realities, the only realities in being were first the city, that throbbed and roared yonder in a belated frenzy of defence and secondly the aeroplanes hurling inexorably towards them over the round shoulder of the world.

At first their mood had been one of exalted confidence, a great pride had possessed them, a pride in one another for the greatness of the issues they had challenged. At first he had walked the room eloquent with a transitory persuasion of his tremendous destiny. But slowly uneasy intimations of their coming defeat touched his spirit. There came a long period in which they were alone. He changed his theme, became egotistical, spoke of the wonder of his sleep, of the little life of his memories, remote yet minute and clear, like something seen through an inverted operaglass, and all the brief play of desires and errors that had made his former life. She said little, but the emotion in her face followed the tones in his voice, and it seemed to him he had at last a perfect understanding. He reverted from pure reminiscence to that sense of greatness she imposed upon him. 'And through it all, this destiny was before me,' he said; 'this vast inheritance of which I did not dream.'

Insensibly their heroic preoccupation with the revolutionary struggle passed to the question of their relationship. He began to question her. She told him of the days before his awakening, spoke with a brief vividness of the girlish dreams that had given a bias to her life, of the incredulous emotions his awakening had aroused. She told him too of a tragic circumstance of her girlhood that had darkened her life, quickened her sense of injustice and opened her heart prematurely to the wider sorrows of the world. For a little time, so far as he was concerned, the great war about them was but the vast ennobling background to these personal things.

In an instant these personal relations were submerged. There came messengers to tell that a great fleet of aeroplanes was rushing between the sky and Avignon. He went to the crystal dial in the corner and assured himself that the thing was so. He went to the chart room and consulted a map to measure the distances of Avignon, New Arawan, and London. He made swift calculations. He went to the room of the Ward Leaders to ask for news of the fight for the stages – and there was no one there. After a time he came back to her.

His face had changed. It had dawned upon him that the struggle was perhaps more than half over, that Ostrog was holding his own, that the arrival of the aeroplanes would mean a panic that might leave him helpless. A chance phrase in the message had given him a glimpse of the reality that came. Each of these soaring giants bore its thousand half savage negroes to the death grapple of the city. Suddenly his humanitarian enthusiasm showed flimsy. Only two of the Ward Leaders were in their room, when presently he repaired thither, the Hall of the Atlas seemed empty. He fancied a change in the bearing of the attendants in the outer rooms. A sombre disillusionment darkened his mind. She looked at him anxiously when he returned to her.

'No news,' he said with an assumed carelessness, in answer to her eyes.

Then he was moved to frankness. 'Or rather – bad news. We are losing. We are gaining no ground and the aeroplanes draw nearer and nearer.'

He walked the length of the room and turned.

'Unless we can capture those flying stages in the next hour – there will be horrible things. We shall be beaten.'

'No!' she said. 'We have justice – we have the people. We have God on our side.'

'Ostrog has discipline – he has plans. Do you know, out there just now I felt – . When I heard that these aeroplanes were a stage nearer. I felt as if I were fighting the machinery of fate.'

She made no answer for a while. 'We have done right,' she said at last.

He looked at her doubtfully. 'We have done what we could. But does his depend upon us? Is it not an older sin, a wider sin?'

'What do you mean?' she asked.

'These blacks are savages, ruled by force, used as force. And they have been under the rule of the whites two hundred years. Is it not a race quarrel? The race sinned – the race pays.'

'But these labourers, these poor people of London – !'

'Vicarious atonement. To stand wrong is to share the guilt.'

She looked keenly at him, astonished at the new aspect he presented.

Without came the shrill ringing of a bell, the sound of feet and the gabble of a phonographic message. The man in yellow appeared. 'Yes?' said Graham.

'They are at Vichy.'

'Where are the attendants who were in the great Hall of the Atlas?' asked Graham abruptly.

Presently the Babble Machine rang again. 'We may win yet,' said the man in yellow, going out to it. 'If only we can find where Ostrog has hidden his guns. Everything hangs on that now. Perhaps this – '

Graham followed him. But the only news was of the aeroplanes. They had reached Orleans.

Graham returned to Helen. 'No news,' he said. 'No news.'

'And we can do nothing?'

'Nothing.'

He paced impatiently. Suddenly the swift anger that was his nature swept upon him. 'Curse this complex world!' he cried, 'and all the inventions of men! That a man must die like a rat in a snare and never see his foe! Oh, for one blow! . . .'

He turned with an abrupt change in his manner. 'That's nonsense,' he said. 'I am a savage.'

He paced and stopped. 'After all London and Paris are only two cities. All the temperate zone has risen. What if London is doomed and Paris destroyed? These are but accidents.' Again came the mockery of news to call him to fresh inquiries. He returned with a graver face and sat down beside her.

'The end must be near,' he said. 'The people it seems have fought and died in tens of thousands, the ways about Roehampton must be like a smoked beehive. And they have died in vain. They are still only at the sub stage. The aeroplanes are near Paris. Even were a gleam of success to come now, there would be nothing to do, there would be no time to do anything before they were upon us. The guns that might have saved us are mislaid. Think of the disorder of things! Think of this foolish tumult, that cannot even find its weapons! Oh, for one aeropile – just one! For the want of that I am beaten. Humanity is beaten and our cause is lost! My kingship, my headlong foolish kingship will not last a night. And I have egged on the people to fight – .'

'They would have fought anyhow.'

'I doubt it. I have come among them – '

'No,' she cried, 'not that. If defeat comes – if you die – . But even that cannot be, it cannot be, after all these years.'

'Ah! We have meant well. But – do you indeed believe – ?'

'If they defeat you,' she cried, 'you have spoken. Your word has gone like a great wind through the world, fanning liberty into a flame. What if the flame sputters a little! Nothing can change the spoken word. Your message will have gone forth. . . .'

'To what end? It may be. It may be. You know I said, when you told me of these things – dear God! but that was scarcely a score of hours ago! – I said that I had not your faith. Well – at any rate there is nothing to do now. . . .'

'You have not my faith! Do you mean – ? You are *sorry*?'

'No,' he said hurriedly, 'no! Before God – *no*!' His voice changed. '*But* – . I think – I have been indiscreet. I knew little – I grasped too hastily. . . .'

He paused. He was ashamed of this avowal. 'There is one thing that makes up for all. I have known you. Across this gulf of time I have come to you. The rest is done. With you, too, it has been something more – or something less – '

He paused with his face searching hers, and without clamoured the unheeded message that the aeroplanes were rising into the sky of Amiens.

She put her hand to her throat, and her lips were white. She stared before her as if she saw some horrible possibility. Suddenly her features changed. 'Oh, but I have been honest!' she cried, and then, '*Have* I been honest? I loved the world and freedom, I hated cruelty and oppression. Surely it was that.'

'Yes,' he said, 'yes. And we have done what it lay in us to do. We have given our message, our message! We have started Armageddon!

But now – . Now that we have, it may be our last hour, together, now that all these greater things are done. . . .'

He stopped. She sat in silence. Her face was a white riddle.

For a moment they heeded nothing of a sudden stir outside, a running to and fro, and cries. Then Helen started to an attitude of tense attention. 'It is – ,' she cried and stood up, speechless, incredulous, triumphant. And Graham, too, heard. Metallic voices were shouting 'Victory!' Yes it was 'Victory!' He stood up also with the light of a desperate hope in his eyes.

Bursting through the curtains appeared the man in yellow, startled and dishevelled with excitement. 'Victory,' he cried, 'victory! The people are winning. Ostrog's people have collapsed.'

She rose. 'Victory?' And her voice was hoarse and faint.

'What do you mean?' asked Graham. 'Tell me! *What?*'

'We have driven them out of the under galleries at Norwood, Streatham is afire and burning wildly, and Roehampton is ours. *Ours!* – and we have taken the aeropile that lay thereon.'

For an instant Graham and Helen stood in silence, their hearts were beating fast, they looked at one another. For one last moment there gleamed in Graham his dream of empire, of kingship, with Helen by his side. It gleamed, and passed.

A shrill bell rang. An agitated grey-headed man appeared from the room of the Ward Leaders. 'It is all over,' he cried.

'What matters it now that we have Roehampton? The aeroplanes have been sighted at Boulogne!'

'The Channel!' said the man in yellow. He calculated swiftly. 'Half an hour.'

'They still have three of the flying stages,' said the old man.

'Those guns?' cried Graham.

'We cannot mount them – in half an hour.'

'Do you mean they are found?'

'Too late,' said the old man.

'If we could stop them another hour!' cried the man in yellow.

'Nothing can stop them now,' said the old man. 'They have near a hundred aeroplanes in the first fleet.'

'Another hour?' asked Graham.

'To be so near!' said the Ward Leader. 'Now that we have found those guns. To be so near – . If once we could get them out upon the roof spaces.'

'How long would that take?' asked Graham suddenly.

'An hour – certainly.'

'Too late,' cried the Ward Leader, 'too late.'

'*Is* it too late?' said Graham. 'Even now – . An hour!'

He had suddenly perceived a possibility. He tried to speak calmly, but his face was white. 'There is one chance. You said there was an aeropile – ?'

'On the Roehampton stage, Sire.'

'Smashed?'

'No. It is lying crossways to the carrier. It might be got upon the guides – easily. But there is no aeronaut – .'

Graham glanced at the two men and then at Helen. He spoke after a long pause. '*We* have no aeronauts?'

'None.'

'The aeroplanes are clumsy,' he said thoughtfully, 'compared with the aeropiles.'

He turned suddenly to Helen. His decision was made. 'I must do it.'

'Do what?'

'Go to this flying stage – to this aeropile.'

'What do you mean?'

'I am an aeronaut. After all – . Those days for which you reproached me were not altogether wasted.'

He turned to the old man in yellow. 'Tell them to put the aeropile upon the guides.'

The man in yellow hesitated.

'What do you mean to do?' cried Helen.

'This aeropile – it is a chance – .'

'You don't mean – ?'

'To fight – yes. To fight in the air. I have thought before – . An aeroplane is a clumsy thing. A resolute man – !'

'But – never since flying began – ' cried the man in yellow.

'There has been no need. But now the time has come. Tell them now – send my message – to put it upon the guides.'

The old man dumbly interrogated the man in yellow, nodded, and hurried out.

Helen made a step towards Graham. Her face was white. 'But – How can one fight? You will be killed.'

'Perhaps. Yet, not to do it – or let someone else attempt it – .'

He stopped, he could speak no more, he swept the alternative aside by a gesture, and they stood looking at one another.

'You are right,' she said at last in a low tone. 'You are right. If it can be done. . . . You must go.'

He moved a step towards her, and she stepped back, her white face struggled against him and resisted him. 'No,' she gasped. 'I cannot bear – . Go now.'

He extended his hands stupidly. She clenched her fists. 'Go now,' she cried. 'Go now.'

He hesitated and understood. He threw his hands up in a queer half-theatrical gesture. He had no word to say. He turned from her.

The man in yellow moved towards the door with clumsy belated tact.

But Graham stepped past him. He went striding through the room where the Ward Leader bawled at a telephone directing that the aeropile should be put upon the guides.

The man in yellow glanced at Helen's still figure, hesitated and hurried after him. Graham did not once look back, he did not speak until the curtain of the antechamber of the great Hall fell behind him. Then he turned his head with curt swift directions upon his bloodless lips.

XXIV

The Coming of the Aeroplanes

Two men in pale blue were lying in the irregular line that stretched along the edge of the captured Roehampton stage from end to end, grasping their carbines and peering into the shadows of the stage called Wimbledon Park. Now and then they spoke to one another. They spoke the mutilated English of their class and period. The fire of the Ostrogites had dwindled and ceased, and few of the enemy had been seen for some time. But the echoes of the fight that was going on now far below in the lower galleries of that stage, came every now and then between the staccato of shots from the popular side. One of these men was describing to the other how he had seen a man down below there dodge behind a girder, and had aimed at a guess and hit him cleanly as he dodged too far. 'He's down there still,' said the marksman. 'See that little patch. Yes. Between those bars.' A few yards behind them lay a dead stranger, face upward to the sky, with the blue canvas of his jacket smouldering in a circle about the neat bullet hole on his chest. Close beside him a wounded man, with a leg swathed about, sat with an expressionless face and watched the progress of that burning. Gigantic behind them, athwart the carrier lay the captured aeropile.

'I can't see him *now*,' said the second man in a tone of provocation.

The marksman became foul-mouthed and high-voiced in his earnest endeavour to make things plain. And suddenly, interrupting him, came a noisy shouting from the substage.

'What's going on now,' he said, and raised himself on one arm to stare at the stairheads in the central groove of the stage. A number of blue figures were coming up these, and swarming across the stage to the aeropile.

'We don't want all these fools,' said his friend. 'They only crowd up and spoil shots. What are they after?'

'Ssh! – they're shouting something.'

The two men listened. The swarming new-comers had crowded densely about the aeropile. Three Ward Leaders, conspicuous by their black mantles and badges, clambered into the body and appeared above it. The rank and file flung themselves upon the vans, gripping hold of the edges, until the entire outline of the thing was manned, in some places three deep. One of the marksmen knelt up. 'They're putting it on the carrier – that's what they're after.'

He rose to his feet, his friends rose also. 'What's the good?' said his friend. 'We've got no aeronauts.'

'That's what they're doing anyhow.' He looked at his rifle, looked at the struggling crowd, and suddenly turning to the wounded man. 'Mind these, mate,' he said, handing his carbine and cartridge belt; and in a moment he was running towards the aeropile. For a quarter of an hour he was a perspiring Titan, lugging, thrusting, shouting and heeding shouts, and then the thing was done, and stood with a multitude of others cheering their own achievement. By this time he knew, what indeed everyone in the city knew, that the Master, raw learner though he was, intended to fly this machine himself, was coming even now to take control of it, would let no other man attempt it. 'He who takes the greatest danger, he who bears the heaviest burthen, that man is King,' so the Master was reported to have spoken. And even as this man cheered, and while the beads of sweat still chased one another from the disorder of his hair, he heard the thunder of a greater tumult, and in fitful snatches the beat and impulse of the revolutionary song. He saw through a gap in the people that a thick stream of heads still poured up the stairway. 'The Master is coming,' shouted voices, 'the Master is coming,' and the crowd about him grew denser and denser. He began to thrust himself towards the central groove. 'The Master is coming!' 'The Sleeper, the Master!' 'God and the Master!' roared the voices.

And suddenly quite close to him were the black uniforms of the revolutionary guard, and for the first and last time in his life he saw Graham, saw him quite nearly. A tall, dark man in a flowing black robe, with a white, resolute face and eyes fixed steadfastly before him; a man who for all little things about him had neither ears nor eyes nor thoughts. . . . For all his days that man remembered the passing of Graham's bloodless face. In a moment it had gone and he was fighting in the swaying crowd. A lad weeping with terror thrust against him, pressing towards the stairways, yelling 'Clear for the aeropile!' The bell that clears the flying stage became a loud unmelodious clanging.

With that clanging in his ears Graham drew near the aeropile, marched into the shadow of its tilting wing. He became aware that a number of people about him were offering to accompany him, and waved their offers aside. He wanted to think how one started the engine. The bell clanged faster and faster, and the feet of the retreating people roared faster and louder. The man in yellow was assisting him to mount through the ribs of the body. He clambered into the aeronaut's place, fixing himself very carefully and deliberately. What was it? The man in yellow was pointing to two aeropiles driving upward in the southern sky. No doubt they were looking for the coming aeroplanes.

That – presently – the thing to do now was to start. Things were being shouted at him, questions, warnings. They bothered him. He wanted to think about the aeropile, to recall every item of his previous experience. He waved the people from him, saw the man in yellow dropping off through the ribs, saw the crowd cleft down the line of the girders by his gesture.

For a moment he was motionless, staring at the levers, the wheel by which the engine shifted, and all the delicate appliances of which he knew so little. His eye caught a spirit level with the bubble towards him, and he remembered something, spent a dozen seconds in swinging the engine forward until the bubble floated in the centre of the tube. He noted that the people were not shouting, knew they watched his deliberation. A bullet smashed on the bar above his head. Who fired? Was the line clear of people? He stood up to see and sat down again.

In another second the propeller was spinning, and he was rushing down the guides. He gripped the wheel and swung the engine back to lift the stem. Then it was the people shouted. In a moment he was throbbing with the quiver of the engine, and the shouts dwindled swiftly behind, rushed down to silence. The wind whistled over the edges of the screen, and the world sank away from him very swiftly.

Throb, throb, throb – throb, throb, throb; up he drove. He fancied himself free of all excitement, felt cool and deliberate. He lifted the stem still more, opened one valve on his left wing and swept round and up. He looked down with a steady head, and up. One of the Ostrogite aeropiles was driving across his course, so that he drove obliquely towards it and would pass below it at a steep angle. Its little aeronauts were peering down at him. What did they mean to do? His mind became active. One, he saw held a weapon pointing, seemed prepared to fire. What did they think he meant to do? In a moment he understood their tactics, and his resolution was taken. His momentary lethargy was past. He opened two more valves to his left, swung round, end on to this hostile machine, closed his valves, and shot straight at it, stem and wind-screen shielding him from the shot. They tilted a little as if to clear him. He flung up his stem.

Throb, throb, throb – pause – throb, throb – he set his teeth, his face into an involuntary grimace, and crash! He struck it! He struck upward beneath the nearer wing.

Very slowly the wing of his antagonist seemed to broaden as the impetus of his blow turned it up. He saw the full breadth of it and then it slid downward out of his sight.

He felt his stem going down, his hands tightened on the levers, whirled and rammed the engine back. He felt the jerk of a clearance, the nose of the machine jerked upward steeply, and for a moment he seemed to to be lying on his back. The machine was reeling and staggering, it seemed to be dancing on its screw. He made a huge effort, hung for a moment on the levers, and slowly the engine came forward again. He was driving upward but no longer so steeply. He gasped for a moment and flung himself at the lever again. The wind whistled about him. One further effort and he was almost level. He could breathe. He turned his head for the first time to see what had become of his antagonists. Turned back to the levers for a moment and looked again. For a moment he could have believed they were annihilated. And then he saw between the two stages to the east was a chasm, and down this something, a slender edge, fell swiftly and vanished, as a sixpence falls down a crack.

At first he did not understand, and then a wild joy possessed him. He shouted at the top of his voice, an inarticulate shout, and drove higher and higher up the sky. Throb, throb, throb, pause, throb, throb, throb. 'Where was the other aeropile?' he thought. 'They too – .' As he looked round the empty heavens he had a momentary fear that this machine had risen above him, and then he saw it alighting on the Norwood stage. They had meant shooting. To risk being rammed headlong two thousand feet in the air was beyond their latter-day courage. The combat was declined.

For a little while he circled, then swooped in a steep descent towards the westward stage. Throb throb throb, throb throb throb. The twilight was creeping on apace, the smoke from the Streatham stage that had been so dense and dark, was now a pillar of fire, and all the laced curves of the moving ways and the translucent roofs and domes and the chasms between the buildings were glowing softly now, lit by the tempered radiance of the electric light that the glare of the day overpowered. The three efficient stages that the Ostrogites held – for Wimbledon Park was useless because of the fire from Roehampton, and Streatham was a furnace – were glowing with guide lights for the coming aeroplanes. As he swept over the Roehampton stage he saw the dark masses of the people thereon. He heard a clap of frantic cheering, heard a bullet from the Wimbledon Park stage tweet through the air, and went beating up above the Surrey wastes. He felt a breath of wind from the south-west, and lifted his westward wing as he had learnt to do, and so drove upward heeling into the rare swift upper air. Throb throb throb – throb throb throb.

Up he drove and up, to that pulsating rhythm, until the country beneath was blue and indistinct, and London spread like a little map traced in light, like the mere model of a city near the brim of the horizon. The south-west was a sky of sapphire over the shadowy rim of the world, and ever as he drove upward the multitude of stars increased.

And behold! In the southward, low down and glittering swiftly nearer, were two little patches of nebulous light. And then two more, and then a nebulous glow of swiftly driving shapes. Presently he could count them. There were four and twenty. The first fleet of aeroplanes had come! Beyond appeared a yet greater glow.

He swept round in a half circle, staring at this advancing fleet. It flew in a wedge-like shape, a triangular flight of gigantic phosphorescent shapes sweeping nearer through the lower air. He made a swift calculation of their pace, and spun the little wheel that brought the engine forward. He touched a lever and the throbbing effort of the engine ceased. He began to fall, fell swifter and swifter. He aimed at the apex of the wedge. He dropped like a stone through the whistling air. It seemed scarce a second from that soaring moment before he struck the foremost aeroplane.

No man of all that black multitude saw the coming of his fate, no man among them dreamt of the hawk that struck downward upon him out of the sky. Those who were not limp in the agonies of air-sickness, were craning their black necks and staring to see the filmy city that was rising out of the haze, the rich and splendid city to which 'Massa Boss' had brought their obedient muscles. Bright teeth gleamed and the glossy faces shone. They had heard of Paris. They knew they were to have lordly times among the 'poor white' trash. And suddenly Graham struck them.

He had aimed at the body of the aeroplane, but at the very last instant a better idea had flashed into his mind. He twisted about and struck near the edge of the starboard wing with all his accumulated weight. He was jerked back as he struck. His prow went gliding across its smooth expanse towards the rim. He felt the forward rush of the huge fabric sweeping him and his aeropile along with it, and for a moment that seemed an age he could not tell what was happening. He heard a thousand yelling, and perceived that his machine was balanced on the edge of the gigantic float, and driving down, down; glanced over his shoulder and saw the backbone of the aeroplane and the opposite float swaying up. He had a vision through the ribs of sliding chairs, staring faces, and hands clutching at the tilting guide bars. The fenestrations in the further float flashed open as the aeronaut tried to right her. Beyond, he saw a second aeroplane leaping steeply to escape the whirl of its heeling fellow. The broad area of swaying wings seemed to jerk upward. He felt his aeropile had dropped clear, that the monstrous fabric, clean overturned, hung like a sloping wall above him.

He did not clearly understand that he had struck the side float of the aeroplane and slipped off, but he perceived that he was flying free on the down glide and rapidly nearing earth. What had he done? His heart throbbed like a noisy engine in his throat and for a perilous instant he could not move his levers because of the paralysis of his hands. He wrenched the levers to throw his engine back, fought for two seconds against the weight of it, felt himself righting, driving horizontally, set the engine beating again.

He looked upward and saw two aeroplanes glide shouting far overhead, looked back, and saw the main body of the fleet opening out and rushing upward and outward; saw the one he had struck fall edgewise on and strike like a gigantic knife-blade along the windwheels below it.

He put down his stern and looked again. He drove up heedless of his direction as he watched. He saw the wind-vanes give, saw the huge fabric strike the earth, saw its downward vans crumple with the weight of its descent, and then the whole mass turned over and smashed, upside down, upon the sloping wheels. Throb, throb, throb, pause. Suddenly from the heaving wreckage a thin tongue of white fire licked up towards the zenith. And then he was aware of a huge mass flying through the air towards him, and turned upwards just in time to escape the charge – if it was a charge – of a second aeroplane. It whirled by below, sucked him down a fathom, and nearly turned him over in the gust of its close passage.

He became aware of three others rushing towards him, aware of the urgent necessity of beating above them. Aeroplanes were all about him, circling wildly to avoid him, as it seemed. They drove past him, above, below, eastward and westward. Far away to the westward was the sound of a collision, and two falling flares. Far away to the southward a second squadron was coming. Steadily he beat upward. Presently all the aeroplanes were below him, but for a moment he doubted the height he had of them, and did not swoop again. And then he came down upon a second victim and all its load of soldiers saw him coming. The big machine heeled and swayed as the fear-maddened men scrambled to the stern for their weapons. A score of bullets sung through the air, and there flashed a star in the thick glass wind-screen that protected him. The aeroplane slowed and dropped to foil his stroke, and dropped too low. Just in time he saw the wind-wheels of Bromley hill rushing up towards him, and spun about and up as the aeroplane he had chased among them. All its voices wove into a felt of yelling. The great fabric seemed to be standing on end for a second among the heeling and splintering vans, and then it flew to pieces. Huge splinters came flying through the air, its engines burst like shells. A hot rush of flame shot overhead into the darkling sky.

'Two!' he cried, with a bomb from overhead bursting as it fell, and forthwith he was beating up again. A glorious exhilaration possessed him now, a giant activity. His troubles about humanity, about his inadequacy, were gone for ever. He was a man in battle rejoicing in his power. Aeroplanes seemed radiating from him in every direction, intent only upon avoiding him, the yelling of their packed passengers came in short gusts as they swept by. He chose his third quarry, struck hastily and did but turn it on edge. It escaped him, to smash against the tall cliff of London wall. Flying from that impact he skimmed the darkling ground so nearly he could see a frightened rabbit bolting up a slope. He jerked up steeply, and found himself driving over south London with the air about him vacant. To the right of him a wild riot of signal rockets from the Ostrogites banged tumultuously in the sky. To the south the wreckage of half a dozen air ships flamed, and east and west and north the air ships fled before him. They drove away to the east and north, and went about in the south, for they could not pause in the air. In their present confusion any attempt at evolution would have meant disastrous collisions. He could scarcely realize the thing he had done. In every quarter aeroplanes were receding. They were receding. They dwindled smaller and smaller. They were in flight!

He passed two hundred feet or so above the Roehampton stage. It was black with people and noisy with their frantic shouting. But why was the Wimbledon Park stage black and cheering, too? The smoke and flame of Streatham now hid the three further stages. He curved about and rose to see them and the northern quarters. First came the square masses of Shooter's Hill into sight from behind the smoke, lit and orderly with the aeroplane that had landed and its disembarking negroes. Then came Blackheath, and then under the corner of the reek the Norwood stage. On Blackheath no aeroplane had landed but an aeropile lay upon the guides. Norwood was covered by a swarm of little figures running to and fro in a passionate confusion. Why? Abruptly he understood. The stubborn defence of the flying stages was over, the people were pouring into the under-ways of these last strongholds of Ostrog's usurpation. And then, from far away on the northern border of the city, full of glorious import to him, came a sound, a signal, a note of triumph, the leaden thud of a gun. His lips fell apart, his face was disturbed with emotion.

He drew an immense breath. 'They win,' he shouted to the empty air; 'the people win!' The sound of a second gun came like an answer. And then he saw the aeropile on Blackheath was running down its guides to launch. It lifted clean and rose. It shot up into the air, driving straight southward and away from him.

In an instant it came to him what this meant. It must needs be Ostrog in flight. He shouted and dropped towards it. He had the momentum of his elevation and fell slanting down the air and very swiftly. It rose steeply at his approach. He allowed for its velocity and drove straight upon it.

It suddenly became a mere flat edge, and behold! he was past it, and driving headlong down with all the force of his futile blow.

He was furiously angry. He reeled the engine back along its shaft and went circling up. He saw Ostrog's machine beating up a spiral before him. He rose straight towards it, won above it by virtue of the impetus of his swoop and by the advantage and weight of a man. He dropped headlong – dropped and missed again! As he rushed past he saw the face of Ostrog's aeronaut confident and cool and in Ostrog's attitude a wincing resolution. Ostrog was looking steadfastly away from him – to the south. He realised with a gleam of wrath how bungling his flight must be. Below he saw the Croydon hills. He jerked upward and once more he gained on his enemy.

He glanced over his shoulder and his attention was arrested by a strange thing. The eastward stage, the one on Shooter's Hill, appeared to lift; a flash changing to a tall grey shape, a cowled figure of smoke and duct, jerked into the air. For a moment this cowled figure stood motionless, dropping huge masses of metal from its shoulders, and then it began to uncoil a dense head of smoke. The people had blown it up, aeroplane and all! As suddenly a second flash and grey shape sprang up from the Norwood stage. And even as he stared at this came a dead report, and the air wave of the first explosion struck him. He was flung up and sideways.

For a moment the aeropile fell nearly edgewise with her nose down, and seemed to hesitate whether to overset altogether. He stood on his wind-shield wrenching the wheel that swayed up over his head. And then the shock of the second explosion took his machine sideways.

He found himself clinging to one of the ribs of his machine, and the air was blowing past him and *upward*. He seemed to be hanging quite still in the air, with the wind blowing up past him. It occurred to him that he was falling. Then he was sure that he was falling. He could not look down.

He found himself recapitulating with incredible swiftness all that had happened since his awakening, the days of doubt the days of Empire, and at last the tumultuous discovery of Ostrog's calculated treachery. He was beaten but London was saved. London was saved!

The thought had a quality of utter unreality. Who was he? Why was he holding so tightly with his hands? Why could he not leave go? In such a fall as this countless dreams have ended. But in a moment he would wake. . . .

His thoughts ran swifter and swifter. He wondered if he should see Helen again. It seemed so unreasonable that he should not see her again. It *must* be a dream! Yet surely he would meet her. She at least was real. She was real. He would wake and meet her.

Although he could not look at it, he was suddenly aware that the earth was very near.

THE SHAPE OF
THINGS TO COME

CONTENTS

INTRODUCTION

The Dream Book of Dr Philip Raven

The unexpected death of Dr Philip Raven at Geneva in November 1930 was a very grave loss to the League of Nations Secretariat. Geneva lost a familiar figure – the long bent back, the halting gait, the head quizzically on one side – and the world lost a stimulatingly aggressive mind. His incessant devoted work, his extraordinary mental vigour, were, as his obituary notices testified, appreciated very highly by a world-wide following of distinguished and capable admirers. The general public was suddenly made aware of him.

It is rare that anyone outside the conventional areas of newspaper publicity produces so great a stir by dying; there were accounts of him in nearly every paper of importance from Oslo to New Zealand and from Buenos Aires to Japan – and the brief but admirable memoir by Sir Godfrey Cliffe gave the general reader a picture of an exceptionally simple, direct, devoted and energetic personality. There seems to have been only two extremely dissimilar photographs available for publication: an early one in which he looks like a blend of Shelley and Mr Maxton, and a later one, a snapshot, in which he leans askew on his stick and talks to Lord Parmoor in the entrance hall of the Assembly. One of his lank hands is held out in a characteristic illustrative gesture.

Incessantly laborious though he was, he could nevertheless find time to assist in, share and master all the broader problems that exercised his colleagues, and now they rushed forward with their gratitude. One noticeable thing in that posthumous eruption of publicity was the frequent acknowledgements of his aid and advice. Men were eager to testify to his importance and resentful at the public ignorance of his work. Three memorial volumes of his more important papers, reports, memoranda and addresses were arranged for and are still in course of publication.

Personally, although I was asked to do so in several quarters, and though I was known to have had the honour of his friendship, I made no contribution to that obituary chorus. My standing in the academic world did not justify my writing him a testimonial, but under normal circumstances that would not have deterred me from an attempt to sketch something of his odd personal ease and charm. I did not do so, however, because I found myself in a position of extraordinary embarrassment. His death was so unforeseen that we had embarked upon a very peculiar joint undertaking without making the slightest provision for that risk. It is only now after an interval of nearly three years, and after some very difficult discussions with his more intimate friends, that I have decided to publish the facts and the substance of this peculiar cooperation of ours.

It concerns the matter of this present book. All this time I have been holding back a manuscript, or rather a collection of papers and writings, entrusted to me. It is a collection about which, I think, a considerable amount of hesitation was, and perhaps is still, justifiable. It is, or at least it professes to be, a Short History of the World for about the next century and a half. (I can quite understand that the reader will rub his eyes at these words and suspect the printer of some sort of agraphia.) But that is exactly what this manuscript is. It is a Short History of the Future. It is a modern Sibylline book. Only now that the events of three years have more than justified everything stated in this anticipatory history have I had the courage to associate the reputation of my friend with the incredible claims of this work, and to find a publisher for it.

Let me tell very briefly what I know of its origin and how it came into my hands. I made the acquaintance of Dr Raven, or, to be more precise, he made mine, in the closing year of the war. It was before he left Whitehall for Geneva. He was always an eager amateur of ideas, and he had been attracted by some suggestions about money I had made in a scrappy little book of forecasts called *What is Coming?* published in 1916. In this I had thrown out the suggestion that the waste of resources in the war, combined with the accumulation of debts that had been going on, would certainly leave the world as a whole bankrupt, that is to say it would leave the creditor class in a position to strangle the world, and that the only method to clear up this world bankruptcy and begin again on a hopeful basis would be to scale down all debts impartially, by a reduction of the amount of gold in the pound sterling and proportionally in the dollar and all other currencies based on gold. It seemed to me then an obvious necessity. It was, I recognize now, a crude idea – evidently I had not even got away from the idea of intrinsically valuable money – but none of us in those days had had the educational benefit of the monetary and credit convulsions that followed the Peace of Versailles. We were without experience, it wasn't popular to think about money, and at best we thought like precocious children. Seventeen years later this idea of appreciating gold is accepted as an obvious suggestion by quite a number of people. Then it was received merely as the amateurish comment of an ignorant writer upon what was still regarded as the mysterious business of 'monetary experts'. But it attracted the attention of Raven, who came along to talk over that and one or two other post-war possibilities I had started, and so he made my acquaintance.

Raven was as free from intellectual pompousness as William James; as candidly receptive to candid thinking. He could talk about his subject to an artist or a journalist; he would have talked to an errand boy if he thought he would get a fresh slant in that way. 'Obvious', was the word he brought with him. 'The thing, my dear fellow' – he called me my dear fellow in the first five minutes – 'is so obvious that everybody will be too clever to consider it for a moment. Until it is belated. It is impossible to persuade anybody responsible that there is going to be a tremendous financial and monetary mix-up after this war. The victors will exact vindictive penalties and the losers of course will undertake to pay, but none of them realizes that money is going to do the most extraordinary things to them when they begin upon that. What they are going to do to each other is what occupies them, and what money is going to do to the whole lot of them is nobody's affair.'

I can still see him as he said that in his high-pitched remonstrating voice. I will confess that for perhaps our first half-hour, until I was accustomed to his flavour, I did not like him. He was too full, too sure, too rapid and altogether too vivid for my slower Anglo-Saxon make-up. I did not like the evident preparation of his talk, nor the fact that he assisted it by the most extraordinary gestures. He would not sit down; he limped about my room, peering at books and pictures while he talked in his cracked forced voice, and waving those long lean hands of his about almost as if he was swimming through his subject. I have compared him to Maxton plus Shelley, rather older, but at the first outset I was reminded of Svengali in Du Maurier's once popular *Trilby*. A shaven Svengali. I felt he was *foreign*, and my instincts about foreigners are as insular as my principles are cosmopolitan. It always seemed to me a little irreconcilable that he was a Balliol scholar, and had been one of the brightest ornaments of our Foreign Office staff before he went to Geneva.

At bottom I suppose much of our essential English shyness is an exaggerated wariness. We suspect the other fellow of our own moral subtleties. We restrain ourselves often to the point of insincerity. I am a rash man with a pen perhaps, but I am as circumspect and evasive as any other of my fellow countrymen when it comes to social intercourse. I found something almost indelicate in Raven's direct attack upon my ideas.

He wanted to talk about my ideas beyond question. But at least equally he wanted to talk about his own. I had more than a suspicion that he had, in fact, come to me in order to talk to himself and hear how it sounded – against me as a sounding-board.

He went on to discuss various other collateral suggestions of mine, which were also, he said, of the 'obvious' class. He offered me a series of flattering insults. He said he found a certain mental simplicity I possess very refreshing. He was being tormented by the ways things were going behind the fronts – and behind the scenes. Everybody, he declared, was busy fighting the war or planning to best our enemies or allies after the war; everybody was being so damned subtle that they were forgetting every clear realization they had ever had, and nobody, with the exception of a few such onlookers and outsiders as myself, was putting in any time in working out the broad inevitabilities of the process. With these others it is always what trick X will play next, and what will be Y's dodge, and whether the Z's will stand this, that, or the other thing that is put upon them – if it is put in this, that, or the other way to them. But, of course, none of this was essential. In the long run only the essentials mattered.

'In the long run,' said I.

'In the long run. And not such a very long run either in these days.'

I accepted that.

Gradually I warmed to his intellectual glow. What were the essentials? On that issue I was as keen as, if less outspoken than, he. 'What is *really* happening now?' I asked.

'Yes,' he agreed, in manifest delight: 'What is *really* happening now? Damn them! Not one of them asks that question. That's where you are so good, that's where you are worth while. The others all think they know so well that they can afford to be shut and sly about it. They can't.'

He called me then a Dealer in the Obvious, and he repeated that not very flattering phrase on various occasions when we met. 'You have,' he said, 'defects that are almost gifts: a rapid but inexact memory for particulars, a quick grasp of proportions, and no patience with detail. You hurry on to wholes. You have to see things simply or you could not see them at all. Consequently you cannot endure any conventional elaborations, any side-shows, needless complexities, indirect methods, diplomacies, legal fictions and tactful half-statements. It's a joy to rattle on to you and feel there's no complications. It isn't, I think, that you have the power to take up all those things in your stride; I won't flatter you like that; no – but you have the intuitive sense to drop them in your stride. There's the secret of your simplicity; you come as near stupidity as wisdom can. How men of affairs must hate you – if and when they hear of you! They must think you an awful mug, you know – and yet you get there! Complications are their life. *You* try to get all these complications out of the way. You are a stripper, a damned impatient stripper. I would be a stripper too if I hadn't the sort of job I have to do. But it is really extraordinarily refreshing to spend these occasional hours stripping events in your company.'

The reader must forgive my egotism in quoting these comments upon myself; they are necessary if my relations with Raven are to be made clear and if the spirit of this book is to be understood. I met him upon an unusual side that he could afford to reveal to very few other persons. That is my point. 'If I generalized to other people as I do to you,' he said, 'if I talked as plainly, my reputation as an expert would go up – like a battleship hit in the magazine.'

I was, in fact, an outlet for a definite mental exuberance of his which it had hitherto distressed him to suppress. In my presence he could throw off Balliol and the Foreign Office – or, later on, the Secretariat – and let himself go. He could become the Eastern European Cosmopolitan he was by nature and descent. I became, as it were, an imaginative boon companion for him, his disreputable friend, a sort of intelligent butt, his Watson. I got to like the relationship. I got used to his physical exoticism, his gestures. I sympathized more and more with his irritation and distress as the Conference of Versailles unfolded. My instinctive racial distrust faded before the glowing intensity of his intellectual curiosity. We found we supplemented each other. I had a ready unclouded imagination and he had knowledge. We would go on the speculative spree together.

Finally it may be he started out to take me on the greatest speculative spree of all. I am quite open to the idea that this book is nothing more than that. It is well to bear that in mind in weighing what I have next to tell about this anticipatory History of his.

Among other gifted and original friends who, at all too rare intervals, honour me by coming along for a gossip is Mr J. W. Dunne, who years ago invented one of the earliest and most 'different' of aeroplanes, and who has since done a very considerable amount of subtle thinking upon the relationship of time and space to consciousness. Dunne clings to the idea that in certain ways we may anticipate the future, and he has adduced a series of very remarkable observations indeed to support that in his well-known *Experiment with Time*. That book was published in 1927, and I found it so attractive and stimulating that I wrote about it in one or two articles that were syndicated very extensively throughout the world. It was so excitingly fresh.

And among others who saw my account of this *Experiment with Time*, and who got the book and read it and then wrote to me about it, was Raven. Usually his communications to me were the briefest of notes, saying he would be in London, telling me of a change of address, asking about my movements, and so forth; but this was quite a long letter. Experiences such as Dunne's, he said, were no novelty to him. He could add a lot to what was told in the book, and indeed he could *extend* the experience. The thing anticipated between sleeping and waking – Dunne's experiments dealt chiefly with the premonitions in the dozing moment between wakefulness and oblivion – need not be just small affairs of tomorrow or next week; they could have a longer range. If, that is, you had the habit of long-range thinking. But these were days when scepticism had to present a hard face to greedy superstition, and it was one's public duty to refrain from rash statements about these flimsy intimations, difficult as they were to distinguish from fantasies – except in one's own mind. One might sacrifice a lot of influence if one betrayed too lively an interest in this sort of thing.

He wandered off into such sage generalizations and concluded abruptly. The letter had an effect of starting out to tell much more than it did. 'Are you coming through Geneva on your way to Italy?' it wound up. 'If so, we might talk.'

When, however, I talked to him in Geneva – it was hot and we took a motor launch and had dinner at a pleasant restaurant on the lake shore beyond the waterspout – he would say scarcely a word about any glimpses he had had into futurity. He was dull and depressed that day. I never found out exactly what it was had robbed him of his customary exuberance. I asked him at last outright whether he hadn't something to tell me about seeing into the future. He seemed to have forgotten his letter altogether. '*What* is there to see in the future?' he asked, hunched in his chair. 'I haven't the guts for it.'

'These people here mean nothing,' he vouchsafed. 'Nothing at all.'

Afterwards we fell talking about the speculative boom that was then at its height in America. He said it was essentially an inflation of credit by bulling securities. While it lasted there would be a kind of prosperity, but there was nothing behind it but faith. At any time someone might start a selling that would collapse the whole thing. 'And once they start a collapse over there . . .'

He let a grimace and a gesture of his lean long hand finish his sentence.

'It's a card castle,' he said, and then with the groan of a tired man: 'I can't even find a metaphor to-day. It's a card castle that will fall – like ten million tons of bricks.'

And I remember another sentence of his.

'What I cannot understand is the levity of human beings – their incurable levity. This Geneva is the home of Calvinism. I used to think the Calvinists at least had some conception of the seriousness of life.'

He shook his head slowly and suddenly a gleam of humour lit up his sombre eyes for a moment. 'It was liver,' he said. 'Everyone who comes to Geneva gets liver.'

'So that's what's the matter!' said I.

'Liver and lethargy. Predestination. Do nothing. Attempt nothing. And burn any heretic who attempts salvation by works. . . . *You* hope by nature, you know. It's just the luck of your glands. They would have burnt you here without hesitation three centuries ago.'

Between endocrines and theology, whatever experiments with time he had been making were forgotten.

Afterwards I thought of the Dunne idea again, and I connected it so little with Raven's abortive confidences that I made up a short story, *Brownlow's Newspaper*, about a man into whose hands there fell an evening journal of fifty years ahead – and of all the tantalizingly incomplete intimations of change, such a scrap of the future would be sure to convey. Brownlow, whom I imagined as a cheerful and self-indulgent friend, came home late and rather alcoholic, and found this paper stuck through his letter-slit in the place of his usual *Evening Standard*. He found the print, paper and spelling rather queer; he was surprised by the realism of the coloured illustrations, he missed several familiar features, and he thought the news fantastic stuff, but he was too tired and muzzy to see the thing in its proper proportions, and in the morning when he awoke and thought about it, and realized the marvellous glimpse he had had into the world to come, the paper had vanished for ever down the dust-chute. This story was published in a popular magazine – the *Strand Magazine*, if I remember rightly – and Raven saw it. He wrote to me at once.

You are joking about a serious possibility (he wrote). *You are making a fairy tale of something that can happen.*

Then he turned up in London, dropped into my study unexpectedly and made a clean breast of it.

'This Dunne business,' he began.

'Well?' said I.

'He has a way of snatching the fleeting dream between unconscious sleep and waking.'

'Yes.'

'He keeps a notebook by his bedside and writes down his dream the very instant he is awake.'

'That's the procedure.'

'And he finds that a certain percentage of his dream items are – sometimes quite plainly – anticipations of things that will come into his mind out of reality, days, weeks, and even years ahead.'

'That's Dunne.'

'It's nothing.'

'But how – nothing?'

'Nothing to what I have been doing for a long time.'

'And that is . . . ?'

He stared at the backs of my books. It was amusing to find Raven for once at a loss for words.

'Well?' I said.

He turned and looked at me with a reluctant expression that broke into a smile. Then he seemed to rally his candour.

'How shall I put it? I wouldn't tell anyone but you. For some years, off and on – between sleeping and waking – I've been – in effect –

reading a book. A non-existent book. A dream book if you like. It's always the same book. Always. And it's a history.'

'Of the past?'

'There's a lot about the past. With all sorts of things I didn't know and all sorts of gaps filled in. Extraordinary things about North India and Central Asia, for instance. And also – it goes on. It's going on. It keeps on going on.'

'Going on?'

'Right past the present time.'

'Sailing away into the future?'

'Yes.'

'Is it – is it a *paper* book?'

'Not quite paper. Rather like that newspaper of your friend Brown-low. Not quite print as we know it. Vivid maps. And quite easy to read, in spite of the queer letters and spelling.'

He paused. 'I know it's nonsense.'

He added, 'It's frightfully real.'

'Do you turn the pages?'

He thought for a moment. 'No, I don't turn the pages. That would wake me up.'

'It just goes on?'

'Yes.'

'Until you realize you are doing it?'

'I suppose – yes, it is like that.'

'And then you wake up?'

'Exactly. And it isn't there!'

'And you are always *reading*?'

'Generally – very definitely.'

'But at times?'

'Oh – just the same as reading a book when one is awake. If the matter is vivid one *sees* the events. As if one was looking at a moving picture on the page.'

'But the book is still there?'

'Yes – always. I think it's there always.'

'Do you by any chance make notes?'

'I didn't at first. Now I do.'

'At once?'

'I write a kind of shorthand. . . . Do you know – I've piles of notes *that* high.'

He straddled my fireplace and stared at me.

'Now you've told me,' I said.

'Now I've told you.'

'If I had known this before, I wouldn't have written *Brownlow's Newspaper*.'

'Naturally. My fault for not telling you plainly sooner.'

His lank hand waved all that aside.

'Can't I see some of the notes?'

'Illegible, my dear sir – except to me. You don't know my shorthand.
I can hardly read it myself after a week or so. But lately I've been
writing it out – some I've dictated.'

'You see,' he went on, standing up and walking about my room, 'if
it's – a reality, it's the most important thing in the world. And I haven't
an atom of proof. Not an atom. Do you – Do you believe this sort of
thing is possible?'

'*Possible*?' I considered. 'I'm inclined to think I do. Though what
exactly this kind of thing may be, I don't know.'

'I can't tell anyone but you. How could I? Naturally they would say I
had gone cranky – or that I was an impostor. You know the sort of
row. Look at Oliver Lodge. Look at Charles Richet. It would smash my
work, my position. And yet, you know, it's such credible stuff. . . . I tell
you I believe in it.'

'If you wrote some of it out. If I could see some of it.'

'You shall.'

He seemed to be consulting my opinion. 'The worst thing against it is
that I always believe in what the fellow says. That's rather as though it
was *me*, eh?'

That in effect was our conversation. I was left half incredulous, half
attracted. My disposition was to believe that between sleeping and
waking he did actually see this book, but that it was not in any sense a
real book; it was the creation of his own hard thinking about man's
past and present and future. He was, I supposed, projecting his own
speculations. His bold, far-ranging mind, severely repressed and kept
within narrow limits in his official work, was escaping in this fantasy,
was indulging in the free play of its possibilities. I was only the recipient
of a fraction of his mental overflow. This was the rest. He was not
content with simply answering my original question, What is really
happening? If one knows what is really happening one knows what is
going to happen. His brain was taking the business out of his hands and
carrying interpretation on to prophecy. It is a logical development. That
is still the most acceptable explanation of this history that follows. Even
as a speculation it merits attention. But, I must insist, it is not a perfect
explanation. There are one or two little things that do not fit into that.

He did not send me any of his notes, but when next I met him, it was
at Berne, he gave me a spring-backed folder filled with papers. Afterwards he gave me two others. Pencilled sheets they were mostly, but
some were evidently written at his desk in ink and perhaps fifty pages
had been typed, probably from his dictation. He asked me to take great
care of them, to read them carefully, have typed copies made and return
a set to him. The whole thing was to be kept as a secret between us. We
were both to think over the advisability of a possibly anonymous

publication. And meanwhile events might either confirm or explode various statements made in this history and so set a definite value, one way or the other, upon its authenticity.

Then he died.

He died quite unexpectedly as the result of a sudden operation. Some dislocation connected with his marked spinal curvature had developed abruptly into an acute crisis.

As soon as I heard of his death I hurried off to Geneva and told the story of the dream book to his heir and executor, Mr Montefiore Renaud. I am greatly indebted to that gentleman for his courtesy and quick understanding of the situation. He was at great pains to get every possible scrap of material together and to place it all at my disposal. In addition to the three folders Raven had already given me there were a further folder in longhand and a drawerful of papers in his peculiar shorthand evidently dealing with this History. The fourth folder contained the material which forms the concluding book of this present work. The shorthand notes, of which even the pages were not numbered, have supplied the material for the penultimate book, which has had to be a compilation of my own. Generally Raven seems to have scribbled down his impressions of the dream book as soon as he could, before the memory faded, and as he intended to recopy it all himself he had no consideration for any prospective reader. This material was just for his own use. It is a mixture of very cursive (and inaccurate) shorthand and, for proper names and so forth, longhand. Punctuation is indicated by gaps, and often a single word stands for a whole sentence and even a paragraph. About a third of the shorthand stuff was already represented by longhand or typescript copy in the folders. That was my Rosetta Stone. If it were not for the indications conveyed by that I do not think it would have been possible to decipher any of the remainder. As it is, I found it impossible to make a flowing narrative, altogether of a piece with the opening and closing parts of this history. Some passages came out fairly clear and then would come confusion and obscurity. I have transcribed what I could and written up the intervals when transcription was hopeless. I think I have made a comprehensible story altogether of the course of events during the struggles and changes in world government that went on between 1980 and 2059, at which date the Air Dictatorship, properly so called, gave place to that world-wide Modern State which was still flourishing when the history was published. The reader will find large gaps, or rather he will find large abbreviations, in that portion, but none that leave the main lines of the history of world consolidation in doubt.

And now let me say a word or so more about the real value of this queer 'Outline of the Future'.

Certain minor considerations weigh against the idea that this history that follows is merely the imaginative dreaming of a brilliant publicist.

I put them before the reader, but I will not press them. First of all this history has now received a certain amount of confirmation. The latest part of the MS dates from September 20th, 1930, and much of it is earlier. And yet it alludes explicitly to the death of Ivar Kreuger a year later, to the tragic kidnapping of the Lindbergh baby, which happened in the spring of 1932, to the Mollison world flights of the same year, to the American debt discussions in December 1932, to the Hitlerite régime in Germany, the Japanese invasion of China proper in 1933, the election of President Roosevelt II, and the World Economic Conference in London. These anticipations in detail I find a little difficult to explain away. I do not think that they are of such a nature that they could have been foretold. They are not events that were deducible from any preceding situation. How could Raven have known about them in 1930?

And another thing that troubles me much more than it will trouble the reader is the fact that there was no reason at all why Raven should have attempted a mystification upon me. There was no reason on earth or in heaven why he should have lied about the way in which this material came to him and he wrote it down.

If it were not for these considerations, I think I should be quite prepared to fall in with what will no doubt be the general opinion, that the writing of this History was deliberately chosen by Raven as an imaginative outlet. That it is indeed a work of fiction by a late member of the Geneva Secretariat with unusual opportunities for forming judgments upon the trend of things. Or, let us say, a conditional prophecy in the Hebrew manner produced in a quasi-inspired mood. The style in which it is written is recognizably Raven's style, and there are few of those differences in vocabulary and locutions that one might reasonably expect in our language a hundred and seventy-odd years from now. On the other hand, the attitude revealed is entirely inconsistent with Raven's fully conscious public utterances. The idiom of thought at least is not his, whatever the idiom of expression. Either his marginal vision transcended his waking convictions or we have here a clear case of suppressions making their way to the surface.

The centre of perspective in this history is as remote from Geneva as it can well be. It floats in a rarer and wider air than the tired atmosphere of that mountain-girdled lake. Its scope is extravagantly wider and uncompromising, and Geneva is above all a place for arrangements and bargaining. Officially Raven was a believer in and a supporter of the League of Nations. The writer of the history details the life and death of the League of Nations with unconcealed contempt and tells of its inglorious end. The attitude towards existing institutions and the leading personalities of to-day affects me as outrageous. My editorial pen has had some prolonged hesitations between what I consider to be my duty to my author and my regard for one or two distinguished friends. The reader may well ask in dismay: 'Is this what posterity will think of them?'

Or alternatively: 'Is this what Raven really thought of the world?' One name alone among those who have been prominent in our time escapes to a certain extent the indictment of this history – the name of Nicolai Lenin. And this although this grim history presently reveals the arrest and relative failure of the creative impulse in Russia. An immense pity pervades this long record of the battle of reason with ignoble folly – there is no other book in the world so full of pity, unless it be Winwood Reade's *Martyrdom of Man* – but all the admiration is for obscure dispositions in ordinary minds and for the work and sacrifices of anonymous men and women. This is a history of unknown heroes. Is that what history is going to be?

There are three possible views about this book. Either it may be a cold-blooded fabrication of Raven's, which he tried to cheat me into accepting as a sort of revelation – this I reject absolutely – or it is largely a product of his subconscious mind, a work of inspiration, as our fathers would have called it, which came up precisely as he said it came up, to his consciousness between sleeping and waking, perplexing him just as much as I am perplexed by its vividness and assurance. Or, thirdly, it is really what he believed it to be, a part of a universal history for students of the year AD 2106. I cannot decide between the two latter alternatives. But one thing is certain: the third choice, a real history from the perspective of that year, is the form in which it is presented. That is what it claims to be. That, I think, is the spirit in which it can be read most agreeably.

Accepting it then as a real history, it is still difficult to imagine the type of reader aimed at by the writer (or writers). It is elementary; it is explicit; but it is not written down to a quite young and unfurnished intelligence. It may be designed for use in what a Scottish educationist would call the 'college' stage. It seems to me to be addressed to a student much better trained in the elements of philosophy and biological science, graver, more alert and keener to learn, than the average youth of to-day. But it is often quite frankly instructive in its manner. Such a higher level of learner is only what is to be expected from the substance of the record. And there is much more attention given to operating forces and much less to mere events than would be the case in a contemporary students' history. (It is tantalizing, for instance, to learn of a great London landslide and fire in 1968 only in various passing allusions.) There are studies of typical personalities, but it is relatively very free from anecdotalism. It is much more scientific. There are gaps in this history, but they are not enigmatic gaps. I have made only the barest intimations where these gaps occur. The reader will notice ever and again little jumps of a dozen or a score of years or so.

I must admit that at first, while I was still under the impression that the whole thing was a speculative exercise, I was tempted to annotate Raven's text rather extensively. I wanted to take a hand in the game. In fact I did some months' work upon it. Until my notes were becoming more bulky than his history. But when I revised them I came to the conclusion that many of them were fussy obtrusions and very few of them likely to be really helpful to an intelligent and well-informed contemporary reader. The more attracted he was by the book, the more likely he was to make his observations for himself; the less he appreciated it, the less he was likely to appreciate a superincumbent mass of elucidation. My notes might have proved as annoying as the pencillings one finds at times in public-library books to-day. If the history is merely a speculative history, even then they would have been impertinent; if there is anything more in it than speculation, then they would be a very grave impertinence indeed. In the end I scrapped the entire accumulation.

But I have had also to arrange these chapters in order, and that much intervention was unavoidable and must remain. I have had indeed to arrange and rearrange them after several trials, because they do not seem to have been read and written down by Raven in their proper chronological sequence. I have smoothed out the transitions. Later on I hope to publish a special edition of Raven's notes exactly as he left them.

We begin here with what is evidently the opening of a fresh book in the history, though it was not actually the first paper in the folders handed to me. It reviews very conveniently the course of worldly events in recent years, and it does so in what is, to me, a novel and very persuasive way. It analyses the main factors of the great war from a new angle. From that review the story of the 'Age of Frustration', in the opening years of which we are now living, flows on in a fairly consecutive fashion. Apart from this introduction the period covered by the actual narrative is roughly from about 1929 AD to the end of the year 2105. The last recorded event is on New Year's Day 2106; there is a passing mention of the levelling of the remaining 'skeletons' of the famous 'Skyscrapers' of Lower New York on that date. The printing and publication probably occurred early in the new year; occurred – or should I write 'will occur'?

H.G.W.

BOOK I

Today and Tomorrow:
The Age of Frustration Dawns

I

A *Chronological Note*

In the nineteenth and twentieth centuries the story of mankind upon this planet undergoes a change of phase. It broadens out. It unifies. It ceases to be a tangle of more and more interrelated histories and it becomes plainly and consciously one history. There is a complete confluence of racial, social and political destinies. With that a vision of previously unsuspected possibilities opens to the human imagination. And that vision brings with it an immense readjustment of ideas.

The first phase of that readjustment is necessarily destructive. The conceptions of life and obligation that have served and satisfied even the most vigorous and intelligent personalities hitherto, conceptions that were naturally partial, sectarian and limited, begin to lose, decade by decade, their credibility and their directive force. They fade, they become attenuated. It is an age of increasing mental uneasiness, of forced beliefs, hypocrisy, cynicism, abandon and impatience. What has been hitherto a final and impenetrable background of conviction in the rightness of the methods of behaviour characteristic of the national or local culture of each individual becomes, as it were, a dissolving and ragged curtain. Behind it appear, vague and dim at first, and refracted and distorted by the slow dissolution of the traditional veils, the intimations of the type of behaviour necessary to that single world community in which we live to-day.

Until the Chronological Institute has completed its present labours of revision and defined the cardinal dates in our social evolution, it is best to refer to our account of the development of man's mind and will throughout this hectic period of human experience to the clumsy and irrelevant computation by centuries before and after the Christian Era that is still current. As we have explained more fully in a previous book [*Nothing of this is to be found in Raven's notes.* – ED.], we inherit this system of historical pigeon-holes from Christendom; that arbitrary chequerwork of hundred-year blocks was imposed upon the entire Mediterranean and Atlantic literatures for two thousand years, and it still distorts the views of history of all but the alertest minds. The young student needs to be constantly on his guard against its false divisions. As Peter Lightfoot has remarked, we talk of the 'eighteenth century', and we think of fashions and customs and attitudes that are character-istic of a period extending from the Treaty of Westphalia in 1642 CE [Christian Era] to the Napoleonic collapse in 1815 CE; we talk of the 'nineteenth century', and the pictures and images evoked are those of the gas-lighting and steam-transport era, from after the distressful years of post-Napoleonic recovery to the immense shock of the World War in 1914 CE. The phase 'twentieth century', again, calls forth images of the aeroplane, the electrification of the world and so forth; but an aeroplane was an extremely rare object in the air until 1914 (the first got up in 1905), and the replacement of the last steam railway train and the last steamship was not completed until the nineteen-forties. It is a tiresome waste of energy to oblige each generation of young minds to learn first of all in any unmeaning pattern of centuries and then to correct that first crude arrangement, so that this long-needed revision of our chronology is one that will be very welcome to every teacher. Then from the very outset he or she will be able to block out the story of our race in significant masses.

The Chronological Institute is setting about its task with a helpful publicity, inviting discussion from every angle. It is proposing to divide up as much of the known history of our race as is amenable to annual reckoning into a series of eras of unequal length. Naturally the choice of these eras is the cause of some extremely lively and interesting interchanges; most of us have our own private estimates of the values of events, and many issues affecting the earlier civilized communities remain in a state of animated unsettlement. Our chronology is now fairly sure as to the year for most important events in the last 4,000 years, and, thanks largely to the minute and patient labours of the Selwyn-Cornford Committee for Alluvial Research, to the decade for another hundred centuries. So far as the last 3,000 years are concerned, little doubt remains now that the main dividing points to be adopted will be *first* the epoch of Alexander and the Hellenic conquests which will begin the phase of the great Helleno-Latin monetary imperialism in the Western World, the *Helleno-Latin Era*. This will commence at the crossing of the Hellespont by Alexander the Great and end either with the Battle of the Yarmuk (636 CE) or the surrender of Jerusalem to the Caliph Omar (638 CE). *Next* will come the epoch of Moslem and Mongol pressure on the West which opened the era of feudal Christen-dom vis-à-vis with feudal Islam: the *Era of Asiatic Predominance*. This ends with the Battle of Lepanto (1571 CE). Then *thirdly* there will follow the epoch of the Protestant and the Catholic (counter) Reforma-tions, which inaugurated the era of the competing sovereign states with organized standing armies: the *Era of European Predominance*, or, as it may also be called, the *Era of National Sovereignty*. Finally comes the catastrophe of the World War of 1914, when the outward drive of the new economic methods the Atlantic civilizations had developed gave way under the internal stresses of European nationalism. That war, and its long-drawn sequelae, released the human mind to the potentialities and dangers of an imperfectly Europeanized world – a world which had unconsciously become one single interlocking system, while still obsessed by the Treaty of Westphalia and the idea of competing sovereign states. This mental shock and release marks the beginning of the *Era of the Modern State*. The opening phase of this latest era is this Age of Frustration with which we are now about to deal. That is the first age of the Era of the Modern State. A second age, but not a new era, began with the Declaration of Mégève which was accepted by the general common sense of mankind forty-seven years ago. This closed the Age of Frustration, which lasted therefore a little short of a century and a half.

The date upon the title-page for the first publication of this History is 2106 CE. Before many editions have been exhausted that will be changed to Modern Era (ME) 192 or ME 189 or ME 187, according to whether our chronologists decide upon 1914, the date of the outbreak of the Great War, or 1917, the beginning of the social revolution in Russia, or 1919, the signing of the Treaty of Versailles, as the conclusive opening of the Age of Frustration and the conflict for world unity. The second date seems at present to be the more practicable one.

In 1914 CE the concept of an organized world order did not seem to be within the sphere of human possibility; in 1919 CE it was an active power in a steadily increasing proportion of human brains. The Modern State had been conceived. It was germinating. One system, the Soviet system in Russia, was already claiming to be a world system. To most of the generation which suffered it, the Great War seemed to be purely catastrophe and loss; to us who see those hideous years in perspective and in proportion to the general dullness and baseness of apprehension out of which that conflict arose, the destruction of life and substance, unprecedented as they were, has none of that overwhelming quality. We see it as a clumsy, involuntary release from outworn assumptions by their reduction to tragic absurdity, and as a practically unavoidable step therefore in the dialectic of human destiny.

I I

How the Idea and Hope of the
Modern State First Appeared

The essential difference between the world before the Great War and the world after it lay in this, that before that storm of distress and disillusionment the clear recognition that a world-wide order and happiness, in spite of contemporary distresses, was within the reach of mankind was confined to a few exceptional persons, while after the catastrophe it had spread to an increasing multitude, it had become a desperate hope and desire, and at last a working conviction that made organized mass action possible.

Even those who apprended this idea before the epoch of the Great War seem to have propounded it with what impresses us to-day as an almost inexplicable timidity and feebleness. Apart from the great star of Shelley, which shines the brighter as his successors dwindle in perspective, there is a flavour of unreality about all these pre-war assertions of a possible world order. In most of them the Victorian terror of 'extravagance' is dominant, and the writer simpers and laughs at his own suggestions in what was evidently supposed to be a very disarming manner. Hardly any of these prophets dared believe in their own reasoning. Maxwell Brown has recently disinterred a pamphlet, *The Great Analysis*, dated 1912, in which a shrewd and reasoned forecast of the primary structure of the *Modern State*, quite amazingly prescient for the time, was broached with the utmost timidity, without even an author's name. It was a scheme to revolutionize the world, and the writer would not put his name to it, he confesses, because it might make him ridiculous.*

Maxwell Brown's entertaining *Modern State Prophets Before the Great War* is an exhaustive study of the psychological processes by which this idea, which is now the foundation of our contemporary life, gradually ousted its opposite of combative patriotism and established itself as a practicable and necessary form of action for men of good-will a century and a half ago. He traces the idea almost to its germ; he shows that its early manifestations, so far from being pacific, were dreams of

---

* Here for once the editor knows better than the writer of the history. This pamphlet was written by William Archer, the dramatic critic, and reprinted under its author's name with a preface by Gilbert Murray in 1931. Apparently the book collectors of the years ahead are going to miss this book. – ED.

universal conquest. He tells of its age-long struggle with everyday usage and practical common sense. In the first of his huge supplementary volumes he gives thousands of quotations going back far beyond the beginnings of the Christian Era. All the monotheistic religions were, in spirit, World-State religions. He examines the Tower of Babel myth as the attempt of some primordial cosmopolitan, some seer before the dawn, to account for the divisions of mankind. (There is strong reason now for ascribing this story to Emesal Gudeka of Nippur, the early Sumerian fabulist.)

Maxwell Brown shows how the syncretic religious developments, due to the growth of the early empires and the official pooling of gods, led necessarily to monotheism. From at least the time of Buddha onward the sentiment of, if not the living faith in, human brotherhood always existed somewhere in the world. But its extension from a mere sentiment and a fluctuating sympathy for the stranger to the quality of a practicable enterprise was a very recent process indeed. The necessary conditions were not satisfied.

In the briefer studies of human innovations that preceded his more important contributions to human history Maxwell Brown has shown how for the past ten thousand years at least, since the Cro-Magnards stamped their leather robes and tents, the art of printing reappeared and disappeared again and again, never culminating in the printed book and all its consequences, never obtaining a primary importance in human doings, until the fifteenth century (CE); he has assembled the evidence for man's repeated abortive essays in flying, from the fourth dynasty gliders recently found at Bedrashen, the shattered Yu-chow machine and the interesting wreckage, ornaments and human remains found last year in Mirabella Bay. (These last were first remarked in 2104 CE after an earthquake in the deep-sea photographs of the survey aeroplane *Crawford*, and they were subsequently sought and recovered by the divers of the submarine *Salvemini* belonging to the Naples Biological Station. They have now been identified by Professor Giulio Marinetti as the remains of the legendary glider of Daedalus and Icarus.) Maxwell Brown has also traced the perpetual discovery and rediscovery of America from the days of the Aalesund tablets and the early Chinese inscriptions in the caves near Bahia Coqui to the final establishment of uninterrupted communications across the Atlantic by the Western Europeans in the fifteenth century CE. In all there are sixteen separate ineffectual discoveries of America either from the east or from the west now on record, and there may have been many others that left no trace behind them.

These earlier cases of human enterprise and inadequacy help us to understand the long struggle of the Age of Frustration and the difficulty our ancestors found in achieving what is now so obviously the only sane arrangement of human affairs upon this planet.

The fruitlessness of all these premature inventions is very easily explained. First in the case of the transatlantic passage; either the earlier navigators who got to America never got back or, if they did get back, they were unable to find the necessary support and means to go again before they died, or they had had enough of hardship, or they perished in a second attempt. Their stories were distorted into fantastic legends and substantially disbelieved. It was, indeed, a quite futile adventure to get to America until the keeled sailing ship, the science of navigation, and the mariner's compass had been added to human resources.

Then again, in the matter of printing, it was only when the Chinese had developed the systematic manufacture of abundant cheap paper sheets in standard sizes that the printed book – and its consequent release of knowledge – became practically possible. Finally the delay in the attainment of flying was inevitable because before men could progress beyond precarious gliding it was necessary for metallurgy to reach a point at which the internal combustion engine could be made. Until then they could build nothing strong enough and light enough to battle with the eddies of the air.

In an exactly parallel manner, the conception of one single human community organized for collective service to the common weal had to wait until the rapid evolution of the means of communication could arrest and promise to defeat the disintegrative influence of geographical separation. That rapid evolution came at last in the nineteenth century, and it has been described already in a preceding chapter of this world history. [*Not recorded by Raven.* – ED.] Steam power, oil power, electric power, the railway, the steamship, the aeroplane, transmission by wire and aerial transmission followed each other very rapidly. They knit together the human species as it had never been knit before. Insensibly, in less than a century, the utterly impracticable became not merely a possible adjustment but an urgently necessary adjustment if civilization was to continue.

Now the cardinal prominence of the Great War in history lies in this, that it demonstrated the necessity of that adjustment. It was never considered to be necessary before. Recognition lagged behind accomplishment. None of the pre-war World-State Prophets betrays any sense of necessity. They make their polite and timid gestures towards human unity as something nice and desirable indeed but anything but imperative. The clearest demand for world-wide cooperation before the war came from the Second International. And even after the war, and after the vague and vacillating adumbration of a federal super-state by the League of Nations at Geneva, most of even the most advanced writers seem to have been still under the impression that the utmost adjustment needed was some patching up of the current system so as to prevent or mitigate war and restrain the insurrectionary urge of the unprosperous.

Even the Communist movement, which, as we had told already, had been able by a conspiracy of accidents to seize upon Russia and demonstrate the value of its theories there, lapsed from, rather than advanced towards, cosmopolitan socialism. Its theories, as we have shown, were hopelessly inadequate for its practical needs. The development of its ideology was greatly hampered by the conservative dogmatism imposed upon it by the incurable egotism of Marx. His intolerance, his innate bad manners, his vain insistence that he had produced a final doctrine to put beside Darwinism, cast a long shadow of impatience and obduracy upon the subsequent development of Communism. He was bitterly jealous of the Utopian school of socialism, and so, until Lenin faced the urgencies of power, the 'orthodox' Marxist took a quite idiotic pride in a planless outlook. 'Overthrow capitalism,' he said, and what could happen but millennial bliss? Communism insisted indeed upon the necessity of economic socialization, but – until it attained power in Russia – without a glance at its technical difficulties. It produced its belated and ill-proportioned Five Year Plan only in 1928 CE, eleven years after its accession to power. Until then it had no comprehensive working scheme whatever for the realization of socialism. Thrown back on experiment, it was forced to such desperately urgent manoeuvres, improvizations and changes of front, and defended by such tawdry and transparent apologetics, that the general world movement passed out of its ken.

The reader of this world history knows already how the moral and intellectual force of the Communist Party proved unequal, after the death of Lenin, to control or resist the dictatorship of that forcible, worthy, devoted and limited man, the Georgian, Stalin. The premature death of the creative and adaptable Lenin and the impatient suppression by Stalin of such intelligent, troublesome, but necessary types as Trotsky – a man who, but for lack of tact and essential dignity, might well have been Lenin's successor – crippled whatever hope there may have been that the Modern State would first emerge in Russia. Terrible are the faithful disciples of creative men. Lenin relaxed and reversed the dogmatism of Marx, Stalin made what he imagined to be Leninism into a new and stiffer dogmatism. Thereafter the political doctrinaire dominated and crippled the technician in a struggle that cried aloud for technical competence. Just as theological disputes impoverished and devastated Europe through the long centuries of Christendom, and reduced the benefits of its unifying influence to zero, so in Russia efficiency of organization was prevented by the pedantries of political theorists. The young were trained to a conceit and a xenophobia, indistinguishable in its practical effects from the gross patriotism of such countries as France, Germany, Italy or Scotland.

Because of this subordination of its mental development to politics, Russia passed into a political and social phase comparable, as Rostovtzeff pointed out at the time in his *Social and Economic History of the*

Roman Empire, in its universal impoverishment and its lack of any critical vigour to the well-meaning but devitalizing autocracy of the Emperor Diocletian. From its very start the Russian revolution failed in its ambition to lead mankind. Its cosmopolitanism lasted hardly longer than the cosmopolitanism of the great French revolution a dozen decades earlier.

This almost inevitable lag of the constructive movement in Russia behind Western developments was foreseen by the shrewd and penetrating brain of Lenin even in the phase of its apparent leadership (*see* No. 3090 in the thirteenth series of the Historical Documents Collection, *Left Wing Communism*). But his observation found little or no echo in the incurably illiberal thought of the Marxian tradition.

It was in Western Europe especially that the conception of the organized and disciplined World-State as a revolutionary objective ultimately grew to its full proportions. At first it grew obscurely. In 1933 any observer might have been misled by the fact of the Fascist régime in Italy, by the tumult of the Nazi party in Germany, by similar national-socialist movements in other countries, and by the increase in tariff barriers and other restraints upon trade everywhere, to conclude that the cosmopolitan idea was everywhere in retreat before the obsessions of race, creed and nationalism. Yet all the while the germs of the Modern State were growing, everywhere its votaries were learning and assembling force.

It needed the financial storm of the years 1928 and 1929 CE and the steadily progressive collapse of the whole world's economic life, of which this storm was the prelude, to give the World-State prophets the courage of their convictions. Then indeed they began to speak out. Instead of the restrained, partial and inconclusive criticism of public affairs which had hitherto contented them, they now insisted plainly upon the need of a world-wide reconstruction, that is to say of a world revolution – though 'revolution' was still a word they shirked. The way in which this increased definition of aim and will came about is characteristic of the changing quality of social life. It was not that one or two outstanding men suddenly became audible and conspicuous as leaders in this awakening. There were no leaders. It was a widespread movement in human thought.

In a second huge supplementary volume Maxwell Brown has assembled the substance of a precise study of fifty typical writers and speakers in Europe and America, and he gives a list of nearly two thousand who yield parallel results which remain filed for reference in the Encyclopaedia Library. In each case, guarded, limited and tentative suggestions give place to more and more outspoken and lucid statements of the world situation. For ten years from 1917 onward these typical people are saying mildly what might be done; then suddenly they begin to say more and more plainly what had to be done. It was a general movement of opinion affecting all the more intelligent people in the world. Whatever interchange of ideas occurred is now untraceable. The development was too rapid to establish priorities. Opinion appears now to have moved in line abreast.

The conclusions upon which all these intelligent people were converging may be briefly stated. They had arrived at the realization that human society had become one indivisible economic system with novel and enormous potentialities of well-being. By 1931 CE this conception becomes visible even in the obstinately intellectualist mind of France – for example, in the parting speech to America of an obscure and transitory French Prime Minister, Laval, who crossed the Atlantic on some now undiscoverable mission in that year; and we find it promptly echoed by such prominent loud speakers as President Hoover of America and Mr Ramsay MacDonald, the British Prime Minister.

That idea at any rate had already become sufficiently popular for the politicians to render it lip service. But it was still only the intelligent minority who went on to the logical consequences of its realization; that is to say, the necessity of disavowing the sovereignty of contemporary governments, of setting up authoritative central controls to supplement or supersede them, and of putting the production of armaments, the production of the main economic staples, and the protection of workers from destructive under-payment beyond the reach of profit-seeking manipulation.

Yet by 1932–33 this understanding minority was speaking very plainly. These immense changes were no longer being presented as merely desirable things; they were presented as urgently necessary things if civilization was to be saved from an immense catastrophe. And not merely saved: the alternative to disaster, they saw even then, was not just a bleak and terrified security. That was the last thing possible. There was no alternative to disorder and wretchedness, but 'such an abundance, such a prosperity and richness of opportunity,' as man had never known before. (These words are quoted from a Scottish newspaper of the year 1929.) Enlightened people in 1932 CE were as assured of the possibility of world order, universal sufficiency and ever increasing human vitality as are we who live to-day in ample possession of our lives amidst the practical realization of that possibility.

Clearness of vision did not make for the happiness of the enlightened. Their minds were tormented not simply by contemporary fears and miseries, but by the sure knowledge of a possible world of free activity within the reach of man and, as it were, magically withheld. They saw hundreds of millions of lives cramped and crippled, meagrely lived, sacrificed untimely, and they could not see any primary necessity for this blighting and starvation of human life. They saw youthful millions drifting to lives of violence, mutilation and premature and hideous deaths. And beyond was our security, our eventfulness and our freedom.

Maxwell Brown, in a chapter called 'Tantalus 1932', cites forty instances of these realizations. But the legendary Tantalus was put within apparent reach of the unattainable by the inexorable decrees of the gods. Mankind was under no such pitiless destiny. The world-wide Modern State shone bright upon the living imaginations of our race within a decade of the Great War, absurdly near, fantastically out of reach. For a century of passionate confusion and disorder that Modern State was not to be released from potentiality into actuality.

It is to the story of these battling, lost and suffering generations, the 'generations of the half-light', that we must now proceed.

For the first time in history the mind of man was really attempting to control his destiny. Hitherto usage, tradition, external necessity, accident, had furnished the unchallenged framework within which he had devised his explanations and his consolations. He had resisted any clear knowledge of his own nature and romanced about his destiny. He had evaded responsibility for his stresses and disasters by putting his faith in over-ruling gods; he had clung to arbitrary rules of conduct against all reason, and he had persecuted and sought to destroy every sceptical thinker, every heretical experimentalist in conduct, who disturbed the equanimity of his submission. He preferred familiar miseries to the mental torture of novel effort. Now through a complex of enlightening accidents, and especially through the jumbling together of a hundred different and discordant cultures in one world-wide mutuality of discredit and destruction, the vision of reality was forcing itself upon him. And with an ever-widening sweep of change even his mean submissiveness gave him no sense of security any more. Effort was before him and the goad behind. He was compelled to ask in spite of himself what indeed he was, and with that, in spite of his deep conservatism, he began to realize all that he might be.

When now we look back to the scattered and diverse individuals who first give expression to this idea of the modern World-State which was dawning upon the human intelligence, when we appraise their first general efforts towards its realization, we need, before we can do them anything like justice, to attempt some measure of the ignorances, prejudices and other inertias, the habits of concession and association, the herd love and the herd fear, with which they had to struggle not only in the society in which they found themselves, but within themselves. It is not a conflict of light and darkness we have to describe; it is the struggle of the purblind among the blind. We have to realize that for all that they were haunted by a vision of the civilized world of to-day, they still belonged not to our age but to their own. The thing imagined in their minds was something quite distinct from their present reality. Maxwell Brown has devoted several chapters, and a third great supplementary volume, to a special selection of early Modern State Prophets who followed public careers. He showed conclusively that in the third and fourth decades of the twentieth century (CE) there was a rapidly increasing number of men and women with a clear general conception of the possibilities of the modern world. He gives their written and spoken words, often astoundingly prescient and explicit. And then he traces out the tenor of their lives subsequent to these utterances. The discrepancy of belief and effort is a useful and indeed a startling reminder of the conditioned nature of the individual life.

As he writes: 'In the security and serenity of the study, these men and women could see plainly. In those hours of withdrawal, the fragile delicate brain matter could escape from immediacy, apprehend causation in four dimensions, reach forward to the permanent values of social events in the space-time framework. But even to the study there penetrated the rumble of the outer disorder. And directly the door was opened, forthwith the uproar of contemporary existence, the carnival, the riot, the war and the market, beat in triumphantly. The raging question of what had to be done that day scattered the fine thought of our common destiny to the four winds of heaven.'

Maxwell Brown adds a vivid illustration to this passage. It is the facsimile of the first draft by Peter Raut, the American progressive leader, of the Revolutionary Manifesto of 1937. It was indisputably a very inspiring document in its time, and Raut gave the last proof of loyalty to the best in his mind by a courageous martyrdom. But in the margin of this draft one's attention is caught by a maze of little figures; little sums in multiplication and addition. By his almost inspired gift for evidence and through the industry of his group of research assistants, Maxwell Brown has been able to demonstrate exactly what these sums were. They show that even while Raut, so far as his foresight permitted, was planning our new world, his thoughts were not wholly fixed on that end. They wandered. For a time the manifesto was neglected while he did these sums. He was gambling in industrial equities, and a large and active portion of his brain was considering whether the time had arrived to sell.

A more illuminating instance of what social psychologists have called the 'divided mind' of the intellectuals in the twentieth century of the Christian Era could scarcely be imagined. In the middle years of the nineteenth century there was a primitive form of entertainment in Western Europe and America called 'Dissolving Views'. Crudely coloured pictures were thrown on a screen by a double-barrelled arrangement of lenses called a 'Magic Lantern'. A picture would be projected first by the right-hand lens of the contraption and then the light would be shifted to the left-hand side, so that the picture cast by one half of the apparatus faded as the other became brighter. The real became a phantom and vanished and the faint intimations of its successor became at length the only reality visible. Apparently this is where our ancestors found the 'magic' effect. At a certain phase it must have been hard to determine which details were advancing and which were receding realities, or of any part of the ensemble whether it was real. It was very much after the fashion of this artless Victorian wonder-toy that faith in established institutions and usages faded and the idea of the Modern State dawned upon the intelligence of mankind.

III

The Accumulating Disproportions of the Old Order

But this analogy of the Age of Frustration to the old-fashioned Dissolving View must not be carried too far. The Modern State was indeed becoming conscious of itself and consciously endeavouring to realize itself, but the sixty-odd sovereign states which divided the world among themselves were by no means disposed to dissolve away in its favour. It was not a case of one thing always growing stronger and another always growing weaker. In the opening decade of the twentieth century there did indeed seem to be some intimations of such a pacific orderly supersession; there were many things that could be interpreted as the gradual establishment of a world community amidst the formal patchwork of governments and cultures. But they were superficial and secondary in relation to the preoccupations that were presently to resist and reverse them.

Let us consider some of the main appearances that disposed many minds to expect a world community in those days. In the first place a very considerable financial unity had been achieved. The credit of the City of London ran to the ends of the earth, and the gold sovereign was for all practical purposes a world coin, exchangeable locally for local expenditure within relatively slight fluctuations. Economic life was becoming very generalized. Over great areas trade moved with but small impediments, and the British still hoped to see their cosmopolitan conception of Free Trade accepted by the whole world. The International Institute of Agriculture in Rome was developing an annual census of staple production and reaching out towards a world control of commodity transport. Considerable movements and readjustments of population were going on, unimpeded by any government interference. Swarms of Russian Poles, for instance, drifted into Eastern Germany for the harvest work and returned; hundreds of thousands of Italians went to work in the United States for a few years and then came back with their earnings to their native villages. An ordinary traveller might go all over the more settled parts of the earth and never be asked for a passport unless he wanted to obtain a registered letter at a post office or otherwise prove his identity.

A number of minor but significant federal services had also come into existence and had a sound legal standing throughout the world, the Postal Union for example. Before 1914 CE a written document was delivered into the hands of the addressee at almost every point upon the planet, almost as surely as, if less swiftly than, it is to-day. (The Historical Documents Board has recently reprinted a small book, *International Government*, prepared for the little old Fabian Society during the Great War period by L. S. Woolf, which gives a summary of such arrangements. He lists twenty-three important world unions dealing at that time with trade, industry, finance, communications, health, science, art, literature, drugs, brothels, criminals, emigration and immigration and minor political affairs.) These world-wide cooperations seemed – more particularly to the English-speaking peoples – to presage a direct and comparatively smooth transition from the political patchwork of the nineteenth century, as the divisions of the patchwork grew insensibly fainter, to a stable confederation of mankind. The idea of a coming World-State was quite familiar at the time – one finds it, for instance, as early as Lord Tennyson's *Locksley Hall* (published in 1842); but there was no effort whatever to achieve it, and indeed no sense of the need of such effort. The World-State was expected to come about automatically by the inherent forces in things.

That belief in some underlying benevolence in uncontrolled events was a common error, one might almost say *the* common error, of the time. It affected every school of thought. In exactly the same fashion the followers of Marx (before the invigorating advent of Lenin and the Bolshevist reconstruction of Communism) regarded their dream of World Communism as inevitable, and the disciples of Herbert Spencer found a benevolent Providence in 'free competition'. 'Trust Evolution,' said the extreme Socialist and the extreme Individualist, as piously as the Christians put their trust in God. It was the Bolshevik movement in the twentieth century which put will into Communism. The thought of the nineteenth-century revolutionary and reactionary alike was saturated with that confident irresponsible laziness. As Professor K. Chandra Sen has remarked, hope in the Victorian period was not a stimulant but an opiate.

We who live in a disciplined order, the chastened victors of a hard-fought battle, understand how superficial and unsubstantial were all those hopeful appearances. The great processes of mechanical invention, which have been described in our general account of the release of experimental science from deductive intellectualism, were increasing the power and range of every operating material force quite irrespective of its fitness or unfitness for the new occasions of mankind. With an equal impartiality they were bringing world-wide understanding and world-wide massacre into the range of human possibility.

It was through no fault of these inventors and investigators that the new opportunities they created were misused. That was outside their range. They had as yet no common culture of their own. Nor, since each worked in his own field, were they responsible for the fragmentary irregularity of their discoveries. Biological and especially social invention were lagging far behind the practical advances of the exacter, simpler sciences. Their application was more difficult; the matters they affected were so much more deeply embedded in ordinary use and wont, variation was more intimate, novelties could not be inserted with the same freedom. It was easy to supplant the coach and horses on the macadamized road by the steam-engine or the railway, because it was not necessary to do anything to the road or the coach and horses to bring about the change. They were just left alone to run themselves out as the railroad (and later the automobile on the rubber-glass track) superseded them. But men cannot set up new social institutions, new social and political and industrial relationships, side by side with the old in that fashion. It must be an altogether tougher and slower job. It is a question not of ousting but of reconstruction. The old must be converted into the new without ceasing for a moment to be a going concern. The over-running of the biologically old by the mechanically new, due to these differences in timing, was inevitable, and it reached its maximum in the twentieth century.

A pathological analogy may be useful here. In the past, before the correlation of development in living organisms began to be studied, people used to suffer helplessly and often very dreadfully from all sorts of irregularities of growth in their bodies. The medical services of the time, such as they were, were quite unable to control them. One of these, due to what is called the Nurmi ratios in the blood, was a great overproduction of bone, either locally or generally. The sufferer gradually underwent distortion into a clumsy caricature of his former self; his features became coarse and massive, his skull bones underwent a monstrous expansion; the proportions of his limbs altered, and the leverage of his muscles went askew. He was made to look grotesque; he was crippled and at last killed. Something strictly parallel happened to human society in the hundred years before the Great War. Under the stimulus of mechanical invention and experimental physics it achieved, to pursue our metaphor, a hypertrophy of bone, muscle and stomach, without any corresponding enlargement of its nervous controls.

Long before the Great War this progressive disproportion had been dimly recognized by many observers. The favourite formula was to declare that 'spiritual' – for the naïve primordial opposition of spirit and matter was still accepted in those days – had not kept pace with 'material' advance. This was usually said with an air of moral superiority to the world at large. Mostly there was a vague implication that if these other people would only refrain from using modern inventions so briskly, or go to church more, or marry earlier and artlessly, or read a more 'spiritual' type of literature, or refrain from mixed bathing, or work harder and accept lower wages, or be more respectful and obedient to constituted authority, all might yet be well. Beyond this sort of thing there was little recognition of the great and increasing disharmonies of the social corpus until after the Great War.

The young reader will ask, 'But where was the Central Observation Bureau? Where was the professorial and student body which should have been recording these irregularities and producing plans for adjustment?'

There was no Central Observation Bureau. That did not exist for another century. That complex organization of discussion, calculation, criticism and forecast was undreamt of. Those cities of thought, full of serene activities, came into existence only after the organization of the Record and Library Network under the Air Dictatorship between 2010 and 2030. Even the mother thought-city, the World Encyclopaedia Establishment, was not founded until 2012. In the early twentieth century there was still no adequate estimate of economic forces and their social reactions. There were only a few score professors and amateurs of these fundamentally important studies scattered throughout the earth. They were scattered in every sense; even their communications were unsystematic. They had no powers of enquiry, no adequate statistics, little prestige; few people heeded what they thought or said.

Maybe they deserved nothing better. They bickered stupidly with and discredited each other. They ignored or wilfully misunderstood each other. It is impossible to read such social and economic literature as the period produced without realizing the extraordinary backwardness of that side of the world's intellectual life. It is difficult to believe nowadays that the writers of these publications, at once tediously copious and incredibly jejune, were living at the same time as the lively multitude of workers in the experimental sciences who were daily adding to and reshaping knowledge to achieve fresh practical triumphs. From 1812 CE, when public gas-lighting was first organized, to the outbreak of the Great War, while the world was being made over anew by gas, by steam, by oil, and then by the swift head-long development of electrical science, while the last *terrae incognitae* were being explored and mapped, while a multitude of hitherto-unthought-of elements and compounds and hundreds of thousands of new substances were coming into use, while epidemic diseases were being restrained and driven back, while the death rate was being halved, and the average duration of life increased by a score of years, the social and political sciences remained practically stagnant and unserviceable. Throughout the century of material achievement there is no single instance of the successful application of a social, economic or educational generalization.

Even the attempt to bring social institutions within the range of genuine scientific enquiry did not begin until after the Great War. It is on record that a chair of 'Social Biology' was set up in the London School of Economics and Political Science in 1930, and there are some allusions to a chair of Social Psychology in the same college. But here our sources are obscure. In the great London landslip of 1968, due to the weight of new buildings piled up on the northern slope, when the bed of the Thames buckled up and the Second Fire of London ensued, a vast mass of material perished, including the irreplaceable treasures of the British Museum, and among other grave, if lesser, losses were all the records of this interesting institution in Clare Market. But certainly that chair of Social Biology was the first of its kind in the European world.

Because of this belatedness of the social sciences, the progressive dislocation of the refined if socially limited and precarious civilization of the more advanced of the eighteenth- and nineteenth-century sovereign states went on without any effectual contemporary understanding of what was straining it to pieces. The Europeans and the Americans of the early twentieth century apprehended the social and political forces that ravaged their lives hardly more clearly than the citizens of the Roman Empire during its collapse. Plenty and the appearance of security *happened*; then débâcle *happened*. There was no analysis of operating causes. For years even quite bold and advanced thinkers were chased by events. They did not grasp what was occurring at the time. They only realized what had really occurred long afterwards. And so they never foresaw. There was no foresight, and therefore still less could there be any understanding control.

IV

Early Attempts to understand
and deal with these Disproportions:
The Criticisms of Karl Marx and Henry George

There are, however, one or two exceptions to this general absence of diagnosis in the affairs of the nineteenth and twentieth century of the

Christian Era which even the student of general history cannot ignore. Prominent among them is the analysis and forecasts of economic development made by Karl Marx and his associates.

In any case Marxism would have demanded our attention as a curious contemporary realization of the self-destroying elements in the business methods of the nineteenth century; but its accidental selection as the ostensible creed of revolutionary Russia after the Tzarist collapse gives it an almost primary importance in the history of kinetic ideas.

Karl Marx (1818–83) was the son of a christianized Jewish lawyer of Treves, of considerable social pretensions; he had an excellent university career at Bonn and Berlin, assimilated the radical thought of his time and became the lifelong friend of the far more modest and gifted Friedrich Engels (1820–95), a Lancashire calico-dealer. Under the inspiration of Engels and the English socialist movement of Robert Owen, Marx elaborated the theory of economic development which is the substance of Marxism. It is embodied in a huge unfinished work, *Das Kapital*, and summarized in a *Communist Manifesto* (1848) drawn up by Engels and himself. (These, and indeed all his writings, together with an able digest and summary, are to be found in the *Library of Historical Thought*, vols. 17252–9.) His chief merit lies in his clear recognition of the ultimate dependence of social and political forms and reactions upon physical necessity ('the Materialist Conception of History'). His chief fault was his insane hatred of the middle classes (bourgeoisie), due mainly to his pose as a needy aristocrat and embittered, it may be, by his material and intellectual dependence on the trader Engels. His own attempts to apply his theories by conspiracy and political action were inept and futile. He died in London a disappointed and resentful man, quite unaware of the posthumous fame that awaited his doctrines. It was the organization of his followers into the disciplined Communist Party and the modernization of his doctrines by the genius of Lenin that made his name a cardinal one in history.

It is interesting to consider his general propositions now in the light of accomplished events and note the hits and misses of those heroic speculations – heroic, that is to say, measured by the mental courage of the time.

Nowadays every schoolboy knows that the essential and permanent conflict in life is a conflict between the past and the future, between the accomplished past and the forward effort. He is made to realize this conflict in his primary biological course. Therein he comes to see and in part to understand the continual automatic struggle of the thing achieved, to hold the new, the new-born individual, the new-born idea, the widening needs of the species, in thrall. This conflict, he is shown, runs through all history. In the old classical mythology Saturn, the Conservative head-god, devoured all his children until at last one escaped to become Jove. And of how Jove bound Prometheus in his turn every lover of Shelley can tell. We need only refer the student to the recorded struggles in the histories of Republican Rome and Judæa between debtor and creditor; to the plebeian Secessions of the former and the year of Jubilee of the latter; to the legend of Joseph in Egypt (so richly interpreted now through the minute study of contemporary Egyptian documents by the students of the Breasted Commemoration Fund); to the English Statute of Mortmain; to Austen Liverwright's lucid study of *Bankruptcy Through the Ages* (1979), to remind him of this perennial struggle of life against the creditor and the dead hand. But Marx, like most of his contemporaries, was profoundly ignorant of historical science, and addicted to a queer 'dialectic' devised by the pseudo-philosopher Hegel; his ill-equipped mind apprehended this perennial antagonism only in terms of the finance of the industrial production about him; the entrepreneur, the capitalist, became the villain of his piece, using the prior advantage of his capital to appropriate the 'surplus value' of production, so that his share of purchasing power became more and more disproportionately great.

Marx seems never to have distinguished clearly between restrictive and productive possessions, which nowadays we recognize as a difference of fundamental importance. Exploitation for profit and strangulation for dominance, the radical son and the conservative father, were all one to him. And his proposals for expropriating the profit-seeking 'Capitalist' were of the vaguest; he betrayed no conception whatever of the real psychology of economic activities, and he had no sense of the intricate organization of motives needed if the coarse incentive of profit was to be superseded. Indeed, he had no practical capacity at all, and one is not surprised to learn that for his own part he never earned a living. He claimed all the privileges of a prophet and all the laxity and indolence of a genius, and he never even completed his great book.

It was the far abler and finer-minded Lenin (1870–1924, in power in Russia after 1917), rather than Marx, who gave a practical organization to the revolutionary forces of Communism and made the Communist Party for a time, until Stalin overtook it, the most vital creative force in the world. The essential intellectual difference between these two men is explained very clearly by Max Eastman (1895–1980), whose compact and scholarly *Marx and Lenin* is still quite readable by the contemporary student. In his time Lenin had to pose as the disciple and exponent of Marx; it was only later that criticism revealed the subtle brilliance of his effort to wrest a practical common sense out of the time-worn doctrines of the older prophet.

Another nineteenth-century writer, with perhaps a clearer realization of the strangulating effect of restrictive property as distinguished from the stimulating effect of exploitation, was Henry George (1839–97), an American printer who rose to great popularity as a writer upon economic questions. He saw the life of mankind limited and dwarfed by the continual rise in rents. His naïve remedy was to tax the landowner, as Marx's naïve remedy was to expropriate the capitalist, and just as Marx never gave his disciples the ghost of an idea for a competent administration of the expropriated economic plant and resources of the world, so Henry George never indicated how, in the world of implacable individualism he advocated, the taxing authority was to find a use for its ever-increasing tax receipts.

We can smile to-day at the limitations of these early pioneers. But we smile only because we live later than they did, and are two centuries and more to the good in our experience. We owe them enormous gratitude for the valiant disinterestedness of their life work.

Our debt is on the whole rather for what they got rid of than for what they did. The broad outlines of the world's economic life are fairly simple as we see them frankly exposed to-day, but these men were born into an atmosphere of uncriticized usage, secrecy, time-honoured misconceptions, fetishisms, working fictions – which often worked very badly – and almost insane suppressions of thought and statement. The very terms they were obliged to use were question-begging terms; the habitual assumptions of the world they addressed were crooked and only to be apprehended with obliquity and inconsistency. They were forcing their minds towards the expression of reality through an intricate mental and moral tangle. They destroyed the current assumption of permanence in established institutions and usages, and, though that seems a small thing to us now, it was a profoundly important release at the time. The infantile habit of assuming the fixity of the Thing that Is was almost universal in their day.

The Marxist doctrines did at least indicate that a term was necessarily set to economic development through profit-seeking, by the concentration of controlling ownership, by the progressive relative impoverishment of larger and larger sections of the world population and by the consequent final dwindling of markets. The rapid coagulation of human activities after 1928 CE was widely recognized as a confirmation of the Marxian forecast and, by one of those rapid mental leaps characteristic of the time, as a complete endorsement of the Communist pretension to have solved the social problem.

Unembarrassed as we are now by the mental clutter of our forefathers, the fundamental processes at work during the distressful years of the third and fourth decade of the century appear fairly simple. We know that it is a permanent condition of human well-being that the general level of prices should never fall, and we have in the Currency Council a fairly efficient and steadily improving world-organ to ensure that end. A dollar, as we know it to-day, means practically the same thing in goods, necessities and satisfactions from one year's end to another. Its diminution in value is infinitesimal. No increase is ever allowed to occur. For the owner of an unspent dollar there is neither unearnt increment nor unmerited loss. As the productive energy of our species rises, the dollar value of the total wealth is arranged to increase steadily in proportion, and neither is the creditor enriched nor robbed of his substantial expectation nor the debtor confronted with payments beyond his powers.

There remains no way now of becoming passively wealthy. Gambling was ruthlessly eradicated under the Air Dictatorship and has never returned. Usury ranks with forgery as a monetary offence. Money is given to people to get what they want and not as a basis for further acquisition, and we realize that the gambling spirit is a problem for the educationist and mental expert. It implies a fundamental misunderstanding of life. We have neither speculators, shareholders, private usurers or rent lords. All these 'independent' types have vanished from the earth. Land and its natural resources are now owned and administered, either directly or by delegation, by a hierarchy of administrative boards representing our whole species; there are lease-holding cultivators and exploiting corporations with no right to sublet, but there is no such thing as a permanent private ownership of natural resources making an automatic profit by the increment of rent. And since there is, and probably always will be now, a continual advance in our average individual productive efficiency by which the whole community profits, there follows a continual extension of our collective enterprises, a progressive release of leisure, and a secular raising of the standard of individual life to compensate for what would otherwise be a progressive diminution in the number of brains and hands needed to carry on the work of the world. Human society, so long as productive efficiency increases, is *obliged* to raise its standards of consumption and extend its activities year by year, or collapse. And if its advance does not go on it will drop into routine, boredom, viciousness and decay. Steadfastly the quantity and variety of things *must* increase.

These imperative conditions, which constitute the ABC of the existing order, seem so obvious to-day that it is with difficulty we put ourselves in the place of these twentieth-century folk to whom they were strange and novel. They were not yet humanized *en masse*; they still had the mentality of the 'struggle for existence'. It is only by a considerable mental effort, and after a careful study of the gradual evolution of the civilized mentality out of the chaotic impulses and competition of an originally very unsocial animal, that we can even begin to see matters with the eyes of our predecessors of a century and a half ago.

V

The Way in which Competition and Monetary Inefficiency strained the Old Order

In the twentieth century of the Christian era there was still no common currency by which to measure and carry on the world's economic exchanges. Those transactions were not merely apprehended inexactly because of this; they were falsified, and it did not seem possible that there would ever be an effective simplification. It is true that during what is known as the First Period of General Prosperity, from 1850 CE until 1914, there was a kind of working world-system of currency and credit, centring upon the City of London and based on the gold pound; but this was a purely accidental growth, made workable by successive gold discoveries which prevented too disastrous a fall in prices as productive efficiency increased, and by the circumstances that gave the insular English a lead in the development of steam transport on land and sea and real incentives towards a practical propaganda of world free trade.

That first gleam of cosmopolitan sunlight waned as it had waxed, without any contemporary apprehension of the real forces at work, much less any attempt to seize upon them and organize them in permanence. The financial ascendancy and initiative of the City of London crumbled away after the war and nothing appeared to take its place. In any case, this quasi-cosmopolitan system based on the gold sovereign, and owing its modicum of success to continual increments in the available gold, would have wilted as the world's gold supplies gave out, but the strangulation of the world's industry after the war was greatly accelerated by the gold hoarding of the Americans and French.

And during all that phase of opportunity there was no substantial effort to take hold of the land, sea and natural resources of the planet and bring them from a state of fragmentary, chaotic and wasteful exploitation into a general scheme. There remained sixty-odd 'sovereign' governments, each claiming a supreme control of all the natural wealth of the areas within its frontiers, and under these governments, under conditions that varied with each, there were private corporations and individuals with a right to deal more or less freely with the fragment upon which they had established a grip. Everywhere the guiding principle in the exploitation of the minerals, sunshine and power resources of the globe was the profit of single or associated private individuals, and the patchwork governments of the time interfered in the profit scramble only in favour of their nationals against their foreign rivals. Yet for nearly a hundred years, because of the fortunate influx of gold and inventions, this profit-seeking system, linked to the metallic monetary system, sufficed to sustain a very great expansion and enlargement of human life, and it was hard to convince the mass of men, and still harder to convince the prosperous manufacturers, traders, miners, cultivators and financiers who dominated public affairs, that this was not a permanent system and that the world already needed very essential modifications of its economic methods. A considerable measure of breakdown, a phase of dismay, fear and distress, was necessary before they could be disillusioned.

The nineteenth century had for its watchwords 'individual enterprise and free competition'. But the natural end of all competition is the triumph of one competitor. It was in America that the phenomena of Big Business first appeared and demonstrated the force of this truism; at a score of points triumphant organizations capable of crushing out new competitors and crippling and restraining new initiatives that threatened their predominance appeared. In Europe there was little governmental resistance to industrial alliances and concentrations in restraint of competition, and they speedily developed upon a scale that transcended political frontiers, but in the United States of America there was a genuine effort to prevent enterprises developing on a monopolistic scale. The conspicuous leader of this preventive effort was the first President Roosevelt (1858–1919) and its chief fruit the Sherman Anti-Trust Act (1890), which proved a rich mine for lawyers in the subsequent decades.

These great consolidations, which closed the phase of free competition, were so far effective in controlling trade and arresting new developments that Hilary Hooker, in his *Studies in Business Coagulation During the First Period of General Prosperity*, is able to cite rather more than two thousand instances, ranging from radium and new fruits and foodstuffs to gramophones, automobiles, reconstructed households, artificial moonlight for the roadways by the countryside, and comfortable and economical railway plant, in which ample supplies or beneficial improvements were successfully kept off the market in the interests of established profit-making systems. After 1900 CE again there was a world-wide cessation of daily newspaper initiative and a consequent systole of free speech. Distribution, paper supply and news services had fallen into the hands of powerful groups able and willing to crush out any new types of periodical, or any inimical schools of public suggestion. They set about stereotyping the public mind.

These same profit-making systems in possession also played a large part in arresting competition from countries in which they were less completely in control, by subsidized political action for the maintenance of protective tariffs. Long before the world breakdown became manifest, the experience of the ordinary consumer so far belied the sanguine theory that free competition was a mode of endless progress that he was still living in a house, wearing clothes, using appliances, travelling about in conveyances, and being fed with phrases and ideas that by the standard of the known and worked-out inventions of the time should have been discarded on an average, Hooker computes, from a quarter to half a century before. There was labour unemployed and abundant material available to remedy all this, but its utilization was held up by the rent-exacting and profit-earning systems already in possession.

The lag in modernization added greatly to the effects of increased productive efficiency in the disengagement of those vast masses of destitute unemployed and unemploying people which began to appear almost everywhere, like the morbid secretion of a diseased body, as the twentieth century passed on into its third decade.

VI

The paradox of Over-Production and its Relation to War

This so-called 'paradox of over-production' which figures so largely in the loose discussions of the 'post-war' period was in its essence a very simple affair indeed. Just as the inevitable end of a process of free competition was a consolidation of successful competitors and an arrest of enterprise, so the inevitable end of a search for profit in production was a steady reduction of costs through increased efficiency – that is to say, a steady decrease of the ratio of employment to output. These things lie so much on the surface of the process that it is almost incredible to us that, wilfully or not, our ancestors disregarded them. Equally inevitable was it that these necessary contractions of enterprise and employment should lead to an increase in the proportion of unemployable people. Geographical expansion and a rising standard of life among both the employed and possessing classes, together with the stimulating effect of a steady influx of gold, masked and tempered for half a century this squeezing-out of an increasing fraction of the species from its general economic life. There were nevertheless fluctuations, 'cycles of trade' as they were called, when the clogging machinery threatened to stall and was then relieved and went on again. But by the opening of the twentieth century the fact that the method of running human affairs as an open competition for profit was in its nature a terminating method was forcing itself upon the attention even of those who profited most by it and had the most excuse for disregarding it, and who, as a class, knew nothing of the Marxian analysis.

We know now that the primary task of world administration is to arrest this squeezing-out of human beings from active economic life by the continual extension of new collective enterprises, but such ideas had still to be broached at that time. The common folk, wiser in their instincts than the political economists in their intellectualism, were disposed to approve of waste and extravagance because money was 'circulated' and workers 'found employment'. And the reader will not be able to understand the world-wide tolerance of growing armaments and war preparations during this period unless he realizes the immediate need inherent in the system for unremunerative public expenditure. Somewhere the energy economized had to come out. The world of private finance would not tolerate great rehousing, great educational and socially constructive enterprises on the part of the relatively feeble governments of the time. All that had to be reserved for the profit accumulator. And so the ever-increasing productivity of the race found its vent in its ancient traditions of warfare, which admitted the withdrawal of a large proportion of the male population from employment for a year or so and secreted that vast accumulation of forts, battleships, guns, submarines, explosives, barracks and the like which still amazes us. Without this cancer growth of armies and navies the paradox of over-production latent in competitive private enterprise would probably have revealed itself in an overwhelming mass of unemployment before even the end of the nineteenth century. A social revolution might have occurred then.

Militarism, however, alleviated these revolutionary stresses by providing vast profit-yielding channels of waste. And it also strengthened the forces of social repression. The means of destruction accumulated on a scale that wellnigh kept pace with the increase in the potential wealth of mankind. The progressive enslavement of the race to military tyranny was an inseparable aspect, therefore, of free competition for profits. The latter system conditioned and produced the former. It needed the former so as to have ballast to throw out to destruction and death whenever it began to sink. The militarist phase of the early twentieth century and the paradox of over-production are correlated facets of the same reality, the reality of the planless hypertrophy of the social body.

It is interesting to note how this morbid accumulation of energy in belligerence and its failure to find vent in other directions became more and more evident in the physiognomy of the world as the twentieth century progressed. The gatherings of mankind became blotched with uniforms. Those admirable albums of coloured pictures, *Historical*

Scenes in a Hundred Volumes, which are now placed in all our schools and show-places and supplied freely to any home in which there are children, display very interestingly the advent, predominance and disappearance of military preoccupations in the everyday life of our ancestors. These pictures are all either reproductions of actual paintings, engravings or photographs, or, in the case of the earlier volumes, they are elaborate reconditionings to the more realistic methods of our time of such illustrations as were available. Military operations have always attracted the picture-maker at all times, and there are plentiful pictures of battles from every age, from the little cricket-field battle of the Middle Ages to the hundred-mile fights of the last Great War, but our interest here is not with battles but with the general facies of social life. Even in the war-torn seventeenth century the general stream of life went on without any manifest soldiering. War was a special occupation. While the battles of the English Civil War, which set up the first English Republic (1649–60), were in progress, we have evidence that hunting and hawking parties were busy almost within sound of the guns. The novels of Jane Austen (England, 1775–1817) pursue their even way without the faintest echo of the land and sea campaigns in progress. Goethe in Weimar (the German literary 'Great Man' during the 'Great Man' period of literary thought in Europe, 1749–1832) could not be bothered by requests for supplies of wood and food for the German troops before the battle of Jena, and was very pleased to meet his 'enemy alien' Napoleon socially during that campaign.

We rarely see the monarchs of the eighteenth century depicted in military guise; the fashion was for robes and majesty rather than for the spurs and feathers of the Bantam warrior-king. It was the unprecedented vehemence of the Napoleonic adventure that splashed the social life of Europe with uniforms, infected feminine fashions, and even set plump princess colonels, frogged with gold lace and clutching bare sabres, joggling unsteadily at the heads of regiments. There was a brief return towards civilian attire with the accession of the 'domesticated monarchs', Louis Philippe in France and Victoria in Great Britain; they marked a transient reaction from Napoleonic fashions; but from the middle of the nineteenth century onward the prestige of the soldier resumed its advance and the military uniform became increasingly pervasive. Flags became more abundant in the towns and 'flag-days' dotted the calendar. There was never a crowd pictured in Europe after 1870 without a soldier or so.

The Great War greatly intensified the military element in the street population, not only in Europe but America. Various corps of feminine auxiliaries were enrolled during that time and paraded the world thereafter in appetizing soldierly outfits. In the United States, except at Washington, or when there was a parade of civil war veterans, a soldier in uniform had been hitherto the rarest of birds. He would have felt strange and uncomfortable. He would have offended the susceptibilities of a consciously liberated people. The Great War changed all that. When Germany was disarmed after the war, a Nazi movement and a Reichsbanner movement supplied the needed colour until a German's freedom to get into properly recognized livery was restored. The pattern of half-military, half-civilian organizations in uniform had already been spread about the world between the South African War (1899–1901) and the Great War by the Boy Scout movement.

Of the Nazi movement, the Italian Fascisti and the Polish Brotherhood at least there will be more to tell later. The black and brown shirts may be cited here as instances of the visible breaking-down of the boundaries between military and civil life that went on during and after the World War.

Hitherto war had been a marginal business, fought upon 'fronts', and the ordinary citizen had lived in comparative security behind the front, but the bombing, gas-diffusing aeroplane, and later the long-range air torpedo, changed all that. The extended use of propaganda as a weapon, and the increasing danger of social mutiny under war stress, had also its share in making the entire surface of a belligerent country a war area and abolishing any vestiges of civil liberty, first during actual warfare and then in view of warfare. The desirability of getting everyone under orders, under oath, and subject to prompt disciplinary measures, became more and more manifest to governments.

So within a century the appearance of the human crowd changed over from a varied assembly of incoordinated free individuals to a medley of uniforms. Everybody's dress at last indicated function, obligation and preparedness. The militarization of the European multitude reached a maximum during the Polish wars. About 1942 gas masks, either actually worn or hanging from the neck, were common for a time, and so, too, were the small sheath-knives which were to be used in disposing of fallen aviators who might still be alive. Patella metal hats and metal epaulettes to protect the head and body against a rain of poisoned needles also appeared. Some civilians became far more formidable-looking than any soldiers.

The military authorities of those days were much perplexed by the problem of giving the general population protective apparatus and light weapons that would be effective against the military enemy and yet useless for the purposes of insurrection. For in spite of the most strenuous suppression of agitation in those troubled decades, the possible revolt of humanity against warfare, the possibility of complete 'loss of morale', however illogical and incoherent, was felt by the professional soldiers as an increasing menace.

Along the streets of most of the old-world cities there presently appeared the characteristic yellow (or in France blue, and in America red-and-white-striped) air-raid pillars with their glass faces, only to be broken into and used after an official alarm, which contained respirators and first-aid sets for possible gas victims. It is also to the same period we have to ascribe the multiplication of vivid and abundant direction signs at every street corner, set so as to throw a minimum of light upward and pointing the way to gas chambers and hospitals. It was a 'gas-minded' world in the 'forties. The practical suppression of other vivid and illuminated street signs was a natural corollary to this preoccupation.

In the first half of the twentieth century the cities blazed with advertisement. It was the period of maximum advertisement. The pictures of the Great White Way of New York, Piccadilly Circus, the Grands Boulevards of Paris and so forth, with their polychromatic visual clamour, still strike us as distractingly picturesque. There was much flood-lighting after 1928. Then progressively the lights were turned down again and that visual clamour died away. As the air threat returned, 'lights out' became at last imperative, except for the vivid furtive indications of refuge and first aid we have just mentioned.

War fear spread very rapidly after 1930. Darkness recaptured the nocturnal town. 'Night-life' became stealthy and obscure, with an increasing taint of criminality. All civil hospitals and all private doctors had disappeared from the world by 1945, and the health services were only legally demilitarized again after 2010. The amalgamation of the military and civil hospital and medical services began in France as early as 1933. By 1945 every doctor in the Old World was, in theory at least, on a quasi-military footing; he wore a distinctive uniform, was subject to stringent discipline, and his premises, as well as the hospitals, bore the characteristic black and yellow chequerwork. All nurses were similarly enrolled. Finally the general public was enrolled for health treatment as common patients under oath. By 1948 in such towns as had sufficiently survived the general social demoralization to enforce such regulations, it was impossible to take a chill or break an ankle without at once falling into the category of patients and being numbered, put into a black-and-yellow uniform and marched or carried off for treatment. Theoretically this system of treatment was universal. In practice neither the uniforms or the doctors were available. For regulation and militarization were going on in that period against an immense counter-drive towards social disintegration. The more humanity got into uniform, the shabbier the uniforms became.

Before the Polish struggle, general architecture was very little affected by military needs. The militarization of costume preceded the militarization of scenery. Even barracks and such-like army buildings were erected by army architects as a simple vulgarization of ordinary housing patterns, a mere stiffening up, so to speak, of the common 'jerry-built' house. There still survive for our astonishment pictures of Victorian Military Gothic and Victorian Military Tudor, produced under the

British War Office. They display homes fit for drill-sergeants. The military mind had to be roused by the experiences of the Polish conflict to the profound reconstruction of the ordinary town that had become necessary if it was still to be taken seriously. Before then, fortification scarcely affected the urban scene at all, even in the case of a fortified town. Previously a fortress had been just an ordinary civil town surrounded at distances of from three to fifty miles by forts, strong points, trench systems and the like. Now it was realized, first in Berlin, and then in Danzig, Warsaw, Paris and Turin, and after that by the whole world, that air warfare demanded not merely fortification round a town, but, much more imperatively fortification *over* a town. The world, which had been far too stupid to realize in 1930 that the direct way out of its economic difficulties lay in the modernization and rebuilding of its houses, set itself, in a state of war panic after 1942, to as complete a revision of its architecture in the face of bombs and gas as its deepening impoverishment permitted. What it would not do for prosperity, it attempted belatedly out of fear.

The first most obvious undertaking was the construction of those immense usually ill-built concrete cavern systems for refuge, whose vestiges are still to be visited by the curious tourist at Paris and Berlin (the London ones have all fallen in, the collapse beginning after the great landslip and fire), and close upon this came the cessation of tall building and the concentration of design upon the vast (and often dangerous) carapace roof and its gigantic supporting pillars and foundation rafts. Only the ever-deepening poverty, the increasing industrial disorganization and the transitoriness of that last war-phase saved all the towns in the world from being thrust completely under such squat massive coverings.

So strong were the influences of that time that even up to 2020 the tendency of architectural design was to crouch. Hardly any mass of buildings erected between 1945 and the end of the century lifts up its head and looks the world in the face. That period has been called, not unjustly, Second Egyptian. And this was so in spite of the multiplying opportunities for grace and lightness afforded by the supersession of steel-frame buildings by the strong and flexible neo-concrete materials that were already available. How timidly they were used! We grovel no longer, because we are ceasing to fear each other. The soaring, ever improving homes in which we live to-day would have sent our great-grandfathers scurrying to their cellars in an ecstasy of terror.

VII

The Great War of 1914–18

There is a monstrous tedious accumulation of records concerned with the World War. The Catalogue of Historical Material stored at Atacama gives a list of 2,362,705 books and gross files, up to date, and of these over 182,000 deal exclusively or largely with the causation of the war. Nothing could bring home to the student the profound difference in mental equipment between ourselves and the men and women of that period than a visit to the long silent galleries of that great library of dead disputes and almost completely forgotten records. He will see hardly a visitor along the vistas of that shining framework of shelves; a quiet cleaner or duster perhaps will be visible, scrutinizing the condition of the material, or a young revisionist student patiently checking some current summary – or a black cat. For the rest, above, below, to right and left is a clean and luminous stillness; papers at rest.

In one large section of this sere honeycomb the student will find the records of the 'war guilt controversy' that agitated the world for decades after the Peace of Versailles. Let him draw out a seat anywhere and take down a file or so at hazard and turn over its pages. He will be able to read almost all of it nowadays, whatever the original language, because practically all the collection has now been interleaved with translations into Basic English. And it will seem to him that he is reading the outpourings of lunatics, so completely have the universal obsessions of that time been exorcized since.

Had 'Germany' planned the war? Was 'France' the guilty party? Had 'Britain' much to answer for? With difficulty will the student let down his mind into the fantastic world of extinct imaginations in which these strange personifications, as monstrous and incredible as the ancient gods of India, were treated as real and morally responsible individuals, hated, trusted, feared and loved. The war was, in immediate fact, an aimless and fruitless slaughter upon the altars of these stupendous deities, the wounding and mutilation of perhaps twenty million human beings, and a vast burning-up of material wealth. In the crazy fancy of our ancestors it was a noble and significant struggle. Happily we need not revive their craziness here. The question of 'war guilt' was never settled. It ceased to be pursued, it was neglected, it floated away into the absurd, and little but those three hundred feet or so of forgotten books and gross files remain to testify to its vanished importance.

The causation of the struggle was, indeed, perfectly simple. It arose naturally and necessarily from that irregular and disproportionate growth of human appliances as compared with the extension of political and social intelligence we have already described.

The new means of communication and transport, and the new economic life which demanded the products of every zone and soil for its purposes, were necessitating the reorganization of human affairs as a World-State, and since the world was already parcelled up among sixty-odd competing sovereign governments there were only two possible courses open to mankind, either to arrange the coalescence of these governments by treaty and rational arrangements to meet the new need, or to allow a steadily intensified mutual pressure to develop into more or less thinly disguised attempts at world conquest. In the decades before the war the British, French, German, Russian, Japanese and American systems were all, as the word went then, 'imperialist' – all, that is, attempting to become World-States on a planet on which obviously there was room only for one single World-State. Nothing of the sort had been apparent when the methods of European statecraft had been devised. These vaster possibilities had yawned open after-wards. The eighteenth and nineteenth centuries were centuries of small restricted wars for limited advantages. In the twentieth century the scale of war expanded beyond any limit and the advantages to be won by it disappeared. But the politicians and diplomatists played their time-honoured game against each other with a sort of terrified inevitability. They were driven; they had no control, or at least none of them seemed to have had the vigour and imagination to attempt a control. They were driven by the economic necessity we have explained in the previous section. They had to arm preposterously. They had to threaten. They had to go through with the business.

These forces account for the outbreak and universality of the Great War, but they do not account for its peculiar frightfulness. For that it is necessary to realize that, though governments expanded only against an enormous pressure of mutual restraint, no limitations had been set to the hypertrophy of financial and industrial enterprises. These last were under the sway of a relentless and unrestrained progress; they expanded, invented, urged and sold; they brought weapons of a strange and terrible effectiveness to the settlement of what were in comparison small and antiquated disputes. To that hypertrophy of the armourer we will return presently, because the Great War was really only a first revelation of this peculiar disproportion between economics and politics, and the evil still went on in an exaggerated form after the formal conclusion of the struggle at the Peace of Versailles (1919). But let us first tell what needs to be known of the details of the Great War.

How little that is now! There is a vast literature both of fiction based on experience and of personal reminiscence about it, and some of it is admirably written; almost any of it may be read for interest and edification, and hardly any of it need be read with scholarly precision. The picture of the outbreak of the war still touches us. There was a curious unconsciousness of the grossness of the menace in events, even on the part of myriads doomed to suffer and die in a few months' time. Many of the stories told begin with a holiday party or a country-house gathering or some such bright setting. The weather that August (1914) was exceptionally fine.

The details of the struggle itself were as horrible and distressing as they were inconsequent, and there is no need whatever for anyone but the specialist to master their sequence in detail. The old-fashioned history, with its lists of names, dates, battles and so on, was designed rather to supply easily marked material for examinations than to give any sense of the historical process. Examinations have long passed out of educational practice; they have gone to join the 'globes' and the abacus, the slate and the cane in the scholastic limbo, but their memory is preserved in the popular game of 'examination papers', when people write down as fast as they can and as much as they can about some suddenly selected subject.

Few of us could write even a brief account now of the World War. The names of such generals as Haig, Kitchener, French, Joffre, Foch and Ludendorff, to take names at random, and such battles as Tannenberg, the Marne, the Somme, Passchendaele, the Falkland Isles, Jutland and so forth, mean nothing and need mean nothing to the ordinary citizen to-day. He does not know whether French was really French or not, nor whether Foch was a Frenchman or a German. He inclines to the latter view. He does not know who won or lost these conflicts and he does not care. He has not even a sporting interest in it. They were not lively fights. Nearly all the commanders concerned had dull and unattractive personalities and the business was altogether too unwieldy for them. Most of their operations were densely stupid, muddled both in conception and execution. One would as soon listen to a child reciting not very accurately and at endless length the deals and tricks of some game of cards it has played, or imagines it has played, as read their memoirs – packed as they too often are with self-exculpation, personal resentments and malice. Faint, faded, immense and far-off tragedies, these struggles that were to have astounded posterity have already gone far towards complete effacement in any but a few specializing minds, are hardly more vivid now in our collective consciousness than the battles of the Peloponnesian War – or the campaigns and conquests of Tamerlane. They had nothing of the primary historical importance and strategic splendour which have restored the gigantic military conceptions of Genghis Khan to an integral place in our ordinary educational curriculum.

For the rodomontade of the conflict the curious cannot do better than glance through the eager narrative of Winston Churchill's *World Crisis*.

There one finds all the stereotyped flourishes and heroisms of nine-teenth-century history from the British point of view; the 'drama of history' in rich profusion, centred upon one of the most alert personalities in the conflict. He displays a vigorous naïve puerility that still gives his story an atoning charm. He has the insensitiveness of a child of thirteen. His soldiers are toy soldiers and he loves to knock over a whole row of them. He enjoyed the war. He takes himself and all the now forgotten generals and statesmen of the war with a boyish seriousness. He passes grave judgments of their tragic fooleries and distributes compliments and blame, often in the most gracious manner, convinced that he is writing for a meticulously admiring and envious posterity. They would read, they would marvel. He was the sort of man who believed that when he begot children he created an audience. He was misled by the excitement of his own reading of history. He not only measures for us the enormous gulf between the mentality of his times and our own, but he enables us to bridge that gulf with an amused and forgiving sympathy.

A less attractive spirit displays itself in the memoirs of such figures as Ludendorff, Bülow, Clemenceau, Fisher, Foch, and so through the whole category of war leaders. The war was the supreme event in the lives of most of these men, and apparently they were never able to think of anything else afterwards. They had none of the recuperative inno-cence of Churchill, his terrier-like interest in everything. They all took to writing furiously in their declining years and no other pens could have damned them so completely. They are grown-up and yet under-developed persons; as adult as old chimpanzees; they cannot claim Churchill's benefit of schoolboy, and there is a real horror in their wrinkled meannesses and envies, their gross enthusiasms and their sincere bloodthirstiness and hate. Most of their mutual recriminations are too incomprehensible to be of the slightest interest now; spite and twaddle are still spite and twaddle even if drenched with blood. The most accessible sample for the contemporary reader is *The Life and Diaries of Field-Marshal Sir Henry Wilson, Bart., G.C.B., D.S.O.*, a lean, unsightly man of infinite energy, gusto and vanity, who played a very prominent rôle in bringing about and carrying out the catastrophe. It is the latest reprint in the Historical Documents Series; it is richly illustrated and abundantly annotated, and with it are bound up the brilliantly scornful criticisms of Wilson's contemporary, Sir Andrew Macphail, and Stephen Freudheim's more scientific analysis of him as the supreme type of the 'soldierly mind'.

For the grimmer actualities of the struggle there is a vast and sombre literature. It has been summarized in the last fifteen years by the Historical Bureau in its *War Pictures for Posterity by Pen, Pencil and Camera.* Everyone should turn over those strange incredible records of endurance, callousness, devotion and insane courage to learn something of the extremes to which men and women like ourselves can be pushed by the grim forces of social compulsion.

The earlier volumes deal chiefly with the psychology of the more than half civilized citizens of the Atlantic and North European states suddenly precipitated into a maelstrom of destruction. We see the urban crowds demonstrating and cheering in the streets of the capital cities, the floods of youths coming from their work to 'join up', the wonder and unimaginative fierceness and heroism of the opening stage. Then come the first contacts, the villages in flames, the wild shooting of curious bystanders as spies and guerillas, realizations of horror and a wave of fear, the invaded populations in flight, black crowds with their pitiful impedimenta streaming along darkling roads, going they know not whither. The rifles and machine-guns rattle, the guns thud, and the cheering adventurousness of the advancing armies as they blunder heavily into contact passes into a phase of astounded violence and hardship. The new war was like no war that had ever been before. The French upon their eastern front went forward to the attack with immense élan, in bright uniforms and to the historical inspiration of the 'Marseillaise'. They were massacred. They lost a third of a million men in three weeks. The Germans poured through Belgium, more than a million strong, to be stopped and stunned with Paris almost within their grasp. The pictures show the smiling landscape of eastern Belgium, France and east Prussia in July 1914, and the same countryside a couple of months later – torn, scored and trenched, defiled with bloody heaps of litter that were once clothed bodies, an anguish of countless thousands of unclean, hungry, exhausted, cruelty-wrung human beings.

These bands of contact, these regions of filthy pain and tumult, spread. Presently there were 'war zones' reaching from the North Sea to the Alps and across Eastern Europe, strange regions in which every house was a ruin, every tree a splintered trunk, where millions of crouching men went to and fro in trenches and ditches furtively like rats, and the ragged dead lay unburied. There day and night the superfluous energy of a profiteering economic system, denied all other outlet by its own preconceptions and the rigid historical traditions in which it was blinkered, blew itself away in the incessant concussions of mines, bombs and guns and a continual destruction of human life.

Presently newly invented weapons, hitherto untried, came to extend and intensify the struggle. The aeroplane, and that primitive 'navigable' the Zeppelin, carried the war behind the fronts and attacked the civilian population in the cities. We see the explosive and incendiary bombs bursting into the dirty little urban homes of the time, blowing to rags the bed-rid grandmother and the baby in the cradle; we see the panic-stricken crowds seeking the shelter of cellars and excavations and the drainlike railway 'tubes' of the time. In the early stages of the air-war only explosives and inflammatory substances were used, but as the struggle progressed the art of using gas bombs developed, and an agonizing suffocation was added to the nocturnal chances of flame and explosion and death among fallen ruins for the non-combatant at home. The submarine, also, was a novelty of the Great War, and a very searching novelty. It was used first to sink fighting ships, and then it was turned against all sea-going craft. We have vivid descriptions of the sinking of the *Lusitania* without warning and the drowning of 1,198 men, women and children. She was, by the standards of the time, a great and luxurious ship, and a sort of symbolism was found by the writers of this period in this sudden descent from light, comfort and confidence into a desperate and hopeless struggle in the waters of the night. All the achievements of nineteenth-century civilization seemed to many to be following in the downward wake of the *Lusitania*.

Service in these early submarines strained men to the breaking point. They were essentially engines of war, they had all the defects of inventions at an early stage, and none of the security and comfort of the great submarine barges that are used to-day for the Mediterranean and Atlantic Ridge mines and for general deep-sea exploration. These, with their beautifully adjusted pressure systems and their limitless vertical range are calculated rather to mislead than enlighten us as to the capabilities of the primitive submarines of the Great War. The latter were able to descend safely only to a depth of a hundred metres; below that the pressure became too much for them and their plates gave and leaked. When they leaked the salt water was apt to affect the accumulators and chlorine gas was released to torment and suffocate the crews. Below a hundred and fifty metres these fragile contrivances crumpled up altogether and were destroyed. The air in them became foul when they submerged, in spite of the compressed oxygen they carried, and the continual condensation of exhaled moisture gave them a peculiar clammy discomfort. They could move about under water for a couple of days by means of their electric batteries, but then it was necessary to come to the surface and run their oil-combustion engines for some hours to recharge. Armed with guns and packed with mines, bombs, torpedoes and other explosives, they set out to harass and destroy the surface shipping of the enemy.

It was a difficult and almost fantastically dangerous task. Submerged, they were invisible, but also they were blind. Near the surface they could get a limited view of what was going on by means of a periscope. On the surface they had the range of outlook of any other surface boat, but all the risks a surface boat must take. So under conditions of extreme discomfort and partial asphyxiation the crews of these strangely formidable and strangely fragile contrivances groped their way towards their victims. To see the quarry fairly they had to come to the surface, and that exposed them to gunfire. If their thin steel skins were pierced by a single shot they could no longer go under. Often when submerged they betrayed their whereabouts unwittingly by bubbles of gas and escapes of oil.

At first, in spite of their limitations, the submarines proved a very deadly weapon, more particularly in the hands of the Central European Powers. They destroyed a great multitude of ships and drowned many score thousands of men. Then slowly the methods used against them improved. They were hunted by a special flotilla, and among other ships by the 'Q' boats, armed vessels disguised as harmless merchantmen. These lured them to the surface and then let down sham bulwarks and opened fire upon them, so that after a time they no longer dared emerge to challenge even the most harmless-looking craft. Explosive mines were moored in their possible tracks and mine-armed nets set across harbours and channels. They were also watched for by aeroplanes and special airships whose signals guided the destroyers to their quarry. Ingenious listening contrivances were invented to locate them. They were shot at on the surface, rammed, and pursued by 'depth-charges' which could strain their plates and disable them even when exploded scores of metres away.

Such, briefly, were the conditions of submarine warfare in the years 1917–18. And yet to the very end of the war men could be found to carry it on, to destroy and drown and be in their turn hunted and destroyed. The building and launching of submersibles never ceased. Men went down in them to chilly confinement, to the perpetual anxiety of mine or ram, to the quivering menace of the distant depth-charge, to the reasonable probability of a frightful death beyond all human aid. Few submarines returned to harbour ten times; many went out new upon their first voyage never to return. Two hundred of them were lost by the Germans alone; each loss a tragedy of anguish and dismay in the deeps. Towards the end it was claimed by their antagonists that the crews were losing morale. Once or twice an undamaged submarine that had been cornered surrendered, and the new commanders showed a growing tendency to return to port for minor repairs or other slight pretexts. But on the whole, such is the unimaginative heroic submissiveness of our species, the service was sustained. The Germans supplied most of the flesh for this particular altar; willing and disciplined, their youngsters saluted and carried their kit down the ladder into this gently swaying clumsy murder-mechanism which was destined to become their coffin.

Their obedience brings us to one of the most fundamental lessons that the Great War has for us: the extreme slowness with which the realization of even the most obvious new conditions pierces through the swathings of habitual acceptance. Millions of human beings went open-eyed to servitude, bullying, hardship, suffering and slaughter without a murmur, with a sort of fatalistic pride. In obedience to the dictates of the blindest prejudices and the most fatuous loyalties they did their

372   THE SHAPE OF THINGS TO COME

utmost to kill men against whom they had no conceivable grievance, and they were in their turn butchered gallantly, fighting to the last. The *War Pictures* volumes dismay our imaginations by portraying a series of wholesale butcheries, many of them on a stupendous scale, of men who died facing their enemies. After the great slaughter of the French at the outset of the war, and a mighty killing of Russians at the Battles of Tannenberg and the Masurian Lakes, there was during what was called the deadlock period, the period of trench warfare, a diminution of the losses upon the West. Hostilities sank down to a gusty conflict of shell-fire, rifle assassinations, and raids with bombs and bludgeons. In the East, however, the Russians ran out of ammunition, and held their trenches only by a great martyrdom of men; they lost well over a million before the end of 1914, and yet they continued to obey orders. A series of minor campaigns broke out in regions from the main centres of contact. There is a horrible account in the *Pictures* of the sufferings of some thousands of British common soldiers taken prisoners at Kut, in Mesopotamia. (Their generals and other officers, however, who had arranged that particular capitulation, were honourably and comfortably entertained by their captors the Turks.) There is no effective expression of resentment by the British troops on record.

In 1916 and 1917 there were spasmodic renewals of hostilities on a large scale by the British and French in France. Newly trained British armies were made to advance in close formation by generals who, unless they were imbeciles, could have had no doubts of the fate to which they were sending their men. If they were not imbeciles then they were criminally unwilling to learn and soul-blind to suffering and waste. The mentality of these men is still a matter for discussion. The poor boys they commanded were marched forward shoulder to shoulder in successive waves of attack, and so advancing they were shot to pieces by the enemy machine-guns. Out of battalions of six or seven hundred, perhaps a hundred would struggle through the defensive fire and come to bomb-throwing, bayonet-thrusts and surrender in the German trenches. Small isolated groups of them in shell-holes and captured positions fought on for days. So perished the flower of an entire school generation, collected from hundreds of thousands of homes, more or less loved, more or less cared for and more or less educated; it had been enlisted, trained, sent out to the battlefields at enormous cost, to be left at last in the desolated spaces between the armies, lying in heaps and swathes to rot and be rat-eaten. For months afterwards, as the photographs show, thousands of them were to be seen sprawling in formation as they fell, just as if their ranks were still waiting to leap again to the attack. But as the observer drew nearer he realized their corruption. He discovered bony hands, eyeless sockets, faces far gone in decay.

The British commander-in-chief in his despatches did not fail to extol the courage of his lost battalions and to represent this monstrous exploit as a victory. Some mile or so of ground had been gained in that July offensive and less than 12,000 prisoners had been taken. Twice as many British were left prisoners in German hands, but this the despatches ignored.

The appalling nature of this particular disaster leaked out only very slowly. The British censorship at least was efficient and the generals, however incapable in other respects, lied magnificently. The Channel crossing made it particularly easy to hide events from the British public. And it had a peculiar effect on the British troops; it gave them a feeling of being in another and a different world from 'home', a war-world in which such cruel and fantastic things could be natural. This monstrous massacre was, indeed, contrived and carried through, not simply without a revolt, but with scarcely an audible protest on the part of either the parents, relations, friends or surviving comrades of those hosts of wasted victims.

The commanders of the Russian armies in Austria, Armenia and elsewhere were announcing equally costly and heroic triumphs and the Germans and Austrians were issuing the most valiant and excessive contradictions of their claims. They, too, were losing hideously enough, though in a lesser proportion than their opponents. The next year (1917), the British, gallant and docile as ever, with only very slightly improved tactics, were going again into great offensives.

But now the French troops began to manifest a livelier intelligence. They were amidst familiar things, nearer their homes and less cut off from subversive influences than the British. A certain General Nivelle, at that time French Commander-in-Chief, made what Churchill calls an 'experiment', which resulted altogether in the loss of nearly a couple of hundred thousand men. It involved the advance of masses of infantry into intense fields of fire. In an hour, said Lieutenant Ybarnegaray (in a debate in the French Chamber, June 1917), they were reduced to a crowd 'running like madmen', all formations and distinctions lost. Provision had been made for less than 15,000 wounded. There were seven times as many. Most of the casualties never received the most elementary attention for three days. The result was gangrene, amputation and death for thousands. Then came the first intimation that there were limits to human obedience. A French divison ordered into action to continue this futile holocaust refused to march. Churchill says this was 'deeply disquieting' to the authorities, and no doubt it pained and distressed every intelligent amateur of war. This particular division was cajoled into a change of mind. It took part in the fighting, says Churchill, 'without discredit', but the spirit of its resistance spread.

The next sign of sanity in this world torture was the collapse of the grotesque Russian autocracy. We have already told of the mental and moral decay of the Tzardom in our general study of the degeneration of monarchy. [*Non inventus.* – ED.] Abruptly this profoundly rotten government collapsed into nothing; its vast domains became a various disorder, and for some months phantom imitations of Western revolutionaries, inspired by memories of the first French revolution or by legends of British parliamentary wisdom, occupied the capital. The one certain fact in the situation was the accumulated disinclination of the Russian people for any further warfare. But this first republican government under an eloquent lawyer politican, of no great directive force, Alexandre Kerensky, was unable to either carry on the war or to end it. A subdued but spreading clamour for 'peace by negotiation' in all the combatant countries ensued, a clamour that active repression and the most rigorous concealment in the Press failed to silence. There was an attempt to call a sort of peace conference of Radicals at Stockholm, and then a second revolution in Russia which carried a small and resolute Communist organization to power – carried it to power simply and solely because there was no other organized alternative, and because it promised peace plainly and surely – peace on any terms. The Russian armies melted away at its signal; the men streamed home. The German military authorities in the East found the trenches before them undefended, and with every courtesy of war, as one soldier to another, welcomed the Russian officers of the old régime, taking refuge from the belated resentment of their own men.

In 1917 mankind seemed already to be awakening from the war-nightmare. Mutinies broke out in sixteen separate French army corps, 115 regiments were involved, divisions elected soldiers' councils and whole regiments set out for Paris to demand a reasonable wind-up of the struggle. The one last hope of the despairing soldiers, said Pierre Laval, had been Stockholm. That disappointment had made life unbearable. But the storm abated with the entry of the United States of America into the war, and the powers in control of the Western World were still able to pursue their dreadful obsessions for another year.

War Pictures for Posterity by Pen, Pencil and Camera devotes a whole volume (xxi) to the tragedy of a special Russian infantry corps in France. Fifteen thousand Russians had been sent thither in 1916 to be equipped and armed and put into the line with the French armies. Many of these poor lads scarcely knew the difference between a Frenchman and a German, and the ostensible objects of the war were quite beyond their understanding. But they heard of the revolution in their own country and they resolved to consider their attitude with regard to it. They elected representatives and put it to the vote whether they should continue to fight, which meant for them to take part in that 'experiment' of Nivelle's known to be in preparation at the time. They chose what seemed to them the generous part and went into the battle. The French command used them ruthlessly, and nearly 6,000 were killed or wounded. The rest came out of the line and mutinied. They would fight no more. Thereupon these defenceless men were surrounded by trust-

worthy French troops, a great concentration of guns was assembled, fire
was opened upon them suddenly and they were massacred. Horrible
photographs of the details of this – photographs hidden away at the
time from the authorities and brought to light later – are given in the
summary already cited.

For nearly a year the French lost confidence in the morale of their
own men and dared make no more great attacks, but their allies offered
up another 400,000 men in the battle of Passchendaele and accounted
for 300,000 Germans, and in the spring the Germans made a vast
multitudinous attack in the West which succeeded at first and then
collapsed, whereupon their antagonists, reinforced by new armies from
America, waded back through blood to a dreadful final victory. The last
nine months of the conflict saw more slaughter than any preceding year.
From March 21st 1918, to November 11th in the same year the British
suffered 830,000 casualties, the French and Belgians 964,000 and the
Germans 1,470,000. There were also 2,000,000 American troops
brought to Europe before the end, and of these more than half were
actually engaged in the fighting. Their casualties were certainly not less
than 350,000. Portugese and other contingents from the most unexpected quarters also contributed to that culminating death-roll, but it is
impossible for us now to give exact numbers for these minor forces.

These are the gross figures of warfare. But *War Pictures* devotes three
volumes, perhaps the most horrible of all, to the presentation of various
details of the fighting in which these vast multitudes suffered and
perished. These three volumes are like the microscopic slides in a
specimen book of anatomy, which show us from a selected scrap of
tissue the texture of the whole. Little figures stand out enlarged, chosen
by the hazard that they wrote or talked or carried a camera, to represent
the nameless millions who have left no record. We have accounts of
men who were left to lie out for days between the lines, tortured by
thirst and stifled by the stench of their own corruption, and yet who
survived to tell the tale. We have the stories of men who fell into heaps
of rotting dead, and lay there choking, and of men who were gassed.
The tortures of gas were already many and various, and most of the
mixtures then used left tormenting weaknesses in the system for the rest
of life. We have descriptions of the rude surgery of the time and
abstracts of the mental disorders through which minds fled from reality.
There are also some dreadful pictures of mutilated men, faceless,
crippled, grotesquely distorted, and an autobiography of one of the
blinded (*Outstaying My Welcome*, by Fritz Schiff, 1923). Scores of
thousands of unhappy fragments of humanity had to be hidden away in
special institutions until they died, they were at once so terrifying and
so pitiful and hopeless. The world forgot them even while they lived.

The distortion of souls was even more dreadful than the distortion of
bodies. One of the most lurid items in that dreadful assemblage of

realities is a lecture on the use of the bayonet, which chanced to be printed, reprinted later by anti-war propagandists and so preserved for us, delivered by a certain Sergeant-Major to a class of English cadets in training. To us he is incredible in his ferocity; we are almost forced to believe he was drunk or mad, until we realize from the 'laughter' that punctuated his utterances, from the hearty thanks of his commanding officer, and the 'three cheers' which merely rewarded him at the conclusion of his discourse, that he was merely expressing the spirit of war service as it was then understood.

'If you see a wounded German,' he said, 'shove him out and have no nonsense about it.'

He was all against taking prisoners – and for murdering them after surrender. He told with sympathy and approval of how a corporal under him butchered a group of German boys. 'Can I do these blokes in, sir?' asked the corporal, pointing to a bunch of disarmed enemies.

'Please yourself,' said the sergeant-major. . . .

When they had been 'done in', the honest corporal, a released convict from Dartmoor prison, came back to the sergeant-major very gratified and honoured, and, still in favour, discussed the technical difficulties of withdrawing a bayonet quickly in order to be ready for the 'next fellow'.

That was, that is, the spirit to which war brings a human being. That gallant Sergeant-Major had abundant equivalents in every army engaged. We are able to quote an English document, freely published. Participants in many other countries had less freedom. On the whole the English were as gentle as any other soldiers. But fear and bloodlust, it is plain, wipe out all the slowly acquired restraints and tolerance of social order very quickly and completely from any breed of men. History must not be written in pink and gilt. Prisoners and wounded were not simply neglected and ill-treated and 'shoved out'. Many were actually tortured to death – either by way of reprisals or in sheer wanton cruelty. There is also a series of photographs of foully mutilated bodies, mutilated and indecently displayed while they were dying or immediately after they were dead. Those millions marched indeed right out of civilization, right out of any sort of human life as we know it to-day, marched down to something viler than mere bestiality, when they marched into the war zone.

After the summer of 1918, which brought with it the certainty of ultimate defeat, the combatant energy of Germany evaporated. Everywhere there was distress and hunger due to a rigorous blockade. The discipline of the land relaxed; the country behind the front was infested by stragglers; the Higher German Command found itself now, like its antagonists, unable to rely upon the men to advance, found itself unable to rely upon their resistance to an enemy attack. They became eager to surrender – taking the off-chance of meeting experimental corporals from Dartmoor on the way.

Wherever there was still loyalty and obedience, however, men were still callously sacrificed by the Higher Command. *War Pictures* (vol. xxvii, 23842 *et seq.*) show the German machine-gunners in their pits, on the defensive against advancing British and American troops. These men allowed themselves to be drugged and chained to their weapons, and so continued to fire and kill until the attack came up to them. Then they found small mercy. They were bayoneted or their brains were beaten out. They paid for the inventions of their masters. They paid for the hatred of Germany the introduction of poison gas had evoked in every attacking army. Such residues of senseless devotion availed nothing against the massive pressures that were at last exhausting Germany. In November the Kaiser, the War Lord, was in flight; a humiliating Armistice had been concluded and the German armies were streaming home in disorder, incoherently revolutionary.

Upon that phrase, 'incoherently revolutionary', our account of the main war may very well end. Here we will only allude to the defeat and demoralization of the Italian armies after the battle of Caporetto, when 800,000 were either killed, wounded, taken prisoner, or (sensible fellows) 'went home'. Nor will we describe the naval battles, of which the chief and last was Jutland. It was the last, because afterwards the German admirals were faced by the threat of mutiny if they essayed another fight. Whether it was or was not a victory for the British was never exactly determined. The controversy died out during the Polish wars.

The *War Pictures* volumes give many photographs and accounts of these naval encounters. We have, for example, a whole series of snapshots of a British cruiser in the Battle of Jutland, the *Defence* steaming at full-speed-ahead to attack and finish up a smashed and sinking German battleship, the *Wiesbaden*. The onrush of that fierce mechanism is terrific. It seems invincible and overpowering. It has an undeniable splendour. Then suddenly a series of blinding flashes show the *Defence* has been hit by the fire of some other German battleship coming to the help of her sister ship, and in a moment she has blown up and gone; she is no more than a mounting unfolding column of smoke and flying fragments, including, we realize with an effort, the torn and scalded bodies of eight hundred men. Then a welter of littered tumbled water. . . .

There is no end to the multitude of such pictures.

But let us return to our phrase 'incoherently revolutionary'. That is the key to the whole human situation at that time. The distaste for the war throughout the world was enormous, if not in its opening phases, then certainly before the second year was reached. It bored; it disgusted. Its events had none of the smashing decisiveness that seizes the imagination. Even the great naval battle of Jutland was, from the point of view of spectacle, a complete failure. None the less, for a very simple reason a comparatively small minority of resolutely belligerent persons was able to keep this vast misery going. On the one hand the war was in accordance with the ruling ideas of the time, while on the other the hundreds of millions whose astonishment and dismay deepened daily, as horror unfolded beyond horror, had no conception of any alternative pattern of life to which they could turn as a refuge from its relentless sequences.

To cry, 'End the war!' ended nothing, because it gave no intimations of what had to replace belligerent governments in the control of human affairs. The peace the masses craved for was as yet only a featureless negative. But peace must be a positive thing, designed and sustained, for peace is less natural than warfare. We who have at last won through to the Pax Mundi know how strong and resolute, how powerfully equipped and how vigilant, the keepers of the peace must be.

VIII

The Impulse to Abolish War:
The Episode of the Ford Peace Ship

One quaint expedition, grotesque and childish and yet an augury of greater things to come, flits very illuminatingly across the dreadful record of these war years. It is the voyage of a passenger steamship from New York to Norway. The dark curtains of oblivion fall in heavier and heavier folds before the thundering battleships of the twilit Battle of Jutland; their forgotten names sink back into a vague general impression of huge flame-spouting masses that rush through smoke and mist to their fate; only a specialist can tell us now whether the *Lützow* or the *Friedrich der Grosse*, the *Lion*, or the *Iron Duke*, the *Vanguard* or the *Colossus* perished with its complement of men or staggered out of that battle. They have become monstrous irrelevances. There is nothing but their size, and the smashing and drowning of hundreds of men in them, to make them more significant to us now than an exploding casket of fireworks. But steaming its way across the Atlantic a few months before Jutland was fought came this other ship, a passenger boat of the Scandinavian-American line, the *Oscar II*, whose voyage remains to this day important and interesting, because in the most simple and artless fashion it mingled the new conceptions of life that were coming into being with all the prevalent weaknesses of the time. The *Oscar II* is better known in history as the Peace Ship of Henry Ford. It is a gleam of tragic comedy amidst the universal horror.

This Henry Ford was a very natural-minded mechanical genius, without much education or social sophistication, a great friend of, and kindred spirit with, that Edison whose career has been traced in the chapter of human history dealing with the development and exploitations of inventions at the close of the nineteenth and the beginning of the twentieth century. Born and brought up in a period of economic expansion, Ford took economic expansion as if it were a necessity inherent in things, and never began to doubt continual progress until he was a man of over seventy. That was his good fortune. That gave him the confidence to design an automobile as sound and good and cheap as could be done at that time, and to organize the mass production of his pattern with extraordinary energy and skill, because his mind was untroubled by the thought that there could be a limit to the number of possible purchasers. He marketed his 'flivver', or 'tin lizzie', as it was affectionately called, in enormous quantities, and in consequence he revolutionized the road transport and town planning of America. He changed the shape of every growing town by enabling the small householder to live further from the work and business centre than had ever been possible before. He did more than any other single man to drive the horse not only from the road but, by making farm tractors, from the fields. He created factories at Dearborn that even to-day seem vast. He became enormously rich and an outstanding 'character' in the world, and particularly in America. And he remained curiously simple and direct in his outlook upon life.

The first effect of the Great War upon him, as on a vast proportion of the English-speaking peoples, was incredulous amazement. He had known there were armies and sovereign nations in the world, but apparently he had never supposed they would fight. He felt there must be some mistake. He exchanged views with other Americans in a similar phase of astonishment. By the beginning of 1915 they had accumulated a sufficient mass of evidence from the belligerent countries to convince them that great masses of people in these countries were as amazed and as anxious to end the widening bloodshed and brutalization as the neutral onlookers. There had been deputations to the President (President Wilson), who was at that time, in harmony with his country, highly pacificist, and there was a widespread ambition that the United States should evoke some sort of permanent arbitration council alone, or in concert with the other Powers still neutral, which should stand, so to speak, on the edge of the battlefield and continue to offer its mediatory services to the warring governments until they were accepted. There was the suggestion of a deputation to Europe to further this idea, and the question arose how should it go across the Atlantic. Ford offered to charter a ship to take it.

Then his peculiar imagination seized upon his own offer. He would make this ship a spectacular ship; it should be the 'Peace Ship'. It should take a complement of chosen delegates to Europe in such a blaze of publicity that at its coming the war would be, as it were, arrested, to look at it. Its mere appearance would recall infuriated Europe to its senses. 'I want to get those boys out of the trenches,' said Ford. 'They don't want to fight, and would be only too glad to shake hands with each other.' At the back of his mind there seems to have been an idea of calling a general strike at the fronts. 'Out of the trenches by Christmas, never to return again,' was his brief speech at a public meeting in Washington in November. All sorts of eminent and energetic people were invited to join the mission. He sought the overt approval of the President, but the President was far too seasoned a politican to squander his publicity upon this 'gesture' of Henry Ford's. He was meditating a gesture of his own later on.

American life at that time had its conspicuous popular stars, who embodied its ideals of greatness and goodness. Some of them are still for various reasons remembered by the historian, Jane Addams and Thomas Edison, for example, William Jennings Bryan (the 'Last Creationist') and Luther Burbank. These names are still to be found even in the Lower School Encyclopaedia. Ford tried to include them all in one meteoric shipload. The governors of all the states in the Union were also invited, groups of representative university students, and so on. The Historical Collection at Atacama has gathered all the surviving originals or replicas of Ford's invitations, and the replies in which these outstanding individuals hesitated over or evaded his proposals. Several were only prevented by sudden attacks of ill-health at the very last moment from joining him. And there was a number of newspaper reporters, cinema operators and other photographers, stenographers, typists, translators, interpreters, baggage masters and publicity agents who made no trouble about coming. A certain Madame Rosika Schwimmer, an Hungarian lady, gleams forth and vanishes again from history as the organizing spirit of this selection. A vast multitude of adventurers and crazy people offered to assist when Ford's project was made public, and many were only prevented with the utmost difficulty from coming aboard the *Oscar II*.

There is still material for a great writer in the details of that expedition, but our interest here is neither with the expedition as a whole nor with Ford or the other persons concerned in it as personalities, but with this idea that flamed and faded, this idea of *an appeal against war to human sanity*. And with the vicissitudes of that idea.

The first thing to note is that it evoked response, and a very wide response. Eminent people, both in America and Europe, with their popularity to consider, found it advisable to be sympathetic, even if unhelpful. President Wilson, for example, was sympathetic but unhelpful. All the pretentious weathercocks of the Western World swung round towards it. We have every indication indeed of a very considerable drive towards a world pax in these years. But presently the weathercocks began to waver and swing away.

Why did they waver? From the first there was a sustained, malignant antagonism to the project. This grew in force and vigour. The American Press, and in its wake the European Press, set itself to magnify and distort every weakness, every slight absurdity, in the expedition and to invent further weaknesses and absurdities. A campaign of ridicule began, so skilful and persistent that it stripped away one blushing celebrity after another from the constellation, and smothered the essential sanity of the project in their wilting apologies. While Ford and his surviving missioners discussed and discoursed on their liner, the newspaper men they had brought with them concocted lies and absurd stories about their host – as though they were under instructions.

We know now they were under instructions. The Historical Documents Series makes this perfectly plain.

As students disentangle strand after strand of that long hidden story, we realize more and more clearly the tortuous dishonesty, the confused double-mindedness, of the times. The export trade of the United States was flourishing under war conditions as it had never flourished before. Munitions of every sort were being sold at enormously enhanced prices to the belligerents. Such great banking houses as Morgan and Co were facilitating the financial subjugation of Europe to America, through debts for these supplies. It is clear that American finance and American Big Business had not foreseen this. They had no exceptional foresight. But suddenly they found themselves in a position of great advantage, and by all their traditions they were bound to make use of that advantage. And Ford in his infinite artlessness, 'butting in', as they said, 'on things that were not his business', was setting out to destroy this favourable state of affairs.

There was just enough plausibility in this endeavour to make it seem dangerous. Ford could not be ignored; his available publicity was too great for that. He was by no means beneath contempt; so he had to be made contemptible. With an earnestness worthy of a better cause, the American Press was launched against him. And it was one of the strange traditions of the American Press that a newsman should have no scruples. The ordinary reporter was a moral invert taking a real pride in his degradation. No expedient was too mean, no lie, no trick too contemptible if only it helped thwart and disillusion Ford.

And they did thwart and disillusion him. They got him wrong with himself. This half-baked man of genius, deserted by his friends, lost confidence in his project. He began to suspect his allies and believe his enemies.

We have to accept the evidence preserved for us, but even with that evidence before us, some of the details of that Press campaign appear incredible. There are a hundred gross files of newspaper cuttings at Atacama, and some of the most amazing are reproduced in the selected Historical Documents. The reporters and writers, who were aboard as Ford's guests, invented and sent home by wireless fantastic reports of free fights among the members of the mission, of disputes among the leaders, of Ford being chained to his bed by his secretary, of mutinies and grotesque happenings. Ford was told of and could have prevented these radio messages being sent – it was his ship for the time being – but a kind of fanaticism for free opinion – even if in practice that meant free lying – restrained him. 'Let them do their darnedest,' he said, still valiant. 'Our work will speak for itself.'

But presently he caught the influenza, a lowering disease long since extinct but very rife in that period, and, under the clumsy medical attention of the day, he arrived in Europe deflated and tired, physically and morally, prepared now to believe that there was something essentially foolish in the whole affair. He had been drenched in ridicule beyond his powers of resistance, and he was giving way. He gave way.

'Guess I had better go home to mother,' said Mr Ford, sick in bed in Christiania, and kept to his room, though all Norway was agog to greet and cheer him.

But his movement went on by the inertia it had gained. His delegation was received with great enthusiasm in Norway and subsequently in Sweden, Switzerland, Denmark and Holland, those small sovereign European states which contrived so dexterously to keep out of the conflict to the end. People in those countries were evidently only too eager to believe that this novel intervention might help to end the war. If Ford was discouraged, some of his associates were of more persistent material. They held great public meetings in Sweden, Holland and Switzerland, and the repercussion of their activities certainly had a heartening effect on the peace movement in Germany and Britain. They contrived to get speech with a number of politicians and statesmen, and they roused the watchful hostility of the German and British war authorities – for the military chiefs of both sides regarded this mission very properly as an attack on war morale. A Neutral Conference for Continuous Mediation came into being – very precarious being – in Stockholm. It is claimed that it checked a movement to bring Sweden into the war on the side of the Germans.

Then gradually the Ford Organization for Peace lost prominence. It was overshadowed by greater movements towards negotiation, and more particularly by the large uncertain gestures of President Wilson, who, re-elected as 'the man who kept the United States out of the war', brought his people from a phase of hypocritical pacifism and energetic armament into the war in 1917. Before that culmination the Peace Ship bladder had collapsed altogether. Its last typist and photographer and clerk had been paid off, and Ford himself was already doing all that was humanly possible to draw a blanket of oblivion over that unforgettable Peace Ship. But the records have been too much for him.

He had not led his expeditionary force in Europe, even nominally, for more than five weeks. He had kept to his Norwegian hotel, avoided his more enthusiastic associates, started a vigorous reduction of his financial commitments, and finally bolted home. He deserted. He left his hotel at Christiania, stealthily, at five o'clock in the morning, and, in spite of the pleadings of those of his party who, warned at the last minute, tumbled out of bed to protest, he got away. Before the year was out he had ceased even financial support, and the various men and women who had abandoned careers and positions and faced ridicule and odium in complete faith in his simplicity were left to find their way back to their former niches or discover fresh ones.

Now what had happened to his great idea? What strange reversal of motive had occurred in the brain and heart of this Peace Crusader? There the curious historian must needs speculate, for that brain and heart have gone now beyond all closer scrutiny.

It has to be noted first that while the Peace Ship was on the Atlantic something very significant was going on at Washington. The swiftly growing munition industries of America had discovered that a home market for their products, a home market of superior solvency, might be added to the vast demands of the fighting nations overseas. America, it was argued, might keep out of the war – well and good – but neverthless America must be 'prepared'. The United States must arm. The President had weighed this proposal with a due regard for the votes and Press support that would come to him at the next election; he had weighed it very carefully as became a politician, and after some resistance he consented that America should be 'prepared'. Munitions should be assembled, troops should be drilled. Flags began to wave – and the United States flag was a very intoxicating one – and drums and trumpets to sound. Military excitement stirred through that vast pacific population and rose.

And Ford had a mighty industrial plant hitherto engaged in pouring out motor-cars and agricultural material, but capable of rapid adaptation to the production of war material. It was his creation; it was his embodiment. It was all that made him visibly different from any other fellow in the street. His friends and family had certainly watched his abandonment of business for world affairs with profound misgiving. It may have been plain to them before it was plain to him, that if he stood out of this 'preparedness' movement as he threatened to do, other great plants would arise beside his own, to produce war material indeed at first, but capable when the war was over of a reverse transformation into great factories for the mass production of motor-cars and the like.

In France this transference from munitions to automobiles was actually foreseen and carried out by the Citroën organization. It is impossible that this prospect could have escaped Ford.

But in his haste he had declared himself against preparedness. He had threatened to hoist an 'international flag' over his works in the place of the Stars and Stripes. . . .

It is clear that in that one lively brain all the main forces of the time were at work. It had responded vividly and generously to the new drive towards a world pax. Lochner (*America's Don Quixote*, 1924) reports him thus on his sailing from New York:

'Have you any last word to say?' a journalist enquired.

'Yes,' he replied. 'Tell the people to cry peace and fight preparedness.'

'What if this expedition fails?' ventured another.

'If this expedition fails I'll start another,' he flashed without a moment's hesitation.

'People say you are not sincere,' commented a third. . . .

'We've got peace-talk going now, and I'll pound it to the end.'

And afterwards came those second thoughts. When, in 1917, the United States entered the war, the Peace Ship was a stale old joke and the vast Ford establishments were prepared and ready for the production of munitions.

Ford was a compendium of his age. That is why we give him this prominence in our history. The common man of the twentieth century was neither a pacificist nor a war-monger. He was both – and Ford was just a common man made big by accident and exceptional energy.

The main thread in the history of the twentieth century is essentially the drama of the indecisions manifested in their elementary plainness by Ford on board his Peace Ship. That voyage comes therefore like a tin-whistle solo by way of overture to the complex orchestration of human motive in the great struggle for human unity that lay ahead.

IX

The Direct Action of the Armament Industries in Maintaining War Stresses

We must now say something about the direct activities of the hypertro-phied 'armament firms' in bringing about and sustaining the massacres of the Great War. A proper understanding of that influence is essential if the stresses and martyrdoms of the middle years of the twentieth century are to be understood.

These 'armament firms' were an outcome of the iron and steel industry, which in a few score years between 1700 and 1850 grew up – no man objecting – from a modest activity of artisans to relatively gigantic possibilities of production. This industry covered the world with a network of railways, and produced iron and then steel steamships to drive the wooden sailing ships off the seas. And at an early stage (all this is traced in full detail in Luke Zimmern's *Entwickelung und Geschichte von Kruppismus*, 1913; *Hist. Doc.* 393112) it turned its attention to the weapons in the world.

In a perpetual progress in the size and range of great guns, in a vast expansion of battleships that were continually scrapped in favour of larger or more elaborate models, it found a most important and inexhaustible field of profit. The governments of the world were taken unawares, and in a little while the industry, by sound and accepted methods of salesmanship, was able to impose its novelties upon these ancient institutions with their tradition of implacable mutual antagonism. It was realized very soon that any decay of patriotism and loyalty would be inimical to this great system of profits, and the selling branch of the industry either bought directly or contrived to control most of the great newspapers of the time, and exercised a watchful vigilance on the teaching of belligerence in schools. Following the established rules and usages for a marketing industrialism, and with little thought of any consequences but profits, the directors of these huge concerns built up the new warfare that found its first exposition in the Great War of 1914–18 and gave its last desperate and frightful convulsions in the Polish wars of 1940 and the subsequent decade.

Even at its outset in 1914–18 this new warfare was extraordinarily uncongenial to humanity. It did not even satisfy man's normal combative instincts. What an angry man wants to do is to beat and bash another living being, not to be shot at from ten miles distance or poisoned in a hole. Instead of drinking delight of battle with their peers, men tasted all the indiscriminating terror of an earthquake. The war literature stored at Atacama, to which we have already referred, is full of futile protest against the horror, the unsportsmanlike quality, the casual filthiness and indecency, the mechanical disregard of human dignity, of the new tactics. But such protest itself was necessarily futile, because it did not go on to a clear indictment of the forces that were making, sustaining and distorting war. The child howled and wept and they did not even attempt to see what it was that had tormented it.

To us nowadays it seems insane that profit-making individuals and companies should have been allowed to manufacture weapons and sell the apparatus of murder to all comers. But to the man of the late nineteenth and early twentieth centuries it seemed the most natural thing in the world. It had grown up in an entirely logical and necessary way, without any restraint upon the normal marketing methods of peace-time commerce, from the continually more extensive application of new industrial products to warfare. Even after the World War catastrophe, after that complete demonstration of the futility of war, men still allowed themselves to be herded like sheep into the barracks, to be trained to consume, and be consumed, by new lines of slaughter goods produced and marketed by the still active armament traders. And the accumulation of a still greater and still more dangerous mass of war material continued.

There is a queer little pseudo-scientific essay by a Bengali satirist (Professor K. Chandra Sen, 1897–1942) among the *India* series of reprints, professing to be a study of the relative stupidity of the more intelligent animals up to and including man. He is concerned by the fatuity with which the mass of humanity watched the preparation of its own destruction during this period. He considers the fate of various species of penguins which were then being swept out of the world – the twentieth century was an age of extermination for hundreds of species – and infers a similar destiny for mankind. He begins with the slaughter of the penguins; he gives photographs of these extraordinary creatures in their multitudes, gathered on the beaches of Oceanic islands and watching the advance of their slayers. One sees them scattered over a long sloping shore, standing still, or waddling about or flapping their stumpy wings while the massacre goes on. They seem to be vaguely interested in the killing of their fellows, but in no way stirred either to flight or resistance. (No thorough scientific observations, we may note, were ever made of penguin mentality, the revival of experimental psychology comes too late for that, and we are left now to guess at what went on in these queer brains of theirs during these raids. There is evidence to show that these creatures had curiosity, kindliness, sympathy and humour; and they were eminently teachable. They stood quite high in the scale of bird intelligence. And yet they permitted their own extinction.) They were not so much a-mental, Professor Sen insists, half seriously, half mockingly, as defective and wrong. They were capable of many idea systems but not of the idea of social preservation. He suggests, too, that the same was true of the sea elephants which were also very rapidly destroyed. (The last of these were murdered later 'to make a record' by a Japanese lunatic with a craving for an 'immortal Name' when the protective patrol was withdrawn during the 'revolt of the sea pirates' in 1985 CE.) But after Professor Sen has weighed every possible case, he still awards the palm for complaisant social stupidity to man.

With a fine parody of the social research methods of that time, he gives various photographs of what he calls the 'human penguins' of that early twentieth century, waddling in their sleek thousands to see battleships launched, to rejoice over reviews and parades, to watch their army aeroplanes stunting in the sky. Side by side he gives photographs of penguin assemblies that, either by happy accident or skilful rearrangement, are absurdly parallel. He gives lists of shareholders in the armament firms, including the current President of the Free Church Council, an Anglican bishop, a great multitude of other clergymen, artists, judges and every sort of gentlefolk. He quotes extensively from the Hansard records of various pre-war debates in the British House of Commons (in a debate on the Naval Estimates early in 1914, Philip Snowden, the radical socialist who afterwards became Viscount Snowden, was particularly explicit), showing that the nature of the danger was clearly seen and clearly and publicly stated. Only it was not *felt*. It is upon that little difference between factual apprehension and the kind of apprehension that leads to effective action that our interest concentrates here.

Why did humanity gape at the guns and do nothing? And why, after the Great War, after that generation had seen over twenty million human beings perish painfully and untimely, did it still go on doing nothing adequate to the occasion? With the preparations still mounting up and the horrible possibilities of war increasing under its eyes? The great Cradle of Bethlehem Steel Corporation of America in 1929 was revealed as actively opposing naval disarmament at the Geneva Conference of 1927. At any rate it was asociated with three shipbuilding companies who were sued by a Mr Shearer, who claimed to have been given that task, for fees alleged to be due to him. There seems to have been little dispute that he had been so employed; the case turned upon the extent of his services and the amount of his fees. Nothing was done by the penguins either to the companies concerned or to Mr Shearer. A few expressed indignation; that was all. Just as now and then no doubt a bird or so squawked at the oil-hunters. (For a detailed account and references see *The Navy; Defence or Portent*, by C. A. Beard, 1930; reprinted Hist. Doc. Series 4270112.)

The clue lies in the fact that there was practically no philosophical education at all in the world, no intelligent criticism of generalizations and general ideas. There was no science of social processes at all. People were not trained to remark the correlations of things; for the most part they were not aware that there was any correlation between things; they imagined this side of life might change and that remain unaltered. The industrialists and financiers built up these monstrous armaments and imposed them on the governments of the time with a disregard of consequences that seems now absolutely imbecile. Most of these armament propagandists were admirable in their private lives: gentle lovers, excellent husbands, fond of children and animals, good fellows, courteous to inferiors, and so on. Sir Basil Zaharoff, the greatest of munition salesmen, as one sees him in the painting (ascribed to Orpen) recently discovered in Paris, with his three-cornered hat, his neat little moustaches and beardlet, and the ribbon of some Order of Chivalry about his neck, looks quite a nice, if faintly absurd, little gentleman. Those shareholding bishops and clergy may, for anything we know to the contrary, have had charming Christian personalities. But they wanted their dividends. And in order to pay those dividends, the dread of war and the need of war had to be kept alive in the public mind.

That was done most conveniently through the Press. You could buy a big newspaper in those days, lock, stock and barrel, for five or ten million dollars, and the profits made on one single battleship came to more than that. Naturally, and according to the best business traditions, the newspapers hired or sold themselves to the war salesmen. What was wrong in that? Telling the news in those days was a trade, not a public duty. A daily paper that had dealt faithfully with this accumulating danger would quite as naturally and necessarily have found its distribution impeded, have found itself vigorously outdone by more richly endowed competitors, able because of their wealth to buy up all the most atttractive features, able to outdo it in every way with the common reader.

It wasn't that the newspaper owners and the munition dealers wanted anyone hurt. They only wanted to sell equipment and see it used up. Nor was it that the newspapers desired the wholesale mangling and butchering of human beings. They wanted sales and advertisements. The butchery was quite by the way, an unfortunate side issue to legitimate business. Shortsightedness is not diabolical, even if it produces diabolical results.

And even those soldiers? Freudheim, in his analysis of the soldierly mind, shows a picture of that Sir Henry Wilson we have already mentioned arrayed in shirt-sleeves and digging modestly in the garden of his villa during a phase of retirement, and the same individual smirking in all his glory, buttons, straps and 'decorations', as a director of military operations. It is an amazing leap from the suburban insignificance of a retired clerk to god-like importance. In peace-time, on the evidence of his own diaries, this Wilson was a tiresome nobody, an opinionated bore; in war he passed beyond criticism and became a god. One understands at once what a vital matter employment and promotion must have been to him. But so far as we can tell he desired no killing *as* killing. If he had been given blood to drink he would probably have been sick. Yet he lived upon tanks of blood.

These professional soldiers thought of slaughter as little as possible. It is preposterous to say they desired it, much less that they gloated over it. It might have fared better with their men if they had thought of it more. They had an age-old sentimental devotion to their country, a solemn sense of great personal worth in their services, an orgiastic delight of battle. And they did not see, nor want to see, what was beyond their occupation. Their religious teachers were quite ready to assure them they were correct in all they did and were.

The senescent Christian Churches of that age had indeed a very direct interest in war. A marked tendency to ignore or ridicule the current religious observances had become manifest, but under the stresses of loss and death people turned again to the altar. It is easily traceable in the fiction of the time. The despised curate of the tea-cups and croquet lawn became the implicitly heroic 'padre' of the sentimental war stories.

The problem that confronted the growing minority that was waking up to the perils and possibilities of our species in the third and fourth decades of the twentieth century was this: How in the first place to concentrate the minds of people out of this distraction and diffusion, how to bring them to bear upon the crude realities before them, and then how to organize the gigantic effort needed to shake off that intermittent and ever more dangerous fever of war and that chronic onset of pauperization which threatened the whole world with social dissolution.

There was no central antagonist, no ruling devil, for those anxious spirits to fight. That would have made it a straight, understandable campaign. But the Press with a certain flavouring of pious intentions was practically against them. Old social and political traditions, whatever the poses they assumed, were tacitly against them. History was against them, for it could but witness that war had always gone on since its records began. Not only the current Bishop of Hereford, and the current President of the Free Church Council, caught with their dividends upon them, but their Churches and the Catholic Church, and indeed all the Christian Churches, in spite of their allegiance to the Prince of Peace, were quietly competitive with, or antagonistic to, the secular world controls that alone could make a healthy world peace possible. The admission of the insufficiency of their own creeds to comfort or direct would have been the necessary prelude to a new moral effort.

And the idea of the naturalness and inevitability of war was not only everywhere in the world around those few forward-looking men who knew better, it was in their blood and habits. They were seeking how to attack not a fortress, but what seemed a perpetually recuperative jungle of mixed motives, tangled interests and cross-purposes, within themselves as without.

X

Versailles: Seed Bed of Disasters

The formal war, against the Central Powers, the 'World War', ended on November 11th, 1918 CE in the defeat and submission of the Central Powers. There was a conference at Versailles, in the same palace in which triumphant Germans had dictated peace to France after a previous war in 1870–71. There was a needlessly dramatic flavour in this reversal of the rôles of the two countries. It was now France and her allies who dictated, and naturally the ideas of a romantic restoration and a stern and righteous judgment dominated the situation. The assembled Powers sat down to right the wrongs and punish the misdeeds of their grandparents. Even at the time it seemed a little belated. But threading their proceedings we do find quite plainly evident the developing conflict between historical tradition and the quickening sense of human unity in the world. If the World-State was not present at the conference, its voice was at any rate 'heard without'.

By this time (1919 CE) there was indeed quite a considerable number of intelligent people in the world who had realized the accumulating necessity of a world government, and a still larger multitude, like that Henry Ford we have described, who had apprehended it instinctively and sentimentally, but there was no one yet who had had the intellectual vigour to attack in earnest the problem of substituting a world system for the existing governments. Men's minds and hearts quailed before that undertaking. And yet, as we now know so clearly, it was the only thing for them to do. It was the sole alternative to an ever-broadening and deepening series of disasters. But its novelty and vastness held them back. Irrational habit kept them in the ancient currents of history.

To us they seem like drowning men who were willing to attempt to save themselves by rallies of swimming, floating, holding on to straws and bubbles, but who refused steadfastly, in spite of the proximity of a ladder, to clamber out of the water for good and all.

Hardly any of them in their ideas of a world system dared go beyond a purely political agreement for the avoidance of war. Five decades of human distress were still needed before there was to be any extensive realization that belligerence was only one symptom, and by no means the gravest symptom, of human disunion.

The American President Woodrow Wilson, of all the delegates to the Peace Conference, was the most susceptible to the intimations of the future. The defects and limitations of his contributions to that settlement give us a measure of the political imagination of those days. He brought what was left of the individualistic liberalism that had created the American Republics to the solution of the world problem. None of the other participants in these remarkable discussions – Clemenceau (France), Lloyd George (Britain), Sonnino (Italy), Saionji (Japan), Hymans (Belgium), Paderewski (Poland), Bratianu (Roumania), Bénès (Bohemia), Venezelos (Greece), Feisal (Hedjaz), and so on through a long list of now fading names – seemed aware that, apart from any consideration of national advantage, humanity as a whole might claim an interest in the settlement. They were hard-shell 'representatives', national advocates. For a brief interval Wilson stood alone for mankind. Or at least he seemed to stand for mankind. And in that brief interval there was a very extraordinary and significant wave of response to him throughout the earth. So eager was the situation that all humanity leapt to accept and glorify Wilson – for a phrase, for a gesture. It seized upon him as its symbol. He was transfigured in the eyes of men. He ceased to be a common statesman; he became a Messiah. Millions believed him as the bringer of untold blessings; thousands would gladly have died for him. That response was one of the most illuminating events in the early twentieth century. Manifestly the World-State had been conceived then, and now it stirred in the womb. It was alive.

And then for some anxious decades it ceased to stir.

Amidst different scenery and in different costumes, the story of Wilson repeats the story of Ford, the story of a man lifted by an idea too great for him, thrown up into conspicuousness for a little while and then dropped, as a stray leaf may be spun up and dropped by a gust of wind before a gale. The essential Wilson, the world was soon to learn, was vain and theatrical, with no depth of thought and no wide generosity. So far from standing for all mankind, he stood indeed only for the Democratic Party in the United States – and for himself. He sacrificed the general support of his people in America to party considerations and his prestige in Europe to a craving for social applause. For a brief season he was the greatest man alive. Then for a little while he remained the most conspicuous. He visited all the surviving courts of Europe and was fêted and undone in every European capital. That triumphal procession to futility need not occupy us further here. Our concern is with his idea.

Manifestly he wanted some sort of a world pax. But it is doubtful if at any time he realized that a world pax means a world control of all the vital common interests of mankind. He seems never to have thought out this job to which he set his hand so confidently. He did not want, or, if he did, he did not dare to ask for, any such centralized world controls as we now possess. They were probably beyond the range of his reading and understanding. His project from first to last was purely a politician's project.

The pattern conceived by him was a naïve adaptation of the parliamentary governments of Europe and America to a wider union. His League, as it emerged from the Versailles Conference, was a typical nineteenth-century government enlarged to planetary dimensions and greatly faded in the process; it had an upper chamber, the Council, and a lower chamber, the Assembly, but, in ready deference to national susceptibilities, it had no executive powers, no certain revenues, no army, no police, and practically no authority to do anything at all. And even as a political body it was remote and ineffective; it was not in any way representative of the peoples of the earth as distinguished from the governments of the earth. Practically nothing was done to make the common people of the world feel that the League was theirs. Its delegates were appointed by the Foreign Offices of the very governments its only conceivable rôle was to supersede. They were national politicians and they were expected to go to Geneva to liquidate national politics. The League came into being at last, a solemn simulacrum to mock, cheat and dispel the first desire for unity that mankind had ever betrayed.

Yet what else was possible then? If Wilson seemed to embody the formless aspirations of mankind, there can be no dispute that he impressed the politicians with whom he had to deal as a profoundly insincere visionary. They dealt with him as that and they beat him as that. The only way to have got anything more real than this futile League would have been a revolutionary appeal to the war-weary peoples of the earth against their governments, to have said, as indeed he could have said in 1918, to the whole world that the day of the World-State had come. That would have reverberated to the ends of the earth.

He was not the man to do that. He had not that power of imagination. He had not that boldness with governments. He had the common politician's way of regarding great propositions as a means to small ends. If he had been bolder and greater, he might have failed, he might have perished; but he failed and perished anyhow; and a bolder bid for world unity might have put the real issue before mankind for ever and shortened the Age of Frustration by many decades.

What he did do was to reap an immediate harvest of popular applause, to present to human hope a white face rigid with self-approval, bowing from processional carriages and decorated balconies, retiring gravely into secret conference with the diplomatists and politicians of the old order and emerging at last with this League of Nations, that began nothing and ended nothing and passed in a couple of decades out of history.

It was a League not to end sovereignties but preserve them. It stipulated that the extraordinarily ill-contrived boundaries established by the Treaty in which it was incorporated should be guaranteed by the

League for *evermore*. Included among other amiable arrangements were clauses penalizing Germany and her allies as completely as Carthage was penalized by Rome after the disaster of Zamia – penalizing her in so overwhelming a way as to make default inevitable and afford a perennial excuse for her continued abasement. It was not a settlement, it was a permanent punishment. The Germans were to become the penitent helots of the conquerors; a generation, whole generations, were to be born and die in debt, and to ensure the security of this arrangement Germany was to be effectually disarmed and kept disarmed.

Delenda est Germania was the sole idea of the French (*see* Morris Henbane's *Study of Pertinax*, 1939), and the representatives of the other Allies who were gathered together in the Paris atmosphere and working amidst the vindictive memories of Versailles were only too ready to fall in with this punitive conception of their task. It was the easiest conception; it put a hundred difficult issues into a subordinate place. It always looks so much easier to men of poor imagination to put things back than to carry them on. If the French dreaded a resurrection of the German armies, the British feared a resurrection of the German fleet and of German industrial competition. Japan and Italy, seeking their own compensations elsewhere, were content to see the German-speaking peoples, who constituted the backbone of the Continent, divided and reduced to vassalage.

The antiquated form of Wilson's ideas produced still more mischievous consequences in the multiplication of sovereign governments in the already congested European area. Deluded by the vague intimations of unity embodied in the League, Wilson lent himself readily to a reconstruction of the map of Europe upon strictly nationalist lines. The Polish nation was restored. Our history has already studied the successive divisions of this country in the eighteenth century. It is a great region of the Central Plain, whose independent existence became more and more inconvenient as the trade and commerce of Europe developed. Geography fought against it. It was a loose-knit union of individualistic equestrian aristocrats dominating a peasantry. But its partition between Russia, Prussia and Austria was achieved with the utmost amount of brutality, and after the Napoleonic wars a romantic legend about this lost kingdom of Poland seized upon the sentiment of France, Britain and America. These rude nobles and their serfs, so roughly incorporated by the adjacent states, were transfigured into a delicate, brave and altogether wonderful people, a people with a soul torn asunder and trampled underfoot by excessively booted oppressors. The restoration of Poland – the excessive restoration of Poland – was one of the brightest ambitions of President Wilson.

Poland was restored. But instead of a fine-spirited and generous people emerging from those hundred and twenty years of subjugation and justifying the sympathy and hopes of liberalism throughout the world, there appeared a narrowly patriotic government, which presently developed into an aggressive, vindictive and pitiless dictatorship, and set itself at once to the zestful persecution of the unfortunate ethnic minorities (about a third of the entire population) caught in the net of its all too ample boundaries. The real Poland of the past had been a raiding and aggressive nation which had ridden and harried to the very walls of Moscow. It had not changed its nature. The Lithuanian city of Vilna was now grabbed by a *coup de main* and the south-eastern boundary pushed forward in Galicia. In the treatment of the Ukrainians and Ruthenians involved in liberation, Poland equalled any of the atrocities which had been the burden of her song during her years of martyrdom. In 1932 one-third of the budget of this new militant Power was for armament.

Not only was Poland thus put back upon the map. As a result of a sedulous study of historical sentimentalities, traditions, dialects and local feelings, a whole cluster of new sovereign Powers, Czecho-Slovakia, Yugo-Slavia, Finland, Esthonia, Latvia, Lithuania, an attenuated Hungary and an enlarged Roumania, was evoked to crowd and complicate the affairs of mankind by their sovereign liberties, their ambitions, hostilities, alliances, understandings, misunderstandings, open and secret treaties, tariffs, trade wars and the like. Russia was excluded from the first attempt at a World Parliament because she had repudiated her vast war debts – always a matter of grave solicitude to the Western creditor, and – strangest fact of all in this strange story – the United States, the Arbitrator and Restorer of Nations, stood out from the League, because President Wilson's obstinate resolve to monopolize the immortal glory of World Salvation for himself and his party had estranged a majority of his senators.

The Senate, after some attempts at compromise, rejected the Covenant of the League altogether, washed its hands of world affairs, and the President, instead of remaining for ever Prince of Everlasting Peace and Wonder of the Ages, shrank again very rapidly to human proportions and died a broken and disappointed man. Like Ford, the United States returned to normal business and the Profit and Loss Account, and the Europeans were left with the name of Wilson written all over their towns, upon streets, avenues, esplanades, railway stations, parks and squares, to make what they could of this emasculated League he had left about among their affairs.

If Russia and Germany in their character of Bad Peoples were excluded from the League, such remote peoples as the Chinese and the Japanese were included as a matter of course. It was assumed, apparently, that they were 'just fellows' of the universal Treaty-of-Westphalia pattern. The European world knew practically nothing of the mental processes of these remote and ancient communities, and it seems hardly to have dawned upon the conferring statesmen that political processes rest entirely upon mental facts. The League, after much difficulty, and after some years' delay, did indeed evolve a Committee of Intellectual Cooperation, but so far as its activities can now be traced, this was concerned with dilettante intellectualism only; there is no indication that it ever interested itself in the League as an idea.

Considering all things in the light of subsequent events, it would have been well if the League of Nations had committed hari-kari directly the United States Senate refused participation, and if the European Powers, realizing their failure to stabilize the planet at one blow, had set themselves at once to the organization of a League of Conciliation and Cooperation within the European area. The League's complete inability to control or even modify the foreign policy of Japan (modelled on the best nineteenth-century European patterns) was the decisive factor in its declension to a mere organization of commentary upon current affairs.

As its authority declined the courage and pungency of its reports increased. Some of the later ones are quite admirable historical documents. Gradually the member governments discontinued their subsidies and the secretariat dwindled to nothing. Like the Hague Tribunal, the League faded out of existence before or during the Famished Fifties. It does not figure in history after the first Polish war, but its official buildings were intact in 1965, and in 1968, and for some years later, they were used as auxiliary offices by the Western branch of the Transport Union.

The imposition of vast monetary payments upon Germany was the only part of the settlement of Versailles that dealt with the financial and economic life of our race. Astounding as this seems to us to-day, it was the most natural oversight possible to the Versailles politicians. Political life was still deep in the old purely combatant tradition, still concentrated upon boundaries and strategic advantages; and it was extraordinarily innocent in the face of economic realities. The mighty forces demanding economic unification, albeit they were, as we have shown, the real causes of the Great War, were ignored at Versailles as completely as if they had never existed.

Only one outstanding voice, that of the British economist J. M. Keynes (*Economic Consequences of the Peace*, 1919), was audible at the time in protest and warning against the preposterous dislocation of credit and trade involved in the reparation payments. There was no arrangement whatever for the liquidation of the debts piled up by the Allies *against each other* (!), and no economic parallel to the political League of Nations. No control of economic warfare was even suggested. The Americans, Wilson included, were still in a stage of financial individualism; they thought money-getting was an affair of individual smartness within the limits of the law; and the American conception of law was of something that presented interesting obstacles rather than effectual barriers to enlightened self-seeking. The contemporary American form of mutual entertainment was a poker party, and that great people therefore found nothing inimical in sitting down after the war to play poker, with France and Great Britain as its chief opponents, for the gold and credit of the world.

It was only slowly during the decade following after the war that the human intelligence began to realize that the Treaty of Versailles had not ended the war at all. It had set a truce to the bloodshed, but it had done so only to open a more subtle and ultimately more destructive phase in the traditional struggle of the sovereign states. The existence of independent sovereign states *is* war, white or red, and only an elaborate mis-education blinded the world to this elementary fact. The peoples of the defeated nations suffered from a real if not very easily defined sense of injustice in this Treaty, which was framed only for them to sign, and sign in the rôle of wrongdoers brought to book. Very naturally they were inspired by an ill-concealed resolve to revise, circumvent or disregard its provisions at the earliest possible opportunity. The conquering Powers, on the other hand, were conscious of having not only humiliated their defeated enemies but thrust them into a state of exasperated disadvantage. The thought of a *revanche* was equally present therefore to the victors, and instead of disarming as the Germans were compelled to do, they broke the obligations of the Treaty and retained and increased their military establishments.

The armament firms and their newspapers naturally did all they could to intensify this persistence in an armed 'security'. Any disposition on the part of the French public, for instance, to lay aside its weapons was promptly checked by tales of secret arsenals and furtive drilling in Germany. And the narrow patriotic forces that guided France not only kept her extravagantly armed against her fallen foe, but carried on a subtle but ruthless financial warfare that, side by side with the American game, overcame every effort of Germany to recover socially or economically.

Moreover, the conquering Powers, so soon as they considered their former antagonists conclusively disposed of, turned themselves frankly, in full accordance with the traditions of the sovereign state system, to the task of getting the better of each other in the division of the spoils. Their 'Alliances' had brought about no sense of community. Already within a year of the signing of the Peace Treaty of Versailles heavy fighting was going on in Asia Minor between the Greeks and the Turks. The Greeks had British encouragement; the French and Italians had supported the Turks. It was a war of cat's-paws. This war culminated in a disastrous rout of the Greeks and the burning of the town of Smyrna. This last was a quite terrible massacre; multitudes of women and children were outraged, men and boys gouged, emasculated or killed; all but the Turkish quarter was looted and burnt. The quays in front of the flaming town were dense with terror-stricken crowds, hoping against hope to get away upon some ship before they were fallen upon, robbed, butchered, or thrust into the water.

A little before this the Turks had driven the French out of the ancient province of Cilicia, and had completed the extermination of that ancient people the Hittites or Armenians. During the war or after the war mattered little to the Armenians, for fire and sword pursued them still. Over two million died – for the most part violent deaths.

Fighting still went on after the Great Peace in the north and south of Russia and in eastern Siberia; and China became a prey to armies of marauders. Poland seized Vilna, invaded eastern Galicia and fought Russia in the Ukraine, and a raid of patriotic Italians expelled a mixed Allied garrison from Fiume.

Presently there was a dreadful famine in south-east Russia which neither America nor Europe was able to alleviate. Always before the war a famine in any part of the world had exercised the philanthropic element in the Anglo-Saxon community. But philanthropy had lost heart. There was a faint but insufficient flutter of the old habits in America but none in Britain.

Such was the peace and union of the world immediately achieved by the Conference of Versailles.

A number of unsatisfactory appendices and patches had presently to be made to correct the most glaring defects and omissions of the Treaty. Constantinople, which had been taken from the Turks and held by a mixed force of the Allies, was restored to them in 1923 after the Smyrna massacre and some warlike gesticulation between them and the British.

In drawing the boundaries of the new and revised states of the European patchwork there was the utmost disregard of economic common sense; peasants would find themselves cut off from winter or summer pasture or from market towns which had been developed by their needs. Great foundries and chemical and metallurgical works were separated from the ores and deposits on which they relied. Vienna, once the financial and business centre of all south-east Central Europe, was decapitated. Most fantastic and, as it proved, most disastrous of all the follies of Versailles was the creation of the free city of Danzig and what was called the Polish Corridor.

Let us note a point or so about this latter tangle to illustrate the mental quality of the Conference at its worst. Here more than anywhere else did the simple romantic idea that the Germans were Bad, and that anyone opposed to the Germans was without qualification Good, rule the situation. The Poles were Good, and they were the chosen of the Allies, the particular protégés of the sentimental historian from America. He had come to put down the mighty from their seats and to exalt the humble and the meek. The hungry and eager were to be filled with good things and the rich, the erstwhile rich, were to be sent empty away. Germany, like Dives in hell, was to look up and see Poland like Lazarus in Woodrow Wilson's bosom. Not only were the Good Poles to be given dominion over Ruthenians, Ukrainians, Jews (whom particularly they detested), Lithuanians, White Russians and Germans, they were to have also something of profound economic importance – 'access to the sea'.

On that President Wilson had been very insistent. Switzerland had done very well in pre-war Europe without access to the sea, but that was another story. The difficulty was that by no stretch of ethnic map-colouring could Poland be shown to border on the sea. A belt of Pomeranians and Germans stretched across the mouth of the Vistula, and the only possibility of a reasonable trading outlet to the sea, so far as Poland needed such an outlet – for most of its trade was with its immediate neighbours – was through an understanding with that belt of people. That would have been easy enough to arrange. At the mouth of the Vistula stood the entirely German city of Danzig. It lived mainly as an outlet for Polish trade, and it could prosper in no other way. There was no reason to suppose it would put any difficulties in the way of Polish imports and exports. It was an ancient, honest, clean and prosperous German city. Ninety-six per cent of its inhabitants were German.

This was the situation to which the Conference of Versailles, under the inspiration of that magic phrase 'access to the sea', turned its attention. Even the profound belief of the Conquerors that there were no Germans but bad Germans could not justify their turning over Danzig itself to Polish rule. But they separated it from Germany and made it into a 'free city', and to the west of it they achieved that 'access to the sea' of Wilson's, by annexing a broad band of Pomeranian territory to Poland. (This was the actual 'Corridor' of the controversies.) It had no port to compare with Danzig, but the Poles set themselves to create a rival in Gdynia, which should be purely Polish, and which should ultimately starve the trading Germans out of Danzig.

And to keep the waters of the Vistula as pure and sweet for Poland as the existence of Danzig at the estuary allowed, the peace-makers ran the Vistula boundary between Poland and east Prussia, not in the usual fashion midway along the stream, but at a little distance on the east Prussian side. (Jacques Kayser, *La Paix en Péril*, 1931; Hist. Doc., 711711.) So that the east German population, the peasant cultivator, the erstwhile fisherman, the shepherd with his flocks to water, was pulled up by a line of frontier posts and a Polish rifle within sight of the stream. Moreover, that eastward country was flat and low-lying and had hitherto been protected from floods and a relapse to marsh conditions by a line of dykes. The frontier cut that line five times, and, since the Poles had no interest whatever in these defences, they fell rapidly out of repair. Further along the boundary cut off the great towns of Garnsee and Bischofswerder from their railway station.

But we must not lose ourselves in the details of this exasperating settlement. The maximum of irritation developed in the absurd Corridor itself. The current of traffic had hitherto run to and fro between east and west, the trend of the railways was in that direction; the traffic in the north and south direction had come to Danzig along the great river. Now the Poles set themselves to obstruct both these currents and to wrench round all the communications into a north and south direction avoiding Danzig. Every German going east or west found himself subjected to a series of frontier examinations, to tariff payments, to elaborate delays, to such petty but memorable vexations as that all the windows of an express train passing across the Corridor should be closed, and so forth, and the city of Danzig, cut off from German trade, found its Polish business being steadily diverted to Gdynia. French capital was poured into Gdynia and into its new railway to the south, so that French financial interests were speedily entangled in the dispute.

The indignity and menace of Danzig burnt into the German imagination. That Corridor fretted it as nothing else in the peace settlement had fretted it. It became a dominant political issue. There was an open sore of a similar character in Upper Silesia; there was a sore in the Saar Valley; there was the sore of an enforced detachment from Austria; there were many other bitter memories and grievances, but this was so intimate, so close to Berlin, that it obsessed all German life.

Within a dozen years of the signing of the Treaty of Versailles the Polish Corridor was plainly the most dangerous factor in the European situation. It mocked every projection of disarmament. It pointed the hypnotized and impotent statescraft of Europe straight towards a resumption of war. A fatalistic attitude towards war as something terrible indeed but inevitable, which had already been evident among the politicians of Europe before 1914, reappeared and spread.

History had an air of repeating itself. Nobody made any definite suggestions about any of these open sores, but there was scarcely a politician of the period who could not claim to have been very eloquent on various occasions against war – with, of course, a skilful avoidance of anything that could be considered specific, controversial, unpatriotic or likely to wound the susceptibilities of the Powers immediately concerned.

XI

The Impulse to Abolish War:
Why the League of Nations failed to
Pacify the World

Before we leave that bleak and futile idealist, Woodrow Wilson, altogether, we will draw the attention of the student to the essential factors of his failure. The defects of his personality must not blind us to the impossibility of his ambition. His narrow egotism, the punitive treatment of the Central Powers and so forth, merely emphasized a disadvantage that would have been fatal to the launching of any League of Nations at that time. There had been an insufficient mental preparation for a world system to operate. No ideology existed to sustain it. The World-State, the Modern State, was still only a vaguely apprehended suggestion; it had not been worked out with any thoroughness and the League was the most hasty of improvisations.

It needed the life scheming of De Windt and his associates, which we shall presently describe; it needed a huge development and application of the science of social psychology, before the supersession of the chaos of sovereign states by a central control was even a remote possibility. Wilson thought he could get together with a few congenial spirits and write a recipe for human unity. He had not the slightest inkling of the gigantic proportions, the intricacy, intimacy and profundity, of the task that was opening before him. He attempted to patch up the outworn system of his time and pass it off as a new one. He did not dream of the monetary reconstruction, the need for a thorough-going socialism throughout the world, and for a complete revolution in education, before the peace and security of mankind could be established. Yet, narrow and blind as he was, he seems to have been in advance of the general thought of his age.

This premature and ineffectual League was a hindrance rather than a help to the achievement of world peace. It got in the way. It prevented people from thinking freely about the essentials of the problem. Organizations of well-meaning folk, the British League of Nations Union, for example, came into existence to support it, and resisted rather than helped any effectual criticism of its constitution and working. They would say that it was 'better than nothing', whereas a false start is very much worse than nothing. In the post-war decade, the amount of vigorous constructive thought in the general mind about world politics was extraordinarily small. It was only when the unsufficiency of the League had passed beyond any possibility of dispute that men began to take up the abandoned search for world unification again.

A dozen years later the Modern State movement was still only foreshadowed in sketchy attempts to find a comprehensive set of general formulae for liberal progressive effort. The pacifists, communists, socialists and every other sort of 'ists' who gave a partial and confused expression to human discontent had still to be drawn together into understanding and cooperation. Most of their energy was wasted in obscure bickerings, mutual suspicion and petty and partial tentatives. The middle of the century had been passed before there was any considerable body of Modern State propaganda and education on earth.

XII

The Breakdown of 'Finance' and Social Morale after Versailles

The unprecedented range and destruction of the World War were, we have pointed out, largely ascribable to the hypertrophy of the world's iron and steel industry relatively to the political and social concepts of the race. But in the first 'post-war' decade the stresses of other disproportionate developments began to make themselves manifest at various other weak points in the loosely linked association of our species. The war from the economic point of view had been the convulsive using up of an excess of production that the race had no other method of distributing and consuming. But the necessities of the struggle, and particularly its interference with international trading, which had evoked factories and finishing processes in many undeveloped regions hitherto yielding only raw or unfinished materials, had added greatly to the gross bulk of productive plant throughout the world, and so soon as the open war-furnaces ceased to burn up the surplus and hold millions of men out of the labour market, this fact became more and more oppressively apparent. The post-war increase in war preparation, which went on in spite of endless palavering about disarmament, did not destroy men, nor scrap and destroy material, in sufficient quantity to relieve the situation.

Moreover, the expansion of productive energy was being accompanied by a positive contraction of the distributive arrangements which determined consumption. The more efficient the output, the fewer were the wages-earners. The more stuff there was, the fewer consumers there were. The fewer the consumers, the smaller the trading profits, and the less the gross spending power of the shareholders and individual entrepreneurs. So buying dwindled at both ends of the process and the common investor suffered with the wages-earner. This was the 'Paradox of Over-production' which so troubled the writers and journalists of the third decade of the twentieth century.

It is easy for the young student to-day to ask, 'Why did they not adjust?' But let him ask himself who there was to adjust. Our modern superstructure of applied economic science, the David Lubin Bureau and the General Directors' Board, with its vast recording organization, its hundreds of thousands of stations and observers, directing, adjusting, apportioning and distributing, had not even begun to exist. Adjustment was left to blind and ill-estimated forces. It was the general interest of mankind to be prosperous, but it was nobody's particular interest to keep affairs in a frame of prosperity. Manifestly a dramatic revision of the liberties of enterprise was necessary, but the enterprising people who controlled politics, so far as political life was controlled, were the very last people to undertake such a revision.

With the hypertrophy of productive activities there had been a concurrent hypertrophy of banking and financial organization generally, but it had been a flabby hypertrophy, a result of the expansion of material production rather than a compensatory and controlling development.

It is so plain to us to-day that the apportionment of the general product of the world for enterprise or consumption is a department of social justice and policy, and can be dealt with only in the full light of public criticism and upon grounds of claim and need, that it is difficult for us to understand the twentieth-century attitude to these things. We should no more dream of leaving the effectual control in these matters in private profit-seeking hands than we should leave our law courts or our schools to the private bidder. But nothing of the sort was plain in 1935 CE. That lesson had still to be learnt.

The story of banking and money in the early twentieth century has so much in it verging upon the incredible that it has become one of the most attractive and fruitful fields for the student of historical psychology. The system had grown up as a tangle of practice. It was evolved, not designed. There was never any attempt to gauge the justice or the ultimate consequences of any practice, so long as it worked at the time. Men tried this and that, did this and that, and concealed their opinions of what the results might be. Reserve was essential in the system. So little was the need for publicity in this universal interest understood that the most fundamental decisions affecting the common man's purchasing power and the credit of industrial undertakings were made in secret, and the restriction and stimulation of trade and work went on in the profoundest obscurity. Neither in the ordinary courses of the schools and universities was there any instruction in these essential facts. The right of private enterprise to privacy was respected in the Churches, the law courts and private practice alike. Men found themselves employed or unemployed, cheated of their savings or better off, they knew not why. Instead of the clear knowledge of economic pressures and movements that we have to-day, strange Mystery Men were dimly visible through a fog of baffling evasions and mis-statements, manipulating prices and exchanges.

Prominent among these Mystery Men was a certain Mr Montagu Norman, Governor of the Bank of England from 1920 to 1935. He is among the least credible figures in all history, and a great incrustation of legends has accumulated about him. In truth the only mystery about him was that he was mysterious. His portrait shows a slender, bearded man, dressed more like a successful artist or musician than the conventional banker of the time. He was reputed to be shy and, in the phraseology of the time, 'charming', and he excited the popular imagination by a habit of travelling about under assumed names and turning up in unexpected places. Why he did so, nobody now knows. Perhaps he did it for the fun of doing it. He gave evidence before an enquiry into finance in 1930 (the Macmillan Committee), and from that and from one or two of his public speeches that have been preserved it is plain that he had what we should now consider an entirely inadequate education for the veiled activities in which he was engaged. Of human ecology he betrays no knowledge, and his ideas of social and economic processes are not what we should now recognize as adequate general ideas even for an ordinary citizen. Indeed his chief qualification for his darkly responsible post was some practical experience acquired in association with various private banking firms before he entered the service of the Bank of England. This experience was acquired during what we know now to have been a period of quite accidental and transitory expansion of human wealth. Plainly he did not even bring a blank mind to his task. He had a mind warped and prejudiced by gainful banking under abnormal conditions. Yet for a time he was regarded as an 'expert' of almost magical quality, and during the convulsions of the post-war period he was able to dictate or defeat arrangements that enriched or impoverished millions of people in every country in Europe.

Another big obscure financial force in the war and post-war periods was the complex of great private banking ganglia of which Morgan and Co., with its associated firms, was the most central and most typical. This particular firm carried on its business upon a scale that completely overshadowed many minor governments. The loans it made or refused, confirmed or shattered régimes. Its founder, J. P. Morgan, a queer combination of Yankee 'gentleman' and German junker, whose innate acquisitiveness overflowed in great collections of pictures and 'art' objects generally, had died before the outbreak of the war, but a phrase he used in a dispute with President Roosevelt the First was taken up later and made into a deadly critical weapon against the whole private banking world. 'Roosevelt,' he protested, 'wants all of us to have glass pockets!'

A second President Roosevelt was presently to revive that demand.

Nothing could better betray the habit of deep gainful manoeuvrings than that phrase. Morgan was never dishonest and always disingenuous. That was the rule of his game. Opaque pockets he insisted upon, and hidden motives, but also the punctual performance of a bargain. His tradition lived after him. His firm became an octopus of credit. The interweaving bargains it made hung like a shadowy group of spiders' webs about European life. It did its work of strangulation by its nature and without malice, as a spider spins. No contemporary could apprehend it. The particulars of any particular situation could only be unravelled vaguely by a normal enquirer after many months of study.

Interacting with such mystery systems as these of the banking world were other dark figures and groups, controlling vast industrial activities, obsessing and perverting spending power. There was, for example, that Mystery Man of Mystery Men, Sir Basil Zaharoff, the armaments salesman, still the delight of our schoolboy novelists, and Ivar Kreuger, who created an almost world-wide system of lucifer match monopolies, lent great sums to governments and was finally caught forging big parcels of bonds. He then staged a suicide in Paris to escape the penalty of fraud. (We have to remember that in those days the lucifer matches we now see in museums were consumed by the billion. There was no other handy source of fire, and their manufacture and distribution was on the scale of a primary industry.) Kreuger, unlike Morgan, was not a man of the acquisitive type; he neither hoarded nor collected; he kept nothing, not even the law, but he built lavishly and gave away money for scientific research. (The discovery of Pekin Man, a memorable incident in early archaeology, was, for instance, made possible by his gifts.) Morgan forestalled and accumulated; Kreuger robbed and gave. When Morgan spent his gains he bought 'Old Masters', manuscripts and suchlike indisputably genuine and valuable junk; when Kreuger dispersed the moneys that had been entrusted to him he made the most extraordinary experiments in decorative art, in electric lighting and fantastic building. But each operated unchecked. So obscure was the financial machinery of the time that for some months Kreuger was able to pass off as genuine a package of forged Italian bonds amounting to about half a million dollars, and to obtain advances upon them from reputable lenders. To-day a trick of such a character would be detected, were it possible, in the course of a single day by the ordinary checking of the Transactions Bureau. But nowadays no one would have any reason for attempting anything of the sort. The lives of these Mystery Men and of the various groups of speculators (the Balkan Gang, e.g.) who manipulated the exchanges of the various national currencies of Eastern Europe, and of a great number of other profit-seeking groups and individuals who were thrusting about amidst the machinery of exchange, are to be found in *Lives of Mischief* (Financial Volumes) taken out of the *Dictionary of Biography*. The very best of them were men who waylaid gain or sought adventures in a fog. Most of them were as active and as blind to the consequences of their activities as voles who perforate a dyke.

In the files of the financial papers of this period, when the movements of gold were of vital significance to the prices of commodities and the credit of everyone in the world, one sees such headings as 'Unknown Buyer Takes Two Millions in Gold' or, less exactly, 'Gold Bought by Unknown Buyer'. Then all the little manipulators of money would be set peering and spying and guessing and rigging their businesses to the possible shift of equilibrium this dark intimation might portend.

Other Mystery Men, Mystery Men *ex officio*, were the various Ministers of Finance, of whom perhaps the British Chancellor of the Exchequer was most typical. Every year there was a vast amount of whispering and hinting, peeping and calculating and going to and fro, about the National Budget and the readjustment of taxation for another twelvemonth. An arithmetical mystery called 'balancing the Budget' had to be performed. Business would be held up as the great revelation drew near; gambling operations, insurance operations, would multiply. The wife, the family, the intimates and secretaries of the Man of Destiny, went about the world sealed, enigmatical, oracular, profoundly important with his reflected importance. At last the great day dawned. The legislature would assemble in unusual force, excited and curious. The Witch Doctor, with his portfolios of Obi, would take his place in the House of Commons, rise portentously, begin the 'Budget Speech'.

No Budget Speech was complete without its 'surprises'. Could anything witness more vividly to the chaotic casualness of the twentieth century? Anything might be taxed; anything might be relieved; anyone might shift the weights about. In the economic darkness of the time it did not seem to matter. The marvel is that the system staggered on for so long.

How amazing, how fantastic, was that condition of affairs! It is as if one of the great transatlantic liners of the period had careered across the ocean with its passenger decks and cabins brightly lit, its saloons and bars in full swing, while down below its essential machinery, manifestly with something going wrong with it, had no arrangements for illumination at all and was served by men (some of them masked), working without a foreman or any general directions, by the light of an occasional match or a treasured but rather worn-out electric torch, or altogether in the dark, upon the great cranks and swiftly sliding shafts that beat and circled about them.

From the very cessation of the fighting in 1918 and onward it was manifest that this machinery was seriously out of gear. The economic history of the time is a story of swerves and fluctuations of the most alarming kind, each one more disconcerting and disastrous than its predecessor. In the decades before the war, though there were certainly variations in the real value of the different currencies they were variations within moderate limits, and the rise or fall went on through comparatively long periods, but after the war there commenced a series of movements in exchange and prices unprecedented throughout the whole period of prosperity. Currencies rose and towered above others and broke like Atlantic waves, and people found the good money in their banks changed to useless paper in a period of a few months. It became more and more difficult to carry on foreign trade because of the increasing uncertainty of payment, and since there was scarcely a manufacturing industry that had not to obtain some material from abroad, the entanglement of foreign trade often involved a strangulation of production at home. Trade and industry sickened and lost heart more and more in this disastrous uncertainty; it was like being in an earthquake, when it seems equally unsafe to stand still or run away; and the multitudes of unemployed increased continually. The economically combatant nations entrenched themselves behind tariffs, played each other tricks with loans, repudiations, sudden inflations and deflations, and no power in the world seemed able to bring them into any concerted action to arrest and stop their common dégringolade.

The opening years of the second third of the twentieth century saw *Homo sapiens* in the strangest plight. The planet had a healthier and more abundant human population than it had ever carried before, and it lacked nothing in its available resources to give the whole of this population full and happy lives. That was already the material reality of the position. But through nothing in the world but a universal, various muddle-headedness, our species seemed unable to put out its hand and take the abundance within its reach. As we turn over the periodicals and literature of the time the notes of apprehension and distress increase and deepen. The war period of 1914–18 was full of suffering, but also it was full of excitement; even the dying on the battlefields believed that a compensatory peace and happiness lay close ahead. The survivors were promised 'homes fit for heroes'. But the Depression of 1930 and onward was characterized by its inelasticity; it was a phase of unqualified disappointment and hopelessly baffled protest. One lived, as one contemporary writer put it, in 'a world bewitched'.

The economic consequences of this monetary disorganization followed hard upon it, but the deeper-lying destruction of social morale
and its effects were manifested less immediately. The whole world
system heretofore had been sustained by the general good behaviour of
common men, by the honesty and punctuality of clerks, workers of
every sort, traders, professional men. General security depended upon
habitual decent behaviour in the street and on the countryside. But the
common man behaved well because he had faith that his pay was a safe,
if sometimes a scanty, assurance of a certain comfort and dignity in his
life. He imagined an implicit bargain between himself and society that
he should be given employment and security in exchange for his law-
abiding subordination, and that society would keep faith with his
savings. He assumed that the governments would stand by the money
they issued and see that it gave him the satisfactions it promised him.
He was not a good boy for nothing. Nobody is. But now in various
terms and phrases all over the world millions of men and women were
asking themselves whether it 'paid' to be industrious, skilful and law-
abiding. The cement of confidence in the social fabric from 1918
onward was more and more plainly decaying and changing to dust. The
percentage of criminal offences, which had been falling through all the
period of prosperity, rose again.

XIII

1933: 'Progress' comes to a Halt

So we bring the history of mankind to that great pause in social
expansion which concluded the first third of the twentieth century. The
year 1933 closed in a phase of dismayed apprehension. It was like that
chilly stillness, that wordless interval of suspense, that comes at times
before the breaking of a storm. The wheels of economic life were
turning only reluctantly and uncertainly; the millions of unemployed
accumulated and became more and more plainly a challenge and a
menace. All over the world the masses were sinking down through
distress and insufficiency to actual famine. And collectively they were
doing nothing effectual in protest or struggle. Insurrectionary socialism
lurked and muttered in every great agglomeration. But insurrection
alone could remedy nothing without constructive ideas, and there was
no power and energy yet behind any such constructive ideas as had

appeared. The merely repressive forces, whatever their feebleness in the face of criminality, were still fully capable of restraining popular insurrection. They could keep misery stagnant and inoperative.

Everywhere, in everything, there was an ebb of vitality. A decline in the public health was becoming perceptible. A diminishing resistance to infections and a rise in the infantile death-rate was already very evident in the vital statistics after 1933.

War was manifestly drawing nearer, in Eastern Asia, in Eastern Europe; it loitered, it advanced, it halted, and no one displayed the vigour or capacity needed to avert its intermittent, unhurrying approach.

Still the immense inertias of the old order carried things on. Under a darkling sky, the majority of people were going about their businesses according to use and want. The unprofitable industries still carried on with reduced staffs; the shop-keepers opened their shops to a dwindling tale of customers; the unemployed queued up at the Labour Exchanges by force of habit, and some at least got a job; the landlord's agent no longer collected the rent that was due but called for an instalment of his arrears; the unfed or ill-fed children went sniffing to chilly schools to be taught by dispirited teachers on reduced salaries, but still the schools were not closed; the bankrupt railways and steamship lines ran diminished but punctual services; hotels stayed open not to make profits but to mitigate losses; the road traffic lost something of its newness and smartness and swiftness, but still it flowed; the crowds in the streets moved less briskly, but, if anything, these sluggish crowds were more numerous, and the police, if less alertly vigilant, maintained order.

There had been a considerable if inadequate building boom after the Peace of Versailles, but after 1930 new construction fell off more and more. Yet some builders found work, necessary repairs were attended to, burnt-out houses were reconditioned, for example. In 1935 and 1937 the world was swept by influenza epidemics of unusual virulence. The lowered resistance, already noted by the statisticians, was now made conspicuous by this return towards mediaeval conditions; but the doctors and nurses stuck to their duties stoutly and the druggists and undertakers, whose affairs had long since been reorganized on Big Business lines, profited.

Pictures of life in the shadows during this phase of devitalization are not very abundant, nor do they convey the essential misery into which a whole generation was born, in which it lived and died. One sees the rows of dilapidated houses, the wretched interiors and shabbily clad men and women standing about. In these pictures they seem always to be just standing about. Descriptive journalism brings the student nearer to the realities of a life without space, colour, movement, hope or opportunity. There were a number of 'enquiries' made, more particularly by the British, American and French newspapers, and the tale they tell is always a tale of wheels slowing down to a stoppage, of factory gates being closed, of smokeless chimneys and rusting rails. Here is a vivid contemporary vignette, to show how things were with millions of human beings during this strange phase of human experience. It is from the pen of H. M. Tomlinson (1873–1969) one of the best of English descriptive writers.

'I chanced upon a little town above Cardiff last week. It was by pure chance; I had never before heard of the place. It is typical of these valleys, so never mind its name. It could have many names. Its population is, or was, about 6,000. Its people have faced trouble before – less than twenty years ago over 300 of its men perished in a mine explosion. We won't say the town got over that, for I spoke to those for whom the calamity is an abiding horror. It was a terrific defeat for them in the war upon Nature, but survivors returned to the struggle and said no more about it.

'When first I saw the town from a distance, with the bleak, bare uplands about it, I was reminded of the towns, once familiar, that were too near the battle-line in France. It was midday, and sunny, yet this colliery town was silent and so still that it seemed under a spell.

'As a fact, it *is* under a spell. It is, in a way, dead. But its people cling to the empty shell of it. Where else can they go?

'At first sight no people could have been there. Buildings in the foreground were in ruins. The gaunt pit-head gearing evidently had not moved for an age. The gaps in the blackened walls of the power-house suggested a home of bats and owls.

'The first man I met when I reached the end of its main street and saw then that the shops were not only closed, but abandoned, was standing on the kerb, a man in the middle years, shrewd, but haggard, his clothes brushed till they were threadbare.

'"What's the matter with this town?" I asked.

'"On the dole."

'"Are you out too?"

'"Of course I'm out."

'"How long?"

'"He was silent. He held up five fingers."

'"Months?"

'"Years."

'"Are all the men here the same?"

'"Most of them. And won't go back."

'He led me up a mound of refuse, where a goat was eating paper, and we had a near view of the colliery itself. "That's the reason we won't go down again," he said. "How would you work it?"

'Whether by design or rust a steel footbridge had fallen across the wide railway track which went to the pit-head. A deflected stream guttered down between the metals, which were overgrown with grass and stagnant marsh stuff. The outbuildings were a huddle of dilapidations. It looked haunted. "Some men I knew," muttered my guide, "are still down here. There they'll stop. They've been there nineteen years now. Would you call them lucky?"

'Two thousand five hundred men came out of the principal colliery five years ago. That is why the shops are shut, long rows of them with whitewashed windows and doorways filled with dust and straws. The woodwork of many houses had been taken for firewood. Even the Cooperative store is shut, as well as the pawnshop. Thrift and thriftlessness mean the same thing in this town, where I noticed that even Noncomformist chapels, with broken windows, had been left to the rats and birds.

'Worse than the dismal shops and broken buildings are the groups of shabby men, all neat and tidy, standing listless and silent at the street corners, waiting.

'Waiting for what? Nothing. There is nothing to come. . . .

'They are doomed, these parents, to watch a generation grow up with thin bones and a shadow on its mind. Their children learn the signs of the slow death about them when they should be at play; children that have no childhood.

'Their homes are in a graveyard of human aspiration. . . .'

The Press and literature of that period make curious reading. It varied between a bleak, insincere optimism and hopeless desperation. An undignified viciousness and a jeering humour invaded popular art and literature; 'strong' in manner and in flavour rather than in any grasp upon the realities of contemporary life. There was also an abundant production and consumption of reassuring and deliberately 'cheerful' books, a movement towards religious mysticism and other-worldliness and a marked tendency towards repressive puritanism. Excesses of libertinism provoke censorious and superstitious suppression; the two things are correlated aspects of a decline in human dignity. In the face of its financial and political perplexities mankind was becoming neurasthenic.

All neurasthenia has apparently unaccountable elements. To us to-day, it seems incredible that the way out of all these distresses was not plainly seen and boldly taken. There was a blindness and an effortlessness that still exercise the mind of the social psychologist. The way was so plain that it was visible, it was indicated by hundreds of intelligent and detached observers as early as the thirties of the twentieth century. Maxwell Brown, in his study of the Modern State idea, has two supplementary volumes of citations to this effect. Such phrases, for example, as 'Cosmopolis, Inflation and Public Employment' (from a British provincial newspaper article in 1932) do state, in general terms at any rate, the line of escape for the race. These are crude, ill-defined terms, but manifestly they have in them the shape of the ultimate reconstruction. 'Cosmopolis' foreshadows our rational world controls, 'Inflation' was a plain indication of our present complete restraint upon the aggravation of debts and fluctuations of price level; 'Public Employment' was our ancestors' conception of socialist enterprise.

But before the exodus to peace and freedom could be achieved, such scattered flashes of understanding had to ignite a steadier illumination. The conception of revolutionary world reconstruction had to spread from the few to the many, spread to them not merely as an idea and as a suggestion, but in such force as to saturate their minds and determine their lives. Then, and then only, could the necessary will-power be marshalled and directed to the effective reorganization of earthly affairs.

A struggle for sanity had to take place in the racial brain, a great casting-out of false assumptions, conventional distortions, hitherto uncritized maxims and impossible 'rights', a great clearing-up of ideas about moral, material and biological relationships; it was a struggle that, as we shall see, involved the passing of three generations. To an analysis of the factors and decisive forces in this struggle our history must next address itself.

Something between eight and ten thousand million human lives in all were lived out during the Age of Frustration. Compared with the average lives of to-day, they were shorter and far less healthy; nearly all of them had long phases of such infection, maladjustment and enfeeblement as are now almost outside man's experience. The great majority of them were passed laboriously in squalid or dingy surroundings, in huts, hovels, cottages, tenements and cellars almost as dismal as the ancestral cave and nearly as insanitary. A minority who could command the services of 'domestics' lived in relative comfort and even with a certain freedom and luxury, at an enormous cost to the rest. This prosperous minority dwindled after 1931. It had vanished in Russia after 1917.

There was a diminishing sense of personal security in the world, an enervating fear and uncertainty about the morrow, through the ensuing years. There was what we find now an almost incredible amount of mutual distrust, suspicion, irritation and quarrelling. Only a small proportion of the world's population lived to be peacefully and gracefully old in this phase of deterioration. Disease or a violent death became the common end again. One of the first general histories that was ever written was called The Martyrdom of Man (Winwood Reade, 1871). In the Age of Frustration it seemed to many that that martyrdom was mounting to a final hopeless agony.

Yet in the welter there were also laughter, sympathy, helpfulness and courage. Those fretted and painful lives interwove with threads of great brightness. Out of that medley of human distresses, out of the brains of men stressed out of indolence and complacency by the gathering darkness and suffering about them, there came first the hope, then the broad plan and the effort, and at last the achievement of that fruitful order, gathering beauty and happy assurance, in which we live to-day.

BOOK II

The Days After Tomorrow:
The Age of Frustration

I

The London Conference:
The Crowning Failure of the Old Governments;
The Spread of Dictatorships and Fascisms

In the preceding chapters we have explained how the old order of the nineteenth century, the Capitalist System as it was called, came to disaster in the second and third decades of the twentieth century because of the disproportionate development of its industrial production, the unsoundness and vulnerability of its monetary nexus, and its political inadaptability. It had no inherent power of recovery, and there was no idea of a new order, sufficiently developed, to replace it. Necessarily therefore the tale of disaster went on.

The only mechanisms in existence for collective action, and that only in disconnected spurts, were the various sovereign governments. Most of these at the outset of the war were either parliamentary monarchies or parliamentary republics. The parliaments were elected upon a very preposterous system by the bulk or all of the population. The age was called the Age of Democracy. Democracy did not mean then what it means now, an equal opportunity for every human being according to his ability and the faculty to which he belongs to serve and have a voice in collective affairs. Nor did it mean the fraternal equality of a small community. It expressed a political fiction of a very extraordinary kind: that every subject of the contemporary state was equally capable of making whatever collective decisions had to be made.

The great republics of a remoter antiquity, the Carthaginian, the Athenian, the Roman, for example, were all essentially aristocratic. Democratic republics, that is to say republics in which every man was supposed to share equally in the government, in the rare instances when they occurred at all before the end of the eighteenth century, were, like Uri, Unterwalden or Andorra, small and poor and perched in inaccessible places. The world at large knew nothing of them. Their affairs were equally small and well within the scope of a common citizen's understanding.

Then with the Era of European Predominance came a turning-point in human affairs, that outbreak of books and discussion in the fifteenth century, a period of great animation and confusion when the destructive criticism of faiths and loyalties got loose. The release of new economic forces strained the old feudal order to breaking. Exploration and merchandizing, new financial conditions, industrial development, created new types of men, uncertain of their powers, needing and demanding free play. They did not know clearly what they wanted; they did not know clearly how they differed from the men of the old order, nor had they any conception of such a structural reform of human relations as Plato had already pictured nearly two thousand years before them. His plan for a devoted and trained order of rulers was unknown to them, though More had tried to revive it. They were simply responding to the facts about them. They chafed under an hereditary aristocracy, and they distrusted an absolute king.

Essentially the movement that evolved the phraseology of nineteenth-century democracy was a revolt against 'birth' and 'privilege', against the monopolization of direction and advantages by restricted and generally hereditary classes in accordance with definitely established dogmas. Because this revolt was the revolt of a very miscellaneous number of energetic and resentful individuals not definitely organized, mentally or socially, it came about that at a quite early stage of the new movement it took the form of an assertion of the equal political rights of all men.

It was not that these sixteenth- and seventeenth-century Radicals were for government by the general mass; it was that they were antagonistic to established classes and rulers. They constituted a vigorous insurgent minority rousing, so far as it could, and trailing after it the apathetic majority of submissive mankind. That was always the character of these democratic movements of the Age of European Predominance. The multitude was supposed to be demanding and deciding – and all the time it was being pushed or led. The individuality of the popular 'leaders' of those centuries stands out far more vividly than the kings and ecclesiastics of the period. Only one or two such hereditary monarchs as William Prince of Orange, or Frederick the Great of Prussia, figure as conspicuously on the record as – to cite a miscellany of new types – Cromwell, Voltaire, Mirabeau, Washington, Gladstone, Robespierre, Bonaparte or Marx.

Later on (in England, America, Scandinavia, Germany, Finland, e.g.) in just the same way a minority of dissatisfied and aggressive women struggling for a rôle in affairs inflicted the vote upon the indifferent majority of women. But their achievement ended with that. Outside that sexual vindication, women at that time had little to contribute to the solution of the world's problems, and as a matter of fact they contributed nothing.

Research in social psychology is still only beginning to unravel the obscure processes by which faith in 'democracy' became for the better part of a century the ruling cant of practically all America and the greater part of Europe. There was often a profound internal disingenuousness even in those who were known as 'Thinkers' in that age. They were afraid in their hearts of stark realities; they tried instinctively to adapt even their heresies to what seemed to them invincibly established prejudices. Their primary conception of democracy was of some faraway simple little republic of stout upstanding men, all similar, all practically equal in fortune and power, managing the affairs of the canton in a folk-meeting, by frank speech and acclamation. All the old-world democracies, up to and including the Republic of Rome, were ruled, in theory at least, by such meetings of all the citizens. The people, it was imagined, watched, listened, spoke, and wisdom ensued.

The extension of this ideal to the large communities of the new world that was replacing the feudal order involved such manifest difficulties and even such absurdities that mysticism was inevitable if the people was still to be supposed the sovereign of the community. But there was so strong and widespread a dread that if this supposition was not maintained privilege, restriction, tyranny would come back that the mystical interpretation was boldly adopted. At any cost those old inequalities must not return, said the adventurers of the dawning capitalist age, and, flying from one subjugation, they hurried on to another.

They found the doctrine of man's natural virtue as expounded by Rousseau extraordinarily helpful and effective. The common man, when he is not beguiled by Priest or King, is always right. The Common People became therefore a mystical sympathetic being, essentially a God, whose altar was the hustings and whose oracle the ballot box. A little slow and lumpish was this God of the Age of European Predominance, but, though his mills ground slowly, men were assured that they ground with ultimate exactitude. And meanwhile business could be carried on. You could fool some of the people all the time and all the people some of the time, said Abraham Lincoln, but you could not fool all the people all the time. Yet for such crucial purposes as bringing about a war or exploiting an economic situation, this was manifestly a quite disastrous degree of foolability.

And the situation naturally evolved a Press of the very highest fooling capacity.

This belatedly inevitable Divinity proved now to be altogether too slow-witted for the urgent political and economic riddles, with ruin and death at hand, which pressed upon our race as the twentieth century unfolded. The experience of the futile Disarmament and Economic Conferences of 1932 and 1933, the massive resistance in every national legislature to any but the most narrow egotism in foreign policy, the inability of the world as a whole to establish any unanimity of action in face of swift economic collapse, revealed the final bankruptcy of Parliamentary Democracy.

The inability of the world's nominal rulers to shake off their lifelong habit of speaking to, or at, a vaguely conceived crowd of prejudiced voters, and their invincible repugnance from clear statement, frustrated every effort towards realism. They recoiled from any suggestion of definitive or novel action on the plea that their function was purely representative. Behind them all the reader feels the sprawling uneasy presence of that poor invertebrate mass deity of theirs, the Voter, easily roused to panic and frantic action against novel, bold or radical measures, very amenable to patriotic claptrap, very easily scared and maddened into war, and just as easily baffled to distrust and impotence by delays, side issues, and attacks on the personalities of decisive people he might otherwise have trusted. An entirely irresponsible Press, mercenary or partisan, played upon his baser emotions, which were so easy to play upon, and made no appeal whatever to his intelligence or his conscience.

The Voter, the Mass, which was neither educated nor led, the Voter without any sincere organizations of leadership anywhere, is the basal explanation of the impotence of those culminating conferences. The World Economic Conference in London was by far the more significant of the two. Armament and disarmament are symptoms and superficial, but economic life is fundamental. This London gathering has been made the subject of a thousand studies by our social psychologists. Many of its contradictions still perplex us profoundly. The men who assembled had just as good brains as anyone to-day, and, as an exhaustive analysis by Moreton Canby of the various projects advanced at the Conference proves, they had a substantial understanding of the needs of the world situation, yet collectively, and because of their haunting paralysing sense of the Mass and Press behind them and of their incalculable impulses and resentments, they achieved an effect of fatuity far beyond the pompous blunderings of Versailles.

Primarily the London Conference was a belated effort to repair the vast omissions of that earlier gathering, to supplement the well-meaning political patchwork of Wilson by some readjustment of the monetary and economic dislocations he had been too limited to foresee or too weak to avoid. Wraithlike conceptions of some vague monetary League of Nations at Bâle, and some Tariff Council and Assembly, drifted through the mists of the opening meeting. And History, with its disposition to inexact repetition, made one of the principal figures of this second world assembly also a President of the United States, belonging also to the Democratic party and according to the ritual of that Party invoking the name of Jefferson as the Communists invoked the name of Marx or the Muslim Mahomet. This was Roosevelt II. He leaves a less vivid impression than his predecessor because he did not impend for so long upon the European scene. But for some months at least before and after his election as American President and the holding of the London Conference there was again a whispering hope in the world that a real 'Man' had arisen, who would see simply and clearly, who would speak plainly to all mankind and liberate the world from the dire obsessions and ineptitudes under which it suffered and to which it seemed magically enslaved. But the one thing he failed to do was to speak plainly.

Drawing wisdom from Wilson's personal failure, he did not come to London and expose himself and his conversation to too close a scrutiny. He preferred to deal with the fluctuating crises in London from his yacht, *Amberjack II*, in Nantucket Harbour, through intermittent messages and through more or less completely authorized intermediaries. *Amberjack II* has become almost as significant a ship in the history of human affairs as the Ford Peace Ship. Significant equally in its intentions and in its inadequacies.

Everywhere as the Conference drew near men were enquiring about this possible new leader for them. 'Is this at last the Messiah we seek, or shall we look for another?' Every bookshop in Europe proffered his newly published book of utterances, *Looking Forward*, to gauge what manner of mind they had to deal with. It proved rather disconcerting reading for their anxious minds. Plainly the man was firm, honest and amiable, as the frontispiece portrait with its clear frank eyes and large resolute face showed, but the text of the book was a politician's text, saturated indeed with good will seasoned with much vague modernity, but vague and wanting in intellectual grip. 'He's good,' they said, 'but is this good enough?'

Nevertheless hope fought a stout fight. There was no other personality visible who even promised to exorcize the spell that lay upon the economic life of the race. It was Roosevelt's Conference or nothing. And in spite of that disappointing book there remained some sound reasons for hope. In particular the President, it was asserted, had a 'Brain Trust'. A number of indisputably able and modern-minded men were his associates, such men as Professors Tugwell, Moley and Dickinson, men whose later work played a significant part in that reconstruction of legal and political method which was America's particular contribution to Modern State ideas. This 'last hope of mankind', it was credibly reported, called these intimates by their Christian names and they called him 'Guv'nor'. He was said to have the modesty and greatness to defer to their studied and matured opinions. Observers, still hopeful, felt that if he listened to these advisors things might not go so badly after all. He was at any rate one point better than the European politicians and heads of State who listened only to bankers and big-business men.

But was he listening? Did he grasp the threefold nature of the problem in hand? He understood, it seemed, the need for monetary inflation to reduce the burthen of debt and over-capitalization; he was apparently alive to the need for a progressive expansion of public employment; and so far he was sound. Unless, which is not quite clear, he wavered between 'public' and 'publicly assisted', which was quite another matter. But was he sound upon the necessity that these measures should be world-wide or practically world-wide? He made some unexpected changes of attitude in these respects. Were these changes inconstancies or were they tactical manœuvres veiling a profoundly consistent and resolute purpose? Was it wise to be tactical when all the world was in need of plain speech and simple directive ideas? His treatment took on a disconcertingly various quality. He listened, it seemed, to his advisors; but was he not also listening to everybody? He was flirting with bimetallism. No medicine, it seemed, was to be spared.

The Conference opened with a stout determination to be brilliant and eventful; the hotels were full, the streets beflagged, the programme of entertainments was admirable, and even the English weather seemed to make an effort. The opening addresses by the King of England and his Prime Minister Ramsay MacDonald make very curious reading to-day. They express an acute recognition of the crucial condition of human affairs. They state in so many words that the failure of the Conference will precipitate world disaster. They insist upon the necessity for world cooperation, for monetary simplification and a resumption of employment; and in all that we admit they had the truth of the matter. But they make not the faintest intimation of how these desirable ends are to be obtained. They made gestures that are incomprehensible to us unless they had an inkling of the primary elements of the situation. And then immediately they turned away to other things. That mixture of resolve and failure to attack is what perplexes us most. If they saw the main essentials of the situation they certainly did not see them as a connected whole; they did not see any line of world action before them.

Cordell Hull, the chief of the United States delegation, was equally large and fine. The grave and splendid words – shot with piety in the best American tradition – that he inscribed upon the roll of history were as follows: 'Selfishness must be banished. If – which God forbid! – any nation should wreck this Conference, with the notion that its local interests might profit, that nation would merit the execration of mankind.'

Again Daladier, the French Prime Minister, opened with extremely broad and sane admissions. He insisted strongly on a necessity which the two opening English speeches had minimized, the necessity, the urgent necessity, for a progressive development of great public works throughout the world to absorb the unemployed and restore consumption. The Americans in the second week seemed to be coming in line with that. But after this much of lucidity the Conference fell away to minor issues. Apparently it could not keep at so high a level of reality. The pressure of the Mass and the Press behind each delegate began to tell upon him. The national representatives began to insist with increasing explicitness that national interests must not be sacrificed to the general good, and in a little time it became doubtful if there could be such a thing as the general good. The World Economic Conference became by imperceptible transitions a World Economic Conflict just as the League of Nations had become a diplomatic bargain mart. All the fine preluding of the first seances withered to fruitlessness because the mind of the world had still to realize the immense moral and educational effort demanded by those triple conditions that were dawning upon its apprehension, and because it was still unwilling to accept the immense political pooling they indicated. The amount of self-abnegation involved was an insurmountable psychological barrier in the way of the representatives present. It would have meant a sacrifice of the very conditions that had made them. How could men appointed as national representatives accept a pooling of national interests? They were indeed fully prepared to revolutionize the world situation and change gathering misery to hope, plenty and order, but only on the impossible condition that they were not to change themselves and that nothing essential to their importance changed. The leading ideas of the Conference were cloudily true, but the disintegrative forces of personal, party and national egotism were too strong for them.

It is a very curious thing that the representatives of Soviet Russia did nothing to enlighten the obscurity of the world riddle. It is still argued by many writers that the Bolshevik régime was the direct precursor of our Modern World-State as it exists to-day. But there was no direct continuity. The Modern State arose indeed out of the same social imperatives and the same constructive impulses that begot Marxism and Leninism, but as an independent, maturer, and sounder revolutionary conception. The Soviet system certainly anticipated many of the features of our present order in its profession of internationalism, in its very real socialism, and particularly in the presence of a devoted controlling organization, the Communist Party, which foreshadowed our Modern State Fellowship. But there was always a wide divergence in Russia between theory and practice, and Litvinoff, who spoke on behalf of that first great experiment in planning, was too preoccupied with various particular points at issue between his country and the western world, trading embargoes and difficulties of credit, for example, to use the occasion as he might have done, for a world-wide appeal. He did nothing to apply the guiding principles of Communism to the world situation. Here was a supreme need for planning, but he said nothing for a Five Year or Ten Year Plan for all the world. Here was a situation asking plainly for collective employment, and he did not even press the inevitability of world-socialism. Apparently he had forgotten the world considered as a whole as completely as any of the capitalist delegates. He was thinking of Russia versus the other States of the world as simply as if he were an ordinary capitalist patriot.

The claims of the other delegations were even more short-sighted and uninspired. Since there was a time-limit set to their speeches, they compressed their assertions of general humanitarian benevolence to a phrase or so and then came to business. Only Senator Connolly, from the Irish Free State, protested against the blinkered outlooks of his fellow speakers and pleaded for a consideration of 'every possible theory, however unorthodox'. But his own speech propounded no substantial constructive ideas. He was too obsessed by an embargo that England had put upon Irish exports, and to that he settled down. . . .

The whole idea of the Modern World-State, Moreton Canby insists, is to be traced, albeit in a warped and sterilized form, alike in the expressed idea-systems of the Americans, the British, the French and the Russians at the Conference. In the American statements it is wrapped about and hidden by individualist phrases and precautions, in the British it is overlaid by imperialist assumptions, in the Russian it is made unpalatable by the false psychology and harsh jargon of Marxism. In the first the business man refuses to change and get out of the way, in the second the imperialist administrator, and in the third the doctrinaire party man. Athwart every assertion of general principles drive the misty emotions of patriotism, party and personal association. Yet for all that it is indisputable that the Modern World-State was definitely adumbrated at London in 1933. Like a ghost out of the future its presence was felt by nearly everyone, though the worst phases of the Age of Frustration had still to come, though generations of suffering had still to lapse, before it could appear as the living reality of human political life.

The ghost, says Canby, did not materialize, because there was no material. Every large country in the world was feeling its way towards the essentials of a permanently progressive World-State, but none was yet within reach even of its partial and local realization. Roosevelt II and his eleventh-hour effort to reconstruct America he finds particularly interesting. The President was plainly aware of the need to relieve debt by inflation, but he was unable to check the dissipation of the liberated energy in speculation. He was dealing with men trained and saturated in the tradition of poker, to whom a solemn cunning had become a second nature, and he was asking them (with occasional fierce threats) to display an open-faced helpfulness. He had no proper civil service available to control large public works; it was impossible to change the American technicians at one blow from quasi-financial operators to a candid, devoted public salariat. So he tried to induce profiteers to forgo profits and organize their industries on altruistic lines by dire threats of socialization which he had no managing class to enforce. And he was as ignorant of British or European mentality and as little able to get to an understanding with it as Wilson had been before him. It was a mutual misunderstanding, but his manners were self-righteous and provocative. He began to scold long before the Conference was over. By 1935 everyone was pointing to a sort of contrasted parallelism between America and Russia. Each was manifestly struggling towards a more scientifically organized state, and each was finding the same difficulty in reconciling productive efficiency in the general interest with primarily political control. Technician and politician had still to be assimilated one to the other. Each great dictatorship was at war with the speculator and the profiteer. Each professed a faint hope of cosmopolitan cooperation and then concentrated practically and urgently upon the establishment of an internal prosperity. But they started towards that common objective from opposite poles of productive efficiency and social assumption. Roosevelt started from the standpoint of democratic individualism and Stalin from that of Marxist Communism. The British system and the other intermediate countries of the world struggled to be conservative in the chaos of financial collapse. No solvent had yet been devised to synthesize the good will in the world.

The London Conference rose to no such dramatic climax as the signing of the Peace Treaty at Versailles. It rose to nothing. It began at its highest point and steadily declined. If Versailles produced a monster, London produced nothing at all. Never did so valiant a beginning peter out so completely.

There are abundant intimations in the Press of the time (see Habwright's *The Sense of Catastrophe in the Nineteen Thirties,* a summary of quotations in the Historical Documents Series 173192) of a realization that the political and economic morale of that age was played out, and that almost any casual selection of men would have been at least as adequate as this gathering of old-world political personages to face the vast impending disasters before our race. For at any rate these men had already been tried and tested and found wanting. Mr Ramsay MacDonald indeed, the British premier, the fine flower and summary of professional politics, rolled his r's and his eyes over the Conference and seemed still to be hoping that some favourable accident out of the void might save him and his like from the damning dissection of history. For a time, in the opening glow of the assembly, with the clicking photographers recording every studied gesture, with the attentive microphones spreading out and pickling for ever his fine voice and his rich accent, with bustling secretaries in sedulous attendance, with the well-trained gravity of the delegates and particularly the well-matured high seriousness of those adepts in public appearance, the Americans, to sustain him, this last sublimation of democratic statesmanship may really have believed that some kind of favourable incantation was in progress under his direction. He must have felt that or he could not have remained there talking. Incantations had made him. By the sheer use of voice and gesture he had clambered from extreme obscurity to world prominence. If he did not believe in incantation there was nothing left for him to believe in. He must have clung to that persuasion to the end. But if that was his state of mind at the time, it could hardly have survived the comments and criticisms of the next few months. Surely then he had some sleepless nights in which even his private incantations failed.

The World Economic Conference lost its brilliance in a week or so. The City, which had been so flushed with hope that for a time its price lists, all pluses, looked like war-time cemeteries, relapsed into depression. The World Slump did not wait for the Conference to disperse before it resumed. At the outset London had been all blown up and distended by bright anticipations, so that it was like one of those little squeaking bladders children play with, and like one of those bladders, so soon as the blowing ceased, it shrank and shrivelled and ended in a dying wail of despair.

As Habwright puts it, by July 1933 intelligent men and women everywhere were saying two things. Of the assembled rulers and delegates they were saying: 'These people can do nothing for us. They do worse than nothing. They intensify the disaster.' And in the second place it was demanded with a sort of astonishment: 'Why have historians, sociologists and economists nothing to tell us now? There may indeed be some excuse for the failure of politicians under democratic conditions. But have our universities been doing nothing about it? Is there indeed no science of these things? Is there no knowledge? Has history learnt nothing of causes, and is there no analysis of the social processes that are destroying us?'

To which the professors, greatly preoccupied at that particular date in marking honours papers in history and social and political science, made no audible reply.

Before the end of the thirties it was plain to all the world that a world-wide social catastrophe was now inevitably in progress, that the sanest thing left for intelligent men to do was to set about upon some sort of Noah's Ark to salvage whatever was salvageable of civilization, so that there should be a new beginning after the rising deluge of misfortune had spent itself. A few prescient spirits had been saying as much for some years, but now this idea of salvage spread like an epidemic. It prepared the way for the Modern State Movement on which our present order rests. At the time, however, the general pessimism was little mitigated by any real hope of recovery. One writer, quoted by Habwright, compared man to a domesticated ape, 'which has had the intelligence and ability to drag its straw mattress up to the fire when it is cold, but has had neither the wit nor the foresight to escape the consequent blaze'. Habwright's brief summary of the financial operations that went on as the sense of catastrophe grew justifies that grim image very completely.

The conviction that Parliamentary Democracy had come to an end spread everywhere in that decade. Already in the period between the vacillation in international affairs after Versailles and the warfare of the Forties, men had been going about discussing and scheming and plotting for some form of government that should be at least decisive. And now their efforts took on a new urgency. There was a world-wide hysteria to change governments and officials.

At its first onset this craving for decisiveness had produced some extremely crude results. An epidemic of tawdry 'dictatorships' had run over Europe from Poland to Spain immediately after the war. For the most part these adventures followed the pattern of the pronunciamentos of the small South American republics, and were too incidental and inconsquent for the student of general history to be troubled about them now. But there followed a world-wide development of directive or would-be directive political associations which foreshadowed very plainly the organization of the Modern State Fellowship upon which our present world order rests.

The Fascist dictatorship of Mussolini in Italy had something in it of a more enduring type than most of the other supersessions of parliamentary methods. It arose not as a personal usurpation but as the expression of an organization with a purpose and a sort of doctrine of its own. The intellectual content of Fascism was limited, nationalist and romantic; its methods, especially in its opening phase, were violent and dreadful; but at least it insisted upon discipline and public service for its members. It appeared as a counter movement to a chaotic labour communism, but its support of the still-surviving monarchy and the Church was qualified by a considerable boldness in handling education and private property for the public benefit. Fascism indeed was not an altogether bad thing; it was a bad good thing; and Mussolini has left his mark on history.

In Russia something still more thorough and broader came into operation after 1917. This was the Communist Party. It was the invention of Lenin; he continued to modify and adapt its organization and doctrine until his untimely death in 1924. While he lived Russia's experiment really seemed to be leading the world in its flight towards a new order from the futile negations and paralysis of Parliamentary government. It is still profoundly interesting to note the modernity of many aspects of the early Bolshevik régime.

This modernity achieved under the stress of urgent necessities and Lenin's guidance was attained in spite of many grave difficulties created by the Marxist tradition. Marx, who was a man of what the psychologists of the middle twenty-first century used to call 'blinkered originality', never saw through the democratic sentimentalities of the period in which he lived. There had been a tendency to exclude the privileged classes from the True Democracy of Common Men even at the dawn of the modern democratic idea, and he and his followers intensified and stereotyped this tendency in their own particular version of deified democracy, the Proletariat. The Proletariat was just Pure Masses, and mystical beyond measure.

But at the outset the actual Russian revolution was under the control of the intensely practical and intensely middle-class Lenin, and he took care that the great social reconstruction he had in mind was equally secured against the risk of paralysis through mass inertia and the risk of overthrow through mass panic. His ostensibly 'democratic' government of Soviets, the Soviet pyramid, was built up on a hierarchic scheme that brought the administration face to face only with seasoned representatives who had been filtered through an ascendant series of bodies. Moreover, he established a very complete control of education and the Press, to keep the thought of the nominally sovereign masses upon the right lines. And to animate and control the whole machine he had his invention of the Communist Party.

This Communist Party, like the Italian Fascisti, owes its general conception to that germinal idea of the Modern State, the Guardians in Plato's *Republic*. For if anyone is to be called the Father of the Modern State it is Plato. The Members of the Communist Party were extremely like those Guardians. As early as 1900 critics of democratic institutions were discussing the possibility of creating a cult primarily devoted to social and political service, self-appointed, self-trained and self-disciplined. The English-speaking Socialist movement was debating projects of that kind in 1909–10 (see *Fabian News* in Historical Documents for those years), but it needed the dangers and stresses of the postwar European situation to produce types of workers and young people sufficiently detached, desperate and numerous to unite effectively into a permanent revolutionary control.

From its beginnings the Communist Party, though it was not divided into 'faculties' and remained political rather than technical in spirit, resembled our own Modern State Fellowship in its insistence upon continuous learning and training throughout life, upon free criticism within the limits of the party, upon accessibility (under due limitations) to all who wished to serve in it, and upon the right to resignation from its privileges and severities of all who wished to return to comparative irresponsibility. But the conditions which created the Russian Communist Party made it inevitably Marxist, and even after a thorough Leninization Communism, that characteristic final product of middle-nineteenth-century radicalism, still retained many of its old sentimentalities, reverting indeed more and more towards them after Lenin's death and the rule of the devoted but unoriginal, suspicious and overbearing Stalin.

There was a heavy load of democratic and equalitarian cant upon the back of the Russian system, just as there was a burthen of patriotic and religious cant upon the Italian Fascist. Even the United States Constitution did not profess democratic equality and insist upon the inspired wisdom of the untutored more obstinately than the new Russian régime. Although hardly any of the ruling group of Russians were of peasant or working-class origin – there were far more politicians from that social level in the public life of Western Europe and America – there was a universal pretence of commonness about them all. They spat, they went unshaved and collarless. They pretended to be indifferent to bourgeois comfort. It was ordained that at the phrase 'Class-War' every knee should bow. When the Communist leaders quarrelled among themselves, 'bourgeois' or 'petty bourgeois' was the favourite term of abuse, none the less deadly because it was almost invariably true. Long years were to pass before any movement whatever in the direction of the Modern State system was quite free from this heritage of cant.

One unfortunate aspect of this entanglement of the new experiment in Russia with the social envies and hatreds of the old order was its inability to assimilate competent technicians, organizers and educators into its direction. In its attempt to modernize, it refused the assistance of just the most characteristically modern types in the community. But since these types had a special education and knew things not generally known, it was difficult to accord them proletarian standing. In Russia therefore, as in America, the politician with his eloquence and his necessary and habitual disingenuousness still intervened and obstructed, if he did not actually bar, the way to a scientific development of a new economic and social order.

Manifestly Stalin learnt much from his difficulties with the Five Year Plan of the evil of subordinating technical to political ability, and a speech of his upon the Old and New Technical Intelligenzia made in June 1931 (Historical Documents Series, *Stalinism*, XM 327705) is a very frank admission of the primary necessity in the modern community of the 'non-party' man of science and of special knowledge. Unhappily the hand of the party politician in Russia was strengthened by the untrammelled activities of those strange protectors of Marxist authority the Checka, which became later the G.P.U. So from 1928, the date of the First Five Year Plan, in spite of a great driving-force of enthusiastic devotion, Russia went clumsily, heavily and pretentiously – a politician's dictatorship, propaganding rather than performing, disappointing her well-wishers abroad and thwarting the best intelligences she produced. When her plans went wrong through her lack of precise material foresight, she accused, and imprisoned or shot, engineers and suchlike technical workers.

A further bad result of this ineradicable democratic taint of the Soviet system was the widening estrangement of the Russian process from Western creative effort. Instead of being allies they became opponents.

As the challenge of social disintegration became more urgent in the Atlantic countries, it became plainer and plainer that such hope as there was for the salvaging of a reconstructed civilization from a welter of disaster lay in the coordinate effort of intelligent, able and energetic individuals of every nation, race, type and class. A revolution was certainly needed, but not a revolution according to the time-worn formula of street battles and barricades, not a class war. A revolution in the very character of revolutions had to occur. There was no need for insurrectionary revolution any longer, since now the system was destroying itself. The phase for boldly constructive revolution had arrived, and at every point where constructive effort was made the nagging antagonism of the Class War fanatic appeared, to impede and divide. (See, for example, Upton Sinclair on this conflict, in *The Way Out*, 1933, in the series of reprints under his name, Historical Documents Series, *History of Opinion*.)

The waste of creative energy was enormous, not only in Russia but all over the world. Multitudes of young men and women in every civilized community, the living hope of the race, dissipated their generous youth and vigour in bitter conflicts upon a purely doctrinaire issue. The poison of nationalism was abroad to complicate their reactions. Many turned against progress altogether and sought to thrust the world back to some imaginary lost age of virtue. So they became Ku Klux Klansmen, Nationalists, Nazis. All felt the natural youthful impulse towards large, effective, vehement action. All meant well. They were one in spirit though they suffered from a confusion of tongues. The idea of the Modern State could not for a long time make itself clear to their imaginations largely because the conspicuous self-contradictions of Russia stood in the way.

Russia seemed to lead, it sought to lead in its acts and deeds, and it lied. Meanwhile, surviving very largely because of this distraction of creative forces, the elderly methods of Parliamentary Democracy and the elderly Nationalist Diplomacy remained in possession of the greater part of the Western World, and the social collapse it was powerless to arrest continued.

II

The Sloughing of the old Educational Tradition

Faber in his interesting and suggestive *Historical Analyses* (2103) discusses how far the wars, depressions, pestilences, phases of semi-famine and periods of actual starvation, in the hundred years before 2014, were necessary, and how far, with the resources then available, they might have been avoided by mankind. He takes the view that the encumbrance of tradition was so great that for all that period this martyrdom of our kind was inevitable. He argues that without the sufferings of these generations men's minds could never have been sufficiently purged of their obstinate loyalties, jealousies, fears and superstitions; men's wills never roused to the efforts, disciplines and sacrifices that were demanded for the establishment of the Modern State.

Faber applies his criticism more particularly to this so-called decadence of education after (*circa*) 1930. It has hitherto been usual to treat the ebb of school-building and schooling that took place then as a real retrogression, to rank it with the fall in the general standard of life and the deterioration of public health. But he advanced some excellent reasons for supposing that, so far from being an evil, the starvation and obliteration of the old-world teaching machinery was a necessary preliminary to social recovery.

The common school, he insists, had to be born again, had to be remade fundamentally. And before that could happen it had to be broken up and wellnigh destroyed. He sweeps aside almost contemptuously the claim that the nineteenth century was an educational century. We are misled, he argues, by a mere resemblance between the schools and universities of the past and the schools and post-school education of the modern period. Both occupy the time of the young, and we do not sufficiently appreciate the fact that what they are doing with the young is something entirely different. Our education is an introduction to the continual revolutionary advance of life. But education before the twenty-first century was essentially a conservative process. It was so rigorously and completely traditional that its extensive disorganization was an inevitable preliminary to the foundation of a new world.

The word education has come now to cover almost all intellectual activities throughout life except research and artistic creation. That was not its original meaning. It meant originally the preparation of the young for life. It did not go on even in extreme cases beyond three or four and twenty, and usually it was over by fourteen! But we draw no line at any age, as our ancestors did, when learning ceases. The general information of the public, public discussion and collective decisions, all fall within the scope of our educational directorate. All that was outside what passed for education in the early twentieth century.

What people knew in those days they knew in the most haphazard way. The privately owned newspapers of the period told the public what their readers or their proprietors desired; the diffusion of facts and ideas by the early cinema, the sound radio and so on was entirely commercialized for the advertisement of goods in America, and controlled and directed in the interests of influential politicians in Great Britain; book-publishing, even the publication of scientific works, was mainly speculative and competitive, and there was no such thing as a Centre of Knowledge in the world.

It is remarkable to note how long mankind was able to carry on without any knowledge organization whatever. No encyclopaedia, not even a bookseller's encyclopaedia, had existed before the seventeenth century, for the so-called Chinese Encyclopaedia was a literary miscellany, and there was no permanent organization of record even on the part of such mercenary encyclopaedias as came into existence after that date. Nor was there any conception of the need of a permanent system of ordered knowledge, continually revised until the twentieth century was nearing its end. To the people of the Age of Frustration our interlocking research, digest, discussion, verification, notification and informative organizations, our Fundamental Knowledge System, that is, with its special stations everywhere, its regional bureaus, its central city at Barcelona, its seventeen million active workers and its five million correspondents and reserve enquirers, would have seemed incredibly vast. It would have seemed incredibly vast to them in spite of the fact that the entirely unproductive armies and military establishments they sustained in those days of universal poverty were practically as huge.

We are still enlarging this Brain of Mankind, still increasing its cells, extending its records and making its interactions more rapid and effective. A vast independent literature flourishes beside it. Compared with today, our species in the Age of Frustration was as a whole brainless: it was collectively invertebrate with a few scattered ill-connected ganglia; it was lethargically ignorant; it had still to develop beyond the crude rudiments of any coordinated knowledge at all.

But not only was general knowledge rudimentary, casual, erroneous and bad. Faber's case against the old education is worse than that. Knowledge was explicitly outside education, outside formal schooling altogether. The need for a sound common ideology is a Modern State idea. The old, so called 'Elementary' schools, Faber shows, did not pretend to give knowledge. So far as directive ideas were concerned, they disavowed this intention. He quotes a very revealing contemporary survey of the situation in America by Dr G. S. Counts (*The American Road to Culture*, 1930) in which the complete ideological sterilization of the common schools of the Republic is demonstrated beyond question. The sterilization was deliberate. So far as the giving of comprehensive information about life went, says Faber, there was absolutely nothing valuable destroyed during this period of educational collapse, because nothing valuable had as yet got into the curricula. The history taught in these popular schools was pernicious patriotic twaddle; the biology, non-existent or prudish and childish – the 'facts of sex', as they were called, were for example *taught* by dissecting flowers – and there was no economic instruction whatever. The nineteenth-century 'education' was not enlightenment; it was anti-enlightenment. Parents, political and religious organizations, watched jealously that this should be so. He quotes school time-tables and public discussions and gives samples of the textbooks in use.

The decline in scientific research, moreover, during this age of systole, Faber insists, has been greatly exaggerated. Although there was certainly a considerable diminution in the number of actual workers through the destruction of private endowments and what was called 'economy', and although there was also a considerable interference with the international exchange of ideas and a slacking down in pace at which ideas grew, there was no absolute interruption in the advance of ordered science even through the worst phases of the social breakdown. Research displayed a protean adaptability and indestructibility. It shifted from the patronage of the millionaire to the patronage of the war lord; it took refuge in Russia, Spain and South America; it betook itself to the aeroplane hangars, to rise again in due time to its present world-predominance. It had never been pampered under the régime of private capitalism. All through that First Age of Prosperity pure research had lived from hand to mouth. As soon as it paid, says Sinclair Lewis in *Martin Arrowsmith*, it was commercialized and it degenerated. When the bad times came the parasites of science fell away, but the genuine scientific worker, accustomed to scanty supplies, tightened his belt a little more and in all sorts of out-of-the-way places stuck to his job.

What really did break up in this period between 1930 and 1950 was a systematic schooling of the masses which had developed steadily during the nineteenth century. Beyond the elements of reading, speech and counting, this was no more and no less than a drilling in tradition. There had been some reforms, more particularly in method, some advance in the teaching of infants (though this was sacrificed early in the economy flurry), and a few exceptional schools emerged, but this was the character of the typical school of the time. A progressive multiplication of this kind of school had indeed gone on in nearly every country in the world even up to the outbreak of the Great War. The proportion of 'literates' who could at least read increased steadily. After that the rate of advance (except in Russia after 1917, where popular teaching was only beginning) fell stage by stage to zero. But what was ebbing was not really knowledge or instruction at all, but a training in the binding traditions of the old society.

The story of what used to be called 'the conflict between religion and science' belongs mainly to the history of the nineteenth century, and we will not tell again here how the fairly stable structure of Christian belief and disciplines was weakened by the changes in values that ensued from the revelation of geological and biological horizons in that period. Before 1850 more than ninety-nine per cent of the population of Europe and America believed unquestioningly that the universe had been created in the year 4004 BC. Their intellectual lives were all cramped to the dimensions of that petty cellule of time. It was rather frightening for them to break out. They succumbed to mental agoraphobia. The student knows already of the difficulties experienced by the Christian ministry during those years of mental release and expansion in 'symbolizing' the Fall and Atonement, which had hitherto been taught as historical facts, and of the loss of confidence and authority that came through this unavoidable ambiguity. The ensuing controversies thundered and died away into mutterings and ironies, but the consequences of these disputes became more and more evident in the succeeding generations. They evinced themselves in a universal moral indefiniteness. The new and old cancelled out.

The accepted Christian world outlook, both that prescribed by the Catholic Church and that of the various dissentient Protestant sects, had carried with it a coarse but fairly effective moral imperative. Hell was the *ultima ratio* of good behaviour. The Churches, although badly damaged in argument, were well endowed and powerfully entrenched in the educational organization. Their practical resistance to the new views proved to be more effective than their controversial efforts. People had the social habit of belonging to them and entrusting their children to them. There were no other teachers ready; no other schools. So the traditional orthodoxies were able to obstruct the development of a modern ethic in harmony with the new realizations of man's place in space and time, in spite of the loss of much of their former power of unquestionable conviction.

Gradually throughout the First Age of General Prosperity the relative value of their endowments diminished, and they lost intellectual and moral prestige. But it was only with the economic landslides of the post-war period that their material foundations gave way completely. For a time these great organizations share in the common disaster, and when at last under new auspices a restoration of production occurred they recovered nothing of their proportional importance. Their old investments had vanished. They suffered with other landlords in the general resumption of estates by the community. By 1965 CE it was no longer possible for an ordinary young man to get a living as a minister of any Church. Holy orders, since they implied an old-world outlook, were also a grave encumbrance for an ambitious teacher. It was extraordinary with what facility the priests and parsons changed their collars and vanished into the crowd with the progressive disappearance of their endowments. The organized Christian Churches pass out of history at last almost as quickly as the priesthood of Baal vanished after the Persian conquest. There is considerable plausibility in Faber's contention that they could have disappeared in no other way.

It has been usual to treat the extensive destruction of social morale which characterized this period as due to the interregnum between the fading out of the Christian ethic and the moral and intellectual establishment of modern conduct. Faber questions that boldly. He admits that the morale of Western civilization was built up very largely by Christian agencies, but he denies that they were sustaining it. He ascribes its evaporation almost entirely to the destruction of social confidence which we have noted already as a natural consequence of the wild fluctuations of economic security and monetary values at that time. Men ceased to respect society because they felt they were being cheated and betrayed by society.

III

Disintegration and Crystallization in the Social Magma: The Gangster and Militant Political Organizations

The dissolutions and regroupings of people that were going on through this period have always attracted the attention of the social philosopher. The common man had lost his faith in a friendly God, his confidence in social justice and his educational and social services. He was out of employment and stirred by unsatisfied appetites. The time-honoured life of work and family interests had become impossible for a growing majority.

What we now call social nucleation was failing; the grouping of human beings in families and working communities was not going on. They became restive and troublesome. The social confidence and

discipline that had prevailed throughout the nineteenth century deteriorated very rapidly. There was a swift fall in social security.

Phases of fever have occurred time without number in human history,
phases of unsettlement and confused motivation, clottings and drives
and migrations of population. Periods of tranquil assurance are the
exception thoughout the ages. But in the past it has usually been the
exhaustion of food supplies, pestilence or some cruel invasion that has
broken up the social texture and made humanity lawless again. This
new disintegration was of a different character. It was due in the first
place to an increase rather than a diminution of material and energy in
the social scheme. It was a process of expansion which went wrong
through the inadequacy of traditional law and government.

The disintegrative forces were already evident in the eighteenth
century; they became very conspicuous in the French revolution and the
subsequent social and political disturbances, but they only rose to a
plain domination of the controlling forces after the World War.

In the seventeenth century, when population was thin and hardly
anyone moved about, it had been possible to keep order by means of a
village constable, to try the malefactor by a local magistrate and jury
which knew him thoroughly and understood his position and motives.
Dogberry and Shallow sufficed. But the economic growth of the
eighteenth century increased the size of towns and the traffic on the
newly made roads between them without any corresponding increase in
the forces of order. It produced, therefore, the urban mob, the footpad,
the highwayman and the brigand. The local constable was unequal to
these new demands; the local magistrate as inadequate. There was a
phase of increasing crime.

After the failure of a régime of savage punishment uncertainly
inflicted, after the excesses of the first French revolution, after phases of
mob violence in every European capital, and endless other manifestations of this outpacing of social control, the machinery of government
did by an effort adjust itself to the new conditions. More or less
modernized police forces appeared throughout the world and inaugurated a new phase of order and security, a phase which reached its
maximum in the years before the Great War. For a time then the world,
or at any rate very considerable areas of it, was almost as safe as it is
today. An unarmed man could go about in reasonable security in most
of Europe, India, China, America. Nobody offered him violence or
attempted open robbery. Even the policeman in the English-speaking
and Western European communities carried no weapon but a
truncheon.

But the World War broke down many of the inhibitions of violence
and bloodshed that had been built up during the progressive years of
the nineteenth century, and an accumulating number of intelligent,
restless unemployed men, in a new world of motor-cars, telephones,

plate-glass shop windows, unbarred country houses and trustful social habits, found themselves faced with illegal opportunities far more attractive then any legal behaviour-system now afforded them. And now after the world slump that insanity of public economy which runs like a disease through the story of the age prevented any prompt enlargement and modernization of the existing educational, legal or police organizations. The scale and prestige of the law-court and police-court dwindled as the problems presented to them by the vast irregular developments of that period of stress and perplexity increased.

So the stage was set for a lawless phase. The criminal was liberated from parochialism and reactionary economies long before his antagonist the policeman, and he experienced all the invigoration and enlargement of that release. The criminal grew big while the law, pot-bound in its traditional swathings, was unable to keep pace with him.

The criminal records of this disorderly interlude make strange reading today. Things that were terrible enough at the time appear to us now as they recede into the past through a thickening, highly refractile veil of grotesqueness and picturesque absurdity. We read about them, as we read about mediaeval tortures or cannibal feasts or war atrocities or human sacrifice, with a startled incredulity. We laugh now; it is all so *impossible*. Few of us actually realize these were flesh-and-blood sufferings that living men and women went through only a century and a half ago.

The criminals of the more fortunate countries of the European system, during that First Age of General Prosperity before the World War, like the few cases of intolerable behaviour with which society deals today, had constituted a small abnormal and diminishing minority, for the most part mental defectives or at best very inferior types. The majority of their offences were emotional or brutish offences. There was some stealing and a steady proportion of swindling in business, not sufficient to disturb the social order at all seriously. But as the morale of the old order dissolved, this ceased to be the case. Increasing numbers of intelligent and enterprising people found themselves in conflict with society because, as they argued very reasonably, society had cheated them. Patriotism too, they felt, had cheated them and given them nothing but poverty and war. They had never had a fair chance. They looked after themselves and left the community to look after itself. They fell back on the nearer loyalties of their immediate associates.

Your 'pal' at any rate was close at hand. If he 'let you down', you had a fair chance to 'get at' him. Little gang-nuclei came into existence, therefore, wherever unassimilated elements of the population were congested and humiliated or wherever intelligent men festered in unemployment and need.

In 1900 European society in particular was still nucleated about the family group in relation to a generally understood code of lawful behaviour. In 1950 its individuals were either nucleated into gangs, groups or societies or dissolved into crowds, and the influence and pretence of any universally valid standard of good conduct had disappeared.

Robbery is the first great division in the catalogue of antisocial offences. Every efficient government in the past reserved to itself the sole right of dispossession, and every intelligent government exercised that right with extreme discretion. In the past of unregulated private ownership the filching of portable objects and raids upon unguarded possessions were always going on. In Great Britain, in which country the highest levels of social order were attained during the First Age of General Prosperity, stealing (with which we may include various forms of embezzlement and fraud) remained the chief offence upon the list. Almost all the others had become exceptional. But whenever there was a dip in the common prosperity, more active methods of robbery appeared to supplement the ordinary theft. The snatcher began to take his chance with bags and watches. The enterprise of the burglar increased. Then came the simple hold-up under threats, or robbery with assault. In a world of general confidence, unarmed and unaccompanied people were going about everywhere wearing valuable jewellery and carrying considerable sums of money. But that atmosphere of confidence could be rapidly chilled. Even in later-nineteenth-century Britain there were epidemics of robbery by single men or by men in couples, the 'garrotters' of the sixties, for example, who assaulted suddenly from behind and seized the watch and pocket-book. They would clap a pitch plaster over their victim's mouth. There were brief phases when the suburban regions even of London and Paris became unsafe, and at no time were any but the more central regions of some of the great American cities secure. This kind of thing increased notably everywhere after the World War.

There were manifest limits to this hold-up business. It was something that extinguished itself. There had to be a general feeling of practical security for that type of robbery to prosper. There had to be people to rob. Robbery from the person is an acute and not a chronic disease of communities. So soon as the footpad became too prevalent people ceased to carry so many valuables, they shunned lonely or dark streets and roads, they went about in company and began to bear arms. The epidemic of hold-ups passed its maximum and declined.

The criminally disposed soon learnt the importance of association for the exploitation of new lines of effort. With a more alert and defensive and less solitary type of victim, the casual criminal developed into the planning criminal. In every country multiplying nuclei of crime began to work out the problems of that terroristic gang discipline which is imperative upon those who combine to defy the law. In Europe the intensifying tariff wars put an increasing premium upon the enterprise of the smuggler, and in smuggling enterprises men readily developed those furtive secret loyalties, those sub-laws of the underworld, which proved so readily applicable to more aggressive efforts. In America the repressive laws against alcohol had already created the necessary conditions for a similar morbid organization of gang systems, which had become readily confluent with the older associations for political corruption and terrorism. As the economic breakdown proceeded throughout the thirties and forties of the twentieth century, ordinary social security diminished even more rapidly in America than in Europe. But everywhere a parallel dégringolade was going on. Now it would be the criminal forces in one country and now those in another which were leading in novel attacks upon the law-abiding citizen of the decaying order.

The hold-up in force became bolder and more frequent. History repeated itself with variations. In the place of the highwayman of the seventeenth and eighteenth centuries came the motor-car bandit and the train-robber. Trains-de-luxe were successfully held up by armed bands, first of all in Eastern Europe and America and then very generally. These were operations involving the concerted action of a dozen men or more, who had to be sure of their 'get away' and with a market for their loot. Country houses and country clubs full of wealthy guests presently began to be attacked – the telephones cut and the whole place systematically looted. Restaurants, gambling-clubs and other resorts of people with full pocket-books were also raided with increasing efficiency. Local banks and bank branches became insecure. Until the nineteenth-thirties a town bank had a large open handsome office with swinging doors, low counters and glass partitions. Ten years later the face of the bank had changed: the clerks were protected by steel defences, they were armed with revolvers, and they parleyed with the customer through small pigeonholes that could be promptly closed.

This change in the scale and quality of aggressive crime was reflected in public manners and display. The wearing of jewellery, gold watch-chains, expensive studs and suchlike challenges to poverty declined, costume became more 'buttoned up' and restrained. Hip-pocket weapons spread from America to Europe. Women's dress and ornaments, though if anything they improved in their artistic quality, diminished in intrinsic value. Everywhere there was a diminution of social ostentation. Houses with narrow exterior windows and well equipped with steel doors, locks, bolts and bars, were preferred to those candidly exposed to sunlight and exterior observation. The window displays of the town shops became more guarded.

The need for protection and the dread of conspicuousness affected automobile design. The common automobile of the middle twentieth century was a sullen-looking pugnacious beast. And its occupants were in harmony with it. Before the World War the spectacle of a broken-down vehicle or any such trouble by the wayside would induce almost any passing car to stop and offer assistance. Under the new conditions people feared a decoy. They would refuse to stop after twilight, and even in the daytime they sometimes hurried on, though injured or apparently injured people might be lying by the roadside.

Travel diminished very rapidly under such conditions. There is some difficulty about the statistics, but between 1928 and 1938 the number of pleasure travellers upon the roads and railways of continental Europe fell by something over, rather than under, eighty per cent. There were, of course, other causes at work besides the general insecurity of movement in producing this decline; there was a general impoverishment also which disposed people to stay at home. But the major factor was insecurity.

The roads were less and less frequented as they became unsafe. Many fell out of repair, and the old road-signs and petrol pumps, now dear to our school-museum collectors, vanished one by one from the landscape.

Improvements in robbery were only one group of the criminal developments in progress. A much more distressful aspect was the organization of terroristic blackmail, at first directed against individuals and then against whole classes in the community. As people ceased to travel to be robbed, the robber had to pursue them to their homes. Here again American inventiveness and enterprise led the world. By imperceptible degrees the ordinary prosperous citizen found his life enmeshed in a tangle of threats and vague anxieties. Even during the prosperous period there had been an element of menace in the lives of the American well-to-do; their securities had never been quite secure and their positions never perfectly stable. But now over and above the ever increasing instability of possessions and income came the increasing need to buy off molestation. Breaking through the now inadequate protection of the police appeared silently and grimly and more and more openly the blackmailer, the kidnapper and the gang terrorist.

A particularly cruel form of attack upon unprotected private people was the threatening and kidnapping of young children. It had a minor grotesque side in the stealing and ransoming of pet animals. Many hundreds of children had been stolen, hidden away, and brought back for reward before the abduction and murder of the child of Colonel Lindbergh, a long-distance aviator very popular in America, called general attention to this increasing nuisance. Nothing effective, however, was done to control these practices, and in the bad years that followed 1930 kidnapping and the threat of kidnapping increased very greatly, and spread to the old world. It was organized. Men and women were spirited away, intimidated by threats of torture, held captive. If the pursuit was pressed too hard they disappeared and were heard of no more. Assassinations multiplied. Bodies of men set themselves up almost without concealment under such names as Citizens' Protection Societies, or Civil Order Associations. The man who wanted to be left alone in peace, he and his household, was pressed to pay his tribute to the gang. Or he would not be left in peace. And even if his particular 'protectors' left him in peace, there might still be other gangs about for whom they disavowed responsibility and with whom he had to make a separate deal.

It was not merely the well-to-do who were worried and levied upon in this fashion. An increasing proportion of minor workers and traders found it necessary to pay a percentage of their gains or earnings to escape systematic persecution. 'Trouble' was the characteristic American word. 'You don't want to have trouble,' said the blackmailer, gently but insistently.

The new generation grew up into a world of secret compromises and underhand surrenders. The common man picked his way discreetly through a world of possible trouble. No one dared live who was not a member (and servant) of a Union of some kind. It was a return to very ancient conditions, conditions that had prevailed for ages in China, for instance, and in Sicily and Southern Italy. But it was a relapse from the freedom and confidence of the better days at the close of the nineteenth century. It was a contraction of everyday human happiness.

Kidnapping was not confined to kidnapping for ransom. There had always been a certain irrepressible trade in the beguiling and stealing of young persons for sexual prostitution, and this also increased again. Workers were kidnapped, and the intimidation of workers in factories became bolder and less formally legal. There was a great release of violence in personal quarrels, and in particular crimes of revenge multiplied. In a phase of dwindling confidence and happiness, people of spirit no longer recoiled from the tragic ending of oppressive situations. They took the law into their own hands. They began to fight and kill, and they were no longer inevitably overtaken by the law.

The remaining rich, the financial adventurers who still appeared, the prominent political leaders, the transitory 'kings' of the underworld, all surrounded themselves with bodyguards. Types recalling the hired 'bravos' of the Italian cities of the later Middle Ages and the Samurai of the Japanese noblemen reappeared as the hefty private attendants of the wealthier Americans. After the economic slump had fairly set in the posse of needy retainers became a universal practice with all who could afford it. They protected the person and the home. They supplemented the police.

The transition from a protective to an aggressive bodyguard was inevitable. Leading American bootleggers were the chief offenders, but the example was contagious. 'Brawling' of retainers reappeared first in America, Germany and Ireland. These brawls were usually small street battles, or conflicts at race meetings and suchlike gatherings, or side issues to political meetings and processions. It was a courageous politician who would face an audience after 1938 unless he knew that his men were about him and posted at strategically important points in the meeting. And he would be wearing a mail undervest or suchlike protection of his more vital parts. There are hundreds of such garments in our museums.

No man, woman or child that 'mattered' went about 'unshadowed' after 1940. After the middle nineteenth century women had made great advances towards personal freedom. About 1912 a pretty girl in her teens might have taken a knapsack and marched off alone through the northern states of Europe or America in perfect safety, unmolested. All this freedom vanished during the age of insecurity. Women ceased to go about without an escort even in the towns. It was not until 2014 that there was any real return towards the former common liberties of the young and weak and gentle. There was on the part of women, as the novels of the time reveal, a survival of social fear in human life, the fear of going alone, until the middle of the twenty-first century.

After 1945 a fresh aspect of insecurity appears in the records. There is mention of unsafe roadside hotels, and a great increase not simply of streets, but of whole districts and villages where 'things happened', people disappeared, and it was inadvisable for strangers to go. Some of these criminally infected areas did not recover their reputations for three quarters of a century. The *dangerous* big hotel with its secret lifts, passages, ambushes and sinister private rooms is still the delight of our popular romancers; it loses nothing in elaboration as it recedes into the past.

The psychology of the twentieth-century policeman has been made the subject of a whole group of historical studies. There was no connection in those days between the policeman and either the educational or medical services. This association which appears so inevitable to us today would have seemed insane to the organizers of the first police forces in the eighteenth and nineteenth centuries. The policeman, for them, was to be an animated barrier and signpost, capable of leaping into action at the sight of assault, petty larceny or unseemly behaviour. Beyond that very little initiative was expected from him. He took into custody people who were 'given in charge'. Above him were officers, usually of a different class, and associated with the force was a group of criminal enquiry experts, who were quite capable of handling most of the offences against the law that prevailed in the era before the extensive introduction of rapid transit, power machinery and mass production. This pattern of police force worked fairly well up to the beginning of the twentieth century. Except in districts where sexual prostitution was rife it remained fairly honest. It maintained a fairly high level of liberty, security of property and social order for a century. Only when the control of morals or political intervention was thrust upon it did it prove unequal to the strain.

And then, as the greater community of the World State began to struggle clumsily and painfully out of traditional forms, we see police control again outpaced by its task. It gives way. 'Why,' the student asks, 'was this police organization unable to keep pace with the new stresses? Why were the ruling people of that time so incapable of fitting it to the new demands upon it?' We have already indicated the main lines of the answer. Just when the need for a fundamental refashioning of the police of the world was becoming urgent, came also, first that exacerbation of international hostilities, of 'secret service' and espionage to render any broad international handling of the problem impossible, and secondly that desperately foolish sacrifice of life to the creditor which seems to be the inevitable conclusion of any social system based on acquisition.

The Profit-Capitalist System was absolutely incapable of controlling the unemployment it had evoked and the belligerence it stimulated. It stagnated on its hoards. It fought against inflation and it fought against taxation. It died frothing economies at the mouth. It killed the schools on which public acquiescence rested. Impartially it restricted employment and the relief of the unemployed. Even on this plain issue of its police protection it economized. Impossible, it said, to plan a new police when we cannot even pay for the police we have.

And so the desperate fight of an essentially nineteenth-century pattern of police organization, under-financed, inadequately equipped, divided up, controlled by small-scale, antiquated national or parochial authorities, in many cases rotten with corruption, against the monstrous forces of disorganiztion released by the irregular hypertrophies to social development was added to the other conflicts of that distressful age.

In spite of a notable amount of corruption and actual descents into criminality, the general will of most of the police forces seems to have remained sound. Most but not all. Most of these organizations did keep up a fight for order even when they were in a process of dissolution. They did keep up their traditional war against crime. But their methods underwent a considerable degeneration, which was shared, and shared for the same reason, by the criminal law of the period. Police and prosecutor both felt that the dice were loaded against them, that they were battling against unfair odds. Their war against crime became a feud. It grew less and less like a serene control, and more and more like a gang conflict. They were working in an atmosphere in which witnesses were easily intimidated and local sympathy more often than not against the law. This led to an increasing unscrupulousness on their part in the tendering and treatment of evidence. In many cases (see Aubrey Wilkinson's *The Natural History of the Police Frame-up*, 1991) the police deliberately manufactured evidence against criminals they had good reason to believe guilty, and perjured themselves unhesitatingly. Wilkinson declares that in the early twentieth century hundreds of thousands of wrongdoers were 'justly condemned on false evidence', and that they could have been condemned in no other way.

But the apologetics of Wilkinson for the police break down when he comes to the next aspect of their degeneration under stress. We have all read with horror of the use of torture in mediaeval practice and shuddered at the fact that there were even special machines and instruments in those days, the rack, the thumbscrew, the boot and so forth, for the infliction of pain. But there remains little doubt now that the police of the twentieth century, fighting with their backs to the wall against enormous odds, did go very far towards a revival of torture against those they believed to be social dangers. It is a difficult as well as an ugly task to disentangle this story now, but sufficient fact emerges to show us that in the general decay of behaviour that was going on, not merely casual blows and roughness of handling, but the systematic exhaustion, pestering, ill-treatment and actual torment of persons under arrest in order to extort confessions and incriminating statements became prevalent.

There is no real distinction in nature between the processes that led up to this chaotic nucleation of human beings about gangs and organizations for frankly criminal purposes and those which led to protective associations for the illegal maintenance of security and order and again to those much wider allegiances within the state such as the nationalist Sokols in the Austrian provinces that became Czecho-Slovakia, the Irish Republican organizations, the Ku Klux Klan in America, the multitudinous secret societies of India, China, and Japan, the Communist Party which captured Russia, the Fascist who captured Italy, the Nazis who captured Germany, all of which pursued on bolder and bolder scales large intimidatory and revolutionary economic and political ends. All these were structurally great gangster systems. Instead of specific immediate blackmail they sought larger satisfactions; that is all the difference. Even when the organization as a whole had large conceptions of its function, it was apt to degenerate locally into a mere boss or bully rule. All these forms of recrystallization within the community, large and small, arose because of the inadaptability and want of vigour and cooperation in the formal governing, economically directive and educational systems. Because there was no foresight to ensure continuity in the growth of institutions, there were these unpremeditated and often morbid growths, expressive of the accumulating discomfort and discontent and of the need for a more intimate, energetic and fruitful form of human association.

It is paradoxical but true that the civilized human society of the later nineteenth and earlier twentieth centuries broke up because of the imperative need of human beings to live in active combination. It was pulled to pieces by its own new cohesions. Until there was a complete, satisfactory and vigorous World-State organization potentially in being, the continuation of this breaking up and reassembling of social energy was inevitable. It was like the break-up of caterpillar organs in the cocoon to form the new structures of the imago.

Even the Modern State Fellowship itself, so far as many of its nuclei were concerned, was at first of this nature, a coalescence of all these varied technicians who realized that employment would vanish, that everything they valued in life would vanish, with the spread of social disorder. They constituted protective and aggressive gangs with an unexampled power of world-wide cooperation. Their confluence became the new world.

The demoralization of the world's sea life, thanks to the surviving vestiges of naval power, was far less rapid and complete than the spread of disorder on the land. It was only after the series of naval mutinies towards the end of the last European war that the ancient practice of piracy was resumed. Even then ships could still be policed and a recalcitrant ship brought to book much more easily than the black streets of a town. One or two pleasure liners were boarded and held up in out-of-the-way ports in the thirties, but in no case did the assailants get away with their plunder. In 1933 the Chinese fleet had disintegrated into shipfuls of adventurers offering their services by wireless to the various governments who divided the country. But these stray warships did little mischief before they were bought, captured or sunk by the Japanese.

A Canadian pleasure liner, *The King of the Atlantic*, on one of the last holiday voyages to be made, was seized on the high seas by an armed gang in 1939, and an attempt was made to hold its passengers to ransom. They were all to be killed if the pursuit was pressed home. In the face, however, of a combined attack by American sea and air forces, at that time still efficient though greatly in arrears with their pay, the hearts of the gangsters failed them and they surrendered ignominiously.

No ship of over 9,000 tons was ever captured by pirates. This relative maintenance of orderliness at sea was due to special conditions – the then recent discovery of radio communications, for example. It out-lasted the practical cessation of shipbuilding in the forties and an immense shrinkage in the world's shipping.

Nor did new types of criminal appear in the air until after the third European conflict, and then not overwhelmingly. Here again was a field of human activity, essentially simple and controllable. For a time indeed the aeroplane was the safest as well as the swiftest method of getting about the world. For some years after the practical cessation of general land travel the infrequent aviator still hummed across the sky, over dangerous city and deserted highroad, over ruined country houses and abandoned cultivations, recalling the memory of former disciplines and the promise of an orderly future.

There were fewer aeroplanes just as there were fewer ships, and, because of the general discouragement of enterprise, there was little change of type, yet the skies, like the high seas, remained practically outside the range of the general social débâcle until well past the middle of the century. The need for aerodromes, for repairing and fuelling, held the dwindling body of aviators together. Air outrages at the worst phase were still scattered and disconnected events. And it was in the air at last and along the air routes that the sword of a new order reappeared.

IV

Changes in War Practice after the World War

The science and practice of warfare during this Age of Frustration, having now no adequate directing and controlling forces over it, pursued, in its development, a preposterous and dreadful logic of its own.

In 1914, at the outbreak of the World War, military science had been a pretentious and backward lore. The War Offices, as we have told, had allowed the armament industry to put enormously outsize weapons into their hands, but they had made none of the necessary mental adjustments needed to meet this change of scale. All the land commanders engaged in that struggle with scarcely an exception were still fighting clumsily according to the obsolete tradition of nineteenth-century warfare. They were still thinking in terms of frontal attack, outflanking, the break-through and so forth. We have told as briefly as we could the horrors of the ensuing harvest. The Admiralties, forewarned perhaps by their engineers, showed a livelier discretion and for the most part hid away their costly fleets from the disasters of combat in strongly defended harbours, and allowed them to emerge only on one or two wild occasions for battles so inconclusive that they were prolonged as controversies for years afterwards and remain undecided to this day. The submarine, the minefield, the aeroplane, the primitive 'tank', organized propaganda to weaken war will, a tentative use of gas, and the replacement of many of the elder commanders as the war proceeded did something to modify land fighting, but to the very last, when the general collapse of 'morale' led to the armistice, the professional soldiers were clinging to the idea that nothing fundamental had happened to the methods of their ancient and honoured profession.

All this changed after the Peace of Versailles. A spirit of unrest entered into both the War Offices and Foreign Offices of the world. They were invaded by a consciousness of great changes none the less potent because it was belated and had accumulated. The younger generals who had been through the war could not put out of their minds memories of attacks from overhead, gas attacks, tank actions, and, above all, the loose ungentlemanly comments of temporary officers of practical ability and unmilitary habits of mind. These younger generals aged in their turn, and as they aged they succeeded to positions of authority. They came into power repeating perpetually: 'We must keep pace with the times.'

A phase of extreme innovation succeeded the conservatism of the older generation. Everywhere the War Offices stirred with novel conceptions of strange inventions, secret novelties and furtive systematic research. Everywhere the obscure reports of spies and informants, carefully fostered by the armament dealers affected, stimulated this forced inventiveness.

It was realized that the old warfare had in fact perished in a state of lumpish hypertrophy in the trenches. It had indeed been a 'war to end war' – and the old war was done for. The new warfare had to replace it – and quickly. The Foreign Offices demanded it. They could not do without war of some sort. Sovereignty was war. The traditional state was an organization against foreigners resting on the ultimate sanction of belligerence. They could imagine no other state of affairs, for to begin with that would have involved imagining themselves non-existent. The Thirties and Forties of the century teemed with furtive and grotesquely hideous researches to discover and develop the methods of the New Warfare. For the only alternative to further war was the abandonment of state sovereignty, and for that men's minds were altogether unprepared.

The changes in war method that went on between 1900 and 1950 CE, with the possible exception of the introduction of firearms between the twelfth and sixteenth centuries, were far greater than anything that had ever happened since the earliest men hit and scuffled in their first rude group encounters. For endless ages the main conflict had been the 'battle', the encounter of bodies of men on foot or on horseback. The infantry had been the traditional backbone of the army, and (except when the Huns and the Mongols refused to play according to the rules) the cavalry was secondary. Artillery was used only for 'preparation' before the attack. So fought Rameses, so Alexander, so Caesar, so Napoleon. The glorious victories during the romantic ages of human warfare all amounted to battles of practically the same pattern, to a great central battering with pikes, swords, bayonets, maces or suchlike implements, a swiping, pushing, punching, pelting, stabbing, poking and general clapperclawing amidst a shower of comparatively light missiles, that went on at longest for a few hours, and ended in a break, a flight, a cavalry pursuit and a massacre. This 'open warfare' alternated, it is true, with long sieges, less sportsmanlike phases, in which the contending hosts refused battle and squatted unwholesomely in excavations and behind walls, annoying each other by raids and attempts to storm and break through, until hunger, pestilence, the decay of discipline under boredom, or the exasperation of the surrounding population broke up the party. Non-combatants suffered considerable temporary and incidental molestation during warfare; there was a certain amount of raping and looting, devastation to destroy supplies, pressed labour and spy-hunting on a scale which amounted in most cases to little more than an exacerbation of normal criminality. Wholesale devastation, such as the break-up of the irrigation of Mesopotamia by the Mongols, or the laying waste of Northumbria by William the Conqueror of England, was, when it occurred, a measure of policy rather than a war measure. War had to go on for many decades before it could produce such disorganization as that of Asia Minor in the wars between Byzantium and Persia. The Islamic invasions were at first made additionally disagreeable by religious propaganda, but this was speedily replaced by discriminatory taxation. The long-distance campaigns of Roman, Hunnish and Mongol armies again spread various once localized infectious and contagious diseases very widely; but the total influence of the old warfare upon human destiny was enormously exaggerated by the nationalist historians of the old régime. It was of infinitely less importance than migration. The peasant life went on unchangingly, squalid and laborious, as it had been going on for the majority of human beings since agriculture began. The various 'Decisive Battles of the World' were high points in that fantasy of the pedants, the great 'drama of the empires', with which they befogged the human mind for so long during its gropings from the peasant state of life towards a sane and orderly way of living.

But with the Napoleonic wars the soldier began to invade and modify the texture of normal life as he had never done before, by conscription, by unprecedented monetary levies, indemnities and taxes that dislocated economic processes; and conversely, quite uninvited by the soldier, as we have shown, the expanding forces of power industrialism and of mass manipulation through journalistic and other sorts of propaganda, invaded both the military field and the common life. War, which had been like the superficial ploughing of our ancestors, became a subsoil plough, an excavator that went deeper and deeper, that began presently to deflect underground springs and prepare extensive landslides.

The Generals of the World War were all in the position of inexperienced amateurs in charge of vast mechanisms beyond their power of control. War, which formerly had been fought on the flat along a 'front', suddenly reached through and over the contending armies, and allowed no one to stand out of it any more. The New Warfare, it was already being remarked by 1918, was a war of whole populations, from which all respect for the non-combatant was vanishing. People said this, and some few even tried to understand in detail what it meant. And now all over the world military gentlemen, many of them still adorned with the spurs, epaulettes, froggings, buttons, stripes, ribbons, medals, residual scraps of armour and suchlike pretty glories of the good old times, set themselves most valiantly to work out the possibilities and methods of the New Warfare.

Courage was always the better part of the military tradition, and nothing could exceed the courage with which these men set themselves throughout this period to overtake the march of invention, to master engineering and engineers, chemistry and chemists, war correspondents and newspapers editors, biology, medicine, and even finance, in their efforts to keep that ancient war idea, the idea of the battling sovereign state, alive. As we have seen, the schools stood loyally by them; they had the support of the armament industries, and, less wholeheartedly perhaps, the approval of the old religions and of the old royalties and loyalties. Their activities were profoundly stupid, but the grotesque horror of their achievements, the distress and unhappiness of three generations of our race, are still recent enough to mask their ludicrous quality.

The literature of the military science of this period is a copious one, and perhaps the best survey of it all is Fuller-Metsch's *The Ideas of the New Warfare in the Middle Twentieth Century* (2001). Therein the writer sets himself to three enquiries: 'For what did they suppose they were going to fight?' 'How were they going to fight?' And, 'What did they consider would constitute a definitive end and winding-up of their fighting?'

The answer he gives is a composite one. No single individual seems to have grasped the New Warfare in its entirety. With a solemn pedantry, a pretentious modesty, each 'expert' dealt with his own department and left it to Fate to put the assembled parts together into a whole. But what the composite soldier of 1935 was contemplating rather foggily seems to have been very much as follows. He conceived the world as divided up among a number of governments or Powers. These were the sovereign states as the Treaty of Westphalia (1642) presented them. All these powers were competitive and passively or actively hostile. The intervals when the hostility was active were wars. The intervals of recuperation and preparation were peace. War was a cessation of a truce between the belligerents, a cessation arising out of an irreconcilable dispute or clash of interests, and the objective then of each Power was to impose its Will upon its enemy. In the days before the twentieth century this imposition of Will was done more or less professionally by the governments and armies. One or other Power took the offensive, crossed its borders and marched on the enemy seat of government. After various operations and battles the capital would be captured or the invader driven back to his own, and a peace made and a treaty signed more or less in accordance with the Will of the victor. Boundaries would be adjusted in accordance with that Will, colonies transferred, indemnities arranged for; the victorious Power expanded and the defeated shrivelled. The people of the unsuccessful Power would be very much ashamed of themselves. To the end of the nineteenth century this formula was observed.

But by the time of the World War much more than the disappearance of the 'front' and the increasing entanglement of the erstwhile non-combatants was happening to this procedure. The Powers were losing their definite identities. The fine question of what constituted a responsible government capable of imposing a Will, or giving in to it, arose. In Russia, for example, was the new Communist régime responsible for the obligations of the Autocracy? Was Germany, were all the Germans, to be held responsible for Krupp-Kaiser militarism? Was a dummy Sultan in Constantinople, or Kemal Pasha in Angora, the proper authority to consent to the dismemberment of Turkey? Again, the United States of America had come gaily into the war and then declined effective participation in President Wilson's settlement. He had not, it seemed, been a plenipotentiary. Was that behaving as a Power should behave?

Still further perplexities arose about the laws of war. If the front was abolished, if civilians were to be bombed from the air, what became of the right of professional soldiers to shoot franc-tireurs and destroy their homes? It was as if the arena of a football match were invaded by the spectators, who began kicking the ball about, chasing the referee, and declining to keep any score as between the original sides in the game.

The military authority recoiled from these devastating riddles of the new age. Such issues, he decided, were not for him. There had always been sides in a war, and there must still be sides. It was for the politicians to define them. He fell back on his fundamental conception of a Power 'imposing its Will' upon another Power, but using now, in addition to the old invasion and march on the capital, the new methods of propaganda, blockades and attacks behind the front, and all the latest chemical and aerial devices to 'undermine the morale' of the enemy population and dispose its government to yield. In the end there must be a march, it only a concluding professional march, through the goal or capital of the losing side. He refused to entertain the inevitable problem of an enemy government not yielding but collapsing, and leaving no responsible successor. That was not his affair. Presumably in that case the war would continue indefinitely.

Nor was it his business to enter into the financial aspects of the matter, to estimate any ratio whatever between the costs of the New

Warfare and the material advantages to be exacted when the Will of the conqueror was imposed. In that regard he was excessively modest. He could not be expected to think of everything. His business was to prepare the best and most thorough war possible, with all the latest improvements, and quite regardless of cost, for his Power. It was for his government to find out how to pay for and use the war he had prepared for it. Or to use it partially. War, just war itself, was the limit of his task.

Research for the latest improvements soon led the now almost morbidly progressive military mind to some horrifying discoveries. Some of the soldiers concerned were certainly badly scared by the realization of what evils it was now possible to inflict in warfare. It leaked out in their speeches and books. But they kept on. They kept on partly because they had a stout-hearted tradition and refused to be dismayed, but mainly no doubt for the same reason that the Christian priests and bishops who had lost their faith still stuck to their Churches – because it was the only job they could do. Throughout the three decades that followed the Congress of Versailles, thousands of highly intelligent men, specialist soldiers, air soldiers, engineering soldiers, chemical, medical soldiers and the like, a far ampler and more energetic personnel than that devoted to the solution of the much more urgent and important financial riddles of the time, were working out, with unstinted endowments and the acquiescence and approval of their prospective victims, patiently, skilfully, thoroughly, almost inconceivably, abominable novelties for the surprise and torture of human beings.

None of these experts seems to have been more than mediocre; it was an age of mental and moral mediocrities; and even within the accepted limitation we have already noted, none of them seems to have worked out the New Warfare as a whole complete process. Groups of men working in secrecy, immune from outer criticism, naturally conspire not only against the foreigner but against each other, and most of the men in decisive positions were rather men skilled in securing appointments and promotion than inspired specialists. A certain lumbering quality in their devices ensued.

In Great Britain a group of these experts became exceedingly busy in what was called mechanical warfare. The British had first invented, and then made a great mess of, the tank in the World War, and they were a tenacious people. The authorities stuck to it belatedly but doggedly. In a time of deepening and ever bitterer parsimony their War Office spared no expense in this department. It was the last of all to feel the pinch. The funny land ironclads of all sizes these military 'inventors' produced, from a sort of armoured machine-gunner on caterpillar wheels up to very considerable mobile forts, are still among the queerest objects in the sheds of the vast war dumps which constitute the Aldershot

Museum. They are fit peers for Admiral Fisher's equally belated oil Dreadnoughts.

The British dream of the next definitive war seems to have involved a torrent of this ironmongery tearing triumphantly across Europe. In some magic way (too laborious to think out) these armoured Wurms were to escape traps, gas poison belts, mines and gunfire. There were even 'tanks' that were intended to go under water, and some that could float. Hansen even declared (see *The Last War Preparations*, xxiv, 1076) that he had found (rejected) plans of tanks to fly and burrow. Most of these contrivances never went into action. That throws a flavour of genial absurdity over this particular collection that is sadly lacking from most war museums.

The British and the French experts, and presently the Germans, also worked very hard at the fighting aeroplane – the British and Germans with the greatest success; the aerial torpedo, controllable at immense distances, was perfected almost simultaneously by the Italians and the Japanese. The French mind, for all its native brilliance, was hampered by its characteristic reluctance to scrap old plant for new. It was the German, American and Russian experts who went furthest with the possibilities of chemical attack. The disarmament of Germany necessarily forced its military authorities to concentrate on an arm that could be studied, experimented upon and prepared unknown to the outer world, and the Russians were forced to take up parallel enquiries because of their relative industrial poverty. The Germans had been first to use gas in the Great War, and they remained for a long time the war gas pioneers. But after the Great War much attention was given to this arm in America through the influence of the chemical industry. Biological warfare, that is to say the distribution of infectious diseases, was also extensively studied, America and the Central Europeans in this case leading the way.

Even before the Central European fighting in 1940 and the subsequent years, the distribution of various disease germs was no longer a merely theoretical possibility. Little containers, made to look like fountain pens, were already being manufactured. The caps could be removed to expose soluble ends, and then they could be dropped into reservoirs or running streams. Glass bombs also existed for use from aeroplanes, railway-train windows and so forth, which would break on hitting water. There are specimens in the Aldershot Museum. The enrolment and territorial organization of medical men and trained assistants to inoculate threatened populations went on with increasing vigour after 1932.

But there was a certain hesitation about the use of disease germs. It is easy to distribute them but hard to limit their field of action, and if prisoners (military or civilian) were still to be taken and towns and territory occupied, a well-launched pestilence might conceivably recoil with deadly effect upon its users. Bacterial warfare seemed, even to the specialists who studied it, a very improbable method for any but an heroically vindictive population in the hour of defeat. Nevertheless it was thought best to have it worked out. Except for the distribution of malignant influenza in Kan-su and Shensi by the Japanese during their efforts to tranquillize North China in 1936, 'without proceeding to extremities', its use was never officially admitted. Other alleged instances of its deliberate employment by responsible Powers have been shown by the researches of the Historical Bureau to have been due either to the unauthorized zeal of subordinates or to the activities of those religious fanatics who became so prevalent during the period of confusion after 1945. The acclimatization of the mosquito transmitting yellow fever in India in 1950, which did so much to diminish the population of that peninsula, has never been explained. It is generally supposed to have been accidental.

So far as method and invention went, what was called 'Gas Warfare' ran very parallel to bacterial warfare. Its beginning and end is now a closed chapter in the history of the human intelligence and will. It is surely one of the strangest. It set its stamp upon the clothing and urban architecture of the age. It ranks in horror with the story of judicial torture or the story of ritual cannibalism, but its inhumanity is more striking because of its nearness to our own times. Like those older instances, it brings home to us the supreme need for sound common general ideas to hold together human activities. It tells how thousands of clear and active minds, each indisputably sane, could, in an atmosphere obsessed by plausible false assumptions about patriotic duty and honour, cooperate to produce a combined result fantastically futile and cruel.

The people engaged in this business were, on the whole, exceptionally grave, industrious and alert-minded. Could they revisit the world to-day individually we should probably find them all respectable, companionable, intelligent persons. Yet in the aggregate they amounted to an organization of dangerous lunatics. They inflicted dreadful deaths, hideous sufferings or tormented lives upon, it is estimated, about a million of their fellow creatures.

Most of the lethal substances prepared for gas warfare purposes have passed altogether out of general knowledge. They are either never manufactured now or they are produced upon rare occasions and under proper control for the purposes of physiological research. The old devices and appliances for their distribution seem nowadays like grotesque anticipations of many of the features of the large-scale agricultural and hygienic operations that are carried out to-day. The treatment of locust swarms by air attack, the spraying of the reafforested regions against various tree diseases, the regular cleansing and stimulation of our grain and root crops are all subsequent rationalizations of these practices of the Age of Frustration.

Faber, that Calvinistic optimist, with his doctrine that the bad is all to the good in this maddest of all conceivable worlds, thinks that all these big-scale methods were 'enormously stimulated' by the crazy inventiveness of the war period. But then he has also suggested that the aeroplane would not have come into general use for many years without war stimulation. We venture to think he carries his doctrine of the attainment of wisdom through imbecility too far. It is really only a modernization of Charles Lamb's story of the invention of the roast pig. It had the touch of Rasputinism, this revival of the ancient heresy that one must sin *thoroughly* before one can be saved.

Much more after the gas-war pattern were the campaigns (2033 and 2035) against rats and mice that finally cleansed the world of the lurking poison of that mediaeval terror, bubonic plague, and the distributions of 'festivity gas' that were permitted in various regions in 2060. The countervailing use of benign-gases as a subsidiary to the suppression of the depressing cometary toxins of 2080 will also occur to the reader. The oxygenation of council chambers, factories, playing-fields and similar loci demanding special brightness and activity, and the use of Padanath Tagore's Lotus Gas in the Himalayan rest valleys, we may note, are also claimed by Faber as part of the legacy of gas warfare.

One or two of the offensive substances actually manufactured for war purposes are now utilized in relation to very special and specially protected processes in our industrial plants. The preparation of some of them is a major felony. They were a very various miscellany, for every chemical possibility was ransacked to find them. Very few of them were actually gases. Many were volatile liquids or even finely divided solids, which were to be sprayed or dusted over positions in enemy occupation. Dr Gertrud Woker, in a paper on this subject contributed to an enquiry by the Inter-parliamentary Union in 1931, gave a useful summary of the existing state of knowledge at that time. In conjunction with various colleagues (*What would be the Character of a New War?* Historical Documents 937, 205), she allows us to form an estimate of what was actually being contemplated by contemporary military experts. Except for one important exception, her list covers all the main types of poison gas substances that were actually prepared. This spate of investigation culminated about 1938. By that time the entire field had been explored. After that there were improvements but no major innovations.

After 1940 even military research was restricted by the increasing financial paralysis. In 1960 no plants capable of producing material for gas warfare on a sufficiently abundant scale were operating.

Of gases actually tried out in the World War itself, the chief seem to have been chlorine and various chlorine compounds (phosgene, Green Cross gas, chloropicrin and so forth). These attacked and destroyed the lung tissue. Chlorine was used by the Germans as early as April 1915 at Ypres, when 6,000 men were killed by it; it was soon abandoned, because it was so immediately irritating that its presence was detected at once, and precautionary measures could be taken. The other gases in this class got to work less frankly. Presently the victim began to cough. Then as the destruction of the bronchioles and alveoli of the lungs went on, he retched and suffocated and coughed up blood and tissue. He died amidst his expectorations with a visage blue and bloated and blood-stained froth on his lips. If by good luck he survived, he survived with his lungs so injured that he easily fell a victim to tuberculosis or suchlike disease. Most of this group of gases had their own characteristic complications. One series, for instance, would attack the nervous system, causing wild excitement, terror, convulsions, screams and paralysis. Thousands of men had already died in agony from Green Cross gas during the World War, and the plans of some of these experts involved the massacre of whole populations in the same atrocious fashion. Green Cross gas was used, but not in sufficient strength to be very deadly, in the Polish bombing of Berlin in May 1940, and in a more concentrated form in the aerial torpedoes that were sent from Germany to Warsaw. It had been used also at Nankin in 1935 and in the Chinese reprisal at Osaka.

Yellow Cross gas, or mustard gas, was much more insidious and also more cruel and murderous. It was not really a gas; it was a volatile liquid. When cold, it spread unsuspected in a thin film over the ground, getting on to boots and clothing, being carried hither and thither. Slowly, as it vaporized, its presence was revealed. Discomfort came, a horrible suspicion, fear and then coughing and retching. It involved quite frightful and hopeless suffering. Steadily but surely it killed every living substance with which it came into contact; it burnt it, blistered it, rotted it away. One part of mustard gas in five million of air was sufficient to affect the lungs. It ate into the skin, inflamed the eyes; it turned the muscles into decaying tissue. It became a creeping disease of the body, enfeebling every function, choking, suffocating. It is doubtful if any of those affected by it were ever completely cured. Its maximum effect was rapid torture and death; its minimum prolonged misery and an abbreviated life. The gases used in the fighting in North China in 1934–37 and in the Chinese raids upon Japan were mostly of this group. And an evacuation of Berlin in 1946 was brought about by the threat of Yellow Cross bombs.

[They were actually dropped, but, either through accident or by the insubordination of the chemists employed by the Poles, they smashed ineffectively. It was one of the most striking instances of what appears to have been the pacifist sabotage that helped to end the formal warfare in Central Europe. Five of the chemical workers concerned were shot and seventeen given long sentences of imprisonment, but none of the records of their trial has survived.]

Allied rather than competing with these gases of the Green and Yellow Cross categories, Dr Woker cites the Blue Cross group. These substances were essentially direct nervous irritants in the form of an almost impalpable dust. They could penetrate most of the gas masks then in use, and produced such pain, so violent a sneezing and nausea, and such a loss of self-control that the victim would tear off his mask, so exposing himself to the Green or Yellow vapours with which Blue Cross was usually associated.

All these torments had been extensively inflicted already during the World War, but after its conclusion the secret activities of the various poison gas departments were sustained with great energy. It took them nearly twenty years even to open up the main possibilities of their speciality. One substance, which played a large part in the discussions of the time, was 'Lewisite,' the discovery of a Professor Lewis of Chicago, which came too late for actual use before the end of 1918. This was one of a group of arsenical compounds. One part of it in ten millions of air was sufficient to put a man out of action. It was inodorous, tasteless; you only knew you had it when it began to work upon you. It blistered as much as mustard gas and produced a violent sickness.

Other war poisons followed upon this invention, still more deadly: merciful poisons that killed instantly, and cruel and creeping poisons that implacably rotted the brain. Some produced convulsions and a knotting up of the muscles a hundred times more violent than the once dreaded tetanus. There is a horrible suggestiveness in the description of the killing of a flock of goats for experimental purposes in these researches: 'All succumbed to the effect of the gas except three, *which dashed their brains out against the enclosure.*' And to assist these chemicals in their task of what Dr Woker calls 'mass murder' there was a collateral research into incendiary substances and high explosives to shatter and burn any gas-attack shelter to which a frightened crowd might resort.

Dr Woker's summary does not include Kovoet's invention of the Permanent Death Gas in 1934. Its composition is still a secret and its very complicated preparation a felony. This compound, although not absolutely permanent, decomposed with extreme slowness. It was in itself neither a gas nor a poison. It was a heavy, rather coarse-grained powder. It evaporated as camphor does, and as it evaporated it combined with oxygen to form a poison effective when diluted with fifty million times its volume of air. Its action was essentially of the Lewisite type. This was actually used in the first Polish War to cut off East Prussia. A zone of territory from a mile to three miles wide along the whole frontier was evacuated and dusted with Permanent Death

Gas. East Prussia became a peninsula accessible only from Lithuania or by sea. In spite of the heaviness of the grains, the winds finally widened this band of death to about fifteen miles in width and carried its lethal influence into the suburbs of Danzig.

This murdered region was not re-entered, except by a few specially masked explorers, until after 1960, and then it was found to be littered with the remains not only of the human beings, cattle and dogs who had strayed into it, but with the skeletons and scraps of skin and feathers of millions of mice, rats, birds and suchlike small creatures. In some places they lay nearly a metre deep. *War Pictures* has two photographs of this strange deposit. Vegetation was not so completely destroyed; trees died and remained bare and pickled; some grasses suffered, but others of the ranker sort flourished, and great areas were covered by a carpet of dwarfed and stunted corn-cockles and elecampane set in grey fluff.

A curious by-product of Permanent Death Gas is what is now known as the Sterilizing Inhalation. This was first made by accident. A Chinese Vindication Society organized an air raid on Osaka and Tokio in 1935 after the great Green Cross raid on Nankin in that year. It was intended to strike terror into the Japanese mind. Permanent Death Powder was to have been used, but because of the haste and danger of the preparations the Chinese had not tested it out, and here again, either by accident or design, things went wrong; the formula, it seems, had been falsified. Consequently, when the raid was made – all the machines employed were brought down on their way home – nothing ensued but a temporary fever accompanied by retching and purging.

There was much derision of the unfortunate aviators in Japan. It was only some months after that the Western World learnt that the medical services of both towns were reporting a complete cessation of early pregnancies. Not a litter of kittens or puppies had appeared for weeks, mares were no longer foaling nor cows in calf. Mice and rats vanished. The sterilization in all cases was permanent. But birds were not affected for reasons that Crayford-Huxley has since made clear. The sparrows multiplied enormously and the hens still clucked triumphantly in these childless cities.

In some way the Chinese chemists had blundered upon one of those rare sub-radiant gases known as Pabst's Kinetogens, which affect the genes. A whole series of these are now known to biologists, chiefly through the work of Pabst and his assistants, and most of the more extraordinary flower sports and new aberrant animal types in our experimental gardens are due to their employment; but for a long time, until indeed Pabst took up the subject with an insight all his own, only the Sterilization Inhalation was known. Most of the campaigns in the Forties of the twenty-first century against contagious rodents made an extensive use of this gas wherever regions could be isolated from human intrusion, and the day may not be distant when it will have important eugenic applications.

But the Japanese experience produced even a graver sensation throughout the world than the actual slaughter of the victims would have occasioned. The militarist class in Japan was as deeply sentimental as the Western equivalent in Europe, and as resolute that the common people should not only die but breed fresh battle fodder for their country. Until the patriots realized that the Chinese supply of this stuff was limited, they lived in horror. They saw themselves stripped bare of subject lives. They saw themselves extinct in the hour of victory. There was a great clamour about the world for the extensive application of this new find during the fiercer war years; there are proposals on record (*Hate Eugenics*, Historical Documents 5752890 and seq.) to apply it from the air to Palestine, Arabia, Ireland, the whole of China and the African Continent in part or as a whole. But mankind was saved from any such catastrophe by the fact that the first production of Sterilizing Inhalation was essentially accidental. It had been prepared furtively, its makers were untraceable, and the proper formula was not worked out and made controllable until our insane world was well in the grip of the harsh humanity of the Air Dictatorship.

How all these hideous devices of the New Warfare were to be brought together to effect the definitive subjugation of the Will of a belligerent Power was apparently never thought out, or, if it was, the plans were kept so secret that now they have perished with their makers. After the millions had choked, after the cities were a stench of dead bodies – what then?

Perhaps the artistic interest of the business precluded such remote considerations. All we can disentangle now of this gas warfare, as its experts contemplated it, consists of projects of mere mischief and torture. They seem imbued with much the same wanton destructiveness as that displayed by some of the younger specimens among the Loando-Mobi chimpanzee hybrids.

Yet some of these plans are amazingly thorough up to a certain point – up to the point where one asks, 'But *why*?' For instance, in the Marine War Museum in the Torcello Lagoon there are no fewer than half a dozen raider submarines built for four different great Powers, and all specially designed as long-distance bases for gas warfare. They carried no guns nor ordinary fighting equipment. They had practically unlimited cruising range, and within them from five to nine aeroplanes were packed with a formidable supply of gas bombs. One of them carried thirty long-range air torpedoes with all the necessary directional apparatus. There were four different types of gas mixture in the bombs, but they differed little in character and efficiency. The smallest of these raiders carried enough of such stuff to 'prepare' about eight hundred square miles of territory. Completely successful, it could have turned most of the London or New York of that time, after some clamour and running and writhing and choking, into a cityful of distorted corpses. These vessels made London vulnerable from Japan, Tokio vulnerable from Dublin; they abolished the last corners of safety in the world.

These six sinister monsters gleam now in the great gallery side by side, their poison fangs drawn, their mission abandoned, the grim vestiges, the uncontrovertible evidence of one nightmare among the many nightmares of hate and evil that afflicted the human brain during the Age of Frustration. There they are. Men made them – as men made the instruments of torture during the previous dark ages. Even amidst the happy confidence of our present life it is well that we should remember that, given different conditions, men technically as sane as ourselves could design and make these things.

There is something revolting in these details. We have given enough for our purpose. History must not be made a feast of horror. From first to last gas warfare destroyed very painfully between one and one and a quarter million lives that might have been fruitful and happy. That much mischief was done. They suffered and they have gone. The gist of our story is that, after the humiliation and quickening of the military mind by the ineptitudes of the World War, belligerent science did not so much progress as lose itself in the multiplicity of its own inventions. It developed one frightful and monstrous contrivance after another, to dismay and torment mankind, to spread ill health and hate, to demoralize and destroy industrial life, to make whole countries uninhabitable and loosen every band that held men together in orderly societies, but it made no steps at all to any comprehensive and decisive conduct of war. With no plan for the future, with no vision of the world as a whole at all, these thousands of furtive specialists, these 'damned ingenious patriots', as Isaac Burtonshaw (1913–2003) called them, went on accumulating, here frightful explosives, there stores of disgusting disease germs, and there again stores of this or that fantastically murderous gas.

No comprehensive plan held any of these centres of evil together into one premeditated whole, as, for instance, the military preparations of the Hohenzollern Empire were held together by a clear and deliberate scheme of conclusive warfare. Beneath the vulgar monarchist claptrap of the German effort of 1914 there was indeed a real scheme for the reorganization and modernization of civilization about a Teutonic nucleus according to Teutonic ideals. It may have had its fatuous elements, but it was logical and complete. But war planning never recovered that completeness after 1914; never got back to the same logical foundations. After that belligerence lost its head. It still went on as everything else went on in those days – by inertia. But it had no longer any idea of what it was up to.

Yet over all the world these incoherent mines were prepared, and they might well have exploded, had their release been simultaneous, into such an outbreak of disorderly evil as staggers the contemporary imagination. It is conceivable that they might have destroyed mankind. It would have needed no change in the essential conditions but only a rearrangement of the determining accidents to have brought about that final catastrophe.

This menace of a chaos of disasters and aimless cruelties hung over a disorganized and unprotected world for three-quarters of a century. It is what some historians call the Period of Maximum Insecurity, from 1935 to 1965. Here and there quite monstrous things occurred – at Nankin, Pekin, Osaka, Berlin, Warsaw, for instance; things terrible enough to hearten and steel the better elements in humanity for the achievement of that world peace towards which all these forces were urging it. Fortunately for mankind the two fundamental evils of traditionalism were just sufficient to neutralize each other during this long period of the incubation of the Modern State. The greed of the creditor balanced the greed of the armament dealer. As armaments grew more and more costly, the possible purchasers grew poorer and poorer. If Economy starved and hampered many good things in human life, it did at least finally take all vigour and confidence out of the development of the New Warfare. The Chemical Armament industry followed the other typical institutions of the old order into the general social liquidation which wound up the bankrupty of Private Profit Capitalism.

V

The Fading Vision of a World Pax: Japan reverts to Warfare

We have shown already how Parliamentary Democracy necessarily abolished real leaders in public affairs and substituted a strange type of pseudo-leader, men who were essentially *resultants,* who made nothing, created no forces, met no emergencies, but simply manoeuvred for position, prestige and the pettier rewards of power. They followed the collapse of the decaying order without an effort to arrest its decay. Why indeed should they have made an effort? They were representatives of the popular will, and if there was no popular will . . .

We have already considered the behaviour of this amazingly ineffective collection of men in face of the financial dislocation that was choking the economic life of the race. It is doubtful if a single one of them ever gave a month's continuous study to the plain realities of that situation. And in the face of the accumulating stresses created by the maladjustments of Versailles, this galaxy of humbugs to whom democracy had entrusted the direction of human affairs – humbugs unavoidably, for the system insisted upon it regardless of the best intentions – was equally enigmatical and impotent. Along the eastern frontiers of Italy and Germany the open sores festered. No one sought to heal them. In the Far East the conflict between Japan and China, failing a European protest, became frankly a formal war. Every world event cried louder than the last for collective action, and there was no collective action. The League of Nations appointed commissions of enquiry and produced often quite admirable analyses of hopeless situations.

No one knew how to arrest the grim development of the situation. The chiefs of states repeated the traditional gestures, as though these were all that could be expected of them. But the patterns of history served them no more. They found themselves like men who attempt to gesticulate and find their limbs have changed to cloud and rock.

Of all the 'Powers' of that time the behaviour of Japan was the most decisive. In 1931 an internal revolution in that country had put political power into the hands of a patriotic military group, diplomatically unscrupulous and grossly sentimental according to the distinctive Japanese tradition, and this coterie set itself now with extraordinary energy and an equally extraordinary lack of authentic vision to caricature the aggressive imperialisms of the nineteenth-century Europeans. The mind of this ruling group was still intensely romantic, still obsessed by those ideas of national dominance and glory which had passed already so fatally over the intelligence of Christendom. Their military initiatives were quasi-Napoleonic, their diplomatic pretences and evasions modelled on the best European precedents. It was 'Japan's turn' now.

The investigation of just what these Japanese Imperialists imagined they were doing has greatly exercised our historical research department. But it is indeed only a special instance of the general riddle of what any 'Power', regarded as a mentality in itself, imagined it was doing in that age. Only a century and a half has passed since those Japanese columns were marching into one Chinese town after another, and today our psychologists confess themselves baffled by an enterprise that was manifestly undertaken by men like ourselves and yet had already assumed a quality of absolute insanity. Why did these very intelligent people behave in that fashion?

The clue lies in the extraordinary ease with which distasteful reality can be repressed by the human mind, and in the atmosphere of grotesque but flattering illusions in which these people were living. Just as in the West the bankers, economic experts, responsible statesmen, would not realize the complete smash to which their fiscal and financial methods were plainly heading until the smash had actually come, so these Japanese militarists could not see the inevitable consequences of their continental adventures. They could not see behind them a miserable peasantry breeding itself down to the basest subsistence; a miserable urban proletariat deteriorating physically and morally; they could not estimate the mutterings of revolt in all their sweated and driven industrial centres; they could not understand the protests of their own fine and growing intelligentzia.

Even the steady fall of the national credit abroad and the increasing economic stresses of the land aroused no misgivings of hallucination. Japan in her headlong pursuit of Western precedents was rapidly reproducing all the revolutionary conditions of the West. All that was lost upon her leaders. The one thing they could see clearly was that China was disorganized, that she was struggling with great difficulty to discover a new method of collective living to replace her ancient slack imperialism, and that by all the rules of the international game this was Japan's opportunity. They thought that, in very much the same way that the disorganization of the Empire of the Great Mogul had laid India bare to the piratical enterprise of the Europeans and permitted the establishment of the unstable aimless Indian Empire of the British, so now Fate had invited them to an equally glorious opportunity, to a parallel Japanese domination of the most or all of Asia. Who could tell where their imperial adventure would end – or whether it would have an end? The mirage of limitless power and glory opened out before them, as it has opened out to all empire-builders since the world began.

They were reckoning without the New Warfare, reckoning without modern industrialism, without the paradoxical self-destructiveness of Private Capitalist enterprise, without Russia, without America, without the superior mass, the traditional unity and mental obduracy of the Chinese population. They were thinking as a Pomeranian Junker or a British general from that 'hotbed of Imperialists', Ulster, might have thought before 1914. It was an archaic megalomania – that led to the killing of about three million combatants, an extreme social disintegration in China, and the final collapse of the Japanese monarchy.

In the special histories of this struggle, the student who needs or desires the knowledge may find the detailed particulars of the Japanese aggressions from 1931 onward which grew at last into the formal invasion of China proper; the tentative of Shanghai, the invasion of Manchuria and the establishment of the puppet kingdom of Manchukuo (1932), the attack on Shanhaikwan which led to the penetration of the Great Wall, the invasion of China Proper from the north and the march on Pekin. The operations up to that point were largely on the pattern of the old warfare as it had been practised up to 1914. The Chinese were poorly equipped and had little modern material; the Japanese found it unnecessary to make any excessively expensive efforts to attain their objectives.

All this earlier fighting went on to an accompaniment of protests from the quite powerless League of Nations at Geneva. A 'Lytton Report' prepared by a commission of enquiry is to be found in the Historical Documents Series (2067111). But counter-balancing these remonstrances were the ambiguous utterances of the British Foreign Office, the support of the French armament industry and its Press, the overt support of a great group of American banks and their newspapers. In view of these divisions, the Japanese militarists had every reason to disregard Western criticism altogether.

In 1935 the Japanese occupied Pekin and Tientsin. They set up a second puppet monarchy in Pekin. But they found very great difficulty in holding the country, particularly to the south and east of these centres. Manchuria, Inner Mongolia and Shansi remained seething with bandits and rebel bands, and the still unoccupied valley of the Yang-tsze-kiang remained fighting with an increasing unity under the leadership of the reorganized Kuomintang. In no part of China or Manchuria was it safe for a Japanese to go about alone, and a rigorous economic boycott, sustained by an omnipresent terrorism, continued. The Kuomintang was a directive association created by the great Chinese revolutionary Sun Yat Sen, and it had gone through various vicissitudes; it had a rough general resemblance to the Communist Party and the various European fascisms, and, like them, it sustained a core of conscious purpose throughout its community. It had no vital centre, no formal head; it was a thing of the mind, unquenchable by military operations. And under the stress of this resistance it had become violently patriotic and xenophobic.

In 1936 Japan already had more than a million and a half men scattered between the Manchurian frontier and Canton, where a third landing had been made, and still her hold upon China hardly extended beyond the range of her guns and the glitter of her bayonets. She had bombed Nankin twice on an extensive scale, Pekin before its surrender, and Wuchang and Hankow, with Yellow Cross bombs. Hundreds of thousands of people had been slaughtered, but the great invertebrate body of China seemed able to endure such losses with a stoicism impossible in a more highly organized state. In return the 'Vindication of China' Society astonished the world by suddenly bombing and, through an error in the gas mixture, *sterilizing* Osaka and Tokio.

No one knew of these Chinese air forces until they appeared in action. The machines had come from Sweden by way of Russia. But nearly every Western country was supplying contraband of war to the Chinese. Unaccountable hostile aeroplanes with untraceable bombs appeared in the sky and came humming over the sea to Japan. Then in 1935 a Japanese transport blew up and sank in the Gulf of Pe-chih-li.

In 1936, three Japanese liners were destroyed by mines of unknown origin within fifty miles of port. War supplies of all sorts got into China from Soviet Russia in the north and from the French and British possessions in the south, and the help and sympathy of America became more and more manifest as the vast imperial ambitions of the Japanese leaders became unmistakable. Western feeling had at first been acutely divided between distrust of Japan and the desire to see China restored to order on capitalist lines and saved from Communism. But with every Japanese advance European and American feeling veered back towards China. Australia and New Zealand appealed to the Washington government for a joint guarantee to supplement the Imperial tie in 1937. They were advocating a mutual guarantee of all the Europeanized regions of the Pacific. For a time it seemed as though the Western world might be guided to a sort of unity by the flares of Japan. But the unforgettable humiliations inflicted upon Central Europe after the war still rankled sufficiently to prevent that.

Even before the launching of the definitive conquest of China there had been considerable economic and social stress in Japan. The earlier successes, the easy capture of Pekin and the failure of an adequate Chinese army to materialize, had filled the island empire with patriotic enthusiasm and hope; the war was brought to a victorious conclusion three times, and each time it broke out again. No invader ever conquered Russia to the end, and no one ever completed the conquest of China. Always beyond the subjugated provinces appeared other provinces swarming with hostility. Szechwan and the south supplied inexhaustible support and supplies for the Kuomintang resistance. It seemed at last as though there could be no peace any more in China until the invaders fought their way through to Tibet.

War weariness descended upon Nippon. The peasants saw their sons marching off, never to return, and shortages of ordinary commodities deepened to famine. There was already vigorous 'Stop the War' agitation in Japan in 1935; there were continual strikes in Nagoya and hundreds of casualties, and afterwards there began a frantic dumping of accumulated goods abroad, to pay not merely for munitions but for such now vitally essential imports as Australian meat and Canadian and American corn. The war was starving the home field of men and it was destroying the productivity of large areas of China. The social structure of Japan proved to be far too primitive to emulate the miracles of economy performed by the Germans during the World War. The confidence and credit of Japan sank steadily. Foreign loans became no longer possible even at such exorbitant rates as 14 or 15 per cent. And still there was no end in sight.

The Japanese militarist had gone too far to recede. Behind them they had a suffering population that might rapidly become vindictive, and about the arena of the struggle watched Russia, America and Europe.

According to the best traditions of their culture, these national leaders resolved on a supreme military effort, a march in overwhelming force into the central province of Hupeh. Colossal preparations were made, and every able-bodied Japanese who was not already enrolled was called up. This was to be 'a blow at the heart'.

A convergent march from Nankin, Shantung, and Canton was planned. This dispersal of the bases was justified by the necessity for living on the country as far as that remained possible. There were railways in existence from Canton and Shantung, but they were difficult to protect, and, apart from them, there was such an utter want of practicable roads that by the time the Japanese were in Hupeh a third of their forces were trailed out upon their lines of communication making roads, and the equipment of heavy guns and munitions they had been able to bring up was very little superior to that of the Chinese, who were still fighting with all the wealth of Szechwan at their backs and the almost overt sympathy of the West. The three great Japanese armies effected their junction in a loose ring round Wuchang – a ring that was for a time slowly drawn tighter and then ceased to contract. A deadlock ensued, a deadlock of mutual exhaustion. Neither up nor down the river was the closure of the ring complete. Throughout 1938, Japan waited for good news from the long crescent of trenches about Wuchang, and waited in vain. Pestilence broke out in July and defeated the utmost sanitary and medical efforts of the invaders. Then early in 1939 they began their retreat to Nanking, with transport disorganized, with mutiny growing, with all the country rising about them.

The horrors of that retreat have never been fully told. The three Japanese armies at their maximum strength had numbered well over two million of men; but probably about a million or less remained fit enough for the retreat. Famine was far more deadly with them than the Chinese guerillas; the exhausted wretches fell out along the line of march and waited stoically for the end; few prisoners were taken; the Chinese had no food even if they had had mercy to give quarter, and the fallen were left to perish in their own time. The broken remnant that assembled at Nankin did not greatly exceed a hundred thousand, and still smaller bodies from the lines of communication fought their way homeward to the north and south. The rest of these two million lay in the vast cemeteries of Puki and Ki-chow, or they had been drowned in the floods, or their bodies were littered as they had dropped and crawled over the sad monotonous landscape of the Chinese hills. At Nankin the weary and dispirited survivors realized that Japan was now also at war with the United States and that Osaka and Nagoya were in the hands of Communist Committees.

For some weeks the Japanese army sprawled inactive in its former cantonments to the west of Nankin. Then it revolted, shot many of its officers, declared for the social revolution and fraternized with the

Chinese Red Army which had marched in under its nose from Hangchow and taken control of the city proper.

The entry of the United States into the Eastern War, which did so much to complete the demoralization of militarist Japan, was the climax of a prolonged wrangle about the supply of mines and submarines to the Chinese, that became more and more acute after the sinking of a Japanese transport in the gulf of Pe-chih-li.

It is only recently that the full history – which is also a very tedious and disputatious history – of the sea war against Japan has been worked out. Every contemporary record was falsified at the time; every event hidden completely or elaborately camouflaged. It is now fairly evident that not merely did private firms manufacture mines and build submarine mine-layers but that the various European navies under the plea of economy sold out a large proportion of quite modern and valid undersea craft for 'breaking up' to agents and dealers acting for South American intermediaries. The submarines, either intact or so 'broken up' that they could easily be reconstructed, went to various Peruvian and Chilian ports and thence found their way across the Pacific to the Philippines. The Philippine Islands were quasi-independent, but the Manila declaration of President Roosevelt II in 1937 had practically extended to them the protection of the Monroe Doctrine, and the Japanese had never had the surplus energy necessary to challenge this informal protectorate. Now these islands became the base for vexatious attacks upon their overseas trade and sea communications.

The naval situation in the Pacific was a complicated one. To the east of the Philippines lie the Ladrones, a scattered group of volcanic islands, of which the largest, Guam, had been assigned to the United States of America by the Treaty of Versailles and was adminstered as a part of the American Navy, while the rest were held by Japan under a mandate. (The Powers previously in possession had been first Spain and, after 1899, Germany.) The Japanese were bound by treaty not to fortify their holdings, but as the situation grew tense they seem to have ignored this restriction, at least to the extent of establishing submarine bases. Now that the situation was growing tenser the state of affairs above and under water between the Ladrones, the Philippines and the Asiatic mainland became darker and more dangerous. There was a threatening concentration of the American Fleet between Guam and the Philippines to ensure the neutrality of the latter, a patrolling concentration of the Japanese along the Chinese coast, and an obscure activity of privateering submarines and ambiguous shipping, which smuggled munitions and supplies and raided weak points of the Japanese communications.

Above water a submarine, like any other ship, can fly a flag and claim the respect due to its nationality, but mines fly no flags, and under water a submarine may be able to recognize the coded signals of a co-national but has no means at all of distinguishing a neutral from an enemy.

Mistakes and pseudo-mistakes were inevitable. Two American submarines disappeared in 1936. Then several Japanese submarines vanished from the Ladrone archipelago. Disputes that broke out in neutral cafés came to a murderous end in the depths. The American navy took matters into its own hands. By 1937 an informal naval war had developed in the Western Pacific.

Neither Power hurried on to an actual declaration of war. America, in spite of, or perhaps because of, the bold experimenting of Roosevelt II was in a state of deepening economic and political disorder, and Japan was putting forth her utmost strength for that disastrous 'blow at the heart' in China. But many of the more conservative influences in the United States saw in a Pacific war a saving distraction of public attention and public energy. There was an agitation to re-annex the Philippines, and after the Japanese failure to hold Wuchang the drive towards open war became uncontrollable.

The particulars of the brief, destructive and indecisive naval war that followed need not occupy us here. The battle fleets met in the Western Pacific and separated after two days of gunfire and heavy losses. Ammunition gave out, it seems, on the Japanese side. At any rate they drew off in the twilight under a smoke-screen. The Americans claimed the victory because they were able to go on to Manila, while the Japanese withdrew to the protection of their minefields and submarines and were never able to emerge again for lack of material. Both Powers were now in a state of deepening domestic stress, and their war, in a technical sense, never ended. That is to say, there was no final treaty as between two Powers, because both had in effect collapsed. They fell apart. Social revolution swept the conflict off the stage.

[The student will be reminded, by this inconclusive termination, of the almost incessant, dreary and futile wars of Byzantine and Sassanid that devastated Asia Minor for three centuries and did not so much come to an end as suffer effacement from history by the sponge of Islam.]

The social disintegration of Japan, once it had begun, was very rapid. The great mass of the population, the peasants, had been scarcely affected by the process of Westernization, and they lapsed very readily into the same unprogressive variant of Communism as their equivalents in Kwantung, Chekiang and Fukien had adopted. A small Westernized intelligentzia with many internal feuds and doctrinal disputes struggled, not very effectively, in the larger towns to turn this merely insurgent Communism into modern and constructive paths after the Moscow pattern. Fragmentation when it came was swift and thorough. Militarism degenerated into brigandage and local feudalism. Here and there some scion of the old nobility reappeared with his attendant Samurai as a ganster boss.

In the space of a few years all Asia from the Pacific to Persia seemed to be sliding back to political and social chaos, to hand-to-mouth civilization, destitution and endemic pestilence. For the greater part of India and most of Further India were also now drifting back to barbarism. There also the phrases and the insubordination, if not the spirit and methods, of Communism had captured vast multitudes who had remained completely unaffected by other European ideas. It was Communism without any Five Year Plan or indeed any conception of a plan. It was the class-war in its ultimate crudity. It killed moneylenders and tax-collectors with gusto and elaboration. It evolved strange religious fanaticisms, and it abandoned sanitation as 'boujawai', the accursed thing. The imperial power in India was not overthrown; rather it was stripped of effective prestige and receded to an immense distance. The princes remained formally 'loyal', though in some cases they tacitly annexed 'disturbed districts' adjacent to their proper dominions. Localities and local adventurers improvised a sort of social order at a low level and with a continually completer disregard of any central authority.

VI

The Western Grip on Asia Relaxes

The recession of the directive influence of the half-modernized European imperialisms in Asia went on steadily. Even as early as 1929 the spread of a peasant Communism similar to that which had obtained so strong a hold upon the popular imagination in China was causing grave alarm to the Indian government. The seizure and trial of a group of British and Indian agitators at Meerut, and the extravagantly heavy sentences passed upon them in 1933, showed both the gravity of these fears and the unintelligent clumsiness with which the situation was being met.

For the British Empire there was to be no such decline and fall as happened to Rome. Instead it relaxed, as we shall now describe, to nothing.

Unhappily, before it relaxed in India it had, as in Ireland, a brief convulsive phase of 'firmness'. . . .

[*Here several sheets from Raven's MS appear to be missing.*]

VII

The Modern State and Germany

A question of primary importance in human history is this: Why were the lessons of the Great War, and the subsequent economic and social disorders, lessons which seem to us to-day to be as starkly plain as lessons could be – why were these lessons lost upon every one of the great communities of thought into which the world was divided? British thought, French thought, American thought, German, Russian, Italian thought, seem in our retrospect to ring the changes upon every conceivable sequence of prejudice and stupidity. Why was Wilson's start towards world unification not followed up? Why after 1932 was there no vigour to reconstruct the League of Nations, when all the world was crying for some central authority to unify money and economic life? Why did the Age of Frustration last so long? We have already noted some of the controlling causes, the mercenary Press, the vast anti-social private interest, the heavy weight of tradition, the reactionary quality of schoolmasters, the social disintegration due to economic demoralization. But even these malignant influences, taken all together, do not seem sufficient for this blindness in the general intelligence of our race towards the obvious elements of its situation.

Behind all these conditions making for failure there was something else: there was an intrinsic weakness in the forces of reconstruction, there was a fundamental lack. *It was impossible for the world to get out of its difficulties because it had no definite complete idea of what it wanted to get out to.* It had ideas, yes, more than enough, but they were confused and often mutually contradictory ideas. A drowning man cannot save himself by swimming unless he has something solid to which he can swim. The deficiency was not moral nor material, it was intellectual. There was the will for salvation and the material for salvation, but there was no plan of salvation. The world had no definition of an objective. That had still to be made plain to it.

It will make this matter clearer if we consider the mental and emotional phases of one typical culture community of central importance at that time, the German. Stories similar in essence, if widely different in detail, could be given of the French, Anglo-Saxon, Russian and Spanish-speaking communities. The feature they had in common was this, a failure to realize that there could be no salvation now unless it was a comprehensive salvation. They were attempting to do severally and with a jostling competitiveness what could only be done with the utmost difficulty in unison. That meant for every one of them the paralysing influence of a war threat, extreme economic instability, incapacity for dealing with morbid financial conditions, and a consequent state of mental 'worry' that made every move inaccurate and untimely.

It is only when we realize the sapping of that aggressive energy that had wellnigh Europeanized the whole world before the World War that we can understand the length of the Age of Frustration. Certain facts of fundamental importance to the continued health of our world community have to be stressed. Europe could not lead the world to unity when the world seemed dying to be led to unity, because Europe itself was profoundly disunited. The World War was merely the explosion of tensions that had been straining below the surface throughout the whole First Period of World Prosperity. Before the European peoples, who by 1920 amounted to a quarter of the whole human race, could resume the exploring, experimenting and civilizing rôle they had played for two centuries, it was necessary that they should be purged of a chronic mental disease – a disease which had, it seemed, to rise to an acute phase and run its enfeebling and devastating course before it could be treated: the disease of hate.

Although each year in the Thirties saw the international tension in Europe increasing, it was only in 1940 that actual warfare broke out. All Europe was 'mined' for ten years before that time, but the very consciousness of that fact, if it did not hold back the drift towards war, increased the gravity of its onset. That ingenious contrivance of President Wilson's, the Polish Corridor, Poland's 'access to the sea', was the particular mine that exploded first. But it was only one of a series of accumulating detonations which were destined to blow the still creaking ineffective League of Nations, and indeed nearly every vestige of the unfortunate Treaty of Versailles and its subordinate 'settlements', out of the way of human readjustment.

The mental phases of that great body of Europeans who used the German language summarize the world situation. The history of Europe from 1900 to 1950 could be told in a study of the German brain alone, its torment and the reactions it evoked in the peoples about it. It was a brain of outstanding vigour and crudity. It aroused admiration, envy and fear. Its achievements in material science were magnificent; its energy of industrial organization was unparalleled. Its mathematical and psychological ineptitudes were redeemed by the Jewish intelligences entangled in its meshes. Compared with the Anglo-Saxon brain its political thought was unsupple, and it had neither the extreme lucidity of the French intelligence, the boldness of the Italian, nor the poetic power of Spain and Russia. It had these conspicuous limitations. Its obstinate association with a stupidly arrogant monarchism and a woolly tangle of preposterous racial pretensions stood in the way of sympath-

etic cooperation with any other cultural system. It had failed conspicuously to assimilate the non-German subject populations involved in its
political web. It had intensified the defensive nationalism of the French;
its tactless challenge upon the sea had terrified and exasperated the
British; it had roused even America to a wary disapproval and a final
hostility. Russia it had never won, but then in the huge carcass of pre-
revolutionary Russia there was very little to be won anyhow. (There
was indeed no real national self-consciousness in Russia before the
Soviet régime; there was only Dostoievsky and the Tzar.) Assertive
ungraciousness had been the chief factor in Germany's isolation and the
cause of its defeat in the World War.

Yet after defeat this afflicted German mentality, if only on account of
a certain toughness and vigour it possessed, remained still the central
reality and the central perplexity of the European system. War and
disaster could not alter the fact that the backbone of Europe, the most
skilled, industrious, teachable and intelligent block of its population,
spoke and thought German. What might happen to it, what would
happen to it, should have been the primary preoccupation of every
intelligent statesman. For if Germany had gone right everything would
have gone right. But there were no statesmen sufficiently intelligent to
consider anything of the sort. Germany had had a phase of pride and
megalomania. It had been immensely disillusioned, it had thrown off its
glittering imperialist headship, it had accepted military defeat. It had
even passed through a phase of humility. At first it did not hate
conspicuously. Amidst great difficulties the new republic displayed
creative courage, moderation, a dawning sense of the significance of
world politics.

Creative, forward-looking minds turned to Germany with an entirely
pathetic hopefulness. 'Now we shall see what Germany can do,' they
said. 'Be patient with Germany.' All the world scolded France for her
inveterate distrust. Given courage and generosity abroad and leadership
at home, this great mass of Teutonic brains might have taken up the
task of the Modern State then, and fallen into cooperation with the rest
of a disillusioned but renascent world. It might even have led in the
work of reconstruction, and 1918 might have been the opening year of
a phase of world renewal.

But that was not to be. The world had still to reap a harvest of
disunion through sixty tragic years. At home leadership came to
Germany too late. Stresemann mastered his lesson too slowly and died
too soon. Brüning was betrayed by Hindenburg's mental decay. And
abroad it seemed to the Germans that there was nothing but war-
stained and vindictive enemies. They looked for friends and saw only
Foreign Offices. We have told already how the rôle of only sinner in a
world of outraged saints was thrust upon Germany by the Conference
of Versailles. She was to be permanently enfeebled, restrained and

humiliated. German babies yet unborn were expected to be born penitent about the war. They were to gasp for their first breath under the smacks of an unforgiving world.

How all the good effort in Germany was thwarted, how the nets of suspicion held her down, would make a long and intricate story. At last these losers of the World War became as violent and frantic as stifled creatures fighting for air. Only by a feat of imagination can we now put ourselves in their places. Everything seemed to be making for the strangulation of Central Europe. The young energetic men in the defeated countries were to be given no share in the rebuilding of their shattered world. That was to be reserved for the new generation of the conquerors. They were to live in an atmosphere of punishment, toiling, heavily taxed, and outlawed from the advancement of civilization to the very end of their days. That they should recover prosperity or achieve great things would be an offence.

Naturally life so circumscribed was bitter and lapsed very easily towards vice, apathy or blind revolt. There is a remarkable novel in the Historical Documents Series (*Fabian*, by Erich Kastner, 1932) which renders the individual aspect of this phase of German life very vividly. Another novel almost equally vivid and illuminating is *Kleiner Mann, was nun?* by Hans Fallada, 1932.

These conditions of mind, this tied and stifled outlook upon life, were, it must be admitted, by no means confined to the German-speaking peoples. The intelligent and ambitious young Indian or Egyptian or negro, the intelligent young man of any subordinate, handicapped and restrained people or class – and this covered perhaps two-thirds of the youth of our race in these days – participated in the same distress of a foreordained inferiority and futility. But the young German had recent memories of hope and pride and a greater fund of resentment and aggressive energy. He had no tradition of inferiority and subservient adjustment.

Unhappily no teachers or leaders arose to point him on to his legitimate rôle in the replacement of the current disorder by the Modern World-State. The Hohenzollern régime and the stresses of the war had stood in the way of his attaining anything like the cosmopolitanism of, say, the English and Americans. His new republicanism was superficial and half-hearted, and in the schools and universities the teachers and leaders of the old militarist régime were still living, active and malignant. The Press and all the organizations of instruction and suggestion stood out of the revolution and showed themselves only too eager and skilful in restoring a pre-war fierceness. The futility of the new Germany was their text. 'This is not German,' they insisted. 'Go back to the old Imperialism,' they said, 'and try again.' The spirit of the women about the new generation, mothers and sweethearts alike, was for the most part one of passionate indignation.

An acute contemporary observer, L. B. Namier, pointed out that it was almost a law in history that war-strained and defeated countries should relapse towards violent patriotism between twelve and fifteen years after the war in which they suffered concluded. He suggested that this was precisely the time when the children who, without any participation in the realities of warfare, had felt all the strain and bitterness of defeat and all the hatred of the enemy would have grown up to manhood. These children became the energetic stratum in the population by 1933.

It was at this phase in European history that the rise of Hitlerism occurred. Adolf Hitler, as the decisive product of Germany in labour, is one of the most incredible figures in the whole of history. He must have astonished even the teachers and writers who had evoked him. We can study his personal presence from a hundred different angles in Vol. 30112 of the *Historical Portrait Gallery*, and it is that of an entirely commonplace man, void of dignity, void of fine quality. We can hear his voice, we can hear him persuading, exhorting and attempting to reason, from the numerous steel-tape records that were made of his speeches. It is a raucous, strained voice, talking violently but incoherently. It is the voice of a vulgar, limited, illiterate man, lashing himself to fierceness, shouting, threatening, beating his fists at the window, smashing the furniture about him, to escape from perplexity and despair. He was perfectly simple and honest in his quality. And that was perhaps the secret of his career. He gave vent to the German overstrain. He is the voice of Germany losing control.

He denounced foreigners, Jews, cosmopolitans, Communists, Republicans, owners of property and leaders in finance with raucous impartiality, and nothing is so pleasing to perplexed unhappy people as the denunciation of others. Not their fault, their troubles. They have been betrayed. To Fallada's question, 'Little Man, what now?' his answer was, 'Massacre Jews, expel foreigners, arm and get more arms, be German, utterly German, and increase and multiply.'

One has to remember that he never carried with him even an absolute voting majority of the German public. But the people permitted him to seize power and shatter their republic, stifle public discussion and destroy their liberties. They had no energy to resist him. They had no conception left in their fagged and hope-starved brains of any finer rôle than that which his bawling nationalism, his violent campaign against Communists and imaginary Communistic plots, against Jews, speculators and Liberals, presented to them. The treason of the senile Hindenburg to the Republic that had trusted him, conduced inestimably to the adventurer's success.

Hitler's exploit in seizing Germany and turning it back towards reaction was modelled on Mussolini's precedent. But intellectually he was far inferior to that strange figure. He took all that was worst in the

Fascist régime and never rose to the real constructive effort or the competent industry of his prototype. One little point that illustrates his general ignorance and essential feeble-mindedness was the adoption of the Swastika, the running cross, as the emblem of the Nazis. This brisk, silly little sign is of very old origin, and, as we have noted in the earlier stages of this summary of history, its ornamental use was one of the associated characteristics of that type of Neolithic culture, that culture of brownish and dark-white warm-water peoples, from which the early civilizations sprang. It is hardly known in connexion with the so-called 'Nordic', or with the negro peoples, and it is in no way expressive of an 'Aryan' culture. Old writers used to declare it was the 'symbol' of the sun, but it seems to have signified little beyond a certain cheerfulness. It took the place of an idea in the muddled heads of the Nazis and they treated it with immense solemnity and wore it on their banners, clothes, proclamations and wherever else they could. Arden Essenden, when it was revived in Europe during the struggle for the air control, called it the 'idiot's own trade mark', and it has certainly had a fatal attraction for many second-rate imaginative types.

So for a time, under a hubbub of young blackguards in brown shirts and Swastika badges, Germany, just when her rather heavy but persistent and faithful mind would have been of primary value in mankind's struggle with the world problem, passed out of the intellectual commonweal of mankind. Her real mind went into exile, in America, in England, in Switzerland, in irony or in hiding. She missed her proper share in the unification of mankind in the twentieth century, just as she missed her share in the Europeanization of the world in the eighteenth and nineteenth. At home this National Socialism sought destructively to construct, sought to restore her former scientific prestige and industrial efficiency by boasting, exhortation, intolerance, outrage and compulsion. It was a pitiful and tragic phase, the dementia of a great nation. The story of German life during this interval is a rowdy and unhappy story – a story of faction fights and street encounters, demonstrations and counter-demonstrations, of a complicating tyranny of blackmailing officials, and at last of an ill-managed and unsuccessful war, that belied the innate orderliness of the Teutonic peoples. There was a progressive increase of secret vice and furtive dishonesty, the outcome of hopelessness. The number of people killed or seriously injured in riots and civil conflicts in Germany, or murdered for political reasons, between 1932 and 1936 amounted to something over rather than under thirty thousand.

VIII

A Note on Hatred

*[This section was in a detached fascicle,
but its place seems to be here. – ED.]*

The student of history will find it almost impossible to understand the
peculiar difficulties of political life as it was lived until about a hundred
years ago, nor will he grasp the essential differences between what was
called education in those days and the educational processes we are still
developing to-day, unless he masters the broad facts about these systems
of hatred that dominated the group relationships of mankind right up
to the assertion of the Modern State. We have given the main particulars
of the issue between the Germans and the Poles, but that is only one
striking and historically important instance of a general condition. We
could give fifty such chapters. Nearly everywhere populations were to
be found steeped in and moved by mass hatreds of a volume and
obduracy outside any contemporary human experience.

All these hatreds arose out of the same essential causes. Two or more
population groups, each with its own special narrow and inadaptable
culture and usually with a distinctive language or dialect, had been by
the change of scale in human affairs jammed together or imposed one
upon another. A sort of social dementia ensued. In the absence of a
common idea of community, civilized motives gave place to instinctive
hostilities and spasmodic impulses.

Wherever there were mingled populations these hates were found,
and, except in the Basque country, Wales and Lapland, they were
intense enough to be of primary political importance. South and east of
Bohemia there seemed no boundary to the realms of hate. The Magyar
hated the Slav, the Slav the Italian, the Roumanian the Russian.
Religious differences, the mischief of priests, cut up even racial solidari-
ties; the Catholic Slav hated the Orthodox Slav and the Orthodox
Greeks in Macedonia were hopelessly divided among themselves. Over
all the ancient domain of the Sultan, through Persia, through India,
hates extended. Islam was rent by two ancient hate systems. These mass
hatreds were accepted in a kind of despair by even the wisest. They
defied the policies of statesmen absolutely. They were supposed to be
beyond human contol.

It is extraordinary how recent is the intelligent mitigation and
suppression of hatred. Our ancestors did not envisage this as a control-

lable mental disease. They did not know that it was possible to get through life without hatred, just as they did not know that the coughs and colds that afflicted them and most of the phenomena of senility were avoidable.

But it is amazing to think how submissively human beings allowed their lives to be spoilt by controllable things – until almost within living memory. It was not only against hate and envy that they made no effort. They left their poor nerves bare and unprotected from an endless persecution by man-made afflictions. Up to 2010 they lived in towns that were crazy with noise; there was practically no control of offensive sounds, and the visual clamour of advertisments died out only in the needy decades that preceded the Air Dictatorship. But then it was still hardly more than a century that there had been sufficient light upon the towns and highways to drive away the blackness of night and overcast weather. In northern climates in the winter before the twentieth century people lived between the nocturnal dark and a dismal grey half-light which they called daylight, not seeing the sun often for weeks together.

And before the nineteenth century it is clear to anyone who can read between the lines that mankind *stank*. One has only to study the layout and drainage of their houses and towns, their accommodation for washing, their exiguous wardrobes, the absence of proper laundry organization and of destructors for outworn objects; to realize that only usage saved them from a perpetual disgust and nausea. No wonder that, quite apart from their bad food and loathsome cooking, they coughed, spat, ached, went deaf and blind and feeble, in a continual alternation of lassitude and mutual irritation.

These conditions of life have gone one after another and almost imperceptibly. Few of us realize how different it was to be a human being only a few hundred years ago. It is only when we take our imaginations with us back into the past that we realize how evil to nose, eye, ear and soul the congregation of human beings could be. And necessarily, inevitably, because of the ill-interpreted protests of body and mind against this mode of existence, they hated – almost at haphazard. We have in Swift's *Gulliver's Travels* (1726) the cry of one man of exceptional intelligence and sensibility who discovered himself imprisoned as it were in the life of the eighteenth century and could find neither outlet nor opiate. The reek of the kennels of a mediaeval town was nothing to the stench of hatred in the popular Press of the twentieth century. The ordinary newspaper of that time was not so much a news sheet as a poison rag. Every morning the common man took in fresh suggestions of suspicion and resentment and gratified his spite with bad news and malicious gossip.

Hatred, we know, is a morbid, infectious and preventable relapse to which the mammalian cerebrum, and particularly the cerebrum of the social types, is prone. It is a loss of rational control. It is caused normally by small repeated irritations of the cerebral cortex. The contagion may occur at any phase before or after maturity, and acute attacks predispose the brain for recurrence and may run together at last into a chronic condition of vindictive disapproval.

Once hatred has established itself to that extent it seems to be ineradicable. The patient seeks, often with the greatest ingenuity, occasion for offence, and finds a profound satisfaction in the nursing of resentment and the search for reprisals and revenges. He has what he calls his 'proper pride'. He disapproves of his fellow creatures and grudges them happiness. Our current education is framed very largely to avert and anticipate this facile contagion, but the Press of that time subsisted by its dissemination, in the interests of reactionary forces. We are as sedulous now for cleanliness and ventilation in our mental as in our physical atmosphere. The contrast between a contemporary crowd and the crowds depicted by Hogarth or Raphael is not simply in the well-clad, well-grown, well-nourished and well-exercised bodies, the absence of rags and cripples, but in the candid interested faces that replace the introverted, suspicious and guarded expressions of those unhappy times. It is only in the light of this universal malaria that human history can be made comprehensible.

And now this great German mind stretching across the centre of Europe in seventy million brains was incapable of auto-therapy, and let its sickness have its way with it. It would not recognize that it suffered from anything but a noble resentment. Least of all peoples was it able to entertain those ideas of world-wide cooperation, of the World-State, which were still seeking their proper form and instrument. It was a deeper hate altogether than the fear-begotten hate of the French. In both these antagonized countries cosmopolitan sanity went begging, but most so in Germany.

The fluctuations in German hatred during the Thirties were curiously affected by subconscious currents of discretion. Though Germany was fiercely belligerent in spirit, her armament still lagged behind that of her neighbours; her Hitlerites snarled and threatened, but rather against Poland than France, and when the tension became too great it found relief by outrages upon Communists, Pacificists and intellectuals and by an exacerbated persecution of those whipping-boys of the Western civilization, the Jews. From the accession of Hitler to the chancellorship of the Reich in 1933 onward, not only looting and massacre, but legalized outrage became an ever present menace in the life of the German Jew.

Faber speaks in his studies of political psychology of the 'hate map' of the world. The intensity of the colouring of such a map would vary widely. The English-speaking states (except for Ireland, that erstwhile 'island of evergreen malice', which is now the most delightful and welcoming of summer resorts) and the Spanish-speaking communities felt hate far less intensely than the peoples of the continental European patchwork. They were less congested, they were free from acute alien interference, they had more space to move about in, and the infection was not so virulent. For two decades Spain and Spanish South America (after the Peruvian Settlement) sustained indeed a more liberal and creative mentality than any other region of the world. The Spanish contribution, beginning with Unamuno and Ortega Y. Gasset and going onward through a long list of great names, was of increasing importance in the building up of the Modern World-State.

Russia, we may note, was never so constructive mentally as Spain. She had not now the same wealth of freely thinking and writing men. She had no surplus of mental energy to philosophize. She ecstasized, prophesied or dogmatized. Such brain discipline as she had was used up in her sprawling technical efforts. But she again was not a malignant country. Young Russia was taught to hate indeed, but to hate a dissolving enemy, the Wicked Imperialist. Even in that hate there was an element of humorous caricature. When in due course the Wicked Imperialist faded away to the quality of a nursery Ogre, he took with him most of the hatred out of Russia. Hate, except in brief vivid spurts, does not seem congenial to the Russian temperament.

Few people in 1940 realized that the essential political trouble in the world, as distinguished from its monetary malaise, was this endemic disease, and still fewer had the boldness of mind even to think of the drastic cleansing and destruction of infected social institutions and economic interests and accumulations that was needed if the disease was ever to be stamped out. Meanwhile along the tangled frontiers of Central and Eastern Europe the sores festered and the inflammation increased.

Among the more frequent methods of releasing hatred in the more troubled communities were aggressive demonstrations inviting or involving violence, attacks on representative buildings, such as embassies and consulates, the defilement of flags, statues and other symbols (in India the slaughter of sacred or forbidden animals such as cows or pigs in holy places), quarrels picked in cafés and restaurants, beatings-up, assassinations, the throwing of bombs and crackers into parties and gatherings of the objectionable nationality, or into law courts, religious buildings and other unsuitable places for an explosion, firing at sentinels and across boundaries. Along the Adriatic coast it would appear there was an exceptionally strong disposition to insult the characteristic Italian respect for statues and pictures.

This was of recent origin. At the Congress of Versailles Italy had been bilked by her French and British allies of a considerable amount of the Dalmatian coast-line – to which indeed neither she nor they had any right, but which nevertheless had been promised to her in the secret engagements that had brought her into the World War. Her patriots had never ceased to resent this nor the Yugo-Slav peoples, who held the coveted districts, to fear a forcible annexation. There had been much propaganda about the dispute. One prominent argument on the Italian side was that the Republic of Venice (of which Rome was the natural heir) had formerly dominated this coast, and, in proof of this, appeal was made to the public buildings in the towns of the disputed regions, which everywhere bore the insignia of their Italian founders and particularly the distinctive lion of Venice. For that was the Fascist fantasy: wherever the Venetian lion had made its lair or the Roman eagles cast their shadows, from Hadrian's Wall in England to Mesopotamia, the Fascisti claimed to rule.

This contention, though taken calmly enough by the English, French, Spanish, Turks and other emancipated peoples, was bitterly resented by the populations more immediately threatened, and particularly did it arouse resentment and hatred along the Dalmation coast. For the young and excitable Slav, those sculptured lions and archaic eagles, those antique vestiges, were robbed of their artistic and historical charm; they took on an arrogant contemporary quality and seemed to demand an answer to their challenge. His response was to deface or mutilate them.

Already in 1932 there were bitter recriminations between Rome and Belgrade on this score, and in 1935 and again in 1937 fresh trouble arose. The later occasions were not simply matters of chipping and breaking. These heraldic and highly symbolic animals were now painted, and painted in such a manner as to bring them into grave contempt. And the outrages were not confined to heraldic animals. Portraits and images of Mussolini were also adorned all too often with pencilled moustaches, formidable whiskers, a red nose and other perversions of his vigorous personality.

Such vexatious modes of expression were in constant evidence in all the inflamed areas. To us they seem trivial, imbecile, pre-posterous, but then they were steeped in tragic possibility.

The reader must picture for himself, if he can, how things went in the brain of some youngster growing to manhood in one of these hate regions, the constant irritation of restrictions, the constant urge to do some vivid expressive thing, the bitter, unconsoling mockery against the oppressor, and at last the pitiful conspiracy, the still more pitiful insult. He must think of the poor excitement of getting the paint-pot and the ladder, of watching the receding police patrol, the tremulous triumph of smearing the hated object. That perhaps was the poor crown of life for that particular brain. Then the alarm, the conflict, the flight, a shot, a wound, straw and filth in a prison cell, the beatings and the formal punishment, the intensified resolve to carry on the resistance. There was nothing to think of then but the next outrage, the next riot. So very often the story went on to wounds and death, the body crumpled up on a street pavement and trampled under foot or put against a wall to be shot, and then the rotting away and dispersal of that particular human brain with all the gifts and powers it possessed. That was all that life could be for hundreds of thousands of those hate-drenched brains. For that they came into being, like flowers that open in a rain of filth.

A Natural History of Cruelty has recently been published by Otto Jaspers (2085–), a lineal descendant of that Professor Jaspers of Heidelberg University under whom De Windt studied and to whose *Die geistiger Situation der Gegenwart* De Windt was greatly indebted. Cruelty in the twentieth century is treated in considerable detail, and it makes very terrible reading indeed. Happily it is not considered a necessary part of a general education to probe under those dark processes of the human mind which make the infliction of horrible pain and injuries a relief to otherwise intolerable mental distresses. The psychologist, however, must acquaint himself with all those facts; he cannot fully understand our intricate minds without them, and the practical disappearance of deliberate cruelty from our world to-day makes the horror literature of the World War and World Slump periods a mine of essential material for his investigations. One or two glimpses we have given the student. If he has any imagination he will be able to expand those hints for himself into an infinitude of mutilations, tortures and wanton violence.

The older psychologists were disposed to classify cruelty as a form of sexual aberration – in ordinary speech we still use their old word Sadistic – but this attribution is no longer respected by contemporary authorities. Cruelty goes far beyond the sexual field. Just as hate is now understood to be a combative fear compound, the stiffening up of a faltering challenge, which may become infectious, so cruelty is regarded as a natural development of effort against resistance, so soon as the apprehension of frustration exceeds a certain limit. It is a transformation of our attempt to subdue something, usually a living thing, to our will, under the exasperation of actual or anticipated obduracy.

This interpretation makes it plain why the breakdown of the private capital economic and political system and the world-wide uncertainty, dismay and want which ensued was followed by wave after wave of unprecedented cruelty. In 1900, a visitor from another sphere might reasonably have decided that man, as one met him in Europe or America, was a kindly, merciful and generous creature. In 1940 he might have decided, with an equal show of justice, that this creature was diabolically malignant. And yet it was the same creature, under different conditions of stress.

There were many thousands of suicides between 1930 and 1940 – suicides of sensitive men and women, who could endure the dreadful baseness and cruelty of life no longer. Yet in the records of the reviving world of 1980 there is scarcely a mention of atrocious conduct towards human beings or animals. It was not a change of nature; it was a change of phase. Millions of people who had actually killed, massacred, tortured, were still alive – and they were behaving now quite reasonably and well. Most of them had forgotten their own deeds more or less completely. Hope had returned to human life. The frantic years were past.

IX

The Last War Cyclone, 1940–50

The drift to war in Europe became more powerful with the elimination of Japan and the United States from the possibility of intervention, and with the deepening preoccupation of Britain with Indian disorder and with the Black Revolt in South Africa. The last restraints upon continental hatreds had gone. The issues simplified.

War came at last in 1940. The particular incident that led to actual warfare in Europe was due to a Polish commercial traveller, a Pole of Jewish origin, who was so ill advised as to have trouble with an ill-fitting dental plate during the halt of his train in Danzig. He seems to have got this plate jammed in such a fashion that he had to open his mouth wide and use both hands to struggle with it, and out of deference to his fellow passengers he turned his face to the window during these efforts at readjustment. He was a black-bearded man with a long and prominent nose, and no doubt the effect of his contortions was unpleasing. Little did he realize that his clumsy hands were to release the dogs of war from the Pyrenees to Siberia.

The primary irritant seems to have been either an orange-pip or a small fragment of walnut.

Unhappily, a young Nazi was standing on the platform outside and construed the unfortunate man's facial disarrangement into a hostile comment upon his uniform. For many of these youths were of an extreme innate sensibility. The flames of patriotic indignation shot up in his heart. He called up three fellow guards and two policemen – for, like the Italian Fascisti, these young heroes rarely acted alone – and boarded the train in a swift and exemplary mood. There was a furious altercation, rendered more difficult by the facts that the offending Pole knew little or no German and was still in effect gagged. Two fellow travellers, however, came to his help, others became involved, vociferation gave place to pushing and punching, and the Nazis, outnumbered, were put off the train.

Whereupon the young man who had started all the trouble, exasperated, heated and dishevelled, and seeing that now altogether intolerable Jew still making unsatisfactory passes with his hands and face at the window, drew a revolver and shot him dead. Other weapons flashed into action, and the miniature battle was brought to an end only by the engine-driver drawing his train out of the station. The matter was complicated politically by the fact that the exact status of the Danzig police was still in dispute and that the Nazis had no legal authority upon the Danzig platform.

By itself this distressing incident might have been arranged without the outbreak of a European war. The moribund League of Nations might have been invoked or even the mummified Hague Tribunal galvanized into activity; either institution was still fully capable of dealing with, let us say, a Polish dentist who might have been treated as the culpable party, traced, punished and made the scapegoat of Europe. But that would have needed a certain good will on the part of the Powers directly involved, and at that time no such good will was forthcoming.

For eight years now the German mind had been working up for a fight over the Corridor, and the rearmament of Germany, overt and secret, had been going on. Both France and Poland had been watching the military recovery of Germany with ever-deepening apprehension, and the military authorities of both countries were urgent that a blow should be struck while they were still disproportionately stronger. Time after time it seemed that the crisis had come, and time after time nothing more than a stock-exchange tornado had occurred. Now the last reasons for patience had disappeared. The tension had risen to a point at which disaster seemed like relief and Europe was free to tear itself to fragments.

Such a situation was the inevitable climax to every 'armed peace' in the old belligerent world. At some point there was an irresistible logic in 'Strike now before they get too strong'. That had been an underlying motive of primary force in the British readiness to fight in 1914. They were eager to strike before the ever-growing German fleet equalled their own. So they ended an intolerable tension. The Germans had 'asked for it', they said. 'Better now than to-morrow.'

Now again Germany had 'asked for it' and Poland was leaping to the occasion. The War Offices pressed their bell buttons. The printing machines of Paris, London and New York were still busy with various misstatements about the murdered commercial traveller, while the Polish and German air patrols were in conflict all along the fatal boundary. That dental plate apparently began to feel uncomfortable about one o'clock in the afternoon of Friday, January 5th, 1940. On Saturday, about three o'clock in the afternoon, Michael Koreniovsky, the Polish ace, after a brilliant fight with three antagonists, fell flaming out of the sky into the crowded Langgasse of Danzig and set fire to the Rathaus.

The first Polish air raid on Berlin and the unresisted 'demonstration flight' of two hundred French air squadrons in formation over Bavaria and West Prussia followed. The Germans seem to have been taken completely by surprise by this display of immense and immediate preparedness. They had not thought it of the French. But they had the quickness of apprehension to decline an air battle against odds, and the French flew home again. The fighting on the Polish-German frontier continued.

The authorities in Paris were uncertain whether they were disappointed or relieved by the non-resistance of their old enemies. A smashing air victory over Germany would have been very satisfactory and conclusive, but these aeroplanes were also wanted at home to cow the ever-increasing domestic discontent. An indecisive battle – and that was always possible in the air – might have produced serious internal stresses.

For a week of years from the resumption of armament by Germany in 1933, the diplomatic centres of the world had been watching the steady onset of this conflict and had been doing nothing to avert it. Now London, Washington, Madrid and Geneva became hysterically active. There was a mighty running to and fro of ambassadors and foreign ministers. 'Delay,' said Geneva; though there had already been twenty years of delay.

'Localize the conflict' was a phrase that leapt into vivid prominence. It found favour not only in the neutral countries, but in Paris and Berlin. In effect 'localize the conflict' meant this: it meant that Paris should scrap her engagements to Poland and leave the Poles to make what sort of arrangements they could between Germany and Russia. For Russia now, by an enigmatical silence combined with a prompt mobilization of the Red Army, became almost immediately an important piece in the developing international game.

And Paris had soon very excellent reasons for not pushing a conflict with Berlin to extremities. The first Frenchman to be killed in the New Warfare had been killed already. And he had been killed in the Maritime Alps, shot by the bullet of an Italian patrol.

On Sunday night, January 7th, while the Polish aeroplanes were dropping gas bombs on Berlin, the Italians were administering the same treatment to Belgrade. At the same time an identical note had been dispatched from Rome to all the Powers giving Italy's reasons for this decisive blow. It seemed that between Friday evening and Sunday morning there had been a violent recrudescence of Yugo-Slav irreverence. The Fascist agents who had to supply the material for grievance and indignation had in fact overdone their task to the pitch of caricature. On Saturday the entire Italian population found itself roused from its normal preoccupation with its daily budget by the terrible intelligence of Mussolini everywhere made bibulous and ophthalmious with red paint, of Venetian lions coloured as indelicately as baboons and of shamefully overdecorated Roman eagles. Eloquent and dishevelled young Fascists, often in tears, protested at every street corner against these intolerable indignities and called for war. The cup of Yugo-Slav iniquity was full. It was only in later years that astounded students, tracing these outrages to their sources, realized how excessively that cup had been filled to justify the Fascist invasion.

Once the Polish and Italian forces had crossed their boundaries the other states of Eastern Europe did not wait even to produce an insult before launching their offensives. The whole crazy patchwork of Versailles dissolved into fighting – the joyless, frantic fighting of peoples full of hate and fear, led blindly to no ends that anyone could foresee. For two straining years the theory of localizing the conflict held Russia and France out of the fight. A 'formula' was found by which France undertook not to intervene on the side of her erstwhile allies, on the understanding that Russia by way of compensation also refrained from any action against them. Moreover, the trade in munitions was to be carried on 'impartially'. It was a flimsy formula to justify a diplomatic default, but it kept warfare away from the Western front of Germany for two distressful years. The persistent shooting by Italians over the French boundary was difficult to explain away, and indeed it was not so much explained away as quietly disregarded. The air fleets of France paraded at intervals, to the increasing irritation of all her immediate neighbours, but on the whole as a restraining influence. The demonstration chilled the foreigner and assuaged the hotheads at home.

From the outset there was far less enthusiam for this 'localized' European war of 1940 than had been displayed by the populations of the belligerent countries in 1914. What enthusiasm was displayed was confined to the inexperienced young of the middle and upper classes, the youth of the Fascisti, Nazi, 'public schoolboy' and scoutmaster type. They went about, shouting and urgent, in a heavy, sullen and apprehensive atmosphere. No nation 'leapt to arms'. The common soldiers deserted and 'fell out' incessantly, and these shirkers were difficult to punish, since the 'deserter mentality' was so widespread, more particularly in the peasant armies of Eastern Europe, that it was impossible to shoot offenders. One Posen battalion went into battle near Lodz with thirty-nine officers and fifty-seven men.

From the first 'economies' marched with the troops. From the first there was a threadbare needy quality about the struggle. General orders insisted upon 'a restrained use of ammunition'.

The actual fighting was, however, on a much higher level, mechanically and scientifically, than the Japanese war in China. The military authorities had good roads, automobiles, camions, railways, rolling stock, electrical material, guns of all sorts, and great air forces available. Behind the fronts were chemical and other munition factories in good working order. If there were no longer infantry battles there were some brilliant conflicts of technicians. The prompt cutting off of East Prussia from any help from main Germany by the Permanent Death Gas was an operation far above the technical level of any Eastern operations. It was stategically silly but technically very successful.

The first offensive against Berlin was also planned with modern equipment and the maximum of contemporary military science. It was to be another 'blow at the heart', and the Polish general staff relied upon it as firmly as the Germans in 1914 had relied upon their march on Paris. Unfortunately for the Poles, it had been necessary to consult a number of 'experts' in preparing this advance; there were leakages through France, through the Czech and Swedish munition makers, through Russia, and through domestic treason, and the broad outline of the plan was as well known and understood in Berlin as it was in Warsaw. The great gas raid on Berlin was indeed terrifying and devastating, but the rush of tanks, great caterpillar guns and troops in motor transport was held and checked within sixty miles of the German capital by an ingenious system of poison-gas barriers – chiefly Lewisite and Blue Cross – wired mines and 'slime pits' of a novel type in the roads and open fields. A cavalry raid to the north between Berlin and the sea failed disastrously amidst wire, gas and machine-guns; nearly forty thousand men were killed, wounded or taken prisoner. Moreover, there had been mistakes in the manufacture of the gas masks worn by the Polish troops, and several brigades gave way to the persuasion that they had been sold and betrayed. The main Polish masses never came into actual contact with the German troops, and only their great numerical superiority in aeroplanes saved their repulse from becoming a rout.

The Polish armies rallied and, according to the secondary plan prepared for any such failure, extended themselves and dug themselves in along a line between Stettin and the Bohemian frontier. Behind the barrier they began a systematic reduction of Silesia. Every night an air battle raged over both Berlin and Warsaw. It was often an indecisive battle. The Poles had the numerical superiority, but the German machines were more efficient and better handled. But the Poles had far more of the new aerial torpedoes – which could go to an assigned spot two hundred miles away, drop a large bomb and return – than their adversaries.

Bohemia, like France, had mobilized but did not immediately enter the war. The Czecho-Slovak armies remained in their mountain quadrilateral or lined out along the Hungarian front, awaiting the next turn in the game. Austria also remained excited, but neutral.

The Southern war opened brilliantly for the Italians, and for some weeks it went on without any formal connexion with the Polish conflict. Bulgaria, Albania and Hungary also declared war upon Yugo-Slavia, the Italian air forces 'darkened the sky', and few of the towns in Croatia and Serbia escaped an aerial bombardment. The Italian fleet set itself to capture the ports and islands of Dalmatia. But the advance of the Italian troops into the hills of Slavonia and Croatia was not as rapid as had been expected. Six weeks passed before they were able to fight their way to Zagreb.

The country was a difficult one, ill adapted to the use of gas or mechanism; there was no central point at which a decisive blow could be struck; and the population had a long tradition of mountain warfare. It did not affect these sturdy peasants whether the townsmen were bombed or not. They never gave battle; they never exposed themselves in masses, but their bullets flew by day and night into the Italian encampments. The defenders went to and fro between their fields and the front. Munitions poured in for them through Roumania, which, with a big Red Army on its Bessarabian frontier and its own peasants recalcitrant, remained also ambiguously, dangerously, and yet for a time profitably, out of the struggle. The Hungarians crossed the Yugo-Slav frontier and threatened Belgrade, but the mass of their forces faced towards Czecho-Slovakia and awaited further events.

A curious pause in the fighting occurred at the end of the year. The frantic efforts of Prague, London and Paris to call a halt were temporarily successful. The invaders of Germany and Yugo-Slavia remained upon enemy territory, but neutral zones were improvised and there was a cessation of hostilities. An eleventh-hour attempt was made to stop the war by negotiation and keep the two conflicts from coalescence. There were weeks during which this seemed possible. Both Germany and Poland were of two minds about continuing the war now that the Polish advance was held, and Italy hoped to be left in possession of Dalmatia without an irksome campaign of further conquest. It was as if the spirit of civilization had once more come near to awakening from its hallucinations and had asked, 'Why on earth is this happening to us?'

The British Cabinet thought the occasion opportune for a conference at Vevey to revise the Treaty of Versailles 'finally'. The pacific speeches of Duff-Cooper, Hore-Belisha, Ellen Wilkinson and Randolph Churchill echoed throughout Europe and were brilliantly supported by Benito Caruso and Corliss Lamont in America. The Pope, the Archbishop of Canterbury, the Non-conformist Churches, the President of the Swiss Republic and the able and venerable President Benes swelled the chorus of remonstrance. France, which had been growing steadily more pacificist after her social conflicts in 1934–35, found able spokesmen in Louchère and Chavanne. Once again we are reminded of the impulses of Henry Ford and Wilson. Once again the concept of a World Pax flickered in the human imagination and vanished. This time it was a fuller, more explicit and more unanimous chorus than that which had cried aloud in 1916-17. Yet at the time it was hardly more effective. Vevey prolonged the truce throughout 1941 until June, but it could settle nothing. The military authorities, having had a breathing-time, became impatient. With a mutually destructive malice the fighting was resumed 'before the harvest could be gathered'.

Vevey failed because the constructive conception of the Modern State had no representative there. It was just another gathering of national diplomatists who professed to seek peace, and yet who set about the business with all those antiquated assumptions of sovereignty that were bound to lead to a revival of the conflict. The fantasy of some 'balance of power' was as near as they ever came to a peace idea. Such a balance was bound to sway from year to year and from day to day. Whatever the common people and men of intelligence were thinking, the experts now wanted to see the war fought to a finish. 'The Germans hadn't been beaten enough' was all too acceptable to the munition dealers and the Press in France and Scandinavia. 'The Italians have their hands full in Yugo-Slavia.'

The British and Americans, who hoped to keep out of the conflict to the end, had experienced an exhilarating revival of exports and found their bills against the belligerents mounting very hopefully. Once more Tyneside echoed to hammering; steel, iron and chemical shares boomed and the iron and steel industry, like some mangy, toothless old tiger, roused itself for the only quarry it had now the vigour to pursue – man-eating. It had long ceased to dream of new liners or bridges or railways or steel-framed houses. But it could still make guns and kill. It could not look far enough ahead to reckon whether at last there would be any meat on the man's bones. The only countries that really wanted peace, enduring peace, were Czecho-Slovakia and Austria, which stretched out between the two combatant systems and had possible enemy frontiers on every hand. The human will for peace as it found expression at Vevey was still a tangled and ineffective will.

The fighting revived almost simultaneously in the Polish Ukraine, where the peasants had revolted and were evidently fighting with Soviet officers and equipment, and in a vigorous surprise attack upon the Polish lines to free the German soil from the invader. The Germans had been working night and day during the truce to equalize conditions in the air; they produced new and swifter aeroplanes and a particularly effective machine-gun, and for some weeks there was such aerial fighting as was never seen before or since.

Gradually the Germans established a sufficient ascendancy to bring their bombers and gas into play. Lodz and Warsaw were terrorized and the civilian population evacuated and the Polish line broken so as to restore communications with Silesia. And then the conflict broadened.

Lithuania, evidently with Russian encouragement, seized her old city of Wilna, and Austria linked the Northern and the Southern struggle by entering both wars as the ally of Germany and Italy. Germany declared her final union with Austria. Very swifty now the remaining European states followed one another into the cauldron. Hungary attacked Eastern Czecho-Slovakia without a declaration of war 'to restore her legitimate boundaries', and brought the army frameworks of Roumania into the field against her. Thereupon Russia announced the impossibility of maintaining her understanding with France in the face of these events, and the Red Army advanced on Lemberg. Macedonia was already a seething mass of fighting, village against village; Bulgaria entered the 'South Slav' alliance and assailed Albania, and Greece seized Rhodes, which had been up to that time held by Italy.

So France saw her ancient policy of 'security', of setting state to balance state and allying herself with a countervailing state at the back of every antagonistic neighbour, work out to its necessary conclusion. Gladly would her business men and her peoples now have rested behind her immensely fortified frontiers and shared the profits of neutrality and munition-selling with the British and Americans, but her engagements were too binding. After one last ambiguous attempt on the part of London, Washington and Geneva to avert the disaster, France declared war against the Central European alliance in 1943.

On the face of it the new war resembled the World War of 1914-18. It seemed to be an attempt to reverse or confirm the Versailles settlement. It had an air of being the same sort of siege of Central Europe. But now Italy was in close alliance with the Teutonic powers; Belgium, in a state of extreme industrial distress, was out of the war; Britain stood aloof; and in the place of her former Allies France had to help – rather than be helped – by the band of states from the Corridor to the Black Sea and the Balkans which the Quai d'Orsay had toiled so painfullly to knit into an anti-German alliance.

Russia, however, was a doubtful ally of the Central Powers; she was not operating in concert with them; she was simply supporting the new Soviet republics in Eastern Poland and Bessarabia. There the Red Army halted. The old enthusiasm for a World Revolution had faded out of the Russian imagination. Marxism had become so Russianized that it feared now to take in too large a contingent of Western adherents. The Kremlin was content to consolidate the kindred Slav Soviets and then rest. Japan and China and the American continent remained out of the mêlée, concentrated on their own social difficulties.

It would be possible for a superficial student to regard all this merely as a rearrangement of the familiar counters of sovereign state politics. But in reality the forces in collision were profoundly different. France, in spite of her internal social stresses, was still a capitalist community of the nineteenth-century type, with democratic parliamentary forms and irresponsible finance and industrialism. Save for the teaching of a sentimental patriotism, her young people were mentally unorganized. Her allies were peasant states with governments of the royal or parliamentary form, and, if anything, more old-fashioned. But the Central Powers were all of the new Fascist pattern, more closely knit in its structure and dominated by an organization of the younger spirits, which claimed to be an élite.

Except for the fundamentally important fact that these Fascisti were intensely nationalist, this control by a self-appointed, self-disciplined élite was a distinct step towards our Modern State organization. These various Fascisti were destined to destroy their own states and disappear because of their essentially shallow and sentimental mentality, their inability to get outside nationalist traditions and coalesce; there is no direct continuity between them and our modern educational and administrative system; but there was nothing like them in the World War of 1914-18 anywhere, and they are noteworthy, as the Russian Communist Party (in spite of its proletarian formula) is noteworthy, for their partial but very real advance on democratic institutions. Amidst the chaos, that organized 'devotion of the young' on which our modern community rests was clearly foreshadowed in these Central European states. The idea of disciplined personal participation in human government was being driven into the mentality of the new generation.

Until something more convincing appeared, it had to crystalize, disastrously enough, about such strange nuclei as the theatrical Mussolini and the hysterical Hitler. It had to be patriotic because that was the only form in which the State then presented itself. But after these first crystallizations had been shattered and dissolved in the war disasters that now ensued, the idea was still there, this idea of banded cooperation ready to be directed to greater ends. Youth had ceased to be irresponsible in all the Fascist countries.

Not only were these new wars unlike their predecessors in the fact that they were not, so far as the Central Powers were concerned, wars of the democratic masses, but also they were quite unprecedented in the range and quality of the fighting. We have already indicated some of the main differences between the New Warfare and the Old. These now became accentuated by the extraordinary way in which the boundaries of the battling states interdigitated. In the first spurt of conflict there was indeed a 'front' between Poland and Germany; but after 1943 there was no front, no main objective, and no central idea to the storming destruction that spread over Europe.

The Poles tried to draw a line of Permanent Death Gas across East Brandenburg before their withdrawal to Posen, but their collapse came too swiftly, and they were able only to poison three small areas of no strategic importance. After 1943 the war became mainly a war in the air, with an increasing use of gas and landing raids, raids rather than invasions, to seize, organize and hold advantageous positions. A bitter and intense naval struggle went on in the Mediterranean to cut off reinforcements and supplies between North Africa and France, but there was little molestation of the Atlantic traffic of France.

There was never an Aerial Trafalgar, never an Air Ecnomus. War in three dimensions does not afford those channels, straits, narrow seas, passes, main roads, by which an inferior force may be brought to a decisive battle, and indeed to this day it is uncertain which side was absolutely predominant in the air. It was a war of raids and reprisals, and no large decisive operations were attempted. A big German infantry push into Posen was held by gas and slimes, and a French invasion of Italy got no further than Turin.

The complete exhaustion of the adversary, materially and morally, became the only possible road to any sort of victory. Once more the tormented populations were urged to sustain a 'war of attrition'. 'It is the man who holds out half an hour longer than the other who wins' was translated into every European language. The attacks on social order increased in malignancy as the impossibility of any military decision became manifest. Crops and forests were deliberately fired, embankments smashed, low-lying regions flooded, gas and water supplies destroyed. The aviators would start off to look for a crowd and bomb it. It became as cruel as the fighting of ferrets.

There was still, in spite of a decade of financial dislocation and industrial depression, a vast amount of mechanical material in Europe; everywhere there were factories strongly protected against air attack and skilfully camouflaged. Moreover, all the chief belligerents had sufficiently open frontiers for the importation of material, so long as anything compact and valuable could be wrung out of their nationals by tax or levy, to pay for such supplies. The goods crossed the frontier at night; the cargoes were piloted into unlit harbours. Every able bodied adult not actually in the fighting forces was pressed to work at excavations for bomb shelters and the reconstitution of buildings against gas and high explosive. Much of this also was night work. Recalcitrance and shirking were punished by a deprivation of rations. There is a grim picture by Eglon Callet called 'Security at Last', of which the reader may have seen reproductions. A chain gang of emaciated and ragged Frenchmen is working under the lash in a tunnel. In the foreground one who had fainted is being given a stimulant; another, past help, dies untended.

In comparison with the abundant literature of personal experiences in the World War, at least so far as the Western front was concerned, there are remarkably few records either of combatant or non-combatant adventures during the Fighting Forties. The big air raids seem to have been altogether horrible. They were much more dreadful than the air raids of the World War. They began with a nightmare of warning maroons, sirens, hooters and the shrill whistles of cyclist scouts, then swarms of frantic people running to and fro, all pride and dignity gone, seeking the nearest shelter and aid, and they ended for most of their victims in an extremity of physical suffering.

We have already given some intimation of the nature of those torture deaths. In nearly every case the organization of refuges and gas masks broke down. In many cases there had never been a real provision, but only sham visors and sham bomb-proof buildings to allay 'premature' panic and 'keep up the popular morale'. None of these great raids was ever reported in the newspapers that still struggled on into the war years. Even in America the publication of any detail was treated as 'pacificist propaganda against recruiting'.

There is a descriptive letter from Berlin after an air raid, undated and signed 'Sinclair', which is believed by most competent critics to have been written by Sinclair Lewis the novelist (1885–1990). One passage may be quoted:

– 'We went down Unter den Linden and along the Sieges Allee, and the bodies of people were lying everywhere, men, women and children, not scattered evenly, but bunched together very curiously in heaps, as though their last effort had been to climb on to each other for help. This attempt to get close to someone seems to be characteristic of death by this particular gas. Something must happen in the mind. Everyone was crumpled up in the same fashion and nearly all had vomited blood. The stench was dreadful, although all this multitude had been alive twenty-four hours ago. The body corrupts at once. The archway into the park was almost impassable. . . .'

So we get one glimpse of how peaceful town-bred people might die a century and a half ago.

The individual stories of the actual fighting in that last warfare are no more ample than the non-combatant descriptions. There was little inducement for anyone to write about it in the subsequent decades; there was not the same high proportion of literate men as there was in the Western armies during the Great War; there was a less artless interest in what was happening and more running away, desertion, apathy, drunkenness, raping, plundering and malignant cruelty, which are not things of which men leave records. The whole world was less sensitive than it had been thirty years before; if it suffered more grossly it suffered less acutely. In 1914–15 many of the British and German rankers kept diaries from day to day. This shows a sense of personality and a receptiveness to events quite outside the sullen fatalism, shot with gleams of primitive exaltation or fury, which seems to have been the prevalent state of mind in the armies of the Forties.

In the Historical Documents Series there is a diary of a Japanese officer who was killed in the retreat from Wuchang. Failing any European material of the same kind, it may perhaps be quoted here to show how it felt to fight in the last war of all. It is not, however, a very vivid document. He was an intellectual, a socialist and a strong believer in the League of Nations, and his record is mainly a series of hostile criticisms in cipher of the superior command. But in the latter half these dissertations die out. The diary becomes a broken record of what he found to eat and drink and how he fought against influenza and dysentery. He seems to have had a company of men with him; he notes twice when he contrived a haul of food for them, and he jots down names as they are killed or missing. There are also figures that may be a note of his diminishing ammunition. He was already badly starved when he was killed. As he weakened he seems to have found his rather complicated cipher too difficult to use, and he lapsed first into bad English and then into plain Japanese. The very last item is an unfinished poem, a fragment in the old style, which might be rendered as follows:

> Almond blossom in the spring sunshine,
> Fuji-Yama gracious lady,
> Island treasure home of lovely things,
> Shall I never see you again? . . .

Something, death perhaps, prevented the completion of his naïve verses. He and his detachment were probably overtaken and done to death near Kai-feng.

In none of these later war memoirs is there anything to recall that queer quality of the 1914-18 stories, of men who felt they were going out from absolutely sure and stable homes and cities, to which with reasonable good fortune they would return – and live happily ever afterwards. The mood then was often extraordinarily brave and tender. The men of this late cycle of wars felt that there would be no such home-coming. They knew that they went out to misery and left misery in active possession at home. Their war was not an expedition; it was a change for ever. The memoirs of the airmen who did so much destruction are amazingly empty. They note fights, but quite flatly. 'Put down two Polaks', for example; 'a close shave'; but they do not seem to have had an inkling of the effect of the bombs they dropped upon the living flesh below. Many of these young men survived to become Modern State aviators and to serve the Air and Sea Control after 1965. But though some wrote well of their later experiences, none of them has left any useful documents for the history of the war time. The historian turns to his dates, maps and totals again from this meagre salvage of the hopes, fears, dreads, curiosities and agonies of the millions who went through that age of cruel disaster, doubtful whether he is sorry or thankful that most of that welter of feeling and suffering has vanished now as completely as though it had never been.

After 1945 the signs of exhaustion multiplied. Such despair had come to the souls of men that even defensive energy failed. They lay starving in their beds and hovels and let the bombs fall about them. But a whiff of gas could still cause a panic, a headlong rush of tormented people coughing and spitting through the streets to the shelter pits. Influenza with its peculiar intensity of mental depression came again repeatedly after 1942, and in 1945 came cholera. These epidemics, though they seemed grave enough at the time, were the mere first scouts of that great 'Raid of the Germs' which was in preparation for disunited humanity. It was as if they were testing the defensive organization of mankind.

Except for air warfare, Britain and the North European neutrals were suffering almost as acutely as if they were actually at war. They had poured munitions into Europe and reaped a harvest of bad debts. After the first economic exhilaration due to this spate of employment, the exports from Great Britain, which had once been the pioneer of free world trade and cosmopolitan thought, dwindled to insignificance; the erstwhile creditor of the world could not collect such debts as were still due to her, and could not pay therefore for the food supply of her dwindling but still excessive population. Her former sanitation had rotted to filthiness under a régime of relentless saving. Housing in that disagreeable climate had passed from congestion to horror. The first cholera epidemic found her in the throes not only of famine but of civil disorder, controlled and suppressed by her highly mechanized army and by the still very powerful habits of orderliness and subordination in her people. Never, since the Black Death of the fifteenth century, had the British Isles known such a pestilence. And yet that cholera was only the precursor of the still more terrible experiences that were to follow it in the subsequent decade.

Slowly but surely the spirit of protest and mutiny spread through Europe. That growing despairful insubordination that had done so much to bring about the winding up of the World War in 1918 reappeared in new forms. But because now war was no longer primarily an infantryman's business, mass mutiny, such as had crippled the French offensives after 1917, taken Russia out of the war, and led to the final German collapse, had not now the same disabling effect. There were not the same big aggregations of men under exasperating discipline and in touch with 'subversive' suggestions. Power had passed over to the specialized forces – to the aviators and war technicians. By the use of small bombs, machine-guns and the milder gases they could 'handle' and disperse mass meetings and 'tranquillize' insurgent districts in a manner that would have been inconceivable to the street-barricade revolutionaries of the later eighteenth century.

Even strikes in the munition factories were no longer so effective as they had been, because even there the increased efficiency of power production had ousted the comparatively unskilled worker in his multitudes. For the same reason the propaganda of insurrectionary class-war Communism, though it now dominated the thought of nine-tenths of the European peasants and workers, found unexpected obstacles in its attempts to seize control of affairs. It could not repeat the Russian social revolution because the new conditions were entirely different. The Bolshevik success had been possible only through the backwardness of Russia and the absence of a technically educated social stratum. The unrest and insubordination of the common people in Central and Western Europe could and did produce passive resistances and local revolutionary movements, but it found opposed to it a whole system of aviators, mechanics, technicians, scientific workers and so forth who had learnt from Red Russia what sort of direction and planning to expect from a proletariat led by party politicians. Whatever they thought about their own governments – and already they were beginning to think in a very fresh and vigorous fashion about them – it was not towards democratic Communism that the minds of the scientific and technical workers were turning.

Nevertheless, with the help of organizers from Russia, the protest of humanity against the prolongation of the New Warfare took for a time the form of Communist risings. In 1947, in Marseilles, St Etienne, Paris, Barcelona, Milan, Naples, Hamburg, Lodz and Glasgow there were mutinies of troops under arms and risings sufficiently formidable to sustain provisional soviets for periods varying from a week to several months. The Hamburg and Glasgow soviets were the best organized and held out longest, collapsing only after considerable bloodshed. Almost everywhere there were minor incidents of the same character. And the formal suspension of the war by the responsible governments concerned was certainly due more than anything else to their terror of a general social revolt. As the material organization of the system was shattered, as the behaviour of the technicians became uncertain, the threatening visage of the class-vindictive proletarian drew nearer and nearer to the face of the stockbroker, the war-monger, the banker, the traditional ruler.

It took nearly three years to end the last war. The Conference of London in 1947 did its best to work out a stable settlement of Europe on the lines of the Versailles Treaty, but the politicians and diplomatists were still incapable of the frankness and generosity needed. Face-saving was so much more important than life-saving to these creatures that they actually allowed the now pointless hostilities to be renewed in 1948.

In the spring of 1949, however, at Prague, President Benes achieved what had seemed to be the impossible, and brought the fighting to an end. He did this by inventing a phrase and suggesting instead of a treaty, a 'Suspension of Hostilities'. Each Power was to remain in possession of the territory it occupied, and there was to be no further fighting pending the assembly of an unspecified Conference to be organized later. Influenza, cholera, and at last maculated fever, the progressive enfeeblement of economic life and new developments of human relationship, prevented that Conference from ever meeting. The Benes Suspension of Hostilities became a permanent suspension. It endures to this day.

X

The Raid of the Germs

That same dearth of detailed description which takes the colour out of the history of the last wars becomes even more apparent in the records of the epidemics that made any resumption of that warfare impossible. Diaries, letters and descriptive writing were out of fashion; there were other things to do and no surplus energy in the brain. It is as if the micro-organisms had taken a leaf out of the book of the Foreign Offices and found in mankind's confusion an opportunity for restoring the long-lost empire of the germs.

The attack began in the best style without a declaration of war. The first line of advance consisted of a variety of influenzas, impoverishing fevers, that were highly infectious and impossible to control under war conditions. The depleted strength of the belligerent populations, a depletion due to their reduced and disorganized nourishment and the collapse of their sanitary services, gave these infections full scope; they killed some millions and diminished the already lowered vitality of the great populations still further. That lowering of the general vitality was far more important than the actual mortality. Cholera and bubonic plague followed, and then, five years and more later, when the worst seemed to have passed, came the culminating attack by maculated fever.

This obscure disease, hitherto known only as a disease of captive baboons, seems to have undergone some abrupt adaptation to the kindred habitat of the human body; possibly there was some intermediate host which prepared the bacilli for their attack on mankind. Or it may be that the preceding epidemics had changed some hitherto defensive element in human blood. We are still quite in the dark upon these points because at that time there were no doctors or biologists with the leisure to record observations, even had they had time to make them, and scientific publications had ceased to appear anywhere.

The disease appeared first in the vicinity of the London Zoological Gardens and spread thence with incredible rapidity. It discoloured the face and skin, produced a violent fever, cutaneous irritation and extreme mental distress, causing an uncontrollable desire to wander. Then the bodily energy vanished in collapse and the victim lay down and died. The fever was not simply infectious through water, but transmitted by the almost impalpable scabs scratched off by the sufferer. Wind, water and the demented sick carried it everywhere. About half humanity was vulnerable, and so far as we know now all who were vulnerable took it, and all who took it died.

So the world's malaise culminated in the terrible eighteen months between May 1955 and November 1956, at which latter date Nature with a pitiless but antiseptic winter came to the rescue of the human remnant. No effectual cure was ever devised for this fever and no helpful palliative. It swept the whole world and vanished as enigmatically as it came. It is still a riddle for pathologists. It no longer affects even the surviving baboon population, so that investigators can make no cultures, nor attempt any experiments. There is no material. It came, it destroyed, and it seems to have at last committed suicide with some unknown anti-body of its production. Or the real disease, as Mackensen believes, may have been not the maculated fever at all, but the state of vulnerability to its infection. That vulnerability had spread unsuspected throughout the world, he thinks, in the Warring Forties. The actual pestilence was not the disease but the harvest of a weakness already prepared.

History is like the individual memory in this, that it tends to obliterate disagreeable experiences. One of the most nonsensical things that was ever said was that a country is happy that has no history. On the contrary, it is only the really secure and prosperous phases that have left anything like sufficient material for historical reconstruction. We know of the pleasant social life of all the centuries of abundance in Egypt; we know the greatness and conquests of Assyria; the court-life of Ajanta and Central Asia is pictured for us to share; but the days of military disaster leave nothing but a band of ashes, and the years of pestilence merely break the continuities of the record. There is a good account of the Plague of London (1665) written by Defoe (1659–1731), and the unwary reader has to be warned that that account was compiled and fabricated many years after the event by an ingenious writer who was not even an eyewitness. There is a painting by Raphael of the plague in Rome which is similarly reminiscent. Most of the great plagues of history took their dead and departed unportrayed. What concerns history is the subsequent social and economic dislocation. On that Clio becomes copious again. What goes on again matters to her, but what is dead is dead.

The flowering prosperity of the nineteenth and early twentieth centuries has left us an almost uncontrollable mass of record about people who knew nothing except hearsay of the more frightful experiences of mankind. We have novels, letters, diaries, memoirs, pictures, photographs and so on by the million. But there survives hardly a letter, no pictures, and not a book or newspaper to throw light on those years 1955 and 1956, little more than a century and a third ago, which were certainly the most terrible through which our race ever passed. What was written at the time was destroyed as infectious. Afterwards it was left for a new generation of Defoes and Stephen Cranes to contrive a picture.

The descriptions of Cable, Nath Dass, Bodesco and Martini seem to be fairly justifiable, and to these fictions the reader is referred. They ring the changes upon not only villages but towns and cities with none but dead men and women in them; people lying unburied and gnawed by packs of hungry dogs and solitary cats; in India the tigers and in Africa the lions came into the desolate streets, and in Brazil the dead population of whole districts was eaten chiefly by wild hog, which multiplied excessively. Rats swarmed, and with an unwonted boldness threatened even the immune.

One terror which is never omitted is the wandering of the infected. Nothing would induce them to remain in bed or hospital; nothing could keep them from entering towns and houses that were as yet immune. Thousands of these dying wanderers were shot by terror-stricken people whom they approached. That dreadful necessity horrifies us to-day as much as that other grim act of self-protection: the survivors in the boats of the big steamship *Titanic* which struck an iceberg in 1912 beating at the knuckles of the drowning men and women who clung to the sides and threatened to swamp them. For a while, under such desperate and revealing stresses, man ceased to obey the impulses of a social animal. Those of the population who resisted the infection – and with maculated fever the alternatives were immunity or death – gave way to a sort of despair and hatred against the filthy suffering around them. Only a few men with medical, military, priestly or police training seem to have made head against the disaster and tried to maintain a sort of order. Many plundered. On the whole, so far as the evidence can be sifted, women behaved better than men, but some few women who joined the looters were terrible.

The nightmare came and passed.

In January 1957 people were walking about in the deserted towns, breaking into empty houses, returning to abandoned homes, exploring back streets littered with gnawed bones or fully-clad skeletons, and they were still unable to realize that the wrath of Nature was over and life still before them.

Maculated fever had put gas warfare in its place. It had halved the population of the world.

XI

Europe in 1960

The more avanced student of history finds it necessary to work out in detail the local variations of the process by which the great patchwork of empires and nationalist states set up during the Age of European Predominance lost its defining lines, lost its contrasted cultures and its elaborate traditions, and ceased to divide the allegiance and devotion of men of good will. It was still standing – a hollow shell in 1933; in 1966 it had gone. It crumpled up, it broke down; its forms melted together and disappeared.

For the purposes of general education, the intricate interplay of personalities and accidents in this world débâcle can be passed over, as we pass over the details of the Great War or of Napoleon's various military campaigns, and as Gibbon, the author of the *Decline and Fall of the Roman Empire* (published between 1776 and 1788) passed over a thousand years of Byzantine court life. Nowadays that sort of history has become a mine for those admirable biographical studies which are ousting the old romantic novel from the entertainment of our leisure so soon as our imaginations have passed beyond the purely romantic stage. All that is needed for our present purpose is some understanding of the broader forces that were operating through this lush jungle of human reactions.

The tempo of human affairs increases continually, and the main difference between the decline and fall of the Roman system and the decline and fall of the world rule of private-profit capitalism in the twentieth century lies in the far more rapid onset and development of the later collapse. A second important difference is the much livelier understanding of what was happening on the part of the masses involved. Each of these two great depressions in the record of human well-being was primarily a monetary breakdown, due to the casual development of financial and proprietary law and practice without any reference to a comprehensive well-being, and to the lag in political and educational adaptation which left the whole system at last completely without guidance. But while the former débâcle went to the pace of the horse on the paved road and of the written and spoken word, the phases of the new downfall flashed about the globe instantaneously and evoked a body of thought and reaction out of all comparison greater than the Roman precedent. So we see only a much compressed and abbreviated parallelism. From the demoralization of the deflated Roman Empire by the great plagues at the end of the second century of the Christian era, to the reappearance of commerce, industry, art and politeness in the cities of the thirteenth and fourteenth centuries, was well over a thousand nerveless years; from the invasion of Belgium by the Germans in 1914 to the return of general material prosperity under the Air dictatorship after 2010 was roughly a century.

The mental process, if for this reason alone, was much more continuous. It got to its conclusions while still in contact with its premises. The first world collapse was spread over a number of generations, each one oblivious of the experiences of its predecessor, but the larger and swifter part of the second world collapse fell well within the compass of a single long life. People who could remember the plentiful and relatively stable times between 1924 and 1928 as young men and women were still only at the riper end of middle age in 1960. Many who were children at the onset of the Hoover Slump were taking an active part in affairs in the days of the first international police, the Police of the Air and Sea Ways. It was possible to grasp what was happening as one whole. It is doubtful if any Roman citizen under the Empire ever grasped what was happening.

Nevertheless in each case there was a parallel obliteration of old ideas, the same effacement of boundaries, the same destruction of time-honoured traditions, the lapsing of debts and obligations, the disappearance of religious and educational organizations, the impoverishment of favoured and privileged classes, the recrudesence of lawlessness, the cleansing disillusionment. Each was the effectual liquidation of a bankrupt civilization preparatory to a drastic reconstruction.

We will now take a sort of rough cross-section of the world at about the date of 1960 CE, and consider the condition of the main masses of the world's population and the great forces at work among them. In the light of subsequent events we can realize that there was already a very considerable convergence of conditions going on throughout the middle decades of the century. But it may be doubted whether that was evident at the time. The goal towards which the fundamental bionomic forces were driving was everywhere the same, but the particulars varied widely with the geographical, ethnic and traditional circumstances, and their immediate interpretations were even more diverse.

We have viewed the events of the Era of European Predominance as the outcome of an uncontrolled irregularity in growth, of economic hypertrophy in a phase of political and cultural atrophy. An immense increase in the energy of human society had occurred which had relieved itself partly in a great multiplication of the human population (Europe from 180 to 420 millions between 1800 and 1914, says Werner Sombart, in spite of a great emigration), partly in a monstrous exaggeration of warfare, and less considerably in an increased fullness and speed of the individual life. But, as we have related, the forces of conservativism and functional resistance embodied in the creditor and legal systems were presently able to give pause to the release of fresh energy. For the second time in human experience the inadaptable quality of the financial and proprietary organization produced a strangulation and an arrest.

The money and credit organization of the prosperity of the nineteenth century differed in many respects from, and was more elaborate than, the Roman, but its life history was essentially the same. It wound itself up in the same fashion. First came a vast expansion and increase of private fortunes and then destructive taxation. So far history repeated itself. The European system, like the Roman system before it, impoverished itself finally by the violent expenditure of its vast windfall of energy. It repeated the same blind story of wastage, but with the unprecedented headlong facilities science afforded it. It ran through its available fortune and was helplessly in debt in a few decades. The height of its expenditure was between 1914 and 1950. Thereafter the pace was less catastrophic.

Regarded even as destruction, the New Warfare proved in the end to be a failure. It went to pieces when it was attempted. It did not kill as it might have killed – which is why the reader is alive to read this history. The actual battles of the European wars in the Forties – the purely military operations, that is to say – in all their ramifications cost mankind hardly a quarter of the battle slaughters of 1914–18. And yet they mark the highest level of scientific fighting ever attained by mankind. The Asiatic troubles had been more destructive because they were nearer the barbaric level, but even there the actual deaths in warfare are estimated as under nine million. Of these, nearly five million are to be ascribed to the final offensive of Japan in 1938, the deadlock in Central China, the desperate fighting with the Kuomintang levies west of Hankow, and the subsequent retreat.

Man had fallen as short as all that of the magnificent horrors he had anticipated. He had failed to raise war to its ultimate mechnical level. The social and political dislocation following upon these two main struggles was indeed proportionately far greater than the disorder of 1917–19, but warfare was its prelude rather than its cause. This New Warfare, which the prophets had said would end in a scientific massacre of mankind, passed insensibly into a squalor of political fiascos, unpayable debts, unsubscribed loans, scrapped machinery, insurrection, guerilla and bandit conflicts, universal hunger and the great pestilences. Gas warfare and air war faded out of the foreground of human experience, dwarfed and overwhelmed by the more primitive realities of panic, famine and fever. The ultimate victor in the middle twentieth century was the germ of maculated fever. The main causes in the fall of the world's population from about two thousand million in 1930 to a little under half that total in 1960 were diseases or simple starvation, arising directly from the complete economic collapse. Where war slew its millions in a few great massacres, pestilence slew its hundreds of millions in a pitiless pursuit that went on by day and night for two terrific years.

As Imhoff has said, there is no single European history of these Famished and Pestilential Fifties which followed so swiftly on the war years; there are ten million histories. The various governments created by the Treaty of Versailles were for the most part still legally in existence throughout this age, but with the monetary cessation they had become so faded and ineffective that they had ceased to have any great influence on everyday life. Some, like the British and the French, limited their activities to efforts – generally quite futile efforts, at tax-collecting; they went on finally in a way which will remind the student of the old tribute-levying Empires before the Helleno-Latin period. They interfered spasmodically with local affairs, but for the most part they let them drift. They ignored or compromised with active resistance. The British government was still, it seems, paying arrears upon its various loans, in 1952, to such stockholders as it was able to trace. The records are obscure; the payments seem to have been made in a special paper currency without real purchasing power. Other governments, like the Italian and Spanish, carried on as real administrative bodies within restricted areas. Rome, for instance, remained in fairly effective control of the triangle marked out by Genoa, Florence and the Mediterranean Coast, and Barcelona and Madrid kept order throughout most of the Peninsula except the Sovietized Spanish Riviera, Portugal and Andalusia.

The process in America was roughly parallel. Detachment was easier so soon as the bankrupt railways ceased to operate there, because the distances between population centres were greater and the capacity of the people for local autonomy much greater. They were still not a century from pioneering. The railways never resumed after the pestilence. The authority of the Federal Government of the United States shrank to Washington, very much as the Eastern Empire shrank to Byzantium, but Washington had none of the vitality of Byzantium, and it was already a merely historical capital long before the revival of tourism towards 2000. Germany as a unity did not survive the Polish wars, and Berlin dwindled rapidly to the status of a group of villages amidst the ruins of the Polish aerial bombardments.

The practical effacement of these bankrupt political systems in a few years, the equally rapid drying up of general transport and communications, the crescendo of the monetary breakdown, the speedy degeneration of military organizations, threw back the tasks of social order upon such local and regional leading as still existed. They found themselves astonishingly called upon. In Europe, as all over the world throughout this extraordinary decade, towns, cities, rural districts, discovered themselves obliged to 'carry on' by themselves. The plague only drove home that imperative need. The municipal authorities organized such health services as they could against the infection, or gave way to emergency bodies that took things out of their hands. When the plague disappeared, they were like shipwrecked sailors on a strange island; they had to reconstitute their shrunken economic life. They used old authority for new needs and old terms for new things. Here it would be an energetic leader who called himself the Mayor or the Duke, here a resolute little band, self-styled the Town Council or the Citizens' Union. Here 'advanced' terminology prevailed, and it was a 'Soviet of Workers' which took control. In effect the latter would be very similar to a Citizen's Union. Its chief distinction was its consciousness of being in a new social phase.

There was the most extraordinary variation in the political structure of this phase of dislocation, and a flat contradiction between the actual and the 'legal' controls. Across Southern Germany, Poland and North France, the prevalent impression was one of social revolution, and soviets were in fashion. But they were very different in character from the original local Russian soviets. It was possible to find a Communist district referring itself vaguely to Moscow, lying side by side with another that was under the control of its former owners and employers and professed to be, and often was, still in communication with the national government in the capital. An uneasy truce would be maintained between these theoretically antagonistic systems. Deputations would go for authority in various disputes – arrears of taxes in hand – to Westminster, Paris or Rome, very much as the barbarian chiefs of the Early Mediaeval period would upon due occasion refer to Byzantium or Rome. Local conflicts and revolutions were constantly occurring. They were recognized at the capitals only as local riots and municipal readjustments.

Scattered through this disarticulating Europe were the vestiges of the old militarism, broken fragments of unpaid armies with irreplaceable weapons and a dwindling supply of ammunition. They consisted of the officers who were soldiers by profession, and the levies who had not been disbanded or who had refused to be disbanded because there was no employment for them outside the ranks. These men had their officers very much under control because of the great facilities for desertion. In some cases these shrivelled military forces were in contact with the capital and the old legal government, and conducted, or attempted to conduct, tax requisitions and suchlike surviving functions of the old order; in other instances they became frankly brigand forces, though often with high-sounding titles, Public Order Guards or the Emergency Army. Most merged with the local police of aggressive Mayors or councils. Small wars of conquest went on in the early Sixties. Old empires and sovereign states reappeared, in duplicate or triplicate, and vanished or became something else. After 1960 there were even quasi-military forces levying contributions, keeping a sort of order, and professing to be Modern State nuclei. They would occupy the old barracks and accommodation of garrison towns.

In the Forties these soldiers had been raw recruits. In the following decades those who remained in their old formations became formidable middle-aged rascals in patched and shabby and supplemented uniforms. Some of the commandants had gained control of local aerodromes and local munition factories, but everywhere the military found themselves more and more out of sympathy with the technical workers they needed to make these acquisitions effective. They degenerated to the level of the nineteenth-century infantry and were at last glad to get even a few thousand roughly made cartridges to replenish their supply.

Under the necessity of doing things for themselves, people did things for themselves that they had left to the central government for a century. Even during the World War, and in the year or so of stress that followed it, various French Chambers of Commerce had supplemented the deficiency in small change by local token coinages. Now this practice reappeared widely. Today our museums contain hundred of thousands of specimens of these improvised European coins of lead, nickel, tin and all sort of alloys, *jetons* or checks of wood, and tons of signed, printed paper notes, useful in the local market, acceptable for rents and local taxes, but of no avail at all at a distance of a few score miles. The local bank manager as often as not would improvise a local credit system in cooperation with the local solicitor; the doctors would contrive a way of getting along without the Home Office. There were still printers' establishments in most centres of population, and for some years local periodicals, often of considerable originality, appearing weekly or monthly and printed on the roughest and most variable paper, supplied all that remained alive of the European Press. But their foreign news amounted to little more than rumour. The great Press agencies were bankrupt and dead; the telegraph organization was out of gear.

Save in a few exceptional centres, the diffusion of news by radio died out completely. The manufacture of receiving sets was entirely disorganized. From 1930 to 1970 the 'ether' for all except special purposes of air transport was still. There is a long and interesting study in the Historical Record Series of the vicissitudes of posts, telegraphs and telephones between 1950 and 1980. There seem to have been extraordinary survivals. Apparently London, Paris and Rome were in telephonic communications almost without a break, and the news of the great London landslide was telephoned to Madrid and thence radioed to Buenos Aires in 1968. But that may have been a revival connected with the new Air and Sea Control.

The disappearance not only of radio sets but of an enormous variety of small conveniences and appliances was extraordinarily rapid after the collapse of world trade. Photography, for instance, was wiped out almost at once. The bicycle became rare, and the old pneumatic tyre was replaced by a thin solid one of often very badly adulterated 'remade' rubber. Electric lighting flickered out and vanished for want of the proper material for filaments. All electrical material deteriorated, and tramway systems either fell into complete disuse or returned to horse traction.

Ordinary life had been lowering its standards bit by bit from the World War onward. First one thing went and then another. Neither in the British nor the French provinces did the housing of the common people recover from the cessation of building during the actual warfare. Except in places like Berlin or Vienna where there had been a vigorous outbreak of post-war building which provided accommodation in excess for the shrunken population, the mass of Europeans were even more congested and dirty in their domestic accommodation than they had been before the conflict, though indeed they never sank to the immemorial squalor and poverty of the Chinese and Indian towns. Cleanliness diminished at such a pace as to be noted even by the newspapers after 1933. There are constant complaints of the dirtiness of the streets and the bad repair of the roads, and regretful comparisons with the trim orderliness of twenty years before.

Clothing declined with housing. The clothing trade shrank steadily per head of population for nearly forty years. The city crowds, in spite of the more and more abundant uniforms (until 1950), lost nearly all their former brightness and élan. People patched up their old clothing for want of new, and rags became increasingly common. The supply of boots was very restricted. The mass production of boots had been commandeered at the outbreak of the war and was never turned back to commercial use because of the complete financial ruin that ensued. But the old-fashioned shoemakers had been driven off the face of Europe long before by this mass production, and so throughout the Famished Fifties the Europeans were very painfully shod. Spain had the best boots and France and Britain took to sandals – and chilblains. A certain manufacture of footwear went on in some centre in Bohemia, now untraceable, and next to Spain ranked Central Europe in the order of shoe welfare. There was an extreme scarcity of hats everywhere.

There was also a universal decline in the little comforts and accessories of life to which the world had grown accustomed. Except in a few favoured regions where it was actually grown, tobacco disappeared. The mass production of cigarettes died out, and those who smoked, smoked pipes of substitute. Real tea became a great rarity, and sugar was scarce. Dietetic diseases and diseases of under-nutrition increased.

During the strain and effort of the Great War most of the Europeans had already learnt something of contrivance and makeshift. Now they were to have a decade of domestic management under difficulties. The Germans were already familiar with the word Ersatz; there was much technical knowledge and ability diffused among them; and it is indisputable that they contrived to keep much nearer comfort than the rest of the world during these dismal years. They devised substitute leather, substitute cotton, substitute coffee and tea, substitute tobacco, substitute quinine and opium, and a very respectable list of other substitute drugs.

At the other extreme were the shiftless Irish. Until the return of production their physical misery was very great indeed. One observer doubted if there were a million yards of new cloth produced in that country between 1950 and 1960. 'They live,' he reported, 'on buttermilk, potatoes, whisky and political excitement. They have contrived garments of woven straw, often very picturesquely dyed, which they call Early Erse and of which they boast inordinately, and they warm themselves by means of fires of peat and dung and a great warmth of mutual invective.' This sounds quite barbaric. Yet it is to this period that we owe the graceful – though, according to a recent Historical Documents report, rather rickety – Church of the Atonement, built on the site of the Dublin Royal College of Science after that had been suppressed by the Censorship of 1939 for 'teaching biology in a manner tending to disintegrate the Holy Trinity'.

The student must be more or less familiar with the representations of this period in that useful compilation *Historical Scenes in a Hundred Volumes*, and he has probably read a number of romances and stories of this time. Actual photographs are least abundant in the later fifties and early sixties. There were still plenty of cameras in the world, but the supply of films seems to have died out after 1955, and there are hardly any but slow wet-plate exposures after that time for nearly ten years. We get only a few score of such animated snapshots as were abundant during the preceding decades, and there are no European cinematograph films at all. Neither was there much sketching except of single figures, and so the editors have had to supplement their material by very carefully studied drawings and photographed restorations made at a later date.

There are six interesting snapshots of scenes in Lyons in 1959. Someone seems to have found a spool of film and been able to develop it. One shows the big central square, the Place Bellecour as it was called, on a market day. Earlier pictures show a big bronze equestrian figure of

Louis xiv, but this had already disappeared, probably it had been melted for its metal; and the windows of some of the big buildings, formerly hotels and hospitals, in the background have the empty frameless look of gutted houses. But the scene is quite a busy one. It was probably the monthly market, and there is a considerable amount of cattle, numerous horses being traded, hurdled sheep, many goats and a row of pig-pens. The people are mostly peasants wearing straw hats and either very old coats or in some cases shawls wrapped about them. Townspeople are still wearing the clothing of the Thirties, shabby and patched, and there are three market officials or magistrates in the old-world top hat. In the foreground a bearded man leads a couple of oxen harnessed to a small 'runabout' car in which a corpulent woman sits in front with a crate of ducklings while behind is a netted calf. The lady smiles broadly at the camera, unaware that she is smiling at posterity.

Another of these snapshots shows a bowls competition in the deserted railway station. It is clearly a festive occasion, and several games are in progress. The rails have disappeared from the tracks, which have been levelled for the game, and the ponies and mules of the players are tethered on the platform in a long line. The doors of the various bureaus have been taken away, but the inscriptions *Chef de Gare, Salle d'Attente, Restaurant*, are still faintly visible. There are two long tables on one of the middle platforms on which simple refreshments are being served. A third picture shows a crowd staring at the ruins of a row of houses which have just collapsed down a steep slope in what is apparently the district know as Fourvière. Here two bearded men in the unmistakable uniform of the old Alpini are keeping order. We know as a matter of fact that the Lyons municipality at that time had three regiments of these soldiers quartered in barracks. They are wearing sandals supplemented by cloth strips that are twisted round their legs, and their cloaks are in good condition.

Three others of these photographs give us a glimpse of the state of affairs in a disused silk factory. Up to the time of the economic collapse, the silk manufacture at Lyons was still largely that produced by the silkworm, but the supply of raw material seems to have died out more or less completely in the Rhône valley, and the shrinkage of trade and then the war diminished the importation of the reeled-up thread. But silk was needed in the manufacture of shells, and probably there were special efforts to maintain the supply up to the last. This particular establishment seems to have been carrying on a diminished output until the Lyons commune in 1951. Then no doubt it was abruptly abandoned. One photograph shows a great heap of paper litter among weaving-machines shrouded in spiders' webs and fine dust. In a third a wild cat crouches among the spindles of a spinning-machine and spits at the unwanted intruder. The machinery has all the complicated clumsiness characteristic of twentieth-century mechanism. Apparently a window of some sort was opened or a blind drawn back to make this particular photograph, for the picture is blurred with a multitude of whirling moths, most of them out of focus, evidently just stirred up.

These particular pictures are valuable because of their authenticity. There are also two contemporary dry-plate pictures of the Café Royal, the big restaurant of the Grand Hotel of Stockholm, deserted and still intact. They are oddly suggestive of two pictures of the ruins of the Baths of Caracalla in Rome as they appeared a hundred years earlier. And there is also a photograph of the remains of the old dining-room of the Hotel Métropole at Brighton in England before it was undermined and fell into the sea. But all the rest of the pictures given in *Historical Scenes* between 1955 and 1963 are arranged pictures. The Transport organization was running scores of aeroplanes and radio communications were restored long before the complex manufacture of photographic apparatus and material was set going again.

There are some very interesting restorations of conditions in London showing the empty streets and the vacant tumbledown warehouses of the city after the pestilence. The pictures of the corridors of the hotels in the Strand turned into hospital wards are very impressive. So too is the sketch of a great fight between the cow-keepers and the potato-growers for the possession of Hyde Park and Kensington Gardens in which three hundred people were killed. The dreadful pictures of the bodies of plague victims floating down the Thames and accumulating in the Pool of London, however, are now said to be exaggerated.

We try in the midst of our present securities to imagine the phases of anxiety, loss, incredulity and reluctant acquiescence through which the minds of hundreds of millions of Europeans passed, day by day, from the general comfort of the Twenties, through the shocks, fear, horror, rage and excitement of the war cycle, into this phase of universal impotence and destitution. The poor perhaps had a less vivid apprehension of disaster than the rich. Even in the days of General Prosperity, as it is called, they had at the best what we should consider very dull, drab, irksome lives. Even though they mostly ate sufficiently, they ate badly, and there was never a stage of universal decent housing at any time for them. They went from bad to worse. They passed from toil to unemployment and lethargy. But the middling sort passed from good to bad, from something one might almost consider tolerable living to the hopeless neediness of the masses.

A class that went through great unhappiness everywhere during this period was the class of elderly and 'retired' persons and persons of 'independent means' (and no responsibilities) which had expanded so enormously during the First Age of General Prosperity. This superfluity of prosperous humanity had spread itself out very pleasantly over the world, oblivious of the exertions that sustained social discipline and ensured its security. Insensibly it had taken the place of the old

administrative and directive noblesse and country gentry. The investment system during its period of steady efficiency had relieved this social
stratum of every bother. There were great areas of agreeable country,
residential districts, given up to this 'well-off' society, to its gardens,
which were often delightful, its golf-courses, race-courses, mountain
sport centres, parks, country clubs, plages, and hotels. It wilted a little
during the World War, but revived again very hopefully in the decade
of hectic and uncertain expansion that followed. Then, as the Great
Slump developed its grim phases, this life of leisure passed away.

The Phase of Economy is really a misnomer. There was really no
economy; there was strangulation and inaction through a cessation of
expenditure. Nobody – unless it was a dexterous speculator on a falling
market – grew richer, or even relatively richer. The only profits appeared
in bank balance sheets. As the malady of arrest spread, traffics declined,
enterprise died out, borrowing states and corporations suspended
payments, and these children of good fortune, these well-off people,
found themselves confronted at the same time by a suspension of
payments and more and more urgent charitable appeals. Their bankers
and solicitors informed them that first this trusted prop and then that
was in arrears or default. The waters of repudiation rose, submerging
security after security. If they sold out and hoarded, some fluctuation in
exchange might still engulf great fractions of their capital. 'Whatever
else may be falling off, sleepless nights are on the increase,' a financial
paper remarked in 1933. The head full of self-reproach that tossed on
the crumpled pillow in the villa marked time with the fretting of the
unemployed who worried in the stuffy cold of the slum.

We have the *Diary of Titus Cobbett*, who rode on a bicycle from
Rome and along the Riviera to Bordeaux in 1958. He had begun life as
an art dealer, and had served the British Inland Revenue for some years
as a valuer of furniture, pictures and the like. His tour seems to have
been a journey of curiosity. He complains bitterly of the difficulty of
changing money between Genoa and Bordeaux. He seems to have had
some obscure diplomatic or consular function, but of that he is too
discreet to speak. Perhaps he was sent to make a report, but if so there
is no record of his instructions.

His description of that smitten coast is still very interesting reading.
He had, as a young man with good connections, known Monte Carlo
well in the twenties, and the places he visited were often those at which
he had stayed as a guest. He records the abandonment of hundreds of
lovely châteaux, locked-up, unsaleable, abandoned, in the keeping
perhaps of some old domestic, or frankly looted by the people of the
district, once delightful gardens whose upkeep had become impossible,
blind tangles of roses, oleanders, pomegranates, oranges, cypresses,
palm trees, agaves, cacti and weeds; unremunerative hotels allowed to
fall into ruins, broken-down water-conduits washing away the roads,

bungalows taken over by the peasants. Something of the same swift desolation must have come upon the Campagna and the villadom of the Bay of Naples during the ebb of Roman vitality, but this had been a swifter decline. The roads, he says, were very variable, but a great number of the road signs and roadside advertisements were still making their mute appeal to a vanished traffic. As he rode along wondering whether he would find a reasonably clean and hospitable shelter for the night, he read, he says, picked out in metallic knobs that answered brightly to his oil lamp:

```
          H  TEL  S  LEN  ID
          CU  SINE  RENOM
   T  T  LE  C  NFOR  M    RNE
```

Whither had host and guests departed? Where were the owners and tenants of these villas and gardens; the bright clientèle of the pleasure resorts? Many of them no doubt were already dead, for the Riviera owners had been mostly middle-aged and oldish people. The rest were back in their own countries leading impoverished lives, full of tiresome reminiscences, lost in the universal indigence.

Cobbett visited the ruins of the old Casino at Monte Carlo, and the younger Sports Club. The ceiling of the American Bar had fallen in a few days before his visit. 'They looked small,' he says. 'When I was young they had seemed tremendous places.'

The celebrated garden in which suicidal gamblers used to put an end to their troubles was overgrown with mesembryanthemum.

Yet there was one exception to this general decadence, and our observer stresses the significance of that. Air traffic was still going on. Between Rome and Marseilles he notes very precisely that he saw thirteen aeroplanes going east or west, beside two that he heard before he got up in the morning. 'I doubt if I should have seen so many twenty-five years ago,' he writes, and goes on to enlarge, very illuminatingly, on the revival of trade and the possible revival of order these throbbing mechanisms portended. At Nice and at Marseilles he noted there was shipping – 'not mere fishing boats but ships of a thousand tons or more'; and at Nice they were building a bigger ship – he estimated it as a three-thousand tonner. We have no other records of shipbuilding between 1947 and 1962. Long before 1940 the building of very big ships had ceased to be a 'a paying proposition' and it is fairly certain that no sea-going ships whatever, big or little, were built anywhere in the world in the early fifties. Year by year the transport system of the bankrupt planet had been sinking into disuse. It is only nowadays that our historical students are attempting to work out statistical charts of that swift decadence.

Cobbett also notes with surprise and hope a stretch of railway (operated by lever trolleys and a petrol engine or so) between the port of Marseilles and some inland quarries. He was clearly under the impression that no railways were operating in the world any longer. So soon as the traffic had sunken to a level below the possibility of paying subsistence wages, maintaining the permanent way and meeting running expenses, it had been impossible even for speculative buyers to handle these once valuable properties. They had become old junk on the landscape, tracks of torn and rusty rails smothered in agaves and wild flowers. He mentions the beauty of the viaducts of the old Sud de France, and tells how he bicycled along the footworn side-path of the Paris-Lyon-Méditerranée in preference to the road. The peasants had used the derelict railway as a convenient iron-mine, and few rails remained. Most of the sleepers had been used for fuel.

At Fréjus there was an aerodrome, and here he describes a very illuminating conversation with a Spanish-American aviator who had served first with the Poles, then with the Germans, and finally with the French during the warfare. Cobbett was impressed by the evident revival of trade, and suprised to find rubber, spices, mercury and block-tin among the commodities coming by air from the East, while clocks, watches, compasses, knives, needles, buttons, hardened glass and the like were going back in exchange. Most of the trade was barter, and the profits were so considerable that there seemed every reason to expect a steady expansion of the service.

He seems to have learnt for the first time of the developing combination of air-merchants, who were mostly aviators surviving from the war. They had already organized a loose world union, it seems, and were keeping the airways and air lights in order.

Cobbett remarked on the shippng revival he had noted.

'We shall have to watch that,' said the aviator significantly.

'You take passengers?'

'When they can pay a passage.'

'But this is civilization coming back!' cried Cobbett.

'Don't believe it! It's a new civilization beginning.'

And he seems to have opened Cobbett's eyes for the first time to some of the ideas that were already taking shape in such brains as his. 'World Empire?' he said. 'That's an old idea! The men who hold the air and the transport hold the world. What do we want with empires and that stuff any more?'

Cobbett was greatly impressed by this conversation. He went on across France to Bordeaux, where it seems some sort of money awaited him, thinking this over and jotting down his thoughts. He makes one sound and interesting parallel between this new World Transport

Organization and those Hansa Merchants who played such an important rôle in the revival of civilization about the Baltic and North Europe
generally after the Roman collapse. 'After all,' reflects Cobbett, 'we
have never given organized transport and trading its proper importance
in history.'

At Bordeaux he sold his bicycle and was able to get a passage in an
aeroplane to Le Bourget (an aerodrome of old origin near the ruins of
Paris) and thence to fly to Hendon. His plane landed at Le Mans for an
exchange of goods. His delight to escape from the rough roads he had
been riding is infectious.

He described the recovery of the devastated French forests in the form
of scrub, and he peered down at the little peasants' clearings that were
appearing in groups and patches round the old towns. He sees the
aviators and mechanics at the aerodromes with new eyes, and he learns
from them of the way in which World Transport was picking up and
reinstating metallurgical and electrical works. He has an eye for the
beauty of Le Mans cathedral, which he had seen and admired in his
student days, and which he rejoices to find intact, and he describes that
early monument to the pioneers of aviation in the Place below which
still survives. Amiens cathedral also was uninjured at that time.

His diary ends on a melancholy note. Apparently he had not visited
England for some years, and he is shocked by the ruinous desolation of
the outer suburbs of London. Plainly he had lived in and loved London
as a boy. A part of Hyde Park, in spite of the opposition of the squatter
cultivators, had been converted into an aerodrome, but he found the
rebuilding of the central region haphazard and unpleasing. He objects
to the crowding of heavy buildings, with their vast anti-aircraft cara-
paces of cement, at the centre, due to the decay of surburban traffic
facilities. It looked, he says, like a cluster of 'diseased' mushrooms.
'When shall we English learn to plan?' he asks, and then with an odd
prophetic gleam he doubts whether the northern slope of the Thames
depression, so ill drained and so soft in its subsoil, can carry this
lumpish mass of unsound new buildings to which the life of the old city
was shrinking.

Only ten years later his fears were to be justified. The bed of the
Thames buckled up and the whole of the Strand, Fleet Street, Cornhill
and, most regrettable of all, the beautiful St Paul's Cathedral of Sir
Christopher Wren, so familiar to us in the pictures and photographs of
that age, collapsed in ruin and perished in flame. The reader who has
pored over *Historical Scenes in a Hundred Volumes* – and what child
has not? – will remember the peculiar appearance of the old Waterloo
Bridge, crumpled up to a pent-house shape, and the grotesque obliquity
of the Egyptian obelisk, once known as Cleopatra's Needle, that
venerable slab of hieroglyphics, cracked and splintered by air-raid

shrapnel, which slanted incredibly for some years before it fell into the banked-up water of the Lambeth-Chelsea lake.

XII

America in Liquidation

The preceding sections have given a general view of the course of history in the Old World during the middle decades of the twentieth century. Even in Europe certain regions, as we have noted, stand rather aloof from the essential drama, following a line of development of their own, less tragic and intense than that of the leading Powers. Spain, for example, the new Spain that was born in 1931, has the rôle of an onlooker, an onlooker much preoccupied with his own affairs. Still more noticeable is the non-participation of both Latin- and English-speaking America in these passionate and violent happenings. They suffered parallel economic, political and social stresses, but within their own limits. After the financial storms of the early thirties, the shocks that came to them from the European troubles affected them less and less. They took up their particular aspect of the decline and fall of private capitalism and worked it out in their own way.

Yet the fact that they did share in that decline and fall brings out very clearly a fact that was sometimes disputed in the past: *the immediate causes of the world collapse in the twentieth century were first monetary inadaptability, secondly the disorganization of society through increased productivity, and thirdly the great pestilence.* War was not a direct cause. The everyday life of man is economic, not belligerent, and it was strangled by the creditor. Had the world been already one state in 1900, and had it still been an economy of private accumulation with a deflating currency, it would have collapsed in very much the same fashion that it did collapse. Had it been cut up into a hundred belligerent states at that time, but with a monetary system that restrained the creditor and allowed industrial development without limit, it might have released sufficient energy to have gone on with its wars for another century or so before it reached the goal of mutual extermination. The monetary collapse was the most immediate factor in the world's disorganization, enfeeblement and famine. Without it man might have pursued a far longer and more strenuous career to massacre and suffocation. On the whole it was perhaps well for him that progress tumbled over finance in the nineteen-thirties.

The futility of all the early anti-war movements becomes understandable only when we grasp the essential importance of a sane monetary nexus. On this we have insisted throughout, we have elucidated the connexion of the creditor and traditional antagonisms from half a dozen angles, and nothing could emphasize and drive home the lesson more than the parallelism of the American and Old-World experiences.

From the days of their first political separation from the European system the American communities had gone through their own series of developmental phases, independent of and out of rhythm with the course of events in the Old World. Independent – and yet not completely independent, because they were upon the same planet. Throughout the nineteenth century the American mind, in north and south alike, was saturated with the idea of *isolation*. It was taught in the schools, in the Press, in every political utterance of a general import, that the New World was indeed a new world, an escape from the tyranny of ancient traditions to peace, liberty, opportunity and a fresh life for mankind. It had to avoid all 'entangling alliances' with Old-World states and policies, forget the inveterate quarrels and hatreds of Europe even at the price of forgetting kinship and breaking with a common culture, and work out and set the example of a more generous way of living. From the days of George Washington to the days of Woodrow Wilson, in spite of the Civil War and much grave economic trouble, the American mind never abandoned its belief in its own exemplary quality and its conception that towards the rest of the world its attitude must be missionary and philanthropic. It realized that it knew many things very simply, but it had no doubt it knew better.

Throughout the nineteenth century both America and Europe expanded enormously, economically, biologically. America was profoundly impressed by her own growth and disposed to disregard the equal pace of European progress. Assisted by a tremendous immigration from Europe, the population of the United States increased by about 80 millions in a hundred years. But in spite of that tremendous emigration, Europe during that period added 240 millions to her multitudes. The American cherished a delusion that he had 'got on' relatively to Europe. His life had in fact expanded, concurrently with the European's, and through the working of ideas and inventions and the importation of human energy from the older centres. In his unimpeded continent the different elements in the expansion increased at rates that did not correspond with the European process. He was living in a similar progressive system, but he was more and more out of phase with transatlantic developments.

And throughout that century inventions in transport and communications were 'abolishing distance' and bringing points that had formerly been months apart into a few hours' or a few moments' distance from one another.

The resulting alternations of intimacy and remoteness across the Atlantic constitute one of the outstanding aspects of twentieth-century history. It is like two great and growing tops that spin side by side. They approach, they touch and clash, they wobble and fly apart. Or it is like two complexes of machinery, destined ultimately to combine into one world mechanism, whose spinning wheels attempt to mesh and fail to mesh and jar with a great shower of sparks and splinters and separate again. From the end of the nineteenth century onward the unifying forces of life were tending to gear America with Europe. By the middle of the twentieth century any observer might have been forgiven the conclusion that the intergearing had failed.

We have already given great prominence in this history to the figures of Henry Ford, Woodrow Wilson, and the second Roosevelt, Franklin Roosevelt. We have told of the magnificent advance upon Europe and the subsequent recoil of America within and about them. A brief but competent contemporary book by an American publicist, Frank H. Simonds, *Can America stay at Home?* (1933) surveys the question of isolation very illuminatingly as it appeared in the opening years of the great economic slump which closed down for good and all the wild freedoms of Acquisitive Private Capitalism. He shows how the phases of approach and repulsion succeeded one another from the first imperialist enterprises of Roosevelt 1 (Theodore Roosevelt, 1901–9) onward; how impossible it seemed for America either to keep out of Old-World affairs or to mingle frankly in them. It expressed its virtuous opinions and would not back them. It insisted upon moral judgments and would not take responsibility. In European eyes, to quote Simond's new historical phrase, 'American concern for peace appeared a transparent endeavour to combine the mission of John the Baptist with the method of Pontius Pilate'. The explanation lay in just that mixture of liberal modernity and naïve crudity in the American intelligence on which we have laid stress.

From its beginning the American republic was a break with history, a new thing, far newer, having regard to its period, than the Soviet Republic of Lenin, and from its beginning it was failing to go on with its newness, failing to develop and intensify its ideas. It evolved a body of higher schools and cultivated men to think itself out only after more than a century of independence; in the interim it left its mass education to underpaid teachers and repetitive women. It grew bodily, immensely, and for more than a century it lived on imported brain-food. The result was this rawness, this immense sense of its mission and this want of any subtlety or vigour in its conduct. Wilson's foolish preachments and arrangements, so foolish and yet so saturated with the wisdom of world peace, were perhaps the highest expression of the American mind of his time.

The American mind even in the nineteenth century was not an ignorant mind; it was an immensely uneducated mind. If it was clumsy, it was also free. Its religious 'revivalism' was exactly parallel to its political fluctuations. We find in the stories and studies of authentic American life such features as camp-meetings and organized emotional campaigns for repentance and conversion. We think of firelit scenes, of harsh preaching and lusty chanting. These waves of popular feeling, these gatherings, often in the woods, with their hymn-singing, their exhortation, their shouts of penitence and exultant belief, the mindless exaltation and the subsequent mindless deflation of American spiritual life, were precisely reflected in these booms and slumps of the American world mission. Only with the shock of world economic disaster did the real social and political thinking of America rise to its full vigour. The retreat of the United States from the imbroglio of European affairs as the great depression intensified was marked by a new, more vigorous determination to grip the essentials of social life.

And certainly there was everything to stimulate thought in the internal situation. The dégringolade was at first more rapid even than in Europe. The industrial edifice had been reared to giddier heights of mass production and fell more heavily. In 1928 the United States of America still believed itself the most prosperous country in the world; in 1933 its unemployed were more hopeless and formidable than those of any other continent. But they made no organized effort of revolt; they had no revolutionary formula to bring them together. They revolted as individuals and gangs and became criminals. Society was not overthrown, but it crumbled rapidly to dust and disorder. The crime wave, the financial stress, the frantic efforts to economize, and all the consequent strangulation of popular eduction and the dissolution of confidence, order and intercommunication – that sequence which we have already traced in general terms manifested itself most severely and typically in this vast, comparatively unhistorical area. Roosevelt II struggled gallantly, but he came too late to stop the rot.

In America as in Europe a phase of fragmentation set in. It was not a smash to which one can give a definite date, but every day there was something happening in the direction of dissolution. In America as in Europe State governments became insolvent phantoms making feebler and feebler efforts to collect taxes, and the Federal authority in Washington faded away, if not as completely as the League of Nations in Europe, at any rate in a comparable manner. We have the same phenomena of municipalities becoming autonomous, and provisional controls, Citizens' Unions, Law and Order Societies, Workers' Protection Associations and plain Workers' Soviets (in New Mexico and Arizona) springing into activity here, there and everywhere. In the Blue

Mountains and on the Pacific coast small republics had already isolated themselves in 1945 and were carrying out a strange blend of Methodism, 'Technocracy' and the Douglas Plan, and Utah had become a practically autonomous Single-Tax State and had restored Mormonism of the original type as the State religion. But there had been no formal secession from the Federal Union anywhere.

There is in the Records a description of Washington in the year 1958, by a former attaché of the British Embassy there. (All the Ambassadors of the British Empire had been replaced by 'consolidated consuls' in 1946.) He describes a visit to the White House, where he was entertained at lunch by President Benito Caruso. The President was carrying on although his term had expired because his successor elect had disappeared on his way to the capital in the Allegheny Mountains. There had been considerable confusion about the last election, and two Secession Presidents who were disputing possession of the State of New York after a conflict over the Yonkers Ballot Boxes had cut off communications with New England altogether.

The President received his visitor very cordially and asked many very sympathetic and intelligent questions about the European situation. He spoke very hopefully of the American outlook. The 'return to Normalcy', he said, was the last in sight. There had been a restoration of the steamboat traffic on the Mississippi, and cotton was going through to the north again in spite of the political unrest. A hundred and forty automobiles had been sent to South America alone in the year 1956–7 in the place of only seventy-two for the previous year. The new quinine-coffee barter system was working well. He looked forward now to a steady upward movement in business affairs. The Hoover Slump had, he admitted, lasted much longer and had gone much lower then had been expected, and it had tried the people to the utmost, but they had faced their trials in a manner worthy of the fathers of the republic. He concluded with the compliments usual then between the two great divisions of the English-speaking peoples.

The lunch was plain but ample. There was excellent pork and a variety of vegetables which the President with genuine democratic frankness boasted he had raised himself with the help of his negro 'secretariat' in the pig-pens and garden at the back of the White House. The duties of the secretariat seem to have been in the household rather than the office. They had been appointed for abstruse political reasons, and several of them were unable to read. Mrs Caruso, a very pleasant lady of Irish extraction, was disposed to dwell on the difficulties of housekeeping in Washington in view of the increasing unpunctuality in the collection of the Federal revenue, but the President checked her, evidently considering these domestic matters a reflection upon the solvency of the nation.

At that time only about a third of the States were actually represented by Congressmen in the Assembly. The rest had found it either too expensive or unnecessary to send delegates. A member was in possession of the house, a tattered individual, reciting some lengthy grievance; there were no reporters visible, and nobody was listening to him. Apparently this man was trying to 'talk out' some legislative proposal, but the visitor could not find anyone who could explain the situation precisely.

The visitor dined on the following day with the eloquent, vital and venerable Senator Borah from Idaho (1865–1970). He was in excellent form, and talked throughout the meal. Indeed, he talked so ably that his visitor was unable to ask him several questions previously prepared for him. He too was extremely hopeful for his country. He admitted that there had been a marked decline in the grosser welfare of America during his lifetime. He would not quarrel with statistics. In tons of coal and steel, in miles of railway run, in the mass production of motor-cars and commodities generally, it was possible to institute unfavourable comparisons with the past. 'But man does not live by bread alone,' said America's Grand Old Man. 'Let us look a little nearer the heart of things.'

That heart, it seemed, had never been sounder. The pestilence, like everything that came from God, had been 'wholesome'. The standard of life was, he maintained, higher than it ever had been, having regard to the nobler aspects of things. Fewer bathrooms there might be, at least in working order, but there was far more purity of mind. In his younger days there had been a lamentable lapse into luxurious indulgence and carelessness on the part of the free people of the States, but all that was past. America was nearer now to the old Colonial simplicity, honesty and purity than she had ever been.

A little inconsecutively the Senator went on to denounce the dishonesty of Europe and the disingenuousness of European and particularly of British diplomacy. He seemed for a time to be repeating long-remembered speeches and to have forgotten how completely British diplomacy had lapsed. He had apparently heard the word 'attaché' before he began to talk, and that had sent his mind back to old times. He returned to the present situation. The United States, he insisted, had gone through far blacker phases in its early history. A hundred and fifty-four years ago Washington had been burnt by a victorious British army. Nothing of the sort had occurred during the present depression – if it could still be spoken of as a depression. Even at the darkest hour in this great Hoover Slump nobody had ever thought of burning Washington.

Later on this same traveller visited the University of Chicago, Columbia University, Harvard and a number of other centres of intellectual activity. His comments are shrewd and intelligent, and fall in very conveniently with our examination of the mental reactions that even then were rapidly producing a new and more sinewy American consciousness amidst the ruins of its ancient laxity.

These institutions were naturally in a most varied state of adjustment to the new conditions. Not all were progressive. Harvard reminded him of what he had read of the ancient lamaseries of Tibet. There was practically no paper to be got for note-taking or exercises, and the teaching was entirely oral and the learning done by heart. The libraries were closely guarded against depredations, and the more important books were only to be inspected in locked glass cases. A page was turned daily. The teachers varied in prestige with the number of their following. They either sat in class-rooms and under trees and lectured, or they went for long walks discoursing as they went to a rabble of disciples. They varied not only in prestige but physical well-being, because it was the rôle of these students to cultivate food for their masters and themselves in the college grounds and produce woven clothing and sandals in the Technical and Art Buildings. Some literary production was going on. The more gifted students wrote verses on slates, and these, if they were sufficiently esteemed by the teaching staff, were written up on the walls or ceilings of the building. The atmosphere was one of archaic simplicity and studied leisure. The visitor was entertained by President Eliot, a tall distinguished-looking elderly man in a toga, who had inherited his position from his grandfather. There was a large open fire in the room, which was lit by tallow candles which two undergraduates continually snuffed. The President talked very beautifully over his simple soup, his choice Maryland claret and a cornucopia of fruit and nuts, and the conversation went on until a late hour.

The impression of Nicholson, the visitor, was one of an elegant impracticability. The simple graciousness of the life he could not deny, but it seemed to him also profoundly futile. He seems, however, to have concealed this opinion from the President and allowed him to talk unchallenged of how Harvard had achieved the ultimate purification and refinement of the Anglican culture, that blend of classicism and refined Christianity, with a graceful monarchist devotion.

'There is a King here?' asked the visitor.

'Not actually a King,' said the President regretfully. 'We have decided that the Declaration of Independence is inoperative, but we have been unable to locate the legitimate King of England, and so there has been no personal confirmation of our attitude. But we have an attitude of loyalty. We cherish that.'

The chief subjects of study seem to have been the Ptolemaic cosmogony, the Homeric poems, the authentic plays of Shakespeare, and theology. The scanty leisure of the students did not admit of a very high standard of gymnastics, and they seem to have abandoned those typical American college sports of baseball and football altogether. The President spoke of these games as 'late innovations'. One chief out-of-door employment seems to have been wood-cutting and felling.

This glimpse of graceful and idealistic pedantry is interesting because it left so few traces for later times. It depended very much on the personality of the President himself, and after his death at an advanced age, and the hard winters of 1981 and 1983, this ancient foundation seems to have been completely deserted and allowed to fall into ruin.

Both Columbia University and Chicago were in violent contrast to Harvard. Here the influence of the new De Windt school of thought was very evident, and the traditions of Dewey, Robinson, the Elmer Barnes couple, Raymond Fosdick, Beard and their associates were still alive. Although New York City was already abandoned and dangerous because of the instability of its huge unoccupied skyscrapers, there was still considerable trading on the Hudson River and some manufacturing activity. The great iron bridges were still quite practicable for pack horses and mules, and, affording as they did a North and South line of communication of quite primary value, they gave the place a unique commercial importance. The industrial workers there and in Chicago were in close contact with the college staffs, and they were working with very great energy at what they called 'The General Problem of Recovery'.

'They don't,' writes Nicholson, 'admit that civilization has broken down. They talk here just as they did in Washington, of the Hoover Slump. I never met people so confident that somehow and in some fashion things will pick up again. There is nothing like this at home. One night there was a tremendous crash and an earthquake. A huge pile called 'Radio City' had collapsed in the night. In the bright keen morning I went out to the Pantheon, and there a crowd of people was watching the clouds of dust that were still rising, and listening to the occasional concussions that marked minor fallings-in. Were they in the least downhearted? Not at all. 'There's a bit more liquidation,' said a man near me. 'We have to get these things off our hands somehow.'

Nicholson gives a fairly full account of the curricula of both Columbia and Chicago. He is greatly struck by the equipment of the scientific laboratories and the relative importance of experimental work. 'I felt almost as though I was back in 1930,' he says, 'when I visited the Rockefeller chemical laboratory.' But still more was he struck by the advanced state of the sociological work. 'They are producing a sort of lawyers who are not litigators,' he writes. 'I think the new law stuff they are doing here is the most interesting thing about the place. It isn't what my father would have recognized as law at all. It's the physiology and pathology of society and social therapeutics arising therefrom. There are one or two men here, Hooper Hamilton and Rin Kay for instance, whose talk is a liberal education. They won't hear any of the rot we deal out at home about the Sunset of Mankind.'

That was his key observation, so to speak. But it is interesting to note that the reduction of Basic English to practicable use was also being made. Spanish and English were already on their way to become the interchangeable languages they remained throughout all the earlier twenty-first century. The teaching of French had fallen off very greatly, and the old classical studies (Greek and Latin), to judge by his complete silence about them, had been completely abandoned.

Our tourist flew from Chicago to the Ford Aerodrome at Dearborn, saw the ruins of the main factories and the reconstructed settlement, and spent some days with the Technological School there and in the still very imperfectly arranged Museum of American Life. It was startling to see some scores of square miles of closely cultivated land round the open space of the Aerodrome and to learn that an old Ford idea of dividing the time of the staff between agricultural production and mechanical work was still in effective operation. There were associated textile and boot factories in Detroit. There was still an output of some thousand-odd automobiles a year and a 'few hundred' (!) aeroplanes. And there was a small but healthy radio department.

'We keep in touch,' said the Director. 'We don't interfere with people, and we are not interfered with. We are running all that is left of the distance letter post.... Yes, Canada and Mexico as well. Nobody bothers us now about the boundaries, and we don't bother. When trade was at its worst we sat tight, cultivated our farms, and did experiments.'

The Henry Ford, that 'great original' whose adventure of the Peace Ship has been chosen to mark a turning-point in our history, had long since played out his part, but the Director mentioned in these papers seems to have been his son Edsel, carrying on the initiatives of his finely simple-minded parent.

That the place was able to 'sit tight and carry on' was no empty boast. The visitor from a slovenly world dwells on the 'tidiness' of everything. The Edison workshop was still in the original state as it had been re-erected by Henry Ford; there or in the Museum Nicholson was shown the first phonograph and the first telephone ever made, and the earliest experimental automobiles and aeroplanes.

'It is as recent as that, ' he tells us he said. 'In the lifetime of ourselves and our fathers we have seen the beginning, the triumph, and the collapse of the greatest civilization that the world has ever seen. We have spanned the whole history of mechanical mass production.'

'Not a bit of it,' said the Director. 'It's hardly begun.'

There followed a long conversation the gist of which the visitor seems to have written down immediately in dialogue form. Its interest for the student of history lies in the fact that here again we have evidence of the way in which amidst the world-wide collapse into misery, disorder and incoherent peasant life the vitality of the mechanical transport system was manifesting itself. We can put the talk of the Dearborn director side by side with that of the European aviator reported by Titus Cobbett. There is the same realization of the final death of the old order. 'All that king business and congress business is as dead as mutton,' said the Dearborn director. 'And the banking business is deader.'

'And what is coming?' asked the visitor.

'*That*,' said the director, and pointed to a mounting aeroplane inaudible and almost invisible in the blue.

BOOK III

The World Renascence:
The Birth of the Modern State

I

The Plan of the Modern State is Worked Out

In the preceding chapters the culmination, the dislocation and the collapse of the private capitalist civilization has been told. It has been a chronicle of disaster, wherein particular miseries, the torment and frustration of thousands of millions, are more than overshadowed by its appalling general aimlessness. We have seen the urge towards unity and order, appearing and being frustrated, reappearing and again being defeated. At last it reappeared – and won. The problem had been solved.

The world was not able to unify before 1950 for a very simple reason: there was no comprehensive plan upon which it could unify; it was able to unify within another half-century because by that time the entire problem had been stated, the conditions of its solution were known, and a social class directly interested in the matter had differentiated out to achieve it. From a vague aspiration the Modern World-State became a definite and so a realizable plan.

It was no great moral impulse turned mankind from its drift towards chaos. It was an intellectual recovery. Essentially what happened was this: social and political science overtook the march of catastrophe.

Obscure but persistent workers in these decades of disaster pieced together the puzzle bit by bit. There is a fantastic disproportion between the scale of the labourers and the immense consequences they released. The psychology of association, group psychology, was a side of social biology that had been disregarded almost entirely before the time of which we are writing. People had still only the vaguest ideas about the origins and working processes of the social structure in and by which they lived. They accepted the most arbitrary and simple explanations of their accumulated net of relationships, and were oblivious even to fundamental changes in that net. Wild hopes, delusions and catastrophes ensued inevitably.

If you had interrogated an ordinary European of the year 1925 about the motives for his political activities and associations and his general social behaviour, he would probably have betrayed a feeling that your enquiry was slightly indelicate, and if you overcame that objection, he would have talked either some nonsense about the family as the nucleus of social organization, a sort of expansion of brothers and cousins, kith and kin to the monarch, the Sire of the whole system, or he would have gone off in an entirely different direction and treated you to a crude version of Rousseau's Social Contract in which he and the other fellows had combined under agreed-upon rules for mutual defence and aid. The betting would have been quite even as to which of these flatly contradictory explanations he would have given.

He would have said nothing about religious ties in 1925, though fifty years earlier he might have based his whole description on the Divine Will. He would have betrayed no lucid apprehension of the part played by the money nexus in gearing relationships; he would have been as unconscious as his Roman predecessor of the primary social importance of properly adjusted money. He would have thought it was just stuff you earnt and handed out and got things for, and he might have added rather irrelevantly that it was 'the root of all evil'. He would certainly have referred to the family idea when his patriotism was touched upon, if not before, to justify that tangle of hates, fears and consequent and subordinate loyalties; he would have talked of 'mother country' or 'fatherland'. If he practised any craft or skill, he might or might not have had his mind organized in relation to his profession or trade union, but there would be no measure between that and his patriotism, either might override the other, and either might give way before some superstitious or sexual complex in his make-up.

Incidentally he would have revealed extensive envy systems and social suspicion and distrust systems, growing up at every weak point like casual fungi. Everything would be flavoured more or less with the chronic hatred endemic everywhere. And all these disconnected associations from which flowed his judgments and impulses he would have regarded as natural – as natural as the shape of his ears; he would have been blankly unconscious that the education of school and circumstances had had anything to do with his accumulation.

On millions of minds equipped in this fragmentary fashion, uninformed or misinformed and with no internal connectedness, the institutions of the world were floating right up to the middle of the twentieth century. Tossing at last, rather than merely floating. Men called themselves individualist or socialist, and they had not the beginnings of an idea how the individual was and might be related to society; they were nationalist and patriotic, and none of them could tell what a nation was. It was only when these institutions began to batter against each other, and leak and heel over, and show every disposition to go down altogether, that even intelligent men began to realize how haphazard, sentimental and insincere were their answers to the all-important question: 'What holds us together and sustains our cooperations?'

This prevalent superficiality and ignorance about socializing forces was the necessary reflection of a backwardness and want of vigour in academic circles and the intellectual world. The common man, busied about his petty concerns, did not know or think about collective affairs, because at the time there existed no knowledge or ordered thought in an assimilable form to reach down and stimulate his mind. The social body was mentally embryonic from the top downward. That it was possible to demonstrate a complete system of social reactions, and to state the necessary idea of the Modern State in convincing and practically applicable terms, had still to penetrate to the minds not merely of the politicians and statesmen, but of the psychologists, historians and so-called 'economists' of the time.

In 1932 Group Psychology was at about the same level of development as was physical science in the days of the Marquess of Worcester's *Century of Inventions* (1663). It was still in that vague inconclusive phase of 'throwing out' ideas. It was no more capable of producing world order than the physical science of 1663 could have produced an aeroplane or a steam turbine. The ordinary man seeking guidance in the dismay of the Great Slump (see Emil Desaguliers' *Ideas in Chaos and Society in Collapse*, 2017) was confronted with a sort of intellectual rummage sale. He had believed that somewhere somebody knew; he discovered that nobody had ever yet bothered to know. A dozen eminent authorities with the utmost mutual civility were giving him every possible and impossible counsel in his difficulties, suavely but flatly contradicting each other. They were able to do so because they were all floating on independent, arbitrary first assumptions without any structural reference to the primary facts of human ecology.

Nevertheless certain primary matters were being rapidly analysed at that time. The general understanding of money, for example, was increasing rapidly. Desaguliers notes about a hundred and eighty names, including the too-little-honoured name of that choleric but interesting amateur, Major C. H. Douglas (*Works* in the Historical Documents, Economic Section B. 178200), who were engaged in clearing away the conception of a metallic standard as a monetary basis. They were making it plain that the only possible money for a progressive world must keep pace with the continually increasing real wealth of that world. They were getting this into the general consciousness as a matter of primary importance.

But they were proposing the most diverse methods of realizing this conception. The 'Douglas Plan' appealed to the general social credit, but was limited by the narrow political outlook of the worthy Major, who could imagine bankers abolished but not boundaries. In America an interesting movement known as 'Technocracy' was attracting attention. Essentially that was a soundly scientific effort to restate economics on a purely physical basis. But it was exploited in a journalistic fashion and presented to a remarkably receptive public as a cut-and-dried scheme for a new social order in which social and economic life was to be treated as an energy system controlled by 'experts'. The explicit repudiation of democratic control by the Technologists at that date is very notable. The unit of energy was to be the basis of a new currency. So every power station became a mint and every waterfall a potential 'gold-mine', and the money and the energy in human affairs remained practically in step. Another important school, represented by such economists as Irving Fisher and J. M. Keynes, was winning an increased adherence to the idea of a price index controlling the issue of currency.

It was a phase of disconnected mental fermentation. Many of those who were most lucid about monetary processes were, like Douglas and Keynes, still in blinkers about national and imperial boundaries; they wanted to shut off some existing political system by all sorts of artificial barriers and restraints from the world at large, in order to develop their peculiar system within its confines. They disregarded the increasing flimsiness of the traditional political structure altogether. They were in too much of a hurry with their particular panacea to trouble about that. And if the money reformers were not as a rule cosmopolitans, the cosmopolitans were equally impatient with the money reformers and blind to the primary importance of money.

A third class of intelligences stressed the urgent necessity for great public enterprises to correct the paradoxical increase of unemployment consequent upon the increase of productivity that had taken the shiftless world by surprise. That was an independent maladjustment. But thinkers of this school were apt to disregard the importance of monetary rectification. As to who was to control the more complicated methods of mutual service proposed, the world money and the world socialism and so forth, there was an even greater diversity of outlook and an even greater conflict of mental limitations. As Desaguliers says in his summary: 'People could not get out of the sinking social vessels in which they found themselves for the simple reason that nothing but the imperfectly assembled phantom of a salvage ship was yet in sight, a large rudderless, powerless promise, so to speak, standing by.'

Only very knowledgeable people could have foretold then how nearly this phase of throwing out bright but disconnected ideas was drawing to its end, and how rapidly the consolidation of social and educational science into an applicable form was to go forward, once it had begun. The rush of correlated social discoveries and inventions to the rescue of mankind, when at last it was fairly started, was even more rapid and remarkable than the release of steam and electrical energy in the nineteenth century. It went on under difficulties. Perhaps it was quickened and purified by those very difficulties.

Gustave De Windt's great work, *Social Nucleation* (1942), was the first exhaustive study of the psychological laws underlying team play and *esprit de corps*, disciplines of criminal gangs, spirit of factory groups, crews, regiments, political parties, churches, professionalisms, aristocracies, patriotisms, class consciousness, organized research and constructive cooperation generally. It did for the first time correlate effectively the increasing understanding of individual psychology, with new educational methods and new concepts of political life. In spite of its unattractive title and a certain wearisomeness in the exposition, his book became a definite backbone for the constructive effort of the new time.

De Windt worked under all the handicap of the intellectual worker in that uncomfortable time. Much of his writing, like that of Marx and Lenin, was done in the British Museum in London, but he was expelled from England during a phase of xenophobia in 1939, and he was not allowed to return from Holland to his 'beloved Bloomsbury' until 1941. He was slightly gassed during the ninth Polish air raid on Berlin, and this no doubt accelerated his death in Bloomsbury, the tuberculous London slum in which his book was completed.

Much has been done since to elaborate and correct the broad generalizations he established. But his name stands with those of Plato, Galileo, Newton, Darwin and Robert Owen as marking a real step forward in the expression and expansion of human ideas. Such men are all in their various dimensions something more than themselves, like stones that have become surveyors' datum marks. After 1950 De Windt's doctrines and formulae spread with great rapidity, in spite of the disturbed state of the world – assisted and enforced indeed by the disturbed state of the world.

Few people read De Windt nowadays, just as few people read Plato or Bacon or Charles Darwin or Adam Smith or Karl Marx, but what he thought has been built into the general outlook of mankind. What he established is now platitude, but in his time very much of what he had to say would still have seemed heresy and fantasy, if it had not been for the patient massiveness, the Darwinesque patience, with which he built up his points.

The most important features of his teaching were, first, that he insisted with an irrefutable rigidity upon the entirely artificial nature of the content of the social side of a human being. Men are born but citizens are made. A child takes to itself what is brought to it. It accepts example, usage, tradition and general ideas. All the forms of its social reactions and most of its emotional interpretations are provided by its education.

'Obviously,' the reader will say. But it is essential to the understanding of history to realize that before De Windt's time this was not obvious. Moral values, bias and prejudice, hatreds and so forth were supposed to come 'by nature'. And consequently the generation about him had grown up in a clotted mass of outworn explanations, metaphors, mythologies and misleading incentives, and the misshapen minds

reflected and condoned the misshapen social order. His rôle in intellectual history is primarily that of a strong arm sweeping a terrible litter of
encumbrance aside, and replacing it by a clearly defined structure. He
restored again to credibility what Plato had first asserted: that, however
difficult, it was possible to begin again at the beginning with uninfected
minds. And having cleared his ground in this way he proceeded to build
up the imperatives of that sane progressive education and life for
mankind which now opens out about us.

He brought home clearly to the general intelligence firstly that the
monetary method of relationship was essential to any complex productive society, since it was the only device that could give personal choice
and freedom in return for service. It liberated economic relationships.
But money was not a thing in itself, it was a means to an end, and its
treatment was to be judged entirely by its attainment of that end. It had
indeed grown out of a barterable commodity, a thing in itself, silver or
gold or the like, but it had ceased to be this, and it was the difficulties
in the transition of money from the former to the latter status that had
released those diseases of the economic system which had in succession
first destroyed the Roman imperialism and then the European sovereign
states. A completely abstract money, a money as abstract and free from
association with any material substance as weight or measure, had to
be contrived for mankind. Human society could not be saved from
chaos without it. It had to be of world-wide validity; its tokens and
notes had to be issued to maintain a practically invariable price index,
and it had to be protected by the most stringent laws against any form
of profit-making manipulation. He demonstrated that not merely forgery, but every form of gambling and speculation had to be made major
offences under a criminal code. He showed that usury was unnecessary.
He unravelled the old entanglements by which new production had
hitherto been saddled with permanent debts for its promotion and
experiments. He made profit-making banking, that Old Man of the Sea,
get off the back of enterprise. He eliminated every excuse for its profits.
Banking was a public function. The distribution of credit was a vital
part of government.

The New Banking of the twenty-first century grew up along the lines
he established for it. To-day it is our system of public book-keeping, a
part of our state statistical organization, a clearing-house of obligations
and a monetary record of the accumulating surplus of racial energy,
which the world-controls apportion to our ever expanding enterprises.
It is entirely public and entirely gratuitous. It is hard to realize that it
was ever allowed to be a source of private and secret profit. We register
a man's earnings and spending as we register births and deaths. Our
money is fundamentally a check on these publicly kept private accounts.

But this desideratum of a sufficiency of invariable money was only a
'foundation need', a quantitative basis for the establishment of vital

relationships, or, in De Windt's terminolgoy, for 'social nucleation'. So soon as money was put in order it ceased to be necessary to trouble about money, just as it is needless to think about light and air in a properly lit and ventilated room.

For a couple of centuries before De Windt, the family, which had been the common social cellule throughout the whole agricultural age of mankind, had been losing its distinctness, had been dissolving into larger systems of relationship, more especially in the Northern and Western communities. It had been losing its economic, its mental, and its emotional autonomy at the same time. In the nineteenth century this dissolution of the family had gone on very rapidly indeed. The domestication of women, and their concentration upon children and the home, had diminished greatly.

By general sentiment, the instinctive factor in family unification had always been overrated. In effect, that instinctive bond dissolves long before the children are thirteen or fourteen. After that age the binding force of parent to child and vice versa is not instinct, but affection, convenience, habit, and tradition. And that convenience, usage, and tradition had dwindled. Put to the test of exterior attractions, family solidarity had weakened not only in the West, but also, as Asia had been Westernized, in Turkey, India, China and Japan. This was so essentially, even more than apparently. The family home remained generally as a meeting-place and common domicile for parents and children, but it ceased to be a vehicle of tradition, it ceased to train and discipline. It ceased to do so for the simple reason that these functions were now discharged with far more emphasis, if with less intensity, by exterior agencies. Citizens were begotten in the home but they were no longer *made* in the home.

De Windt drew a vivid contrast between the home life of a Central European family in the late eighteenth century, with the father reading the Bible to his assembled offspring, conducting daily prayer, watching over, reproving and chastising his sons and daughters up to the age of sixteen or seventeen and even controlling their marriage, and the loosely associated family structure in the early twentieth century.

This structural dissolution was universally recognized long before the time of De Windt, but it was left for him to emphasize the need for a planned 'renucleation' in the social magma that arose out of this dissolution. The popular school, the experiences and associations of industrialized production, the daily paper and so forth, had knocked the strength out of the mental and moral education of the home and put nothing in its place. The sapping forces had not, in their turn, been converted into 'organic forces'. In default of these, minds were lapsing towards crude and base self-seeking and entirely individualistic aims.

These contemporary emotional suggestions and haphazard ideologies were not good enough, he preached, to make a human being a tolerable social unit. Social tissue was not to be made and coordinated on such lines. The stars in their courses were pointing our race towards the organized world community, the Modern State, and if ever that goal was to be attained, if the reorganization of the species was not to collapse, degenerate, and perish by the wayside, then the individual mind throughout the world had to be educated, had to be disciplined and equipped, definitely and sufficiently to this end. That would not come by nature. The social side of the individual had to be oriented deliberately. 'Society is an educational product.'

For the race to get to this Modern State as a whole it had to get there as so many hundreds of millions of human beings, all individually aware of that as the general objective at which their lives aimed. The Modern State could not arrive as an empty form with all humanity left behind it. Every teacher, every writer, every talker, every two friends who talked together constituted a potential primary nucleus in a renascent social system. These nuclei had to be organized. Their existence had to be realized, and they had to be brought into effective cooperation.

It is hard nowadays to realize that once upon a time such commonplaces as these were not commonplaces, and that in the very days when De Windt was writing, multitudes of well-meaning people were attempting to assemble 'movements' for social reconstruction and world revolution out of the raw, unprepared miscellany of the contemporary crowd. It was with extreme reluctance that impatient reformers turned their minds from impossible *coups d'état* and pronunciamentos, strikes against war and booby millennia, to this necessary systematic preliminary renucleation of the world. The immediate task seemed too narrow and intense for them and its objective too high and remote. 'It is no good asking people what they want,' wrote De Windt. 'That is the error of democracy. You have first to think out what they ought to want if society is to be saved. Then you have to tell them what they want and see that they get it.'

And further, he urged, if you cannot start nucleation everywhere, then at least you can start it close at hand. 'Get the nuclei going. Be yourself a nucleus.' From the beginning of life, nuclei have begotten nuclei. The Modern State, which had to be evoked everywhere, could be begun anywhere.

Another point that was new in his time, so far as Western civilization went, was his insistence upon the greater importance of adolescent education and his denial of the primary right of the parent to shape his offspring according to his fancy. The 'renucleation' of society had to be complete. The 'nuclei' which were ultimately to become the sole education and disciplinary units of a new-born society would be in the first place, and usually, intensive study circles and associations for moral and physical training. Their social and political activities were to be secondary exercises, subordinated to a primary mental, moral and bodily training. He searched the social disorder about him for favourable conditions for the pioneer nucleations. He looked to factories, laboratories, technical schools, public services, hospital staffs, to banded men and women of all sorts, for the material for his nucleation. He insisted that the impulse to build up a social order was instinctive. Wherever there was social confusion the crude efforts to get together into a new directive order appeared.

He pointed to the Sokols, Nazis, Fascists, Communist Party members, Kuomintang members of his time, as the first primitive intimations of the greater organization that was coming. They had the spirit of an élite class, although they wasted it more or less upon the loyalties and prejudices of the past. People are not leading these young men, he argued; 'they are taking advantage of the instinctive needs of these young men. Try to realize what it is that they are – however blindly – seeking.'

Like St Paul, the founder of Christianity, speaking to the Athenians – he quotes the passage – he said: 'That Unknown God, whom ignorantly ye worship, him declare I unto you.' He was declaring the as yet unknown Modern State.

Intensively De Windt's teaching was a theory of education; extensively it was the assertion of the Modern State. These were inseparable aspects of the same thing. 'A community is an education in action', he declared. And with a complete continuity he carried up his scheme of social structure through every variety of production organization, control and enterprise. Men were to 'fall in and serve this end.'

Borrowing a word from Ortega Y. Gasset, but going boldly beyond that original thinker, he declared that 'plenitude' of life was now only to be attained by living in relation to the Modern State. All other living was 'waste, discontent and sorrow'. It was becoming impossible to retain self-respect, to be happy within oneself, unless one was 'all in' upon that one sound objective. The old loyalties, to flag, to nation, to class, were outworn and discredited. They had become unreal. They did not call out all that was in a man, because now we saw their limitations. They could no longer keep up the 'happy turgidity' of life. They could not be served 'with a sure and untroubled soul'. They would certainly leave a man in the end 'deflated, collapsed into an aimless self'. In the past men could live and live fully within their patriotisms and their business enterprises, because they knew no better. But now they knew better.

Finally De Windt set himself diametrically against one of the direst concepts of Parliamentary Democracy, a concept that still had enormous influence in his time, and that was the idea of the 'Opposition'. 'Criticize,' he wrote, 'yes, but do not obstruct.' If a directive organization is fundamentally bad, he taught, break it and throw it away, but rid your minds altogether of a conception of see-saw and give and take as a proper method in human affairs. The Parliamentary gang Governments, that were then in their last stage of ineptitude, were rotten with the perpetual amendment and weakening of measures, with an endless blocking and barring of projects, with enfeebling bargains and blackmailing concessions. Against every directive body, every party in power, sat another devoting itself to misrepresenting, thwarting, delaying, and spoiling, often for no reason or for the flimsiest reasons, merely for the sake of misrepresenting, thwarting, delaying and spoiling, what the governing body was attempting to do, in the hope of degrading affairs to such a pitch of futility as to provoke a change of government that would bring the opposition into power. The opportunities of profit and advancement afforded in such a mental atmosphere to a disingenuous careerist were endless.

All this tangle of ideas had to be swept aside. 'About most affairs there can be no two respectable and antagonistic opinions,' said De Windt. 'It is nonsense to pretend there can be. There is one sole right way and there are endless wrong ways of doing things. A government is trying to go the right way or it is criminal. Sabotage must cease. It has always been one of the ugliest vices of advanced movements. It is a fundamental social vice.'

His discussion of the difference between Criticism and Opposition is one of those classics that few people read. It is a pity, because it is a very good specimen of twentieth-century English prose. The right to criticize and the duty of well-wrought criticism are fundamental to modern citizenship. He considered how that right and duty had been ignored by the shallow mentality of Italian Fascism and how fatally they had been entangled with the suppression of malignancy in Russia. He analysed the reckless irresponsibility of censorship in the Western communities. There was no law anywhere to restrain conspiracies, on the part of religious, political, or business bodies, for the suppression of publications. His warnings against the suppression of opinion were not so immediately effective as his general revolutionary project. Many people did not realize what he was driving at. In practice the conflict of world order with the opposition spirit, during the struggle to maintain the Air Dictatorship, was to lapse again and again into the suppression of honest criticism. In practice it was found that criticism and suggestion passed by insensible degrees into incitement and the insurrectionary propaganda.

This clear-cut revolutionary scheme of De Windt's was vividly new and tonic to the energetic young men of the middle twentieth century. We summarize here its main constructive conceptions in spite of its present platitudinousness. It is unnecessary to tell in any detail his far-sighted schemes to link his nuclei into a world propaganda, because by insensible degrees that organization has grown into the educational system of our world to-day. This history and indeed every textbook in use in the world could well be dedicated to him. And his complex and very detailed anticipations of the process of a world revolution need not detain us here (his Book V, *The New World in the Body of the Old*, contains most of this), because we can now tell of that vast reconstruction itself.

In some respects he was remarkably prescient, in others he estimated human reactions inaccurately and even incorrectly. The reconstruction of human affairs involved some very rough work from which he would have recoiled. None the less he put all the main structural factors in the establishment of the Modern State so plainly and convincingly before his fellow-men that soon thousands and presently millions were living for that vision, were bringing it out of thought into reality. He made it seem so like destiny that it became destiny.

For some years his views spread very slowly. An increasing number of people knew about them, but at first very few made serious efforts to realize them. One man after another would say, 'But this is right!' and then, 'But this is impossible!' De Windt was dead before his school of thought became a power in the world. Like Karl Marx, he was never to know of the harvest he had sown.

In our description of the failure of the League of Nations we have noted how foredoomed that experiment was, because nowhere among either the influential men of the time nor among the masses was there any sense of the necessity and the necessary form of a new world order. The statesmen, diplomatists and politicians of the time impress us as almost incredibly blind to things that are as plain as daylight to us now, and it is hard for us to believe that that blindness was not wilful. It was not. They could not see it. We read their speeches at conference after conference until their voices die away at last in the rising tide of disaster, and we almost cry out as we read: 'You idiots! Wasn't world control there just under your noses? And was anything else but disaster possible?'

The answer is that it was not precisely under their noses. Slowly, laboriously, with perpetual repetitions and slight variations, the Obvious had to be got into and spread and diffused in the human mind. It is De Windt's peculiar claim to human gratitude, not that he discovered anything fresh, but that he so built up and fortified the Obvious that not the most subtle and disingenuous mind, nor the biggest fool who ever sentimentalized and spouted, could escape honestly from its inexorable imperatives.

II

Thought and Action;
The New Model of Revolution

It is a wholesome check upon individual pride that no single man and indeed no single type of man is able both to conceive and carry through the simplest of our social operations. Even the man who cultivates the earth and grows food cannot make the productive implements he uses or select the seeds and plants that yield him increase. Defoe's queer story of Robinson Crusoe is an impossibly hopeful estimate of what a single man, with only a little flotsam and jetsam from the outer world, and in unusually benign climatic conditions, could on a desert island contrive to do for his own comfort and security. Still more does this interdependence of men and different types apply to the complex processes that now, in this Age of Maximum Insecurity, were demanded, if the new generation was to escape from the economic and institutional wreckage amidst which it found itself, and create the social order in which we live to-day.

First came the intellectuals, men living aloof from responsibility, men often devoid of the qualities of leadership and practical organization. Like De Windt they planned everything and achieved no more than a plan. Such men are primarily necessary in the human adventure, because they build up a sound diagnosis of events; they reveal more and more clearly and imperatively the course that lies before the race and in that task their lives are spent and justified. Then it is that the intelligent executive type, capable of concentration upon a complex idea once it is grasped, and resisting discursiveness as a drag on efficiency, comes into action. Their imaginative limitation is a necessary virtue for the task they have to do. No man can administer a province successfully if he is always wandering beyond its frontiers. The rather unimaginative forcible type is the necessary executive of a revolution, and the benefit of a revolution is entirely dependent upon the soundness of the ideology with which he has been loaded.

Because of this necessity for complementary types of revolutionary, history does not produce any modern equivalents to the legendary figures of Solon, Moses or Confucius in its story of the coming of the Modern State. De Windt was not so much a creator as a summarizer, a concentrator, a lens that gathered to a burning focus the accumulating mental illumination of his day.

The light of understanding that lit the fires of this last revolution came from no single brain. It came from ten thousand active and devoted minds, acting and reacting upon one another, without order or precedence; it was like the growth of physical and biological science that preceded it, something that happened as a whole, something that happened not in any single consciousness but in the consciousness of the race.

We have already noted how far back the first germination of the World-State idea can be traced; we have shown how the forces of economic life drove towards it in the nineteenth century. We have displayed it working as a quasi-instinctive aspiration in the brains of Henry Ford and Woodrow Wilson. With De Windt's *Social Nucleation* we see it made concrete, with all its essential structures projected and all its necessary conditions laid down, a practicable proposal. The World-State has ceased to be a cloudy aspiration and it has become a plan. Forceful men could adopt it.

A distinct change in the quality of those who were promoting the movement for the Modern State became very evident even before the War Cycle of the Forties. It was now sufficiently 'thought out' for men of resolute character to incorporate it in their personal lives. It was passing over from the reflective to the energetic types. Its earliest propagandists had been largely reflective and practically ineffective individuals; a miscellany of pacificists whose dread and detestation of war was overwhelming and who had the intelligence to realize that war can only be avoided by establishing a World Pax; a number of writers, 'pure' scientific workers, young sociologists, economists and the like and 'intellectuals' from the working class movement. Now a multitude of engineers, architects, skilled foremen and industrial organizers, technicians of all sorts, business men and captains of industry, were also beginning to 'talk Modern State' and put in an increasing proportion of their time and attention to its advocacy.

The transition is easily explicable. The increasing social disorder was driving men of the vigorous practical type out of satisfactory employment. During the First Age of Prosperity, and during the false recovery after the World War, such men had been able to find ample work agreeable to their temperaments in the immense industrial development of the time. They had organized great businesses, vast production; they had exploited the incessant stream of inventions; they had opened up the natural resources of hitherto backward regions. They had carried production far beyond the consuming power of human society. So long as all this enterprise could go on, it did not seem necessary to them to trouble about the political and monetary methods of their world. Now and then some of them showed a certain restiveness at the banking network; our typical original-minded industrial Henry Ford, for instance, had two vigorous tussles with the bankers during his career;

but generally the phenomena of political and financial strangulation only began to compel their serious attention after the great Hoover Slump (the thirty Year Slump) was well under way.

Then they began to think, talk and write about the social order with the energy of men accustomed to handle large affairs and work for immediately tangible results. The vast experiment of Soviet Russia aroused their technical jealousy and a sort of envious impatience both at its opportunities and its incapacities. And the young men coming on from the abundant technical schools of the time, stirred by the books and talk and omnipresent hopes and memories of the immediate past, and looking for adventure and achievement in material enterprise, realized very rapidly that the lights of opportunity upon their paths were being turned down in a manner at once mysterious and exasperating.

The revolutionary movement in the nineteenth century had seemed to such men a tiresomeness of slacking workers, aided and abetted by critics like Ruskin, artists like William Morris, playwrights like Bernard Shaw and suchlike impracticable and unconvincing people. It was associated in their minds with sham Gothic, yellow-green draperies, long hair, anti-vivisection and vegetarianism. There was scarcely a man of scientific or technical eminence on the revolutionary side before 1900. But by the third decade of the twentieth century two-thirds of the technicians, scientific workers and able business organizers were talking active revolution. It was no longer to be a class insurrection of hands; it was to be a revolt of the competent. Their minds were feeling round for ideas. They found in such books as De Windt's exactly what they wanted. They began to set about the evocation of the Modern World-State in no uncertain fashion.

A revolution in revolutionary ideas had occurred. The protean spirit of Revolution had cut its hair, put on blue overalls, made blue prints for itself, created a New Model, and settled down to work in a systematic fashion.

III

The Technical Revolutionary

The existence of this large number of scientific and technical workers in the Western communities and their rapid and lively apprehension of the breakdown about them is one of the profoundest differences between the second and the first Decline and Fall.

We find no real equivalent at all to them in the Roman story. There were great numbers of artisans without any science, steeped in tradition; and quite out of touch with these artisans there were a few small groups of ineffective philosophers whose speculations were finally swamped by the synthesis of Christianity. Artisan and philosopher were in different worlds. The philosopher has left it on record that he despised the artisan. Probably the artisan despised the philosopher in equal measure so far as he knew about him; but he has not left it on record. Neither artisan nor philosopher seems to have had any awareness of the broad social forces that were destroying the common security in which he went about his affairs, and turning the Empire into a battling ground for barbarian adventurers.

It is doubtful if at any time the imperial court or the imperial civil service had any real conception of any sustained decline. Nineteenth- and twentieth-century historians, as Ogilvy and Freud point out in their *Roman History* (2003 and revised by Pan Chow Liang 2047), were all too apt to imagine any up-to-date intelligence for such emperors as Julius Caesar, Octavius, Marcus Aurelius or Domitian. They represented them as scheming and planning on almost modern lines. But there is no proof of any such awareness in the Latin record. One large element in that old Roman world that would surely have displayed some sense of the needs of the time, if anywhere there had been that sense, was the universally present building industry. It did hold on in a way throughout the decline and fall, but consciously it did nothing politically.

Students are still working out the preservation and continuation of the art and mystery of the masons into the Middle Ages. There was a great loss of knowledge but also a real survival. The mediaeval freemasons who built those flimsy but often quite beautiful Gothic cathedrals it is now such a task to conserve carried on a tradition that had never really broken with that of the pyramid-builders. But they had no sense of politics. They had a tradition of protective guild association similar to the Trade Unions of the Capitalist age, they interfered in local affairs in order to make jobs for themselves, but there is no sign that at any time they concerned themselves with the order and stability of the community as a whole. Their horizons were below that level of intelligence.

Now the skilled and directive men of the collapsing order of the twentieth century were of an altogether livelier quality. Their training was not traditional but progressive, far more progressive than that of any other class. They were inured to fundamental changes in scope, method and material. They ceased to be acquiescent in the political and financial life about them directly they found their activities seriously impeded. Simultaneously with the outbreak of that very expressive and significant word 'Technocracy' in the world's Press (1932–33) we find, for instance, a Professor of Engineering, Professor Miles Walker, at a meeting of the British Association for the Advancement of Science, boldly arraigning the whole contemporary order by the standards of engineering efficiency. Everywhere in that decadence, amidst that twilight of social order, engineers, industrialists and professors of physical science were writing and talking constructive policies. They were invading politics. We have already noted the name of Professor Soddy as one of the earlier men of science who ceased to 'mind his own business', and took up business psychology.

At first these technicians and business men were talking at large. They did not immediately set about doing things; they still assumed that the politicians and monetary authorities were specialists with sound and thorough knowledge in their own departments, as capable of invention and adaptation as themselves; so that they did no more than clamour for decisive action – not realizing that the very conditions under which bankers and politicians lived made them incapable of varying their methods in any fundamental fashion. But this grew plain as disaster followed disaster. A new type had to assume authority if new methods were to be given a fair chance. New methods of government must oust the old. An increasing proportion of the younger men, abandoning all ideas of loyalty to or cooperation with the old administration institutions, and with an ever clearer consciousness of their objective, set themselves to organize nuclei after the De Windt pattern and to link these up with other nuclei.

The movement spread from workshop to workshop and from laboratory to laboratory with increasing rapidity all over the world. Al Haran estimated that already in 1960 seven-eighths of the aviators were Modern State men, and most of the others he says were 'at least infected with these same ideas'. Such infection went far and deep.

Wherever there was little or no repression the development of this movement to salvage civilization went on openly. But to begin with it encountered some very serious antagonisms. The military element had always been disposed to regard the man of science and the technican as a gifted sort of inferior. The soldier in his panoply ordered them to do their tricks, and they did their tricks. That was the idea. The behaviour of both types during the World War did much to confirm this assumption of their docility. The Peace of Versailles came before there was any serious disillusionment. The nineteenth-century scientific man had been a very lopsided man; often he had proved himself a poor conventional snob outside his particular investigation.

'The sciences,' as Simon Azar remarked, 'came before Science'; the scientific outlook was a late result and not a primary cause of the systematic pursuit of knowledge. It was a discovery and not a starting-point. Science taught the men who served it, and the pupil learnt more than the teacher knew. There was and is an incessant conflict in the scientific world between achievement and fresh enquiry, and in the nineteenth and early twentieth centuries it was acute. The older men suspected younger men with broader ideas and hindered their advancement. They wanted them all to work in specialist blinkers. But after the World War the world of pure and applied science found itself obliged to think about things in general, and, as the Great Slump went on without surcease, it thought hard. The technicians, because of their closer approach to business and practical affairs generally, were considerably in advance of the 'pure' scientific investigators in this application of constructive habits of thought to political and social organization.

Even during the Chinese warfare there were intimations that chemists, engineers and doctors might have different ideas from the military. After the Tokio sterilization fiasco, and still more so after the failure of the eleventh gas offensive upon Wuchang to produce adequate results, the Japanese military authorities began to enquire into the possibility of 'expert sabotage', and their enquiries had a certain repercussion upon the relations of 'scientific' military men to real scientific and technical experts in Europe. There was an attempt to distinguish between experts who were 'loyal' and experts who were 'subversive'. More often than not it was the latter who were the brilliant and inventive men. Uncritical loyalty was found to go with a certain general dullness. The authorities found themselves in a dilemma between men who could not do what was wanted of them and men who would not.

A campaign against pacifist, disturbing and revolutionary ideas had been gathering force during the thirties. It became a confused and tiresome persecution in the later Forties. But it was ineffective because it was incoherent. Attempts to weed the staffs and students of technical schools and to reduce the teaching profession to docility failed, because there seemed to be no way of distinguishing what was essential science from what was treasonable thought. The attempt to destroy freedom in one part of a man's brain while leaving other parts to move freely and creatively was doomed to failure from the outset.

IV

Prophets, Pioneers, Fanatics and Murdered Men

History, especially general history, is prone to deal too much with masses and outlines. We write that 'all Germany' resented an insult, or the 'hopes of Asia' fell. But the living facts of history are changes in thought, emotion and reaction in the minds of thousands of millions of lives.

In the preceding sections we have spoken in general terms of 'concepts of combination' developing; of ideologies dissolving and giving place to other ideologies like clouds that gather and melt and pass across the mental skies of mankind. In the books before those sections we traced the growing awareness of a possible World-State in the thoughts of men throughout two thousands years of slow awakening. But the presentation is incomplete until we have turned our attention, for a chapter at least, from the broad sweep of opinion and the changing determination of the collective will to the texture of individual experiences, the brain storms, the tormented granules, which shaped out these massive structural developments.

One must draw upon the naive materials of one's own childhood to conceive, however remotely, the states of mind of those rare spirits who looked first towards human brotherhood. One must consider the life of some animal, one's dog, one's cheetah or one's pony, to realize the bounded, definite existence of a human being in the early civilizations. The human life then was just as set in its surroundings as any animal's. There was the town, the river, the cultivations, the distant hills, the temple, near friends and strange distant enemies constituting a complete and satisfying *all*. The gods were credible and responsible, taking all ultimate responsibility off your shoulders; the animals had souls like yourself, as understandable as yourself, and the darkness and shadows were haunted by spirits. In that sort of setting unnumerable generations lived and loved and hated and died. Everything was made familiar and understandable by the trick of personification. You brought the stranger into your family; you made it a member of your group. Earth was a mother and the sun a great father of glory marching across the sky.

It is a marvellous intricate history to trace how the human mind began to doubt, to pry and question, to penetrate the curtains of assurance and fancied security that enclosed it. Perhaps it was rather torn out of its confidence than that it fretted its way out by any urgency of its own.

The Hebrew Bible, which Christianity preserved for us, is a precious record of uneasy souls amidst the limited conditions of these ages before mechanism or travel or logical analysis. It tells how man came out of the Eden of unquestioning acceptance and found perplexity. It gives us intimate glimpses of states of mind that were typical of what went on in hundreds of thousands of struggling brains. They were beginning to note thorns and weeds, toil and insecurity of life. They made great efforts to explain their growing sense that all was not right with the world. They had to dramatize the story. They had as yet only 'personification' as a means of apprehending relations and causes. They had no way of getting hold of a general idea except by imagining it as a person. Strange thoughts frightened them. They seemed exterior to them. They dared not even say, 'I think'; they had to say, 'I heard a voice', or the 'Word of the Lord came to me'. Enormous effort therefore was needed to pass from the thought of a patriarchal tribal God to a mightier overriding God. Men did not unite communities; they identified their Gods. Monotheism was the first form of the World-State in men's minds.

What a desperate deed it was for some inwardly terrified man to lift up his voice against the local elders and the local idol, proclaiming, 'There is no God but God'! The reactions of his fellows, living still within the framework of accepted beliefs, to this attempt to break out to wide relations, were scorn, amusement, irritation, dislike or horror and superstitious fear. We have the story of Mohammed recorded, and of his fight with the gods of Mecca, but that was a late and sophisticated instance of something that happened in innumerable times and places; the challenge of the man 'inspired' by his new idea to the social mental nest out of which he was breaking.

Men who saw the light and spoke were only one species of a larger genus of human beings whose minds worked differently from the common man's or were simply more feverishly active. The others were eccentrics or downright madmen. One sort was hardly to be told from another, for both were sayers of incredible things.

The beginning of written record in the millennium before Christ shows a long tradition already established for the treatment of these odd, disturbing exceptions. So far as we can peer into the past we find the tranquillity of the everyday community broken by these troubled troublesome individuals who went about, living queerly, saying unusual and disconcerting things, inciting people to behave strangely, threatening divine anger, foreboding evils. There was a disposition to buy them off with a sort of reverence – and disregard. Inferior and unhappy people might find an interest and excitement in their strange announcements and suggestions. But rulers did not like them, comfortable people disliked and feared them. They irritated, they terrified contented people. They seemed perverse, and many of them plainly were perverse. If they went too far mankind turned on them and they were ill-treated and mobbed and ridiculed; they were cast into prisons; beaten and killed.

The ones that mattered most seemed always, by our present standards, to have had something to say that was at once profoundly important and yet not quite true or not quite truly said. Disciples, sometimes in great multitude, respond to their enigmatical utterances. When they died or were killed men were left asking, 'What exactly did he say? What exactly did he mean?' the inspired words became very readily riddles for interpreters and matter for pedantry. They were phrased and rephrased, applied and misapplied, tried out in every possible and impossible way.

Nowadays we find a common quality in all these madmen, prophets, teachers and disturbers of the mental peace. The species was learning to talk and use language. The race was, as it were, trying to think something out; was attempting to say something new and enlarging to itself. It was doing this against great resistance. Its intellectual enterprise was playing against its instinctive fear of novelty. Some of these teachers died terribly, were flayed or burnt or tortured to death. One hung on a cross and died of physical weakness some hours before the two felons who were his hardier fellow sufferers, leaving a teaching compounded of such sweet and fine ideas of conduct, such mystical incomprehensibleness, such misleading inconsistency, that it remained a moral stimulus and an intellectual perplexity, a jungle for heresies and discoveries, for millions of souls for two millennia.

Vainly does one try nowadays to put ourself into the mind of the prophet led to execution. We know the value of what he did, it is true, but what did he think he was doing? The secret of such personifying, urgently seeking brains seems hidden from us now for ever.

In the busier and more prosperous social phases of history such disturbers are less evident; in times of change, and especially when there was also a release of social energy, when conflicting traditions ground and wore upon each other, these troubled and troublesome minds seemed to have multiplied. The days of the vast unstable Roman imperialism abounded in efforts to say something new and profound about life. Everywhere there were new worships, because a worship still seemed the only form in which a new idea and way of life could be conveyed from mind to mind. Everywhere the puzzled sprawling human race was trying to say something, some magic word to resolve its perplexities and guide it to peace.

With the Renascence of learning and the onset of organized science the actual number and the actual proportion of enquiring and innovating minds increased greatly. The effort of the racial mind to master the conditions of its being was renewed on a multitudinous scale. But now the disturbers of equanimity no longer appear as wild-eyed prophets; they no longer claim that the Word of the Lord is upon them. Abstract and logical thought has pervaded the mind of the race and such personification is no longer needed. They do not denounce the old gods; they analyse them. Moreover, now that we approach modern times and deal with more and more abundantly recorded events, we begin to realize with a living understanding and sympathy what was going on in the minds of the innovators and to feel in touch with the immeasurable heroisms and unnumerable tragedies of those later pioneers, those rebels, critics, revolutionaries who were thrusting, more or less intelligently, against the acceptances and inertias amidst which they lived, towards a saner, more comprehensive and more clearly apprehended racial idea.

So far no completely masterly digest has been made of the millions of biographies and tons of other material that tell of the mental seething of the world from the seventeenth century of the Christian Era onward. If the old-world prophets are too rare and remote for our understanding, the modern revolutionaries are almost too close and abundant for us to stand back and see them clearly. Vast studies have been organized of various portions of the field; Roger Cuddington and his associates' *Studies of Protestant Thought in Holland, the Rhineland, Switzerland and Britain from the Seventeenth to the Nineteenth Century* give, for instance, a picture of one wide area and period, in which the fermentation arose first in a religious form and owed much to the clash of Jew and Gentile; while Margrim's *Early Forms of Anarchism and Socialism* is a very successful attempt to realize the ideas and personalities from which the modern criticism of rule and property derived. With the help of such works as these, and with some luck among the biographies, we do contrive at last to get down close to an imaginative participation in those individual reactions which in the aggregate remade the human community in the form we know to-day.

Every one of these personal stories, if it were told completely, would have to begin with a child, taking the world for granted, believing its home, its daddy and mummy to be right and eternal. It confronted a fixed and established world with no standard of comparison in past or future. It was told its place in life and·what it had to do. Bad luck, discomfort, some shock or some innate unrest was needed to put a note of interrogation against these certainties. Then for those whom destiny has marked for disturbance comes the suspicion: 'This that they have told me isn't true.' Still more disturbing came the possibility: 'This that they do and want me to do isn't right.' And then with a widening reference: 'Things could be better than this.' So the infected individual drifted out of easy vulgar living with his fellows, out of a natural animal-like acceptance of the established thing, to join the fermenting and increasing minority of troubled minds that made trouble.

He began talking to his fellows or he made notes in secret of his opinions. He asked awkward questions. He attempted little comments and ironies. We could conjure up hundreds of thousands of pictures of such doubters beginning to air their opinions in the eighteenth-century world, in the little workshops of the time, in shabby, needy homes, in market-places, in village inns, daring to say something, hardly daring to say anything, unable often to join up the vague objections they were making into any orderly criticism. But in the brown libraries and studies of the period other men were sitting, poring over books, writing with something furtive in their manner, while the pride of contemporary life brayed and trumpeted along the roadway outside. 'What is being told to the people is not true. Things could be better than this.' Men ventured on strange suggestions in university classes; brought out startlingly unorthodox theses.

The infectious interrogations spread. Constituted authority got wind of these questionings and itself came questioning in search of heresy and sedition, with rack and thumbscrew. When we read the books and pamphlets of that awakening phase, writings which seem amidst profuse apologies to half say next to nothing, we get the measure of the reasonable timidities of the time. Men might pay in sweating agony and death for that next-to-nothing they had said.

At first they raised not so much the substance as the form of an interrogation. In the sixteenth century you would have found a number of local accumulations of heresies, but hardly any inkling of the Modern State. Except for some scholar's echo to the *Republic* or *Laws* of Plato, there was no one at all reading and comparing in the field of social and political structure before the seventeenth century. The eighteenth century was, in comparison with its predecessor, an age of voluminous revolutionary thought. Men began calling fundamental ideas and political institutions in question as they had never been challenged since the onset of Christianity. They went into exile for their innovations; their books were burnt; censorships were established to suppress these new ideas. Still they spread and multiplied. The authoritative claim of aristocracy, the divinity of monarchy, tarnished, dwindled, became ineffective under these dripping notes of interrogation. Republics appeared and the first embryonic intimations of socialism.

In our account of the first French revolution and the revolutionary perturbation of the eighteenth century [*No traces of this account are to be found in Raven's papers.* – ED.] we have had to discriminate between the economic and social forces that were forcing political readjustment on the one hand, and the influence of new ideas on the other. We have shown how little these formal changes were planned, and how small a share in these events is to be ascribed to creative intention or mental processes generally. Nevertheless the questioning was drawing closer to reality and the scope of the planning was spreading. We will not tell again of the profound change in men's ideas about private property, private freedom and monetary relationship, that began to find expression in the socialist and communist movements of the age. Our concern here is to emphasize the billions of small wrangles that were altering the collective thought, to summon out of the past, for an instant, an elfin clamour of now silenced voices that prepared the soil for revolution, the not-at-all-lucid propagandists at street corners, the speakers in the little meeting-houses, in open spaces and during work intermissions; to recall the rustle of queer newspapers that were not quite ordinary newspapers; and the handicapped book publications that were everywhere fighting traditional and instinctive resistances. Everywhere the leaven of the Modern State was working – confusedly.

As we have seen, the new conception of a single world society did not come at one blow, perfect and effective, into the human mind. It was not completed even in outline until the days of De Windt, and before that time it was represented by a necessary confusion of contributory material, incomplete bits of it and illogical and misleading extensions of those bits. It had to begin like that; it had to begin in fragments and rashly. There was always a fierce disposition manifested to apply the new incomplete ideas, headlong and violently. The more the sense of insufficiency gnaws at a man's secret consciousness, the more he is in conflict with an inner as well as an outer antagonist, the more emphatic, dogmatic and final he is apt to be. That disposition to bring the new ideas to the test of reality, the urge to assert by experiment, was the chief source of trouble for these ever increasing multitudes of innovating minds. Constituted authority, established usage, have no quarrel with ideas as such; it is only when these ideas become incitation, when they sought incarnation in act and reality, that conflict began.

So all over the world throughout the nineteenth century men were to be found contriving trouble for authority and devising outrages on usage. The light of world reconstruction lit their souls, but often it filtered through thick veils of misconception and had the colourings of some epidemic hate. They dreamt of insurrections, of seizures of power, of organized terror; in practice their efforts dwindled down too often to stupid little murders – often completely irrelevant murders – to shouting and swarming in the streets, to peltings and window-breaking, to blowing in the front doors of government houses and embassies, to the casting of explosives amidst the harmless spectators at public ceremonies.

Before the French revolution there was not nearly so much of such sporadic violence as afterwards. There were a few assassinations by religious or racial fanatics, but usually the older type of political crime was definitely connected with some conspiracy to change the personnel rather than the nature of a régime. The 'Anarchist' outrages of the nineteenth century, however clumsy, were by comparison social criticisms. Behind them, even though vague, exaggerated and distorted, was the hope of a new world order.

Linked inseparably with all these premature expressions of the desire for a new life were the activities of more extensive revolutionary systems: printing-presses in cellars, furtive distribution of papers, secret meetings, the savage discipline of fear-ruled illegal societies, the going to and fro of emissaries – men often with narrow and ill-assorted minds, but nevertheless men with everything to lose and little to gain or hope for by such activities. After we have allowed for every sort of resentment and bitter impulse in them, the fact remains such men were devotees. They were a necessary ferment for the spread of thought.

That increasing revolutionary ferment, in all its tentative aspects, used to be called The Extreme Left. There had never been anything quite like it in the world before. For the most part these men had broken not only with the political and social order of their time, but with its religious beliefs. Between 1788 and 1965, hundreds of thousands of men and thousands of women, far braver than any Moslem fanatics, sustained by no hope of a future life, no hope of any greeting after the sudden blankness of their untimely deaths, and, so far as we can gather now, not even with a clear vision of the full and ordered social life for which they died, stood up sullenly or with a certain sad exaltation to face the firing party or the halter. A hundred times as many endured exile, prisons, ostracisms, beatings, gross humiliations and the direst poverty for the still dimly apprehended cause of human liberation.

They had not even the assurance of unanimity. They were all convinced that there had to be a better world, but they had not the knowledge, they had not the facilities for free and open discussion, to clear up and work out the inevitable outline of their common need. They formulated their ideas dully and clumsily; they went a certain way to truth and then stopped short; they suspected all other formulae than the ones they themselves had hit upon; they quarrelled endlessly, bitterly, murderously, among themselves. Nearly all sooner or later were infected by hate. Often it happened that two men, each of whom had roughly half the justice of things in him, killed each other, when indeed they needed only to put their prepossessions together to get the full outline of a working reconstruction.

Da Silva has called all those who made the revolutions and revolutionary efforts that occurred between 1788 and 1948 the 'revolutionaries of the half-light'. His studies of the tangled history of the new social concepts that broke through the open popular discussion only after the establishment of the Soviet régime in Russia in 1917 constitute a very brilliant work of elucidation and simplification. It is a history of twilight that ends at dawn. In the twenties and thirties of the twentieth century the ordinary man in the street was discussing, cheaply perhaps, but freely, ideas, possibilities and courses of action that no one would have dared to whisper about, would scarcely have dared to think about, two centuries before. He scarcely knew a single name of the pioneers, fanatics and desperadoes who had won this freedom for his mind.

The nature of the conflict was changing. That was very plain by 1940. Where there had been pioneers, there were now systematic explorers and surveyors; the teeming multitudes of our race were still producing devoted and sacrificial types, but the half-light was now a cloudy daylight and the ordered analyses and plans of such men as De Windt were making understandings and cooperations possible that would have been incredible in the nineteenth century. In the nineteenth century revolution was suspected, forbidden, dark, criminal, desperate and hysterical. In the twentieth century it became candid and sympathetic. The difference was essentially an intellectual one; after a vast period of stormy disputation the revolutionary idea had cleared up. The sun of the Modern State broke through.

Revolution still demanded its martyrs, but the martyrdoms were henceforth of a different character. Biographies of revolutionists before the Great War go on by night, amidst a scenery of back streets, cellars, prisons, suspicions and betrayals. Biographies of revolutionists in the final struggle to establish the Modern State go on in full daylight. It is reaction now which has taken to the darkness, to plots, assassinations, and illegal measures. The Modern State propagandist became less and less like an insurgent individual of some alien subject race; he became more and more like a missionary in a savage country, ill-armed or un-armed, and at an immediate disadvantage, but with the remote incalculable prestige of a coming power behind him.

The later death-roll of revolutionaries has fewer and fewer executions in it and an increasing tale of assassinations and deaths in public conflict. A larger and larger proportion of those who died for it were killed either by mobs or in fair and open fighting. And soon the idea of the Modern State had become so pervasive that the battles ceased to be for it or against it; they became, rather, misunderstandings between impatient zealots with a common end. In many conflicts the historian is still perplexed to determine which side, if either, can be counted as fighting for the Modern State.

The analyses of De Windt made immense charities of understanding possible. Creative-minded men, though they hardened against the liar and the cheat, became less and less willing to fight the puerile adherent and the honest fanatic with a tiresome but honestly intended formula. 'There,' they said, 'but for certain misconceptions and resolvable obsessions, go our men,' and set themselves at any risk or loss to the task of conversion. Just as Fascism in its time seized upon the ancient terroristic and blackmailing Mafia in Sicily and partly annexed it, partly changed it and so superseded it, just as the Nazi movement incorporated large chunks of the Communist party in its efforts to reformulate Germany, so now the Modern State fellowship grappled with the world-wide series of organizations which had superseded democratic institutions nearly everywhere, made every effort to capture the imaginations of their adherents and showed the most unscrupulous boldness in seizing their direction whenever it could. The Modern State Movement differed from every preceding revolutionary movement in its immense assimilatory power, due to the clearness of the objectives it set before men's minds.

The difference between the revolutionary before the Great War and the revolutionary after that illuminating crisis is closely parallel to the difference between the old alchemist and the modern man of science; the former haunted by demons, goblins and spirits, warped by symbolic obsessions and cabalistic words and numbers, terribly alone with himself, obsessed with religious fears, by fear of the inquisitor, by fear of the ruler above and of the rabble below, perpetually baffled in his attempts to achieve great things, but full of a dangerous unpremeditated knowledge of poisons and mischievous devices; the latter with a mind released by centuries of analysis and simplification, reassured by the incessant tale of scientific victories, stoically indifferent to popular misrepresentation and equally sure of his universe and himself.

V

The First Conference at Basra: 1965

The conference of scientific and technical workers at Basra in 1965 is regarded by historians as a cardinal date in the emergence of the Modern State. It was organized by the Transport Union, which had begun as a loose association of the surviving aeroplane and shipping operators for mutual aid and protection. The ideas formulated at this conference – and even those were still formulated with a certain tentative or tactful incompleteness – had been gathering force and definition for some time. But this conference was the first to draw up a definite plan of the general human outlook and initiate an organization to carry it out. It marked the transition from thought to action in general affairs.

The idea of using air transport as the combining and directive force for a new synthesis of civilization was already an old and familiar one. It had been in men's thoughts for at least thirty years. A popular story published in 1933, *Man's Mortality* (by the English romancer Michael

Arlen, 1895–1990), for instance, is an amusing fantasy of the world dominated by an air-transport syndicate. It is still a very readable book and interesting in showing the limitations of the educated imagination at that time. The belief in the possibilities of invention is unbounded; air velocities and air fighting are described on a scale that still seems preposterously exaggerated to-day; while on the other hand the inflated stock buying and selling of that period, although it had grown from the merest germ in about a century and a half, is represented as still going on unchanged, and the world's air dictators are gambling dishonestly in stock, and at last 'crash' financially and bolt as though they were just contemporary politicians and mystery men rather than lords of the whole power of the air. In a world of incredible metals, explosives and swiftness, the Stock Exchange, the Bourses, still survive. And there are still Powers and Foreign Policies! Nothing could illustrate better the inability of people at that time to realize the economic and political changes that were then actually tumbling upon them. For some obscure reason mental and moral progress and institutional invention seemed absolutely impossible to them.

An interesting little London periodical of the same time, *Essential News*, has recently been reprinted for graduate students of history in the *Students' Reprint Series*. Its fourth issue (February 4th, 1933) contains a summary of contemporary thought about World Air Control. It cites a complete scheme for the 'International' control of aviators, drawn up by a small French group at the suggestion of M. Henri de Jouvenal under the presidency of M. Pierre Denis. A *Union Aéronautique Internationale* is proposed, a cosmopolitan air transport company. Linked with this and controlled by the poor League of nations, an 'Air Force for Mutual Assistance' was to police the atmosphere. The proposals are so plainly utopian and impracticable in the face of the sovereign state system as to seem insincere. It was only thirty years later, after the common suicide of the sovereign Powers of Europe, that the assembled technicians at Basra could revive the broad conception of this proposal.

This first conference at Basra was distinguished from its predecessors first by its universality and then by the extremely bold and comprehensive proposals for united action it accepted – proposals which were in effect, if not in form, the project for the modern World-State. It was the first of these gatherings attended by considerable American, Chinese and Japanese contingents, as well as the customary European representatives, and the Russian technicians were present in unprecedented strength and unexpectedly united and independent of the political controllers who accompanied them. New Zealand also had reappeared in the world's affairs. There were even two representatives (two schoolmasters in the Social Psychology section) from Iceland, which for most practical purposes had been cut off from the world for over five years.

And one has only to compare the agenda of this and previous assemblies to feel at once the stride forward in the scope and courage of scientific and technical thought that had occurred.

It was a young gathering; the average age is estimated by Amen Rihani as about thirty-three, and five or six women attended in the social and educational branches. A third but very significant feature was the extensive use of that simple and convenient *lingua franca* of the aviators, Basic English. Even the native English-speaking people present did their best to keep their speeches within the limitations of that ingenious idiom.

The master section was still that of General Transport. The body which had organized the gathering was, as has been said already, the Transport Union, originally a purely business body, but the inspiration was that of the Modern State movement, and technicians in medicine, education, agriculture and every main type of industrial production were present. There was much discussion of the upkeep of the world routes and the administrative tasks arising out of that. Nothing could give the student a more vivid sense of the derelict state of the world at that time than the boldness with which this Control took possession of things and pushed its activities into new fields. It was decided, for instance, that all existing aerodromes and landmarks, lights and lighting fields, should be directly under its management. There was no question of purchase; it took them over. Every aeroplane in the world was to be registered, was to carry a distinctive number, respect the common tariff of charges and pay a registration fee to the Control. Airships and aeroplanes which did not do this were to be treated as pirates, denied the use of aerodromes and filling stations, and 'driven out of the air'. They were to be driven out of the air if necessary by an 'air police' which the Control was to organize. Aerodromes or regions that harboured such recalcitrants were to be boycotted.

These proposals were not accepted without discussion. But there was very little protest against what was certainly, from the older point of view, an illegal usurpation of authority. The political members of the Russian contingent offered the chief resistance, and what other opposition appeared was not from aviators, engineers, chemists, biologists or men of that type, but from sociologists and economists of the less advanced schools. The main objection took the form of a question: 'But what will governments say to this?' So far as the Westerners and Chinese were concerned there was a disposition to disregard the possibility of political intervention. 'Wait till it comes,' they said cheerfully. But Soviet Russia and Soviet Japan were at that time much more rankly political than the rest of the world, and they at least had politicians as well as men of skill and science present at this gathering. A long speech was made by the commissar Vladimir Peshkoff, full of the menace of later trouble. He denounced the projected Control as an insidious attempt to restore a capitalist trust in the world. Its psychology would be bourgeois and capitalist. Moscow would never consent to the passage of controlled machines over the vast territories under Soviet control nor allow the exploitation of the resources of Russia in oil and minerals by any outside organization.

'And how will Moscow prevent it?' asked Ivan Englehart, a Russian aviator and aeroplane builder, rising as Peshkoff sat down. 'Is it in nationalism of this sort that the Third International is to end?'

By way of reply Peshkoff leant towards him and spat out in Russian, 'Wait until you return to Moscow.'

'I may have to wait a little time,' said Englehart. 'I am a citizen of the world, and I shall go back to Russia in my own time and in my own fashion.'

'This is treason. Wait until Moscow hears of this!'

'And how and when will Moscow hear of this?'

'Very soon.'

Englehart was standing a few yards from Peshkoff. He shook his head with a sceptical smile. He spoke gently, like a man who had long prepared himself for such an occasion.

'You flew here, Tavarish Peshkoff, in my squadron. How do you propose to return?'

Peshkoff rose to his feet, realized the blank want of sympathy in the gathering, spluttered and sat down again in unconcealed dismay.

Englehart waited for a moment or so and then went on, choosing his words with quiet deliberation, to assure the meeting of the adhesion of the Russian technicians to the projected Control. 'That phantom Proletarian of yours fades with all the other empires and kingdoms,' he said to the political delegates, his colleagues. 'We are only giving shape to a new world order that is already born.'

His speech set the key for most of the subsequent debate.

That establishment of the Control was the backbone discussion, but it was no more than the backbone of a plan that covered the whole future organization of society; upon it was articulated a whole framework of structural proposals. The central section dealt not only with the air network but with the organization of every type of communication. The lighthouses, lightships, sea marks, channels and harbours of the world were suffering from a decade of economy, a decade of wartime destruction and a decade of chaos and decay. The meteorological services were no longer operative. All this had to be restored. The definite abandonment of every type of railroad was accepted as a matter of course. Railways were buried at Basra for ever. And the restoration and reconstruction of production in a hundred essential industries followed also as a necessary consequence of these primary resolutions.

The more the reader scrutinizes the agenda, the more is he impressed by the mildness of the official title of the gathering: 'A Conference on

Scientific and Mercantile Communications and Associated Questions'. It is clear that the conveners resolved to press on with their task of world reorganization as far as they possibly could, without rousing the enfeebled and moribund political organizations of the past to obstruction and interference. The language throughout is that of understatement; the shape of the projects is fearlessly bold. A committee of experts had prepared a very good general survey of the natural resources of the planet, including those of the already suspicious Russia, and the conference set itself unhesitatingly to work out the problems of a resumption of production generally, with an entire disregard of the various proprietary claims that might arise to challenge the realization of these schemes. There was no provocative discussion of these claims; they were ignored. The Air and Sea Control evidently meant to take effective possession not only of all derelict ports, aerodromes, coal-mines, oil wells, power stations and mines, but to bring those in which a certain vitality still lingered into line with its schemes by hook or by crook, by persuasion or pressure. Its confidence in its solidarity with the skilled men working these latter establishments was absolute. Such a solidarity would have been inconceivable thirty years before. Financial adventure had been washed out of the minds of the new generation of technicians altogether. They simply wanted to 'get things going again'. Ideas of personal enrichment were swamped in their universal conviction that their class must now either work together and master the world, or leave it.

So with a modest air of logical necessity, of being driven rather than driving, the Conference spread its planning far beyond the material and mechanism of world intercommunication.

What is this reconstructed transport to carry? How is it to be fed – and paid for? About the air-ports everywhere were tracts and regions sinking back to that primordial peasant cultivation which had been the basis of all the barbaric civilizations of the past. The question of the expropriation of the peasant and the modernization of agricultural production was taken up at Basra at the point where Lenin and Stalin had laid it down, defeated. The Conference was lucidly aware that upon the same planet at the same time you cannot have both an aviator and a starveling breeding peasantry, toiling endlessly and for ever in debt. One or other has to go, and the fundamental objective of the Conference was to make the world safe for the former. The disappearance of the latter followed, not as a sought-after end but as a necessary consequence. And the disappearance of as much of the institutions of the past as were interwoven with it.

In the ideas of their relations to each other and to the world as a whole, these Basra technicians were all what the nineteenth century would have called socialistic. They were so fundamentally socialistic that they did not even raise the question of socialism. It is doubtful if the word was ever used there. They took it for granted that this Control that was growing like a limitless polyp in their minds would be the effectual owner and exploiter of all the aeroplanes, routes, industrial townships, factories, mines, cultivations that were falling into place in their Plan. It would have seemed as unnatural to them that a new Ford or a new Rockefeller should arise to own a factory or a mine personally as that anyone should try to steal the ocean or the air. There it was for the common good, and just as much was industrial plant for the common good.

All these men, it must be remembered, almost without exception, were men of the salaried type of mind. They had been born and brought up in a tradition in which money was a secondary matter. From the beginning of the mechanical age, the men of science, the technical experts, the inventors and discoverers, the foremen and managers and organizers, had been essentially of the salariat. Some few had dabbled in finance and grown rich, but they were exceptions. Before the World War indeed these sort of men had been accustomed to accept the acquisitive and gambling types, the powerful rich and owning people, as a necessary evil. Now they were manifestly a totally unnecessary evil, and without the least vindictiveness or animosity plans were made to do without them and prevent their return. The Basra Conference would as soon have considered a return of Foreign Offices or of Kings or Divinities.

But they had to consider – and this was the work of a powerful section upon which the Americans were exceptionally active – how the wealth of the world that they meant to restore had to be distributed for consumption, and how a close-knit world organization was to be reconciled with personal freedom and particularly with artistic and literary initiatives. This was entitled the Section of Wages, Charges and Supply.

There seems to have been the completest agreement that the only way of combining services with private liberty is by the use of money. Without money there is necessarily a dictation of consumption and a dictation of movement to the worker. He would be given 'what was good for him'. But money generalized the claim of the worker as worker, and the claim of the citizen as shareholder in the commonweal, upon the goods, pleasures, facilities and liberties of life. You take your money and you buy this or that, or go here or there, or do whatever you please. But there were dangers in this invention; twice in history money had failed mankind and a money-linked order had crashed. This time, they thought, mankind had learnt its lesson, and a new money had to be devised that would be, in any large sense, fool-proof, sneak-proof and scoundrel-proof. So much lay beneath the intention of the Section of Wages, Charges and Supply.

This section carried the question of money into regions that would

have seemed quite outside its scope thirty years before. In the Twenties
and Thirties of the century, and indeed into the war troubles of the
Forties, there had been a great volume of discussion about money. Men
had realized its dangers and set themselves, with the energy born of a
sense of crisis, to the analysis of its processes and the invention of new
methods that should prevent the gross accumulation of ownership, the
mischievous manipulation of credit, the relative impoverishment of the
worker and the strangulation of enterprise that had wrecked the second
monetary civilization. Gradually it had been realized that there could be
no Theory of Money that was not in fact a complete theory of social
organization. The Conference set itself now to a prepared and simplified
task.

The interdependence of monetary theory with the general theory of
property and social structure, which had hardly been suspected by their
fathers, was now universally recognized. There was a considerable
contingent of young lawyers present, though it would have amazed the
previous generation beyond measure to find them in the ranks of
technologists and men of science. They knocked the dust of centuries
off the idea of ownership in these very pregnant debates. We have
already mentioned the surprise of Nicholson at the new sort of law
schools he found in America. At Basra the products of these schools
were very much to the fore, together with several older teachers from
the London School of Economics, which flourished until the landslide
in 1968. These new lawyers, with their fundamentally scientific habits
of mind, were amazingly unlike their professional predecessors – those
obstinate, cunning and terrible old sinners who played so large a part in
the economic strangulation of the United States and the frustration of
all the high hopes of their founders. They had completely abandoned
the pretence that the business of the law was to protect private property,
exact debts and maintain a false appearance of equity between man and
man. They knew that justice without equality of status and opportunity
can be nothing more than a sham, and their ideas were already
completely based on our current conception of law as the regulative
system in the network of relationships between the human commonweal
and its subordinate corporations and individuals. They were entirely
contemptuous of any claims, contracts, rules and precedents that
impeded the free expansion of human welfare. Among all the various
types that gathered at Basra, these younger lawyers, in close touch with
the new economists on the one hand and the group psychologists on the
other, and inspired by a political constructiveness of the boldest sort,
were certainly the most remarkable.

It is chiefly to them that we owe the firm assertion by the Basra
Conference of the principle that in a modern community there can be
no individual property in anything but personal belongings and money.
This was thrown out as something too obvious to discuss. Houses and

lands were henceforth to be held on leases of a not too lengthy period, life tenure being the longest. All other tangible things, they assumed, belonged inalienably to the world commonweal – in the usufruct of which every human being was manifestly a shareholder. And it was these younger lawyers also who did the greater part of that task of disentanglement and simplification, which reduced money to its present and only proper use as a check for consumable goods and services, either paid out to the individual, or, in the case of minors and incapables, to the individual's guardians, either as a part of the racial inheritance or else as wages for work in the common service. The world was to be reborn without usury or monetary speculation.

The monetary methods of the world at that time were in a state of such complete chaos that there was no effective system in working order anywhere to present an immediate resistance to the operation of the new ideas. Every region was running its own, often very arbitrary and primitive, system of tokens and checks. But the revival of communications that had made Basra possible was already giving an increasing prestige to what was known as the 'air-dollar'. This was not a metallic coin at all; it was a series of paper notes, which represented distance, weight, bulk, and speed. Each note was good for so many kilograms in so much space, for so many kilometres at such a pace. The value of an air-dollar had settled down roughly to a cubic metre weighing ten kilograms and travelling two hundred kilometres at a hundred kilometres an hour.

This was already an energy unit and not a unit of substance, such as the old-world standards had always been. It marked very definitely that the old static conceptions of human life with limited resources were giving place to kinetic ideas of a continually expanding life. The air-dollar was a unit of energy in terms of transport, and its transformation into the energy dollar of our daily life to-day was already sketched out clearly by the Basra experts, although the actual change over was not accomplished until ten years later.

It was the plain, if unformulated, intention of the new Air and Sea Control to gain possession and exploit all the available sources of energy in the world as soon as possible, to frame its human balance sheet, scale its wages and declare its dividends as the common trustee of mankind, but manifestly if the threat of Peshkoff materialized, and the Russian Soviet system (or indeed any other owning group) was able to remain in effective control of its territorial wealth, the energy dollar would afford a just unambiguous medium for whatever trade was necessary between the competing administrations.

The planning of a new political, industrial, and monetary world scheme still does not measure the full achievement of this First Basra Conference. There was also a strong and vigorous educational section working in close touch with the technicians and the social psychologists.

It made plans not only for the coordination of the surviving colleges and technical schools in the world and for the revivification of those that had lapsed, but it set itself definitely to the task of that propaganda of the idea of the Modern State which is the substantial content of our existing fundamental education. This was dealt with by the Section of Training and Advertisement. Basic English was to lay the foundations of a world lingua franca. Evidently wherever the influence of the Air and Sea Control extended, a new propaganda, a new Press, and new common schools were to extend. There can be little doubt that most of the teachers at Basra already saw quite clearly ahead of them the world-wide mental and social order in which we live to-day. They knew what they were doing. They went back from this gathering encouraged and confirmed, to give themselves to the terrific and exalting adventure before them, to the evocation day by day, and idea by idea, of a new civilization amidst the distressful, slovenly, and still living wreckage of the old.

When the Conference at last dispersed two new realities had appeared in the world, so unobtrusively that it was only slowly that the mass of mankind realized their significance. One was the Central Board, known also as the Air and Sea Control, consolidating the Transport Union, linking with it the other Controls and sections, and having its permanent offices at Basra; the other was the Police of the Air and Sea Ways, at first a modest organization with about 3,000 aeroplanes, a handful of seaplanes, a hundred patrol ships, and a personnel of about 25,000 men. It was a small body judged by the standards either of preceding or subsequent times, but at that period it was by far the most powerful armed force in the world.

VI

The Growth of Resistance to the Air and Sea Control

For nearly ten years the new Air and Sea Control was able to grow and extend its methods and influence without any general conflict. The little breeze between the Russian political control and the technicians did not rise to a storm; instead it died away. Russia was learning wisdom at last and weakening in her resolve to subordinate the modern scientific type of man to his old-fashioned demagogic rival. She had suffered so severely by the miscalculations and convulsive direction of her party chiefs, she was still so ill equipped mechanically, and so poorly provided with aviators, that the old and now mentally weary dictatorship recoiled from a new struggle with these and their associated technical experts. It is to be noted that, in spite of the closest espionage, the creed of the Russian aviators, engineers, and men of science was already the Modern State and not the Dictatorship of the Proletariat, and that her political rulers were beginning to understand this.

So that the new Air and Sea Control, sustained by a multitude of nuclei on De Windt's pattern scattered throughout the world, very much as the Bolshevik political organization had been sustained by the Communist Party, came into existence and spread its ever-growing network about the planet without an immediate struggle. Its revolutionary nature was understood by few people other than its promoters. It grew rapidly. As the Esthonian proverb says: 'One must be born before one's troubles begin.'

The recovery of human prosperity in that decade between 1965 and 1975 was very rapid. It went on side by side with the expansion of the Transport system. By 1970 the Transport Control, the chief of the subsidiaries of the general Air and Sea Control, was running worldwide services that had as many as 25,000 aeroplanes aloft at the same time; it had possessed itself of shipyards on the Tyne, in Belfast, Hamburg, and a number of other points, and was building steel cargo ships by the score; it was creating a new system of high roads for which a number of the old main railway tracks were taken over, and it was running water-power stations, substituting our present chemical treatment of carboniferous strata for the terrible hand coal-mining of the older economy, and it was working oil. It had developed a subsidiary body, the Supply Control, which was rapidly becoming a vaster organization than its parent. This was engaged in producing iron and steel, producing or purchasing rubber, metals, cotton, wool and vegetable substances, and restoring the mass production of clothing of all sorts, electrical material, mechanisms, and a vast variety of chemicals of which the output had been dormant in some instances for twenty years or more.

Never very clearly cut off from the Supply Control was the Food Control, which began ostensibly with the victualling of the Transport Services, and was soon carrying on a vast barter in food materials, its own surplus supplies and commodities generally throughout the world. In all its ramifications these three bodies were in 1970 employing about two million people, to whom wages were paid in the new modern dollars, energy dollars, good for units in transport, housing, and for all the priced commodities handled by the Controls.

The property of all these Controls was vested in the Modern State

Society, which consisted at this time of about a quarter of a million Fellows, who had to be qualified up to a certain level of technical efficiency, who submitted to the Society disciplines during their years of active participation, and received wages varying by about 200 per cent above or below a mean standard, according to their standing. About a quarter of the other employees were student apprentices aspiring to fellowship, and of these the proportion was increasing. The Society had already developed the organization it was to retain for a century. The Fellows were divided into faculties for technical purposes; they voted by localized groups upon local issues and they had a general vote for the faculty delegations to the central council of the Society, which had its first seat at Basra contiguous to the central offices of the Three Controls. The relation of the Society to the Controls was not unlike the relation of the Communist party to the Moscow Government in the early days of the Soviet system; it was a collateral activity of much the same people.

It was the Society itself which at first directed the educational activities of the Modern State Movement. Wherever it had either its own 'nuclei' or found employees of the Controls, it provided an elementary education of the new pattern, which involved a very clear understanding of the history and aims of the Modern State idea, and wherever it had works and factories and a sufficient supply of students, it founded and equipped science schools and technical schools, which included psychology, medicine, group psychology and administration. Gradually a special section of Training and Education was developed under the Air and Sea Control, and this grew into a separate Educational Control. But it never became as distinct from, and collateral to, the Modern State Fellowship as the rest of the Control organizations. One may figure the whole of this world system as a vast business octopus, with the Air and Sea Control as its head and the other Controls as its tentacles. The account-keeping of this octopus centred at Basra, but a rapid development of subsidiary record and statistical bureaus also occurred. Side by side grew the intelligence and research services. By 1970 the world meteorological service was far in advance of anything that had ever existed before.

But already this restoration of communications and circulation was producing effects far beyond the Fellowship and the power of employment of the associated Controls. The ebb in the vitality of human life had already passed its maximum, and now began a restoration of activity everywhere, a fresh movement in the decaying towns, a new liveliness upon the countryside, a general reawakening of initiative, that were to confront the direction of this fast growing nexus of the Modern State with challenges, difficulties, and menaces, that grew rapidly to tremendous proportions.

It had been comparatively easy to spread throughout a prostrate and bankrupt world the new system of air and sea communications and trading that had been evolved. That world was too exhausted by war, famine, and pestilence and too impoverished to support extensive and aggressive political organizations. It was altogether another problem, even with the spreading 'nuclei', the new schools and propaganda, to control and assimilate the populations that now, no longer living in want and insecurity, were beginning to feel a fresh strength and a renewed vigour of desire.

Let us review the world situation about 1975. The Transport Control had usurped a monopoly of air and sea transport and was also monopolizing the use of its own new great roads. This gave it a practical ownership of the trade in staple products throughout the world. It was turning all the surplus products of its activities back, when its salaries had been paid, into strengthening its grip upon the general economy of mankind. By 1975 the Modern State Society counted just over a million Fellows, and in addition it was employing and training two million candidates, it was simply employing another three million, and it had between seven and eight million youngsters in its new schools. They were all, we may note, not only given a sound training in physical science and biology, but were learning world history and so acquiring a world outlook in the place of the more limited views that had hitherto framed the ordinary political imagination, and they were being taught Basic English as a *lingua franca*. In ten wonderful years the Transport Control had grown far beyond the scale of any of the great Trusts or Controls of the opening years of the century. It had created a world currency. But it was still far from 'owning the earth'. Its own produce did not exceed an eighth of all the outside stuff that it bought and sold. Its own production was mainly fuel, metals and mechanisms. Food it bought, timber, vegetable oils, crude rubber, for example. Several hundred millions of human beings were still self-subsisting, quite out of its scheme, or dealing with it only for a few manufactured articles and mass-produced commodities. And other hundreds of millions were rapidly developing, or rather recovering, a collateral productivity in relation to or in rivalry with its activities.

The chief difficulties before the Modern State Movement arose out of this parallel to its own rapid success. It was calling into existence a mass of exterior prosperity far beyond its immediate power of assimilation. Propagandists and teachers, advisory traders and competent directive agents are not made in a day. The strain upon the supply of ability, loyalty, and complete understanding in the movement was already being noted in 1970. In 1972 we hear of a 'scrutiny of qualifications', and new rules were made for the lapsing and expulsion of incompetent and unsatisfactory Fellows. The controlling staff had to be enlarged continually, and the supply of men with the necessary character, knowledge of group psychology and understanding of the constructive theory of the movement was limited.

'Let us serve,' said Fedor Galland, who was already becoming a leading spirit upon the World Council, in a speech that was circulated in 1973; 'let us not fall into factions; let us not group ourselves. We cannot afford bickering; we must not thwart and waste each other. We have done no more as yet than make a start. Remember the strangulation of Russia by Stalin. Remember those excellent chapters of De Windt against the spirit of opposition. The struggle for the Modern State has only begun.'

Here we have the clearest indication that growth strains were already apparent within the structure of the still infantile Modern State.

But if the movement found difficulty in sustaining its internal unanimity, there was at least this in its favour, that outside it there was no single world-wide framework in which antagonisms could concentrate. The old international banking system was dead and gone, and the new order issued its new money and was free to create and dominate the financial organization of things. The old armament-dealing interests were dead and buried. The old nationalist Press systems were dead and already forgotten. It is extraordinary with what rapidity this latter aspect of social life was forgotten, seeing that up to 1940 at any rate it was the primary medium of collective thought and opinion. To-day a copy of a newspaper of any date between 1890 and 1970 is a rare and precious thing, which has to be protected from carbonization in an air-proof wrapper. The central Board controlled most of the new paper supplies as well as the now rapidly reviving telegraphic, telephonic and air transmission system.

The resistances and antagonisms it had to encounter, within its organization and without, were certainly immense, but they were extremely various; the dangers they developed never came together into one united danger, never rose to a simultaneous maximum and produced a supreme crisis. In this respect or that the advance of the Modern State might be fought to a standstill and held, but it was never put entirely upon the defensive, and since it held trade, money and its ever-spreading efficient common schools in its hands, time was always on its side. 'If not today, to-morrow,' said Arden Essenden. 'But better to-day,' said Fedor Galland.

The rapidity with which the Transport Control of 1965 expanded into the Modern State octopus of 1975 accounts for quite another group of difficulties, as well as this initial difficulty of creating a personnel to keep pace with the perpetually elaborated task. This second group of troubles came from the fact that in habit and spirit the old order of things, the old ideas, the old methods, had not had time to die. That old world, blinded and enfeebled by its own errors, had staggered and fallen down in the Thirties and Forties, had lain in a coma in the Fifties. Throughout the Sixties the new world had come into existence. But in the brains of all the men and women alive who were more than forty years old, and in a great majority of these younger, more or less of the old world survived. The revival of human vitality in the Seventies involved not merely a renascence but a restoration. Old things came back to find their habitations still very imperfectly occupied by the new.

Let us consider what form this opposition had taken and what were the more serious survivals of the old order – old 'state of affairs' rather than 'order' – still in active existence about 1975. We shall then have a clue to the history of the next seventy-five years.

The task before the Air and Sea Control was essentially to leaven the whole world to its own pattern. Within its far-flung tentacles it embraced and sought to permeate with its own nature, with the concepts and methods of a commonweal of mutual service, a mass of some thousand and a half million human beings, still carried on by inertias established during thousands of generations. Morowitz calculates that in 1976 about sixty per cent of this mass was living directly upon the seasonal cultivation of the soil, and that two-thirds of this, throughout the temperate zone, was producing mainly for its own consumption and not for trade. He thinks this was a relapse from the state of affairs that obtained about 1910–20. An emancipation from the soil, an abolition of the peasant, had then been in progress for more than a century. Large-scale production, with an abundant use of machines, had so increased the output per head as to liberate (if it can be called liberation) a growing proportion of hands for industrial work or unemployment. But this process had been reversed after 1940. From that date onward there was a drift back of workers to the land, to live very incompetently and wretchedly.

The abolition of the self-subsisting peasant had been the conscious objective of Lenin and Stalin in Russia. The cultivator, with increasing ease, was to produce fundamental foodstuffs far beyond his own needs and to receive for his surplus an ever increasing variety of helps, comforts and amenities. Millions of the cultivators in 1910 were cultivating entirely for the market; they produced cotton, hemp, rubber or what not, and were as dependent on the provision shop for their food as any townsman. The social crash had ended all that. In the Famished Fifties, as Morowitz says, everyone was 'scratching for food in his own patch'. In the Sixties the common way of life throughout the world was again immediate production and consumption. Only under the direction and stimulus of the Transport Control did the workers upon the soil begin to recover the confidence and courage needed to produce beasts only for sale and crops only for marketing.

The ambition of the Modern State Fellowship was to become the landlord of the planet and either to mine, afforest, pasture, and cultivate directly or to have these tasks performed by responsible tenants, or groups and associations of tenants under its general control. But at the outset it had neither the personnel nor the power to carry out so fundamental a reconstruction of human affairs. The comparative failure of the two Five Year Plans in Russia had been a useful warning against extravagant propositions.

The Modern State did not mean, as the old saying goes, 'to bite off more than it could chew'. Its chief missionaries were its traders. They were more abundant than, and they did not need the same amount of training as, the Modern State school-masters and propagandists. They went offering contracts and prices to existing or potential food growers, cotton growers, rubber planters and operable mines; the Control did its best to guarantee sales and prices to any surviving factories, and it trusted to the selective power it had through transport, the new monetary issues, research and technical education to strengthen its grip as time went on and enable it to establish a general order in this world-wide mélange of bankrupt producers and impoverished customers it was restoring to activity.

At first it made no enquiry as to the ownership of goods that were brought to its depots; it paid cash and observed its contracts; it attempted no discriminations between man and man so long as they delivered the goods and traded square. Its nuclei and schools were still propagandist schools in 1975 and quasi independent of the trading, transport and industrial organizations that endowed them. But this was only the first stage in the Modern State undertaking. The next was to be more difficult.

The student of history must always keep in mind the importance of lifetime periods of social and political change. Between 1935 and 1975 was only forty years. Everywhere old systems of ideas were still dominating men's brains and still being transmitted to the young. Old habits of thought, old values, old patterns of conduct, that had been put aside, as it were, just as jewels and fine clothes and many polite usages had been put aside, during the days of dire need and immediate fear, returned with returning self-respect. During the Famished Fifties the full creative scheme of the Modern State won its way to dominate the imaginations of at most a few score thousand minds, whose scientific and technical education had prepared them for it. After that the propaganda had been vigorous, but still, even after the Conference of Basra in 1965, the number of brains that could be reckoned as primarily Modern State makers probably numbered less than a couple of hundred thousand.

The subsequent propaganda was still more swift and urgent, but the new membership was not always of the same thorough quality as the old. The society wanted the services of every man or woman it could incorporate with its Fellowship, but it did not want an inrush of half-prepared adherents, refugees from moral perplexity requiring guidance, ambitious careerists. Every new religion, every church, every organized movement has known this conflict between the desire for expansion and the dread of dilution. On the one hand the Modern State recalled the headlong shallow mass conversions of Christianity and Islam, which had reduced those great faiths to a mere superstitious veneer upon barbarism, and on the other there was the more recent warning of Soviet Russia, morally and intellectually sterilized at last by the eternal espionage, censorship and 'purges' of the G.P.U. The central brain of the Modern State octopus had to steer its world system of organization between the extremes of rash receptiveness and black suspicion. It had to go steadfastly and discreetly and yet it had to go swiftly. If, on the other hand, it found presently that its own Fellowship was not altogether as free as it had been at first from reactionary weaknesses and traditional sentiments, on the other it found that its leading ideas, by virtue of its material successfulness and of continual explicit statement, were spreading far beyond the limits of its nuclei and its organized teaching.

In the economic realm there appeared, even from the first, intimations of a revival of prosperity, a number of developments that the Society, had it had the necessary resources, would gladly have nipped in the bud. It wanted to deal directly with every primary producer. To-day that is how things are. But so soon as there was a new demand for cotton, for rubber, for pork, wheat, rice and the like, a multitude of obliging intermediaries appeared between the negro cotton growers in America, the Sudanese cotton growers, the local folk who went into the largely abandoned rubber plantations to collect rubber again, the wheat farmers and swineherds and ranchmen, and set themselves to collect and handle the produce for the Control buyers and to distribute Control goods by retail in return.

These people, the former business men of the world, emerged from the slums of decaying towns, from municipal offices, from their own reluctantly cultivated corners of land, from the dingy retreats of predatory bands, from small local trading establishments, full of the sense of trade revival. They organized loans to the peasants, contrived advances of material to them, advised them shrewdly, went officiously to the Control agent for instructions.

This sort of intervention did not stop at individuals, nor with advices and promises. In many parts of the world, in townships and counties and small states, where a Town Council or Workers' Soviet or Mayor or Lord of the Manor was in authority, or where mines or plantations lay abandoned and neglected, the reviving breeze of buying produced a violent desire in the minds of men to set other people working for their profit. There were 'Getting to Work Again' fêtes in America in 1969 to 'stimulate local business'.

By 1975, from Manchuria to Cape Colony and from Vancouver to Java, the old state of affairs – peasants in debt, peasants working to pay rent, peasants bringing in goods in arrears, fishermen, miners, factory and gang workers generally, collectors and hunters, the old immemorial economic life of mankind – was recovering vigour. Debt serfdom was returning everywhere. Rents were rising everywhere. Everywhere the increasing surplus product was being intercepted according to time-honoured patterns. Even slavery was reappearing in thinly disguised forms.

It had always been a strong tendency in the old order to utilize the labour of offenders against the law. Forced labour seemed so just and reasonable a punishment that whenever the possibility of using it profitably appeared the authorities set themselves to multiply indictable offences and bring luckless people into unpaid servitude. In the 'classic' age most mines were worked and most galleys propelled by convicts. In the late Middle Ages the Mediterranean shipping waited on the magistrate, and if offenders did not appear in sufficient numbers they had to be sought for. Out of the dimness of the Fifties and Sixties into the returning publicity and activity of this phase of recovery there appeared everywhere local bosses, chiefs and political gangs inciting and driving people to the production of marketable goods. The Supply Control Report of 1976 on 'Conditions of Labour Supplying Goods to Us' notes the existence of convict labour in North and South America on the West Coast of Africa, in Soviet Russia, Central India, North China, Japan, Java and elsewhere, and states that in many districts it is hardly distinguishable from kidnapping.

'The cheapness of human beings', runs the Report, 'is once more impeding the efficient organization of mechanical production. Outside the range of our own services and factories, there are vast and increasing masses of people now living at a standard of life too low and under stresses too urgent for them even to begin to understand the objectives of the Modern State, and, drawing its sustenance from their degradation, there is arising again an intricate tangle of exploiting classes, entrepreneurs, wholesalers, retailers, moneylenders (lending the local coinages and exchanging against our notes), politicians, private and corporation lawyers, investors and landowners, of the most varied types, but all having one common characteristic, that they put profit before service and will resist and drive as hard a bargain as they can with our expanding organization. These things are returning about as fast as we are growing.'

The Transport Control Report of the same year notes another system of troubles arising. Here the attack on Modern State development was more direct. 'We are finding the question of way-leaves an increasing difficulty in the extension of our road net for local and heavy traffic. The world, we are told more plainly every day, is not ours to do with as we like. Everywhere claimants are springing up, renascent corporations, local authorities or private individuals who profess ownership of the soil and demand rents or monetary compensation from us. In some cases, where the local authority was of such a character as to afford a reasonable hope of its ultimate absorption by our organization, we have been able to come to an arrangement by which it has taken over the making and maintenance of the route within the area of its alleged jurisdiction, but in the majority of instances the resistance is much more frankly in the nature of a hold-up. The enquiries of our social psychologists show a widespread desire for simple or disguised bribery on the part of the obstructives, though it has to be admitted that there are many genuine cases of quite disinterested stupidity. Few of them realize clearly that they are demanding bribes or exacting blackmail. They are obsessed by old-fashioned ideas of property; almost anything in existence they imagine can be appropriated as a man's 'own', and then he has an absolute right to do what he likes with his 'own', deny its use to the commonweal, destroy it, let it at a rack rent, hold it for some exorbitant price.

'Rarely have these obstructives the wholehearted support of their communities behind them – so much has to be conceded to the propaganda of the Modern State and to the general diffusion of our ideas and the spontaneous appearance of fresh and kindred idea systems. We are preparing a schedule of obstructives. They vary in scale from the single tiresome litigious individual with an old-fashioned clutching mind, through a long range of associations, cities and provincial councils, to the resuscitated sovereign governments of the war period. Two royal families have been exhumed from their retirement in the German-speaking part of Europe and more, it is said, are to follow. On various of our routes, notably on the Bordeaux-Black Sea road, the old Chinese claim for 'likin' has reappeared. Our lorries have been held up at Ventimiglia, where a 'dogana' has been erected by the Fascist government in Rome, a barrier has been put across the track, and payments have been demanded in the name of the King of Italy. There have also been demands for Octroi dues outside some French and Italian towns.

'A legal committee of the Modern State Faculty of Social Psychology is taking up the question of these new impediments to world revival and unification, and it will prepare a plan of action in the course of the next month. This attempt to revive the proprietary strangulation which ended the old order is irritating and may develop into very grave obstruction. The former world system of ownership and administration was in complete liquidation before 1960, and we have no intention of buying it out at anything above scrap rates. We deny absolutely any claim to enhanced values created by our restoration of production and commerce.'

VII

Intellectual Antagonism to the Modern State

The earliest known histories are dynastic. They are little more than lists of priest-kings and kings and tribes and contributions. With Herodotus history became political. It was only in the eighteenth century (CE) that economic processes came into the story, and only after the time of Karl Marx that their essential importance was recognized. Later still, climatic, biographical and geographical changes were woven into the historical tapestry. Not until the last hundred years have education, cultural influences and psychological sequences generally been given their proper rôle in the human drama.

The most difficult thing in our understanding of the past is to realize, even in the most elementary form, the mental states of those men and women, who seem so deceptively like ourselves. They had bodies on exactly the same pattern as ours, if not so well exercised, well nourished and uniformly healthy; they had brains as capable as ours and as complicated. It is only when we compare their conduct with ours that we realize that, judged by their contents and their habits of reaction, those brains might almost have belonged to another species of creature.

We read incredulously about the public burning of religious heretics, of the torture of criminals to enforce confession, of murders and outrages, of the offence of rape, of the hunting and tormenting of animals for 'sport', of men and women paying money for the pleasure of throwing sticks at a tethered cock until it died, and it is hard to resist the persuasion that our ancestors were insane. Most of us, were we suddenly put back into the London of King Henry VIII would be as frightened, and frightened in the same way, as if we were put into a ward of unattended criminal lunatics. But the brains of these people were no more diseased than ours. Their mental habit systems had been built up on a different framework; and that is the whole difference.

It was perfectly sane men who made the World War, who allowed the private capitalist system to smash itself to fragments in spite of reiterated warnings, and who came near to destroying mankind. If the reader were sent back only for the hundred and seventy years between now and 1933, he would still feel a decided uneasiness about what people might or might not do next. Yet as he fought down his alarm and went about among them he would have found them as completely satisfied of the sanity of their own mental shapes as he was.

Presently he would have found himself trying to adapt himself to those mental shapes. In the end he might come to realize that in his own case also it might be that the things he felt compelled to believe and do, and the things he found impossible to believe and do, though they had served his everyday purposes in his own time fairly well, were no more final in the scheme of things than the ideology that framed the motives and acts of a Roman emperor or a Sumerian slave.

The difficulty in the comparison and understanding of past mental states with our own increases rather than diminishes as we approach the present, because the differences become more subtle and more interwoven with familiar phrases and with values we accept. We cannot keep in mind that meanings are perpetually being expanded or whittled away. We live to-day so saturated in our circumstances, so full of the security, abundance and vitalizing activity of our world-commonweal, that it is hard to realize how recently it was possible for minds of the highest intelligence to call the most fundamental conceptions of our present order in question. Even in the middle twentieth century ideas that now seem so natural and necessary to us that we cannot imagine them disputed appeared extravagant, impossible and offensive to brains that were in their essential quality just as good as the best alive to-day.

In the early half of the twentieth century a great majority of educated and intelligent men and women had no faith whatever in the Modern State; they hated it, feared it and opposed it, and it is doubtful whether the balance was redressed until the twenty-first century was well under way. The Modern State was built up by comparatively mediocre men, upon whom the necessary group of ideas happened to strike with compelling force. As H. Levy insisted in his *Universe of Science* as early as 1932 (Historical Documents: General Ideas Series, 192301), science is a 'social venture' rather than an accumulation of individual triumphs. Both the scientific idea and the idea of the human community were not individual but social products. And the Modern State prevailed because its logic steadily conquered not this man in particular nor that man in particular, but the sense of fitness in the general human intelligence.

Maxwell Brown, in his monumental studies of the growth of the Modern State idea, has made a fairly exhaustive review of the art and literature of the early twentieth century. Except in the writings of a few such sociologists as J. A. Hodson, Harry and Mary Elmer Barnes, James Harvey Robinson, C. A. Beard, Raymond B. Fosdick and a few American and English journalists, and in such alarmist fantasies as Aldous Huxley's *Brave New World*, there is no sense whatever of the immense revolutionary changes that were occurring in the social structure. Bernard Shaw, for example, though classed as a revolutionary writer, never, except in his preposterous *Back to Methuselah*, anticipated. The mass of his work was a witty and destructive commentary upon contemporary things, ending in that petition in bankruptcy, *Too*

True to be Good. He had to a supreme degree the opposition mentality of the Irish.

This estrangement of literature from the Modern State Movement became more marked throughout the Nineteen Twenties and Thirties. As reality became urgent, as war and insolvency descended upon social life, literature, art and criticism recoiled into studies and studios and their own bitter and peculiar Bohemia; they became elaborately stylistic and 'rare', or brilliantly or brutally smutty.

This decadence of literature, says Maxwell Brown, was an inevitable expression of the economic decadence of the Thirties and Forties. He draws an illuminating contrast between the type of mind primarily directed towards aestheticism and the type of mind primarily directed towards science. The 'aesthetic producer', he insists, is dominated by acceptance; he writes for response. The scientific worker aims at knowledge and is quite indifferent whether people like or dislike the knowledge he produces. Aesthetic life therefore is conditioned by the times; science conditions the times.

Literature and art are necessarily time-servers, either abjectly so or aggressively and pretentiously so. They reflect real moods or speculate upon possible moods in the community. It is no good writing books that people will not read or painting pictures from which they merely turn away. Psychology in those days had not developed sufficiently to permit of a scientific analysis of creative work, and such criticism as there was, when it was not a simple release of spite, was essentially an effort either to persuade or to browbeat people into buying books and pictures or listening to music of a type fancied by the critic. It was more bitterly partisan and more propagandist than political discussion.

In the expansive phase of the later nineteenth century the general confidence of the prosperous classes was reflected in a large, hopeful, forward-looking complacent literature, and every critic was, so to speak, an uncle, a prosperous uncle, sitting by the fire, but the sense of contraction and advancing dangers that troubled the patrons of art and literature as the twentieth century unfolded threw a defensive quality over the intellectual world, outside the spheres of science and invention. The progressive note was popular no longer. The reading offered to the people was pervaded by a nagging hostility to new things, by lamentations for imaginary lost loyalties and vanished virtues.

It was not so much that the writers of the time desired civilization to retrace its steps, as that they wished that no more steps should be taken. They wanted things to stop – oh, they wanted them to stop! The underlying craving was for consolidation and rest before more was lost. There was little coherent system in the objections taken; it was objection at large. Mass production was very generally reprehended; science rarely got a good word; war – with modern weapons – was condemned, though much was to be said for the 'chivalrous' warfare of the past;

there were proposals to 'abolish' aeroplanes and close all the laboratories in the world; it was assumed that hygiene, and especially sexual hygiene, 'robbed life of romance'; the decay of good manners since the polished days of Hogarth, Sir Charles Grandison and Tony Lumpkin was deplored, and the practical disappearance of anything that could be called Style. As one nineteenth-century American writer lamented, in suitably archaic English:

> How life hath cheapened, and how blank
> The Worlde is! like a fen
> Where long ago unstainèd sank
> The starrie gentlemen:.
> Since Marston Moor and Newbury drank
> King Charles his gentlemen.

That was the dominant note.

Maxwell Brown gives a volume of material, quotations (*Literature Hangs Back*; Historical Documents: General Ideas Series, 311002) from about four thousand representative books and papers.

As the world emerged again from the sheer desolation of the Famished Fifties and the great pestilence, this purely opposition mentality revived in hundreds of thousands of elderly literate people whose brains had been fitted and turned round in that way for good. It revived because it was all there was to revive in them; and it met with all too ready and natural an acceptance among those endless myriads of cleverish active people who were now trying to get private businesses and private profit systems going before it became too late for ever, between the expanding system of the Transport Control and its collaterals above, and the inarticulate and still needy masses below. They did not realize how much the revival of prosperity was due to the new organization. It was not in their type of mind to want to account for revivals of prosperity. What they desired to do was to take advantage of the 'turn of luck'. To them from the first the Transport Control appeared as a formidable competitor, harsh in spirit and still harsher in method, which had set itself to prevent smaller brighter folk making hay while the sun shone. They were only too eager to see it as a huge, cheap, nasty, vulgar menace to all the jolly little profits and rewards and assurances that were peeping up again in life. For the loyalty and obedience of servants, it offered them ingenious mechanical arrangements; for the labour of respectful toilers, it suggested indifferent and dangerous power machinery. Are we not wise and virtuous enough in ourselves, they asked, that this World Control should come 'tidying us up'?

Manifestly the new order was resolved to 'incorporate' (hateful word!), if it could, all these would-be privileged, would-be irresponsible people. Its face was hard towards them. Its hygienic and educational activies threatened an increasing regulation of their lives. It proposed to rob them of the natural excitements and adventure of gambling and speculation; to deprive them of the legitimate advantages of their foresight and business flair. It threatened them with service; service and ever more service – a rôle, they insisted, that would be unendurably 'monotonous'. They wanted to be good sometimes and bad sometimes and jump from this to that. A 'soulless uniformity' became the bugbear of these recalcitrant minds.

The workers often resented Modern State methods almost as much as their immediate employers. Men have always been difficult to educate and reluctant to submit themselves to discipline, and there was a curious suggestion of the schoolmaster about these fellows of the Modern State nuclei. Dislike of what was at hand helped to conjure up fears of what might lie beyond. Once freedom of business had gone, what rules and regulations might not presently enmesh the wilful individual under the thumb of this one world employer? For instance, the Modern State centres were talking of a control of population; it was easy to see in that a hideous invasion of the most private moments in life. Weights and measures and money today, and wives and parentage tomorrow!

These widely diffused repugnances, fears and antagonisms were enhanced by the difficulties put in the way of aspirants to the Modern State Fellowship and to positions of responsibility in the service of the Controls. Jobs were not for everyone. Rejected candidates to the Fellowship were among the most energetic of Modern State antagonists. By 1970, all over the world, wherever the remains of the old prosperous and educated classes of 'independent' and business people were to be found, appeared associations to combat the activities of the Modern State nuclei. There were Liberty Clubs and Free Trade Associations; there were Leagues of Citizens, Trade Protection Chambers and 'Return to Legality' societies. There were organized religious and patriotic revivals. The Modern State schools were discovered to be immoral, unpatriotic and anti-religious. It was extraordinary how the money-changers hurried to the deserted temples and clamoured for the return of Christ.

Every town and city found someone or other – as often as not it was some elderly lawyer or politician from the old days – keen to revive and protect its privileges. The world heard once more of the rights of peoples and nations to be free and sovereign within their borders. A hundred different flags fluttered more abundantly every day about the reviving earth in the sacred name of freedom. Even men who were engaged in organizing debt-serf cultivation and debt-serf industrialism in the American cotton districts, in the old rubber plantations and in the factories of India, China and South Italy, appeared as generous support-ers of and subscribers to the sacred cause of individual liberty.

The behaviour of the inferior masses showed a wide divergence of reactions. The widespread communist propaganda of the War Years and the Famished Fifties had intensified their natural hostility to the profit-seeking bourgeoisie, and there was little chance of their making common cause with them; but the Modern State Society, with the lessons of Russia before it, had no disposition to exacerbate the class war for its own ends. It knew quite clearly that to appeal to the mere insurrectionary impulse of the downtrodden was to invite the specialist demagogue, sustained by his gang and his heelers, his spies and secret police, to take the chair in the council chamber.

De Windt had driven that point well home. 'Creative revolution cannot cooperate with insurrectionary revolution.' There was to be no flattery of ignorance and inferiority as though they were the keys to an instinctive wisdom; no incitement to envy and jealousy against knowledge and ability. The Modern State meant to abolish toil, and that meant to abolish any toiling class, proletariat, labour mass, serf or slave, whatever it was called, but it had no intention of flattering and using the oafish mental as well as physical limitations it meant to liberate from existence altogether. It took the risk that the forces of reaction would organize strikes and mass resistance against its regulations, its economies of employment, its mechanization, its movements of population and the like, among the other inevitable difficulties of its task.

So the world-stage was set for the triangular drama of the late twentieth and early twenty-first centuries, in which reaction in a thousand forms, and Modern State organization in one, struggled against each other to subjugate or assimilate the more or less passive majority of mankind.

We write in outline, and necessarily in an elementary history it is only the primary lines that can be given. But just as when we enlarge our scale of observation, the broad divisions of a map vanish and countries and divisions become hills, valleys, buildings, forests, roads, and at last, when we come to earth, stones, pebbles, blades of grass and flowers, so this rough division of humanity into three intermingled and intensely interacting multitudes was in reality qualified by a thousand million individual complications.

On the whole the content of people's minds was far more intricate then than it is now. That is a principle the student of history must never forget. The intellectual progress of mankind had been a continual disentanglement and simplification leading to increased grasp and power. These closing decades of the Age of Frustration were still, in comparison with our own time, a time of uncertainties, inaccuracies, mixed motives, irrational surprises and bitter late realizations. There was scarcely an unskilled toiler in the world who was really no more than a passive clod in the hands of his exploiters and employers. There was scarcely a reactionary who did not in some fashion want tidiness and efficiency. And, conversely, there was hardly a Fellow of the

Modern State organization, man or woman, who had not spasms of acute self-seeking and vanity, who could not be doctrinaire, intolerant and vindictive on occasion, who could not be touched by the sentimental and aesthetic values of the old order, and who did not like, love and react to scores of people incurably shaped to the opposition pattern.

The New Fiction of the Eighties and Nineties is enormously preoccupied with this universal battle of ideas and mental habits in people's minds. The simpler novels of the earlier past and the novels of the present day tell of individual character in a set battle between good and bad in a world of undisputed standards; but the novels of those years of social conflict tell of a wild confusion between two sorts of good and two sorts of bad and of innate character distorted in a thousand ways. It was a difficult age. Life still has its endless ironies and ambiguities, but they are as nothing to those amidst which the men of 1970 had to steer their courses.

VIII

The Second Conference at Basra: 1978

The second Conference at Basra, though many of its prominent figures had already played leading rôles in the earlier gathering in 1965, was very different in scale, scope and spirit from that assembly. It was an older gathering. The average age, says Amen Rihani, was a full ten years higher. Young men were still coming into the Fellowship abundantly, but there had also been accessions – and not always very helpful accessions – of older men who had been radical and revolutionary leaders in the war period. Their frame of experience had shaped them for irresponsible resistance. Their mental disposition was often obstructively critical and insubordinate. Many had had no sort of technical experience. They were disposed to throw an anarchistic flavour over schools and propaganda.

Moreover, the great scheme of the Modern State had now lost something of its first compelling freshness. The 'young men of '65' had had ten years of responsible administrative work. They had been in contact with urgent detail for most of that period. They had had to modify De Windt's generalizations in many particulars, and the large splendour of the whole project no longer had the same dominating power over their minds. They had lost something of the professional *esprit de corps*, the close intimate confidence with each other, with which they had originally embarked upon the great adventure of the Modern State. Many had married women of the older social tradition and formed new systems of gratification and friendship. They had ceased to be enthusiastic young men and they had become men of the world. The consequent loss of a sure touch upon primary issues was particularly evident in the opening sessions.

Moreover, the atmosphere of the 1965 gathering had been purely a Modern State atmosphere. Except for the Russian political representatives, there had been no antagonism at all to its general purposes, and there had been few people in Basra who were not Fellows of the Modern State Society or closely sympathetic with its aims. But now the reviving nationalisms, the resuscitating social and commercial interests of the moribund old-world system, were acutely aware of the immense significance of events at Basra, and there had gathered an assemblage of delegations, reporters, adventurers, friends and camp followers of every description, far exceeding the numbers of the actual Fellows. They crowded the Control rest-houses that clustered about the aerodrome, they invaded the offices and residences of the Controls, they stimulated the private enterprise hotels and restaurants that had recently sprung up among the date palms and rice fields of the environs, to an unprecedented congestion and liveliness, and multitudes of them had to be accommodated in tents and houseboats. A number of thirty-year-old hulls of passenger liners were fitted for their accommodation. Observers were reminded of the tourist period of the First Age of General Prosperity when they saw these uninvited visitors, chaffering with the old-world Bagdad carpet traders and Arab nomads who had also been attracted by the gathering.

There would probably have been a far greater multitude drawn to Basra if the Transport Control had not realized in time the social and hygienic dangers of too great a gathering, and had refused passages and limited bookings. Casual individuals were eliminated as much as possible, and all over the world groups of stranded pilgrims found themselves unable to get further on the journey.

The most serious of these invaders were the delegations of enquiry sent by the reawakening sovereign governments of the old order. These were half diplomatic, half official-expert, teams, and they came with the declared intention of challenging the activities of the Controls in their several territories. They proposed to legalize and regulate the Controls. They had no formal standing in the Conference; they had invited themselves and given the Conference organizers notice of their coming. 'Better now than later,' said the Modern State officials, and accepted notice and provided accommodation. 'We have to have things out with them,' Williams Kapek wrote to Isabel Garden (*The Kapek Garden Letters*. Historical Documents Series: Basra II, 9376).

Beside these 'old government' agencies there were a number of parties claiming to represent various new business combines and interests that were setting up in frank competition with the Control monopolies. There were a number of lawyers of the older type, men in sharp contrast and antagonism to the younger legists of the new American school. The contrast of the two types, the older all pomp and dodges and the younger all candour and science, is dwelt upon lengthily by Kapek.

'This Conference is essentially a Conference on Scientific and Mercantile Communications and Associated Questions, similar to that held at Basra in 1965'; so ran a printed notice circulated to all the visitors who could claim any representative status. 'Its discussions are open only to the Fellows of the faculties of the Modern State Society. They are not public discussions and their reports are for the use of Fellows only. But it would be disingenuous to deny that the decisions arrived at may affect the general welfare of mankind profoundly, and since you come to present criticisms, claims and proposals presumably in that interest, the committee of organization of the Conference will do all it can to facilitate meetings between your group and the faculty or faculties affected. Unfortunately the accommodation for meetings in Basra will be greatly strained by the needs of the actual Conference, and the committee can do little to arrange conferences between the immense variety of accredited bodies that have made an appearance, much less to arrange for their pleasures and comforts during the period of this assembly. The committee regrets that it does not consider the proposal of the committee of Bagdad citizens, claiming to represent the government of Irak, to police this unexpected World Fair with 300 Arab policemen, a camel corps of seventy-nine men and six machine-guns, as a practicable one. It has removed this body painlessly to comfortable quarters in the Island of Ormuz, and the Police of the Air and Sea Ways in its recognizable uniform will be alone responsible for order in the ancient province of Bassorah.'

Explicit details of information bureaus, hospital organization, supply and available accommodation followed.

It is difficult to see how else the Central Control could have dealt with this unexpectedly abundant eruption of the old system, but the various delegations and commissions professed to be extremely indignant at their reception. They were of such various and unequal value that they found it impossible to fall into any combined scheme of action. Since their theory was that the Controls and the Modern State organization were nothing more than a sort of world cooperative society, none of them could behave as diplomatic missions to a sovereign power. And consequently they could not regard each other as diplomatic missions. Their powers and authorizations were extremely ill-defined. The bland refusal of the Conference authorities to concede them meeting-places and anything but a very limited use of telephonic, cable and radio communications embarrassed them extremely.

'I met Sir Horatio Porteous, the British Imperial representative, in the street,' writes Williams Kapek. 'He was very eager to get my advice upon a point of etiquette. It seems that we have seized the province of Bassorah from the government of Irak and made prisoners of an alleged local police – those fifty lousy camels and the rest of it I told you about in my last – and that Irak is a mandatory protectorate under Great Britain. He wished to put in a protest somewhere. 'But *where?*' said he.

'I adopted a sympathetic tone. "You see," said Sir Horatio, "this Central Contol of yours isn't any damned thing at all! If it was a provisional government or something . . ."

'I suggested a call on the Air and Sea Police.

'"But they are acting under orders. Who gives the orders? It's all so damned irregular! . . ."'

There was a flutter of calls between the delegations, some 'serious talks' and much drafting of more or less futile minutes, reports and protests. The weather was exceptionally hot and dry and such space and apparatus as was available for exercise and recreation was monopolized by the more energetic Fellows who were taking part in the Conference proper. It was difficult to keep cool, difficult to keep calm; still more difficult to keep well and hopeful. Some few of the intrusive delegates and commissioners took to drinking hard, but the supply of alcohol was severely limited and the police had turned practically all the professional ministers of pleasure out of the province. On the other hand, the Transport Control, in a mood of friendly indulgence, started a special service of pleasure steamers to Bubiyan, outside the jurisdiction of its police, and there a floating little mushroom town of cafés, restaurants, houses of pleasure, music halls and shows of every sort speedily sprung up to minister to the unofficial overflow of the Conference.

'Bubiyan is draining us quite pleasantly,' wrote Williams Kapek, 'and they say there is quite a boom in entertainment for man and beast in Babylon and Bagdad. The old British institution of the *long week-end* flourishes and Babylon gets more and more Babylonian.'

But there were still plenty of outsiders left in Basra to keep the faculties busy.

Meanwhile the Conference was going on behind closed doors. It was clearly recognized that this curious mélange of agents, delegates and officials from without its organization was only the first intimation of the confused antagonisms that were gathering against the new order. The policy of expansion and quiet disregard had lasted long enough. The pretence of being a Conference upon communications and associated matters had to be dropped. The time had come for the Modern State to define itself and clear up its relations to the past out of which it had arisen and to all this world of tradition which was now rapping at its doors.

'Before we disperse,' said Arden Essenden, who presided at the first plenary session, 'we must admit some at least of these delegations, hear them and give them answers to take home with them. But first we have to know our mind much more clearly. What are we now and what do we intend to do? The days before us begin a new chapter in human history. It is for us to choose the heading and plan that chapter now.'

IX

'Three Courses of Action'

There was no dominant individual of the De Windt character and quality at the second Basra Conference. There was no prophetic direction of the deliberations. But there was no want of what used to be called 'leadership', and a number of interesting personalities, the politic Hooper Hamilton; the frank, emphatic William Ryan; the intricate Shilung-tang; M'bangoi, the East African biologist; Rin Kay, the social psychologist – perhaps the finest mind in the gathering; Mohini L. Tagore; Morowitz, the mystical humanist; and Arden Essenden, the fanatic of action, gave point and definition to the differences of opinion.

They were interesting rather than outstanding men, because the general level of intelligence was a high one. The gathering had a personality of its own, wary, resolved to be well informed and to weigh considerations, but essentially determined. The presence of that miscellany of delegations and commissions which besieged the Conference dramatized the world situation and pressed for decisions. 'I feel like one of those old-world jurymen,' wrote Williams Kapek, 'who used to be locked up together until they returned a verdict. And you cannot imagine how hot and dry Basra can sometimes contrive to be.'

De Windt and his school of writers had planned the frame-work of a new world and shown to what social elements one had to look for its evocation, but he had given only the most scanty suggestions for getting rid of the body of the old. Already in 1965 the Modern State people had had a fairly distinct vision of our present order. But few of them had anticipated the diffused toughness of the old corpus and its capacity for counter-revolutionary exertion. That had become oppressively evident by 1975.

Reports on the general situation had been very carefully prepared. They dealt with the various centres at which the spirit of opposition was being organized. Most serious of these were those former sovereign governments and legal systems which had seemed effaced, moribund or prostrate during the desolation of the Famished and Fever-stricken Fifties. In 1965 the only government actively antagonistic to the Controls had been the Soviet government in Russia. That antagonism, curiously enough, was not so great as it had been at first. The technicians of the sovietized regions were ousting the politicans; there was now indeed a working cooperation of Russian transport, communications and production with the world system under the Controls, and there seemed a reasonable prospect of ultimate assimilation. There was no objection being made to people nominally Communists who were also Fellows of the Modern State, and many Russian scientific and technical workers were Modern State Fellows and not members of the Communist party at all. The reports discussed hopefully and analytically the possibility of some similiar process in America and the Far East. There also the political and legal structures did not present insurmountable obstacles to assimilation. The decline of humbug in America was bringing out the fundamental constructive energy of that great synthesis of Western peoples. But elsewhere there was increasing evidence that the sovereign state system and the system of private ownership were fundamentally irreconcilable with the new conceptions.

The reports gave information, which was in many particulars new to most of the assembled Fellows, of the very strenuous attempts that were being made by the reviving national governments in Germany, France, Italy and Great Britain to resume the manufacture of aeroplanes and war material. Whether there was a common agreement among them was doubtful, but the intention to put up air forces and organize aerodromes that should be able to ignore the regulations and refuse the services of the Air and Sea Control was quite plain. They were finding great difficulty in securing the services of competent engineers, mechanics and aviators, but the thing was going on. Every student in the technical schools of the Control who failed a test or an examination, or was penalized for misbehaviour or rejected from the Modern State Fellowship, would turn up presently as a national government expert. And the governments were now setting up their own national technical schools and attempting to bring the schools and laboratories of the Control into the 'national' educational organization. Not only was there a disposition to set up a competing system side by side with the Controls system, but there was a growing tendency to annex the organizations, roads, plant, mines, factories, aerodromes, schools, colleges, laboratories and personnel of the Control that chanced to be within the jurisdiction of the sovereign government concerned. The new Bavarian government, the Windsor Parliament and the government in Rome were all 'arranging to take over' these things within their territories. They were becoming more explicit about it every year. They persisted in regarding the interlocking Controls as a dangerous international Trust.

This was the burthen of the national missions of observation and enquiry which were stewing in the sunshine outside the doors of the Conference – 'in a state of tentative menace', as Williams Kapek put it.

The minor delegations representing groups of owners and organized local interests had this much in common with the national missions, that they proposed more or less frankly to resume possession of properties the Controls had taken hold of and revived, or to impose burthensome charges. They varied like the inmates of a zoological garden in scale and power, but they had one quality in common: an obstructive litigiousness.

In the frankness of its privacy behind its closed doors, the Conference sized up these antagonisms and discussed their treatment. 'There are just three lines of treatment possible,' said Ryan brutally. 'We can treat with 'em, bribe 'em, or rule 'em. I'm for a straight rule.'

'Or combine those ingredients,' said Hooper Hamilton.

The method of treaty-making and a *modus vivendi* was already in operation in regard to Russia. There indeed it was hard to say whether the Communist party or the Modern State Movement was in control, so far had assimilation gone. And the new spirit in the old United States was now so 'Modern' that the protests of Washington and of various state governors against the Controls were received hilariously. Aeroplanes from Dearborn circled over the capital and White House and dropped parodies of the President's instructions to dissolve the Air and Food Trust of America. All over that realist continent, indeed, the Controls expanded as a self-owned business with a complete disregard of political formalities. But the European situation was more perplexing.

'Most of these European sovereign governments are no more than scarecrows,' said William Ryan. 'There's no living people behind them any longer. Leastway, no living people that matter. Call their bluff on them and you'll hear no more about them.'

It was Shi-lung-tang who argued against defiance and stated the case for Bribery.

Bribery in his suave exposition, bribery combined with treaties and tact, became a highly moral amelioration of direct action. He asked the Conference to realize how specialized and rare as yet was its new forward-looking habit of mind. When all the work of the propaganda and schools had been accounted for, it was doubtful if a twentieth part of the race accepted, or if a tenth understood, even in the most general terms, the difference between minds trained to creative conceptions and minds brought up in an atmosphere of defensive acquisitiveness and property accumulation. It would take three or four generations to convert the world to a forward-looking attitude. Either the Modern

State movement had to seize power openly now and inaugurate a tyranny that would have to last as long as it took to turn round the great majority of intelligences into the new direction, or it had to propitiate, compromise and persuade these outer masses – *upon their own lines*.

'These people will never see things as we see them,' he insisted, making strange gestures and repeating his words to emphasize their importance. 'They have to live and die, *on their own lines*. It is not just to impose too much upon them. It is only as they die out that the Modern State form of mind can hope to be in a dominant majority. Their mental vices are incurable. Meet them half-way, make things easy for them. You will save the world three generations of suffering and bitter conflict.'

He unfolded his Machiavellian project. A greedy acquisitiveness was part of the make-up of every energetic old-world type. They were as incurably voracious as dogs. And yet we made good friends and helpers out of dogs. Their loyalties were at best gang loyalties; they were none the less greedy because they did at times hunt in packs. But they had no fundamental instinctive hostility to the Modern State. It was only when the Modern State thwarted their established habits of behaviour that they snarled at it and began to fear it. They could never make a solid front against the Modern State. They could always be played off against each other, one against another; they could be neutralized. The lesson of Russia's harsh repression of her bourgeoisie and professional classes in the Twenties and Thirties was a warning against the miseries and social damage of too sudden and forcible an attempt to change ideals of behaviour. Let the Modern State go more softly and more kindly.

He went on to detailed suggestions. With Russia, Spain and America, bribery need play but a minor rôle. The ruling mentality in these countries was now such that the present working agreements would pass naturally into assimilation in a little while. Elsewhere there was really no permanent harm in recognizing the old claims to sovereign and proprietary rights, and securing such a hold upon leading men that they would keep their hands off the Modern State propaganda and schools and be content with handsome subsidies from the Control services and industries. It would be cheaper than war. 'If they want a little war now and then among themselves – '

In spite of Shi-lung-tang's smiling face, there was audible disapproval at this point.

When he had done, his case for tact and insinuating corruption was knocked to pieces by Rin Kay. 'If we were a Society of Moral Supermen,' he said, 'we might venture to be as disingenuous as this.' But Mr Shi-lung-tang forgot that every Fellow in the Modern State society had two enemies: the acquisitive man outside and the acquisitive man within. The point their Chinese friend missed was the fact that it was much more natural to adopt the behaviour patterns of the old world than to acquire those of the Modern State. The old dispositions were something that was; the new dispositions were something that had to be made and sustained. The inner life of a Modern State Fellow was a sustained effort to be simple and serve simply. That should take him all his time. He could not afford to be intricate and politic. 'We have a difficult enough task before us just to do what we have to do, plainly and honestly. We cannot afford to say and do *this* and mean *that*.' William Ryan supported that with vigour, but Hooper Hamilton spoke long and elaborately on the other side. The spirit of the society was plainly with Kay.

M. L. Tagore, an economic botanist, introduced a new line of thought into the discussion, or rather he revived the line of thought of nineteenth-century mystical liberalism. He said he was equally against bribery, insincere treaties or any use of force. He was old-fashioned enough to be a democrat and a believer in the innate wisdom of the unsophisticated man. And also he believed in the supreme value of truth and inaggressiveness. We must not outrage the sense of right in man, even if that meant the abandonment of our immediate objectives. We had to persuade him. And we had no right to assume that he did not hold himself to be right because his conception of conduct differed from ours. Let the Modern State society go on with the scientific organization of the world, yes, and let us go on with propaganda of its doctrines in every land. But let it not lift a hand to compel, not even to resist evil. He appealed to the missionary successes of early Buddhism and Christianity as evidence of the practical successfulness of spiritual urgency and physical passivity. He concluded in a glow or religious enthusiasm that did not spare him the contemptuous criticisms of the social psychologists who fell upon him tooth and nail so soon as he had done.

These speeches, which are to found in full in the Basra Conference Reports, vols. 371 and 372, were the three salient types of opinion in that gathering. The immense majority were for the active line, for frankness and rule. A not inconsiderable minority, however, wavered behind the leadership of Hooper Hamilton. They felt that there were elaborations, and refinements that did not find expression in the more aggressive speeches, that the use of force could be tempered by tact, and that lucidity towards an objective was compatible with kindliness and concession.

In a number of speeches some of them tried to express this rather elusive conception of compromise; some of them were not too skilful as speakers, they went too far in the opposite direction, and on the whole they tended to drive the movement towards a harder assertiveness than it might otherwise have expressed. The problems of the Russian system and American were abundantly discussed. Russia now was represented only by technicians, and there was abundant evidence that the repressive influence of the Og-pu had waned. Ivan Englehart was again a leading figure. He assured the Conference that there would be no trouble from Moscow. 'Russia,' he said, 'is ready to assimilate. Is eager to assimilate.'

Arden Essenden spoke late in the general discussion; he spoke with a harsh enthusiasm and passionate faith; he carried all the younger men and most of the older ones with him, and he shaped the ultimate decisions.

Some of his phrases are, as people used to say, 'historical'. He said, 'The World-State is not a thing of the Future. It is here and now. It has always been here and now, since ever men said they had a common God above them, or talked, however timidly, of the brotherhood of mankind. The man who serves a particular state or a particular ownership in despite of the human commonweal is a Traitor. Men who did that have always been Traitors and men who tolerated them nursed treason in their hearts. In the past the World-State had been torn up among three-score-and-ten anarchies and a countless myriad of pro-prietors and creditors, and the socialists and cosmopolitans, the true heirs of the race, were hunted like criminals and persecuted and killed.

'Now, through the utter failure of those robbers even to maintain their own social order and keep at peace among themselves, the world has fallen into our hands. Power has deserted them, and we, we here, have Power. If we do not use it, if we do not use it to the fullest, we are traitors in our turn. Are we to tolerate even a temporary revival of the old system? In the name of reason, why? If their brains have got into the wrong grooves – well, we can make fresh brains. Are we to connive with and indulge this riff-raff that waits outside our doors? Go out and look at them. Look at their insincere faces! Look at their furtive hands. Weigh what they say. Weigh the offers they will make you!'

To us to-day that seems platitudinous and over emphatic, but it conveyed the sense of the Conference and it led directly to the general decisions with which its proceedings concluded. The most significant of these was the increase of the Police of the Air and Sea Ways to a million men, and the apportionment of a greatly increased amount of energy to the improvement of their equipment. There was also to be a great intensification and speeding up of Modern State education and propaganda. Provision was also made for the enlistment of auxiliary forces and services as they might be needed for the preservation of order; these auxiliaries were to renounce any allegiance except to the Transport or other Control that might enlist them. The Controls were reorganized, and a central committee, which speedily became known as the World Council, was appointed by them to act as the speaking head of the whole system. The ideas of treaties and contracts with exterior admin-istrations and of any diplomatic dealings with dissentients were aban-doned. Instead it was determined that this central committee, the World Council, should openly declare itself the sole government of the world

and proceed to make the associated Controls the administrative organization of the planet.

Accordingly a proclamation was prepared to this effect and issued
very widely. It was broadcast as well as printed and reprinted from a
multitude of centres. It was 'put upon the ether' everywhere to the
exclusion of other matter. For now the world had its wireless again in
as great abundance already as in the early Thirties. So simultaneously
the whole planet received it. It whipped up the waiting miscellany at
Basra into a foam of excited enquiry. All over the world city crowds or
solitary workers received it open-mouthed. At first there was very little
discussion. The effect was too stunning for that. People began to talk
after a day or so.

We give it as it was issued: a singularly poor piece of prose when we
consider the magnificence of its matter. It seems to have been drafted by
Arden Essenden, with some assistance from Hamilton and amended in
a few particulars by the Council.

'The Council for World Affairs, constituted by the Air and Sea Control
and its associates, declares:

'That between 1950 and 1965 this planet became derelict through
the incapacity of its ostensible rulers and property owners to keep the
peace, regulate production and distribution, and conserve and guide the
common life of mankind;

'That chaos ensued, and

'That it became urgently necessary to build up a new world administration amidst the ruins.

'This the Air and Sea Control did.

'This administration has now been organized about a Central Council
for World Affairs, which is making this statement to you.

'It is the only sovereign upon this planet. There is now no other
primary authority from end to end of the earth. All other sovereignty
and all proprietary rights whatever that do not conduce directly to the
general welfare of mankind ceased to exist during the period of disorder,
and cannot be revived.

'The Council has its air and sea ways, its airports, dockyards,
factories, mines, plantations, laboratories, colleges and schools throughout the world. These are administered by its officials and protected by
its own police, and the latter are instructed to defend these organizations
whenever and wherever it may be necessary against the aggression of
unauthorized persons.

'In every centre of population there are now Modern State nuclei and
Control agents conducting the educational work of the Council and in
reasonable contact with the local economic life, with local enterprises,
local authorities and individuals not yet affiliated to the Modern State
organization. The time has come for all these various quasi-independent

organs of business and adminstration to place themselves in orderly relations to the new Government of the Whole World.

'We are constituting a Bureau of Transition, for the simplification and modernization of the business activities, the educational and hygienic services, production, distribution and the preservation of order and security throughout our one home and garden, our pleasure ground and the source of all our riches – the earth, our Mother Earth, our earth and yours.

'Without haste or injustice and without delay, with a due regard to your comfort, your welfare and your wishes, the Bureau will set itself to bring your life into sound and permanent correlation with the one human commonwealth.'

'It is usurpation!' cried a voice, when the declaration was put to the vote as a whole.

'You decided upon Force,' said Shi-lung-tang. 'I did my best – '

'But this means War!' cried Tagore.

'No,' said Arden Essenden. 'There is no more War. This is not War – nor Revolution. This is the recognition of a Revolution and Government again.'

X

The Life-time Plan

It is still a debatable question how far that hard decisive declaration of the Socialist World-State at Basra was not premature. There are those who consider it the most timely of acts; there are some who believe it should have been made as early as the first Conference in 1965. The discussion became involved with the intellectual and moral conflicts that went on under the Air Dictatorship. It mingles with the controversies of to-day. But certainly, from 1978 onward, the Modern State movement lost something of its pristine mental freshness, lost openness, lost much of that almost irresponsible adventurousness that had flung the network of transport and trading controls so swiftly about the earth. 'We have swallowed the world, but now we have to digest it,' said Arden Essenden. The old defiant repudiation of the past was replaced by a firm and sometimes rather heavy insistence upon the order of the future.

There was nowhere any immediate uprising in response to the proclamation of a World Government. Although it had been plainly coming for some years, although it had been endlessly feared and murmured against, it found no opposition prepared anywhere. Thirteen years had wrought a profound change in Soviet Russia and the large areas of China in association with Moscow. The practical assimilation of Soviet Transport and Communications was almost tacitly accepted. The details of the amalgamation were entrusted to committees flying between Moscow and Basra. All over the world, wherever there was any sort of governing or managing body not already associated with the Modern State System, it fell to debating just how and to what extent it could be incorporated or how it could resist incorporation. Everywhere there were Modern State nuclei ready to come into conference and fully informed upon local or regional issues. The plain necessity for a systematic 'renucleation' of the world became evident. The 'Section of Training and Advertisement' had long since worked out the broad lines of a *modus vivendi* between the old and the new.

That *modus vivendi* is called variously The Life-time Plan or – with a memory of that pioneer effort in planning, The Five Year Plan of the Russian Dictatorship – The Thirty Year Plan. Independent businesses that respected certain standards of treatment by the workers, which would accept a certain amount of exterior control, technical and financial, and which maintained a certain standard of efficiency, were to be accorded not simply tolerance but a reasonable protection. Even if their methods were suddenly superseded by new devices, they were to be kept running until they could be wound up, their products were still to be taken by the Controls. This was far better treatment than was ever accorded superseded producers under the smash-and-grab conditions of the competitive system. In the same way, whenever possible the small owning peasant or the agricultural tenant was not dispossessed; he was given a fixed price for his output, counselled or directed in the matter of improvements and so merged by bearable degrees into the class of agricultural workers. This, as Rupert Bordinesco put it (*Brief Explanation*: Historical Documents Series 1969), gave them 'time to die out'. Because it was an integral part of the Life-time Plan that the new generation should be educated to develop a service mentality in the place of a proprietary mentality. There were to be no independent merchants or independent cultivators under twenty in 1980, none under thirty in 1990 and none under forty in 2000. This not only gave the old order time to die out; it gave the new order time to develop the more complex system of direction, mechanism and delivery it needed soundly and healthily. The lesson of the mental discords and tragic disproportions in the headlong development of the first Russian Five Year Plan – disproportions as monstrous and distressful as the hypertrophies and atrophies of the planless 'Capitalist System' of the nineteenth century – had been marked and learnt.

It did not trouble the World Council that to retain millions of small businesses and tens of millions of small cultivators the whole world over for so long meant a much lower efficiency of production. 'These older people have to be fed and employed,' wrote Bordinesco, 'and now they will never learn or be able to adapt themselves to a novel routine of life. Help them to do their job a little better. Save them from the smart people who want to prey upon them – usurers, mortgagers, instalment salesmen, intimidators, religious or secular; and for the rest – leave them in peace.'

The *Brief Explanation* also drew a moral from the 'Period of Glut' in the Twenties, which preceded the collapse of the Thirties, when the whole world was full of unconsumed goods and unemployed people. This, Bordinesco pointed out, was the inevitable consequence of an unregulated progressive sytem of private enterprise. 'There is no sense in throwing a man out of an employment, however old-fashioned, unless there is a new job for him. There is no sense in bringing children into the world unless there is education, training and useful work for them to do. We have to see that each new generation is arranged numerically in different categories of training and objective from those of its predecessor. The Russians learnt this necessity in their great experiment. As we progress towards a scientific production of primary substances, the actual proportion of agricultural workers, miners, forest wardens, fishermen and so forth in the community must fall. So also the proportion of ordinary industrial workers must fall. The heavy industries will precede the light in that. A certain compensation will be caused by a steady rise in the standard of living and particularly by what De Windt called 'the rebuilding of the world', new cities, new roads, continually renewed houses everywhere.' (This was foreshadowed to a certain extent by the French plan for 'Outillage National' and the German housing schemes in operation as early as the late Twenties, plan and schemes ultimately strangled by the budget-balancing fanatics.) But even that diversion of energy from the production of basic materials and small commodities to big structural undertakings would not suffice to use up the continually released human power in the community. At this point appeared what Bordinesco called the 'enlarging categories', which were to consume more than they gave. There had to be increasing numbers of people engaged in education, in the developing and ordering of knowledge, in experimental science, in artistic production, in making life more abundant and ample. To that expansion no limit could be set.

'We men have a lease of this planet,' runs the *Brief Explanation*, 'for some millions of years. It is foolish not to press on to better life, but it is more foolish to hurry frantically and cruelly. The history of the past two centuries is one sustained warning against the disemployment of men and women for whom there is no other use. Before we teach, our teachers have to learn; before we direct comprehensively, we must have experience in direction. We must always be attempting a little more than we can do, but we must not be attempting the impossible. We must advance without needless delay, but without waste, hurry, or cruelty. Do not be fearful or jealous of the advent of the new conditions. No honest worker, man or woman, has anything to fear from the coming of the Modern State.'

XI

The Real Struggle for Government Begins

But the rulers of the new World-State, as their enlargements of the Air and Sea Police made manifest, were under no illusion that the new order could be established in the world by declarations and 'Brief Explanations', and hard upon its proposals for conferences and assimilations came the organization of its local constabularies and the regulations that made the reorganized nuclei the sole means of communication of independent local authorities, businesses and individuals with the central Controls. In nearly every part of the earth the nuclei had prepared a personnel of sympathizers and auxiliaries, varying in character with local conditions, outside the ranks of the Fellowship. The khaki uniform of the street and road guardians, differing very little then from the one familar to us to-day, appeared as if by magic all over the world, and the symbol of the winged disc broke out upon aeroplanes, post offices, telephone and telegraph booths, road signs, transport vehicles and public buildings. There was still no discord with Russia; there the blazon of the wings was put up side by side with the old hammer and sickle.

Nowhere at first was there any armed insurrectionary movement. We realize from this how complete had been the collapse of the organized patriotic states of the World War period. They had no national newspapers, no diplomats, no Foreign Offices any more. There had been no paper for the former and there had been no salaries for the latter. Lacking vocal organs, nationalism as such was silenced. There were, however, protests, in a considerable variety of ineffectiveness, from local self-appointed bodies, and much passive resistance and failure to comply. But even the removal of the winged sign was infrequent, and usually where that occurred nothing further ensued when the air police came whirring out of the sky to replace it.

This phase of tacit acquiescence was, however, only temporary, until the opposition could gather itself into new forms and phases and discover methods of organization. The elements of antagonism were abundant enough. The Fascist garrison in Rome, claiming to be the government of all Italy, was one of the earliest to make its challenge. It had a number of airmen, unlicensed for various reasons by the Transport Control, and it now sent a detachment of its Black Shirts to occupy the new aeroplane factory outside the old Roman town of Turin, and to seize a small aerodrome and whatever air material was to be found in it at Ostia. The winged disc at these two places was replaced by the national fasces. A proclamation was made and disseminated as widely as the restricted means of publication permitted, calling for an assembly of the old League of Nations and reviving a long-defunct phrase of President Wilson's, 'the self-determination of peoples'. The Kind of Italy, after a diligent search, was found inoffensively farming in Piedmont, and the long-closed palace of the Quirinal was reopened and made habitable for him.

The new air police had been waiting with a certain impatience for provocation of this sort. It had been equipped with a new type of gas bomb releasing a gas called Pacificin, which rendered the victim insensible for about thirty-six hours and was said to have no further detrimental effect. With this it now proceeded to 'treat' the long-resented customs house at Ventimiglia and the factory and aerodrome in dispute.

At Ostia the police planes found a complication of the situation.

An extraordinary ceremony was in progress in the aerodrome. Three new aeroplanes had just been brought hither from the Turin factory, and they were being blessed by the Pope (Pope Alban iii).

For the still vital Catholic Church had always been given to the blessing of implements, shops, boats, bridges, automobiles, flags, guns, battleships, new buildings and the like. It was a ceremony that advertised the Church, gratified the faithful, and did no perceptible harm to the objects blessed. And this particular occasion had been made something of a demonstration against the World Council. The Pope had come; the King and the reigning Duce were present. Sound films made only a few minutes before the arrival of the air police show a gathering as brilliant, with its uniforms and canonicals, as anything that might have occurred before the World War. Choristers in cassocks and charming little lace collars chant, acolytes swing censers; the venerable Holy Father sits on a throne under a canopy, on a large crimson-draped platform. There was a muster of at least three thousand Black Shirts.

The action of the Council commander, Luigi Roselli, was precipitate.

The subsequent enquiry intimates pretty clearly that he betrayed anti-clerical bias. He had been chosen for this task because he was himself an Italian, and so, it was thought, less likely to exacerbate any latent nationalist feeling. (It is an interesting sidelight on the times that the Fascist commandatore on the ground was Mario Roselli, his elder half-brother.) His general instructions had been to seize the aerodrome and the aeroplanes with as little violence as possible. The Pacificin was only to be used in case of armed resistance. But the sight of the cassocks, the birettas, the canopies and ornaments and robes, the sound of chanting and the general ecclesiastical atmosphere were too much for the young man's prejudices. His squadron circled in formation over the aerodrome. The ceremony proceeded with dignity in spite of the noise of his propellers. For it seemed incredible that any human being would dare to gas the Pope.

'Let go,' said Luigi Roselli, too malicious to realize the brutality of his outrage.

The gas containers came crashing into the arena.

'Just for a moment,' says one of the aviators concerned, in a memorable letter, 'the chanting rose louder. They showed pluck, those priests. Hardly one of them broke ranks. Then they crumpled up in their places, drifting down on their knees for the most part. It was queer the way you saw the gas spreading among them; it was like a bed of flowers dying and the death spreading out from a lot of centres. The old boy on the throne didn't turn a hair. He had his hands together and his head bowed. You couldn't tell when it took him. The Fascist guard and the King's party weren't anything like so dignified. They gesticulated, they yelled. They were defiant and all that. And some ran about a bit before the stuff got them.

'Of course, you must understand, the whole lot thought they were being killed. None of them could have known anything of this new stuff. *We* didn't know until a fortnight ago.

'We had no gas masks on our bird, so I didn't take part in the landing party which seized the new 'planes.

'The last I saw of that aerodrome, it looked like some old Turkish carpet, gone threadbare in places but still with some brightish patches. Perfect garden of sleep. I hope nobody robbed any of them before they came to. But Roselli, I believe, dropped proper instructions about it all in Rome. . . .'

Unhappily the raid had not been so completely bloodless as this young man supposed. A youthful priest, Odet Buanarotti, had been struck on the head by one of the glass containers and killed outright. He was subsequently canonized; the last saint and martyr to be inscribed in the Latin hagiography.

[*At this point Raven's written transcript breaks off abruptly*]

BOOK IV

The Modern State Militant

I

Gap in the Text

So far I have been transcribing, with very little correction and no alteration, the text of Raven's dream book as he left it fully written out. But at this point, that fully written out history breaks off. The record of the next seventy or eighty years is represented only by an untidy mass of notes in the perfectly abominable private shorthand Raven used. Then comes the concluding chapter fully written out again.

I cannot say with any certainty why Raven left this very vital part of his story obscure and confused while he went on to the very last part of all. But I have my own ideas of what happened in his brain. In the first place he had a very human impulse to realize the issue of this world revolution that was unfolding in these notes, and it was easier, therefore, because it was more attractive, for him to write out the later part first. And in the next the intervening matter was really much more intricate for him to handle. It had, if I may use the expression, 'come through his mind' with difficulty and against resistances. His general ideas had been prepared for the new wars, for the post-war breakdown and for a world rule based on air power, and they had also been prepared for the steadily progressive World-State of the final phase. But they had not been prepared for the profound and complex mental and spiritual struggles of three-quarters of a century which inaugurated the new order. Those he had not thought out.

Whether it was really a clairvoyant vision he had of a real future textbook of history, or whether all this matter was an eruption from his subconscious mind, hardly affects the manifest fact that all this part came against the grain. One of the strongest arguments for the view that this Outline of the Future was evolved by Raven from his inner consciousness is the fact that there are several passages in which he seems to argue with himself, and that the quiet unhurrying assurance of the earlier and later narratives is not sustained in these middle parts.

I do not think it was mere chance that pulled him up precisely at the point when he came to the gassing of the Pope and the martyrdom of Saint Odet of Ostia. I think that this incident struck him as cardinal, as marking a supremely significant corner which humanity was turning. It was something that had to happen and it was something he had never let his mind dwell upon. It ended a practical truce that had endured for nearly three centuries in the matter of moral teaching, in the organization of motive, in what was then understood as religion. It was the first killing in a new religious conflict. The new government meant to rule not only the planet but the human will. One thing meant the other. It had realized that to its own surprise. And Raven, with an equal surprise, had realized that so it had to be.

Nearly a year earlier the One World-State had been declared at Basra. There already it had been asserted plainly that a new order must insist upon its own specific education, and that it could not tolerate any other forms of training for the world-wide lives it contemplated. But to say a thing like that is not to realize its meaning. Things of that sort had been said before, and passed like musical flourishes across the minds of men. The new government did not apprehend the fullness of its own intentions until this unpremeditated act of supreme sacrilege forced decision upon it. But now it had struck down the very head of Catholic Christianity and killed an officiating priest in the midst of his ministrations. It had gripped that vast world organization, the Catholic Church, and told it in effect to be still for evermore. It was now awake to its own purpose. It might have retreated or compromised. It decided to go on.

Ten days later air guards descended upon Mecca and closed the chief holy places. A number of religious observances were suppressed in India, and the slaughter-houses in which kosher food was prepared in an antiquated and unpleasant manner for orthodox Jews were closed throughout the world. An Act of Uniformity came into operation everywhere. There was now to be one faith only in the world, the moral expression of the one world community.

Raven was taken unawares, as the world of 1978 was taken unawares, by this swift unfolding of a transport monopoly into a government, a social order and a universal faith. And yet the experiment of Soviet Russia, and the practical suppression of any other religion than the so-called Communism that had been forced upon it, might well have prepared his mind for the realization that for any new social order there must be a new education of all who were to live willingly and helpfully in it, and that the core of an education is a religion. Plainly he had not thought out all that such a statement means. Like almost all the liberal-minded people of our time, he had disbelieved in every form of contemporary religion, but he had tolerated them all. It had seemed to him entirely reasonable that minds could be left to take the mould of any pattern and interpretation of life that chanced upon them without any serious effect upon their social and political reactions. It is extraordinary how such contradictory conceptions of living still exist side by side in our present world with only a little mutual nagging. But very evidently that is not going to be accepted by the generations that are coming. They are going to realize that there can be only one right way of looking at the world for a normal human being and only one conception of a proper scheme of social reactions, and that all others must be wrong and misleading and involve destructive distortions of conduct.

Raven's dream book, as it unfolded the history of the last great revolution in human affairs to him, shattered all the evasive optimism, all the kindly disastrous toleration and good fellowship of our time, in his mind. If there was to be peace on earth and any further welfare for mankind, if there was to be an end to wars, plunderings, poverty and bitter universal frustration, not only the collective organization of the race but the moral making of the individual had to begin anew. The formal revolution that had taken place was only the prelude to the real revolution; it provided only the frame, the Provisional Government, within which the essential thing, mental reconstruction, had now to begin.

That precarious first world government with its few millions of imperfectly assimilated adherents, which now clutched the earth, had to immobilize or destroy every facile system of errors, misinterpretations, compensations and self-consolations that still survived to confuse the minds of men; it had to fight a battle against fear, indolence, greed and jealousy in every soul in the world, the souls of its own people most of all, and win. Or it had to lapse. It had to do that within a definite time. If it did not win within that time, then dissension and relapse were inevitable and one more century of blundering and futility would have to be added to the long record of man's martyrdom. This new régime had to clean up the racial mind or fail, and if it failed then in all probability it would leave the race to drift back again to animal individualism, and so through chaos to extinction. Failures in the past had been possible without general disaster because they were partial and local, but this was the decisive world effort.

II

Melodramatic Interlude

I have remarked already how impersonal is this school history of the year 2006 in comparison with the histories of our own time. Politicians and statesmen pass like the shadows of general forces, royalties peep and vanish like mice behind the wainscot. They vanish at last altogether – unobtrusively. Now and then this history picks out individuals, Henry Ford for instance, or De Windt, Winston Churchill or Woodrow Wilson, not as heroes and leaders but as types and witnesses. They manifest streams of tendency in the social brain, systems of ideas at a point of maximum effectiveness.

Then suddenly at this point the history lapses into something like melodrama. For a phase personalities assume such an importance as to seem to dominate the world's affairs, as Caesar and Cleopatra did or Mirabeau and Marie Antoinette. I think some explanatory links must be missing here, some comments that might have pointed the value of this episode in illuminating the play of motive that led to the Air Dictatorship. But let me give it as it came to me.

The Air and Sea Control and the organization of the associated subsidiary Controls had been the work of a group of keen young men, moved to action by the growing disorder of life and directly inspired by De Windt and his school of writers. They had been full of generosity, enthusiasm and confidence. The first World Council elected in 1978 included most of these leaders of '65, now coming to middle age, one or two older acquisitions and only two additions from among the younger men. Arden Essenden, with his vigour of initiative, was not only the chairman but the natural leader of the first World Council. Only Ivan Englehart could compare with him in power of personality. There were finer and nobler minds present, but none others so emphatic and so available for the crude uses of popular admiration.

There was, it seems, a curiosity in the world about Essenden; his name was better known than any of his colleagues; his portrait, though indeed through nothing worse than acquiescence on his part, got into circulation, as newspapers began to abound again. It was the method of the new world government to have no presidential or secretarial signatures to its public announcements; it was stated simply that the 'Control', whichever it was, or the Council suggested, stated, proposed or had decided, and the World-State seal with its winged disc authenticated the document. But the idea spread by impalpable means that Essenden, who was known to have made the decisive speech for immediate world government at the second Basra Conference, might well have put his name whenever that seal appeared. His prestige grew and came back to his ears. There can be no doubt that his consciousness of a vague exterior support affected his attitude towards his colleagues and their common task.

The historians of our textbook, so far as some difficult passages in the stenography can be deciphered, weigh the good and bad effects of this reinforcement of Essenden's natural impatient decisiveness. They bring in other instances and compare him with other dictators. Indisputably there are crises in human affairs so urgent that many worthy considerations and qualifications are better disregarded and overborne rather than that action should be delayed. These critics of our time study the amount of justification that can be made out for Mussolini, for Stalin, Kemal, Hitler and the various other dictators during the economic débâcle of the West, and I find this judgment of posterity very discordant with my own profoundly liberal and Anglo-Saxon prejudices. They stress the hopeless indeterminateness of the preceding parliamentary régime more than I should do.

They do not extend anything like the same charity to Essenden that they do to the earlier dictators. He played the 'strong man' rôle half a century too late. The pattern of development, they decide, had been fully provided by De Windt and his fellow theorists. Essenden, they insist, did not so much lead as 'speak first', and with a needless haste, when the general decision was imminent. He induced the committee to strike too soon and too harshly at the old religious and political traditions that seemed to stand in the way of the Modern State. He found some of his colleagues slow in grasping things that seemed obvious to him. He was impatient and overbearing.

Quite early after the declaration of world sovereignty there were altercations in the committee meetings between him on the one hand and William Ryan and Hooper Hamilton on the other. Shi-lung-tang also becomes an inexplicable thorn in Essenden's side, an enervating influence full of insidious depreciation. We find Rin Kay intervening with a gentle firmness in these disputes and Englehart fretting openly at their dissensions.

This new world government, one must realize, was carrying on under conditions that were often saturated with emotion. There was still much uncertainty in the outlook; and this perhaps let in adventure and romance. The World Council was in effective possession of world power, but not in unchallenged possession. Even in 2000 CE, nineteen-twentieths of mankind were still unassimilated to the organization. If the world was not rebellious it was mutinous, and there were plenty of alert and intelligent people in opposition, estranged people or people shaped to forms of thought altogether uncongenial to the reconditioning of human affairs on Modern State lines.

It was inevitable that these disharmonies between the leading figures at the centre of things, and the similar veins of discord that broke the solidarity of the Fellowship with a thousand intricate streaks and patches of weakness, should find echoes and misinterpretations in the greater world outside the machine. That greater world was still prepared for heroes and villains, ready for blind partisanships and storms of suspicion. It wanted drama in its government. A legend came into being which exaggerated a supposed want of sympathy on the part of Essenden for the 'priggishness' and 'petty tyrannies' of the various Controls. He was supposed to be nobler stuff. He was credited with the intention of taking things into his own hands altogether and ruling the world in a more generous and popular spirit. As the history puts it: 'An autocrat has always been the imaginative refuge of the crowd from hard and competent aristocracy.'

That Arden Essenden ever plotted to realize these dreams there is no evidence at all. No word, much less any deed, is on record to show that he was unfaithful to the Modern State. But there can be no doubt that he felt that he was a fine figure and very necessary to the World Republic. He felt, as Stalin had done before him, that men could not do without him.

And then abruptly women come back into the history. We find a love intrigue flung across the stream of history. I did not notice until I came to this part of the world story how small a part women had played in the drama that began with the World War. In most countries they had been emancipated and given equal political rights with men before that disaster. That achieved, they vanish out of the picture throughout four decades of violence. There were indeed women leaders in the early stages of the Russian revolution, but none filled a decisive rôle. And for all the leadership women exercised between the Twenties and the Eighties they might have been every one of them in kitchen, nursery, hospital, or harem. They lost what little political significance they had when queens went out of fashion. A considerable proportion of the Modern State Fellowship was feminine, but no women occupied decisive positions in the scheme. There were none on the World Council. They were doing vitally important work, educational, secretarial, executive, and the like, but it was ancillary work that did not lead to individual distinction.

But at this point the historian of the year 2106 breaks his inadvertent taboo and two women's names appear, the names of Elizabeth Horthy and Jean Essenden, and we find the threads of human destiny running askew about a story of passionate love and passionate misbehaviour.

Elizabeth Horthy, who caused the downfall and execution of Arden Essenden, was evidently a woman of splendid appearance and unfaltering conduct. She was an air pilot, and she seems to have liked to wear her uniform on occasions when most women would have been in a robe. She knew, says the history, what suited her. She was tall and evidently beautifully made; she 'lifted her chin', it seems; she had a 'broad brow' and a 'serene' face. This I learn from quotations that are given from Essenden's letters to her. They are the letters of a man quite artlessly in love. But there is nothing in the notes to tell us whether she was dark or fair, what colour of eyes looked out from under that 'broad brow', nor what sort of voice she had. Her love letters seem to have been pithy and extraordinarily indiscreet. Of her charm and distinction there can be no doubt. She was one of those women who seem radiant to men. She was 'like sunshine'; she was 'like heartening music'. Again

I quote Essenden. She made men her friends, except for Hooper Hamilton, who manifestly felt some obscure resentment against her.

Now this young woman, with her obvious 'bravery' and a powerful disposition for romance, seems to have come to Basra in the train of William Ryan. It is possible but improbable that she was his mistress. Apparently she took little or no interest in the immense task of the World Revolution except as a suitable background for her exciting personal adventure. She seems to have fallen in love with Essenden at sight and he with her. It may be she came to Basra intending to do that. Something theatrical about him was not too theatrical for her. They were both theatrical. She liked things to be magnificent, and perhaps her taste for magnificence was stronger than her critical powers.

She seems to have given herself to him without hesitation or qualification or concealment. Theirs was – again I quote those artless letters of his – 'the sort of love that flaunts itself like a flag'.

But there was a third principal in this primitive drama, the wife of Essenden, a woman of great energy, great possessiveness and obtrusive helpfulness. It had been her vanity to 'inspire' Essenden. And in the cast of the drama was Ryan, loudly resentful at Essenden 'stealing' his 'air girl', and Hooper Hamilton, inexplicably malignant. We are left to guess at the incidents and details of the drama, which was after all a very commonplace drama, only that it was magnified to the scale of the world stage. It culminated in Jean Essenden bringing a charge before the World Council against her husband of being concerned in a reactionary plot against the Modern State. She had, she said, intercepted letters, though none were ever produced. The historian of the year 2106, reviewing the particulars of the case, declares that there was no real evidence at all of any guilty associations of either Elizabeth Horthy or Essenden with the widespread movement that certainly existed for a monarchist and individualist reaction. But at the time the accusation was all too plausible. In some of her scrawled notes to him it seems Elizabeth called him 'my King'.

Moreover, Jean Essenden repeated the most incredible conversations with her husband: boasts of future glory, dark threats at his colleagues, strange replies to her remonstrances. She at least was an inflexible Modern Republican. Afterwards in a storm of remorse she retracted all this evidence, but only when it was too late. Probably it was half true. Probably it was reality a little refracted in her mind.

It was Hamilton who sealed Essenden's fate. He presided over the Special Court that had been formed to try the case. 'Some of the evidence may be given with a motive,' he said, looking at the white face of the accusing wife. 'But it is a small matter that Essenden should or should not be a party in this conspiracy. His real offence is that he should have allowed this situation to develop, that he should have permitted his attention to wander from the services of the Republic to personal gratifications – personal gratifications and displays. At least he has been guilty of egotism. He has sacrificed himself and the interest of the world that has wrapped about him to an intensely personal drama. The question of his specific guilt is an altogether minor matter. The question before us is not, "What has Essenden done?" but, "What are we going to do about Essenden?" There is need for repression coming; civil war and bloodshed are plainly upon us. This is no time for Great Lovers. Essenden has become ambiguous. He cannot lead us, and – how can we do without him? Things have come to this, Essenden, you are *inconvenient*. Apart from this quarrel of the women, *you are in the way*.'

The notes quote these words from the gramophone records of the trial. For it appears that the historian of the year 2106 could sit at his desk and listen to the steel-band record of the proceedings; note the speeches and mark the inflexions of the voices.

There was a pause, and then Essenden cleared his throat. 'I see that I am in the way.'

It was decided that there should be no open trial and condemnation. That would have precipitated the revolt. A tabloid was to be given to him, and he was to take it privately. He might 'sit in the spring sunshine amidst flowers and green trees' and take it in his own time.

The record was cut deep, it seems, by the scream of Jean Essenden, protesting that that last half-hour should not be spent by the two lovers together.

Through all the years to come those steel ribbons will preserve the shrill intonations of those distressful moments. 'I can't bear *that*!' cried Jean Essenden – down to the end of time.

'No,' Elizabeth's acutal words are given; 'there is no need for you to be hurt any more. Don't be distressed, Jean, any more. It's over. It's all over for ever. I will go now. Out of the court now. I never meant to hurt Arden in this way. How was I to know? There is no need at all for us two even to say good-bye or be together any more. Jean, you couldn't help yourself. You had to do what you have done. But I never meant to hurt you. Or him.'

Those are her words as the shorthand notes give them, but we shall never hear the sound of them. But the man who wrote them down, a century after they were spoken, heard them as he wrote, heard her voice weaken, if it weakened. Was she speaking or was she making a speech? We are left guessing how far these words of hers betrayed her sense of drama or whether it had indeed the simple generosity it may have had.

There is no description of the last moments of Arden Essenden, the man who had drafted the proclamation that founded the World-State. Possibly he did sit for a while in some sunlit garden and then quietly swallowed his tabloid. He may have thought about his life of struggle, of his early days in the years of devastation and of the long battle for the World-State for which he had fought so stubbornly. Or perhaps according to all the rules of romance he thought only of Elizabeth. Much more probably he was too tired and baffled to think coherently and sat dully in the sunshine staring at those flowers which make the colophon to his story. Then the book closed for him. He died somewhere in the North of France, but the notes do not say precisely where.

They are more explicit about the fate of Elizabeth Horthy, who killed herself that day. There was no tabloid for her. She took her nearest way out of the world by flying her machine to an immense height and throwing herself out. She went up steeply. It was as though she was trying to fly right away from a planet which had done with romance. 'The aeroplane ceased to climb; it hung motionless, a quivering speck in the sky, and then began to waver and fall like a dead leaf. It was too high for anyone to see that its pilot had leapt free from it and was also falling through the air. A mere tattered rag of body was found amidst the branches of a little thicket of oak near Chantilly.'

A fortnight after Hooper Hamilton also succumbed to 'egotism' and took an overdose of sleeping-draught at his summerhouse in the Aland Isles.

And with that this novelette-like interlude ends. It is elementary in its crudity. It is out of key with all that precedes it and all that follows. We are told there were other 'stories' about the men of the First Council, but those other stories after this one sample are left to our imaginations. Its immense irrelevance tears the fabric of our history. But through the gap we see the pitiful imagination of humanity straining for a supreme intensity of personal passion.

Did that young woman as she stepped out upon nothingness above the cirrus clouds feel that her life had been worth while? The history calls her 'that last romantic'.

III

Futile Insurrrection

The notes show the historians of 2106 convinced that there was no real complicity between Elizabeth Horthy and the leaders of the Federated Nationalists who now broke out into open revolt. The impression of her character made by her recorded words and deeds is, they argue, quite incompatible with the idea that, if she had indeed been a revolutionary, she would have abandoned her fellow conspirators for a melodramatic suicide because of the execution of Essenden. Far more like her would it have been for her to fly to the rebels in Germany and give herself passionately to avenge and vindicate his memory. But plainly she did not care a rap for the monarchist conspiracy, and it is possible that she did not know of its existence. Both she and Essenden, there can be little doubt, lived and died loyal, in intention at least, to the Modern State.

But it suited the revolt to seize upon her tragedy and use her as one of its symbols, and it was long believed that Essenden had retracted the socialist cosmopolitanism of the Basra Conference in favour of Federated Nationalism. It is interesting to find the legend of the poor old League of Nations presently become more powerful than its living reality, and ironical that it should supply the formula for an attempt to divide up the world again into 'sovereign' fragments. The declaration of the so-called Prince Manfred of Bavaria put the League into the forefront of his promises. Alternatively he spoke of it as a World Federation of Free Peoples, and he promised Freedom of Thought, Freedom of Teaching, Freedom of Trade and Enterprise, Freedom of Religious Profession, Freedom from Basic English, Freedom from Alien Influence everywhere. As a foretaste of these good things, he released a little pogrom in the Frankfurt district where a few professing Jews still lingered.

[*From this point to another which I shall indicate when I reach it I am able to give a fairly trustworthy transcription of the notes* – ED.]

There was never anything that amounted to actual war during this period of disturbance; nothing that could be called a battle. The World Council had the supreme advantage of holding all communications in its hands, and, as military and naval experts could have told the rebels, there is no warfare without communications. Prince Manfred issued some valiant proclamations 'to the World' before he took his tabloid, but since Basic English was repudiated by his movement, they were translated into only a few local languages, printed on stolen paper by hidden hand-presses, and sought after chiefly by collectors. The jamming of the public radio service was mischief rather than revolt. At first there was a certain revival of the manufacture of munitions in factories that had been seized by rebel bands, but generally those ended their output after at most a few weeks under the soporific influence of Pacificin. There were a few deserters from the Air Police and a certain number of small private aeroplanes in nationalist hands; but the network of registration, vigilant police patrols, and the absence of independent aerodromes soon swept rebellion out of the air.

There remained the bomb, the forbidden pistol, the dagger and the ambush. It was these that made the revolt formidable, forced espionage, search raids, restriction of private movement and counter violence upon the World Control, and rendered the last stages of the struggle a grim and indeed a terrible chapter in human history. In narrow streets, in crowds and conferences, in the bureaus of administrations and upon the new roads, lurked the death-dealing patriot. He merged insensibly with the merely criminal organizations of blackmail and crime.

It was this murder campaign, the 'Warfare of the Silenced and Disarmed', as Prince Manfred put it, which stiffened the face and hardened the heart of the Modern State for half a century. It took to 'preventive' measures; it began to suspect and test; that horrible creature, the *agent provocateur*, was already busy again before 2000. He was busy for another decade; he did not certainly vanish from the world until the Declaration of Mégève in 2059, but there is no record of his activity after 2030. And the government which had begun its killing with Arden Essenden and Prince Manfred came to realize the extreme decisiveness and facility of the lethal tabloid. For the grosser forms of execution had given place to this polite method, and every condemned man could emulate the Death of Socrates, assemble his friends if he chose, visit some lovely place, or retire to his bureau. In vain the veteran Rin Kay protested in the committee that, just as he had argued long ago that men were not good enough to be Machiavellian, so now he declared they were not good enough to be given powers of life or death, incarceration or relief over their fellows. 'You murder yourselves when you kill,' he said.

The rebels, however, were killing with considerable vigour and persistence, and their victims had no such calm and grace in their last moments. They were stabbed, shot, waylaid and beaten to death.

'For a terror,' wrote Kramer, 'death must be terrible.'

'For murder,' said Antoine Ayala, 'death must be inevitable.'

In the end the penal code did seem to achieve its end. There were 5703 political murders in 2005, and 1114 in 2007. The last recorded occurred in 2034. The total is over 120,000. But during these twenty-nine years there were 47,066 political executions! Rihani estimates that more than seven per cent of these were carried out upon anonymous, circumstantial, or otherwise unsatisfactory evidence. Most were practically sentences by courts martial. The millennium arrived in anything but millennial fashion.

IV

The Schooling of Mankind

And now again the shorthand notes are troubled, disturbed and almost unreadable, and the resistances of Raven rise up and mingle with the proper text.

It was the age-long issue between faith in compulsion and faith in the good will of the natural man that had invaded the record. It affects me as I transcribe now; I do not see how it can fail to affect any contemporary writer or reader. I get again that flavour, that slight but perceptible flavour of – what can I call it but *inhumanity*? – in the historian's contribution. These men whom we anticipate here are different in their fundamental ideas. This short transition of a hundred and seventy years is marked by a subtle change in the human heart. I wonder if the same kind of difference might not arise if we could bring a good contemporary mind of the early eighteenth century into untempered contact with our thoughts to-day. Would not such a mind find us nowadays rather hard and sceptical about things respected, rather harshly frank about things biological, rather misshapen in our sentimentalities?

It is an old joke to revive such literary characters as Dr Johnson or Addison and make them discuss contemporary things, but generally the fun goes no further than clothing modern reactions in old-fashioned phrases and costume. But in the light of my own response to the harshly lucid, cold, and faintly contemptuous criticism of our present resistances by the writer or writers of this 2106 document I find myself reviewing these old juxtapositions. I see that if we could indeed revive Johnson he would not only strike us as an ill-mannered, offensive, inadaptable and tiresome old gentleman who smelt upleasantly and behaved worse, whose comments on life and events would be wide of the mark and discoloured with the echoes of antiquated controversies, but we should find that his contact with us would be pervaded by an incurable distress at our pace, at our strangely different values, our inhuman humanitarianism, as it would have seemed to him, and our cruel rationality. He who had sat so sturdily against his background of accepted and acceptable institutions, customs, and interpretations would find that background vanished and himself like a poor martyr in the arena with eyes upon him from every direction. Of course he would be hustled off to meet Mr G. K. Chesterton, and that might prove the most painful of all his encounters. For Mr Chesterton, who is posed so often as an avatar of the old doctor, belongs to his own time quite as much as the most futuristic of us all.

I am a hostile critic of present conditions and a revolutionary in essence; nevertheless, I can get on with the people about me because, even though my song is a song of revolt, it is in the same key and tempo as theirs; but I perceive that if I were transferred to this infinitely happier and more spacious world the history of Raven's reveals I should be continually and irreparably, in small things and great things alike, discordant. I should find nobody to get the point of my intelligent observations; I should laugh incomprehensibly, fail to see the jokes that pleased these larger, more vigorous people, and the business of life would hurry past me. All sorts of things I had hoped for and forecast might be there – but in some essential way different and alien to me.

It is one of the things that Raven's notes have taught me that a human mind, an adult human mind anyhow, is much less easily transplanted to a new time and climate than I had been wont to assume. To me, the story of Arden Essenden's bold leadership, his acute self-consciousness, and his uncontrolled love for Elizabeth Horthy seem matter for such another story, let us say, as Meredith's *Tragic Comedians*; but the historian of the year 2106 finds him and her only material from which to dissect out the treacherous egotism of passion. Something in me rebels against that, just as it rebels against the assumption that the World War was a process of sheer waste, its heroisms and sacrifices blind blundering, and its significance out of all proportion less than the social and economic dislocations that caused it.

And now that I come to these disconnected records of the harshly rational schooling of human motives under the Air Dictatorship, records that even Raven found no zest in copying, my distaste is as ineradicable as it is unreasonable. I feel that, but for 'the accidents of space and time', I should have been one of the actively protesting spirits who squirmed in the pitilessly benevolent grip of the Air Dictatorship. But whether it suits my temperament or not, this story, as it came through Raven to me, has to be told.

The men who made the great revolution and unified the world between 1965 and 1978 were men of practically the same mental assumptions as our own. They were in direct mental and moral continuity with our contemporaries. While the reader turns the page, if there is any truth in this history, De Windt, still absolutely unknown, must be working either in Berlin or London upon that Theory of the Nucleated Modern State which was the decisive plan of that final consolidation, publishers must already have read and rejected the preliminary scheme of his great work, and in a year or so from now some Mrs Essenden will be choosing the name of Arden for her boy. It is as close to us as that. The men of the first World Council, therefore, saw both sides of the business and wavered in feeling between our tradition and the new order they were creating. But the subsequent generation which constituted the Air Dictatorship had been shaped from the beginning in the aggressive bright new schools of the Modern State nuclei, they had fed on a new literature, they looked out upon fresh horizons, and their ideology had been determined more than anything else by the social psychologists and 'new lawyers' of the American school. They were starkly constructive. Nuance to them was obscurity and compromise weakness.

It is plain that so far as the future was concerned the first World Council with its rivalries and politics was far less effective than the unobtrusive Educational Control which worked under it during its regime and gradually drew together police, hygiene, schooling, and literature into one powerful nexus of direction. While the World Council was fighting for and directing and carrying on the unified World-State, the Educational Control was remoulding mankind. With the opening years of the twenty-first century (CE) the erstwhile leading figures of the revolution fall back into secondary places or vanish from the limelight altogether, and a simpler-minded, more determined group of rulers comes to the front.

[I resume my transcription here.]

'The world is various enough without artificial variety,' was a leading maxim of the Educational Control which created the men of the Air Dictatorship; and a variant of this maxim was: 'It does not increase the interest of the human assembly to suffer avoidable mental cripples and defectives.' So this body of teachers set themselves to guard new lives, beginning even with pre-natal circumstances, from what they esteemed to be physical and mental distortion. There was no shadow of doubt upon this score for the Educational Control. Every possible human being had to be brought into the new communion. Everyone was to be exposed to the contagion of modernity. Every year now increased the power of the Modern State Fellowship; by 2000, it numbered five million; by 2010 thirteen. Every increase enabled the Educational Control to thrust its enquiring and compelling fingers more and more intimately into the recesses of human life. It had more men and women made to its pattern and a greater force of teachers and inspectors it could trust.

There can be no denying the excellence of the immediate physical results. *Historical Scenes in a Hundred Volumes* witnesses from 1990 onward, not only to the resumption of the advance in the technique of picture-making and the abundance of pictures, but to the restoration of physical welfare. As the student turns over the pages he sees man straighten himself again, grow physically, become more alert. The slouching foot-dragging men and women, the aimless faces, the fattish and lumpish figures of improperly nourished people, the wretched clothing and ignoble makeshift gear of the Second Decline and Fall, disappear; after 1990 clothing is fresh and simple, and after 2010 it begins to be austerely beautiful.

And this was being achieved very largely through what the liberal thought of the nineteenth century would certainly have called 'persecution'. It is plain that the earlier World Council was all too disposed to leave great areas of the planet that did not 'give trouble' alone. The new World Council, which is known also as the Air Dictatorship, would have none of that. There began a systematic attack upon the 'lapsed regions', as they were called from the year 2006 onward. The government set itself in that year to 'tidy up' the still half-barbaric peasant populations of Hayti, Ireland, West and Central Africa, South Italy, American Georgia and its associated states, Georgia in the Caucasus, Eastern Bengal, regions where traditional superstitions, secret societies, magic cults or sacrificial practices showed an obstinate persistence. There was a definite hunt for medicine men, sorcerers, priests, religious teachers, and organizers of sedition; they would be fined or exiled, and parents and others would be fined for 'impeding' the education of their children at the cosmopolitan schools.

Many critics of the Air Dictatorship are of opinion that this was a needless pursuit of dying customs and beliefs that might well have been left to fade out into mere fantasies and affectations. But the new generation of rulers took life too seriously for that. It is an issue that can never be settled, since we can only know what actually occurred.

The old Catholic Church, it seems, was still in existence in these days, the last surviving Christian organization, but it was greatly impoverished, and it had suffered severely from schisms, evidently the result of imperfect communications throughout the dark decades. There was a Pope in Dublin and another in Rome and a coloured Pope in Pernambuco. From the legal point of view the Irish Pope was the most legitimate successor of St Peter. He had been duly elected by the Conclave, but the Fascist organization objected that he was not of Italian origin, his original surname being O'Dowd and his Italian accent imperfect, and the cardinals were intimidated into a new election. Some feud between rival gang organizations in America seems to have been involved in this split, but the details are obscure and need not occupy the student's time here. There was in consequence a division of the American Catholic world between the Dublin and the Roman communion, and this led to a murderous series of feuds, riots, and small local wars. 'Down with the Wop Pope!' said the Irish. One is reminded of that earlier splitting of the Church through the rivalry of the French monarchy and the Central European imperial system that set up a rival Pope in Avignon.

Ireland was the last stronghold of Christianity. The Catholic religion had been compulsory in South Ireland from 1944 until 1980, and the Erse language, although that was largely corrupted by unavoidable

English words and locutions, had also been made obligatory. Overt Birth Control knowledge had been successfully banned, though this produced no effect in the decline in population, and the Modern State nuclei had been boycotted more effectually there than in any other part of the world. The Dictatorship found itself fighting one of its most difficult battles for power with this tenacious people. The Irish came out in revolt all over the world. In Ireland after the maculated fever the population never rose above two millions, but there was a widespread Irish tradition throughout the English-speaking world. Some of the more brilliant and formidable antagonists of this schooling and drilling of our race that was going on, Paidrick Lynd, Arthur Fitzgerald, and Bernard O'Dwyer for example, came from Ireland. Oddly enough none of these three was a Catholic, and Fitzgerald at any rate had suffered a term of imprisonment for blasphemy, but the spirit of opposition was either innate in them or it had become ingrained in their natures.

Let the student note the open alternative at the end of the preceding paragraph. It raises a question that remains unsettled to this day. It is the clue to our contemporary moral problem. The Air Dictatorship, with what was still a very under-developed science of social psychology at its disposal, had come upon one of the obscurest and most debatable of educational problems, the variability of mental resistance to direction and the limits set by nature to the ideal of an acquiescent cooperative world. De Windt, preoccupied by his gigantic schemes for world organization, had treated the 'spirit of opposition' as purely evil, as a vice to be guarded against, as a trouble in the machinery that was to be minimized as completely as possible. The Air Dictatorship was carrying out and did carry out its world settlements on those assumptions. One may well believe that the world could have been unified into one enduring Pax Mundi in no other way. And yet they were faulty assumptions, and in the end they had to be abandoned for subtler and better conceptions of social interaction.

As every practising teacher understands, resistance is a necessary factor in teaching. Soft non-resistant material takes an imprint very readily only to lose it again very quickly. Easy pupils make teaching slipshod. The difficulty but also the soundness of teaching increases with the amount of reaction in the learner. And also resistance involves a certain element of collaboration; the thing learnt becomes a resultant, incorporating elements introduced in the struggle. It is easier to carve cheese than a good piece of wood; every piece of wood has a bias, it has to be dealt with on its own terms, it has to be managed and humoured, but in the end there is no comparison in quality and interest between carved cheese and wood-carving. These are the commonplaces of our educationists. But the defence of the work of the Educational Control is that its repressive measures were aimed not at intrinsic but at artificial resistances left over from the pre-revolutionary age.

In the old world of the early twentieth century there was a vast amount of crude generalization about what were called 'racial' characteristics. There were generalizations about arbitrarily chosen agglomerations of mixed population – the Spanish for example, or 'the West', 'Russia', or the Jews; such generalizations were always unjust and inaccurate and often extremely mischievous. Nowadays we do not write of races any more, but we recognize groups of characteristics, evidently transmitted en bloc as a rule by associated genes, and anthropologists are steadily developing a scientific classification of human types. In few aspects do human beings vary more widely than in their recalcitrance. It is not a simple case that some people are more resistant and some less. There is a wide variation in the life cycle in this respect. Recalcitrance varies with age and sex. It varies with diet. Some types are obdurate as children but afterwards become more reasonable. Generally speaking, passive resistance, unteachableness and obstinacy, but not insurrectionary energy, increase rapidly with age. And in certain populations, of which the Irish was one, there was a powerful access of resistance after adolescence in the male. It rose to the level of absolute refractoriness.

Now the apologists for the 'persecutions' of the Air Dictatorship maintain that its missionary teachers were already quite prepared with the sympathy and finesse needed to teach every type of human being they would encounter in the world. So long as resistance was personal between teacher and learner they welcomed it. At least they said they welcomed it. But when it came to the systematic organization of young people who would otherwise have had indifferent minds, so as to present a mass resistance and subversive opposition to the world order, the Educational Control, it is argued, was justified in hindering and suppressing books, meetings, teachings, agitations. It had the whip hand, and it would have been a sin not to have made use of that advantage. 'We do not suppress individuality; we do not destroy freedom; we destroy obsessions and remove temptations. The world is still full of misleading doctrines, dangerous imitations and treacherous suggestions, and it is the duty of government to erase these'; so ran the uncompromising memorandum issued by the Educational Council in 2017.

'We have to get a common vision of existence, a common idea of right and wrong, established throughout the whole population of the world, and *speedily*,' this memorandum declares. 'Natural instinct is no help in a labyrinth of artificialities. It has to be supplemented by either training or discipline. The better we train, the less need for oppression; the more thoroughly we crush out false presentations and agitations, the more freely, as well as safely, men can live. Things are rushing back headlong to prosperity, and we cannot face abundance and leisure with the present morale of the race. It has to be stiffened up; it has to be drilled to keep ranks.'

In 1955 humanity was suffering throughout the globe from disorder, famine and pestilence; its numbers were declining, and it might well have been supposed that it was driving towards extinction. The change of fortune was swift beyond precedent. As early as 2017 we have this clear intimation that its guides and rulers were contemplating the advance of plenty and an excess of leisure with terror.

Editor's Note

I think that it may make things clearer for the reader here if I give a compact summary of the political forms assumed by the developing world government between 1965 and 2106. The writer of this history of Raven's, writing for his contemporaries, assumed them to be familiar with many institutions for which the readers of this book will be altogether unprepared. Fortunately the relations of the Communist and Fascist Parties to their respective governments give us a helpful parallel to the relations to the World Council, the actual world government after 1965, of what was called the Modern State Movement. It was its incentive and its conscience.

The political structure of the world developed in this fashion:

After the chaos of the war (1940–50) and the subsequent pestilence and 'social fragmentation' (1950–60) there arose, among other attempts to again reconstitute a larger society, a combine of the surviving aviators and the men employed upon the ground plant of their trade and transport. This combine was called *The Transport Union*. It does not appear to have realized its full potentialities in the beginning, in spite of the forecasts of De Windt.

It initiated various conferences of technicians and at last one in 1965, when it was reorganized as *The Air and Sea Control* and produced as subsidiary organs *The Supply Control, The Transport (and Trading) Control,* an *Educational and Advertisement Control,* and other Controls which varied from time to time.

It was this Air and Sea Control which ultimately gave rise in 1978 at the Second Conference of Basra to the *World Council.* This was the first declared and formal supreme government of the world. The Air and Sea Control then disappeared, but its subordinate Controls remained, and coalesced and multiplied as ministries do in existing governments, under the supreme direction of the World Council.

There was no further change in essential political structure between 1978 and 2059, but there was a great change in the spirit and method of that supreme government, the World Council. A new type of administrator grew up, harder, more devoted and more resolute than the extremely various men of the two Basra Conferences. These younger men constituted what our historian calls here the Second Council, though it was continuous with the first. There was a struggle for power involving the deaths of several of the earlier councillors, but no formal change of régime; there continued to be a World Council constituting the supreme government of the world. This Second Council is also referred to as the Air Dictatorship in its earlier years, and later on as the Puritan Tyranny. These are not exact constitutional terms but loose descriptive phrases. The membership of the World Council changed by individuals coming and going, but its character remained singularly uniform for over forty years. It grew more elderly in spite of a few youthful accessions. In 2045 its average age was 61.

This Second World Council endured until a Conference at Mégève in Savoy (2059) reconstituted the world government on lines which are drawn out fairly plainly in the following chapters.

And now for the relations of this series of governing bodies to the World-State Movement.

The ideological developments that inspired these changes were initiated by a group of writers of whom De Windt was the outstanding figure. He built up the project for a World-State in all its essentials in a book on *Social Nucleation* published in 1942. The intrinsic quality of this book has been entirely overshadowed by its importance as a datum point in history. It is a slow laborious book.

It was the seed of the Modern State Movement which furnished the plans of the Air and Sea Control. The Modern State Movement was never a formally constituted government nor anything in the nature of a public administration; it was the propaganda and development of a system of ideas, and this system of ideas produced its own forms of government. The 'Movement' was initially a propaganda and research, and then a propaganda, research, and educational organization. Its active full members were called Fellows; it had a class of dormant members, whose relationship to the active category varied under different conditions and at different periods; and it had a class of neophytes or apprentices, as numerous or more numerous than its active Fellows. It ultimately incorporated the mass of adult mankind (and womankind) in its Fellowship.

It was never divided up into regional bodies. Its Fellows were acceptable at any local centre they happened to visit. Naturally it began mainly as localized nuclei, but those localizations were merely for convenience of propaganda, teaching, and local purposes. The effective subdivision of the Fellowship was into *faculties*, and these again were subdivided into sections and departments. There was to begin with a faculty of scientific research, a faculty of interpretation and education, a health faculty, a faculty of social order, a supply and trading faculty, a number of productive faculties, agricultural, mineral and so on. There were splits and coalescences among these faculties.Their splits and coalescences had a frequent relationship to the splits and coalescences of the Controls, because it was obviously a mental convenience for a faculty or faculties to correspond with one or more Controls.

The faculties and their subdivisions, their sections and departments, possessed electoral central councils, but there never seems to have been a general directorate of the Modern State Movement after the early days in which it was one simple system of propaganda and enquiry nuclei; its nuclei almost from the outset differentiated naturally into faculties, each viewing human affairs from its own angle; the movement as a whole did not require a continuing directive council; there were only conferences when concerted action between diverse faculties was desirable.

There never seems to have been any difficulty in the way of a man or woman belonging to two or more faculties at the same time, and this greatly facilitated the melting of one faculty into another. The Modern State Movement was an 'open order' attack on social structures; it was a solvent and not a mould. The moulds were the Controls.

The faculties and their sections, departments, and so forth developed very unequally; some dwindled to insignificance, and some on the other hand grew to unanticipated proportions and created their own distinctive organization and machinery. This was particularly the case with the social psychology department of the faculty of science, which annexed the whole faculty of training and advertisement by a sheer community of subject. This social psychology department of the faculty of science was given the legal and responsible direction of the Educational Control.

This body of social psychologists and their associates became a great critical and disciplinary organism side by side with the World Council, which ultimately, as will be explained in the following chapters, it superseded.

The world then ceased, it seems, to have any single permanent government at all. It remained under a series of primary Controls dealing with each other by the method of conference, namely the Controls of transport, natural products, staple manufactures, population (housing and increase), social sanitation (police and medicine), education (these two latter were later merged as the Behaviour Control), and the ever expanding activities of scientific research and creative work. So the world which had once been divided among territorial Great Powers became divided among functional Great Powers.

Later a Bureau of Reconciliation and Cooperation seems to have grown up, which decided upon the necessity and method of inter-

Control conferences. It was something rather in the nature of a Supreme Court than of a ruling council.

Most of the old faculties of the Modern State Movement dissolved into technical organizations under these Controls, with the one exception of that former department of the science faculty the department of social psychology, which by 2106 had become, so to speak, the whole literature, philosophy, and general thought of the world. It was the surviving vital faculty of the Modern State Movement, the reasoning soul in the body of the race.

In the end it becomes something like what the early nineteenth century used to think existed under the name of Public Opinion, the consensus of active thought and imagination throughout the world. It is plain that by 2106 this rule by a pervasive intelligence had become an unchallenged success. It was all that was left by way of King, President, or Supreme Government on earth.

This assembling and clearing-up of statements which are otherwise scattered rather perplexingly through the text under consideration will not, I hope, annoy such readers as have already grasped what I have summarized here. I will now return to that text itself.

V

The Text resumes:
The Tyranny of the second Council

The Air Dictatorship is also called by some historians the Puritan Tyranny. We may perhaps give a section to it from this point of view.

'Puritan' is a misused word. Originally invented to convey a merely doctrinal meticulousness among those Protestants who 'protested' against the Roman version of Catholicism, it came to be associated with a severely self-disciplined and disciplinary life, a life in which the fear of indolence and moral laxity was the dominant force. At its best it embodied an honourable realization: 'I shall do nothing worth while and nothing worth while will be done unless I pull myself together and stiffen up my conduct.' If the new Air Dictatorship was schooling the whole with considerable austerity, it was certainly schooling itself much more so.

The code of the first makers of the World-State had been a simple one. 'Tell the truth,' they insisted; 'maintain the highest technical standards, control money and do not keep it, give your powers ungrudgingly to the service of the World-State.' That seemed to leave them free for a good deal of refreshing self-indulgence, and it did. They ate, drank, and were merry, made love very freely, envied and competed with one another for power and distinction, and set no adequate guard upon the growth of rivalries and resentments. Our history has glanced at the fall and death of Essenden, but this is only one episode in the long and complicated history of the private lives of the first world committee. Slowly the details are being elucidated and analysed by a body of historical students. Except that the victims are dead, and cannot hear, the results are as pitiless as the old Christian fancy of the Recording Angel and his Book on Resurrection Day.

They appear as very pitifully human; their sins happened to them, they were taken unawares in phrases of fatigue, by resentment, by sensuality or flattery. Women were attracted by their prestige and offered the reassurance of love to their weaker moments. In many cases the moral downfall was due to the very limitlessness of the devotion with which they first gave themselves to their world task. They worked without rest. Then they would suddenly find themselves worn bare, bankrupt of moral energy. They had made no proper balance between the public task and the inward desire. Outbreaks of evil temper would follow, or phases of indolence or gross indulgence. The Fellowship was disconcerted; the outer world ran with scandal. 'These Fellows,' said their critics, 'are no better than the pretenders and rascals of the old régime. Rin Kay, the wise, is consumed with affection for his little friend, and Ardasher of the experimental aeroplanes makes his young men do dangerous stunts to please a girl. Morovitz is collecting Persian miniatures quite unscrupulously and Fedor Galland spends half his time now making a garden at Babylon.'

The ambitious young men who were little boys when the first conference at Basra was held were educated by teachers who were none the less harshly zealous because they were doing relatively inconspicuous work and had no little friends nor minatures nor gardens to amuse them. These teachers had a lively sense of their leaders' defects and of their own modest but real moral superiority. The youngsters under their teaching were saturated with constructive enthusiasm, but they were trained also to judge and condemn the weaknesses of their spent and tired predecessors. They learnt that the brightness of this new world that had been made for them was in danger from the very men who had made it. The technically more skilful and intensive teaching that had been given them had made them more self-conscious and wary in their behaviour, and far more capable of managing the detail of their lives. They were simple in principle and hard in detail. They had a modern wisdom about diet and indulgence; they regarded lack of fitness as a crime.

The difference is evident in *Historical Pictures*, where one usually sees the older generation dressed either carelessly or picturequely and often self-consciously or gracelessly posed, while the younger men and women in the simpler and plainer clothing that was coming into fashion carry themselves like athletes. Austerity has become a second nature to them. Devotion and the sacrifice of the individual they carried to such a pitch that, for instance, it was considered unseemly for them to have portraits made, and there was no record kept of the names of the chairmen and of the movers of motions in the central committee during their ascendancy. It has needed special research to rescue some of the names of this second generation of world rulers, who set up the Puritan Tyranny and made the Socialist World-State secure. One of the moving spirits was certainly Han H'su and another Antoine Ayala.

They ousted their predecessors without any coup d'état, one by one, through sheer superiority in energy and working power. The great revolution was over; the World-State was in being. But it was not secure. It was a time for just such continuous detailed work as only a naturally able and energetic type with a hard training could hope to do. They were not selected by any voting or politics to fill the Council, they were selected by their own staying and driving power. The milder or subtler types could not keep the pace and fell into less authoritative positions. The influence of certain teachers and groups of teachers was very considerable. Three schools, the Unamuno Foundation at Coimbra, the Columbia University of New York, and the Tokio Social College, accounted for more than a third of the World Council in 2017.

For nearly forty years the new Council, with occasional renewals, worked and kept a whole generation of men and women working. As Aldous Huxley (1894–2004), one of the most brilliant of reactionary writers, foretold of them, they 'tidied up' the world.

There can be no denying the purification and rarefaction of the human scene that was achieved during their sway. They tightened up the disciplines of the Modern State Fellowship, and nevertheless the proportion of the Fellowship increased until it bade fair to become the larger moiety of adult mankind. The mental habits of the Fellowship, its habitual bearing, extended through the whole population. The Tyranny, says Vordin, altered the human face for ever. It closed the mouth and made the lips firmer, made the eyes steadier and more candid, opened the brow, altered the poise of the head, obliterated a number of wrinkles and habits of expression. Portraits of the earlier and later time confirm this generalization. One type of odd-character after another became rare and began to disappear from the human comedy. Rascals and recalcitrants grew old, sat in the sun for a time rather protestingly and vanished. They took many disagreeable and some whimsical casts of countenance with them. Sexual prostitution ceased and eliminated a characteristic defiance from feminine carriage. The trader found he had nothing to trade with and came into the employment of the Supply Control. Gambling, horse-racing, sport, generally went out of fashion, and those queer oblongs of pasteboard, 'playing cards', retired to museums, never to emerge again. Every one of these vanishing interests or practices took its own scores of social types, of 'reaction systems', to use the modern phrase, away with it. Faces ceased to be masks.

Every year the world grew safer for the candid. The need for cunning and wary self-restraint diminished enormously, the habit of making a face a 'mask'. Humanity was extroverted. A lively self-forgetful interest in external things becomes more and more patent. The 'worried' look of the introspective habit of mind disappears. 'Everyone must know plainly,' said the new rulers. 'Men must be perplexed no more.' The old religions could not emulate the moral prestige of the new cult, and even the resentments of the persecution that deprived them of their last shreds of educational influence could not preserve them. For nearly forty years this rule of the new saints, this resolute simplification and smoothing out of life, went on.

History becomes a record of increasingly vast engineering undertakings and cultivations, of the pursuit of minerals and of the first deep borings into the planet. New mechanisms appeared, multiplied, and were swept away by better mechanisms. The face of the earth changed. The scientific redistribution of population began. Yet there was little likeness to the world of to-day, as we know it. No age in human history has left us such strange and uncongenial pictures.

Costume was not unpleasant during this period, because of its simplicity; the human figures in the scene at least are tolerable; but these scientific Puritans also produced some of the clumsiest architecture, the most gaunt and ungainly housing blocks, the dullest forests, endless vistas of straight stems, and the vastest, most hideous dams and power-stations, pylon-lines, pipe-lines, and so forth that the planet has ever borne. But at any rate they flooded the Sahara and made the North African littoral the loveliest land in the world. The productivity of mankind was now advancing by leaps and bounds, in spite of the severe restraint presently put upon the introduction of fresh labour-saving devices; and yet these Puritans were consumed by an overwhelming fear of leisure both for themselves and others. They found it morally necessary to keep going and to keep everybody else going. They *invented* work for the Fellowship and all the world. Earth became an ant-hill under their dominion, clean and orderly but needlessly 'busy'. So harshly had they reacted against the weaknesses of their seniors and so unable were they to mitigate their own self-imposed severities.

Let us cast up the good mankind can attribute to this strange phase of sternness and grim repression. For all the faint masochist and sadistic flavour of its closing years, the good was beyond all measure greater than the evil. 'The obliteration of out-of-date moral values' (the phrase is Antoine Ayala's) 'and the complete establishment of a code of rigorous and critical self-control, of habitual service, creative activity, cooperation, of public as well as private good manners, and invariable truthfulness, were achieved for all time. We grow up so easily now into one free, abundant, and happy world that we do not realize the effort still needed even in the year 2000 to keep life going upon what seem now to us the most natural and simple lines possible. We find it almost impossible to imagine the temptations to slacken at work, loiter, do nothing, 'look for trouble', seek 'amusement', feel bored and take to trivial or mischievous 'time-killing' occupations, that pursued the ill-trained, under-vitalized, objectless common citizen before 2000 CE. Still more difficult is it to realize how subtly these temptations were diffused through the mass and how hard they made a well-directed life. We have to trust the psychological experts about that.'

The New Puritans 'disinfected' the old literature, for example. It is hard to see that now as an urgent necessity. These old stories, plays, and poems seem to us to convey the quaintest and most inexplicable systems of motivation conceivable, and we cannot imagine people being deflected by them; they might as easily be led astray by the figures on a Chinese screen or an Hellenic sarcophagus; but before the persecution those books were, as one censor called them, 'fever rags'. They stood then for 'real life'. They provided patterns for behaviour and general conduct. That queer clowning with insults and repartees, that insincerely sympathetic mocking of inferiors, that denigration of superiors, which constituted 'humour' in the old days, strikes us as either fatuous or malicious. We cannot understand, for instance, the joy our ancestors found in the little blunders and misconceptions of ill-educated people. But then they also laughed at the cripples who still abounded in the world! Equally distasteful now is most of their 'romance' with its false stresses, its unnecessary sacrifices and desperations. 'Romance', says Paul Hennessey, 'is essentially the violent and miserable reaction of weak spirits to prohibitions they cannot fairly overcome.'

We find the books glorifying war and massacre, and the tangled masses of suggestion that elaborated the innate hostility and excitement caused by difference of racial type, so unconvincing that it is difficult to believe that they ever gripped. But they did grip and compel. They drove innumerable men to murders, lynchings, deliberate torture. They dressed the foulest and cruellest of crimes in heroic colours. There had to be a break with these traditions before they could be seen as we see them now. It needed the heroic 'priggishness' of the Air Dictatorship, putting away the old literature and drama for a time, suppressing the suggestion systems of the old religions and superstitions, jailing and segregating men and women for 'hate incitement', ruthlessly eliminating sexual incitation from the lives of the immature and insisting upon a universal frank sexual hygiene, to cleanse the human mind for good and all and inaugurate the unconstrained civilization of to-day. There was no other way to renaissance.

Joseph Koreniovsky has called the Puritan Tyranny 'the cold bath that braced up mankind after the awakening'. Man, he says, was still 'frowsty-minded' and 'half asleep' in the early twenty-first century, still in urgent danger of a relapse into the confused nightmare living of the Age of Frustration. You may call it a tyranny, but it was in fact a release; it did not suppress men, but obsessions. None of us now can fully realize the value of that 'disentanglement from tradition', because now we are all disentangled.

And next to this ruthless 'mental disinfection' of the world, and indeed inseparable from it, we must put the physical disinfection of mankind to the credit of the Air Dictatorship. Between 2000 and 2040 every domicile in the world was either destroyed and replaced, or reconditioned and exhaustively disinfected. There was an immense loss of 'picturesqueness' in that process, and we shiver nowadays when we look at pictures of the white bare streets, the mobile rural living-boxes, the bleakly 'cheerful' public buildings, the plain cold interiors with their metallic furniture, which everywhere replaced the huts, hovels, creeper-clad cottages and houses, old decaying stone and brick town halls, market houses, churches, mosques, factories and railway stations in which our tough if ill-proportioned and undersized forefathers assembled about their various archaic businesses.

But between the same years the following diseases, the names of which abound in the old histories, and the nature of which we can hardly imagine, vanish from the human records: catarrh, influenza, whooping cough, sleeping sickness, cholera, typhus, typhoid, bubonic plague, measles, and a score of other infectious scourges. (Only yellow fever remained as a serious infection after 2050. That demanded the special effort of 2079 for its extirpation.) Syphilis, and indeed all those diseases known as venereal, were stamped out completely in two generations; they were afflictions so horrible and disgusting that their description is not now considered suitable for the general reader. There was a similar world-wide attack on plant diseases and distortions, but of that the student will learn in his Botanical History.

The psychologists who are rewriting human history have still many open questions to settle about the training and early influences that gave the world this peculiar group of rulers, and so the account of its hardening and deterioration remains incomplete. They admit that the Tyranny was in essence a liberation, but they insist that it left vitally important desires in the human make-up unsatisfied. Old traditions and mischievous obsessions were rooted in these desires, and the Tyranny had not been content with an eradication of the old traditions. It had denied the desires. It had pulled up the soil with the weeds. It had exalted incessant, even if pointless, activity above everything else in life.

Overwork, a strained strenuousness, has been a common characteristic of the rulers of mankind in the past. It shows through the Edicts of Asoka, for example, and particularly in Rock Edict VI (*Asoka*, D. R. Bhandarkar, 1932, Classical Historical Studies, 21–118). 'I am never satisfied,' runs the Edict, 'with the exertion or with dispatch of business. The welfare of the whole world is an esteemed duty with me. And the root of that, again, is this, namely, exertion and dispatch of business.' A great majority of the successful Caesars and Autocrats from Shi-Hwang-Ti to Hitler have the same strenuousness – Alexander the Great perhaps was the chief exception, but then his father had done the work before him. Mussolini, the realizer of Italian Fascismo, in his *Talks* to Ludwig (Historical Documents Series 100,319) betrays an equal disposition for single-handed accomplishment and an equal disinclination to relinquish responsibility.

All the chief figures of the Air Dictatorship betray, upon scrutiny, signs of the same drive to do too much and still to do more. They display all the traits of a collective weary conqueror, unable to desist and think and adapt himself. They went on ruling and fighting when their victory was won. They had tidied up the world for ever and still they went on tidying. After their first real successes they manifest an extreme reluctance to bring new blood into the responsible administrative task. They had arisen to power as a group by their usefulness, because they were unavoidably necessary to those original founders of the World-State whom they first served and then by sheer insistence upon performance pushed out of authority and replaced. The three virtues in a ruler according to Han H'su were punctuality, precision, and persistence. But it was a dictum of Paidrick Lynd's that 'indolence is the mother of organization'. They had none of that blessed gift of indolence. When the legacy of work that the first world revolution had left them was exhausted, they brought things at last to the necessity for a final revolution through their sheer inability to organize a direct succession to themselves or to invent fresh undertakings.

That final revolution was the most subtle of all the substitutions of power that have occurred in human affairs, the most subtle and so far the last. The Dictatorship could suppress overt resistance; it could impose obedience to its myriads of injunctions and rules. But it could not suppress the development of general psychology nor the penetration of its own legislative and administrative activities by enquiry and criticism.

The Department of General Psychology had grown rapidly until it had become the most vigorous system of activities in the scientific faculty of the Modern State Fellowship. In its preparatory stages it had taken the place of the various 'Arts' and Law curricula of the old régime. It was the modernization of the 'humanities'. The founders of the World-State had given this particular department of the scientific faculty almost as great a directive and modifying power over both the Educational and Legal Controls as it exercises to-day. Even then it was formally recognized as the responsible guardian in the theory of Modern State organization. It more than realized the intentions of De Windt. It became the thought, as the World Council had become the will, of mankind acting as a whole. And since the education and legal adjustment of the World-State was thus under the direction of a department of research continually advancing, they differed diametrically in character from the education and teaching of the old-world order.

The student cannot keep this difference, this flat contrast, too clearly in mind. He will never understand the historical process without it. The Old Education existed to preserve traditions and institutions. Progressive forces arose as a dissent from it and operated outside its machinery. In the eighteenth, nineteenth, and early twentieth century education was always a generation or so behind living contemporary ideas and the school-master was a drag on mankind. But the New Education, based on a swiftly expanding science of relationship, was no longer the preservation of a tradition, but instead the explanation of a creative effort in the light of a constantly most penetrating criticism of contemporary things. The new schoolmaster showed the way, and the new education kept steadily ahead of contemporary social fact. The difference of the New Law and the Old Law was strictly parallel. If a man of the year 1900 had been told of a progressive revolution led by lawyers and school-masters inspired by scientific ideas, he would have taken it as a rather preposterous joke, but to-day we ask, 'How else can the continuity of a progressive revolution be sustained?'

The failure of the German revolution of 1918 and the relapse of that unfortunate country into the puerility and brutish follies of Hitlerism was entirely due to the disregard of the elementary principle that no revolution could be a real and assured revolution until it has completely altered the educational system of the community. Every effective old-world revolution was a revolt against an established education and against the established law.

The rôle of the modern Education Control in preserving, correcting, and revivifying the progressive process in human affairs had already been manifested by the supersession of the leading personalities of the Basra Conference in the World Council by their successors who became the Air Dictatorship. Now these men in their turn found the instruments of government becoming recalcitrant in their hands and obeying the impulse of unfamiliar ideas. They had cleared and cleansed the site while social science had been preparing the idea of the new structures that were to stand upon it, and now they found themselves confronted by an impulse towards creation and enrichment entirely discordant with their habits of administration. Their subordinates began to send back the instructions given them as 'insufficient and not in accordance with the psychology of the workers' – or other people – 'concerned'. Schemes were condemned by those to whom they were entrusted as unnecessarily toilsome or needlessly ungracious. Workers took matters into their own hands and demanded more pleasant processes or more beautiful results. The committee was disposed at first to insist upon unquestioning obedience. Thereupon the Education Control produced a masterful argument to show 'the social harmfulness of unquestioning obedience'.

There could be no greater contrast in the world than that between the older revolutionary crises in human affairs and this later conflict of wills. The old revolutions were at best frantic, bawling, sentimental affairs in which there was much barricading of roads and destruction of property; people were shot abundantly and carelessly and a new régime stumbled clumsily to responsibility on the ruin and reversal of its predecessor. Such revolutions were insurrections of discontent against established institutions. But this last revolution was the cool and effectual indictment of the world executive by a great world-wide educational system. It was not an insurrection; it was a collateral intervention. The new order arose beside its predecessor, took matters out of its hands and replaced it.

The need for an intolerant militant stage of the World-State had passed. The very reason for the disciplines of the Puritan Tyranny had been dissolved away in the completeness of its victory. But the last men to realize this were the old men who now sat trying to find tasks to keep humanity out of mischief in the bureau of the World Council.

VI

Aesthetic Frustration:
The Notebooks of Ariston Theotocopulos

It is a growing custom of historians, and we have already followed it freely, to vivify their general statements by quotations from contemporary descriptive writers. As histories have disentangled themselves from their primitive obsession about rulers and their policies, they have made a more and more extensive use of private memoirs, diaries, novels, plays, letters, sketches, pictures and the like. Once upon a time washing bills and memorandum books were below the 'dignity of history'. Now we esteem them far above acts of parliament or diplomatic memoranda. And certainly there is no more convenient source of information about current ideas and feeling under the Air Dictatorship than the cipher Note Books of that gifted painter and designer Ariston Theotocopulos (1997–2062). For thirty-seven years until his death, he wrote in these books almost daily, making his own shrewd comments on current events, describing many odd and curious occurrences, noting very particularly his own emotional reactions, and adorning them all with a wealth of sketches, dreams, caricatures and the like, which make the full edition in facsimile, with a translation, among the greatest delights of the book-lover. The bulk of this matter does not concern the student of general history at all, and yet it is possible to pick out from it material for a far clearer realization of life under the second Council than could be derived from a score of abstract descriptions.

The earlier of these volumes are coloured by the irritation of the writer with three particular things: the restrictions upon private flying, his difficulties in finding scope for his genius, and the general want of beauty and graciousness in life. At that time there were no privately owned aeroplanes and no one could act as an air pilot who was not an active Fellow of the Modern State organization and subject to its rules and disciplines. Theotocopulos had an anarchistic soul, and his desire to wander freely above the mountains and clouds, to go whither he liked at his own sweet will, unhampered by any thought of immediate 'service', became an obsession with him. 'If they would let me alone I would give the world something,' he scribbles. 'But what on earth is the good of those blighted old Master Decorators telling me to do this and that? Did I come into the world to imitate and repeat things done already?'

And in another place he notes: 'Some damned official flying overhead on his way to preventing something. It spoilt the day for me. I couldn't *think* any more.'

Then comes a cry of agony. 'The lay-out of all this terracing is wrong. What is the good of putting me to do a frieze of elephants on a wall that ought to come down again? If I do anything good that wall will stay where it is. The better I do it, the more likely they are to keep that wall. And it's wrong. It's wrong. It's wrong.'

A few pages on, one word is all alone by itself: '*Elephants*!'

Then follows a string of caricatures of that animal which Li has characterized as acute biological criticism. Theotocopulos had been vividly interested in elephants, but now he had tired of them. He represents them as diaphanous or altogether transparent, and reveals the distresses of their internal lives. And there is a whole page of incredibly wicked elephants' eyes.

He was working on the rather deliberate decoration of the main-road system then in course of construction, running from Cape Finisterre through North Italy and along the North Black-Sea Dyke to the Crimea and Caucasia. That system has since been deflected from the Ligurian coast northward, but at that time it was made to follow by the sea to Genoa, and thence passed in a great cutting through the mountains to the plain of the Po and so to the still existing Chioggia viaduct. It was one of a not very ably conceived system of world roads that was greatly modified before its completion in our own time, and it was carried out with a massiveness and a solidity of ornamentation that witness to the World Council's incapacity to realize that Change was still going on. Those roads seem to have been planned for all time. They indicated mental coagulation.

Theotocopulos was engaged upon the coast section between the old town of Nice to the old port of Genoa. It was driven in a series of flattened curves that straightened out in places to a right line, cutting brutally through headlands and leaping gulfs and bays in vast viaducts. Above and below the slopes were terraced with natural or imitation marble walls and the terraces were planted with oranges, lemons, vines, roses, olives and agaves. These terraces went up, as Theotocopulos says, 'relentlessly' to the old Corniche Road above, broken only by a few masses of evergreen trees. The ruins of the villas and gardens of the Capitalist era and most of the towns along the coast that Titus Cobbett had visited and described seventy-odd years before had now been cleared away; a few groups of residential buildings occurred here and there, and pretentious staircases, which were rarely used because of the lifts they masked, led down to beaches and holiday places and harbours for pleasure boats and fishermen. These holiday places and the residential buildings were low and solid-looking, after the fashion of the time, and they provoked Theotocopulos to frenzy. He caricatured them and spotted his drawings with indecent words. It is amazing how truthfully he drew them and how ingeniously he distorted them. He represented them as cowering into the earth like the late buildings of the war years, from which they certainly derived their squatness.

'We still dream of air raids and war in the air,' he said, and he speaks elsewhere of 'the inmates of those fortifications. . . . If only I could get hold of an aeroplane and a bomb! Perhaps after all there is some sense in keeping intelligent people like me out of the air, with this sort of stuff about.'

His task unhappily kept him in close contact with all this squat architectural magnificence. He had won distinction at an unusually early age for his brilliant drawings of men and animals; he had a grotesque facility for seeing into bodies and conveying his sense of internal activities; before his time the only anatomy known to artists had been muscular anatomy; and he was set to 'decorate' an ungainly stretch of wall near Alassio with a frieze of elephants. It is necessary to explain that in those days there was the completest divorce in people's minds between aesthetic and mechanical considerations. First you made a thing, they thought, and then you decorated it. It seems almost incredible now, but the engineers of the Air Dictatorship were supposed and expected to disregard all thought of beauty in what they did. If they made something frightful, then the artist was called in to sugar the pill. There, as in so many things, the restless sensitive mind of Theotocopulos anticipated the ideas of to-day. 'Engineers ought to be artists,' he says, 'anyhow; and artists ought to be engineers or leave structural work alone.' This wall of his still exists; his decoration has preserved it, even as he foresaw. It just remains for his sake, a lesson for students and a monument to his still incomparable talent.

'Took a holiday,' he notes one day, 'and rowed about five miles out to sea. These disproportions grow worse as one gets away from them. Never before have I seen anything that got uglier as it receded in perspective. This coast does. The road is too broad and big. There will never be that much traffic. The population of the world isn't increasing and on the whole it rushes about less than it did. One hundred and twelve metres of width! What is this coming torrent of traffic from Finisterre to God knows where? Not a sign of it as yet. Nor ever will be. The little lizards get lost across that glassy surface and die and dry up. Artless earthworms crawl out upon it and perish. One sees them by the thousand after wet weather. No shade for miles. The terraces are badly spaced and the walls that sustain them look gaunt. There is no sympathy in all this straight stuff with the line and movement of the hills behind. They *live*. And this accursed habit of building houses close to the ground! Damn it, don't we build to get away from the ground?'

And then suddenly in big capitals comes one word: 'PROPORTION!'

After that he meditated with his pencil in hand, jotting down his thoughts. 'The clue to life. Not simply beauty. There is no evil but *want of proportion*. Pain? Pain arises out of a disproportion between sensations. Dishonesty? Cruelty? It is all want of proportion between impulse and control. . . .'

It is interesting to trace in the notebooks how he tries over ideas that are now familiar to everyone. He worries between the ideas of proportion and harmony. Then he hits on the discovery that all history is a record of fluctuations in proportion. Today, of course, that is a commonplace. We have told the economic and political history of the twentieth century, for instance, almost entirely as the story of an irregular growth of the elements of life, hypertrophy of economic material going on concurrently with a relative arrest of educational, legal, and political adjustment. The first dim realizations of these disharmonies were manifested by the appearance of 'planning', those various crude attempts to make estimates of quantities in social life of which the Russian Five Year Plan was the first. After 1930, the world was full of Plans, and most of them were amazingly weak and headlong plans.

We learn from these notebooks of Theotocopulos how imperfectly this idea of really deliberate quantitative preparation in the activities of our species was apprehended even in the early twenty-first century. Just as the war complex ran away with men's minds in the war period, so now political unity and uniformity and an extravagant concentration of enterprise upon productive efficiency had outrun reason. The interest of these notebooks lies exactly in the fact they are not the writings of a scientific social psychologist, but of a man who was, except for his peculiar genius and energy of expression, a very ordinary personality. They tell us how common people were taking the peculiar drive of the times, how the general mind was puzzling out its new set of perplexities and asking why, after having abolished war, restored order, secured plenty, defeated the fears and realized the wildest hopes of the martyr generations, it was still so far from tranquillity and happiness.

'Growing pains,' he writes abruptly. 'That was old Lenin's phrase. Is a certain want of proportion unavoidable?'

After that flash in the pan, the notebook wanders off into a dissertation upon Levels of Love, of no importance for our present purpose. But that idea of 'Growing Pains' was working under the surface all the time. Suddenly appear pages of sketches of strange embryos, of babies and kittens and puppies, all cases of morbid hypertrophy. 'Is want of proportion inevitable in all growth? Nature seems to find it so, but she always has been a roundabout fumbler. She starts out to make a leg, and when it comes out a wing she says, "Eureka! I *meant* to do that." But in *designed work*? In engineering for example?'

His mind goes off to the making of castings, the waste in grinding, the problems that arise in assembling a machine.

'Nature corrects the disproportions of growth by varying the endocrines,' he reflects. 'And when a house has got its frames set up and its walls built, we turn out the masons and put in the plasterers and painters. So now. A change of régime in the world's affairs is indicated. New endocrinals. Fresh artisans.'

This particular entry in the notebook is dated April 7th, 2027. It is one of the earliest appearances of what presently became a current phrase, 'change of régime'.

The preoccupations of Theotocopulos with the physical and mental aspects of love, his extraordinary knack of linking physiological processes with the highest emotional developments, need not concern us here, important as they are in the history of aesthetic analysis. For a year or so he is concentrated upon his great 'Desire Frieze' in the Refectory of the Art Library at Barcelona, and he thinks no more of politics. He likes the architects with whom he is associated; he approves of the developments at Barcelona, and he is given a free hand. 'These fellows do as they like,' he remarks. 'A great change from all those damned committees, "sanctioning" this or asking you to "reconsider" that.' Then he comes under the influence of that very original young woman from Argentina, also in her way a great artist, Juanita Mackail. Sketches of her, memoranda of poses and gestures, introduce her. Then he remarks: 'This creature thinks.' So far he has never named her. Then she appears as 'J' and becomes more and more frequent.

'There is something that frightens me about a really intelligent woman. Was it Poe or De Quincey – it must have been De Quincey – who dreamt of a woman with breasts that suddenly opened and became eyes? Horrid! To find you are being looked at like that.'

Following this a page has been torn out by him, the only page he ever tore out, and we are left guessing about it.

An abrupt return to political speculation in the notebooks follows. A number of entries begin, 'J says', or end, 'This is J's idea.'

Then some pages later he repeats: 'This creature thinks. Do I? Only with my fingers. Language is too abstract for me. Or is it true, as she says, that I am mentally lazy. *Mentally lazy* – after I had been talking continuously to her for three hours!'

'It seems all my bright little thoughts don't amount to anything compared with the stuff these social psychologists are doing. I have a lot to learn. I suppose J would schoolmistress anybody.'

The notebooks keep the fragile grace and mental vigour of Juanita Mackail alive to this day. She was the sort of woman who would have been a socialist revolutionary in the nineteenth century, a commissar in Early Soviet Russia or a hard worker for the Modern State in the middle twentieth century. Now she was giving all the time her strongly decorative idiosyncrasy left free to the peculiar politics of the period. It is plain that before she met Theotocopulos she was already politically minded. She had had a feeling that the world was in some way not going right, but her clear perception of what had to be done about it came only with her liaison with him. The notebooks with their frankness and brutality tell not only a very exceptional love story, but what is perhaps inseparable from every worth-while love story, a mutual education. Theotocopulos was her first and only lover. To begin with he had treated her as casually as he had treated the many other women in his life, and then it is plain that, as he began to find her out, his devotion to her became by degrees as great or greater than her devotion to him.

He studied her. He made endless notes about her. We know exactly how she affected him. How he affected her we are left to guess, but it is plain that for her there was at once the magnificence of his gifts and the appeal of his wayward childishness. The former overwhelmed her own. It is plain in her surviving work. The earlier work is the best. He asks twice, 'Am I swamping J? Her stuff is losing character. She is borrowing my eyes. That last cartoon. Am I to blame? It *was* such lovely stuff. Once upon a time.' And he writes: 'This maternity specialization is Nature's meanest trick on women. If they are not going to be mothers, if they *can't* be mothers, why on earth should they be saturated with motherhood? Why should J think more about getting me a free hand to do what I please than she does about her own work? She does. I haven't asked her. Or have I, in some unconscious way, asked her? No, it's just her innate vicious mothering. I am her beloved son and lover and the round world is my brother, and every day her proper work deteriorates and she gets more political and social-psychological on our account.'

From that point onward the trend of these notebooks towards politics becomes very strong. The early volumes express the resentments of an isolated man of extreme creative power who finds himself singlehanded and powerless in an unsympathetically ordered world. The late show that same individuality broadening to a conception of the whole world as plastic material, sustained by a sense of understanding and support, coming into relationship and cooperation with an accumulating move-ment of kindred minds. At last it is not so much Theotocopulos who thinks as the awakening aesthetic consciousness of the world community.

'The change of régime has to be like a chick breaking out of its egg. The shell has to be broken. *But the shell had to be there.* Let us be just. There is proportion in time as well as in space. If the shell is broken too soon there is nothing to be done but make a bad omelette. But if it isn't broken at the proper time, the chick dies and stinks.'

The forty-seventh notebook is devoted almost entirely to a replanning of the subject of his early animadversions, the Ligurian coast. That notebook proved to be so richly suggestive that to-day some of his sketches seem to be actual drawings of present conditions, the treatment of the Monaco headland for example, and the reduction of the terraces. But his dreams of orange-groves are already quaint, because he knew nothing of the surprises in tree form that the experimental botanists were preparing. The forty-ninth notebook is also devoted to planning. 'Plans for a world,' he writes on the first page. 'Contributions.' He seems to have amused himself with this book at irregular intervals. There are some brilliant anticipations in it and also some incredible fantasies. Occasionally, like every prophet, he finds detail too much for him and lapses into burlesque.

There is a very long note of a very modern spirited discussion about individuality which he had with Juanita when apparently they were staying together at Montserrat. The notes are the afterthoughts of this talk, 'shots at statement' as he would have called them, and they bring back to the reader a picture of that vanished couple who strolled just sixty years ago among the tumbled rocks and fragrant shrubs beneath the twisted pines of that high resort, both of them so acutely responsive to the drift of ideas that made the ultimate revolution – she intent and critical, holding on to her argument against his plunging suggestions, like someone who flies a kite in a high wind.

'The individual is for the species; but equally the species is for the individual.

'Man lives for the State in order to live by and through – and in spite of – the State.

'Life is a pendulum that swings between service and assertion. Resist, obey, resist, obey.

'Order, discipline, health, are nothing except to make the world safe for the aesthetic life.

'We are Stoics that we may be Epicureans.

'Exercise and discipline are the cookery but not the meal of life.

'Here as ever – PROPORTION. But how can proportion be determined except aesthetically?

'The core of life is wilfulness.'

So they were thinking in 2046. Have we really got very much further to-day?

VII

The Declaration of Mégève

Theotocopulos and his Juanita were present at the Conference at Mégève which wound up the second World Council. They both seem to have been employed upon the decoration of the temporary town that was erected for this purpose on those upland meadows. The notebooks, in addition to some very beautiful designs for metal structures, contain sketches of various members of the Council and some brilliant impressions of crowd effects in the main pavilion. There is also a sketch of a painting Theotocopulos afterwards made; it appears in all our picture-books of history: the tall presence of old Antoine Ayala, standing close to the aeroplane in which he departed for his chosen retreat in the Sierra Nevada; he is looking back with an expression of thoughtful distrust at the scene of his resignation. The pilot waits patiently behind him. 'Well, well,' he seems to say. 'So be it.' The sinking sun is shining in his eyes, so that they peer but do not seem to see.

The drawing of nine of the World Councillors listening intently to the statement of Emil Donadieu, the secretary of the Education Faculty, is almost equally well known.

It was the most gentle of all revolutions. It might have been a thousand years away from the fighting and barricading, the pursuits and shootings and loose murderings, of the older revolutionary changes. The Council suffered not overthrow but apotheosis. Creation asserted itself over formal construction and conservation. For a decade and more the various Controls had been showing a greater and greater disregard of the Central Council; they had been dealing directly with one another, working out their immense cooperations without the intervention – which was more and more inhibition – of the overriding body. It was the Education Faculty of the Control of Health and Behaviour that had at last provoked the gathering. It had in its own authority set aside the prohibitions on naked athleticism which had been imposed by the Council in its 'general rules of conduct' thirty years before. The matter was a trifling one, but the attention of the Council was drawn to it; and it was decided to choose the occasion for a definite assertion of the Council's authority. Was there still a Supreme Government in the world? was the question posed by the veteran ruling body. Probably it seemed to them quite imperative that there should be a supreme overriding body, and the bland exposition of Emil Donadieu which dispelled this assumption must have been an illuminating revelation to them of the march of human ideas since those days of youthful zeal and vigour when they found themselves directing the still-militant World State.

In those days the need for concentrated leadership had prevailed over every other human consideration. It had been necessary to fight and destroy for ever vast systems of loyalties and beliefs that divided, misled and wasted the energies of mankind. It had been necessary to replace a chaos of production and distribution for individual profit by an ordered economic world system. But once this vast change-over was made and its permanence assured by the reconstruction of education on a basis of world history and social science, the task of a militant World-State was at an end. The task of the World Council was at an end.

'But then who is to govern the world?' asked Eric Gunnarsson, the youngest and most ambitious member of the Council.

'No need to govern the world,' said Donadieu. 'We have made war impossible; we have liberated ourselves from the great anti-social traditions that set man against man; we have made the servitude of man to man through poverty impossible. The faculties of health, education, and behaviour will sustain the good conduct of the race. The controls of food, housing, transport, clothing, supply, initiative, design, research, can do their own work. There is nothing left for a supreme government

to do. Except look up the world it has made and see that it is good. And
bless it.'

'Yes,' said Eric Gunnarsson, 'but – '

These words are registered in the phonograph record of the debate.
And with these two words Eric Gunnarsson, the ambitious young man
who may have dreamt at one time of being President of the World,
vanishes from history.

Donadieu went on to a brief history of government in human affairs,
how at first man could only think in personifications and had to
conceive a tribal God and a tribal King because he could not conceive
of organized cooperation in any other way; how Kings remained all too
individual and all too little social for anything but the narrowest tribal
and national ends, and how therefore they had to be controlled and
superseded by councils, assemblies and congresses, which in their turn
became unnecessary. These ruling bodies clamped men together through
ages of discord until at last the race could be held together in assured
permanence by the cement of a universal education.

But the gist of that debate was embodied in the 'Declaration of
Mégève' with which the Conference concluded its deliberations.

'The World-State now follows all the subordinate states it swallowed
up to extinction; the supreme sovereign government, which conquered
and absorbed all minor sovereignties, vanishes from human affairs. The
long, and often blind and misdirected, effort of our race for peace and
security has at length succeeded, thanks to this great Council that now
retires. It retires with the applause and gratitude of all mankind. And
now in serenity and security we can survey the property it has redeemed
from waste, this planet and its possibilities, our own undeveloped
possibilities too, and all the fullness of life that lies before us. This is the
day, this is the hour of sunrise for united manhood. The Martyrdom of
Man is at an end. From pole to pole now there remains no single human
being upon the planet without a fair prospect of self-fulfilment, of
health, interest, and freedom. There are no slaves any longer; no poor;
none doomed by birth to an inferior status; none sentenced to long
unhelpful terms of imprisonment; none afflicted in mind or body who
are not being helped with all the powers of science and the services of
interested and able guardians. The world is all before us to do with as
we will, within the measure of our powers and imaginations. The
struggle for material existence is over. It has been won. The need for
repressions and disciplines has passed. The struggle for truth and that
indescribable necessity which is beauty begins now, unhampered by any
of the imperatives of the lower struggle. No one now need live less nor
be less than his utmost.

'We must respect the race and each other, but that has been made
easy for us by our upbringing. We must be loyal to the conventions of
money, of open witness, of responsibility for the public peace and health

and decency: these are the common obligations of the citizen by which the commonweal is sustained. We must contribute our modicum of work to the satisfaction of the world's needs. And, for the rest, now *we can live*. No part of the world, no work in the world, no pleasure, except such pleasure as may injure others, is denied us. Thanks to you, Heroic Council; thanks beyond limit to you.'

BOOK V

The Modern State in Control of Life

I

Monday Morning in the Creation of a New World

With the Declaration of Mégève in 2059 CE the Age of Frustration, the opening phase of the Era of the Modern State, came to an end. Let us recapitulate that history in its barest outline. The World-State had appeared dimly and evasively, as an aspiration, as a remote possibility, as the suggestion of a League of Nations, during the World War of 1914–18; it had gathered experience and definition throughout the decades of collapse and disaster; it had formally invaded human politics at the Conference of Basra in 1965 as manifestly the only possible solution of the human problem, and now it had completed its conquest of mankind.

The systematic consolidation of that conquest had begun in earnest after the Second Conference of Basra in 1978. Then the World Council had set itself to certain tasks that had been so inconceivable hitherto that not the most daring sociologists had looked them in the face. They had contented themselves with pious aspirations, and taken refuge in the persuasion that, if they were sufficiently disregarded, these tasks would somehow do themselves. They were tasks of profound mental reconstruction, reconstruction going deeper into the substratum of the individual life than anything that had ever been attempted before. In the first place traditions of nationality had to be cleared away for good, and racial prejudice replaced by racial understanding. This was a positive job against immense resistances. Next a lingua-franca had to be made universal and one or the other of the great literature-bearing languages rendered accessible to everyone. This again was not to be done for the wishing. And thirdly, and most evaded of all three obstacles that had to be surmounted, issue had to be joined with the various quasi-universal religious and cultural systems, Christianity, Jewry, Islam, Buddhism and so forth, which right up to the close of the twentieth century were still in active competition with the Modern State movement for the direction of the individual life and the control of human affairs. While these competing cultures remained in being they were bound to become refuges and rallying-shelters for all the opposition forces that set themselves to cripple and defeat the new order of the world.

We have told already how that issue was joined, and shown how necessary it was to bring all the moral and intellectual training of the race into direct and simple relations with the Modern State organization. After 2020 there is no record of any schools being open in the world except the Modern State schools. Christianity where it remained sacerdotal and intractable was supressed, but over large parts of the world it was not so much abolished as watered down to modernity. Everywhere its endowments had vanished in the universal slump; it could find no supply of educated men to sustain its ministry; the majority of its churches stood neglected and empty, and when the great rebuilding of the world began most of them vanished with all the other old edifices that lacked beauty or interest. They were cleared away like dead leaves.

The story of Islam was closely parallel. It went more readily even than Christianity because its school organization was weaker. It was pinned very closely to the teaching of Arabic. The decadence of that language shattered its solidarity much as the disuse of Latin disintegrated Western Christianity. It left a few-score beautiful mosques as Christianity left a few-score beautiful chapels, churches and cathedrals. And patterns, legends, memories remained over in abundance, more gracious and lovely by far than the realities from which they were distilled.

There had been a widespread belief in the tenacity and solidarity of Judaism. The Jews had been able to keep themselves a people apart, eating peculiar food and following distinctive religious practics, a nation within the nation, in every state in the world. They had been a perpetual irritant to statesmen, a breach in the collective solidarity everywhere. They had played a peculiar in-and-out game of social relationship. One could never tell whether a Jew was being a citizen or whether he was being just a Jew. They married, they traded preferentially. They had their own standards of behaviour. Wherever they abounded their pecularities aroused bitter resentment.

It might have been supposed that a people so widely dispersed would have developed a cosmopolitan mentality and formed a convenient linking organization for many world purposes, but their special culture of isolation was so intense that this they neither did nor seemed anxious to attempt. After the World War the orthodox Jews played but a poor part in the early attempts to formulate the Modern State, being far more preoccupied with a dream called Zionism, the dream of a fantastic independent state all of their own in Palestine, which according to their Babylonian legend was the original home of all this synthesis of Semitic-speaking peoples. Only a psycho-analyst could begin to tell for what they wanted this Zionist state. It emphasized their traditional wilful separation from the main body of mankind. It irritated the world against them, subtly and incurably.

On another score also the unpopularity of Israel intensified in the early twentieth century. The core of the slump process was manifestly monetary. Something was profoundly rotten with money and credit. The Jews had always had and cultivated the reputation of a peculiar understanding and cleverness in monetary processes. Yet in the immense difficulties of that time no authoritative direction came from the Jews. The leading minds of the time who grappled with the intricate problems of monetary reconstruction and simplification were almost all Gentiles. It was natural for the common man to ask, 'Where are the Jews?' It was easy for him to relapse into suspicion and persecution. Were they speculating unobtrusively? It was an obvious thing for Gentile speculators to shift suspicion to this race which gloried in and suffered by its obstinate resolve to remain a 'peculiar people'.

And yet between 1940 and 2059, in little more than a century, this antiquated obdurate culture disappeared. It and its Zionist state, its kosher food, the Law and all the rest of its paraphernalia, were completely merged in the human community. The Jews were not suppressed; there was no extermination; there were world-wide pogroms during the political and social breakdown of the Famished Fifties, but under the Tyranny there was never any specific persecution at all; yet they were educated out of their oddity and racial egotism in little more than three generations. Their attention was distracted from Moses and the Promise to Abraham and the delusion that God made his creation for them alone, and they were taught the truth about their race. The world is as full as ever it was of men and women of Semitic origin, but they belong no more to 'Israel'.

This success – the people of the nineteenth century would have deemed it a miracle – is explicable because of two things. The first of them is that the Modern State revolution was from the first educational and only secondarily political; it ploughed deeper than any previous revolution. And next it came about under new and more favourable conditions. In the nineteenth century the family group had ceased to be the effective nucleus in either economic or cultural life. And all the odd exclusiveness of the Jew had been engendered in his closed and guarded prolific home. There is an immense collection of fiction written by Jews for Jews in the early twentieth century, in which the relaxation of this immemorial close home-training and the clash of the old and modernizing generations is described. The dissolution of Israel was beginning even then.

The task of making the mind of the next generation had been abandoned almost unconsciously, for Jew and Gentile alike, to external influences, and particularly to the newspaper and the common school. After 1940 this supersession of home training was renewed in an extensive form. The Modern State movement had from the outset gripped the teachers, re-created popular education after the dark decades upon its own lines, and arrested every attempt to revive competing schools. Even had he desired it the Jew could no longer be peculiar in the food either of his body or his mind.

The complete solidarity of mankind in 2059, the disappearance of the last shadows of dislike and distrust between varied cults, races, and language groups, witnesses to the profound truth of what Falaise, one of De Windt's editors, has called the Mental Conception of History. The Age of Frustration was essentially an age of struggle to achieve certain plainly possible things against the resistances of a muddled human mind. The Declaration of Mégève was not simply an assertion of victory and freedom for the race, it was the demonstration of its achieved lucidity.

As the curtain of separatist dreams, racial fantasies and hate nightmares thinned out and passed away, what was presented to that awakening human brain? A little sunlit planet, for its external material, bearing what we now realize is not a tithe of its possible flora and fauna, a ball crammed with unused and unsuspected resources; and for the internal stuff of that brain almost limitless possibilities of mental achievement. All that had been done hitherto by man was like the scribbling of a little child before eye and hand have learnt sufficient co-ordination to draw. It was like the pawing and crawling of a kitten before it begins to see. And now man's eyes were open.

This little planet of which he was now at last in mentally untroubled possession was not simply still under-developed and waste; its surface was everywhere scarred and disfigured by the long wars he had waged so blindly for its mastery. Everywhere in 2059 the scenery of the earth still testified to the prolonged war, the state of siege to establish a unified mastery, that had now come to an end. If most of the divisions and barriers of the period of the sovereign states had disappeared, if there were no longer castles, fortifications, boundaries and strategic lines to be traced, there were still many indications that the world was under control and still not quite sure of its own good behaviour. The carefully planned system of aerodromes to prevent any untoward developments of the free private flying that had been tolerated after 2040 was such an indication, and so was the strategic import plainly underlying the needlessly wide main roads that left no possible region of insurrection inaccessible. From the air or on a map it was manifest that the world was still 'governed'. The road system was like a net cast over a dangerous beast.

And equally visible still was the quality of recent conquest in the social and economic fields. As Theotocopulos complained, the Second Council overdid its embankments. It was distrustful even of the waters of the earth. Its reservoirs and rivers had, he says, 'a bullied air'. If the jostling little fields and misshapen ill-proportioned farms, the untidy mines, refuse-heaps, factories, workers, slums and hovels and all the dire squalor of competitive industrialism had long since disappeared from the spectacle, there was still effort visible at every point in the layout of twenty-first-century exploitation. The stripping and burning of forests that had devastated the world so extensively in the middle decades of the preceding hundred years had led to strenuous reafforestation. Strenuous is the word. 'Grow,' said the Council, 'and let there be no nonsense about it.' At the end of the Age of Frustration a tree that was not lined up and lopped and drilled was an exception in the landscape.

Everywhere there was still this suggestion of possible insubordination and the sense of an underlying threat. Man had struggled desperately and had won, but it was only now that he was finding time to consider any but the most immediate and superficial possibilities of his planet.

The air-view as the dispersing delegates from Mégève saw it forty-seven years ago was indeed in the vividest contrast to the world garden in which we live to-day. That clumsy rationality, that real dread of aestheticism, that had haunted the Council to its end, had made the artificial factors in the landscape inelegant and emphatic almost without exception. Bridges and roads 'got there', as Theotocopulos said, 'like charging rhinoceroses'. True that the disposition to squat forms, which came from the age of the air raids, no longer prevailed, but there was a general tendency to make buildings too solid and too big; they had sometimes a certain grandiose boldness, but more often than not there was a touch of military stupidity in the appearance of their piled-up masses. They stood to attention. There was a needlessly lavish abundance of pylons, and they were generally too sturdy.

The enrichment of vegetation which is now world-wide was in operation at that time only in a few experimental areas; in most regions there was still hardly more forest or cultivation than had existed a century and a half before. If the devastation of fellings and fires during the last wars had been replaced by the new straight-ruled, squared-out forests, there was as yet no perceptible rise in the level of the plant community anywhere; what had previously been forest was plantation or forest again, and what had been prairie was still prairie, differing only from the grass prairies of older days in the dwindling contingent of weeds and wild flowers. In spite of the self-complacency of the forestry department of that time, many trees distorted by disease survived, and most were by our standards stunted. To young eyes today this world of our fathers, as they see it in picture book and panorama, has not merely a regimented but a barren look, and its cultivation seems laborious and poor.

Yet compared with the landscape of two centuries ago its aspect was relatively prosperous, spacious and orderly. There is something very touching in the freely expressed response of the nineteenth-century folk to both urban and country landscape and to natural scenery generally.

They did not dream how meagre their descendants were to find the spectacle before them. They had, at any rate, as good cloudscapes and sunsets as we have, and such natural coast scenery as that of Western Scotland was practically the same then as it is today. They would endure irksome travel to see sunlit snowy mountain masses or get to some viewpoint that caught the rhythm of a distant chain. They loved water and woodlands and distant fields in a wide view, and towns they admired chiefly as piled up accumulations seen from a distance. Also they delighted very greatly in the close brightness of flowering hedges, sheets of bluebells, primrose rides, green moss and tendrils and any sort of flower. They pick these things out for appreciation so persistently in their literature and paintings that it is only with an effort we realize how much they were 'picked out', and how dull and repetitive were endless miles of their normal roads and countryside and how flatly forbidding the ordinary aspects of their habitations.

So far as we can reconstruct it now the prevalent note of the nineteenth century scene was weak insipidity, degenerating very easily into a distressful mean ungainliness. America was frost-bitten in the north and slovenly in the south and unkempt everywhere. Happily the shorter-lived, not very healthy or vigorous folk of these days had no standards of comparison, and actual intimations of discontent with nature and the countryside were rare. There is scarcely an admission in nineteenth-century literature that the larger part of the natural world was gaunt, unsatisfactory and utterly unsympathetic. Writers and poets did not dare to admit as much because they had neither the hope nor the energy to make things better. They would not see it in obedience to an elementary psychological law.

But under the Second Council, the criticism not only of man's achievement but of natural insufficiency had become voluminous because neither was felt any longer to be final. It was not only the heavy engineering, the massive buildings and the over-emphasized roadways that those returning delegates threatened with their minds. Much of the land was still unsettled. They looked down on areas of marsh and scrub, bare wildernesses of rock, rainless regions, screes and avalanche slopes. For them as for us it was a world of promise still to be fulfilled.

'Now we can begin on all this,' they said. 'Now we have really to begin.'

I I

Keying up the Planet

It had long been known that the vegetation of earth and sea, on which the volume and vigour of all other life depends, was not nearly commensurate with the available moisture and sunlight. As early as the nineteen thirties it was being pointed out by an English economic botanist, Frederick Keeble (1870–1975, *Collected Works* in the Science section of the Reprints), that there were delays and arrests in the multiplication of diatoms, seasonal grass crops, and other extensive primary vegetable growths, arrests due to the fact that while all other conditions were favourable the supply of assimilable nitrogen was too slow to keep up the growth process. He applied the agricultural lesson of manuring to the whole spectacle of life and insisted that we were living in a 'nitrogen-starved world'. Nitrogen is yielded up by the inorganic world to the uses of life with extreme reluctance. This observation of Keeble's threw a new light for most people on the alleged bounty of nature. Other workers in the same field spread their observations to other elements. Carlos Metom (1927–2014), in a striking passage, compared life on our planet to 'a starveling foal on a barren patch that has never learnt to look for green pasture'.

This fundamental poverty of terrestrial existence can be traced through most of the geological record. Life has been a stinted thing. There were a few periods of exuberance, the period of the Coal Measures for example, when life seemed really to pour upward; but for most of recorded time life nibbled round the outside of a ball of limitless mineral wealth to which it had no key. No individual intelligence could ever penetrate that hidden hoard of plenty. It was only when the collective mentality of Science had arisen and was going on deathlessly from one clarification to another that a far more abundant vegetable basis for animal and human existence came within the range of possibility, and only now that the waste of human energy in warfare and uncoordinated trading and money-getting was at an end for ever, that the realization of that possibility could be attempted. But hundreds of thousands of brains are now alight with the prospect of evoking such a plenty and wealth of life on our planet as the whole universe had never dreamed of before this time.

The Second Council, in the beginning of its long reign, had not a sufficient knowledge of the latent powers of applied biology to anticipate this fundamental enrichment of life. It conceived its rôle to be the working-out of the logical consequences of mechanical invention during the nineteenth and twentieth centuries. The greatest of these consequences were the abolition of distance and the supersession of toil by power machinery. The goal of the Council was to confirm and establish human unity for ever, and to set up a frame of progressive public activities that should provide universal employment and universal purchasing power in the face of a continually increasing industrial efficiency. At first it was preoccupied by the persecuting activities that were needed to secure the world against any reaction towards private monopolization, romantic nationalism, religious eccentricism, and social fission. Then, as its success in this direction passed beyond challenge, as the world community was plainly assured, it found itself confronted by an ever more portentous problem of leisure.

It seemed a natural outlet for the surplus of human energy to provide among other things for an enormous development of scientific research and an exploration of the deeper mineral resources of the earth's crust. The Council assigned something like a third of the resources available for science to biological work, and it does not seem to have occurred to these rulers of the world, preoccupied as they were with the suppression, the excessive suppression, the obliteration even, of deleterious and antiquated separatist doctrines and the refashioning of economic life, that this huge growth of biological enquiry would result in anything more than the extinction of plant and animal diseases, and improvements and economies in cultivation. It was outside the range of their imaginations to anticipate a spate of biological invention that put the spate of mechanical invention which revolutionized the conditions of human life in the nineteenth and twentieth centuries altogether in the shade. Biological knowledge outgrew them just as aesthetic sensibility outgrew them.

From the Thirties of the twenty-first century onward the conservatism of the Second Council had held back an increasing amount of scientific discoveries from practical application. The world was unified; it was supporting its population (which was being kept well below the modest safety line of 2000 million) with absolute ease; its health was at a higher level than nature had ever known before; and it was, so far as the powers in being could manage it, marking time. It was like an adolescent who is still treated as a child. Even the new possibilities of exuberant vegetation were not being released. The areas needed for food supply could have been halved before 2050, but the Council decided that the consequent dislocation of the population would be likely to strain social order, and it kept four or five million people at the healthy but not very entertaining work of agricultural production, while it promoted enquiries for the 'industrial application of marginal excesses of foodstuffs'. It was not only producing, but distributing, staples in 2050 on precisely the lines adopted in 2020. It was restraining educational developments and innovations in building. It had made the world safe for humanity, and it meant to keep the world at that.

In 2047 Homer Lee Pabst published his remarkable researches on the effect upon chromosomes of certain gases derived from the old Steriliz-ing Inhalation made from Permanent Death Gas. These gases are known now as Pabst's Kinetogens, and there is a whole series of them. Their general effect is to produce mutations of various types. They bring about, abundantly and controllably, a variability in life which has hitherto been caused only with comparative rarity by cosmic radiations. By 2050 the biological world was confronted by a score of absolutely new species of plants and – queer first-fruits in the animal world – by two new and very destructive species of rodent. The artificial evolution of new creatures had come within the range of human possibility.

Limitless possibilities opened before the human imagination. The Council gave way to panic. It saw the world it had taken such pains to put in order given over to uncontrollable vegetable and animal mon-strosities. A nightmare of evil weeds and strange beasts dismayed it. Even the human type, it realized, was threatened. The laws restraining experiments upon animals were extended, and every animal novelty produced by Pabst was to be reported upon and destroyed. Plant novelties of decorative or economic value were, however, to be toler-ated. Within his laboratory and experimental grounds Pabst ignored these prohibitions, and the faculty of science increased the endowment of the new experimental genetics. And now that the Supreme Council could no longer interfere, the Transport and General Distribution Control, the newly developed section of the Behaviour Control and the Health Services took up Pabst's results and arranged a conference (2060) for their proper exploitation. A general plan for the directed evolution of life upon the planet was drawn up, a plan which, with various amendments, is in operation to this day.

Most of the 'wild beasts' of our ancestors are now under control in their special enclosures and reservations. There are fifteen Major Parks of over five hundred square miles in which various specially interesting faunas and floras flourish without human interference, except for the occasional passage of some qualified observer on foot or the transit of a specially licensed aeroplane overhead. Adventurous holiday-makers are excluded. The creatures in these areas are less affected by man than were their predecessors. They form a valuable reserve control of the genetic tentatives that are being made upon their more or less captive brethren. The most startling result of these experiments is Dumoric's claim to have restored, by means of carefully bred crosses and the cultivation of atavistic types, extinct ancestral forms of the fallow deer.

One beneficial result of the preoccupation of the Second Council with the problem of employment for idle hands and minds had been the very great advances made in both mineralogical and meteorological science.

It did not realize that the systematic observation of winds and rainfall could possibly upset its orderly world. Indeed, the prospect of forbidding the wind to blow where it listed was entirely after the Council's heart. So, too, the possibility of controlling or drying up volcanoes and earthquakes appealed very strongly to it. Before 2000, man's knowledge of the composition of what he used to call the earth's 'crust' and the mineral resources of the planet beneath that crust was extraordinarily superficial. Geologists relied almost entirely for their knowledge upon surface features, chance exposures, and industrial excavations. But the ever increasing resources available for research made a systematic probing and exploration of the deeper layers increasingly possible. The student will find in any contemporary textbook of Geology an account of the series of beautiful contrivances such as the Shansi borer, the Hull and Watkins 'diviner', and the Noguchi petrograph, which have now made, so to speak, hidden things visible to a depth of twenty-five miles, and there too he will find a description of a score of ingenious devices for isolating blocks of deep-lying rock and bringing their desirable ingredients to the surface. Until a hundred years ago nothing of this sort was even imagined. Instead of employing the energy imprisoned underground to drive what was needed to the surface, the scanty product of the old-world mines was *hauled* up by human or mechanical power from above and the ores and coal and salt were actually hewn out in situ by hordes of sweating, underpaid human beings.

Equally rapid was the progress of meteorology once the Second Council gave its mind to that subject. Practical meteorology was of very recent date. Except for a little work with the barometer from 1643 onward, forecasting began only in the nineteenth century and was not systematically attempted until 1850. An infinitesimal tampering with the composition of the air began in the early twentieth century. Then man found himself able to withdraw nitrogen from it, but this was done only to provide fertilizers, and in such small quantities as to make no appreciable effect upon the composition of the atmosphere. Little more was attempted until the last war, when the local use of substances like the so-called Permanent Death Gas was carried out on a sufficiently big scale to amount to a transitory readjustment of the air over the region poisoned. Then in the thirties of the twenty-first century there was an extensive use of gas on a large scale to destroy locusts, rodents, and various insect pests. Considerable enthusiasm was shown at the time, but one or two unfortunate accidents cooled the zeal of the Council. It was realized that air-mixing for anything but stimulating and purifying purposes must wait upon the achievement of wind control. Air-mixing was put back into the pigeonholes with a gathering number of other gifts from science that the Council deemed premature.

The Joint Commission for replanning the world found itself therefore with three correlated groups of possibility challenging its spirit of adventure. A new flora of several thousand species was awaiting release from the experimental grounds, and this was only the easiest of the apparently limitless possibilities of animal and vegetable variation that experimental biology was taking up. A huge and hitherto unsuspected wealth of mineral substances was ready to come out of the deep-lying rocks and refresh the rather limited and jaded resources of the contemporary soil. And alterations in the composition and movements of the atmosphere were no longer inaccessibly beyond human effort. The obstruction of individual ownership and localized governments had been swept away for ever. In that respect the Second Council had beyond question triumphed. But the very vigour with which it had done its task for man and the world as they were, and still in effect are, had cleared the ground for such an unprecedented inventiveness as is now rapidly altering not only the face but the very substance of life.

The Replanning Commission set about its task with the leisurely energy of a body under no stress of necessity. 'Life is quite good as it is,' runs the Introduction to its Draft Plan. 'But it is part of the fundamental goodness of life that we have as much incessant novelty as we desire at our disposal. Due proportion must be our perpetual care. Want of proportion in the development of new things was the general cause of the great bulk of human suffering and frustration during the past five centuries. We have now an organization of Controls that can restrain anything like the spasmodic mercenary enterprise, without plan or balance, that let loose disaster in the early twentieth century. We can afford to look before we leap and measure within quite close limits the tale of consequences we set going. In the end we may find that there was very considerable justification for the restraint put by our Supreme Council upon the immediate application of recent inventions, and particularly of recent biological inventions, which might otherwise have precipitated very similar but even more fundamental and catastrophic disproportions to those which overwhelmed the capitalist civilization of the nineteenth century.

'The particular field in which we propose a continuation of restraint is in the application of the rapidly advancing science of genetics to the increase of variability so far as human beings, and probably some other of the higher mammals, are concerned. We believe that the general feeling of the race is against any such experimentation at present. Under the Second Council the painless destruction of monsters and the more dreadful and pitiful sorts of defective was legalized, and also the sterilization of various types that would otherwise have transmitted tendencies that were plainly undesirable. This is as far, we think, as humanity should go in directing its racial heredity, until our knowledge of behaviour has been greatly amplified. For an age or so we can be content with humanity as it now is, humanity no longer distressed and driven to cruelty by overcrowding, under-nourishment, infections, mental and physical poisons of every sort. There is a rich mine of still greatly underdeveloped capacity in the human brain as it is, and this we may very happily explore by means of artistic effort, by scientific investigations, by living freely and gaily, for the next few generations. Normal human life can be cleansed, extended and amplified. With that we propose to content ourselves. Even upon this planet we have millions of years ahead before there can be any fundamental change in our environment.

'Directly we turn from humanity to other forms of life it is manifest that a most attractive realm is opening to us. We may have new and wonderful forests; we may have new plants; we may replace the weedy and scanty greensward of the past by a subtler and livelier texture. Undreamt-of fruits and blossoms may be summoned out of non-existence. The insect world, on which so much of the rest of life depends, may be made more congenial to mankind. The smaller fry of life and the little beasts and the birds can be varied now until they all come into a tolerable friendship with ourselves. As our hands lose their clumsiness we may interfere more and more surely with the balance of life. There is no longer fear of abundance now that man is sane.

'Our planning of human activities for the next few generations will involve no fundamental changes at all for humanity. It will be a keying-up of the sort of life for which our race, however darkly, confusedly and unsuccessfully, has always striven. At present deliberate weather-control is too big a task for us, but we believe that a sure weather calendar for a year or so ahead is now becoming possible. An immense series of enterprises to change the soil, lay-out, vegetation and fauna, first of this region and then of that, will necessitate a complete rearrangement of the mines, deep quarries, road network and heavy sea transport of the globe. None of this need be ugly or repulsive, even in the doing; it can be all made intensely interesting. Engineering structure, which was once clumsy and monstrous, is now becoming as graceful as a panther. Industrial enterprises that formerly befouled the world with smoke, refuse and cinder heaps, are now cleaner in their habits than a well-trained cat. The world lay-out of the Second Council, designed apparently for a static society, will be to a large extent swept aside by our new operations. And no doubt our achievements in their turn will give way to still bolder and lovelier enterprises.'

So ran the Introduction to what is known as the Keying-up Plan of 2060. Today we are most of us still immersed in its realization. It has given the world occupation without servitude and leisure without boredom. When we have had enough of our own work for a time we fly off – or walk round the corner – to see what other people are doing. The world is full of interest and delight, from the forest gardens of the Amazons with their sloths, monkeys and occasional pumas and alligators to that playground of the world, the snowfields of the Himalayas.

We can arrange to take a turn with the meteorological observers in the upper air, or tune our lungs for a spell in the deep-sea galleries below the rafts of Atlantis. There we can see the great cephalopods of the middle levels coming for their food or watch the headlong growth of a giant pearl.

We are already so accustomed to grace, beauty and variety in all the details and general forms about us that it is only by turning over the pictures and records of seventy years ago that we realize how relatively uneventful were the first decades of human unity. At first man seems to have been so exhausted by his escape from massacre, disease, economic waste and general futility, and so terrified by the thought of any relapse into the old confusions, conflicts and economic cannibalism, that he was capable of nothing but order. But he gathers courage. It is not only our world that is being keyed up, but ourselves.

III

Geogonic Planning

Among the 'deferred projects' that lie behind our current activities, and second only to the system of schemes for inducing and directing a great increase in human variability, is the complex of plans that have been drawn out to alter the terrestrial contours. Here again is something far too great and dangerous for our present wisdom, but something which it seems inevitable our race will ultimately attempt.

At present, and for many generations yet, we are still the creatures and subjects of geography; the oceans and great mountain chains condition our lives. They determine habitats, which again determine the human type best adapted to live for the greater part of its life in this or that region. Every kind of us, dark or fair, thick-set or slender, black or buff, has its own distinctive best place in which to rear its children and work and rest. It may roam the earth as it will, but only in certain regions is it altogether at home. No type is at home everywhere. There is no universal man. A universal type of man would be possible only on a flat and uniform earth. There is a necessary variety in humanity which no one now desires to diminish.

But the question the modern geographer puts to us is whether there is not a classification of habitats possible, into very desirable, desirable, undesirable, and inimical, and whether a certain modification of the planet-levels operating in conjunction with the restoration of forests now in progress would not greatly increase the desirable habitats, by a redistribution of rainfall, a change in the fall of the surface waters, protection from winds and so forth. A not very considerable rise in the Apennines, for instance, would bring them up to the permanent snow-line and change the character of the entire Italian peninsula. And an increase in desirable habitats may bring with it an increase in the variety of desirable human types.

Yesterday this sort of thing was called 'chimerical', today it is impracticable and unnecessary, because of the volcanic forces that might be released. So far the present the geogonist, like the geneticist, must content himself with dreams – in his case dreams of moulding a fire-spouting, quivering planet closer to the expanding needs of man. His turn to remodel the world will come perhaps in a thousand years or so. There is plenty of time for that.

IV

Changes in the Control of Behaviour

The past forty-eight years have seen very great modifications in the social control of individual behaviour. There has been a very great increase in the science, skill and quality of the teachers throughout the world, but quite apart from that the character and purpose of education and police have changed profoundly.

Education as we understand it today began about the middle of the twentieth century. It had only the slenderest continuity with the education of the preceding age, just as the education of Christendom had only the slenderest continuity with the education of the pagan world. Reading, writing, and counting were taught in all three systems, but beyond that the very objectives were different. Modern education began as propaganda after the time of De Windt, as the propaganda of the Modern State. It sought to establish a new complete ideology and a new spirit which would induce the individual to devote himself and to shape all his activities to one definite purpose, to the attainment and maintenance of a progressive world-socialism, using an efficient monetary system as its normal medium of relationship.

This seemed, and was, a gigantic undertaking. It faced colossal obstacles in ordinary human nature. But it was supremely necessary if human civilization was to continue. The alternative was a relapse through chaotic barbarism to animal casualness and final extinction. Thought and behaviour patterns had to be shaped therefore to subserve this objective, to the relative disregard of any other conceivable purpose. The Modern State became the whole duty of man. This propaganda passed necessarily into a training for public service and a universal public education. The Modern State Fellowship was a trained body pledged to impose its own type of training upon all the world. It proposed to be the New Humanity. It would accept no compromises. It made the whole education framework militant. No other type of school and no other system of teaching was tolerated for more than half a century. Never before was man so directed and disciplined.

The educationists of this period of the First Council and the Air Dictatorship were particularly sedulous to restrain what they called 'aberrant motives'. Austerity in eating and drinking, hardiness, severity in exercise, a jealousy of leisure, and a profound distrust of aesthetic and sensuous gratification, and particularly of sexual excitement, marked the educational ideals of these men who set out to remodel the world. In the early stages of progressive and revolutionary thought in the nineteenth century there had been considerable laxity of private conduct. There had been a revolt against what was called 'Christian morality', and a disposition not simply to condone but encourage indulgence in forms that had hitherto been prohibited. Most of this 'liberalism' in conduct had vanished from revolutionary circles by the second or third decade of the twentieth century. The Modern State Movement, as it developed, was pervaded by a disapproval of every sort of sensuous or emotional affection. The business in hand could not suffer it. It wasted time; it wasted energy. It let in too much intrigue. It undermined the common loyalty. Not even Christianity in its most militant stages was so set against the dissipation of energy in this direction. The new sexual puritanism differed from the old in its toleration of birth control, its disregard of formal marriage, and a certain charity towards the first excesses of youth, but it insisted with even greater vigour upon public decency and upon the desirability of sexual seriousness, enduring connexions, and complete loyalty between lovers. As a result the world was far more monogamous, more decorous and decently busy after 2000 CE than it had ever been before.

Many critics today are disposed to consider the repressions of that time excessive. We are now in a different phase; the militant age is past. They allege that there was a vast amount of secret and solitary vice and moral and mental distortion beneath the cold surface of things during these disciplined years, and they consider that the undeniable harshness and obstinacy of the Second Council as it grew old was a direct result of its puritanism. They do not hesitate to use such terms as masochist and sadist. But this is by no means a unanimous opinion. Equally reputable authorities deny that there was any such seething pit of stifled desires and thwarted motives under the orderly and healthy activities of the constructive time as this new school pretends. In no psychological problem are we still so inadequately informed as in the quantitative estimate of sexual impulse and restraint.

Our investigators work at literature, biographies, diaries, pictorial art, police reports in their intricate attempt to recover the vanished mental states of these departed generations. There seems to be a sort of rhythm in these things. The contrast between present conditions and conditions seventy years ago is paralleled in history by the contrast between English social life in 1855 and 1925. There also we have a phase of extreme restraint and decorum giving way to one of remarkable freedom. We can trace every phase. Every phase is amply documented. There are not the slightest grounds for supposing that the earlier period was one of intense nervous strain and misery. There was a general absence of vivid excitation, and the sexual life flowed along in an orderly fashion. It did not get into politics or the control of businesses. It appears in plays and novels like a tame animal which is not to be made too much of. It goes out of the room whenever necessary. By comparison England in 1920 was out for everything it could do sexually. It did everything and boasted about it and incited the young. As the gravity of economic and political problems increased and the structural unsoundness of the world became more manifest, sexual preoccupations seem to have afforded a sort of refuge from the mental strain demanded by the struggle. People distracted themselves from the immense demands of the situation by making a great noise about the intensifications and aberrations of the personal life. There was a real propaganda of drugs and homosexuality among the clever young. Literature, always so responsive to its audience, stood on its head and displayed its private parts. It produced a vast amount of solemn pornography, facetious pornography, sadistic incitement, re-sexualized religiosity and verbal gibbering in which the rich effectiveness of obscene words was abundantly exploited. It is all available for the reader today who cares to examine it. He will find it neither shocking, disgusting, exciting nor interesting. He will find it comically pretentious and pitifully silly.

It is small wonder that the scattered workers for the Modern State, who were struggling heroically with the huge problems of social dislocation and social reconstruction, developed an antipathy against these aesthetic and sexual preoccupations which robbed them of the help and service of so many hopeful youngsters. The Modern State Movement was unobtrusively puritanical from the outset. After the romantic lapses of the First World Council it became oppressively puritanical.

It was the precedent of the moral disorder of the early twentieth century to which the Educational Control appealed, a hundred and twenty years later, to justify its sustained regulation of private morals and repression of stimulation. It failed to realize the profound difference of the new conditions. The florid ebullition of sexual troubles, sexual refinements and sexual grossnesses in the Age of Frustration had been a natural consequence of frustration. Everywhere in the face of challenges too huge to face, rich and poor alike found themselves aimless, unoccupied, menaced. Ill health was increasing. Drugs, alcohol and sex were available to excite and soothe and deaden their distressed nerves. Good-looking youth, which could not sell its brains or labour, could still find a market for its person. About every nucleus of unjustly acquired wealth or demoralized power prostitution and parasitism festered. What else was there to do in that ugly, unhappy and dangerous world? But the world of 2040 was a busy, keenly interested and healthy world again.

We cannot detail in this general review of history the reluctant lifting of one prohibition after another. We may now go naked, love as we like, eat, drink and amuse ourselves with our work or as we will, subject only to a proper respect for unformed minds. And no harm has been done at all. When the Puritanical Tyranny began, its directors felt they had imprisoned a tiger that would otherwise consume all the plenty and safety they achieved. Very reluctantly indeed, bit by bit and after endless disputes, were their prohibitions relaxed. And no tiger appeared. Properly nourished people do not take to gluttony, properly interested people are not overwhelmed by sex. Instead of a tiger appeared a harmless, quiet, unobtrusive and not unpleasing pussy-cat, which declined to be in any way notable.

Humanity was changing. The threatened outbreak of pornography, abnormality and sex excitation did not occur. But anyone who studies the fiction and drama of the past half-century and compares it with the similar literature of the old world will realize that there are far more personal love and far more happy lovers than ever before, and that physical love to demonstrate loyalty, show preference, enrich association and seal friendship was never so direct and beautiful. Jealousy we have, but it is rarely malicious; desire, but it is rarely vicious. In this as in so many other things progress has meant simplification. The souls we read about of two centuries ago strike us as grotesquely tangled, tormented and nasty souls. Hate mingled with their desires; mercenary considerations were an ever present defilement; they paired dishonestly and mated insincerely.

But while there has been this release from the straitlaced sexual morals of the militant period, in another field there has been no relaxation. The new order can tolerate no tampering with the monetary-property system that holds us all together. Not only is our police incessantly alert against robbery and cheating as the old world understood it, but many gainful practices that 1920 would have considered tolerable or even admirable are suppressed, and are likely to be suppressed for all time. Gambling, the mean desire and device to get the spending of someone else's earnings, is punished as heavily as the forgery of money checks; and all those speculative activities which seemed to be the very texture of the nineteenth-century social order dare not reappear now in any disguise at all. Money is a check for our personal needs, or for the giving of graceful presents. There must be no misuse of money to gain an advantage over another human being, even with that other human being's connivance. There we are still bound. That sort of thing is the vice of cannibalism. Beyond that liberty increases daily.

With a sound education of mind and body and a rigorous and exact protection of property and money from dishonourable impulses, we have found that it is possible to give every human being such a liberty of movement and general behaviour as would have seemed incredible to those militant socialists who ruled the world during the earlier decades of the last century. But it is just because of their stern and thorough cleansing of human life that we can now live in freedom. We may go anywhere in the world now, we may do practically anything that we can possibly desire to do.

V

Organization of Plenty

Just as it becomes increasingly difficult for the teacher of history to convey to each new generation what human feelings and motives were like in a world of morbid infections and unwholesome bodily habits or in a heavily sentimentalized atmosphere of general distrust and insecurity, so also he has to make a most vigorous imaginative effort to recover even the faintest shadow of the pervading vexation, humiliations and straining anxiety that resulted from an almost universal deficiency of common things. Everybody, except a small minority, went short until the close of the twentieth century. Even the rich had to be wary, cunning buyers to satisfy all their fancies and desires. The simplified economic order of our world today runs so smoothly that we hardly think at all about our ordinary needs. Housing, food and clothing wait upon us wherever we go. It is so easily done that we fail to realize the immense cleansing away of obstructive difficulties that had to occur before it could be made so easy.

One of the results of abundance that our ancestors would have found paradoxical is the abolition of encumbrance. But the less there was in the past the more you had to have and hold. Men had to appropriate things because there was not enough to go round. Your home was not simply the place to which you retired for solitude or intimacy; it was a store-house. In the sixteenth or seventeenth century it was even fortified by bars, locks and bolts agains robbers. You got with difficulty, and what you got you kept. The successful man of those days was imprisoned and smothered in accumulations upon which he dared not relax his watchfulness and grip. They were as indestructible as he could make them, for once destroyed or ignored they might prove irreplaceable. Everybody was keeping things, keeping them rather than using them. If they were not wanted now they might be wanted presently. If that successful man desired to vary his urban life he had to possess a country house. In these establishments there had to be a miniature social economy. Much of the food was not only prepared in the personal household, but produced on the private estate. All this had to be managed and watched to prevent waste, slackness and dishonesty. All the clothes the prosperous man might want to wear had to be stored and preserved in presses and wardrobes; his household needed gear against any possible emergency; and all his accumulations had to be guarded against robbers. It was almost as anxious and wearing a job to be rich as to be poor in those days of general insufficiency. And if the rich man travelled, he had to travel in his own coach with his attendants, taking a great burthen of clothing and general luggage with him.

In the relatively plentiful days of the later nineteenth century, which in so many details foreshadowed and yet failed to complete and generalize the conditions of our own time, there was for the prosperous at least a certain alleviation of the burthen of property. The temporary achievement of a limited cosmopolitanism of money and credit, the multiplication of the bourgeoise, the liquidation of ownership by joint-stock undertakings, the increased facilities for communication and movement, made successful people less disposed to sit down amidst their possessions. There was a sustained general effort, which we now find grotesque and irrational, to keep property and at the same time not to be bothered by property. The ideal of success was no longer concrete ownership but purchasing power. Houses, furnishings and so forth changed hands with increased readiness.

Instead of living in great complete houses and dining at home, people lived in smaller houses or flats and dined in collective dining-rooms or restaurants. They gave up having country houses of their own and travelled freely and variously, evoking a vast industry of hotels and hired villas. They travelled lighter – in comparison with preceding centuries, that is. As retail trade organized itself upon big-business lines, the need for the private storage of gear diminished. People bought things when they wanted them, because now they could do so. The big 'stores' of the early twentieth century carried an enormous and greatly varied stock.

In the days of Shakespeare new clothes, new furniture, new houses, new things of all sorts were infrequent; in the early twentieth century there were already intimations of the general fresh newness of our own times. The facilities for scrapping were still poorly developed, and there was much congestion and endless litter about, but renewal and replacement for those who had purchasing power were already well developed. If it had not been for the social catastrophe due to ignorance, individualism, monetary deflation and nationalism that overwhelmed that phase of civilization, the distributing organization of the world might very probably have developed straight on from the system of linked stores as it flourished in America in 1925 to our present conditions. And similarly there was an expansion of hotel life and a belated beginning of portable country houses, clearly foreshadowing our current arrangements.

After the disasters and new beginnings of the middle decades of the twentieth century it was to the patterns of big business at the close of the First Age of Abundance that the direction of the Transport Union recurred. We have told how easily and necessarily that Union became the trading monopoly and finally, as the Air and Sea Control, the actual government of the renascent world. Its counting-houses issuing and receiving its energy notes became the New Banking; its Trading Council became the New Retailing; its Supply Control took over, at last, the productive activities of the world. From the first the new powers were instinct with the idea of mobility. They had no vestiges in their composition of the skimping and saving traditions of the ages of insufficiency. They set about providing as ample and various accommodation for everybody as the ever-increasing production of the planet permitted.

The great distributing stores of the previous age provided the patterns from which the new distribution developed in that age of recovery. Wherever old towns and cities were being reconstructed or new ones appearing about new centres of productive activity the architects of the Air and Sea Control erected their great establishments, at first big and handsome after the old fashion and then more finely planned. At first these stores sold things according to the old method, then gradually in regard to a number of things, to clothing for example, they organized the modern system of exchanging new things for old; the new shoes or garment would be made and fitted to the customer and the old taken away and pulped or otherwise disposed of. Nothing is cobbled nowadays; nothing is patched or repaired. By degrees this method abolished that ancient institution the laundry altogether. That line of fluttering patched and tattered garments so characteristic of old-world village scenery vanished from the earth. New rapid methods of measuring and fitting replaced the tape, scissors and sewing of the old days. In the time of the Hoover Slump men would wear their underclothes for years, having them painfully washed out, dried, ironed and returned weekly, and they would wear their complex outer garments with all the old fastenings, buttons, straps, buckles and so forth, sometimes for many years. They had to be made of dark fabrics with broken patterns to conceal their griminess. The clothing of the Middle Ages was still filthier. Nowadays the average life of our much simpler and brighter outer garments with their convenient zip fastenings is about a week, and such light underclothes as we wear last about three days. We keep no wardrobes of them; the stores are our wardrobes. If the weather changes the stores are ready for us everywhere with wraps or heavier or lighter materials. It must be a remote expedition indeed that needs a change of raiment. We wear less clothing than our ancestors, partly because of our healthier condition, partly because we do not like to hide lovely bodies, but mainly because in the past men wrapped themselves up against every contingency. They wore hats whenever they were not under a roof, socks inside their boots, buttons on their sleeve-cuffs, collars and ties. It seems as though these elaborations became necessary to social prestige because of the general shortage. In an age of scarcity it was a testimonial to one's worth to be fully clad. In the nineteenth century the well-to-do wore gold watch-chains and gloves, which they carried in their hands in hot weather, as further evidence of substantial means.

Housing again, under the Air and Sea Control, took off from the point where the hotel-flat had left it in 1930. There was never any attempt to resume the building of those small permanent houses which were spread so abundantly over England, for example, after the World War. The first task of the new world control was mainly sanitary. Infection lurked everywhere; four decades of social disorder had made every building a decaying disease-trap for the young that were born into it. The Housing Control rebuilt the housing quarters of the rotten old towns in the form of blocks of dwellings, clean, spacious and convenient, but, to our eyes now, very squat and dull. They were from ten to twelve stories high, and very soundly and honestly made. Everywhere they had water, lighting, heating in the colder climates, and sanitation. The picturesquely clustering rural villages were replaced all over the earth by the same type of concentrated house-block, the style and material varying only so far as conditions of climate required it. The villages were literally swept up into these piles. Even where small private cultivation was still going on, the concentration into these mansions occurred and the peasants bicycled out to their properties. Every block had its crèche, its school, its store and its general meeting-rooms.

As we look back on it this supersession of the single separate unlit, undrained and waterless hut or hovel, cottage or little steading seems to have been a swift business, but in reality it took from 1980 to 2030, much more than half the average lifetime, to spread this new conception of housing over most of the world, and by that time in the more advanced regions the older blocks were already being replaced by more beautiful and convenient creations.

Historical Pictures shows us the whole process. We see the jumbling growths of the early phase of the twentieth century; towering apart-ment-houses and hotels struggling up, far above the churches, mosques, pagodas and public buildings, out of a dense undergrowth of slums. Then come arrest and decline. The pictures become as full of ruins, sheds and makeshift buildings as the drawings of Albrecht Dürer. Amidst these appear air-raid shelters with their beetling covers, first-aid pillars with their chequered markings, and anti-aircraft forts. Further ruin ensues and we see life disorganized by the Great Plague.

Then suddenly these stout, squat, virtuous new blocks thrust into the scene and the battered past vanishes. A new Age has begun. The towns grow larger, finer and more varied. The housing blocks are grouped with the expanding stores, public clubs and hotels in parks and gardens near to the aerodrome, and convenient for whatever industry gives the agglomeration its importance. The public club became prominent after 2000 CE, both architecturally and socially. That again was the revival of two old ideas; it was a combination of the idea of the English or American club with the idea of the Baths to which the Roman citizens resorted. Here from the start were grouped the gymnastic and sports halls, dancing-floors, conference rooms, the perpetual news cinema, libraries, reading-rooms, small studies, studios and social centres of the reviving social life.

The twenty-first century rediscovered an experience of the nineteenth and of the first centuries of the Christian Era, a discovery that was also made by Alexander the Great, that it is much easier to build great modern cities in new places than to modernize the old centres of activity. And the more vital these old centres remained the more difficult was their reconstruction, because it meant the interruption and transfer of important activities to new quarters. New York was typical of this lag in rebuilding. Up to quite recently Lower New York has been the most old-fashioned city in the world, unique in its gloomy antiquity. The last of the ancient skyscrapers, the Empire State Building, is even now under demolition in 2106 CE!

This was not because New York has fallen out of things, but, on the contrary, because it was in the van of the new movement. We have already quoted Nicholson's account of its reviving importance in 1960.

A year or so later it became the headquarters of the American branch of the Air and Sea Control, a western equivalent to Basra. The swiftly expanding activities of the new government needed immediate housing, and the gaunt surviving piles of Lower New York were adapted hastily to its accommodation. This kept them going for a time, and then arose a prolonged controversy between rival schools of planning for the reconstruction of that strangely vital city. It is not only true that the poorer the world was the more it was encumbered by property, but also that the more vigorously a place or a building is being used in progessive work the more difficult it is to keep it up to date.

Since the middle of the twenty-first century there has been a world-wide reappearance of the individual home, more particularly on the countryside, by the sea, and amidst forests and mountain scenery. But it has reappeared in a new form. It is not really the same thing as the old cottage and country house.

The idea of a home made of portable material, constructed at some convenient industrial centre and sent to any desired site, was already in the minds of such restless innovators as Henry Ford before the Decline and Fall. The country college, the country house, is an imaginative outlet. For great numbers of men and women comes a phase when the desire for that little peculiar place, with its carefully chosen site, its distinctive long-coveted amenities, its outlet upon the woods, the mountain, the jungle or the sea, has an overpowering appeal. There they will live, dream, work and be happy. Few of the many who had that dream could satisfy it in the old days. Some rare, rich persons, were able to buy land, build elaborately after their desires, make gardens. When they died or became bankrupt other people without the leisure to make their own homes bought the abandoned home. They would far rather have made a place for themselves, but there stood the predecessor's desire in brick or stone, solid and irremovable, and they did what they could, by means of alterations, to eliminate the taste of him.

But as plenty and mechanical power increased, as the new road system made more and more of the earth accessible, as power-cables and water supply spread everywhere, it became easy not only to clear away and obliterate the traces of houses that were done for, but to bring a pleasant individualized country house within the purchasing power of an increasing proportion of the population. The mastery of power in our time is manifested almost as much by its swift scrapping and scavenging as by its limitless productivity. Nowadays a man or woman may hit upon an unoccupied site, spend a few pleasant weeks planning and revising projects and designs, and give his order. In a month his home is ready, in a day or so more the foundation has been laid, and in three or four weeks the dream is realized; the house stands as he wished it to stand, connected to the power mains, supplied with water, furnished to his taste, smiling and ready. It is hardly more trouble than ordering an aeroplane or an automobile.

In its earlier stages the evocation of the preconstructed house was not so rapid, but from the first it was far quicker than the laborious piling up of the old-world builder.

And with an equal facility now a house is cleared away. We no longer think it meet to wear another man's abandoned house any more than we think it proper to wear the clothes of the dead. Clearing away, says Michael Kemal, is the primary characteristic of the Modern Age. The Age of Frustration was essentially an age that could not clear away, either debts, sovereignties, patriotisms, old classes, old boundaries, old buildings, old scores or old grievances. It is only in the past century that man has learnt the real lesson of plenty, that far more important than getting things is getting rid of things. We are rich universally because we are no longer rich personally.

We have mentioned the travelling wealthy man of the seventeenth century, for then only the wealthy aristocrats could travel freely, and we have glanced at the cumbersome impedimenta of his voyage. Compare him with any ordinary man today who decides to take a holiday and go to the ends of the earth. He may arrange with a travel bureau overnight for one or two special accommodations, then off he goes in the clothes he wears. He takes a wallet with his money account, his identification papers and perhaps a memorandum book. He may wear, as many people do, a personal ornament or so that has taken a hold upon his imagination. He may carry something to read or a specimen he wants to show. Whatever else he is likely to want on his way he will find on his way. He needs no other possessions because his possessions are everywhere. We have solved the problem of socializing property, the problem the early twentieth century was unable to solve. We have the use and consumption of material goods without the burthen of ownership.

VI

The Average Man Grows Older and Wiser

The numbers and the quality of the human population have changed very greatly in the past two centuries. Always these things have varied; every animal and vegetable species fluctuates continually in the numbers and quality of its individuals; but it is only recently that these movements have been recorded and examined systematically. The anti-progressives of the early twentieth century loved to assert that 'human nature' never altered; to imagine that the men of the Stone Age felt and thought like bank clerks picnicking in a cave, and that the ideas of Confucius and Buddha were easily interchangeable with the ideas of Rousseau, Karl Marx or De Windt. They were not simply ignorant but misinformed about almost every essential fact in the past experiences and present situation of the race. Only when the twenty-first century was well under way did any consciousness of the primary operating forces in human biology appear in the discussion and conduct of world affairs.

In the year 1800 the total population of the world was under 900 millions, and the average age was about 22. In 1900 the population had doubled and the average age had risen by nearly ten years. In 1935 a maximum was attained of 2000 millions and the average age had mounted to nearly 40. In a hundred years the facilities for intercommunication and physical reaction had increased beyond all measure. But the statesmen, educators and lawyers of that age, as we have shown very plainly in this history, were unaware of any of these differences that had occurred since their methods were developed. They drooled along according to precedent. A set-back for adjustment was therefore inevitable. We have told the broad facts of the crash that began with the war massacres of 1914–18 and culminated in the cycle of pestilences before 1957. In thirty years the population of the earth fell to about one thousand millions or less, and the average age receded to something about 23. This was a stupendous recession, not merely in numbers but in the maturity of the average mind.

Then came the Air and Sea Control of the First and the Second Council with their restoration of hygienic conditions and their scientific planning. The increase of population was watched and restrained for a century, but the average age extended until now it is 62 and still rising. The population total crept back to 1500 millions in 2060 and reached 2000 millions again in 2085. It has become manifest that such a population is no longer unwieldy, and that with the scientific education and behaviour control we now possess a considerable further increase can be contemplated without dismay.

The population of the earth is now 2500 millions, and it will probably be let up to 4000 millions as rapidly as the world is keyed up for its full support and happiness. The danger of such a population swarming dangerously or getting into panics, mental jams, crushes and insanitary congestions grows less and less. The opinion of contemporary authorities is that 4000 millions is an optimum, and that before many decades have passed it will be possible to keep most of those actively and happily alive to something like 90 years of age. But the question of the possibility and advisability of prolonging the individual life more than three or four decades beyond the 'threescore and ten' of the Biblical barbarian is still an open one. It is possible that there is a limit to the memories a brain can carry and to its power of taking new interest in fresh events. There may be a natural death for most people in the future about the age of a hundred or a little more, as painless and acceptable as going to bed and sleeping after a long and interesting day.

These quantitative biological alterations involve the profoundest differences in the quality of every life concerned. It is not simply that each individual has now a justifiable faith that he will live out his life to the end, but that the conditions in which he lives call out quite a different reaction system from that evoked in the past. Before the Middle Ages people thought of their grandparents as older and mightier people, but we think of our ancestors as younger and feebler people. Those earlier generations were like fresh-water fish, living in shallow, saline and readily dried-up water, in comparison with others of the same species living in a deep, abundant, well-aerated and altogether congenial lake. They were continually uncomfortable, constantly stranded by circumstances; they flapped about wildly and died early. Although they were the same in essence, their behaviour, their very movements, were like the behaviour of a different species of being.

Consider the existence of a young man in Shakespeare's time. If he did not die young he aged rapidly. He would be heavy, old and pompous at forty. A swarm of ailments lay in wait for him to emphasize and accelerate his decay. Youth was stuff that would not endure. The beauty and vitality of women were even more evanescent. So they snatched at love and adventure. The world was full of Romeos and Juliets at the crest of their passionate lives in their teens, who nowadays would be in the college stage of education, a score of years away from any conclusive drama. The literature of the time witnesses to a universal normal swift transitoriness. The simple precipitate love story, the jealousy, the headlong revenge and so on makes the substances of drama, romance and poem. That and the grab at spendable wealth: El Dorado, treasure trove or robbery attempted and defeated. A career was made or marred by a week's folly, and there was little time to recover it before the end. It is extraordinarily interesting to note all the things in life that are left out by the Elizabethan literature, and so to measure that smaller brighter circle of interest in that age.

The changing biological conditions between 1840 and 1940 mirror themselves faithfully in the art and reading of the decades. The novel which is at first pervaded by a gay hello to life, which accepts everything as cheerfully as a young animal, which laughs, caricatures and incites, becomes reflective, analytical, purposeful. Life no longer ends at the first rush. The proportion of novels to other books diminishes. The penetration of the individual consciousness by the great social and economic processes that were going on becomes more and more evident. When literature revived at the close of the twentieth century it was an adult literature, expressing the mentality of readers and writers who were fully grown men and women in a planning world that had ceased to be accidental and incoherent. In the novel as it then reappeared there is much more about personal love and the interplay of character but far less (and the proportion continues to diminish) about the primary love adventure.

That diminution of haste and avidity, of the quick egotism and swift uncritical judgment of youth, still continues. The deliberation, serenity and breadth of reference in the normal life increase. The years from thirty to seventy were formerly a sort of dump for the consequences of the first three decades; now they are the main part of life, the years of work, expression and complete self-discovery, to which these earlier stages are the bright, delightful prelude. There was a time when the man or woman over forty felt something of a survivor; he was 'staying on'; relatively the world swarmed with youth, with the swiftness, rivalries and shallowness of youth; the fitness of the ill-protected body had gone already; the elderly people who were 'getting on for fifty' moved slowly and had duller if sounder apprehensions. But now most of us are in the graver years with our bodies and apprehensions unimpaired, and there is no longer the same effect of being rather in the way of a juvenile treat. The Juvenile Treat, the age when even the old aped the young, ended in the World War and the economic collapse. After that came a struggle, at first unconscious and then open and declared, between youth and mental maturity.

In the bad years after the World War for a couple of generations there was a very unhappy relapse towards youthful predominance. The old people had failed to avert the collapse, the legitimate seniors for the new period were dead and broken and morally disorganized, and there was a sort of poetic justice in the stormy release of puerility that ensued. Italy was scourged by its hobbledehoys in black shirts; Russia was ruled by the blue-chinned Young; Ireland was devastated by hooligan patriots; presently Germany, after brooding over its defeat for ten years, had a convulsive relapse to fiercely crazy boyishness in the Nazis. Indian patriotism had a kindred immaturity. The tender years of many of the young revolutionaries executed by the British, outrage our standards of toleration. Everywhere was youthful ignorance with lethal weapons in its hands, conceited, self-righteous, exalted, blind to the tale of consequences. Breaking up things is the disposition of youth, and making is not yet in its experience. Liberalism and the middle-aged had a phase of unprecedented ineffectiveness. There seemed to be no judgment left in the world, and the young, in masks and requisitioned cars, making nocturnal raids, indulging in punitive cruelties, beating, torturing, displaying in equal measure physical recklessness and moral panic, came near to wrecking the whole civilizing process.

It is an interesting task to trace the gradual maturing of these adolescent organizers that seized so much of the control of the world in that age of transitional disorder. There are voluminous books in which Fascism in 1920, Fascism in 1930, and Fascism in 1940, or again Communism in the same decades, is elaborately compared with itself. After all their impatience and sentimentality, their rank patriotism and reactionary cant, we find these youth movements unobtrusively sneaking back to planning, discipline and scientific methods. Millions of young men who began Fascist, Nazi, Communist and the like, blind nationalists and irrational partisans, became Modern State men in their middle years. They became at last instruments to realize the plans and visions of the very men they had hunted, maltreated and murdered in the crude zeal of their first beginnings.

But now youth is well in hand for ever, and when we speak of a man to-day we really mean a different being from a nineteenth-century man. Bodily he is sounder and fitter, almost completely free from disease; mentally he is clear and clean and educated to a pitch that was still undreamt of two centuries ago. He is over fifty instead of being under thirty. He is less gregarious in his instincts and less suggestible because he is further away from the 'home and litter' mentality, but he is far more social and unselfish in his ideology and mental habits. He is, in fact, for all the identity of his heredity, a different animal. He is bigger and stronger, more clear-headed, with more self-control and more definitely related to his fellow creatures.

This is manifest everywhere, but it is particularly visible in such regions as Bengal and Central China. There we find the direct descendants of shrill, unhappy, swarming, degenerate, under-nourished, under-educated, underbred and short-lived populations among the finest, handsomest, longest-lived and ablest of contemporary humanity. This has been achieved without any attempt at Positive Eugenics; it has resulted from the honest application of the Obvious to health, education, and economic organization, within little more than a hundred years. These populations were terribly weeded by the pestilences of the age of disorder and grimly disciplined by the Tyranny. They are now, after that pruning and training, bearing as fine flowers of literary and scientific achievement as any other racial masses.

VII

Language and Mental Growth

(I print this section exactly as Raven wrote it down. It is, the reader will remark, in very ordinary twentieth-century English. Yet plainly if it is a part of a twenty-second-century textbook of general history it cannot have been written originally in our contemporary idiom. It insists upon a refinement and enlargement of language as if it had already occurred, but no such refinement is evident. It must have been translated by Raven as he dreamt it into the prose of today. If he saw that book of his at all, he saw it not with his eyes but with his mind. The actual page could have had neither our lettering, our spelling, our phrasing nor our vocabulary.)

One of the unanticipated achievements of the twenty-first century was the rapid diffusion of Basic English as the lingua franca of the world and the even more rapid modification, expansion and spread of English in its wake. The English most of us speak and write today is a very different tongue from the English of Shakespeare, Addison, Bunyan or Shaw; it has shed the last traces of such archaic elaborations as a subjunctive mood; it has simplified its spelling, standardized its pronunciation, adopted many foreign locutions, and naturalized and assimilated thousands of foreign words. No deliberate attempt was made to establish it as the world language. It had many natural advantages over its chief competitors, Spanish, French, Russian, German and Italian. It was simpler, subtler, more flexible and already more widely spoken, but it was certainly the use of Basic English which gave it its final victory over these rivals.

Basic English was the invention of an ingenious scholar of Cambridge in England, C. K. Ogden (1889–1990), who devoted a long and industrious life to the simplification of expression and particularly to this particular simplification. It is interesting to note that he was a contemporary of James Joyce (1882–1955), who also devoted himself to the task of devising a new sort of English. But while Ogden sought scientific simplification, Joyce worked aesthetically for elaboration and rich suggestion, and vanished at last from the pursuit of his dwindling pack of readers in a tangled prose almost indistinguishable from the gibbering of a lunatic. Nevertheless he added about twenty-five words to the language which are still in use. Ogden, after long and industrious experimentation in the reverse direction, emerged with an English of 850 words and a few rules of construction which would enable any foreigner to express practically any ordinary idea simply and clearly. It became possible for an intelligent foreigner to talk or correspond in understandable English in a few weeks. On the whole it was more difficult to train English speakers to restrict themselves to the forms and words selected than to teach outsiders the whole of Basic. It was a teacher of languages, Rudolph Boyle (1910–59), who contrived the method by which English speakers learnt to confine themselves, when necessary, to Basic limitations.

This convenience spread like wildfire after the First Conference of Basra. It was made the official medium of communication throughout the world by the Air and Sea Control, and by 2020 there was hardly anyone in the world who could not talk and understand it.

It is from phonetically spelt Basic English as a new starting-point that the language we write and speak to-day developed, chiefly by the gradual resumption of verbs and idioms from the mother tongue and by the assimilation of foreign terms and phrases. We speak a language of nearly two million words nowadays, a synthetic language in fact, into which roots, words and idioms from every speech in the world have been poured. K. Wang in a recent essay has shown that there are still specializations of vocabulary. The vocabulary of a score of recent writers of Italian origin chosen haphazard shows a marked preference for words derived from the Latin, in comparison with twenty Eastern Asiatic writers whose bias is Chinese and American. Yet they can all understand one another and they are all in one undivided cultural field.

There are few redundancies in the new English of to-day and tomorrow, and there is an increasing disposition to take synonyms, and what used to be classified as 'rare' or 'obsolete' terms, and re-define them to convey some finder shade of meaning. Criticism, in the form of the Dictionary Bureau, scrutinizes, but permits desirable additions. One can feel little doubt about the increasing delicacy and precision of expression today if we compare a contemporary book with some English classic of the eighteenth or nineteenth century. That is still quite understandable to us, but in its bareness and occasional ineptitudes it seems half-way back to the limitations and lumberingness of Early English or Gothic.

The fuller the terminology the finer the mind. There can be very little doubt that the brain of a twentieth-century man compared with the brain of an ordinary man today, though in no way intrinsically inferior, was a far less polished and well-adjusted implement. It was warped by bad habits, cumbered with a tangle of unsound associations, clogged with unresolved complexes; it was like a fine piece of machinery in a state of dirt and neglect. The modern brain is far more neatly packed and better arranged, cleaner and better lubricated. It not only holds much more, but it uses the larger keyboard of our contemporary language more efficiently. The common man today is apt to find the

philosophers and 'thinkers' of two centuries ago unaccountably roundabout, tedious and encumbered. It is not so much that he finds them
obscure, but that when at last he has dragged the meanings out of their
jungles of statement into the light of day he finds he has thought all
round them.

An interesting and valuable group of investigators, whose work still
goes on, appeared first in a rudimentary form in the nineteenth century.
The leader of this group was a certain Lady Welby (1837–1912), who
was frankly considered by most of her contemporaries as an unintelligible bore. She corresponded copiously with all who would attend to her,
harping perpetually on the idea that language could be made more
exactly expressive, that there should be a 'Science of Significs'. C. K.
Ogden and a fellow Fellow of Magdalene College, I. A. Richards
(1893–1977), were among the few who took her seriously. These two
produced a book, *The Meaning of Meaning*, in 1923 which counts as
one of the earliest attempts to improve the language mechanism. Basic
English was a by-product of these enquiries. The new Science was
practically unendowed, it attracted few workers, and it was lost sight of
during the decades of disaster. It was revived only in the early twenty-
first century.

Then Carl Ratan became the centre of a group of workers inspired by
the idea of making English more lucid and comprehensive and a truly
universal language. His work has expanded into the voluminous organization of the Language Bureau as we know it today. The work of that
Bureau has been compared to the work of the monetary experts who
finally made money exact a hundred and fifty years ago. Just as
civilization was held back for some centuries by the imperfections of
the money nexus, so we begin to realize today that our intellectual
progress is by no means so rapid as it might be because of the endless
flaws and looseness of the language nexus.

An interesting compilation in hand, which promises to become a
veritable history of philosophy and knowledge, is the *Language Discard*.
This project was originally set going by the Dictionary Section of the
Language Bureau, as a mere account rendered of obsolete or obsolescent
terms or terms which have become greatly altered from their original
meaning; but the enquiry into the reasons for these changings and
preferences and abandonments led very directly into an exhaustive
analysis of the primary processes of human thought. A series of words,
'*soul, spirit, matter, force, essence*', for example, were built into the
substance of Aryan and Semitic thought almost from their beginnings,
and it was only quite recently that the exhaustive analyses by Yuan
Shan and his associates of these framework terms made it clear that the
processes of Chinese and Negro thinking were by no means parallel.
Translation between languages, in all matters except matters of material
statement, is always a little loose and rough, but between the ideology

underlying the literature of Eastern Asia or the attempts of Africans to express themselves and that embodied in the ruling language of today the roughness approaches violence. That clash, as it is examined, is likely to produce very extensive innovations in our philosophical (general scientific) and technical nomenclature. We are speaking and writing a provisional language today. Our great-grandchildren will no more think of using many of our terms and turns of expression today than we should think of resorting again to the railway train, the paddle steamboat and the needle telegraph.

This rearrangement of the association systems of the human brain which is now in progress brings with it – long before we begin to dream of eugenic developments – the prospect of at present inconceivable extensions of human mental capacity. It will involve taking hold of issues that are at present quite outside our grasp. There was a time when early man was no more capable of drawing a sketch or threading a needle than a cow; it was only as his thumb and fingers became opposable that the powers of craftsmanship and mechanism came within his grip. Similarly we may anticipate an enormous extension of research and a far deeper penetration into reality as language, our intellectual hand, is brought to a new level of efficiency.

There is not only this sharpening and refinement of the brain going on, but there has been what our great-grandparents would have considered an immense increase in the amount, the quality, and the accessibility of knowledge. As the individual brain quickens and becomes more skilful, there also appears a collective Brain, the Encyclopaedia, the Fundamental Knowledge System, which accumulates, sorts, keeps in order and renders available everything that is known. The Encyclopaedic organization, which centres upon Barcelona, with its seventeen million active workers, is the Memory of Mankind. Its tentacles spread out in one direction to millions of investigators, checkers and correspondents, and in another to keep the educational process in living touch with mental advance. It is growing rapidly as the continual advance in productive efficiency liberates fresh multitudes of workers for its services. The mental mechanism of mankind is as yet only in its infancy.

Adolescence perhaps rather than infancy. It is because the mind of man is growing up that for the first time it realizes that it is young.

VIII

Sublimation of Interest

Not only is the average man today, an older and graver creature than his ancestor of three centuries ago, but he is very differently employed. There has been a great diversion of his interest from the primary necessities of life.

Three centuries ago, well over ninety per cent of the human population was absorbed either in the direct production of necessities or the scramble to get them from their original producers. Direct producers, the peasants and toilers, the entrepreneurs and their managers and directors, and direct distributors accounted for upward of eighty per cent of the human total; the rest were the millions of interveners, usurers, claim-makers, landowners, rentiers, solicitors, speculators, parasites, robbers, and thieves who were deemed necessary to ginger up the economic process. The forces of law, order and education, excluding temporary conscription and levies for military ends, took up five or six per cent of the residue, and a small minority, something under five per cent of the total population, supplied all the artistic effort, the scientific enquiry, the social and political thought, the living soul of the entire social body.

The systems of interest of most people were therefore restricted almost entirely to work and the struggle to possess. They had to think continually of the work they did either for their own profit or for the personal profit, comfort or fantasy of some employer. They had to think of keeping their jobs or of getting fresh ones, and this, in the days of narrowing employment after the Hoover Slump, became at last a monstrous obsession of the brain. What they earned they had to spend carefully or guard carefully, for the rascaldom of business was everywhere seeking to give nothing for something. Sometimes, sick of their narrow lives, they would gamble in the desperate hope of a convulsive enlargement, and for most of them gambling meant disappointment and self-reproach. Add to these worries a little love, a good deal of hate, and a desperate struggle to see it all in a hopeful and honourable light, a desperate hunger to be flattered and reassured, and you have the content of ninety-nine per cent of the human brains that made the world of 1930. They could no more escape from this restricted circle of urgently clamorous interests, hardly ampler than the circle of an animal's interest, than the animals can.

The Modern State has broken this cramping circle of interests for every human being. We are still creatures with brains like our forefathers, corresponding ganglia to ganglia and fibre to fibre, but *we are not using those brains for the same purposes.* The Modern State, by ensuring plenty and controlling the increase of population, has taken all the interests of the food-hunt and the food-scramble, and all the interests of the struggle to down-and-out our human competitors, away from the activities of the individual brain. A relatively small number of specialized workers keep the necessary Controls of these primary preoccupations going. We worry about food, drink, clothing, health and personal freedom no more. The work we *must* do is not burthensome in amount, and it is the most congenial our educational guardians can find for us and help us to find. When it is done we are sure of the result; nobody is left in the world to cheat us or rob us of our pay. We are still competitive, more so perhaps than ever; jealousy still wars with generosity in us; the story of our personal affections is rarely a simple story; but the interest we feel in our work is a masterful interest and not a driven interest, and our competition is for distinction, appreciation and self-approval and not for mutual injury. There has been a release of by far the larger moiety of the mental energy of the normal man from its former inescapable preoccupations.

This steady obliteration of primary motives is manifested most illuminatingly by the statistics of what used to be 'Crime and Punishment', figures of the offences, insubordinations and deliberate outrages upon social order and the consequent punishments and corrective proceedings that are issued by the disciplinary organization of the Behaviour Control. Statistics for the years of decadence are not forthcoming, but there is plentiful material from the comparatively orderly and prosperous period between 1890 and 1930. Great Britain then constituted the healthiest and most law-abiding community in the world, but the figures that emerge to the student of history present what seems to us an appalling welter of crime. Stealing, cheating of every sort, forgery, burglary, robbery with violence, poisoning and other forms of murder, occurred daily. It did not seem as though that thick defilement of wrongdoing about property could ever cease. Innumerable suicides occurred through pecuniary worry. Yet now all these crimes, which filled the jails, arising out of the scramble for money and property in an age of insufficiency, have almost completely vanished from human life. The Behaviour Control Report for 2104 (2105 is not yet available) records 715 cases of stealing for the whole world. In nearly every case the object stolen was some personal work of art, some small jewel, a piece of embroidery, a pet animal, several children, and – in one instance – the bulb of a new variety of lily that aroused the instinct to possess and care for. It is doubtful whether there were many undetected or unreported thefts.

There has not, however, been anything like the same abolition of personal offences. They have diminished. But while the property offences have diminished to the scale of one-ten-millionth of the old-world figures, these others show a reduction in the nature of single instances to former hundreds. Many types in our population are still very easily turned towards sexual lawlessness. Beautiful and attractive people and particularly attractive children are not yet perfectly immune from undesired solicitation, personal persecution, annoying assault and resentful injury. Jealousy is still a dangerous passion, more particularly below the age of forty. The Behaviour Control ascribes nearly 520,000 offences to this group of urgencies, mostly assaults of varying degree of malignity, culminating in 67 murders. There were also 2192 suicides in the total. These figures show only a slight improvement upon the annual average for the previous decade.

Another difficult class of offence which finds no exact parallel in the criminal statistics of former times, unless the British offence of 'malignant mischief' is to be put in this group, are acts of annoyance, destruction, assault and so forth, due to competitive jealousy and the exasperation aroused, often quite unwittingly, by the bearing or achievements of one's fellow creatures. This sort of misbehaviour varies in degree from the black hatred and fury of an uncontrolled egotism to what verges in some cases upon justifiable criticism of slightly fatuous self-complacent behaviour. Four murders, some hundreds of assaults and acts of wanton destruction in this category witness to the fact that this world is still not a Paradise for every type of individual. Either they are bitter by some inner necessity or they have been embittered. Yet when we take the grand total of every misdeed that had to be dealt with last year, counting even the most petty occasions for restoration, warning or reproof, and find it is just three quarters of a million in a world of 2500 million people, we have a quantitative measure of human progress in two brief centuries that justifies a very stalwart confidence in the human outlook. The imagination of man's heart is no longer evil continually. It is only evil occasionally, and the practical task of our social psychologists is to reduce those occasions and provocations.

The abundant release of brain-stuff, the mental plenty which has resulted from the organization of material plenty, is of necessity being directed into new channels. That meagre half per cent or less of creative workers of the old régime, the few curious men who played about with novel ideas, the odd men of leisure who collected 'rarities' and inventions, has grown into a mighty body of enquiry, experiment, verification and record which is becoming now the larger part of the world's population.

We know now certainly what the people of three centuries ago never suspected, that the human brain released from hunger, fear and the other primary stresses is very easily amenable not only to creative and directive desire but also to kindly and helpful impulses. Almost all the people who keep our productive, our distributing and transport services going are there because they find the work entertaining, because they like making the machine work well and helping people. There is a satisfaction in being able to do things skilfully for others that they could not do nearly so well for themselves. The barbers, shoemakers, tailors, dressmakers, hatters, outfitters and so forth in the great stores today are very different people from the rather obsequious, deferential 'inferiors' who made our great-great-grandfathers presentable to the world. Their essential interest is to make their customers sightly and comfortable and not to earn a profit for an employer. The old literature reeks with contempt for barbers and tailors and cobblers, often the contempt of profound resentment. If the common man despised the cobbler, the cobbler pinched his toe and chafed his heel. The barber, it seemed, did no more than cut hair rather badly, and the tailor cut clothes. Except by accident, the barber had ceased to be a barber-surgeon. But nowadays the old-world barber would scarcely recognize himself in the barber-dentist, the kindly expert who sees to our coiffure, gives attention to our teeth, scrutinizes our mouth, hair and skin to detect any evidence of failing health, and sends us on our way refreshed, encouraged or warned. Often his friend the tailor or dressmaker will call in while he deals with us to consider our general bravery and improvement, and suggest variations of our exercise and habits.

The old distributing trades have lost their sharp demarcation from the advisory professions. They are in touch with the guardians of development who have replaced the schoolmasters, nurses, governesses, tutors and so forth of the old time, and with the general advisers who have taken on the tasks of the family solicitor, religious minister, private confessor and general practitioner of the past. These advisory and directive professions probably number two or three times as big a proportion of the whole population as the lawyers, educationists and doctors of the nineteenth century. They merge again into another stratum, the specialist teachers, concerned with developing and imparting skills and building up and maintaining the common ideology. This class again passes by insensible degrees into the worlds of technical work, art, literature and scientific research.

The primary producers and elaborators of material, our agriculturalists, engineers, chemists, transport men and industrial directors, also do their work because they like doing it. It satisfies them. They like their materials, they like their difficulties, they like the order of their days. In spite of an increasing output per head of population and an increasing variety and elaboration of the things we use, socially or individually, the numerical proportion of this section of the human population does not increase. Efficiency still outruns need and desire. The two and a half years of compulsory public service, which is an integral part of our education, supplies a larger and larger proportion of such toil as is still unavoidable.

This release of human energy from primary needs is a process that seems likely to continue indefinitely. And all the forces that have made our world-wide social life and keep it going direct that released energy towards the achievement of fresh knowledge and the accumulation and rendering of fresh experience. There is a continual sublimation of interest. Man becomes more curious, more excited, more daring, skilful, and pleasantly occupied every year. The more we learn of the possibilities of our world and the possibilities of ourselves, the richer, we learn, is our inheritance. This planet, which seemed so stern a mother to mankind, is discovered to be inexhaustible in its bounty. And the greatest discovery man has made has been the discovery of himself. Leonardo da Vinci with his immense breadth of vision, his creative fervour, his curiosity, his power of intensive work, was the precursor of the ordinary man, as the world is now producing him.

IX

A New Phase in the History of Life

From the point of view of the ecologist the establishment of the Modern State marks an epoch in biological history. It has been an adaptation, none too soon, of our species to changing conditions that must otherwise have destroyed it. The immense developments and disasters of the nineteenth and twentieth centuries show us mankind scrambling on the verge of irreparable disaster.

The infinite toil of millions of tormented brains, the devotion and persistence of countless forgotten devotees, gave form and clear purpose in time to what were at first mere flounderings and clutchings towards safety. The threatened race did not fall back into that abyss of extinction which has swallowed up so many of the bolder experiments of life. In pain and uncertainty it clambered past its supreme danger phase, and now it has struggled to such a level of assurance, understanding and safety as no living substance has ever attained before.

By means of education and social discipline the normal human individual today acquires characteristics without which his continued existence would be impossible. In the future, as the obscurer processes of selection are accelerated and directed by eugenic effort, these acquired characteristics will be incorporated with his inherent nature, and his educational energy will be released for further adaptations. He will become generation by generation a new species, differing more widely from that weedy, tragic, pathetic, cruel, fantastic, absurd and sometimes sheerly horrible being who christened himself in a mood of oafish arrogance *Homo sapiens*.

The differences of the coming man from the man of the past will be multitudinous and intricate, but certain broad lines of comparison appear already. We have noted already the difference in the age cycle between ourselves and our ancestors, which has prolonged the youthful phase and shifted on the valid years towards the thirty-five to eighty period, and we have cited also the completer physical development, due to the release of vital energy from the task of resisting various infections, poisons and morbidities of growth. We are probably only in the beginning of very much more considerable physical modification. The aesthetic ideals of the past are likely to play a large part in determining the direction in which these modifications will take us. But these physical developments, important though they must ultimately be, are as yet much less important than the changes in moral form that are manifestly in progress. A brief consideration of these will make a fitting conclusion to this general outline of history.

Essentially they constitute a readjustment of the individual to the racial life. When we go back in time for a million years or so we find our ancestor species in a phase of almost fundamental individualism. Except where sexual life and the instinct system to protect offspring came in, the subman shifted for himself. He had no associates in the food hunt, no allies for defence. He was as solitary an animal as the tiger. From that he passed through stages of increasing sociability. The onset of these stages was made practicable by the retention of immature characteristics into adult life. The same thing is happening to the remnant of the lions to-day. They remain cubbish and friendly now to a much later age than they did a few-score thousand years ago. Man passed through a stage when he was as sociable as a modern lion and on to a phase when he was as sociable as a wolf or hunting dog.

But he did not rest at that. All the conditions of his life favoured the formation of still-larger communities and still-closer interdependence. He became a cultivator, an economic animal, and his communities expanded to thousands and scores of thousands of individuals held together by mutual service. He produced language and religion to bind the will and activities of these aggregations into an effective common policy. The history of mankind, as we unfold it to the contemporary student, is a story of ever increasing communication and ever increasing interdependence. Insensibly the material side of individual freedom was modified into unavoidable cooperation with the community.

Stress must be laid upon that word material. The physical subjugation and socialization of the human animal far outran his moral subjection. The history of mankind is also a history of education and compulsion. It is a record of give and take. Man almost up to the present day has remained at heart still the early savage, caring only for himself, for his sexual life, and, during the few years of their helplessness, his children. He has been willing to associate for aggression or for defence, but only very reluctantly for a common happiness. He has had to barter his freedom for the advantages of collective action, but he has done so against the grain, needing persuasion, pressure and helpful delusions.

The history of mankind has had to be very largely the history of a succession of religious and emotional inventions and reconstructions, to override the inherent distate in the individual for subordination and self-sacrifice. At every opportunity the individual has sought to recover its personal initiatives. Its egotism has battled instinctively of necessity to get the best of the bargain and receive with as little giving as possible.

Man's natural self struggles to do that now as strongly as ever he did. But he struggles now in a better light and more intelligently; he realized what is impossible, and the long conflict of individualism with society has arrived at a rational compromise. We have learnt how to catch and domesticate the ego at an early stage and train it for purposes greater than itself.

What has happened during the past three and a half centuries to the human consciousness has been a sublimation of individuality. That phase is the quintessence of modern history. A large part of the commonplace life of man, the food-hunt, the shelter-hunt, the safety-hunt, has been lifted out of the individual sphere and socialized for ever. To that the human egotism has given its assent perforce. It has abandoned gambling and profit-seeking and all the wilder claims of property. It has ceased altogether to snatch, scramble and oust for material ends. And the common man has also been deprived of any weapons for his ready combativeness and of any liberty in its release. Nowadays even children do not fight each other. Gentleness in difference has become our second nature.

All that part of man's life and interests has been socialized entirely against his natural disposition in the matter. In all those concerns the whole race is now confluent; it is becoming as much a colonial organism as any branching coral or polyp, though the ties that link us are not fleshly bands, but infinitely elastic and invisible and subtle. In the later chapters of this world history we have examined and displayed, with particular attention because of its culminating character, the essential individualism of the World War process, and we have told how, with what difficulty and after what scourgings, our race has been brought to its present phase of organized self-control. This present phase is the victory of creative power working through the individualities of a more intelligent minority, in the face of universal confusion, taking indeed advantage of that confusion to inaugurate our present order. That wilful minority has opened the gates to a power and abundance of existence beyond all former dreaming. But our Modern State has neither absorbed nor destroyed individuality, which now, accepting the necessary restrictions upon its material aggressiveness, resumes at every opportunity its freedom and enterprise upon a higher level of life.

The individuality deprived, or relieved if you will, of its primary instinctive preoccupations with getting and keeping, disillusioned about precedence, personal display and suchlike barbaric vanities, growing continually and swiftly in wisdom and knowledge, has now to go further afield to find itself. No longer a self-sufficient being, at war with all its kind, it has become a responsible part of a species. It has become an experiment in feeling, knowing, making and response.

The body of mankind is now one single organism of nearly two thousand five hundred million persons, and the individual differences of every one of these persons is like an exploring tentacle thrust out to test and learn, to savour life in its fullness and bring in new experiences for the common stock. We are all members of one body.* Only in the dimmest analogy has anything of this sort happened in the universe as we knew it before. Our sense of our individual difference makes our realization of our common being more acute. We work, we think, we explore, we dispute, we take risks and suffer – for there seems no end to the difficult and dangerous adventures individual men and women may attempt; and more and more plain does it become to us that it is not our little selves, but Man the Undying who achieves these things through us.

As the slower processes of heredity seize upon and confirm these social adaptations, as the confluence of wills supersedes individual motives and loses its present factors of artificiality, the history of life will pass into a new phase, a phase with a common consciousness and a common will. We in our time are still rising towards the crest of that transition. And when that crest is attained what grandeur of life may not open out to Man! Eye hath not seen, nor ear heard; nor hath it

---

* This was the phrase of that interesting mystic St Paul (Saul) of Tarsus (2–62 CE *Epistles* with analysis and commentary by Hirsch and Potter in the *Historical Reprints: Development of Ideas Series*), who did so much to pervert and enlarge the simpler cosmopolitan fraternalism of Jesus of Nazareth (4–30 CE) before it was finally overwhelmed and lost in the sacrificial sacerdotalism of formal Christianity. For a brief period before it relapsed the Pauline cult had a curious flavour of Modern State feeling. There was, however, a politic disingenuousness in Paul which betrayed his undeniable intellectual power. He was ambiguous about blood sacrifices, immortality, private property and slavery, to the eternal injury of the Christian movement. It was completely prostituted to usage before the first century was over. See Ivan Mackenzie, *General Elements of Religion* 2103. Mackenzie has an excellent chapter on the anticipation of Modern State ideas by ancient writers, and is particularly interesting on the Superior Person (Generalized or Super Man) of Confucius (551–478 BC) and the *City of God* of St Augustine (354–430).

entered into mind of man to conceive. . . . For now we see as in a glass darkly. . . .

At this point Raven's copied-out manuscript comes to an end – it seems to me a little abruptly. But it is the end; he has written the word 'Finis' here. I will add only one word or so by way of comment. I have called that manuscript a dream book. Was it a dream book or was it indeed, as he declared and believed it to be, a vision of the shape of things to come? Or – there is a third possibility. As dreaming, this book is far too coherent; as vision, incredulity creeps in. But was Raven, too busily employed and too obsessed by the sense of urgency to embark upon a detailed analysis of world development, was he trying nevertheless to sketch out in this fantastic form a general thesis at least about the condition of things to come? If this is neither a dream book nor a Sibylline history, then it is a theory of world revolution. Plainly the thesis is that history must now continue to be a string of accidents with an increasingly disastrous trend, until a comprehensive faith in the modernized World-State, socialistic, cosmopolitan and creative, takes hold of the human imagination. When the existing governments and ruling theories of life, the decaying religious and the decaying political forms of today, have sufficiently lost prestige through failure and catastrophe, then and then only will world-wide reconstruction be possible. And it must needs be the work, first of all, of an aggressive order of religiously devoted men and women who will try out and establish and impose a new pattern of living upon our race.